CHASING THE SUN

CHASING THE SUN

A READER'S GUIDE TO NOVELS
SET IN THE AMERICAN WEST

EDWARD JOSEPH BEVERLY

SUNSTONE
PRESS

SANTA FE

Book and Cover design by Vicki Ahl

Sunstone books may be purchased for educational, business, or sales promotional use. For information please write: Special Markets Department, Sunstone Press, P.O. Box 2321, Santa Fe, New Mexico 87504-2321.

Library of Congress Cataloging-in-Publication Data

Beverly, Edward Joseph, 1934-
Chasing the sun : a reader's guide to novels set in the American West / by Edward Joseph Beverly.
   p. cm.
Includes bibliographical references and indexes.
ISBN 978-0-86534-603-1 (softcover : alk. paper)
1. Western stories--Bibliography. 2. Western stories--Stories, plots, etc. I. Title.
Z1251.W5B48 2008
[PS374.W4]
016.813'54--dc22

2008003453

WWW.SUNSTONEPRESS.COM
SUNSTONE PRESS / POST OFFICE BOX 2321 / SANTA FE, NM 87504-2321 /USA
(505) 988-4418 / ORDERS ONLY (800) 243-5644 / FAX (505) 988-1025

To Francisca, who can read a novel in one lazy afternoon. This lifelong passion for reading has given her a knowledge of our world and its inhabitants that is truly amazing.

Contents

PREFACE

Setting is the unifying feature for the novels included in this reader's guide. The American West, or more precisely the North American West, a land that encompasses a remarkable variety of physical and cultural landscapes, is the backdrop for a wide variety of themes and plots employed by an equally wide variety of novelists.

It is difficult to place boundaries on the West. Its landscapes are varied: the Colorado Plateau, the Llano Estacado, the Sonoran Desert, the Big Thicket, the upper Rio Grande Valley, the brush country of South Texas, the Pacific Coast, the Alaskan tundra, and numerous other unique locales. Some book reviewers, however, contend that the one thing all Western settings have in common is aridity, and wouldn't consider novels set in Missouri or along the Pacific Coast or in other non-arid regions to be Western fiction. Some include stories set in Canada and Alaska; others differentiate these as "Northerns." Some define the West in relation to the movement of the frontier, and include James Fenimore Cooper novels that were actually set in the East. And although the bulk of the literature is set in the Old West, defined roughly as the period between the end of the Civil War and the invention of the automobile, there's a growing body of work set in contemporary times. The books in this guide are all set in states west of the Mississippi, including Alaska. I've also included novels that take place in western Canada and Mexico; both played an important part in our Western frontier experience.

There are recurring themes built around cattle drives, wagon trains, Indian wars, water rights, the Pony Express, and so on that help in classifying the Old West novels as Western fiction. Those set in the New West are concerned with such things as the environment, the struggle to hold onto a vanishing way of life, personal freedom, and individuality; these are also easily recognized Western themes. However, there are many novels that are set in the West, primarily the contemporary urban West, that do not have a recognizable Western theme and are not included in this guide.

Western fiction includes the real cowboy narrative of Will James, the formula Westerns of Max Brand and Frank Gruber, the romantic novels of Zane Grey and Louis L'Amour, the Navajo mysteries of Tony Hillerman, the ethnic novels of Louise Erdrich, the contemporary novels of Edward Abbey, and the genuine literature of Willa Cather and Wallace Stegner.

Since Western fiction covers such a vast geographic, cultural, and thematic landscape, most critical works on the subject are narrowly confined to formula Westerns, regional fiction, or a few chosen writers that academia considers worthy of formal criticism. This guide spans the Western literary landscape.

The material is organized around content such as exploration, trapping, wagon trains, the Indian wars, and contemporary fiction. Each chapter, or category, contains a reader's guide that provides "thumbnail" samples of the literature from early publications to the present, and a short review of one or more novels in that category. The thumbnails are descriptive rather than evaluative. I make no claim to having read every book in this reader's guide. Many thumbnails have been constructed from secondary sources.

The reviews are personal favorites that represent the diversity of the literature. I focus on setting, theme, plot, and characterization and leave the discussion of social or psychological insights and other formal literary criticism to others. A bibliography is included that will guide readers to sources written to any depth that suits their purpose.

The categories I used to group the titles are neither exhaustive nor mutually exclusive. In general, the books are categorized according to subject matter. In the thumbnails, I have tried to indicate the setting and a glimpse of the plot. But the placement of a novel in a particular category is sometimes purely subjective. *The Forests of the Night* (Dial Press, 1974), J. P. S. Brown's story of a Mexican peasant's hunt for a jaguar, is set in the high country of the Mexican Sierras, and could have quite properly been placed in either category

"The Spanish West" or "The Hunters." No attempt was made to balance the titles across categories. "High Noon: The Romantic West," for example, is made up of novels most people call *genre* Westerns. There have been literally thousands of these novels written, and many authors such as Max Brand (Frederick Schiller Faust) wrote a multitude of them, so only a sampling of his and the other more prolific writers' works are included. On the other hand, religion has not been nearly as popular a subject and the entries under "The Glory Trail: The Church in the West" are significantly fewer.

Publication data are given for each entry to assist the reader in tracking down a copy. But in no sense should this guide be considered a bibliography. However, a selected bibliography is appended to assist the reader in further research.

A titles index and an authors index are provided to help in finding specific authors or novels.

1

BEYOND THE GREAT DIVIDE: THE TRAILBLAZERS

INTRODUCTION

Prior to the Lewis and Clark Expedition of 1804-1806 the vast territory between the Mississippi River and the Pacific was virtually unknown. The expedition's purpose, to map a water route from the Mississippi to the Pacific, was not realized. However, the objective itself was proved a myth. But more important, a huge blank space on the map of North America had been filled. The American West, known previously only through rumor and conjecture, had been traversed.

Zebulon Pike, Stephen Harriman Long, and John Charles Frémont are perhaps the best known of those men who conducted explorations in the West in the decade prior to the Civil War. Pike was a soldier and explorer who led an expedition in 1806-07 to determine the extent of the Louisiana Territory's southwestern lands. Long, a major in the elite Army Corps of Topographical Engineers, explored the Platte, Arkansas, and Red rivers in 1820. In 1823, on his most successful expedition, he explored the region between the Mississippi and Missouri rivers. Frémont's prominence as an explorer began in 1842, when he was given the assignment of surveying the Oregon Trail up the Platte River to South Pass. As an officer in the Topographical Corps, he led three expeditions west to map the Oregon Trail and to find a direct route to California.

Also, during the first half of the 19th century, trappers roamed the Rocky Mountain region of the continent, taking beaver and other pelts for the rich markets back east and in Europe. Known as "mountain men," these trappers accumulated information that later greatly aided settlement of the far western frontier. The heyday of the mountain men began in 1822, and during the next 15 years they discovered passes through the Rocky Mountains, including the South Pass to Oregon, explored the Great Basin and far Southwest, and developed several routes to California and Oregon. During this time perhaps as many as 3,000 mountain men operated in the Far West. Jim Bridger, Thomas Fitzpatrick, Kit Carson, Jedediah Smith, and others of their calling contributed greatly to knowledge of the geography of the region.

The best known of the fur traders were General William H. Ashley, who is credited with organizing the Rocky Mountain fur trade, and John Jacob Astor, who founded the American Fur Company. General Ashley's expeditions out of St. Louis in the early 1820s were characterized by brigades of American trappers who lived in the mountains and worked for him or one of his competitors. In 1823 John Jacob Astor formed partnerships with many leading traders in St. Louis and bought up the Missouri River trade. By 1827 he had a virtual monopoly on it. During the period between 1820 and 1840 the the fur trade was at its peak.

The last major exploration occurred in 1869, when Civil War hero John Wesley Powell led an expedition down the Colorado River, solving the mystery of the last "great unknown" in the American West.

The explorers, the mountain men, and the traders opened the West. Historians have thoroughly documented their heroic deeds. These deeds also provide a wealth of material for novels set during this adventurous period of our nation's development. Reviews of three of the best follow the Reader's Guide. Will Henry's evocative *The Gates of the Mountain*, (Random House, 1963) views the Lewis and Clark expedition through the eyes of a young boatman, half-French and half-Pawnee, who is in love with the Shoshone guide Sacajewea. Harvey Fergusson's lyrical *Wolf Song* (Alfred A. Knopf, 1927) is ranked among the classic novels of the mountain men, and David Nevin's *Dream West* (G. P. Putnam's Sons, 1983) is an historical novel based on the life and explorations of John Charles Frémont.

Long before the Americans set their sights to the west, Spanish explorers made significant inroads into the present American Southwest.

Novels of their explorations and influence are discussed in Chapter 13, The Spanish West.

READER'S GUIDE

The Adventures of Captain Bonneville by Washington Irving. 1837. When Captain Benjamin Bonneville set out for the West in 1832, his mission was "to collect information on the geography, geology, and topography of the Country within the limits of the Territories belonging to the United States, between our frontier and the Pacific." He was gone nearly five years, and with mountain man Joseph Rutherford Walker discovered Yosemite, a southern route across the Sierras, and Utah's Bonneville Salt Flats.

Edward Warren by William Drummond Stewart. 1854. This book is an eyewitness account of the beaver trade of the Rocky Mountains and the mountain men, sketched from life by one who shared their times. Sir William Drummond Stewart was a soldier, adventurer, and baronet who spent most of a decade on the plains and mountains of the American West in the 1830's. He published his memoirs of the era in this "novel," which modern scholars have proved to be his autobiography.

Life in the Far West by George Frederic Ruxton. Harper, 1889. A mountain man novel based on the author's personal experiences in the Rocky Mountains during 1846-47.

The Splendid Wayfaring by John G. Neihardt. Macmillan, 1920. A story of the adventures of Jedediah Smith and the Ashley-Henry men, 1822-1831, and their discovery of the central route from the Missouri River to the Pacific Ocean. Smith is the central character, but there is also an emphasis upon his companions, among them Ashley and Henry, builders of the fur industry, and the trapper Hugh Glass.

Man of the Forest by Zane Grey. Harper and Brothers, 1920. In 1920 this Zane Grey mountain man story was the number one best seller. Set in Arizona's Tonto Basin, Grey's familiar themes—survival of the fittest, the balance of nature, and self-preservation—are all present.

Lige Mounts: Free Trapper by Frank Bird Linderman. Charles Scribner's Sons, 1922. In 1822 Elijah Mounts, barely eighteen, shouldered his rifle and walked from his uncle's Missouri farm to Saint Louis to seek his fortune in the fur trade. Linderman's novel is a first-person account, based on a true story and his own trapping experience, of a young man's coming of age among the trappers and Indians in remote Montana.

The Long Rifle by Stewart Edward White. Doubleday, Page, 1923. In 1822 young Andy Burnett left St. Louis, carrying Daniel Boone's long rifle, to make his way across the plains and the Great Divide, eventually to the far side of the Sierras. The first of the *Andy Burnett* series.

Buckskin Brigade by L. Ron Hubbard. Macaulay, 1937. This is an historical adventure loosely based on two entries in the journals of Lewis and Clark referencing a Blackfeet Indian chief who was killed in an encounter with the expedition, and an unnamed white man who was living with the Blackfeet a few miles away.

The Forbidden Ground by Neil H. Swanson. Rinehart, 1938. Set in 1778, this is a story of the fight for the rich fur empire of the American Northwest.

The Big Sky by A. B. Guthrie, Jr. William Sloan, 1947. This mountain man story follows Boone Caudill in 1830 from Kentucky to the wilderness country of the West, where he mastered the skills needed for survival in a hard and savage land. Voted by the Western Writers of America in 1995 the Best Western Novel of All Time. Basis for the 1952 film.

Johnny Christmas by Forrester Blake. William Morrow, 1948. A novel about mountain men set in the 1830s and 1840s on the plains of Texas, the central Rocky Mountains of northern New Mexico and southern Colorado, and the Spanish Trail to California that introduces Blake's mountain man, Johnny Christmas.

Song Before Sunrise by Jonreed Lauritzin. Doubleday, 1948. Set in Acoma, Santa Fe, Canyon de Chelly, and the remote tributaries of the Colorado, this is a tale of a mystical romance between a mountain man and a Spanish-Navajo girl in the time of the Santa Fe trade a century ago.

Wilderness Passage by Forrester Blake. Random House, 1953. Johnny Christmas was a Mountain Man who despised the invasion of his wilderness homeland by the Mormons. That is, until he met the tall, fair-haired wife of the Mormon leader. His love for her nearly lost him the freedom he prized more than life.

Lord Grizzly by Frederick Manfred. McGraw-Hill, 1954. When Hugh Glass was mauled by a grizzly bear and left for dead, he was no longer just a mountain man—he was Lord Grizzly. Deserted by his companions, he lived to crawl an incredible 300 miles to Fort Kiowa on the Missouri River. Then he began his search for the two people who had been left to bury him, but instead had abandoned him.

Pemmican by Vardis Fisher. Doubleday, 1956. In Hudson Bay territory in 1815, rival trading companies were engaged in a deadly feud for trading rights, and Indians were scalping any white man in sight. Against this background, a young trader for the Hudson's Bay Company faced numerous hazards in pursuit of his livelihood.

Yellowstone Kelly by Clay Fisher (Henry Wilson Allen). Houghton Mifflin, 1957. Luther Sage Kelly, of the Yellowstone Valley, was a true legend. Here he searches for Crow Girl, his Absaroka mate, and for her Hunkpapa Sioux captor. Basis for the 1959 film.

Crow Killer by Raymond W. Thorp and Robert Bunker. Indiana University Press, 1958. Mountain man Jeremiah Johnson, who one day discovered his Indian wife and unborn baby murdered by a marauding band of Crow braves, swore revenge upon the entire Crow nation. This is the story of that terrible vengeance. Partial basis for the 1972 film "Jeremiah Johnson."

Tale of Valor by Vardis Fisher. Doubleday, 1958. Fisher's rendering of the Lewis and Clark expedition, told from the viewpoint of each of the principals.

Trask by Don Berry. Viking Press, 1960. Elbridge Trask was a mountain man restlessly seeking a new land to settle. In 1848 the Oregon Coast beckoned. Trask was a restless man and, yearning for change, set out with a young Clatsop Indian and an Indian spiritual leader of the tribe on an extraordinary journey of discovery.

Moontrap by Don Berry. Viking Press, 1962. In 1850 three mountain men—Johnson Monday, Elbridge Trask and Solomon Smith—settled in Oregon's Willamette Valley and become a part of the established community. Old Webb, one of the last of the mountain men, came to the valley to visit his old friends, the companions of his best years. But a personal tragedy of his friend Monday, the changes brought about by civilization, and the hostility of the community violated his sense of justice, and drove him to murder. Spur Award from Western Writers of America.

Follow the Free Wind by Leigh Brackett. Doubleday, 1963. A fictional account of James Beckwourth, the part-black mountain man who led an adventurous life and became a legend on the frontier. Spur Award from Western Writers of America.

Mountain Man by Vardis Fisher. William Morrow, 1965. Subtitled *A Novel of Male and Female in the Early American West.* Based on the actual "Crow Killer" John Johnson, Sam Minard was a mountain man who returned from his traplines one day to find his Flathead Indian wife and unborn child brutally slain. From then on, only vengeance filled his days. Partial basis for the 1972 film "Jeremiah Johnson." National Cowboy and Western Heritage Museum Western Heritage Award. Spur Award winner.

The Great Adventure by Janice Holt Giles. Houghton Mifflin, 1967. By twenty-nine, Joe Fowler was an old-timer among the mountain men who dared the vast wilderness of the Rockies long before the settlers followed. He came west seeking the solitude of the mountains, and to test himself against the hostile Indians and nature.

Give Your Heart to the Hawks: A Tribute to the Mountain Man by Win Blevins. Nash Publishing, 1973. Jim Bridger, Jedediah Smith, James Beckwourth, and Kit Carson are among the legendary mountain men who are in this tribute to their extraordinary way of life.

Charbonneau: Man of Two Dreams by Win Blevins. Nash Publishing, 1975. Jean Baptiste Charbonneau, born in 1805, was the son of French-Canadian fur trapper Touissant Charbonneau and Sacajawea, the young Shoshone who guided the Lewis and Clark Expedition. This is the strange story of how he lived in two cultures, mastered them both, and ultimately was forced to choose between them.

Bloody Hand by Matt Braun. Popular Library, 1975. Jim Beckwourth was born a slave and became a mountain man, living among the Crow Indians in the Wind River Mountains. There he became Bloody Hand, sworn to take a hundred scalps, and become the People's greatest warrior.

Sacajawea by Anna Lee Waldo. Avon Books, 1979. Sacajawea, a young Shoshone Indian woman, won a place in history as the guide for the Lewis and Clark Expedition. This voluminous novel is her story.

The Medicine Calf by Bill Hotchkiss. W. W. Norton, 1981. This novel is based on the life of James Beckwourth, a mulatto mountain man who was captured by the Crow and became one of them. They gave him the name Medicine Calf and he took many wives—as many as eighteen by some counts.

Lewis and Clark: Northwest Glory by James Raymond. Dell, 1981. This novel follows Lewis and Clark and their small band of young American soldiers as they explore the uncharted land of the Northwest.

Fair Land, Fair Land by A. B. Guthrie, Jr. Houghton Mifflin, 1982. The final book in Guthrie's *Big Sky* series, following *The Big Sky* (William Sloan, 1947) and *The Way West* (Houghton Mifflin, 1952). In the mid-1800s, mountain man Dick Summers became disenchanted with the Oregon to which he led a wagon train in *The Way West*. He relocated in what is now Montana, became a discerning conservationist, and sought retribution from his former companion Boone Caudill and companionship with Teal Eye, both from *The Big Sky*.

Carry the Wind by Terry C. Johnston. Jameson Books, 1982. Set in the Grand Tetons, this is the first volume in Johnston's trilogy of trappers and mountain men, Indian fighters, and hardy pioneers.

Valley Men: A Speculative Account of the Arkansas Expedition of 1807 by Donald Taylor. Ticknor & Fields, 1983. A fictional account of an expedition from Natchez up the Arkansas River in 1807. The author based his story on a planned expedition that was canceled, and used the actual cast of characters involved.

From Sea to Shining Sea by James Alexander Thom. Ballantine Books, 1984. In one generation, the Clark family of Virginia fought for our nation's independence, and explored, conquered, and settled the continent from sea to shining sea. This novel recreates their contributions to America, including the Lewis and Clark Expedition.

Streams to the River, River to the Sea by Scott O'Dell. Houghton Mifflin, 1986. The story of the Lewis and Clark Expedition, narrated by their guide Sacajawea. The novel also covers her adventurous life before and after the epic journey. A young reader's novel.

Winter of the Wolf by Jory Sherman. Walker, 1987. For young readers. A mountain man who has been accepted by the Arapaho helps rescue three girls kidnapped by the Indians.

The Yellowstone by Win Blevins. Bantam Books, 1988. From Bantam Books's *Rivers West* series. In 1841, young Robert Burns Maclean became separated from his fellow trappers. He discovered the wonders of the Yellowstone River, its country and its inhabitants. His love affair with the Yellowstone dominated the rest of his life.

Trail by Louis Charbonneau. Doubleday, 1989. President Thomas Jefferson's vision was to explore the vast land west the Mississippi, a wilderness virtually unknown to the white man. The Lewis and Clark Expedition brought his vision to fruition.

Yellowstone by Richard S. Wheeler. Tor Books, 1990. From Wheeler's *Barnaby Skye* series. Yellowstone was wild, untamed country. Barnaby Skye and his Indian wives knew the dangers of that land, and its rules of survival. When Skye hired out to an English lord who wanted to kill buffalo, there was a deadly clash of wills when the Englishman refused to abide by the land's rules.

Buckskins by Albert Booky. Sunstone Press, 1991. A young Virginian adventurer teams up with an older French Canadian trapper in the 1800s and learns the ways of the mountain man. They become guides to the Wyandot Indian nation in its effort to relocate west of the Mississippi, lend assistance to three mountain men who are trapped by the Comanches, and have other adventures that test their survival skills before they settle in the Jicarilla Mountain area and establish a ranch.

The First Mountain Man by William W. Johnstone. Pinnacle Books, 1991. He had come west to the Rockies as a runaway twelve-year-old and grown into a legendary mountain man. Now all he wanted was some companionship at the annual mountain man rendezvous in Popo Agie. But his plans changed for the worse when he rode into Fort Hall and agreed to lead a train of sixty wagons on the last leg of a journey to Oregon.

Wilderness by R. Zelazny and G. Hausman. Tor Books, 1994. John Colter and Hugh Glass survived endless physical torture in the early 19th century in the harsh environment surrounding Yellowstone National Park.

War at Bent's Fort by John Legg. St. Martin's Press, 1994. From St. Martin's *Forts of Freedom* series. In 1833, William and Charles Bent built a trading empire around their adobe-walled fort on the Arkansas River. But then they were caught up in a tragic frontier war that would take one brother's life.

Grand Canyon by Gary McCarthy. Pinnacle Books, 1996. In 1869 John Wesley Powell led a historic expedition down the Colorado River through the Grand Canyon. Seeking his fortune on Powell's epic expedition, William Dunn found short-lived happiness with a beautiful half-Havasupai woman and a perilous career as a rancher and champion of American Indian rights.

Meridian: A Novel of Kit Carson's West by Norman Zollinger. Forge, 1997. Set in the turbulent 1840s, at the time of America's war with Mexico, *Meridian* is based on the exploits of two of the legends of westward expansion: the scout and guide Kit Carson and the explorer John Charles Frémont. The conquest of the vast lands of New Mexico and the province of California by Frémont, Carson, and their band of soldiers and mountain men is recounted.

Mountain Passage by Jason Manning. Signet, 1998. The promise of a new life drew Gordon Hawkes from Ireland to the American frontier. Befriended by a Scots adventurer, Hawkes set off on an excursion into the wilderness. But trouble had a way of following him. Accused of murder in New Orleans and chased by bounty hunters in St. Louis, he was faced with a test of survival. Only in the rugged mountains of the American West did he find his calling.

Yellowstone by Gary McCarthy. Pinnacle Books, 1998. From McCarthy's *National Parks* series. Yellowstone was a mythical land seeded with gold to the California frontiersmen. To the tribes that called it home, it was an unspoiled, sacred ground. Then the pioneers broke through the mountains and plundered it.

Death Rattle by Terry C. Johnston. Bantam Books, 1999. From Johnston's *Titus Bass* series. The beaver trade was ending and mountain man and trapper Titus Bass had to find a new way of making a living. He joined an expedition to Spanish California where they stole horses and mules and drove them back across the Mojave Desert to sell to fur traders. Along the way Titus began to feel his age. Was this his death rattle?

River Walk: A Frontier Story by Rita Cleary. Five Star, 2000. The plot of *River Walk* is based on the Lewis and Clark Expedition. The author attempts to recreate historical figures as they might actually have been. To the entries in the journals of Lewis, Clark, Charles Floyd, John Ordway, Joseph Whitehouse, and Patrick Gass, Cleary adds dialogue and emotion, turning historical facts into drama.

Sign-Talker: The Adventure of George Drouillard on the Lewis and Clark Expedition by James Alexander Thom. Ballantine Books, 2000. A recounting of the Lewis and Clark Expedition (1804-1806), as seen through the eyes of George Drouillard, a half-Shawnee, half-French hunter hired by Lewis and Clark as the first interpreter for their expedition. Drouillard had contempt for the whites because of, among other things, their materialism. But he admired the Indians, sensing a nobility in their character.

Corps of Discovery by Jeffrey W. Tenney. iUniverse, 2002. Under the leadership of Meriwether Lewis and William Clark, the Corps of Discovery crossed the unexplored Louisiana Territory by way of the treacherous Missouri River, then continued on foot into and beyond the Rocky Mountains. Many of the soldiers looked on the expedition as an opportunity to have a grand time, but instead found there were rules to follow and stern discipline.

The Last Canyon by John Vernon. Houghton Mifflin, 2002. When John Wesley Powell set out to run the Colorado River in 1869, he embarked upon the last great journey of exploration on the North American continent. Vernon's novel addresses the quality of Powell's leadership and the scale of his heroism.

So Wild a Dream by Win Blevins. Forge, 2003. The first in Blevins' *Rendezvous* series, this novel is about Sam Morgan, who traveled to the West from Pennsylvania. In 1822, he joined the fur trade with a brigade of fur trappers to complete the first phase of his mountain man education. Spur Award from Western Writers of America.

I Should Be Extremely Happy in Your Company by Brian Hall. Viking Press, 2004. A narrative of the Lewis and Clark Expedition, told from four points of view: Meriwether Lewis, William Clark, Sacajawea, and Toussaint Charbonneau, Sacajawea's French fur trader husband. Spur Award from Western Writers of America.

Love On the Lewis and Clark Trail by Pat Decker Nipper. Syringa Books, 2004. Focusing on Idaho and the expedition's extended stay with the Nez Percé, Nipper blends fact and fiction to tell a story of William Clark's romance with an Indian woman named Tom-sis, translated as Wild Rose.

Dancing with the Golden Bear by Win Blevins. Forge, 2005. From Blevin's *Rendezvous* series. Jedediah Smith planned to explore California, which at that time was still part of Mexico, in search of new country for fur trappers. Sam Morgan and his Crow Indian wife joined Smith's brigade of fur trappers. But when they arrived in California, the Mexican government suspected they were spies for the Americans, and the brigade had to flee.

SELECTED REVIEWS

The Gates of the Mountains
by Will Henry
Random House, 1963

Frank Rivet of La Charrette is listed among the crew of French boatmen of the Lewis and Clark Expedition. His name disappeared from the middle pages of the journal. What happened to him between Fort Mandan and the Pacific? *The Gates of the Mountains* is Will Henry's fictional account of Frank Rivet's adventure, within the historical context of the monumental exploration.

The Lewis and Clark Expedition of 1804-1806 occurred only two decades after the Declaration of Independence. It took their party twenty-eight months to make the trip from St. Louis up the Missouri River, along the edges of today's Kansas, Nebraska, Iowa, through North and South Dakota, across Montana and Idaho, down the Columbia River between Washington and Oregon to the Pacific, then to return, crossing the Rockies, exploring the Marias River to the north and the Yellowstone to the south. They transversed an awesome and dangerous wilderness. They fought the violent, unpredictable

Missouri River. They crossed the bitter-cold Rocky Mountains and navigated the mighty Columbia River. They had to contend with curious, sometimes hostile, Indians. They had to conquer a wilderness.

Henry's Frank Rivet was the son of Achille Rivet, a riverman who had been captured years before by the Shoshone, and the Pawnee woman Antelope, daughter of the Chief, Lame Horse. Frank was young and brash and brave, a skilled riverman in his own right, who joined the expedition for the adventure and with hopes of finding his father. He was liked and championed by Captain Clark, but distrusted by Captain Lewis.

Captain William Clark was a tough looking man, with flaming red hair, the younger brother of Revolutionary War hero George Rogers Clark. He was promised a Captaincy by President Jefferson but was still a Lieutenant. Lewis addressed him as Captain and treated him as an equal, but Clark considered Lewis the Commander. Clark believed if you stood hard and fast with the Indians, they'd never harm you.

Captain Meriwether Lewis was President Jefferson's private secretary. He had an oval face, a small mouth, and a long and slender nose. He was neither handsome nor attractive. Frank could never tell whether Lewis was amused or annoyed. The Indians didn't like Lewis as they did Clark, and Lewis couldn't handle them nearly so well in most cases. But Henry tells us that " . . . in battle pose, in outright hostile confrontation, [Lewis] was, if possible, even more effective than Clark. The difference with the Indians was the contraposition of fear and affection. Clark liked them, Lewis did not; the red brother understood this distinction keenly."

Within the context of the expedition, Frank's love for the Indian girl Sacajawea is the basic plot. Sacajawea was Shoshone. She had been captured by the Minnetarees "five winters gone" as a small girl of eleven. Toussaint Charbonneau, hired by Lewis and Clark as an interpreter for the Minnatarees, had purchased her for five winter-thin ponies and a rusted gun. Charbonneau sent for Sacajawea when he learned the captains sought an interpreter for the Shoshone language. Frank was infatuated from the moment he first saw her:

How may one tell of Sacajawea, or Birdwoman, as the Shoshones translated her name? She was no more than a girl when we first saw her, sixteen summers Charbonneau said, and she was swollen big with the seventh month of her pregnancy. Yet when she came up the bank of the river to stand before Clark and myself at the construction site, and to murmur in her low voice, "I am Sacajewa, my chiefs, the younger wife of Charbonneau," I loved her. When she raised her eyes and looked at me, my heart stopped beating.

Captain Lewis wasn't as impressed. His journal said that Sacajawea showed no signs of distress when recalling her captivity, nor any joy at the prospect of being restored to her country, for "she seems to possess the folly or the philosophy of not suffering her feeling to extend beyond the anxiety of having plenty to eat and a few trinkets to wear."

Frank's friend Captain Clark wanted him to understand the differences between the cultures of the Indian and the white man:

I was shown a Sacajawea that August night over the Goatpen Creek campfire of old Toussaint Charbonneau that I had never seen. Clark had wanted me to see an Indian woman, as she was . . . I saw her begin the evening by killing a fat, friendly puppy, with which I had seen both her and her button-eyed infant laughing and playing that same noonhalt. She seized the squealing mongrel by its hind legs and knocked out its brains against the nearest cottonwood sapling, and dropped it, still jerking, into the kettle of hot stones and steaming water where it would boil, ungutted and unskinned, for our supper.

Henry provides great detail on the Indian cultures encountered by the expedition. Of the Mandans, he wrote that they fell short of what Clark's imagination had pictured. They weren't as tall nor as strong looking as the Teton Sioux, and not nearly as good looking as the Rees. But the Mandan were intelligent and had lively dispositions, and were fundamentally friendly. "And their women, if less comely than those of the Arikara, were no less amorous." The men were easy to talk with, and "one felt immediately that these were civilized Indians and, indeed, civilized men."

Of the Shoshone, he observed that they were a male society. A man purchased or disposed of his women as it pleased him. Male children were seldom corrected and never punished. The girls were less favored, though both sexes were unspeakably spoiled.

Up the Missouri there were wondrous place names: Cheyenne River, Bad River, Grand Detour, Knife River, Land of the Mandan, White Earth, Big Muddy, Bear Paws, Musselshell, Little Manitou, Yellowstone, Prairie of Arrows, Sand Island, Vermilion River, Spirit Mound. There were also magnificent Indian tribal names: Omahas, Poncas, Loups, Pawnees, Sauks, Kaws, Arikaris, Sioux, Mandans, Minnetarees, Gros Ventres, Blackfeet, Bloods, Snakes, Flatheads, Crows. They are all captured in Henry's story.

Will Henry, born Henry Wilson Allen, was a prolific Western writer. He also wrote under the name Clay Fisher. Eight of his 53 novels became motion pictures, and several have won top literary awards, including the coveted Spur Award from the Western Writers of America. *The Gates of the Mountains* stands as one of the best fictional renderings of the fabled Lewis and Clark Expedition.

Wolf Song
by Harvey Fergusson
Alfred A. Knopf, 1927

The mountain man has been celebrated in fiction in such classics as Stewart Edward White's *The Long Rifle* (Doubleday, Doran, 1932), A. B. Guthrie's *The Big Sky* (William Sloan, 1947), Frederick Manfred's *Lord Grizzly* (McGraw-Hill, 1954), and Vardis Fisher's *Mountain Man* (William Morrow, 1965). Harvey Fergusson's *Wolf Song* ranks high in this prestigious list, and is the most lyrical of all the mountain man novels. Consider the opening paragraph:

> Up from the edge of the prairie and over the range rode three. Their
> buckskin was black with blood and shiny from much wiping of
> greasy knives and nearly all the fringes had been cut off their pants
> for thongs. Hair hung thick and dirty to their shoulders. Traps rattled

in rucksacks behind their Spanish saddles and across the pommel each carried a long Hawkins rifle of shining brassbound steel and battered wood stock. Six pack mules bulged with square bales of beaver worth eight dollars a pound in St. Louis and six in the mountains.

One of the three trappers was Sam Lash.

He was a restless a young man reared on a farm in Tennessee. When he had saved a hundred dollars from his first job, Sam headed west to St. Louis. He bought a heavy Hawkins rifle, hired on to a wagon train and wound up in Taos, in what is now New Mexico.

He joined a party of twenty men who were headed for Mexican terriory to trap beaver. At the Rio Grande below Socorro, beaver sign was everywhere. Sam Lash learned to read sign, anchor and bait a trap, set a float stick, and flesh and stretch a pelt.

They summered in the White Mountains, where Sam proved himself. He fought and held his own, hunted and brought in more than his share of meat, learned to track like an Indian, and to plant a ball in his target. He made himself a buckskin shirt and pants, and became a mountain man.

And he fell under the spell of the mountains. He enjoyed the fellowship of his fellow mountain men, hunting and fighting together, and sitting around fires swapping yarns. And he knew the excitement of their annual trip to Taos.

All mountain men, sooner or later, came to Taos. They came from as far north as the Red and as far south as the Gila. Taos whiskey and Taos women were known and talked about on every beaver stream in the Rockies. The town "smelled of dust, horses, and wine, but in the evening it tinkled with hidden music and pattered softly in a strange tongue." In the great sprawling houses where the wealthy Mexicans, or *ricos*, lived, Sam glimpsed pretty women and Indian slaves, and smelled meat, chocolate and wine. He saw men with tall hats and silver spurs ride out on fine horses. They rode arrogantly and did not look at him. It was in Taos that Sam Lash met Lola Salazar.

Don Solomon Salazar, Lola's father, was the most prominent *rico* in Taos. A half a century before, when the Comanche wiped out the first settlement of Taos, a few survivors got to Mexico City. These survivors returned and built the walled town. When the Comanche came again, they were all but annihilated. Don Solomon's father was among those who defeated them.

Along the Rio Grande from Taos to El Paso the Mexicans were in power. The young men had nothing to fight, and were getting fat and lazy. Then the gringos came, trapping beaver in all the Mexican streams against Mexican law. Then they gave *bailes*, or parties, got drunk and danced with the women. Don Solomon detested the gringos.

His daughter Lola was betrothed to Ambrosio Guiterrez, a *rico* who loved horses and women. He was often seen riding lordly among the peons on his prancing sorrel mare, ordering them about. He could have any of the women in Taos except the unmarried daughters of the first families, who were denied to him except in marriage. He had chosen the most beautiful of these to be his wife.

Lola was restless and not looking forward to a life with Ambrosia. He was free to roam while she was bound within four walls. It would be the same when she was married. If she took lovers, he would punish her. He might even cut off her ears. No man ever lost his ears. So when the mountain men rode into Taos, Lola Salazar silently picked Sam Lash as hers. "He was dirty, but he could be washed and his skin would be so white and his hair so golden."

The mountain men held a *baile* and the town came. All kind of women were there, and each wore the best she had. Lola danced with Sam, and she felt to him as fragile as a basket of eggs. She was "gorgeous in a white skirt worked with red and yellow flowers, a silk bodice trimmed with lace and a red and black mantilla over one shoulder. A red paper rose was stuck in her heavy black hair behind one ear." He told Lola if she "ever wanted a fool gringo, she could have him."

Lola later slipped away from her father's house and left with Sam. The mountain men covered their departure. She was afraid to go, but more afraid to be held back by her familiar surroundings. She belonged to the gringo "solely because his hand upon her had stirred her as had no other."

From this point on, *Wolf Song* is a love story—or rather, a story of divided love. Sam was in love with the mountains, and in love with a woman. He quickly learned that "everything that binds a man down goes with a woman." His friend and fellow mountain man Old Rube Thatcher told him if he craved a woman he should buy a squaw who would follow him wherever he chose to go. Rube asked, "What kin a man do with a Mexican woman but set and watch her or go off and leave her?"

The plot revolves around this conflict, but also dwells on the contact between the Anglo-Americans and the Spanish-Americans. While the Indians play a part in Fergusson's novels (there's a deadly duel between Sam Lash and a Cheyenne warrior in *Wolf Song*), his major interest was Anglo-Spanish relations. Their contact provides the theme and drama for most of his work.

Unfortunately, the novel is racist; Mexican and Mexican-American readers will be offended. The dialogue can be excused because it reflects the attitudes of the times. But the third person narration and the author's exposition contain racial slurs that are deeply repugnant.

The historical period that held Fergusson's interest began with the mountain men in Taos and Santa Fe and continued through the breakup of the large Spanish Land Grants. In 1936 his first three novels—*Wolf Song, In Those Days* (Alfred A. Knopf, 1929), and *The Blood of Conquerors* (Alfred A. Knopf, 1921)—were published in one volume as *Followers of the Sun: A Trilogy of the Santa Fe Trail* (Alfred A. Knopf, 1936). The three stories cover almost one hundred years, from the days of the mountain man to the decay of an old Spanish family in Albuquerque.

Fergusson's style is remarkably lyric, with simple but effective images: "They [trout that Sam Lash caught] fell flopping in the grass and danced themselves to death." The deft use of dialect adds texture and local color to the novel: "Hump yourself, you goddam mule! This chile's half froze for liquor! . . . This outfit's bound for Taos!" And Fergusson believed that knowledge of the land is of prime importance to a writer. He said he couldn't write about people if he had never seen the land they lived on: "They had trapped up the South Platte in the fall when cottonwoods was yellow in the bottoms and cold winds blew swarming wildfowl out of the north and early snow tipped blue mountains white." In *Rio Grande* (Alfred A. Knopf, 1933), he wrote "The character of a country is the destiny of its people."

In 1929 Paramount made *Wolf Song* into a popular motion picture starring Gary Cooper and Lupe Velez. It was produced and directed by Victor Fleming.

In his *Guide to Life and Literature of the Southwest* (Southern Methodist University Press, 1952), J. Frank Dobie wrote, "The characters in Harvey Fergusson's *Wolf Song* (1927) are the Mountain Men of Kit Carson's time, and the city of their soul is rollicky Taos. It is a lusty, swift song of the pristine earth." Well said.

Dream West
by David Nevin
G.P. Putnam's Sons, 1983

John Charles Frémont's place in American history is a subject of debate. But there can be no question that he led an adventurous, eventful life: explorer, governor of California, U. S. senator from California, the first Republican candidate for president, Civil War general, terriitoral governor of Arizona—an ideal subject for exciting historical fiction.

Frémont was brilliant, egoistical, unpredictable. He was a man of action; he once told his wife Jesse:

> You might as well know how I am. Truth is, I don't always think
> a great deal about what I do. If it seems a good thing to do, likely
> I'll do it. Lots of situations, you know, don't give you much time to
> think. If you're going to do it, you've got to move fast. Or the chance
> vanishes. That's how I am. I get a feeling about it and I move . . .
> You get to questioning everything you do—and you wind up doing
> nothing.

This philosophy generally served him well and led to his many accomplishments, but it also caused him to tarnish his reputation.

Dream West, David Nevin's first novel, was inspired by his research for *Time-Life's Old West Books,* which convinced him Frémont wasn't the foolish, vain man he was so often described as. Nevin decided to present a better picture, using the broad canvas of an historical novel.

Frémont is best known for his exploring expeditions. Along with Lewis and Clark, Zebulon Pike, and Stephen Harriman Long, he was one of the most prominent of the American explorers in the decade prior to the Civil War. As an officer in the Army's elite Topographical Corps, he led three expeditions west to map the Oregon Trail and to find a direct route to California.

To map the Oregon Trail, Frémont hired Kit Carson as his guide, and they developed a lifelong friendship. Carson was Scotch-Irish, a man of cool temperament and good judgment; he seemed to have been everywhere and to know everyone in the mountains.

In five hard months the expedition traveled to South Pass, the great entryway to the Rocky Mountains, and returned to St. Louis. South Pass was a great swale in the mountains, so wide, Frémont was told, that you couldn't be sure you were there until you found the streams running west.

The second expedition, made up of forty men, mapped the Oregon Trail from South Pass through the dangerous Blackfoot country to the Snake River and down the Columbia to Fort Vancouver, the Hudson's Bay Post. Frémont's mission was complete when he reached Fort Vancouver, but he continued, without any official orders, down along the south flank of the Cascades. The lure of California was strong.

> Folks said the Californios were lazy, but Carson had formed the
> opinion that they were just plain sensible. They worked as hard as
> necessary in a spot the creator had designed especially for good
> living, and the rest of the time they played—rodeos, horse races,
> turkey shoots, bear hunts, and at night, with wine flowing and
> lanterns lit, fandangos and bailes, where the guitars played and pretty
> girls spun their skirts in the air.

Frémont decided to cross the Sierras to Sutter's Fort, just east of Sacramento, against the advice of the experienced mountain men in the party: Carson, Alex Godey, Louie Freniere, and Tom "Broken Hand" Fitzpatrick. They didn't think it could be done in winter. The party left the Columbia with well over a hundred horses and mules. When they arrived at Sutter's Fort, most of the animals were dead, and they were down to one day's supply of mule meat. But Frémont had reached California.

Probably the greatest influence on Frémont's life was his wife Jesse, the daughter of Senator Thomas Hart Benton of Missouri, the self-proclaimed father of *Manifest Destiny* and a Frémont booster. But it was Jesse who ensured Frémont's success and popularity.

Jesse had a flair for rich, evocative prose. The report on the first expedition, dictated by Frémont and written and polished by Jesse, was a promotional masterpiece for westward expansion. The report on the second expedition made an even greater stir. Frémont became the national symbol for Manifest Destiny.

The third expedition was to map a more direct route to California. While in California, Frémont and his men became involved in the 1845 Bear Flag Rebellion—a revolt against Mexican authority by a small group of Americans. The extent of his involvement and the reasons for it are not well understood, but Nevin lays it out clearly—from Frémont's viewpoint. Then a colonel, Frémont was appointed governor by Commodore Stockton, the U. S. Forces Commander. But he was arrested and sent back to Fort Leavenworth for court-martial by General Kearny, Stockton's successor. His transgressions, in Kearny's words, were:

> You broke your word to the Mexican authorities, you seized mounts and provisions from the Californios and paid for them with bogus promissory notes—above all you led an armed force onto foreign soil on the flimsy pretext of a scientific survey, instigated American settlers to rebel against Mexican authority, carried out a campaign of military conquest, and assumed control over all of Northern California without any official authority whatever.

Frémont was found guilty on all of the twenty-two charges brought against him. He was sentenced to be dismissed from the service. The president, on review of the court-martial, reversed the sentence. But Frémont, highly offended, resigned his commission.

His reputation as an explorer continued to grow, undamaged by the trial. The Royal Geographical Society in London awarded him its Founder's Medal for service to geography. Frémont secured private financing and, in

1848-49, tried to map a winter railroad route across the Rockies. Old Bill Williams was hired as guide and the expedition started into the Wet Mountains in late November. Eighteen days later they had used half their planned time, and supplies were dwindling. Bill Williams was lost, even though he wouldn't admit it. The expedition was a disaster and Frémont's reputation as an explorer was sullied.

His political career was as controversial as his western explorations. In 1856, the newly-formed Republican Party made him their first candidate for president. He was defeated in a vicious campaign by Democrat James Buchanan. In 1866, during the Civil War, President Lincoln appointed Frémont a Major General and gave him command of the Western Department. His Civil War record is not rated very high by most historians. He again resigned from the army in anger, and with Jesse returned to California.

When Rutherford B. Hayes was elected president, he appointed the old soldier governor of the Arizona Terriitory, primarily a ceremonial job that paid only $2,000 a year. But, at sixty-five, Frémont loved it. He was up at dawn, riding out with an army escort to explore the countryside. He held this post for five years. This seems a fitting end to the career of an adventurous man who galloped across the American scene, generating controversy wherever he went, and acting immediately in the national interest "if it seemed like a good thing to do."

In 1986, CBS aired a seven-hour miniseries based on Nevin's book, under the same title. Frémont was ably portrayed by Richard Chamberlain, supported by Alice Krige as his wife Jesse. Rip Torn turned in an outstanding performance as Kit Carson. The script closely followed the novel, even the dialogue, and the result is a sweeping, beautifully filmed slice of Western history.

Whatever Frémont's faults in other respects, the testimony of Kit Carson in his autobiography (1826) goes far to establish his reputation as a superb leader of men:

> I was with Frémont from 1842 to 1847. I find it impossible to
> describe the hardships through which we passed, nor am I capable
> of doing justice to the credit which he deserves. But his services to his

country have been left to impartial freemen, and all agree in saying that they were great, and have redounded to his honor, and to that of his country. I can never forget . . . how cheerfully he suffered with his men when undergoing the severest of hardships . . . and I say . . . that no one but he could have surmounted so many obstacles, and have succeeded in so many difficult services.

2

Wagons West!

Introduction

The expression "Manifest Destiny," used to justify U. S. terriorial expansion, came into use in 1845 when a New York edior, John L. O'Sullivan, wrote that it was "the fulfillment of our manifest destiny to overspread the continent allotted by Providence for the free development of our yearly expanding millions." The term was used to justify the Mexican War (1846-48), the Alaska Purchase (1867), and the Spanish-American War (1898)—all of which resulted in huge territorial gains for the United States.

In 1842, John Charles Frémont's first expedition west mapped the Oregon Trail to South Pass, which cuts its way through the Continental Divide at the southern end of the Wind River Mountains in Wyoming. The pass offered an easy traversable route between the Great Plains and California and the Southwest. Frémont's report on the expedition, published in bulk and widely distributed, was a promotional masterpiece for westward expansion. The report on the second expedition, mapping a route from South Pass to Fort Vancouver (in what is now Washington), made an even greater stir. Frémont became the national symbol for Manifest Destiny. The westward trek began in earnest.

During the 1840s and 1850s the Oregon Trail, which stretched about 2,000 miles from Independence, Missouri to Fort Vancouver, carried thousands of American pioneers to the rich farmland of the Willamette Valley in the Oregon country. Other routes west used by the pioneers and merchants were the California Trail, an offshoot of the Oregon that crossed the Sierras and ended in Sacramento; the Mormon Trail to Salt Lake City; and the Santa Fe Trail, a traders' route to Santa Fe that linked up with two southern California routes, the Gila River Trail and the Old Spanish Trail. By 1869, the year the first transcontinental railroad was completed, at least 350,000 emigrants had plodded along just the Oregon Trail.

Pioneer journals, many written by women who made the trip, accurately recorded the trials and tribulations of those historic journeys. They provide an abundant source for historical fiction. The two novels I have chosen to review are A. B. Guthrie's Pulitzer Prize winning *The Way West* (Houghton Mifflin, 1952), a story of an Oregon Trail journey, and Ernest Haycox's *The Earthbreakers* (Little, Brown, 1952), which begins at the end of the Oregon Trail and follows a group of settlers to the rich Willamette Valley of Oregon.

The California Gold Rush of 1849 also lured thousands west over the wagon trails. Novels based on their experiences are included in Chapter 10, Wealth of the West.

READER'S GUIDE

The Prairie by James Fenimore Cooper. Carey, 1827. This is the final chapter in Cooper's *Leatherstocking Tales*, the saga of frontiersman Natty Bumppo, and the only one set in the West. Here the aging hero journeys westward seeking to end his days on the Great Plains, which is still a wilderness. But he becomes involved with an emigrant party, and once more finds himself in confrontation with civilization.

The Covered Wagon by Emerson Hough. D. Appleton, 1922. In this classic novel of the trek west, an 1884 overland caravan of settlers fights its way through hostile Indians en route to Oregon. There are two major battles with the Sioux and with the Crow. Mountain men Bill Jackson, Jim Bridger, Kit Carson, and Caleb Greenwood appear in the story.

On to Oregon! by Honoré Willsie Morrow. William Morrow, 1926. The best-selling children's author Honoré Morrow and her husband founded William

Morrow & Company in 1926 and this was the company's first published title. It is a young readers' novel set in 1848, in which a thirteen-year-old boy, against almost impossible odds, takes his parents' place after they die on the trail and leads his orphaned brother and sisters from Missouri to Oregon. Later reprinted as *Seven Alone* and basis for the 1974 film with that title.

The Land Is Bright by Archie Binns. Charles Scribner's Sons, 1939. The story of a wagon train crossing to the Pacific Northwest on the Oregon Trail in the 1850s.

The Mothers: An American Saga of Courage by Vardis Fisher. Vanguard, 1943. The story of the ill-fated Donner Party and their tragic experiences crossing the Sierra Nevada in 1846-47, narrated from the point of view of the mothers in the group.

Bend of the Snake by Bill Gulick. Houghton Mifflin, 1950. A group of early settlers face great hardships as they travel by wagon train through the American wilderness in an attempt to get to the Oregon Territory. Basis for the 1952 film "Bend of the River."

The Wheel and the Hearth By Lucia Moore. Ballantine Books, 1953. An historical novel about women who came over the Oregon Trail in 1847. Spur Award from Western Writers of America.

Journey by the River by John Prescott. Random House, 1954. Mountain man Aaron Davis leads a wagon train across the Oregon Trail westward toward the Rockies and the Oregon frontier. Spur Award from Western Writers of America.

Winter Harvest by Norah Lofts. Doubleday, 1955. This novel is based on the experiences of the Donner Party, a group of settlers who set out for California in 1846 and met a terrible fate in the Sierra Nevada.

Westering by Irwin R. Blacker. World Publishing, 1958. The families of the covered wagons pushing toward Oregon faced starvation, Indians, and plague.

Voyage to Santa Fe by Janice Holt Giles. Houghton Mifflin, 1962. In the spring of 1823 Judith Fowler drove a team of mules hitched to a light wagon from the settled Arkansas Territory to Santa Fe, the only woman in her husband's wagon train. Johnny Fowler (sometimes known as "Johnny Osage" because of his close friendship with the Osage Indians) planned to make his fortune with the trade goods carried by his mule train.

The Ordways by William Humphrey. Alfred A. Knopf, 1964. The early Ordways came west from Tennessee to Texas, carrying the family tombstone and the bones of their forefathers. They lost a child fording the Red River because of the weight of the tombstone. They were a proud and tough family. Those who came later were just as proud and tough.

The Conestoga People by Jeannie Sommers. Dell, 1979. From Dell's *The Making of America* series. The largest wagon train ever to leave Independence heads west with an assortment of characters that includes a fool for a leader, an inexperienced chief scout, a murderer, a fourteen-year-old tart, a mulatto with a secret white lover, and a man who does not want the wagons to get through.

Bride of the Santa Fe Trail by Jean M. Burroughs. Sunstone Press, 1984. A novel based on Susan Shelby Magoffin's pioneer trip along the Santa Fe Trail in 1846. Magoffin was the first white woman to travel the Santa Fe Trail from Independence, Missouri, to Chihuahua, Mexico—a distance of 1,300 miles.

The Homesman by Glendon Swarthout. Weidenfeld, 1988. More properly categorized as "Wagons East!" When four women on the isolated frontier go mad, a "homesman" has to accompany them back East. Spur Award from Western Writers of America.

Kansas Blue: A Novel of the American West by Dylan Harson. Donald I. Fine, 1993. In the wake of the 1862 Homestead Act, a wagon train of settlers headed west from Fort Leavenworth, Kansas. They had to contend with storms, floods, and outlaws.

Survival: A Novel of the Donner Party by K. C. McKenna. Berkley, 1994. Originally published by Washington Catholic University of America in 1938. This historical novel is the story of a wagon train of people who in July of 1846 started for California, separated from a larger convoy of wagon trains, and took a new, untried route through the Sierras. Trapped by the weather in early November, they found themselves snowbound at the summit while within sight of the pass that they needed to cross, and faced by terrible hardships, some resorted to cannibalism in order to survive. Spur Award from Western Writers of America.

The Overland Trail by Wendy Lee. Forge, 1996. A novel based on the diaries of women who journeyed on the Overland Trail in the late 1840s.

Brides of Prairie Gold by Maggie Osborne. Warner Books, 1996. A wagon master used to transporting guns and whiskey found himself responsible for twelve mail-order brides on a harrowing wagon train journey from Missouri to Oregon.

The Journal of Callie Wade by Dawn Miller, Pocket Books, 1998. This novel is narrated as a series of journal entries and letters written by an 18-year-old Missouri farm girl recording her experiences on a wagon train bound for California in 1859.

Boone's Lick by Larry McMurtry. Simon and Schuster, 2000. The novel follows the Cecil family's arduous journey by riverboat and wagon from Boone's Lick, Missouri, to Fort Phil Kearny in Wyoming. Based on a actual family of 19th century traders and freighters, the plot centers on Mary Margaret Cecil's search for her elusive husband, Dick, to tell him she's leaving him. The search leads to the the discovery of his second and third families.

Snow Mountain Passage by James D. Houston. Alfred A. Knopf, 2001. This is the tragic story of the Donner Party, whose ill-fated journey from Springfield, Illinois, to California during the winter of 1846-1847 ended in cannibalism. James Frazier Reed, one of the leaders of the expedition, killed a man in self-defense and had to leave the party and his family and cross the Sierra Nevada alone. The novel presents a third-person account of Reed's travels as he crisscrosses California in search of a rescue party, and the recollections of his daughter, Patty, who lived through the snowbound nightmare.

A Sudden Country by Karen Fisher. Random House, 2005. An ancestor of the author, Emma Ruth Ross Slavin, was eleven when her family joined the 1847 Oregon migration. From the child's spare notes, Fisher constructed a novel of the westward trek that is centered on Emma's mother, Lucy Mitchell, and James McLaren, a Scottish trapper for the Hudson's Bay Company, whose stories converge on the trail to Oregon.

SELECTED REVIEWS

The Way West
by A. B. Guthrie, Jr.
Houghton Mifflin, 1952

A. B. Guthrie's epic western *The Way West* is historical fiction at its finest. Chronicling the journey of a group of pioneers from Independence, Missouri, to the Willamette Valley of Oregon in the mid-1800s, the Pulitzer Prize novel dramatically depicts their heroic adventure and the hardships they endured. It's an adventure the reader will remember long after he's read the book. As one of the novel's historical characters, mountain man Caleb Greenwood, put it: "Starvin' and thirstin' and nigh drownin' makes rich rememberin'."

Guthrie once remarked that the kind of fiction he was writing is about people: "It isn't event that is important, it is human and individual involvement in and response to event." *The Way West* is made memorable by Guthrie's use of multiple points of view to relate individual involvement. Each character who shares the experience with us has a particular reason for going to Oregon, as well as expectations, fears, regrets. Some are true pioneers; some are swept along by the true pioneers. But each adds a unique personal perspective to the story.

Lije Evans, an easy-going man with physical competence in his stout hands and big frame, told a friend: "No, I ain't been there [Oregon], but I've been here. I ain't satisfied just to work to keep myself up so's I can work some more. There ought to be more to livin' than that." Rebecca Evans went because Lije wanted to. She concluded Oregon was what Lije needed—and what their son Brownie would need later—a chance to find out what he amounted to. Mountain man Dick Summers, first introduced by Guthrie in *The Big Sky* (William Sloan, 1947), had said goodbye to the beaver country and came back to Missouri to farm. But the memories were vivid; he could see far off, beyond the long plains of the Platte, along the Green River that the trappers knew as the Seeds-kee-dee. These memories—and the urging of his friend Lije—

persuaded him to guide the wagon train west. Irvine Tadlock, elected Captain of the train, let himself believe that his obsession with getting to Oregon ahead of the rest was for the welfare of the company. Spindly-looking Henry McBee, a mean-spirited man who talked big to hide his littleness, was taking his brood to Oregon because he thought he might make it in "the promised land." The Fairmans hoped their frail son Tod would respond to the new country. Curtis Mack, out of frustration, brought his frigid wife west in hopes of a more satisfying marriage. The handyman Hig, "a long splinter of a man with a pinched face," went only because he "hankered to go." Brother Weatherby, itinerant preacher, tall and old, whose face showed weather and wear and was solemn with the weight of what he knew, went because he believed God had singled him out to spread the word. And so Guthrie gives us the opportunity to view this historic journey through the eyes of men, women, the young, the old, the strong, the weak, the good, and the not-so-good.

The wagons rendezvoused outside Independence, then moved west over the grasslands of what is now Kansas. Lije Evans watched the train from a gradual slope he had ascended:

> He could see the wagon train winding, the gray-white train
> squirming in its haze of dust. The time was coming on towards noon
> and the train had straggled out. Behind the wagons came the loose
> horses and behind the horses the cattle, with riders back of them and
> to the sides, keeping them in line and pushing them along. Out from
> the wagon, to the windward side so as to be out of the dust, women
> and children were walking . . .

Life on the trail was the story of an ever-more-difficult roadway, of failing supplies, of bone-wrenching weariness, of miseries of every sort. As the pioneers pushed overland, perhaps fifteen miles a day, every day brought a new obstacle to overcome:

> A storm came up that morning—a wretched, all-day rain that
> greased the ground and later soaked it, so that the rearward wagons
> floundered half-stuck in the mud. The rain was cold, slanted by a

chilly breeze. The drivers climbed up in the wagons to escape it and got colder yet for want of exercise and climbed back down and stomped along, their feet misshapen with the clinging mud. But they went on.

And then, there were the Indians.

Trouble with Indians was rare, but they did occasionally draw blood. Brownie Evans had an experience with them he would never forget. Only seventeen, still a boy, he stayed behind the wagon train to carve Mercy McBee's name on Independence Rock. When he descended the rock, he found himself in the midst of a band of Sioux. They were shouting and poking him when

> The shouting died away and the Indians' heads turned. It was Dick Summers like an answer to a prayer, old Dick Summers galloping his horse across the flat, riding straight as a drawn line, his uncovered hair silvery in the sun, Dick Summers not scared of an Indian or a nation.

Summers' rescue of Brownie is the most exciting episode in the novel; it's also the only hostile encounter the train has with Indians.

A newspaperman-turned-author, A. B. Guthrie wrote lean, straightforward prose. However, his metaphorical language, "A new wagon would jolt up from town, and women and young ones would blossom out of it," and his preference for conjunctions rather than commas, "Buffaloes and wolves and grasshoppers with no grass to hop on and rib bones and skulls lying around," give his writing an informal, pleasing tone.

During the heyday of Westerns in Hollywood, Guthrie wrote historical fiction of a believable West. *The Big Sky* launched his career in 1947, and *The Way West*, published in 1949, won the Pulitzer Prize for fiction in 1950. *The Big Sky*, *The Way West*, and *These Thousand Hills* (Houghton Mifflin, 1956) became movies; Guthrie disliked all of them. On viewing *The Way West*, released by United Artists in 1967, it's easy to understand why.

Director Andrew V. McLaglen's ambitious effort fails completely. His lackluster direction is partially to blame, but the big problem is the script. For some reason the screenwriters tinkered with the plot until the overall theme was obliterated. Although most of Guthrie's characters are present, they're barely recognizable. The all-star cast includes Robert Mitchum as Dick Summers, Kirk Douglas as Irvine Tadlock, Richard Widmark as Lije Evans, and Lola Albright as Becky Evans. If the script hadn't been so convoluted, Mitchum and Douglas would have been credible as Summers and Tadlock, but Widmark and Albright were completely miscast. Even with these stellar performers, McLaglen's film lost the sense of history that was in Guthrie's novel.

In his foreword to the Signet Classic edition of Francis Parkman's *The Oregon Trail* (Signet, 1950), Guthrie wrote,

> The reasons for its popularity aren't far to seek . . . it brings to sight and sound and feeling the great and barren valley of the Platte River, where wolves slink and antelopes circle and buffalo lumber and furtive Indians await a chance to steal.

Even so, he regretted Parkman's preoccupation with the day-to-day life of the Indians, where he "let history stream by him while he examined an eddy." *The Way West*, like Parkman's book, exhibits a good eye for detail, but is grand in scope. This could well account for the critical acclaim and popularity of this wonderful story of an extraordinary journey along the Oregon Trail.

The Earthbreakers
by Ernest Haycox
Little, Brown, and Company, 1952

Ernest Haycox was a prolific writer of the formula Westerns, one of the best short story writers ever to address the genre, and toward the end of his short life (1899-1950), the author of fine historical novels. If he had lived longer, he might have written great Western literature. *The Earthbreakers* represents his later work, and shows he was clearly headed in that direction.

The story begins where other novels of the journey west on the Oregon Trail, such as Guthrie's *The Way West* (Houghton Mifflin, 1952), end. A wagon train of four hundred people, after two thousand miles and five months of land travel, made the last ninety miles of their journey to western Oregon by water, through the Columbia Gorge of the Cascades.

The success of this short, perilous journey relied on a spirit of community developed during the overland trek. The settlers' dependence on their neighbors was neither complex nor novel, but in Haycox's hands it held together a riveting story of love, passion, infidelity, violence, and courage.

After reaching the Willamette Valley, men rode off on their personal scouting expeditions. When they returned they took their wagons away and by nightfall fifty square miles had become a settlement. The ordeal of work that followed soon eased the idea of a land of milk and honey.

The settlers worked eighteen-hour days. They quickly built small cabins to meet their immediate need of protection from the weather, then began clearing land, running fence lines, building a barn and a smokehouse, and finally, planting the first crop.

Haycox was born in Oregon and lived and worked there most of his life. His firsthand knowledge shows in his descriptions of the tasks performed, and of the hardships endured. He tells of western Oregon's unique weather:

> You had to get used to the rain in Oregon. The first year was the worst. You weren't entirely dry until the spring. Your bedclothes were always clammy and your iron rusted. In January the winter came, the kind of winter they had left behind them and were lonesome for. Even so, it was a mild thing. The wind blew steadily from the east, bringing sharp temperatures; the ice formed in buckets and glittered as a ragged edge in the slack eddies of the creek. The high mountains grew whiter, the sky was blue, the sun bright and heatless. By early morning the cattle stood stiff-legged at the barn-lot gate, their breath cloudy in the air.

Against this weather and the other obstacles, neighbors helping neighbors becomes an exalted theme.

But the people weren't homogeneous. There were disagreements on many things—the amount of government they needed, in particular. John

Gay, the informal leader of the group, would have preferred "government by a thousand fools to government by one wise man, for at least the thousand fools would be speaking the common wish." Others disagreed. A man named McIver said: "I fear government more than I fear hell. I fear it because I fear the instinct in all men to want something for nothing. I never saw a government that stayed small. They all get big and suck the sap out of the people they serve." Haycox probed both the economics and the social structure of the community, as well as the political struggle, giving us a complete picture of the growth of a pioneer society.

The protagonist is Rice Burnett, a man who had trapped three seasons on the Missouri head waters, but joined the wagon train with plans to be the miller for the new settlement. His antagonist, Cal Lockyear, was also a mountain man, but the mountains had "reduced him to the lean meat of his character." There was a mixture of the unsure and the threatening in him. He "had no cushion of reflection to absorb the shock of his impulses." Cal told Burnett,

> This place will break you before you get it broke. You'll be a damned old man in five years. You need a woman to cook, but she'll drive a hard bargain with you. She'll tie you with a wedding ring and load you with ten kids and you'll not be able to pick up your gun and roam for a hundred miles for the fun of it. God damn these white women, they'll have their way. They wring a man dry and trap him with work; then what's left of him? Squaws are better—they let a man stay a man. There's your white settlement, kids to raise and cows to milk and fences to keep up, and cabin broke men, and women that have got things their own way.

The unavoidable confrontation between Lockyear and the rest of the community pits Burnett against Lockyear in a test of the survival skills they developed as mountain men.

There are numerous acts of courage, some unexpected. John Millard had an outspoken wife who disliked men: "Oh, the egotism of men. You give and you take away, and women ought to be proud to do your slave work and stroke your heads and give you pleasure, and crawl away humble when you don't want them." Millard was looked down on because he couldn't control his wife. Yet, when Mrs. Millard attacked Lockyear and got a bloody nose in return, Millard, without reflection, told her he "would have to kill the man," and eventually confronted Lockyear.

The Millards are only two of the finely etched supporting characters. When Director John Ford bought the screen rights to Haycox's short story *Stage to Lordsburg*, he said he liked the characters. Haycox's ability to develop interesting characters is abundantly evident in this novel. There's Edna Lattimore, who liked men and whose actions were impulsive rather than deliberate. And Bob Hawn, a young mountain man who had been in the country more than six years before the settlers came, a squaw man not accepted by the women of the community. And Veen Lockyear, Cal's crippled brother— smaller, steadier, not afraid of Cal, but no match for him. Harris Iby was six-feet-six of bone and tissue, a gentle giant who never got mad. There are many others. The preacher Lot White is perhaps the best example of Haycox's ability to develop crisp, interesting, sympathetic characters.

> Lot was a short, turkey-cock man with an upper body shaped by his
> blacksmithing trade; his hat, thrust back, showed a half-bald head;
> his eyes were a shade of blue too light for his complexion; his mouth,
> though forceful, was thin enough to be without color, and his jaw
> was stubborn and his words came out with a kind of tumbling effect,
> as though sped by the pressure of other impatient words behind.

Edna Lattimore told Lot not to "come trying to drive the snakes out of me. Go drive your snakes out of men." Lot replied: "It won't do. Man's frail that way. Woman has got to stand above him." Lot told Ralph Whitcomb, a doctor, that if education didn't make a man stand on the right side of things, it had better be destroyed. Whitcomb gathered that Lot believed virtuous ignorance is better than educated doubt. Although Lot knew he wasn't taken seriously by most of his neighbors, his dogged persistence in serving the Lord is both poignant and admirable.

Ernest Haycox's body of work includes some of the finest Western fiction published. Especially notable are the novels *Alder Gulch* (Little, Brown, 1942), *Man in the Saddle* (Little-Brown, 1938), *Border Trumpet* (Little, Brown, 1939), *Bugles in the Afternoon* (Little, Brown, 1944), and Canyon *Passage* (Little, Brown, 1945); and the short stories *Stage to Lordsburg* and *High Wind*. Recreated for the screen as *Stagecoach* (United Artists, 1939), *Stage to Lordsburg* gave a new vitality to the Western film and gained it a new respect from critical audiences.

The Oregon settings of *The Earthbreakers* are extraordinary and the accomplishments of the hardy people who settled there are an important part of our history. Ernest Haycox has made a notable contribution to the literature of the American West with this fine novel.

3

Boots and Saddles: The Army in the West and the Indian Wars

Introduction

The Indian Wars in the West began in 1540 when the conquistadors of Francisco Vazquez de Coronado clashed with Zuni warriors of the pueblo of Hawikuh. They ended three and one-half centuries later, in 1890, when U. S. cavalry troops almost wiped out Big Foot's band of Sioux at Wounded Knee.

In the 1840s U. S. military policy in the West was to keep the travel routes open and protect the settlers. But as their land was invaded, the Indians fought back, attacking both travelers and settlers. In the 1850s the army fought rebellious tribes in the Pacific Northwest, the Sioux and Cheyenne on the Great Plains, the Kiowa and Comanche along the Texas frontier, and the Apache in the Southwest.

During the Civil War soldiers were diverted from the western frontier to support Union forces in the East. Between 1861 and 1865 volunteer forces fought the Navajos of the Southwest and the Great Plains tribes. In 1862 the Minnesota Sioux savagely killed about 800 settlers. At Sand Creek, in Colorado Territory, volunteer troops massacred a band of Cheyenne in 1864.

In 1866, after the Civil War had ended, the Fetterman Massacre occurred when a detachment of soldiers from Fort Phil Kearny, Wyoming, was ambushed on the Bozeman Trail. After a series of treaties in the late 1860s failed to bring peace, the wars that followed were fought to force tribes onto reservations.

There were major conflicts with the Sioux and Cheyenne of the northern Plains from 1876 through 1881. The famed "Custer's Last Stand" at the Little Bighorn occurred on June 25, 1876. Over 200 men under the command of Lieutenant Colonel George Armstrong Custer perished in that engagement. Sioux and Cheyenne resistance ended with the surrender of the Sioux chief, Sitting Bull, in 1881. The Red River War of 1874-75 finally brought peace to the southern Plains and Texas as the Kiowa, Comanche, Cheyenne, and Arapaho accepted life on reservations. Other encounters were the Modoc War of 1872-73, in the California lava beds; the dramatic flight in 1877 of Chief Joseph and the Nez Perce from Idaho across the American Northwest; the Bannock-Paiute uprising of 1878 in Idaho and Oregon; and the Ute outbreak of 1879 in western Colorado. The long and bloody Apache wars of New Mexico and Arizona ended in 1886 when Geronimo surrendered for the last time.

Wounded Knee, the tragic clash of reservation Sioux with U. S. troops in 1890, marked the end of the Indian Wars.

Most early Western fiction treated the American Indians as bloodthirsty savages, with little sympathy for their fight for survival. Elliott Arnold's *Blood Brother* (Duell, Sloan and Pearce, 1947) broke this trend. The better writers began to be more evenhanded in their treatment of the first Americans. Elmer Kelton's *The Wolf and the Buffalo* (Doubleday, 1980) captured the violence of the Comanche Wars in Texas, but presented both sides of the conflicts. These novels provide a good introduction to the literature of the Indian Wars.

READER'S GUIDE

Trooper Ross by Charles King. J. B. Lippincott, 1895. General Charles King (1844-1933) participated in actions against the Apache, the Sioux, the Cheyenne, and the Nez Perce, and drew on his experiences to write many novels and short stories. Trooper Ross is based on an actual event that occurred in Wyoming: the Fetterman Massacre. The protagonist is an officer's son who was unable to compete academically at West Point. He joined the cavalry as an enlisted trooper, determined to work his way up through the ranks.

The Captain of the Gray-Horse Troop by Hamlin Garland. Harper and Brothers, 1902. This novel takes place towards the end of the Indian wars and is about a cavalry action against renegade Indians in eastern Montana. It deals with the abuse of American Indians by cattlemen.

Marion's Faith by General Charles King. J. B. Lippincott, 1911. First published in 1886. Following the events leading up to and culminating with the massacre of Custer's 7th Cavalry at the Little Big Horn, *Marion's Faith* looks at cavalry life from the perspective of the officers and of their wives.

The War Chief by Edgar Rice Burroughs. Burroughs, 1928. Edgar Rice Burroughs enlisted in the 7th Cavalry and saw active service in the Apache country of Southern Arizona. Knowing the country and its people, he wrote two books on the subject: *The War Chief* and *Apache Devil* (Burroughs, 1933). The first of these tells of the rearing of a white boy in the Apache tradition, as the adopted son of Geronimo named Shoz-Dijiji, who would grow into a great war chief with a hatred for all whites. The second continues his story.

Apache by Will Levington Comfort. E. P. Dutton, 1931. Focusing on the life of Mangas Coloradas, the infamous Mimbreño Apache chief who led his warriors in repeated attacks against both white settlements and Army installations, this novel explores his awareness of the disintegration of his people's way of life, and his inability to stop it.

Apache Devil by Edgar Rice Burroughs. Burroughs, 1933. This novel takes the story of Shoz-Dijiji, began in *The War Chief* (Burroughs, 1928), further, as he and Geronimo desperately fight to maintain life and dignity for their people. Following Geronimo's capitulation to the army, the day of the Apache was over. But the old chief's son Shoz-Dijiji—the warrior they called the Apache Devil— slipped away.

Montana Road by Henry Sinclair Drago. William Morrow, 1935. Stephen Glen was a government agent in the Indian country, and knew about their exploitation by traders. And there was a tide of gold-seekers overrunning Indian lands with the first discovery of nuggets in the Black Hills. Then came General Custer, looking for glory, certain that his cavalry could smash the gathering tribes. Glen was caught in the middle.

Broncho Apache by Paul I. Wellman. Macmillan, 1936. Massai was a legendary Apache who escaped from Geronimo's prison train in 1886, and made his way back to Apacheria, where for several years, before finally disappearing, he waged a ruthless single-handed war against whites and Mexicans. Source for the 1954 film "Apache."

The Border Trumpet by Ernest Haycox. Little, Brown, 1939. This novel of the Apache war is notable for its picture of U. S. Army life on the Arizona frontier.

The Habit of Empire by Paul Horgan. Rydal Press, 1939. A narrative of the conquest of New Mexico by Juan de Oñate in 1604, of his death at Acoma and the subsequent destruction of the Pueblo.

The Lieutenant's Lady by Bess Streeter Aldrich. D. Appleton, 1942. In the wake of the Civil War, a young woman traveled from Omaha, Nebraska, up the Missouri River to deliver a "Dear John" letter to a friend's fiance. She subsequently became the wife of the recipient, an army lieutenant. The story is based on the actual diary of an army wife whose husband served on the frontier during a period when settlers were pouring into the West and displacing the Indian tribes.

Bugles in the Afternoon by Ernest Haycox. Little, Brown, 1944. At Fort Abraham Lincoln in Dakota Territory, a sergeant and a lieutenant in the cavalry held a deep hatred for each other. And a further complication, they were under the command of the volatile General George A. Custer, who would lead the 7th Cavalry to its fateful encounter on the Little Bighorn. Source for the 1952 film.

Station West by Luke Short (Frederick D. Glidden). Houghton Mifflin, 1947. A frontier army post stood next to the most lawless town in the West. It had to contend with hardcase miners and gamblers, hostile Indians, and betrayal from within. Source for the 1948 film.

The Great Betrayal by Dorothy Gardiner. Doubleday, 1949. This novel is an account of what happened in 1864 at Sand Creek in southwestern Colorado, when a regiment of cavalry wiped out an encampment of friendly Indians, including women and children.

No Survivors by Will Henry (Henry Wilson Allen). Random House, 1950. The story of the Battle of the Rosebud, Custer's last stand, and Reno and Benteen's fight. Henry shows what General Custer's lonely stand and final moments at the 1876 Battle of the Little Bighorn might have been like.

Sundown Riders by Thomas Thompson. Doubleday, 1950. Set in Oregon, the story centers on events leading up to the Modoc Indian War of 1872-73.

Only the Valiant by Charles Marquis Warren. Bantam Books, 1950. A cavalry officer who was a strict disciplinarian nearly drove his men to mutiny in the course of their attempt in the 1870s to hold a ruined fort in the blistering New Mexico desert against a furious Apache horde. Basis for the 1951 film.

The Apache by James Warner Bellah. Fawcett, 1951. Cuchillo, chief of the Apaches, pronounced a curse upon the white men under the command of Colonel Rattay, and beyond all human understanding, the curse came true.

Red Blizzard by Clay Fisher (Henry Wilson Allen). Simon and Schuster, 1951. Son of a Basque fur trader and an Oglala Sioux squaw, John "Pawnee" Perez didn't belong in either the white or Indian world in the early 1870s. So he made his own place, his own destiny, but still ended up caught between the U. S. Cavalry and three thousand Indians led by Crazy Horse.

Navajo Canyon by Tom W. Blackburn. Doubleday, 1952. A scout is hired by the army to track the Navajo into Canyon de Chelly.

Adobe Walls by W. R. Burnett. Alfred A. Knopf, 1953. In 1874 a handful of buffalo hunters successfully withstood the assault of a large war party of Kiowa-Comanche at Adobe Walls, Texas. The protagonist in this story of the Battle of Adobe Walls is based on historical scout Al Sieber. Basis for the 1953 Paramount film "Arrowhead."

Yellow Hair by Clay Fisher (Henry Wilson Allen).Houghton Mifflin, 1953. In the winter of 1868 George Armstrong Custer set out to fulfill his ambitions for glory. Josh Kelso, a mountain man and Indian scout, would suffer from Custer's foolhardy ambition. During the weeks before the battle of the Washita, Kelso found himself on both sides of the fight.

Cochise of Arizona by Oliver La Farge. Aladdin, 1953. A fictionalized biography of the Apache chief Cochise.

Arrow in the Dust by L. L. Foreman. Dell, 1954. The wagon train's escort was seventy raw recruits, led by a deserter. The nearest settlement was 300 miles to the east. And ahead of them were a thousand Apache and Pawnee. Source for the 1954 film.

The Searchers by Alan LeMay. Harper and Brothers, 1954. The story of two men's quest to find a young girl taken from her Texas plains home by Comanche raiders. Was she alive or dead? This tormenting question drove the searchers on, even as the years passed and success seemed hopeless. Source for the 1956 film.

The Bounty Hunters by Elmore Leonard. Houghton Mifflin, 1954. Soldado, the fiercest of the Mimbres Apache, was the most hunted Indian renegade in the Southwest. He was a deadly challenge worth four dollars a day to track and bring back to the government agency for the contract scout Flynn. To Lazair, he was just a scalp worth a staggering bounty. But these hunters would quickly become the hunted in a desert hell where the Apache reigned.

Scarlet Plume by Frederick Manfred. Simon and Schuster, 1954. Set in south Minnesota in 1862 during the legendary Sioux uprising, this is the story of a young white captive who was determined to survive her ordeal. She developed a passion for a Sioux warrior, her benefactor Scarlet Plume, that crossed all boundaries.

The Brass Command by Clay Fisher (Henry Wilson Allen). Houghton Mifflin, 1955. Based on an actual event, this story occurred during 1873 to 1880 on a lonely army outpost in northwest Nebraska. The Powder River Cheyenne, exiled into the barren Oklahoma Territory, prepared to make a last stand. All that stood in their way was the brass command—a lonely outpost of the U. S. Cavalry at Fort Robinson, Nebraska.

Pillars of the Sky by Will Henry (Henry Wilson Allen). Bantam Books, 1956. A wagon train was ambushed in the Bitterroots and a woman captured. An attempt by an army sergeant to rescue her touched off the bloodiest Indian fighting in the old Northwest Territory. Source for the 1956 film.

Apache Rising by Marvin H. Albert. Fawcett, 1957. Frontier scout Jess Remsberg bravely led a wagon train through hostile territory to Fort Conchos. But underneath his valor, he had an ulterior motive: to settle a score with a man whom he believed killed his wife. Source for the 1966 film "Duel at Diablo."

Modoc: The Last Sundown by L. P. Holmes. Dodd, Mead, 1957. Faced with virtual extinction at the hands of the white man, the Modoc Indians made their final defiant stand in a northern California lava stronghold. It was their last sundown.

Last Stand at Papago Wells by Louis L'Amour. Fawcett, 1957. He was a man without illusions, wealth, or destination. He had killed many men and had made even more enemies. When he found himself holed up at Papago Wells in the Arizona desert, with three women and only a handful of soldiers, and heard the screams of the Apache war party, he needed every one of his deadly skills. Basis for the 1958 film "Apache Territory."

Yellowhorse by Dee Brown. Permabooks, 1958. A cavalry captain was sent to Yellowhorse, a reopened frontier fort. The reactivation of Yellowhorse was a treaty violation calculated to drive the Sioux back on the warpath. The captain was to be a test pilot on a weather balloon, risking his life in the balloon as well as in action against the Sioux raiding Yellowhorse.

Taos by Irwin R. Blacker. World Publishing, 1959. A novel about the Pueblo Revolt of 1680, when the Pueblo Indians of Arizona and New Mexico rebelled against the Spanish and drove them from the area.

Dance Back the Buffalo by Milton Lott. Houghton Mifflin, 1959. In 1889, the defeated Sioux listened to the prophecies of an Indian "Messiah," who preached a ceremonial "ghost dance" that would bring back the vanished buffalo herds and drive the hated white man from Sioux hunting grounds.

The Buffalo Soldiers by John Prebble. Harcourt, Brace, 1959. Set just after the Civil War on the borders of Texas, this is a story of black men, the "Buffalo Soldiers," living and fighting on the outposts of civilization. They had to deal with racial prejudice as well as an extraordinary military ordeal. The protagonist, Lieutenant Garrett Byrne, was a white officer assigned to Fort Sill after the Civil War, and placed in charge of some Negro recruits whose unwelcome mission was to escort a band of Comanche on their last buffalo hunt before they were confined to a reservation. Spur Award winner.

Sergeant Rutledge by James Warner Bellah. Bantam Books, 1960. Developed from the screen play for the 1960 film by Bellah and Willis Goldbeck, from which the John Ford picture of the same name was made. To Troop D, 9th U. S. Cavalry, and its commanding officer, Sergeant Rutledge was a top soldier. But the women and other officers on the post thought he was a black rapist, murderer and deserter.

Comanche Captives by Will Cook. Bantam Books, 1960. Guthrie McCabe, the sheriff of Oldam County, Texas, was hired by the U. S. Cavalry to bring back white captives of the Comanche. He was accompanied on his mission by Lieutenant Jim Gary. All the white captives they discovered had been reduced to brutish animals and the one adolescent boy McCabe did bring back committed a vicious murder and was hanged. Jim Gary rescued the niece of a U. S. Senator, who for five years has been the captive wife of a Comanche. Basis for the 1961 film "Two Rode Together."

From Where the Sun Now Stands by Will Henry (Henry Wilson Allen). Random House, 1960. Told from the viewpoint of a young Indian fighter, this story recounts the saga of 113 days in the summer and autumn of 1877 when Chief Joseph reluctantly led his people in a rear-guard action from the Nez Perce reservation in Oregon to Montana, across more than one thousand miles of trackless mountain country. Spur Award from Western Writers of America.

A Distant Trumpet by Paul Horgan. Farrar, Straus & Cudahy, 1960. This is an historical novel about 1880s cavalry duty in Arizona, seeking to "pacify" the Apache. Source for the 1964 film.

A Thunder of Drums by James Warner Bellah. Bantam Books, 1961. A newly commissioned cavalry officer, the son of a general, is roughly treated by his superior, the commander of an isolated frontier army post. He finally proves himself when the Apache go on a rampage. Basis for the 1961 film.

Nino: The Legend of the Apache Kid by Clay Fisher (Henry Wilson Allen). William Morrow, 1961. Nino had been an enlisted Apache Scout. Now he was the most feared and hunted fugitive in the Arizona Territory, in a savage duel with the U. S. Cavalry.

Savanna by Janice Holt Giles. Houghton Mifflin, 1961. Set in Arkansas Territory, now Oklahoma, this is the story of Savanna Fowler, who was a bride at sixteen and a widow at nineteen. A throwback to both her frontier grandmothers, she successfully operated a string of cavalry trading posts in competition with such experienced and ruthless men as Auguste Chouteau and Sam Houston.

Comanche Captives by Fred Grove. Ballantine Books, 1961. An army lieutenant escorted 300 Comanche prisoners to Fort Sill, four hundred miles through the heart of Indian Territory, with only one platoon—made up of "defectives," or misfits. Spur Award from Western Writers of America.

The Winter War by William Wister Haines. Little, Brown, 1961. An historical novel about the Indian War of Montana in 1876, when General

Nelson A. Miles pursued the Sioux following the Custer defeat at the Little Big Horn. Spur Award from Western Writers of America.

A Time in the Sun by Jane Barry. Doubleday, 1962. In 1870 the Apache were making a last stand against the white men. A white woman and a Mexican girl traveling with her were captured by a raiding party. Victorio, leader of the Mimbrenos tribe, ransomed the Mexican girl but was unwilling to release the white woman. Most of the Apache leaders and some of the Americans who figure in the book are historical personages.

The Border Guidon by Gordon D. Shirreffs. Signet, 1962. A sergeant in the Union army rode out alone from an isolated outpost into the Apache-infested Arizona desert to find and recover a cache of Federal ammunition that had fallen into Confederate hands.

Apache Canyon by Brian Garfield. Bouregy, 1963. The Coyotero Apache in Arizona were on the warpath from Fort Dragoon to the Arrowhead Mountains. A U. S. Army scout, with only a few days left on his contract, had to try to bring them back to the reservation.

Adobe Walls by James Louttit. Avon Books, 1963. In 1874 around a thousand Indians, led by Comanche Chief Quannah Parker, attacked the small buffalo hunters' settlement of Adobe Walls in the Texas Panhandle. Using their big .50 caliber rifles, the hunters withstood repeated attacks over three days.

A Very Small Remnant by Michael Straight. Alfred A. Knopf, 1963. In 1864 Major Ned Wynkoop, commanding officer at Fort Lyon, Colorado, agreed to talk with Chief Black Kettle about the Chief's offer to release four captive white children. He had no way of knowing what calamity would ensue, but Major Wynkoop was one of a small remnant of men who held the founding fathers' vision that a hand of friendship extended to the Indian inhabitants would ensure peaceful settlement of the nation.

The Renegade by Cliff Farrell. Doubleday, 1964. A friend of the Indians' cause finds himself trapped in a bloody uprising of vengeful Cheyenne and Sioux. Spur Award from Western Writers of America

The Branded Man by Hal. G. Evarts. Fawcett, 1965. The Army court-martialed Randall, then branded him with a hot iron, making him an outcast drifting in the hills. But they would need his knowledge of those hills and of the old Indian leader who was holding a dying officer hostage.

Paiute by Sessions S. Wheeler. Caxton House, 1965. A novel about the Indian Wars and gold and silver mining in the Nevada area in 1859-60. It includes the massacre of Major Ormsby and his volunteers by the Paiute at Pyramid Lake in 1860.

Captain Apache by S. E. Whitman. Berkley, 1965. Captain Apache's real name was Captain Cullah Burnett. He was a full-blooded Apache, the protégé of General Ryland, who handed Burnett every dirty job that turned up in the Arizona Territory. Source for the 1971 film.

The Last Warpath by Will Henry (Henry Wilson Allen). Random House, 1966. The Cheyenne and the U. S. Cavalry fought for forty years on the Western plains. Here is a story of the principal adversaries, men like Sherman, Chivington, Custer, Black Kettle, Dull Knife, and Little Wolf, who were engaged in that long confrontation.

The Wolf is My Brother by Chad Oliver. New American Library, 1967. Comanche chieftain Fox Claw had seen the white man ravage his land and slaughter the buffalo. Then Fox Claw and another proud and honorable man, Colonel Bill Curtis of the Twelfth Cavalry, found themselves locked in a deadly struggle. Spur Award from Western Writers of America.

The Red Sabbath by Lewis B. Patten. Doubleday, 1968. General George Armstrong Custer led 225 men of the 7th Cavalry into the valley of the Little Big Horn and one of the bloodiest massacres in American history. This novel recreates the events that led up to that battle. Spur Award from Western Writers of America.

Buffalo Soldier by William Heuman. Dodd, Mead. 1969. An ex-Confederate soldier, now serving in the U. S. Cavalry in the West, learns from the black "buffalo soldiers" that the color of a man's skin is not what makes him a man.

Broken Lance by X. X. Jones. Ballantine Books, 1969. A first sergeant, who had won the Medal of Honor at Gettysburg, refused to shoot Indian women and children in an engagement with the Cheyenne on the Western plains, even when ordered to kill them.

Arrow in the Sun by Theodore V. Olsen. Doubleday, 1969. A band of Cheyenne burned an army paymaster's wagon. Only one soldier and a woman, a former captive of the Cheyenne, survived, and with little prospect of rescue, they were in a desperate situation. Basis for the 1970 film "Soldier Blue."

Valdez Is Coming by Elmore Leonard. Fawcett, 1970. Valdez was a respectful man who wore a suit and a collar. But in another place at another time, he had been a dangerous man. Now he had been pushed too hard by his adversaries, and Valdez was coming for them. Source for the 1971 film.

Kearny Rode West by James Norman. G. P. Putnam's Sons, 1971. The story of Colonel Stephen Watts Kearny's military expedition to California in 1846.

Black Fox by Matt Braun. Fawcett, 1972. A Texas cattleman, a former slave who came West to prove himself the equal of any man, and a Comanche chief who battled to regain the land of his people are the principals in this saga of people fighting for what they believe is theirs. Source for the 1993 television miniseries.

The Last Stronghold: A Story of the Modoc Indian War by Harriett Luger. Young Scott Books, 1972. A young readers book. From November of 1872 to May of 1873, fifty Modoc warriors, in their lava beds stronghold near the California-Oregon border, stood off a force of 1,000 United States soldiers. This is the story of three teenage boys—a young Modoc, a settler's son, and an immigrant soldier youth—whose lives crossed during that conflict.

Mission to the West by Theodore V. Olsen. Doubleday, 1973. The birth of the United States Cavalry was the establishment of the 1st Regiment of the U. S. Dragoons in 1833. Their first mission was an expedition to the Far West to impress the proud plains Indians with a show of mounted might.

Restless Spurs by Archie Joscelyn. Lenox Hill, 1974. A former major in the Civil War, now a lieutenant stationed on the Western frontier, is appalled at the callousness of his superiors toward the Indians, and the atrocities committed against them.

The Hands of Geronimo by Lewis B. Patten. Ace, 1974. Geronimo's renegade Apache were fighting their way toward their stronghold in the Sierra Madre Mountains, with the U. S. Cavalry on their trail. With the Apache was a three-year-old captive white boy.

The Camp Grant Massacre by Elliott Arnold. Simon and Schuster, 1976. In the Arizona Territory in 1871, the settlers of Tucson were subjected to constant attacks by the Apache. First Lieutenant Royal E. Whitman, the army commander at Camp Grant, brokered a truce with Eskiminzin, the Apache tribal chief, and the Indians surrendered their weapons, and settled in a village near the camp. But the townspeople of Tucson, distrustful of the Apache, attacked the village and the army was unable to prevent a massacre.

The Spirit Horses by Lou Cameron. Ballantine Books, 1976. Secretary of War Jefferson Davis knew the French were policing the Sahara with camel troops. To him a desert was a desert, so in 1857 a herd of dromedaries was purchased for the U. S. Army. They bucked like a horse, kicked like a mule, bit like a dog, and spat green slime. But Davis put cavalry troopers on their backs and sent them out to engage the Apache. Spur Award from Western Writers of America.

Bugles on the Bighorn by Jackson Cole (House Name). Popular Library, 1976. From the *Rio Kid* series. Bob Pryor, the Rio Kid, was caught in the same cruel trap as the legendary General Custer and the Seventh Cavalry. He rode to head off the delivery of a deadly cargo of rifles by renegades to the Sioux.

The Court-Martial of George Armstrong Custer by Douglas C. Jones. Charles Schribner's Sons, 1976. What if Custer had survived the Little Big Horn and had lived to stand trial? Would he have emerged as a military genius or a vain glory seeker. Source for the 1977 film. Spur Award winner.

Watch for Me on the Mountain by Forrest Carter. Delacorte, 1978. A story of the Apache leader Geronimo that attributes him with mystic and supernatural powers.

Arrest Sitting Bull by Douglas C. Jones. Charles Scribner's Sons, 1978. Fourteen years after the Sioux Nation's victory at Little Bighorn, the army moved to arrest Sitting Bull, to end the mystic rebellion of the Ghost Dance. This is the story of what really happened to Sitting Bull, who showed his people how to die.

A Creek Called Wounded Knee by Douglas C. Jones. Charles Schribner's Sons, 1978. Custer was dead, but his famed Seventh Cavalry marched into history one more time—to a creek called Wounded Knee—where in 1890 a single shot fired by accident triggered a massacre and one of the most shameful events in American history.

The Trail of the Apache Kid by Lewis B. Patten. Doubleday, 1979. The

Apache Kid was ruthless, even for an Apache. Here he captures the wife of a professional army scout, to use her as bait to lure the scout to his death.

Surgeon to the Sioux by Robert J. Steelman. Doubleday, 1979. The story of a military doctor captured by the Sioux and forced to provide medical treatment to his captors.

That Damn Single Shot by Jim Miller. Fawcett, 1980. An army scout is unhappy with his Springfield 1873 rifle, ruefully known as "that damn single shot," while fighting Sioux and Cheyenne in Wyoming Territory. Then he takes it into a battle called the Little Big Horn.

A Mighty Afternoon by Charles K. Mills. Doubleday, 1980. A novel of the Battle of the Little Big Horn, where on June 25, 1876, in the Black Hills of Montana, six hundred men of the Seventh Cavalry met and engaged a force of two thousand Sioux warriors. This historic battle resulted in the greatest Indian victory and the most devastating Army defeat in the American history.

Comanche Revenge by Jeanne Sommers. Dell, 1981. Book 1 of the *American Indian* series. Cynthia Ann Parker was captured by the Comanche when she was only nine years old. She and a friend, fourteen year old Beth Hutchens, were the sole survivors of a raid that wiped out their families and destroyed their homes. But Cynthia Ann found a new home among the Comanche.

Killdeer Mountain by Dee Brown. Holt, Rinehart and Winston, 1983. A journalist boarded a steamer heading up the Missouri River in 1866, looking for stories for the Saint Louis Herald. He found one in Charles Rawley, Civil War hero and Indian fighter, whose past included: the court-martial of an innocent man; a forced march across a barren plain that ended in massacre; a moment of dishonor in the battle with Indian warriors at Killdeer Mountain; and Rawley's last act, the deed that redeemed him.

Claws of the Eagle by Andrew J. Fenady. Walker, 1984. Army scout Al Sieber tracks the renegade Apache Geronimo for General George Crook.

Snowblind Moon by John Byrne Cooke. Simon and Schuster, 1985. On a remote cattle ranch in Wyoming, in the villages of beleaguered Indian tribes, among the government troops advancing through the bitter winter landscape, the time of the Snowblind Moon heralds the beginning of an apocalyptic clash between the Indians and the whites. Time is running out for Sioux Chief Sun

Horse's people as the U. S. Army rides to force them out of Wyoming onto a barren Dakota reservation. Spur Award from Western Writers of America.

Lords of the Plains by Max Crawford. Atheneum, 1985. The U. S. 2nd Cavalry rolls into Texas in the 1870s with orders to keep the peace and persuade the fierce Comanche to move quietly onto the reservation. The story includes the decisive battle at Palo Duro Canyon.

The Pride of Hannah Wade by Janet Dailey. Pocket Books, 1985. Hannah Wade was a captive of the Apache who survived only because of her will to live. But when she was rescued and returned to her New Mexico home, her husband and friends felt she was soiled and disgraced.

A Mighty Afternoon: A Novel of the Battle of the Little Big Horn by Charles K. Mills. Doubleday, 1985. A character study of soldiers forced to fight an unconquerable foe on his own terms. The true heroes and villains of the Little Big Horn emerge.

Sacred is the Wind by Kerry Newcomb. Bantam Books, 1985. A disgraced Northern Cheyenne warrior strikes against the army commander who betrayed the Cheyenne truce.

Apaches by Oakley Hall. Simon and Schuster, 1986. In New Mexico in the 1880s, in the midst of the bloody Lincoln County War, a band of Bosque Alto Apache planned one last drive to escape the reservation.

Song of the Meadowlark by John A. Sanford. Harper & Row, 1986. A novel set against the background of the 1877 Nez Perce War. Teeto Hoonod, the protagonist and narrator, was at peace with the white settlers in Oregon's Wallowa Valley. But when the peace was broken by the settlers' demands for more land, Teeto and his family, along with 300 warriors and 500 women and children of the Nez Perce nation, began an incredible journey of over 1,700 miles across the Pacific Northwest in an effort to escape to Canada, fighting the pursuing U. S. Army along the way.

Yellowstone Kelly by Peter Bowen. Jameson Books, 1987. Luther "Yellowstone" Kelly was a hunter, trapper, and fighter who fought in both the Civil War and various Indian wars. This novel covers Kelly's experiences as a scout for General O. O. Howard, the Army's war against the Plains Indians, and the tragic last stand of the Nez Perce tribe. Afterwards, Kelly headed for South Africa and the British battle to subdue the fierce Zulu nation.

The Ghost Dancers by Gordon D. Shirreffs. Fawcett, 1987. An army major respects and admires the Apache for their mystical beliefs, for the healing power of their ghost dances, and for their fighting spirit. He goes to war against Mexican scalp-hunters who kill Apache for bounty.

Dodging Red Cloud by Richard S. Wheeler. M. Evans, 1987. Three travelers on the Bozeman Trail took a detour to dodge the infamous Sioux chief Red Cloud. It was September, 1868, and winter was near. As they headed toward the Bridger Cutoff, they realized they had not avoided all obstacles.

Dances with Wolves by Michael Blake. Fawcett, 1988. When Lieutenant John Dunbar was assigned to an abandoned army post after an altercation with a superior, he found himself alone. His only companion was a wolf, with an occasional visit from some roving Comanche. Survival soon forced Dunbar into the Comanche camp, where he learned to admire them. Basis for the 1990 film.

Apache, the Long Ride Home: A Novel of the Old West by Grant Gall. Sunstone Press, 1988. This is the saga of Pedro Bautista, who was captured by the Apache Indians when he was nine years old after a raid on his Mexican village. Adopted into the tribe, he absorbed their culture and survived their eventual confrontation and defeat by American troops.

Campaigning by Jim Miller. Fawcett, 1988. Following an ambush on the Santa Fe Trail, a man was saved from dying by two Indian strangers. The trio was later joined by a former slave, seeking his own destiny in the West. The band joined Kit Carson in his campaign against the Comanche, and also participated in the battle of Adobe Walls.

Broken Eagle by Chad Oliver. Bantam Books, 1989. On the great plains the buffalo were dwindling and the white man claimed the land of the Cheyenne. Yet there were still battles to come, like the Sand Creek Massacre (1864) and the Battle of the Little Big Horn (1876), that would become legends. National Cowboy and Western Heritage Museum Western Heritage Award.

Red Cloud's Revenge by Terry C. Johnston, St. Martin's Press, 1990. From Johnston's *Plainsmen* series. In 1867, Red Cloud's Teton Sioux and Dull Knife's Northern Cheyenne terrorized travelers on the Bozeman Trail. Includes the Hay Field and the Wagonbox fights.

Sioux Dawn: The Fetterman Massacre, 1866 by Terry C. Johnston. St.

Martin's Press, 1990. From Johnston's *Plainsmen* series. When settlers poured into the Sioux's ancestral hunting grounds in the shadow of the Big Horn Mountains, Red Cloud had no choice but to fight. The Fetterman Massacre of 1866 provided the tragic opening for a long and deadly conflict.

The Stalkers: The Battle of Beecher Island, 1868 by Terry C. Johnston. St. Martin's Press, 1990. From Johnston's *Plainsmen* series. Alongside the Republican River in Colorado Territory, a force of fifty seasoned civilian frontiersmen, led by Major George Forsyth, found themselves outnumbered twenty to one by Cheyenne warriors. They survived a nine day siege, sustaining thirty casualties.

Geronimo by Bill Dugan. Harper & Row, 1991. From Dugan's *War Chiefs* series. A novel of the Apache wars and two of the chief protagonists: Geronimo and George Crook, an army general as strong and as determined as the Apache leader.

Devil's Backbone: The Modoc War, 1872-1873 by Terry C. Johnston. St. Martin's Press, 1991. From Johnston's *Plainsmen* series. When Modoc chief Kientpoos (Captain Jack) murdered an American official during peace negotiations, fighting erupted between the Modocs and the U. S. Army. For seven months the Indians waged a bloody war from their natural stronghold in the lava beds, near Tule Lake in the Oregon Territory.

Chief Joseph by Bill Dugan. Harper & Row 1992. From Dugan's *War Chiefs* series. The story of Chief Joseph and the Nez Percé War. In 1877 more than 2,000 troops were in the field against Joseph as he led his people from their homeland in Oregon toward freedom in Canada. But on September 30, in a blizzard in the Bear Paw Mountains, the end of his fight was near.

Sitting Bull by Bill Dugan. Harper & Row, 1992. From Dugan's *War Chiefs* series. Hunkpapa Sioux Sitting Bull was the paramount chief of the thirteen bands of the Sioux Nation. He was responsible for the defeat of Custer at the Battle of the Little Big Horn in 1876.

Crazy Horse by Bill Dugan. Harper & Row, 1992. From Dugan's *War Chiefs* series. Crazy Horse was an Oglala Sioux war chief under the political leadership of Sitting Bull. He was the leader of the Sioux and Cheyenne warriors who swept down on the five companies of Custer's Seventh Cavalry at the Little Big Horn in 1876.

Quanah Parker by Bill Dugan. Harper & Row, 1993. From Dugan's *War Chiefs* series. Following the Mexican War, Texans turned their attention to subduing the Comanche. Quanah Parker, the son of a Comanche chief and a white female captive, had the wisdom to lead his people into coexistence with the Texans.

Blood Song by Terry C. Johnston. St. Martin's Press, 1993. From Johnston's *Plainsmen* series. The Battle of Powder River and the beginning of the Great Sioux War of 1876 erupted in the Black Hills of Dakota when Sitting Bull and Crazy Horse defied the Federal Government and refused to lead the Northern Plains tribes onto the reservation.

Brazos Dreamer: The Story of Major Robert S. Neighbors by Gene Shelton. Doubleday, 1993. From Shelton's *Texas Legends* series. Based on the life of Major Robert Simpson Neighbors, a Texas Indian agent. Major Neighbors, a former Texas Ranger, was caught between two cultures in the turbulent years between the Mexican and Civil Wars.

Libbie: A Novel of Elizabeth Bacon Custer by Judy Alter. Bantam Books, 1994. She was barely a woman when she married the flamboyant George Armstrong Custer. Following her heart, she made a home for her beloved "Autie" in outposts throughout the West as he followed his destiny. This is the story of her own personal battles as she prepared herself for the day she would lose him.

Reap the Whirlwind by Terry C. Johnston. Bantam Books, 1994. From Johnston's *Plainsman* series. The Battle of the Rosebud, June 1876. Brigadier General George C. Crook met the Sioux in what some call Chief Crazy Horse's dress rehearsal for the Little Big Horn.

War at Bent's Fort by John Legg. St. Martin's Press, 1994. First book in the *Forts of Freedom* series. The one thing trappers and traders, westward-bound pioneers, and the frontier soldiers had in common was the frontier fort—a place of safety in a vast and dangerous land. In 1833 William and Charles Bent built a trading empire around their dusty, adobe-walled fort on the Arkansas River. Suddenly the Bents found themselves swept up in a tragic frontier war, a deadly conflict that would take one brother's life.

Treaty at Fort Laramie by John Legg. St. Martin's Press, 1994. From the *Forts of Freedom* series. In 1848, Major Winslow Sanderson, post commander of Wyoming's Fort Laramie, had his hands full with gold-fevered soldiers, dwindling supplies, and keeping peace between wagon trains and the Indians. A major event that transpired in the novel, based on an actual occurrence, was a treaty council involving around 12,000 Indians.

To Die in Dinetah: The Dark Legacy of Kit Carson by John A. Truett. Sunstone Press, 1994. Early in the Civil War, young Terry O'Neill volunteers for assignment at Fort Stanton in rugged New Mexico. He joins the famous Colonel Kit Carson, campaigning against the Apaches and Navajos in the deadly snowstorms of Canyon de Chelly, only to find himself a part of the Navajos' torturous "Long Walk" to imprisonment at Fort Sumner.

The Massacre at Sand Creek by Bruce Cutler. University of Oklahoma Press, 1995. On November 29, 1864, in the early dawn a Colorado militia unit attacked a peaceful encampment of Cheyenne by Sand Creek in southwestern Colorado Territory. They murdered almost 200 men, women, and children. Present in this novel are Colonel John M. Chivington, who planned and led the attack, Captain Silas Soule, the only officer who refused to attack, and Black Kettle, the Cheyenne leader who waved the white flag of peace even as the army was attacking.

Powder River by Ralph Cotton. St. Martin's Press, 1995. From Cotton's *Jeston Nash* series. Jeston Nash was a look-alike cousin of Jesse James, but he was never the desperado he wanted to be. In this story, he joined Chief Red Cloud and the Oglala Sioux in an attempt to win the Powder River Indian War.

The Apache Kid by Phyllis De La Garza. Westernlore Press, 1995. Formally a sergeant in the Apache scouts based on the San Carlos Agency under the command of Al Sieber, the Apache Kid declared war on three nations—the Apache, the Mexicans, and the Americans—following his conviction for murder and subsequent escape.

Marching to Valhalla by Michael Blake. Villard, 1996. A novel of George Armstrong Custer, as viewed from the General's journal.

A Road We Do Not Know: A Novel of Custer at the Little Bighorn by Frederick J. Chiaventone. Simon and Schuster, 1996. This is the story of the Battle of the Little Bighorn as seen through the eyes of ordinary soldiers and warriors.

Winter Woman by F. M. Parker. Pinnacle Books, 1996. Raised on Mississippi riverboats, Jacob Morgan came west to make his fortune as a fur trapper. Driven from his rightful lands by the white invaders, Wolf Voice, a Crow warrior, had been forced to steal and kill in order to survive. On a tributary of the Powder River in the Wyoming Territory, they would come together as enemies in a terrible confrontation.

Not Between Brothers by David Marion Wilkinson. Boaz, 1996. This is an epic tale of Texas that spans four decades—exploring the opposing views of American settlers and Indians battling for a land to call home.

Aymond: A Novel by A. G. Burkhart, Jr. Sunstone Press, 1997. Aymond was captured at the age of five by Comanches, taken by raiding Apaches at eight and rescued unwillingly at twelve by U. S. troopers. He was raised by the whites and college educated. When he returned home he came upon the scene of a bloody massacre made to look like the work of Indians. With the help of a young survivor he set out to bring the murderer to justice.

Wolf Mountain Moon by Terry C. Johnston. Bantam Books, 1997. Colonel Nelson A. Miles leads his tired troops up the Tongue River to the rugged buttes where Crazy Horse, with a thousand Lakota warriors, waits to fight his last battle against the U. S. Army.

Monument in the Storm by John A. Truett. Sunstone Press, 1997. In 1875, Lieutenant Colonel William R. Shafter and his courageous Buffalo Soldiers, dying of thirst on the Staked Plains, discovered a life-saving spring in southeastern New Mexico Territory. As a guide to future settlers seeking water, they built a monument of glistening white rock on a nearby plateau, a spot known today as the community of Monument, New Mexico. Around this landmark, Truett has fashioned a novel about the exciting adventures of Cassandra, a young girl who, in 1875, married an Army captain and forged her way west.

Josanie's War: A Chiricahua Apache Novel by Karl H. Schlesier. University of Oklahoma Press, 1998. In Arizona Territory in 1885, five small bands of Chiricahua Apaches fled the reservation. Three of these bands were led by Chihuahua, Naiche, and Geronimo. The other two were led by Nana and Mangas. This is the story of the last great Apache war as told through the character of Josanie, Chihuahua's older brother, the war captain of his band.

Faraway Blue by Max Evans. Forge, 1999. Here Max Evans tells the story of the Ninth Cavalry's long and bloody campaign against the Warm Springs Apache Chief Nana. The story is based on the real-life exploits of Sergeant Moses Williams, former slave, Civil War veteran, and Medal of Honor-winning buffalo soldier, who was sent in 1879 to pacify the Apache territory of New Mexico. His primary quest was for Nana, whose lightning raids on frontier settlements had practically halted the pioneers expansion into New Mexico and Arizona.

The Contract Surgeon by Dan O'Brien. Lyons Press, 1999. An historical novel based on the friendship between Valentine McGillycuddy, a young army contract surgeon during the Great Sioux War, and Chief Crazy Horse. When Crazy Horse surrendered there was mistrust and treachery on both sides and the chief was fatally wounded. McGillycuddy tried to keep him alive, but could not. National Cowboy and Western Heritage Museum Western Heritage Award.

Lost River: An Epic Novel of the Modoc War by Riddle Paxton. Berkley, 1999. Paxton, a descendent of an intermarriage between Modoc and white during the time of the Modoc War, strives to explain the conflicts between the white settlers and the Modoc Indians that led to the deadly battle in the lava beds stronghold in the late 1800s.

American by Blood by Andrew Huebner. Simon and Schuster, 2000. A young army scout arrived at the Little Big Horn the day following Custer's Last Stand. This novel follows his story from that horrific day until the defeat of the Nez Perce a year later.

The Holy Road by Michael Blake. Villard, 2001. In this sequel to *Dances with Wolves*, set in 1874, it had been eleven years since Lieutenant Dunbar deserted from the army to live among the Comanche. He was Dances with Wolves and had married Stands with a Fist, the captive white woman raised by Indians, and they had three children. When a party of white rangers attacked his village and kidnaped his wife and youngest child, Dances with Wolves went after them in a wild attempt at rescue. In parallel, the novel tells of the conflicts among the Indians regarding whether to fight the white man or to make peace.

The Curse of Destiny: The Betrayal of General George Armstrong

Custer by Romain Wilhelmsen. Sunstone Press, 2001. George Armstrong Custer lived a life of defiance and brilliance until he met his fate at the battle of the Little Big Horn. This novel explores the events—and the unpredictable hand of destiny—that led to that fateful day and Custer's untimely demise.

Lonely Trumpet by Johnny D. Boggs. Five Star, 2002. In 1881 a general court-martial was convened at Fort Davis, Texas, to try Second Lieutenant H. O. Flipper, an officer in the Tenth Cavalry of the U. S. Army, Lieutenant Flipper was charged with embezzlement and conduct unbecoming an officer. Flipper was the first former slave and the only black man to graduate from West Point. His defense attorney, a respected Army officer, viewed the government's case against Flipper as a a conspiracy to remove the only black officer in the U. S. Army.

Moon of the Bitter Cold by Frederick J. Chiaventone, Forge, 2002. In 1866, as the U. S. Army built ever more forts on the Great Plains, Lakota Chief Red Cloud, assembled more than 3,000 warriors to drive the white man out. National Cowboy and Western Heritage Museum Western Heritage Award.

Spark on the Prairie by Johnny D. Boggs. Five Star, 2003. From Boggs' *Guns and Gavel* series. This novel recreates the historic 1871 trial of Kiowa Indians Satanta and Big Tree for the murder of seven teamsters during a raid near Jacksboro, Texas. National Cowboy and Western Heritage Museum Western Heritage Award.

The Sergeant's Lady by Miles Hood Swarthout. Forge, 2003. This is a story of love between an aging army sergeant acout and a rancher's middle-aged divorcee sister, set against the backdrop of the very last raid into Arizona by renegades under Chiricahua Chief Naiche's leadership at the tail-end of the twenty-six year war with the Apache in 1886.

Blood Kin: A Haunting Novel of Early Texas by Henry Chappell. Texas Tech University Press, 2004. Amidst the bloodshed of the Texas Revolution and the early days of the Texas Republic, escalating Indian raids prevented the peace sought by Isaac Webb and other Texans. The Texans wanted land and the Comanche wanted to raid and steal horses and take captives. Issac was appointed a peace emissary to the Comanche by Sam Houston, but was unable to bridge the chasm between them and the Texans.

The Indian Agent by Dan O'Brien. Lyons Press, 2004. A sequel to *The*

Contract Surgeon (1999), this volume continues the fictionalized biography of Dr. Valentine McGillycuddy, a U. S. Army contract surgeon who became friends with Crazy Horse. It begins after the death of Crazy Horse, when McGillycuddy became the agent for the Pine Ridge Indian Reservation. He and Chief Red Cloud had opposing views on almost every subject.

An Obituary for Major Reno by Richard S. Wheeler. Forge, 2004. A chronicle of Custer's last stand from the perspective of Major Marcus Reno, one of Custer's senior officers. History condemned Reno for failing to come to Custer's aid on the day of the massacre in Montana in 1876. In 1889, dying of cancer, a disgraced man who wanted only to regain his honor, Reno granted a last interview to a newspaper reporter, hoping to finally tell his side of the story.

SELECTED REVIEWS

Blood Brother
by Elliott Arnold
Duell, Sloan and Pearce, 1947

Brigadier General George Crook, who finally defeated the Apaches and brought a measure of peace to the territories of Arizona and New Mexico, said the Indians never broke a treaty they made—and the white man never kept one. This is a story of broken treaties and tragic consequences.

When the war between the United States and Mexico ended with the Treaty of Hidalgo Guadalupe in 1848, the U. S. promised to keep the Apaches from raiding into Mexico. The Indians were not a party to the treaty. Then, with the Gadsden Purchase in 1853, the homeland of the Chiricahua Apaches became a part of the United States. Again, the Apaches weren't consulted.

The Chiricahua was the smallest but the fiercest and most feared of the many tribes in the Apache nation. Their traditional home was in the Chiricahua Mountains in what's now southwestern Arizona. Two strongholds in the mountains were their impregnable, rocky havens. A few warriors placed at the narrow entrances could hold off a large enemy force indefinitely. The Mexicans were their traditional enemies.

When the Americans began to pour into the Southwest, Cochise, the great chief of the Chiricahua, met with his brother-in-law, Mangas Coloradas, chief of the Mimbres, the largest Apache tribe. He spoke of his plans to make peace with the ever-increasing population of white men. The Mimbres chief wouldn't join him because the Americans also demanded peace with Mexico, whom Mangas Coloradas hated because Mexicans still collected money from their government for Apache scalps. A Chiricahua warrior named Gokliya also "walked away" from the proposed peace and a small group of warriors followed him. Using the name Geronimo, given to him by the Mexicans, Gokliya would terrorize that section of the Southwest for many years to come.

Nevertheless, Cochise made peace, which held for about four years. But the treachery of a green army lieutenant destroyed the fragile accord, and Cochise swore a war of vengeance. He joined forces with the Mimbres, and in 1862 the Apaches were attacking in forces as high as three hundred at a time.

Throughout the Civil War Cochise dominated Arizona. No white man saw him and remained alive to tell of it. His domain stretched from the Mimbres country in New Mexico across almost all of Arizona, from the Gila River in the North to as far south as his men cared to venture. He became a legend of death and horror.

The fury of the Apache wars provides a dramatic backdrop for a story of friendship between Cochise and Tom Jeffords, a tall, spare, red-bearded ex-army guide.

In September of 1865, some five months after the end of the Civil War, Jeffords resigned his commission as an army scout. He accepted a job supervising the mail between Tucson and Bowie. Because of the Apaches, the mail couldn't get through. They killed the riders and scattered the mail pouches all over the desert.

Jeffords decided to see Cochise. He learned Apache and, at great risk, had an Indian guide lead him to Cochise's temporary camp. Cochise admired bravery above all else, and agreed to listen. Jeffords asked only that the mail be allowed to go through. Since he came to Cochise alone and spoke with a straight tongue, Cochise agreed. They became friends, and later mixed their blood in an Apache ceremony and became blood brothers. They made a pact that allowed mail riders who worked for Jeffords to pass through Chiricahua country unharmed.

On April 30, 1871, in the early hours while the Indians slept, white citizens of Tucson and San Xavier clubbed and stabbed one hundred and eight Arivaipa Apaches to death. Only eight were men, the rest was women and children. This incident became known as the Camp Grant Massacre, and it turned the attention of the country to the Apache problem in Arizona. President Grant sent Major General O. O. Howard to Arizona to find Cochise and make peace. Howard had Tom Jeffords take him to Cochise, who greeted Jeffords warmly, then asked General Howard the purpose of his visit. They negotiated, and Cochise told Jeffords, "I think he speaks with a straight tongue." Cochise insisted the Chiricahuas be allowed to stay in their own country. He also insisted Tom Jeffords be appointed Indian agent. General Howard acceded, and Cochise declared that the white man and the Indian were at peace. And, true to history and the underlying theme of Arnold's novel, the government ignored its obligation under the treaty.

Elliott Arnold captures not only the intensity and the ultimate tragedy of the Apache wars, but he deftly conveys both the beauty and the barrenness of the Arizona setting, and the power it exerts on the people who have to survive in these deserts. And he eloquently describes the little dramas that happened during this time in a far-flung western outpost. For example, the Gadsden Purchase changed Tucson overnight from Mexico to the United States. Arnold wrote of this occasion:

Late on the afternoon of March 9 the Mexican garrison formed for the last time in La Plaza de las Armas with their backs to the sinking sun and then marched in formation across the Calle de la Guardia into La Plaza Militar. Their uniforms were clean and for the first time in a long time every rifle was polished and every bayonet shone. The bugler sounded retreat and the tiny garrison marched down the Calle Real to the main gate and, as the people stood and wept and watched, they evacuated the town and started for Mexico. The natives stared as their country marched away from them.

Following the Gadsden Purchase the American army was garrisoned at Tucson, changing forever the lives of its Mexican residents.

Arnold provides an insight into Apache life, customs, beliefs, and environment. From childhood the Apache male was trained in nothing but the hunt and the raid. He could run seventy-five miles a day through the hard cactus and mesquite-laden country, up and down mountains and canyons, with a tirelessness that was the despair of the Mexicans and Americans who tried to follow them. Fearless in battle, they showed no quarter to an enemy. They often tortured captives. The Chiricahuas captured a Mexican who had sold Apache scalps to his government. They buried him in a hole up to his neck, poured sweet syrup over his head, and squatted in a circle around him and watched the ants engulf his head.

But the Apaches had a sense of humor. They had learned the extreme range of rifles used by the Americans and during rest periods in their frequent encounters they removed themselves out of gun range, which perhaps was no more than two hundred and fifty yards, and then indulged in a favorite form of insult. They lifted their loincloths, exposed their buttocks, and said offensive things.

The main events in the book are true. A number of the smaller events are also true, but the author has woven them into the fictional episodes. Almost all the characters are drawn from history; in most instances real names were used. The characterizations are powerful. Consider Mangas Coloradas:

> He was an imposing man. He was a larger man physically than even
> Cochise, and his largeness was everywhere on him, on his huge
> body, on his bulky arms, his broad legs, and mostly, on his enormous
> head. He had wide, penetrating eyes, and in the center of his gigantic
> head he wore a slender, almost delicate nose, narrow at the bridge
> and broadening on slightly at the nostrils.

Regarded as the elder statesman of the Apache nation, Mangas Coloradas was never a great military leader. His strength lay in the wisdom of his advice at councils and in his diplomacy in dealing with other tribes. After he was killed by American soldiers, his body was exhumed, the head severed and sent to Washington. The brain weighed as much as that of Daniel Webster, and the skull was larger. The skull was sent to the Smithsonian Museum and put on display.

Elliott Arnold broke away from the prevailing view of the Indian in this landmark novel. He viewed the American migration into the Southwest from the Indian's perspective. Though he detailed the injustices the white man visited upon the Indians, he clearly showed why there was hatred on both sides.

Blood Brother was made into the enduring, successful film "Broken Arrow" and later serialized on television. The 1950 20th Century Fox film was directed by Delmer Davis and starred James Stewart as Tom Jeffords and Jeff Chandler as Cochise. The film began a cycle of Westerns that treated the Indian sympathetically.

The Wolf and the Buffalo
by Elmer Kelton
Doubleday, 1980

Elmer Kelton, raised on a Texas Panhandle ranch, has written over forty novels, all set in the American West. Seven won Spur Awards from the Western Writers of America, and that organization voted him the Best Western Author of all Time. Four of his novels won the National Cowboy and Western Heritage Museum's Western Heritage Award.

The Wolf and the Buffalo grew out of a request by the editors of *Reader's Digest Condensed Books* for a novel about the black cavalry in the West. Kelton originally intended to tell the story from the viewpoint of a young black soldier, Gideon Ledbetter, but the role of Gideon's Comanche adversary Gray Horse kept expanding. The result is a sympathetic picture of two opposing forces locked in a struggle to the death.

Fort Sill, in the heart of the reservations, was headquarters for Colonel Benjamin H. Grierson and the black 10th Calvary. Grierson commanded detachments scattered more than two hundred miles south. Gideon was stationed at Fort Concho, one of the 10th Calvary's Texas outposts. Located next to the town of Saint Angelia (present-day San Angelo), it was built on a patch of wide-open, treeless plain at the juncture of the Main and North Concho Rivers. From this isolated post, troopers fanned out to patrol north and west from the Llano Estacado to the Pecos River.

The novel chronicles the monotony of the soldiers' lives on post, the hardships they endured on patrol, and the savagery of their engagements with the Comanche. With sagacious insight, Kelton recounts the injustice that came with being black in a white man's army.

The black units were commanded by white officers. It was said that if an officer wasn't fit for promotion the only way he could move up was to join a black regiment. And although the troopers were there to protect the whites from the Indians—or to take the Indian's land for the whites—they were despised by the people they protected. Virtually everyone in neighboring Saint Angelia wanted the "nigger soldiers" moved out of Fort Concho. But the "Buffalo Soldiers" (so named because of the resemblance between their hair and the buffaloes' shaggy coat) were held in much higher esteem by their Comanche adversaries. Their campaign record was substantial; they fought frequently and hard.

The Wolf and the Buffalo is, in part, the story of how Gideon evolved from a slave to a first-class soldier with a measure of self-respect. Old Colonel Hayworth had never encouraged his slaves to think for themselves. So when Gideon and his friend Jimbo—a wonderful character who was "in constant danger of grinning himself to death"—were freed at the end of the Civil War, they were unable to fend for themselves. Recruited by the army because of Jimbo's skill with horses, they were shipped west to help man the thin line of forts scattered across the frontier. Gideon started out as a clumsy soldier; in his first engagement with the Comanche, his horse bolted and ran away from the troopers' gunfire, toward the Indians. This earned him the embarrassing nickname "Charger" from his commander. But through the tutelage of First Sergeant Essau Nettles, a black soldier who bore himself like the commander-in-chief of all the armies, Gideon learned to stand his ground.

In parallel with Gideon's growth, a young Comanche warrior named Gray Horse came of age. Kelton describes Gray Horse's quest for "personal medicine," some sign of approval by a good spirit, a sign that was needed before a young man could venture out upon the war trail. We're given the Comanche view of warfare, where they "showed no mercy or pity. No wrong could be done to an enemy, whether it was man, woman or child." We watch Gray Horse grow into a warrior that others follow. And within the grander scale of the Plains Indian wars, we watch a deadly engagement between opposing forces led by Gray Horse and Corporal Gideon Ledbetter.

The Indian wars were inevitable. Lieutenant Frank Hollander, Gideon's company commander, put it this way:

> The Indians—the plains tribes, anyway—are too different from us.
> They don't see life in our terms, and we can't see it in theirs. The
> white man gains respect by his work, by what he builds, by what he
> accumulates and keeps. These things mean nothing to the Indians.
> They are warriors. A warrior gains respect by his feats in battle.
> Put an Indian where he can no longer fight, and how is he to live?
> What is he to live for? Where is he to earn respect?. . . . Try to put us
> together and the white man will always covet the Indian's land. The
> Indian will always be looking for a fight so he can gain honor. We're
> incompatible . . .

Elmer Kelton has said it is unfair to judge past generations by the standards of our own times; if we are to condemn our forefathers for taking the land from the Comanches, then we must condemn the Comanches for taking it from the Apaches, and so on. Many won't agree with this philosophy, but most should agree that Kelton is even-handed in presenting both the soldiers and the Indians as products of their era.

Fort Concho is one of the best preserved frontier forts in America. It stands today as a memorial to the soldiers who made West Texas safe for settlement.

4

THE WILD WEST: LAWMEN, GUNFIGHTERS, OUTLAWS, AND FRONTIER JUSTICE

INTRODUCTION

When the "Wild West" is mentioned, certain names and places routinely come to mind: Wyatt Earp, Wild Bill Hickok, Jesse James, Butch Cassidy, Dodge City, Tombstone. There are others, many others, rooted in our culture. Partly myth but based on fact, gunfighting in the Wild West accounts for much of the public's enduring fascination with it.

First there were the cow towns. Thousands of longhorns were driven up the Chisholm Trail from Texas to Abilene, Kansas. From 1867 to 1871, about a million and a half cattle were shipped by rail to processing plants in Chicago and Kansas City. In rapid succession, new railheads such as Wichita, Hays City, Ellsworth, and Dodge City began shipping longhorns east.

After a long, miserable trail drive, contending with lousy food, little sleep, quicksand, stampedes, and the sheer monotony of driving an average herd of twenty-five hundred of the dumbest animals on earth, the cowboys were spoiling for a good time. They found it at the end of the trail, in the gambling and bawdy houses at the railheads. Few places have ever equaled these cow towns in sheer lawlessness.

The exuberant trail drivers fought each other, and the townsmen, whom they usually thought were cheating them. For self-protection, the towns imported professional gunmen. Some of these "shootists" brought law and order and became legends: Wyatt Earp, Wild Bill Hickok, Bat Masterson, Bill Tilghman, Tom Smith, Dallas Stoudenmire, and Ben Thompson. Gunmen of equal notoriety who lived outside the law migrated to the towns: John Wesley Hardin, who feared no man; Clay Allison, a ruthless gunman with a hair-trigger temper; Billy the Kid, who killed his first man at age fifteen; Bill Longley, who had killed thirty-two men by age twenty-seven. There were many others of their ilk, scattered throughout the Wild West.

More boomtowns sprang up. Tombstone, surrounded by rich silver mines, boasted of being the wickedest, most wide-open town in the West. Other towns made the same claim. Gunfighters, some operating in the name of the law and others showing contempt for it, were drawn to these places. Their very presence inspired awe and dread. The towns nurtured the West's reputation as a wild and violent land.

Lawlessness was not confined to frontier towns. Following the Civil War, roving outlaw bands robbed banks, stagecoaches, and trains. The most notorious was Jesse James and his gang, operating in and around Missouri for fifteen years. The James gang inspired Cole Younger and his brothers, as well as the Dalton brothers, who robbed and pillaged in the same area. The Indian Territory, present-day Oklahoma, was terrorized by Bill Doolin and Henry Starr's gangs. During and following the Civil War roving bands of guerrillas, called bushwhackers, harassed Union forces and citizens along the Kansas-Missouri border. In Utah in 1895, Butch Cassidy and his trusted confederate Harry Longabaugh, better known as the Sundance Kid, formed the Wild Bunch, last of the old-time outlaw gangs.

Then there were the range wars. Arizona's Pleasant Valley War was the result of animosity between cattlemen and sheepmen. On September 4, 1887, at Holbrook, Sheriff Commodore Perry Owens killed several men from one of the warring factions in one of the more famous gunfights of the era. Wyoming's Johnson County War started in 1892 when the powerful Stock Grower's Association, based in Cheyenne, declared war on the small ranchers in Johnson County, whom they suspected of rustling their cattle. The Association's "regulators" included cattlemen, stock detectives, and twenty-one hired Texas gunmen. When two suspected rustlers were killed in a dramatic twelve-hour shootout, fighting erupted between the regulators and the small ranchers, led by the Johnson County sheriff. New Mexico's Lincoln County War of 1878 began as a mercantile competition by two rival companies seeking commercial monopoly in the area. The conflict climaxed in Lincoln in July, 1878, with a five day gun battle. Among the participants was young William H. Bonney, yet to gain fame as Billy the Kid.

In the remote Southwest, where there was little if any government, outlaws were brought to justice by a special breed of lawman. They were the rangers, direct agents of the state or territorial government. They recruited tough men who could patrol great distances on horseback, pursuing rustlers and other wanted men along the Mexican border in Texas, New Mexico, and Arizona.

In the end, however, since a peace officer could only fight violence with violence, it was the responsibility of the frontier judges to bring lasting law and order to the Wild West.

No region presented more of a jurisdictional problem than the vast Indian Territory, some 70,000 square miles of wild country. Isaac Parker, judge of the Western District of Arkansas, was the absolute law for the territory for two decades. During his tenure, he sentenced 160 men to the gallows. Sixty-five of his deputy marshals died in the line of duty.

Judge Roy Bean, the self-styled "Law West of the Pecos," never held a post higher than justice of the peace. But beginning with his appointment in 1882, he had a twenty year magisterial reign over his desolate West Texas jurisdiction. He was noted for serving liquor and administering justice simultaneously in his saloon. He tried all cases brought before him, regardless of the charge. Even the Texas Rangers would bring their prisoners to Judge Bean for trial.

Lawmen, outlaws, jurists, rustlers, vigilantes, range wars, and cow towns are fine grist for exciting novels. The Earps' adventures in Tombstone, Arizona, are the subject of Loren D. Estleman's *Bloody Season* (Bantam Books, 1988). *Deadwood* (Random House, 1986), by Pete Dexter, is the story of Wild Bill Hickok's last days in Deadwood, South Dakota. Charles Portis' *True Grit* (Simon and Schuster, 1968) has as its main character a one-eyed old deputy U. S. marshal, working out of Judge Isaac Parker's Western District court, who tracks a killer into the wild Indian Territory. *The War in the Nueces*

Strip (Doubleday, 1989), by historan Don Worcester, follows the heroic deeds of Captain Lee McNelly and his company of Texas Rangers as they fight rustlers and bandits in the border country of south Texas. *Willie Boy: A Desert Manhunt* (Paisano Press,1960), by Harry Lawton, is the true story of a 20th Century manhunt across the Mojave Desert that rang down the curtain on the Wild West.

Reader's Guide

The Scalp Hunters by Thomas Mayne Reid. London: Dean, 1851. English author Captain Mayne Reid (1818—1883) wrote more than fifty books about the American West. This novel, his second, was set in the West from St. Louis to Santa Fe and extended south through El Paso into Chihuahua. It is the story of a Creole who was hired by a scalp hunter to kill Navajos and Apaches for the bounties on their scalps. He left hundreds of bodies in the wilderness as testimony of his skill.

The Sunset Trail by Alfred Henry Lewis. A. L. Burt, 1905. An early fictional biography of Bat Masterson.

Stepsons of Light by Eugene Manlove Rhodes. Houghton Mifflin, 1921. A story of frontier justice and chivalry—where a man would rather face hanging than implicate a woman—in territorial New Mexico in the late 19th century.

The Saga of Billy the Kid by Walter Noble Burns. Doubleday, Page, 1926. A novelized account of the life of Billy the Kid, the notorious southwestern bad man, who was killed by Sheriff Pat Garrett at Fort Sumner, New Mexico, in 1881. Source for the 1930 and 1941 films "Billy the Kid."

Tombstone: An Illiad of the Southwest by Walter Noble Burns. Doubleday, Page 1927. The Arizona silver boom town of Tombstone and the infamous Earp brothers are the subjects of this novelized frontier history.

Wyatt Earp: Frontier Marshal by Stuart N. Lake. Houghton Mifflin, 1931. This is an authorized biography, novelized with dialogue. When this book was published in 1931, Wyatt Earp's status as an American legend was secured.

Robin Hood of El Dorado: The Saga of Joaquin Murrieta, (spelled "Murieta" by some authors) *Famous Outlaw of California's Age of Gold* by Walter Noble Burns. Coward-McCann, 1932. During California's tumultuous Gold Rush, a Mexican outlaw named Joaquin Murrieta tracked and killed his wife Rosita's murderers and defended Hispanos against violence and dispossession by rampaging gold rush miners. Source for the 1936 film "Robin Hood of El Dorado."

The Hash Knife Outfit by Zane Grey. Harper and Brothers, 1933. Set seven years after the Pleasant Valley War between cattlemen and sheepmen in 1880s Arizona. The Hash Knife Outfit was assembled to guard over a million acres of land owned by the Aztec Land and Cattle Company in northern Arizona. This novel dramatizes the band's disintegration and demise.

Gamblin' Man by E. B. (Edward Beverly) Mann. William Morrow, 1934. A novel about Billy the Kid that portrays him as a likeable youth who became a victim of persecution.

The Trusty Knaves by Eugene Manlove Rhodes. Houghton Mifflin, 1934. A novel of corruption overturned in Target (Deming), New Mexico. Target was "a no-good town. What was needed to clean up the town was a group of trusty knaves." Rhodes knew outlaw Bill Doolin, and based his character William Hawkins on the noted outlaw.

Gringo Gold by Dane Coolidge. E. P. Dutton, 1939. A novel based on the life and legends of the California bandit Joaquin Murrieta.

The Ox-Bow Incident by Walter Van Tilburg Clark. Random House, 1940. A novel of frontier justice, carried out by a mob. In 1885, near a small Nevada cow town, a well-liked cowboy was ambushed and murdered by rustlers. The sheriff was away, but a posse was formed, and a struggle began between those calling for vigilante justice, and the few voices insisting on following the law. Basis for the 1943 film.

Trail Town by Ernest Haycox. Little, Brown, 1941. Sheriff Dan Mitchell had been hired to keep law and order in River Bend, a rough and dusty cowtown at the end of a cattle trail from Texas. But he had more trouble with the townspeople who hired him than he did with the cowboys who came up the trail. Source for the 1946 film "Abilene Town."

Pistols for Hire by Nelson Nye. Macmillan, 1941. A novel about Billy the Kid that depicts him as a cold-blooded mercenary who shot people in the back.

Montana, Here I Be! by Dan Cushman. Macmillan, 1950. A famous road agent named Comanche John rode into the Montana town of American Flag. He learned that a hanging was scheduled that night for a man named Comanche John.

The Comancheros by Paul I. Wellman. Doubleday, 1952. Three Texas Rangers found the nest of the Comancheros, white men who raided with the deadly Comanche in their bloody massacres. Basis for the 1961 film.

Billy the Kid by Edwin Corle. Duell, Sloan and Pearce, 1953. A novel about Billy the Kid that portrays him as a steely-eyed, emotionless killer. The source for the film "Pat Garrett and Billy the Kid "

Night Passage by Norman A. Fox. Dodd, Mead, 1955. A disgraced troubleshooter for the railroad had one chance at redemption. He had to get a payroll for the construction crew past a gang of train robbers. One of them was his brother. Basis for the 1957 film.

Who Rides with Wyatt? by Will Henry. Random House, 1955. This novel portrays a vengeance-bent Wyatt Earp who "takes the law into his own hands" as he tracks down his brother's slayers. Source for the 1959 film "Young Billy Young."

The Life and Adventures of Joaquin Murieta, the Celebrated California Bandit by John Rollin Ridge. University of Oklahoma Press, 1955. First published in 1854. Murieta was a shadowy figure, a Spanish-speaking outlaw in the early months of 1853 for whom there exists very little documentation. Ridge's novel is largely an imaginative work written for commercial purposes, a fictionalized biography that established Murieta's image as a folk hero.

The Ballad of Cat Ballou by Roy Chanslor. Little, Brown, 1956. When Cat Ballou saw her parents murdered, she swore vengeance. As the leader of a band of outlaws, she would twice ascend the gallows. Basis for the 1965 film "Cat Ballou."

The Authentic Death of Hendry Jones by Charles Neider. Harper and Brothers, 1956. A novel based on Billy the Kid and the Lincoln County War, thinly disguised with the setting transformed to California. Basis for the 1961 film "One-Eyed Jacks."

Riders of Judgement by Frederick Manfred. Random House, 1957. Set during the bloody range wars of the 1880s in Johnson County, Wyoming, where small ranchers and farmers made a last stand against the cattle barons, who employed crooked politicians and hired guns. Basis for the 2001 Hallmark teleplay "Johnson County War."

Reckoning at Yankee Flat by Will Henry (Henry Wilson Allen). Random House, 1958. Henry Plummer was the sheriff of Virginia City in the wide-open Montana Territory of the mid-1800s. He was also the leader of a gang of road agents, who murdered, robbed and terrorized the whole territory until frontier justice caught up with them.

Warlock by Oakley Hall. Viking Press, 1958. Based on the Wyatt Earp/Tombstone saga. Clay Blaisdale (Earp) is a gunman brought in by a citizens' committee to clean up Warlock (Tombstone). Basis for the 1959 film with the same title.

Sam Bass & Company by Will C. Brown (Scott Boyles). New American Library, 1960. Recounts the rise and fall, in Denton County, Texas, of illiterate outlaw and train robber Sam Bass.

The Daybreakers by Louis L'Amour. Bantam Books, 1960. Tyrel Sackett killed a man in Tennessee, then rode west with his brother Orin. Orin became a peace officer and brought law and order to Santa Fe. Tyrel's fast gun backed him. Partial source for the 1979 Teleplay "The Sacketts."

Honor Thy Father by Robert Roripaugh. William Morrow, 1963. A rancher feuds with his son who supports the homesteaders in Wyoming's 1887 Johnson Couny War, a conflict that could end the cattleman's way of life. National Cowboy and Western Heritage Museum Western Heritage Award.

Time for Outrage by Amelia Bean. Doubleday, 1967. An historical narrative based on the Lincoln County War of New Mexico in 1878, the Tunstall factions versus the McSween factions, with Hendry Brown, Billy The Kid, Jesse Evans, Pat Garrett, and Governor Lew Wallace involved in the drama.

Alias Butch Cassidy by Will Henry (Henry Wilson Allen). Random House, 1968. At sixteen, George Parker, grandson of a Mormon bishop, threw in with Mike Cassidy, a shrewd old bandit who saw something in the boy no one else did. The old bandit was a good judge of men; the brash, smiling kid would carve out a legend of violence and bravery. This is the saga of George LeRoy Parker—alias Butch Cassidy.

Death of a Gunfighter by Lewis B. Patten. Doubleday, 1968. He was a legendary gunfighter, now the marshal in a quiet Texas town. He could handle any bad men who came his way. But then the town turned against him. Basis for the 1969 film.

Captain's Rangers by Elmer Kelton. Ballantine Books, 1969. In 1875, nearly forty years after the Mexican War, Mexicans and Texans were still fighting over ownership of the Nueces Strip. The Cortinista bandits raided at will along the desolate strip. Texas Ranger Captain L. H. McNelly was brought in to keep the peace. His measures were harsh and controversial but effective.

Butch Cassidy, the Sundance Kid, and the Wild Bunch by David King. Popular Library, 1970. Of the old Wild Bunch, Butch Cassidy and the Sundance Kid were the only two left. The rest were in prison or dead. A few steps ahead of the federal marshals, bounty hunters and Pinkertons, traveling with a deceptively demure woman named Etta Place, they made their way to Argentina. But a peaceful, prosperous life in South America wasn't in their future.

The Collected Works of Billy the Kid; Left Handed Poems by Michael Ondaatje. Tor Books, 1970. Ondaatje uses poems and stories to present the personal life—and to journey into the mind—of the notorious outlaw and killer Billy the Kid.

The Man Who Loved Cat Dancing by Marilyn Durham. Harcourt, Brace, 1972. In the Wyoming Territory of the 1880s, a lively woman named Catherine falls into the hands of a gang of outlaws. Their leader is torn between his passion for Catherine and the memories of his dead Indian wife, Cat Dancing. Basis for the 1973 film.

Outcasts of Canyon Creek by Clay Fisher (Henry Wilson Allen). Bantam Books, 1972. The vigilantes of Montana in the mid-1800s were at times a lynch mob. In this story they put their noose on the wrong man.

El Paso by Matt Braun. Fawcett, 1973. It was fitting that El Paso, the rowdiest town on the Texas-Mexican border, hired Dallas Stoudenmire in 1881 as its marshal. He was a no-nonsense lawman, an ex-Texas Ranger who was good with his gun, and was determined to clean up the town that some called the toughest on the Rio Grande.

Breakheart Pass by Alstair MacLean, Doubleday, 1974. A train trip in the Rocky Mountains in the 1870s is the setting for this suspense-adventure tale in which a Federal agent is pitted against villainous thieves. Basis for the 1975 film.

Rockspring by R. G. Vliet. Viking Press, 1974. A tale of the abduction by Mexican outlaws of a 14-year-old pioneer girl in the Nueces River Valley of Texas in the 1830s.

Noble Outlaw by Matt Braun. Pocket Books, 1975. John Wesley Hardin was the worst killer ever to come out of Texas. He may have killed as many as forty men.

I, Tom Horn by Will Henry (Henry Wilson Allen). J. B. Lippincott, 1975. Tom Horn was a famed Arizona cavalry scout, the final tracker of Geronimo, and a Pinkerton detective. This fictional autobiography addresses the question that has haunted both his admirers and detractors through the years: did this extraordinary man kill fourteen-year-old Willie Nickell, or was he framed?

The Shootist by Glendon Swarthout. Doubleday, 1975. John Bernard Books rides into El Paso in 1901, an old shootist (gunfighter) dying of cancer. Rather than die in bed or take his own life, Books chooses his own executioner. Basis for the 1976 film. Spur Award from Western Writers of America.

Cattle Annie and Little Britches by Robert Ward. William Morrow, 1978. An historical novel based on the lives of Jennie Stevens "Little Britches" and Annie McDougal "Cattle Annie" and their association with Bill Doolin and his gang and the Dalton Gang. Basis for the 1980 film of the same title.

The Wind and the Wayward by Georgia Granger. Dell, 1979. From Dell's *The Making of America* series. Set in the last days of the Wild West. Jesse and Frank James, Wild Bill Hickok, the Doolin Gang, and the Rose of Cimarron have roles in this Western saga.

Desperadoes by Ron Hansen. Alfred A. Knopf, 1979. This is the story of the notorious Dalton Gang, from its beginnings to its violent end in Coffeyville, Kansas in 1892. The narrator is Emmett Dalton, the only survivor of the Coffeyville shootout.

Belle Starr by Speer Morgan. Little, Brown, 1979. Belle Starr, unattractive and brazen but smart, was known as the "Bandit Queen of

Oklahoma." This novel is the story of her last tragic months of life before she was assassinated.

Black Marshal by Bill Burchardt. Doubleday, 1981. Judge Isaac Parker commissioned Gar Rutherford (based on Bass Reeves, an actual "black marshal" during that period)) a Federal marshal. Parker thought a black marshal would engender less hatred among the Indian tribes of the Oklahoma Territory than a white lawman. But the judge underestimated the prejudice of whites against Rutherford.

Aces and Eights by Loren D. Estleman. Pinnacle Books, 1981. James Butler "Wild Bill" Hickok was shot in the back while playing poker (holding aces and eights) in Deadwood, Dakota Territory, on August 2, 1876. Here his life is presented from both sides during the trial of his killer. Spur Award winner.

Corey Lane by Norman Zollinger. Ticknor and Fields, 1981. Corey Lane was the legendary sheriff of Chupadera County, New Mexico, a man who could handle anything, even the Apache leader Victorio. Then he became a renegade.

Smash the Wild Bunch by Giles A. Lutz. Walker, 1982. Federal Marshal Evett Nix received orders from Washington to go after Bill Doolin's gang, who had been terrorizing the Oklahoma Territory, and were now hiding out in the tiny town of Ingalls.

The Assassination of Jesse James by the Coward, Robert Ford by Ron Hansen. Alfred A. Knopf, 1983. The life of the Missouri Outlaw Jesse James, and his assassination by Bob Ford, a young member of the James gang who both admired and envied Jesse.

Sam Bass by Bryan Woolley. Corona, 1983. A novel based on the life of the infamous Texas highwayman. Spur Award from Western Writers of America.

Hanging Judge by Elmer Kelton. Bantam Books, 1984. Justin Moffitt was sworn in as the newest deputy marshal to "the hanging judge" Isaac Parker, who lost almost one law officer for every criminal he hanged. Justin was assigned to Marshal Sam Dark, and the two of them had to deal with the vengeance-seeking family of a man Judge Parker had hanged.

The Bounty Hunters by Lee Davis Willoughby (house name). Dell, 1984. From Dell's *The Making of America* series. Jamie McKay killed the men who had raped and murdered his Indian mother. One of the dead men was the son of a wealthy rancher, whose offer of a large reward set Wyatt Earp, Doc Holliday, Ben Thompson, Johnny Ringo, and other gunfighters on McKay's trail.

The Texas Rangers by Lee Davis Willoughby (house name). Dell, 1984. From Dell's *The Making of America* series. In Texas in the 1870s, a small force of Texas Rangers stood against the fierce Comanche, cattle thieves from both sides of the border, and outlaw killers like Sam Bass.

The Old Colts by Glendon Swarthout. Donald I. Fine, 1985. A novel based on Bat Masterson and Wyatt Earp and the last assault on Dodge City. This is the story of two old men looking for one last adventure.

West Wandering Wind by W. R. Garwood and Carl H. Breihan. Doubleday, 1986. Judge Roy Bean, who administered swift and often final justice, became one of the most enduring legends of the Southwest. This novel takes us back to his early years.

Stringer by Lou Cameron. Doubleday, 1987. The first novel in Cameron's *Stringer* series. Stuart MacKail was a "stringer," or part-time newspaper reporter, who worked for the *San Francisco Sun*. In the series, he was dispatched by his editor all over the Old West to write stories on momentious events and colorful characters. In this story he was sent to California to investigate "The Ghost of Sonora," Joaquin Murieta.

Sonny by Jim Miller. Doubleday, 1987. A grizzled frontiersman, working as a cook on John Chisum's Jingblebob Ranch, tries to keep a young hothead from joining up with Billy the Kid during New Mexico's infamous Lincoln County War of 1878.

The Last Narrow Gauge Train Robbery by Robert K. Swisher, Jr. Sunstone Press, 1987. Bill Masterson, Ronnie Wild, Riley Page and Frank Cummings were ex-hippies living outwardly responsible and respectable lives who yearned for the old days of freedom. Finally they decided to do something daring and different: robbing the tourist-crowded narrow gauge train.

Mamaw by Susan Dodd. Viking Press, 1988. A novel based on the life of Zerelda James, the mother of Frank and Jesse James, and of her notorious sons, as seen through the eyes of their mother.

Anything for Billy by Larry McMurtry. Simon and Schuster, 1988. In this fictional tale of Billy the Kid (here called Billy Bone), narrated by an eastern writer named Ben Sippy who wrote Western dime novels, Billy is a homely teenager who kills without remorse, mainly to live up to his growing reputation.

The Saga of Henry Starr by Robert J. Conley. Doubleday, 1989. Henry Starr was a seventeen-year old Cherokee cowboy when he was framed and arrested for a crime he did not commit. He became one of the most notorious criminals of the Old West, best known for robbing two banks in the same town at the same time.

The Lady and Doc Holliday by Preston Lewis. Eakin Press, 1989. A novel about Doc Holliday and legendary Texas gambler Lottie Deno, set in Fort Griffin on the Texas frontier.

What Law There Was by Al Dempsey. St. Martin's Press, 1991. The gold camp of Bannock, Montana, in 1862 was crowded with every type of humanity—good and bad—and they needed a sheriff. The lawman they selected was Henry Plummer, a notorious gunman/outlaw who would organize an efficient and ruthless gang to terrorize and plunder the region. It was then that the Freemasons of Bannack become "What Law There Was."

Kid Curry: The Life and Times of Harvey Logan and the Wild Bunch by F. Bruce Lamb. Johnson Books, 1991. An account of the life of Harvey Logan, a cowboy-outlaw who for a while was one of the original members of Butch Cassidy's "Wild Bunch."

The Gringo Amigo by Gary McCarthy. Doubleday, 1991. An Irish immigrant named Callahan becomes friends with a Mexican named Joaquin Murieta during the California Gold Rush, earning him a reputation as a Gringo Amigo.

Rage in Chupadera by Norman Zollinger. Forge, 1991. In this sequel to *Corey Lane* (Tichnor and Fields, 1981), the story of the legendary sheriff turned renegade, his son returns from the Spanish Civil War to Chupadera County, New Mexico, to find that old hatreds die hard. Spur Award winner.

A Ballad for Sallie by Judy Alter. Doubleday, 1992. Longhair Jim Courtwright had been a marshal in Fort Worth back in the late 1870s, and a fugitive because of a New Mexico killing. In 1886 he returned to Hell's Acre, the roughest part of Fort Worth, where he was a legend. There, outside the

White Elephant Saloon, he and another legend named Luke Short had a deadly encounter.

The Gun Fight by Richard Matheson. M. Evans, 1993. An ex-Texas Ranger, once known as the "fastest gun in the West," put away his gun and tried to settle down. But a young man was goaded by his fiancée and his father into challenging him, an act of vanity that could result in deadly consequences.

Journal of the Gun Years: Being Choice Selections from the Authentic, Never-Before-Printed Diary of the Famous Gunfighter-Lawman Clay Halser, Whose Deeds of Daring Made His Name a By-Word of Terror in the Southwest between the Years of 1866 and 1876 by Richard Matheson. M. Evans, 1993. The plot follows the diaries of a drifter in the Old West who evolves from a Civil War veteran to a ruthless desperado, then lawman, and finally a professional gambler. His story is picked up by newspapers and dime novel writers, and the legend grows, until he is defined by it. Spur Award winner.

Streets of Laredo by Larry McMurtry. Simon and Schuster, 1993. The sequel to McMurtry's *Lonesome Dove* (Simon and Schuster, 1985). Captain Woodrow Call, pushing seventy, now works as a hired gun for the railroad. Set fifteen years after *Lonesome Dove*, the story recounts Call's pursuit of the elusive young Mexican bandit Joey Garza, and the psychopathic manburner Mox Mox. Basis for the 1995 television miniseries.

The Demise of Billy the Kid: The Memoirs of H. H. Lomax by Preston Lewis. Bantam Books, 1994. The first in Lewis' series featuring H. H. Lomax, who wasn't much of a gunfighter, but rather a likable loser who ran into old western celebrities like Billy the Kid and the James Gang.

While Angels Dance: The Life and Times of Jeston Nash by Ralph Cotton. St. Martin's Press, 1994. In a blend of history and fiction, this is the story of Frank and Jesse James, including their time with Quantrill's Raiders and the exploits of the James-Younger gang. The narrator is Jeston Nash, a fictional cousin who rode with them.

Single Tree by Gary D. Svee. Walker, 1994. A story of vigilante justice in Montana in the late 1880s. During this time Montana was cattle country, and where there were cattle, there were rustlers. Vigilantes would hang anyone suspected of rustling, and mistakes were made.

The Pistoleer by James Carlos Blake. Berkley, 1995. The fictional life of notorious gunman John Wesley Hardin, who during his time was the deadliest man in Texas. The novel covers his violent youth, his sixteen years in prison, and the end of his wild days when he was only forty-two.

Doc Holliday's Woman by Jane Candia Coleman. Warner Books, 1995. Based on her diaries, this is the story of Kate Elder, "Big Nose Kate," mistress of the legendary gunfighter, who broke Holliday out of a Texas jail on the night before his hanging, and witnessed his showdown with the Clantons in Tombstone.

Dead Man's Walk by Larry McMurtry. Simon and Schuster, 1995. This is a "prequel" novel to McMurtry's classic *Lonesome Dove* (Simon and Schuster, 1985). Woodrow Call and Gus McCrae are young Texas Rangers in the early days of the Republic. Basis for the 1996 teleplay with the same title.

Jesse James: Death of a Legend. by Will Henry (Henry Wilson Allen). Leisure Books, 1996. Jesse James will always be part man and part myth, the "Robin Hood" of the West. In this novel, he is presented as he was, an outlaw with few redeaming characteristics.

Reflections in a Dark Glass by Bruce McGinnis. University of North Texas Press, 1996. Individuals who knew John Wesley Hardin reminiscence on the life of the gunfighter.

Doc Holliday: The Gunfighter by Matt Braun. St. Martin's Press, 1997. Dr. John Holliday was a dentist by training, a gambler by choice, and a gunfighter by inclination. He drifted across the West, his name associated with some of the deadliest men on the frontier, and never walked away from a fight.

One Last Town by Matt Braun. St. Martin's Press, 1997. Bill Tilghman had a long career as a frontier peace officer. But Cromwell, Oklahoma, an oil boomtown, would be his last town. Source for the 1999 film "If You Know My Name."

Comanche Moon by Larry McMurtry. Simon and Schuster, 1997. This novel completes McMurtry's *Lonesome Dove* saga. It follows Texas Rangers Augustus McCrea and Woodrow Call as they pursue Buffalo Hump, the great Comanche war chief; Kicking Wolf, a Comanche horse thief; and a deadly Mexican bandit king. In a major subplot, their superior, Captain Inish Scull, an eccentric intellectual, engages in a deadly war of wills with the sinister Mexican bandit chief Ahumado. Spur Award from Western Writers of America.

The Spanish Peaks by Jon Chandler. Rogers and Nelsen, 1998. A mountain man tracked his prey, an outlaw family of three with a price on their heads, through the Southern Rockies—the beautiful Huajatolla country where the Spanish Peaks are located.

The Fourth Horseman by Randy Lee Eickhoff. Forge, 1998. A novel based on the life of Doc Holliday, the tubucular dentist turned gambler and gunfighter.

The Kiowa Verdict by Cynthia Haseloff. Five Star, 1998. A novel based on the 1871 Texas state court trial of Satanta, a Kiowa war chief. During the 1860s and early 1870s Satanta's war parties raided northwestern Texas constantly. Spur Award from Western Writers of America.

Gentleman Rogue by Matt Braun, St. Martin's Press, 1999. Luke Short, a noted gambler and deadly shootist, wanted to run honest games with straight odds and build a future in Fort Worth in 1885. But the sporting crowd there had a gold mine; a lucurative business they would defend at any cost. Short had no choice but to fight.

The Tombstone Conspiracy by Tim Champlin. Thorndike Press, 1999. A Rebel officer was left with a deep hatred for everything Yankee at the end of the Civil War. He brought his hatred—and the phantom legion he formed to continue the war on his terms—to the West. The boomtown of Tombstone, Arizona, became their target. Their depredations against Wells Fargo brought a secret agent to Tombstone—the Tombstone of the Earps, Doc Holliday, Sheriff Johnny Behan, and the Clantons.

Storm Riders by Ed Gorman. Berkley, 1999. A roman á clef where a thinly disguised Billy the Kid is offered amnesty by the governor. Gorman takes liberties with names and places in order to explore the myth of Billy and present the reality as he sees it.

The Hell Benders by Ken Hodgson. Pinnacle Books, 1999. The Benders were a family who turned murder into a livelihood. Those who stayed the night at their ramshackle inn outside of Parsons, Kansas, on the Osage Mission Trail, stayed forever, stripped of their belongings and dropped in an old well.

The Buckskin Line by Elmer Kelton. St. Martin's Press, 1999. The complicated plot includes the capture of a white boy by the Comanche in 1840, his rescue and subsequent service as a Texas Ranger. The boy was rescued by a member of a "ranging company" of Texans dedicated to protecting settlers against Indian raids. In its early days the Texas Rangers were poorly paid volunteers without authority other than their own.

Bandit Invincible, Butch Cassidy by Suzanne Lyon. Five Star, 1999. This novel of the famous bandit's life begins with the premise that Cassidy survived the shootout with the Bolivian army and returned to the United States. As an old man, he was living in Wyoming and searching for lost loot and love.

Masterson by Richard S. Wheeler. Forge, 1999. In 1920, Bat Masterson was a successful New York newspaper columnist. His colleagues' persistent questions prompted Bat to examine his past, particularly the Dodge City years and his associations with Doc Holliday and the Earp brothers. Spur Award winner.

Wyoming Wind by Jon Chandler. Five Star, 2000. A novel about the life and death of Tom Horn, a hero of the Spanish-American War and the Apache Indian Wars, who later became a stock detective for some of the biggest cattle ranchers in the West. Stock detectives were essentially killers, hired to eliminate cattle rustlers. But Horn made a mistake. He killed the thirteen-year-old son of a sheepman, and, outside Cheyenne, Wyoming, was hanged

Henry Plummer by Frank Bird Linderman. University of Nevada Press, 2000. Written in 1920 but unpublished until eighty years later, this novel follows the evil deeds of a notorious outlaw and sheriff in the Montana Territory during the mid 19th and early 20th century.

Clay Allison, Legend of Cimarron: A Novel of the Old West by John A. Truett. Sunstone Press, 2000. After the Civil War ravaged their Tennessee home, Clay Allison and his brother, John, left to start a new life in Cimarron, a little town in wild untamed New Mexico Territory. There Clay acquired the reputation of a cold-hearted gunfighter.

The Chivalry of Crime by Desmond Barry. Little, Brown, 2001. A story of Jesse James, his killer Bob Ford, and a young man befriended by Ford in Weaver, Colorado, in 1892. Included in the narrative is Ford's account of James, from his bushwhacking adventures in the Civil War, through his days as one of America's most notorious criminals, up to the moment Ford killed him.

The Master Executioner by Loren D. Estleman. Forge, 2001. For more than a quarter of a century Oscar Stone was the master executioner. He embraced his grisly talent to the exclusion of everything else, and elevated his profession from a vocation to an art. But the darkness of his trade haunted him as he traveled across the American West, dispensing the final act of justice decreed by the courts. National Cowboy and Western Heritage Museum Western Heritage Award.

Manhunt: The Pursuit of Harry Tracy by Bill Gulick. Caxton Press, 2001. On June 9, 1902, Harry Tracy shot his way out of the Oregon State Penitentiary, killing three guards, and a two month, two state manhunt began. King County Sheriff Edward Cudihee swore he would follow Tracy "to the ends of the earth," no matter how far the trail led outside the sheriff's King county jurisdiction.

Bucking the Tiger by Bruce Olds. Farrar, Straus and Giroux, 2001. The tiger in the title is the top card in a faro deck. The protagonist who bucks the tiger in Olds' novel is John Henry "Doc" Holliday, a consumptive dentist who made a name for himself in the Old West as a gambler, pistoleer, faro dealer, and participant in the infamous 1881 "Gunfight at the O.K. Corral" in Tombstone, Arizona.

Gunman's Rhapsody by Robert B. Parker. G. P Putnam's Sons, 2001. Robert B. Parker, well known for his crime fiction, wrote this moody novel on the events leading to the 1881 shootout at the O.K. Corral in Tombstone, Arizona. The gunman in the title is Wyatt Earp, and all the western legends associated with Wyatt—the other Earp brothers, Doc Holliday, Bat Masterson, Clay Allison, and Johnny Ringo—play their parts.

Arm of the Bandit: The Trial of Frank James by Johnny D. Boggs. Signet, 2002. From Boggs' *Guns and Gavel* series. In 1882, after Jesse James was killed by Bob Ford, his brother Frank surrendered and faced trial for murder. But he was so popular that his trial was like a circus. Was Missouri ruled by the arm of the law—or the arm of the bandit?

Billy the Kid: The Legend of El Chivato by Elizabeth Fackler. Sunstone Press, 2003. Billy was a charming, likable kid armed with a cock-eyed smile and a six-gun. He was also a ruthless killer.

Sunset: An Historical Western Novel by Glen Onley. Sunstone Press,

2003. Thirteen-year-old Everett watched his father hanged for murder, then was taken by Deputy Marshal Bass Reeves to Fort Gibson where he became a stable hand until early manhood. Believing an outlaw named Wiley Stuart had committed the murder, Everett hunted him down, but was denied the opportunity to clear his father's name. He drifted to Caldwell, Kansas, worked on a ranch, killed two brothers in a poker game dispute, fled to New Mexico and eventually joined a band of horse thieves.

All Honest Men by Claude and Michele Stanush. Permanent Press, 2003. Although not as well known as the Dalton gang, Jesse James, and Butch Cassidy, the Newton gang were bank and train robbers in the 1920s who stole more money than any of their better known peers.

Law of the Land: The Trial of Billy the Kid by Johnny D. Boggs. Signet, 2004. From Boggs' *Guns and Gavel* series. Sheriff Pat Garrett finally caught up with Billy the Kid on December 23, 1880. Then the Kid went on trial for the murder of a sheriff two years prior. He had evaded the law more times than anyone could count and proved that no jail could hold him. Would he face justice this time?

And Not to Yield by Randy Lee Eickhoff. Forge, 2004. A novel of the life and times of Wild Bill Hickok, including his stints as rancher, gambler, Union soldier, Indian fighter, lawman, baseball umpire, merchant, and actor. Born James Butler Hickok, Wild Bill made his reputation as a gunfighter, and became a legend. National Cowboy and Western Heritage Museum Western Heritage Award.

Pendencia Creek: The Life and Times of a Texas Gunfighter by E. Lee Fisher. Publish America, 2004. A fictionalized biography of Texas gunman John King Fisher, a cousin of the author's grandfather, who controlled the Nueces Strip in Southwest Texas in the 1870s, and provided sanctuary for various outlaws and murderers.

Trouble in Tombstone by Richard S. Wheeler, New American Library, 2004. This novel gives a first person account of Wyatt Earp's Tombstone days, as Wyatt himself might have told it. As he looks back, he tries to understand what went wrong, and why things spiraled out of control.

Robert Clay Allison: Requiescat in Pace by James S. Peters. Sunstone Press, 2007. Cimarron badman legend Clay Allison takes his readers on a ride through his uneven and turbulent life while trying to grab a part his own American dream: a ranch and sons to preserve his name and legacy. But his choice of a short-cut to prosperity by linking with the Santa Fe Ring darkens his future.

SELECTED REVIEWS

Bloody Season
by Loren D. Estleman
Bantam Books, 1988

Tombstone, Arizona, sat in a no-man's land in the late 1870s. With the nearest real law in Prescott and Mexico just a short jump away, cowboys who had settled along the nearby San Pedro River made a lucrative living stealing fat cattle from below the border. They supplemented their income by robbing Wells Fargo stages carrying bullion from local silver mines. Since they owned the sheriff and the local Wells Fargo agent, the area was a bandit's paradise.

The Clantons and the McLaurys had settled along the river in the early 1870s, before Tombstone was born. They were a rough lot. When he first came to the territory, Old Man Clanton was "a hell-driven man, black-bearded and as hard and as quick with his fists as he was with a quotation from the scripture." His oldest son Ike, "bearish and goat-whiskered with a tobacco lump taken root under his right ear," was belligerent and dangerous when drunk. His brother Billy was level-headed and tried to keep Ike out of trouble. Frank McLaury was a bantam "with a short man's short fuse." His brother Tom was "a courtly man," a range banker who made loans from a money belt and depended on his brother to collect them. Tombstone was where they rested, where they drank and gambled and fought.

Into this no-man's land rode the Earps. James, the eldest, had been wounded at Fredericktown, Missouri, in 1861. Virgil, a deputy U. S. marshal, was heavier than his brothers and his heavy handlebars underscored his jowls. Wyatt, tall and lean with the trademark Earp drooping moustaches, steadfastly maintained he was a businessman: "I'll fight no one if I can get away with it. There is no money in fighting." Morgan, in appearance, was Wyatt's twin, three years younger. Warren was the youngest. Virgil, Wyatt, and Morgan would write a bloody chapter in the history of the American West.

Earning his place in history alongside the Earps was Wyatt's friend Doc Holliday, an alcoholic, cadaverous, tubercular dentist, who, at twenty-eight, had been trying to get himself killed for years.

The Earps posed an insidious threat to the good thing the cowboys had in Cochise County. They were nocturnal men, preferring to make their living at the gambling tables to any day work, striving to seize a lion's share of silver from the region without swinging a pick. They soon had business interests in Tombstone, and Wyatt had political ambitions. The Earps had the same needs as the cowboys. The region was rich, but not rich enough to support two rival factions of like determination.

The clash came on October 26, 1881, in what has become known, erroneously, as the "Gunfight at the O.K. Corral."

Ike and Billy Clanton, Frank and Tom McLaury, and a cowboy named Billy Claiborne had gathered on an empty lot thirty yards west of the OK Corral. Billy Clanton and Frank McLaury were armed. Tom McLaury had a rifle in his saddle scabbard. Word reached U. S. Marshal Virgil Earp that the cowboys wanted a showdown. He deputized his brothers Wyatt and Morgan, and Doc Holliday. They started down Fremont Street, by Virgil's orders, to "disarm these jackasses." Sheriff Johnny Behan tried to dissuade Virgil, to no avail.

> Nearing Bauer's they spread out four abreast with ten feet between each man and his neighbor. Morgan and Virgil took the outside while Doc moved to Wyatt's right. Gusts pulled at the flap of Doc's coat, exposing the shotgun in teasing glimpses like white thigh on a variety girl.

When the smoke cleared, Tom and Frank McLaury were dead; Billy Clanton was fatally wounded. Virgil and Morgan Earp were wounded.

Estleman starts his novel with the gunfight and the proximate events that led to it, then backfills the long-standing animosity between the Clanton-McLaury faction and the Earps. There was the Benson stage holdup in 1881, where Wyatt bribed Ike Clanton and Frank McLaury to betray the men he suspected were the robbers, and the betrayal backfired. Sheriff Behan, a friend of the cowboys, spread the rumor that Doc Holliday was one of the bandits. Bad blood developed. Political rivalry between Wyatt, who wanted to be sheriff, and Johnny Behan intensified.

And the aftermath, when "in the loose time between the fall drives and the spring round-up (and in a season when the vaqueros who rode for the grandees below the border were paid eight dollars apiece for the heads of American rustlers), they [the cowboys] trickled in from Galesburg and Charleston on town horses and buckboards and pitched camp outside town or checked in at the Grand Hotel" to see Wyatt Earp and Doc Holliday tried for murder. But the trial didn't end it.

There's a collection of interesting, well-known characters in the novel. In addition to the principals of the gunfight, there are detailed sketches of Big Nose Kate Fisher, Doc Holliday's woman, who would fight with him throughout their relationship, leave, then come back each time, Mattie Blaylock, who shared a house with Wyatt Earp and considered herself Mrs. Earp until she was replaced by Sadie Marcus, who came to Tombstone with a theatrical troupe, took up with Johnny Behan, and left him for Wyatt, and Johnny Ringo, a killer with eyes "as dull and flat as two pennies on a counter" who had studied Homer and Euclid. Other recognizable characters who pass through the novel include Old Man Clanton, Curly Bill Brocius, Deputy Billy Breckenridge, John Clum, Bob Paul, Bat Masterson, Luke Short, and Buckskin Frank Leslie.

Loren D. Estleman is unsurpassed in the genre in descriptive writing, whether it be characterization, setting, or narration. His characters and the events surrounding them speak directly, with little prompting from the narrator. Consider this description of Doc Holliday:

> The nickle-plated Colt's Lightning hurtled into the room towing Doc behind it. He towered there in his tall-crowned hat, the tails of his greatcoat spreading behind him like buzzard wings.

"Where is he?"

The woman was looking, not at the weapon, but at the skull face of the gringo who was holding it, his eyes molten in their sockets. She thought it was Señor Muerte come to claim her children . . .

And this of Wyatt Earp, entering the room where his wounded brother lay: "Wyatt came in then, his eyes blue nailheads in a face nearly as pale as his brothers."

And this description of a posse:

At the West End Corral they selected big chesty mounts built to carry a lot of iron and rode south with Winchesters and shotguns and saddle pistols in scabbards and revolvers under their coats—six grim men with moustaches in wide hats and big coats, who looked like pallbearers.

Estleman is more productive and better known today as a mystery rather than a Western writer. But his novels set in the Old West, particularly those based on well-known characters and events—*Aces and Eights* (Pinnacle Books, 1981), about the death of Wild Bill Hickok and *This Old Bill* (Doubleday, 1984), based on the life of Buffalo Bill Cody, and *Bloody Season*—are noted for their historical accuracy and riveting characterizations.

Respected critics seem to agree. Dale L Walker said Estleman is "one of the two or three best stylists the genre has ever produced." Edward Gorman believes he is the preeminent writer of his time. And so does Martin H. Greenberg: "Estleman is generally considered the best Western writer of his generation."

Deadwood
by Pete Dexter
Random House, 1986

James Butler "Wild Bill" Hickok was a legend in the Old West. Some of his deeds were real and heroic. As an Army scout in 1868, he rescued thirty-four men from an Indian siege in Colorado, galloping through the hostiles to summon help. As a lawman, he kept the peace in Hays City and Abilene, Kansas, killing four men in the line of duty. But there was also make-believe. There was an eye-witness story in *Harper's Weekly* of how Bill had wiped out all ten of the McCandles gang (he actually killed two of them). After that, everything he did was immortalized. Bill saw where it was leading, and let it take him along. He encouraged the stories; he even helped make up some of them.

But his career as a peace officer slid downward. In 1871 in Abilene, he shot into a crowd of rowdy drunks and accidentally killed a policeman. The city council fired him. In 1876, plagued by eye trouble, he wandered to Deadwood in Dakota Territory. This dreary setting and the final days of Bill's eventful life provide the focus for Pete Dexter's cynical novel of the Old West.

Dexter's Wild Bill is a doomed and subtly noble man, weary of living up to the legends others wrote about him. He arrived at Deadwood with his friend Charley Utter. Although Bill and Charley were drunk through most of the novel, Bill never lost his deportment. He was straight and tall and looked purposeful. He had a premonition that Deadwood was his last camp.

Deadwood in the late 1870s was a small town, swollen beyond capacity by the craze for gold. Bill and Charley rode in from the south, downhill:

> The gulch fell out of the mountains, long and narrow, following the Whitewood Creek, where things widened enough for a town sign, that was Deadwood. The place looked miles long and yards wide, half of it tents. The Whitewood joined a smaller creek—the Deadwood—at the south end and ran the length of the town. The mud was a foot deep, and every kind of waste in creation was thrown into the street to mix with it.

On that day, in that light, the hills seemed to Charley "as black as the devil's dream." Against this grim backdrop, Dexter surrounds Bill with whimsical characters who were actually in Deadwood during the time the major events in the plot happened.

Historical characters who appear in the novel include Captain Jack Crawford, self-styled Indian fighter and poet; Agnes Lake, Bill's absentee wife, who came to know her husband only after his death; Bill's best friend Charley Utter, a little dandy who wore pearl-handled pistols and gave people their distance, but didn't give up his own; and Calamity Jane Cannary. The poignant portrayal of Calamity Jane exemplifies the tragicomic characterizations that abound in *Deadwood*.

Jane was a filthy, depression prone prostitute whose love for Bill was both touching and demented. She had told more lies about Bill Hickok than Harper's Weekly. She even said they had been married. Dirt poor and homely, she cried for the most famous and handsome man in the West.

The Deadwood characters and the incidents in which they appear are presented primarily through acrid dialogue. An exchange between bounty hunter Boone May and Sheriff Seth Bullock shows Dexter's wit and skill:

> Boone said, "I got Frank Towles head that's worth two hundred dollars in Cheyenne. I shot him myself in a legal, fair fight, and did the public's welfare. So I don't see why you couldn't jurisdict this manner and give me the two hundred dollars here, so's I don't have to ride all the way back to Cheyenne."
>
> Seth Bullock leaned closer . . . "Frank Towles head isn't worth a nickel in Dakota Territory," he said . . . "I don't know Frank Towles or what he looks like. That could be anybody, and you bring it in here tracking mud and say the town of Deadwood owes you two hundred dollars . . ."
>
> Boone May looked at Bullock a long time . . . "You come and talk to me . . . fast enough when you need somebody killed," he said. "You never mentioned muddy when you wanted somebody tracked down . . ."

I never said killed," Bullock said. "I always said 'apprehended.'"

Boone pointed to the head on the desk. "That's as apprehended as you can get."

Like the dialogue, the narration is crisp and moves the story along briskly. When Charley Utter finds Lurline Monti Verdi, his favorite whore, in bed with Handsome Banjo Dick Brown, the action moves quickly to a conclusion:

> The room was half-lit . . . Charley saw the holster hung
> there, and dropped to the floor . . . Charley never stopped, or thought,
> or saw it happen. One minute he was standing in the doorway, the
> next minute he had Handsome Banjo Dick Brown's jaw locked in
> one arm and was holding the knife against the pulse in his neck.
> In the seconds that had taken, Handsome Dick had reached behind
> himself with his gun and the muzzle was pressed into Charley's leg.
> Charley held him dead still. "I been shot in the leg before,"
> Charley whispered in Handsome Dick's ear, "have you ever had your
> throat cut?"

This wry humor coupled with deadly seriousness is a distinguishing characteristic of Dexter's style

Pete Dexter is best known as a quirky newspaper columnist who won the National Book Club award for his novel *Paris Trout*. *Deadwood* is his first literary foray into the Old West. Let's hope there's much more to come.

True Grit
by Charles Portis
Simon and Schuster, 1968

I saw the film "True Grit" years before I read Portis' novel. I like John Wayne's Western portrayals, and the grizzled Rooster Cogburn was his finest (most film critics don't agree, but the role earned him his only Academy

Award). I didn't anticipate the novel being better than the movie. But it was. The film was so successful in part because screenwriter Marguerite Roberts closely adapted her script to the novel source.

The central characters in the story are U. S. Marshal Rooster Cogburn, young Mattie Ross, Texas Ranger Sergeant Jules LaBoeuf, a drifter named Tom Chaney, and outlaw leader Lucky Ned Pepper.

Cogburn was a deputy marshal for Judge Isaac Parker's U. S. District Court for the Western District of Arkansas having criminal jurisdiction over the Indian Territory. He was a "one-eyed old jasper built along the lines of Grover Cleveland." He's introduced to the reader when he takes the witness stand during the trial of a murderer he had captured:

> Mr. Cogburn: . . . we spotted the two boys and their old daddy, Aaron Wharton . . . I told the old man . . . that we was U. S. marshals . . . He picked up an ax . . .
>
> Mr. Barlow: What did you do?
>
> Mr. Cogburn: I started backing away . . . C. C. Wharton picked up a shotgun . . . . Potter seen him but it was too late . . . Wharton pulled down on him with one barrel and then turned to do the same for me . . . I shot him and when the old man swung the ax I shot him. Odus lit out for the creek and I shot him. Aaron Wharton and C. C. Wharton was dead when they hit the ground. Odus Wharton was just winged.
>
> Mr. Barlow: What happened to Odus Wharton?
>
> Mr. Cogburn: There he sets.
>
> Mr. Goudy: How many men have you shot . . . ?
>
> Mr. Cogburn: Around twelve or fifteen, stopping men in flight and defending myself.
>
> Mr. Goudy: . . . remember that you are under oath . . .
>
> Mr. Cogburn: I believe them two Whartons made twenty-three.

When Rooster was told later that Odus Wharton had escaped and was looking for him he replied: "If he is not careful he will find me."

Mattie Ross' family owned 480 acres of good bottom land on the south bank of the Arkansas River not far from Dardanelle in Yell County, Arkansas, about seventy miles from Ft. Smith. Mattie was fourteen when Tom Chaney shot and killed her father in Fort Smith. She traveled to Fort Smith, had her father's body sent home, and set about finding a man with "true grit" to track down Chaney and bring him to justice in Judge Parker's court. She settled on Rooster Cogburn, and paid him cash money, up front.

Against Mattie's wishes, Rooster allowed Texas Ranger LaBoeuf to join their hunt. Mattie didn't like LaBoeuf, although he was a nice-looking man of around thirty years of age with a "cowlick" at the crown of his head. He looked to be a man of good family. But his manner was stuck-up and he had a smug grin. Mattie thought him "a vain and cocky devil who cultivated his cowlick." The ranger wore two revolvers and Mexican spurs with big rowels. He carried a big-bore Sharps carbine that Rooster said would come in handy if they were jumped by buffaloes or elephants.

Tom Chaney had joined up with Lucky Ned Pepper's gang. Ned was a feisty little fellow, with part of his upper lip missing, courtesy of an earlier meeting with Rooster. With LaBoeuf and Mattie in tow, Rooster tracked the desperados deep into the Indian Nations, near present-day McAlester, Oklahoma.

The plot is pure Western genre, with steady action and exciting climaxes. But the pleasure of reading the novel lies in Mattie's narration and the dialogue. Portis uses late 18th century vernacular, an archaic, formal way of speaking found in pioneer diaries, that's humorously out of place when used by Mattie and her rough-hewn companions and adversaries.

Mattie was a spunky young woman with strong convictions. Today she'd be called assertive, but that implies a disagreeable element of character that wasn't in her makeup. But her opinions and pronouncements were strong and forthright. Speaking of Judge Parker's conversion to Catholicism on his deathbed, she said,

> If you had sentenced an hundred and sixty men to death and had seen around eighty of them swing, then maybe at the last minute you would feel the need for some stronger medicine than the Methodists could make.

Her opinion on drinking was, "I would not put a thief in my mouth to steal my brains." On Rooster, sleeping off a night of drinking, she sniffed,

> I had never seen anyone in bed at ten o'clock in the morning who was not sick but that was where he was.

On men, Mattie proclaimed, "Men will live like billy-goats if they are let alone." She was speaking specifically of Rooster.

Rooster, LaBoeuf, and Mattie mix like oil and water. Mattie is near-perfect (by my standards), Rooster likes to pull a cork and violates all the preconceptions of the Western hero, whereas LaBeouf is a dashing caricature of an Old West lawman. Their dialogue sparkles. LaBeouf tells Mattie:

> Earlier tonight I gave some thought to stealing a kiss from you, though you are very young, and sick and unattractive to boot, but now I am of a mind to give you five or six good licks with my belt.

Mattie responds,

> One would be as unpleasant as the other . . . Put a hand on me and you will answer for it. You are from Texas and ignorant of our ways but the good people of Arkansas do not go easy on men who abuse women and children.

Paramount's fine film was produced by Hal Wallis in 1969. It was directed by Henry Hathaway. In addition to Wayne, the cast included Kim Darby as Mattie Ross, Glen Campbell as LaBoeuf, and Robert Duvall as Lucky Ned Pepper. All gave sterling performances. Some reviewers considered Campbell's performance to be weak, but they likely hadn't read the book. Campbell captured the ranger's character exceptionally well.

In 1969 *Time* magazine commissioned Harry Jackson, a master artist of the American West, to create a sculpture of John Wayne as Rooster Cogburn for a cover portrait. The resulting sculpture, titled *The Marshal*, is genuine Americana and is probably as close as anything to our national image of the Wild West.

The War in the Nueces Strip
by Don Worcester
Doubleday, 1989

In 1874 the Texas Legislature created the Special Force of Texas Rangers, whose task was to tame the infamous Nueces Strip. Their commander was Captain Leander H. McNelly, and the force was known as "McNelly's Rangers."

History has been kind to the Rangers. Walter Prescott Webb documented their incredible exploits, including McNelly's, in *The Texas Rangers: A Century of Frontier Defense* (Houghton Mifflin, 1935), which J. Frank Dobie called, "The beginning, the middle, and end of the subject." Webb used numerous records and the recollection of those who served to write a definitive and exciting history of the famed organization.

There are two other excellent accounts of the feats of McNelly's Rangers: the memoirs of ex-Rangers George Durham and J. A. Jennings. There's some controversy over Jennings' account because his first person narration covers periods when he wasn't with the Rangers.

The War in the Nueces Strip is noted Texas historian, Don Worcester's stirring novel based on the extraordinary accomplishments of Captain McNelly and his men. Worcester's story closely parallels Durham's record, with some minor differences. The narrator is a young ranger named Concho Carter, with similarities to Ranger Bill Callicott, who provided much of the narration for Webb's book. His best friend is George "Josh" Burnham, obviously based on Durham. But the central character, and the focus of the novel, is Captain McNelly.

Lee McNelly was an unlikely choice to lead the Special Force. He wasn't physically impressive, standing only about five-and-a-half feet tall and weighing less than 135 pounds. He was tubercular, and spent long stretches in bed recuperating. His voice was so weak he could hardly be heard. He didn't look or sound like a fighting man.

And his troop, when he first organized it, was nothing to brag about. Concho Carter observed,

We must have been quite a sight when we set out in a column of twos just before sunset. The scouts were out ahead of us on either side of the road. Captain, the lieutenants, and the sergeants rode at the head of the column, and after them came the rest of us following our corporals. We were forty-three in all, counting Captain. Hats were of every kind from Captain's good beaver to Mexican straw sombreros to Josh's floppy brimmed hand-me-down. Mounts ranged from so-so saddle horses and mustangs to Josh's old farm horse. I couldn't see how we'd ever catch up with well-mounted bandidos. We were sure one ragtail, bobtailed outfit, and if looks meant anything we weren't much of a fighting force.

But they would be. They would follow their captain into numerous battles against incredible odds for thirty-three dollars a month in state script. The state supplied food and bullets. The rangers had to provide their own horses, gear, and guns.

The Nueces Strip is a narrow stretch of land that runs between the Nueces River and Mexico from Corpus Christi to Eagle Pass. There was probably more rustling, pillage, and murder in the Strip in the early 1870s than anywhere else on the western frontier. Patrolling the South Texas brush country for outlaws was an exacting task, made difficult by the terrain:

Old Rock [one of McNelly's scouts] was no easy man to follow for he led the way at a lope, splashing through lagunas and climbing up slopes, occasionally heading straight through thorny brush that almost clawed some Rangers out of their saddles. Old Rock was ducking and clinging to the side of his horse now and then like a brush-popper after mossyhorn steers. I'd chased cattle in the brush before, so I just gave my mustang his head and crouched low, ducking under limbs and shielding my face as best I could. The men on big horses really got scratched up. I was sure glad I hadn't swapped my mustang for a big horse . . .

American posses raiding South Texas ranches owned by Mexicans were almost as bad as Juan Cortina's raiders from Mexico. Captain McNelly disbanded them whenever he came across one. He told a rancher named Culver, who was leading a hundred man posse, "I can't prove you're outlaws right now, 'cause I don't know all you've done. But in ten minutes you will be for sure. You'll be reckoned as armed outlaws, and we've been ordered to kill any we find. Tell your men we'll do just that." The posse was disbanded.

At Palo Alto McNelly's Rangers defeated a band of about fifty of Cortina's rustlers and recovered 300 beeves. Only one Ranger was killed. McNelly had the bodies of the bandits stacked like cordwood in the plaza in Brownsville, and ordered Sergeant John Armstrong to arrest anyone who came to identify any of them.

McNelly led his Rangers across the river near Rio Grande City to the Mexican village of Las Cuevas and recovered nearly 400 cattle. He had ignored orders from Washington, invaded Mexico, on foot, and killed the Mexican general in charge—with only thirty men. He arrested the notorious King Fisher and put an end to the infamous Taylor-Sutton feud.

There was criticism of McNelly's methods. He seldom took prisoners; he even had his own hangman. When rustlers were captured and turned over to a sheriff, they always made bond and were back in business right away. "Since there were lots of cattle on the range, finding men near a herd didn't prove they had stolen it. I guess that's why Captain preferred it when outlaws put up a fight. Then he didn't have to make arrests." The Mexicans called the Rangers "El Diablo Tejanos." Only Captain Richard King and other ranchers who were losing cattle supported him.

Walter Prescott Webb said It was unfortunate that McNelly wasn't at the Alamo or Goliad, where his courage would have earned him a more prominent place in Texas history. But as a leader of fighting men, his courage and tenacity set him apart. His rangers could whip three times their number of border bandits. His actions and deeds will long be remembered in Texas.

The recipient of the 1988 Western Writers of America's Saddleman Award for Lifetime Contribution to Western Literature

Willie Boy: A Desert Manhunt
by Harry Lawton
Paisano, 1960

The Willie Boy legend began September 26, 1909, when the Paiute Indian murdered William Mike, a Chemehuevi, on a ranch in Banning, California. He then kidnapped Lolita, the fourteen-year-old daughter of "Old Mike." They fled across the Mojave Desert, pursued by a posse that included Indian trackers from the nearby Morongo Reservation. Lolita impeded his progress, so Willie Boy killed her. He ambushed another posse at Ruby Mountain, killing all their horses and seriously wounding one man. A week later, yet another posse found his body at the site of the ambush. Willie Boy had committed suicide with his last bullet.

Willie Boy's motivation—whiskey, pride, Paiute ritual—that led to the murders is factually presented, with some speculation. But the heart of the story is the pursuit; a manhunt on horseback across a wild and barren California landscape that occurred over two decades after the Western frontier was considered closed.

Banning, the starting point of the story, lies in Southern California, approximately eighty-five miles inland from Los Angeles and twenty-three miles west of Palm Springs. It's situated in San Gorgonio Pass, between the San Bernardino and San Jacinto Mountains, near the edge of the Mojave Desert. Lawton's desert, harsh and desolate, is also a living desert, brought to life with vivid scenes such as this, in which a coyote follows the fleeing Willie Boy and Lolita:

> An old coyote, relying on the acquired cunning of age to fill his belly, trotted in the dim light of early morning along the arroyo bed, stopping once to nibble on a screwbean pod. A chuckawalla scurried across his path and the coyote whirled after it. The squat lizard darted into a crevice in a boulder. The coyote whined around the crack and finally gave up. He loped on, threading his way through sagebrush, and then halted to sniff at a jagged razor of rock in the midst of the sandy wash. Tiny drops of blood clung to the rock. The coyote

lingered over the smell. Then he set off with idle curiosity up the canyon, paw tracks blending with two pair of human footprints.

We follow Willie Boy as he runs for his life. Clara True, the Indian agent whose jurisdiction included both Morongo and the Paiute's home reservation at Twentynine Palms, later wrote, "Willie Boy grew up a desert man, sinewy and healthy. He never had any training except that of the desert . . ." On foot, in a desert where he knew all the seeps and waterholes, he was more than a match for the several mounted posses trailing him. He ate lizards and drank from scum covered, brackish waterholes. During his long flight he covered over five hundred miles on foot, beneath a burning desert sun, where temperatures were sometimes over a hundred degrees.

The posse's harried pursuit made the shooting of Lolita inevitable. "He was Paiute now. The white man was his enemy, and to abandon Lolita to his pursuers would be to allow them to determine his fate . . ." Lawton's Willie Boy did not understand Western ideas of chivalry. He believed he had been driven to kill her; he would erase the memory of the girl from his mind.

The Paiute was pursued by posses from both Riverside and San Bernardino Counties; both had experienced horsemen who were well-equipped. San Bernardino County Sheriff John Ralphs told reporters that he was "taking only men hardened for long distance riding . . . There will be riflemen and . . . high powered rifles enough to wipe out a Japanese army. We'll have long distance field glasses capable of picking out an object the size of a man's head miles away even by moonlight." But they were no match for the lone Paiute on foot.

The riders . . . spurred their horses west. For more than an hour they followed the plodding prints of Willie Boy. He appeared unhurried . . . Gradually the horsemen became conscious that Willie Boy's strides were lengthening. The prints wound among clumps of greasewood.

Reche sensed the meaning of the strides. "We've got him on the run," he yelled. "He's spotted us. Let's go, boys."

They broke into a lope, spreading over a wide area. . .

Hundred degree heat dazzled the sands . . . An hour passed and still they rode, following the unbroken strides of Willie Boy.

The horses were tiring, chests heaving. But the Indian's footprints pounded on ahead. . . . The five horsemen were incredulous.

"I make it about fifteen miles—maybe eighteen," Reche said. "And we never caught a glimpse of him."

The posse that finally cornered him paid such a price that it was difficult for the sheriff to form another to continue the chase.

The manhunt coincided with a visit to nearby Riverside by President Taft. A swarm of reporters converged on San Bernardino. They reported that the president was in "Willie Boy" country and led off their stories with the Willie Boy manhunt, giving it national press coverage. The wire services and newspapers were avid for every detail.

Randolph Madison, from the *Los Angeles Record*, suggested that the shooting of Old Mike was a natural consequence of "marriage by capture," a Paiute ritual. But the killing of Lolita heightened public interest. When the posse brought her body to town, Constable Ben de Crevecouer said, "Shot her down like a dog . . . when she was no more use as a pack animal. Shot her where she dropped—and kept right on. Never stopped." This prompted a sense of outrage across the nation.

Fifty years later journalist Harry Lawton reconstructed the story of Willie Boy. He relied on first person accounts from posse members and relatives and newspaper stories from regional dailies. Even the dialogue was based on actual recollections. A 1969 film, directed by Abraham Polonsky, based on Lawton's "nonfiction novel," was a commercial success and an entertaining, although brooding, Western. It starred Robert Redford, Katharine Ross, with Robert Blake in the title role as Willie Boy.

Historians James A. Sandos and Larry E. Burgess wrote a revised history of the event titled *The Hunt for Willie Boy: Indian-Hating & Popular Culture* (University of Oklahoma Press, 1994). They felt the novel and the film reflected a whites' view and attempted to develop the Indian view and provide rationale for the two brutal murders. There were some minor differences with

Lawton's account—names and tribal relationships—but there was also a major difference. Their evidence suggests Lolita was shot, accidentally, by one of the Indian trackers. It's an interesting piece of historical revision, but not truly convincing.

Harry Lawton wrote in the foreword to his novel, "Whatever one may think of Willie Boy, his feat commands respect. He existed from waterhole to waterhole in temperatures that have killed men in less than a day. During his long flight, he covered more than five hundred miles of desert wilderness on foot, harried by pursuers, beneath a burning sun. As a sheer feat of desert endurance the Willie Boy episode is unparalleled."

Amen!

5

WHOOPI-TI-YI-YO: RANCHING AND TRAIL DRIVES

INTRODUCTION

The ranchers, who laid the foundations of the West as we know it today, were a new breed of businessmen. They became the first settlers throughout most of the vast, empty, and inhospitable regions that had been considered a wasteland. They used the abundant prairie grasses to produce beef and mutton and to raise horses, and opened the land for development by the settlers who followed.

Land was cheap or even free for the taking in the early days, and a number of cattlemen put together great ranches that covered several hundred thousand acres. Some were owned by wealthy cattle barons, such as the Marquis de Morès in the Dakota Territory. Other ranches, like the Matador in Texas, were owned by syndicates. And some enterprising cattlemen, among them Jesse Chisholm and Charles Goodnight, made fortunes rounding up wild Texas longhorns and trailing them north to the railheads in Kansas, and later to the northern plains of Wyoming and Montana. In the heyday of Western ranching from 1866 to 1886, ranchers shipped more than 10 million cattle and one million sheep to markets in the East.

The livestock business spawned our first true national icon—the American cowboy. His heroic impression on his countrymen, and the rest of the world, endures today. He was actually a laborer who spent most of his time tending stock and mending fences, but our exaggerated perception is based on fact. His vocation was dirty and tedious, but it required the courage to ride a horse at breakneck speed while trying to turn a stampeding herd, the perseverance to spend months on a trail drive or a lonely winter at a line camp, and the skill to drag a belligerent 800-pound longhorn steer out of the brush. The roundup and the trail drive broke the boredom of everyday ranch life, and tested his skills and fortitude.

From the earliest days of the conquistadors, sheep had been the chief agricultural product of the Spanish West. But, American ranchers disliked the odor and the bleating of sheep, or "woolleybacks," as they came to be called. Certainly sheep herding was the least glamorous job in the Old West. But sheep were profitable, and by the 1880s many western ranches were raising them. There were even "sheep drives" from Montana to California.

The rangeland provides much material for fiction. There are growing-up stories set in cattle and sheep country. Many plots are based on conflicts such as water disputes, cattle barons versus small ranchers, cattlemen versus sheepmen, and cattlemen versus nesters. The day-to-day life of the cowboy is the theme for numerous novels, as is, to a much lessor degree, that of the sheepherder. The cattle rancher and the sheepman are central to many novels, as are events such as roundups and trail drives, and their struggles to get their herds or flocks through the fierce western winters and summer droughts. There are plots based on cattle trading and land speculation. Many novels view ranching from a woman's point of view. Legendary cattlemen such as Charles Goodnight, Jesse Chisholm, John Slaughter, and John Chisum, along with a Dakota Territory small rancher named Teddy Roosevelt, repeatedly appear. Range wars, Indian raids, cattle rustling, and vigilante actions provide further material. Many mainstream novels, Western romances, young reader novels, and traditional Westerns use the rangeland settings.

In *The Virginian* (Macmillan, 1902), Owen Wister created a new and enduring kind of American fiction. With its publication, the image of the American cowboy was forever changed. Will James's *The Drifting Cowboy* (Charles Scribner's Sons, 1925) is an authentic narrative about working cowboys. Oakley Hall's *The Badlands* (Atheneum, 1978) is built around the conflict between cattle barons and small ranchers in early Montana. Niven Busch's *Duel in the Sun* (William Morrow, 1944) is about family conflict on a ranching empire in the Staked Plains of Texas. *Lonesome Dove* (Simon and Schuster, 1985), by Larry

McMurtry, is a classic trail drive story that breathed life back into the Western novel. *Sam Chance* (Duell, Sloan and Pearce, 1965) is Benjamin Capps' story of an ex-Confederate army sergeant who left Tennessee for Texas and became a cattle baron. Conrad Richter's *The Sea of Grass* (Alfred A. Knopf, 1937) is about ranching on the vast New Mexico plains and it's effect on a rancher's wife. Max Evans' *The Rounders* (Macmillan, 1960) is a humorous novel of contemporary cowboying. These stories are representative of, and some of the best, novels in this category and are reviewed at the end of the chapter.

READER'S GUIDE

A Texas Cowboy by Charles Angelo Siringo. 1885. Subtitled *Fifteen Years on the Hurricane Deck of a Spanish Pony. Taken from Real Life*. Charles Siringo punched cattle for Shanghai Pierce, rode the Chisholm trail, once roped a buffalo, and helped chase Billy the Kid. His story of his years as a cowboy, range detective, and adventurer is one of the first classics about the Old West. Actually *A Texas Cowboy* is an autobiography, but its embellishments, use of dialog, and sheer readability account for its inclusion, along with two subsequent Siringo books, in this guide.

The Wire-Cutters by Mollie E. Davis. Houghton Mifflin, 1899. Inspired by the "Fence Cutting Wars," a destructive competition among Texas ranchers to gain access to water for their herds, *The Wire Cutters* portrays the life of the 19th-century cowboy and is considered by some to be the first Western novel.

The Log of a Cowboy by Andy Adams. Houghton Mifflin, 1903. A true story that shows life on a trail drive as it really was. The drive, from the Rio Grande to the Blackfoot Reservation in Northern Montana, took place in 1882.

The Shepherd of the Hills by Harold Bell Wright. A. L. Burt, 1907. A stranger, a cultured old man with a face marked with sadness, came to the Missouri Ozarks and took on the lowly work of tending sheep. But he was a man with a mission, which no one understood. Basis for the 1919, 1928 and 1941 films.

Wells Brothers: The Young Cattle Kings by Andy Adams. Houghton Mifflin, 1911. During the fierce winter of 1885-86, the young Wells Brothers considered abandoning their land on Beaver Creek in northeastern Kansas.

The Flying U Ranch by B. M. Bower. Dillingham, 1914. Bower's "Happy Family" of cowboys on the Flying U Ranch confront defiant sheepherders who have invaded Montana's Bearpaw country. Source for the 1927 film.

To the Last Man by Zane Grey. Harper and Brothers, 1922. This novel, set in Grey's familiar Arizona Tonto Basin, is based on the famous Graham-Tewksbury feud between Arizona cattlemen and sheepmen. Basis for the 1933 film.

North of 36 by Emerson Hough. D. Appleton, 1923. Events in this novel take place on a trail drive from Caldwell County, Texas, to Abilene, Kansas. The drive outfit includes Alamo, a memorable lead steer, Jim Nabours, an old cowboy foreman and boss of the Del Sol outfit, and Taisie Lockhart, the female owner of the ranch. Source for the 1924 film of the same title, the 1931 film "The Conquering Horde" and the 1938 film "The Texans."

The Wind by Dorothy Scarborough. Harper and Brothers, 1925. Set in West Texas near Sweetwater during the drought years of the 1880s. Letty, the protagonist, was fresh from the green hills of Virginia, and unaccustomed to the relentless wind and the dirt it brought with it like a plague. She was finally driven mad by the wind, the isolation, and the grim marriage she shared with Lige on the godforsaken Cross-Bar Ranch. Source for the 1928 film.

Cowboy by Ross Santee. Hastings, 1928. A plotless narrative about the making of a cowboy out of an East Texas farm boy, who graduated from horse wrangler to cowpuncher before he was twenty. Illustrated by the author.

Riders of the Night by Eugene Cunningham. Houghton Mifflin, 1932. A novel of the Texas range about the romance of a young man and a young woman whose fathers had created the cattle empire bearing the Y brand, and of a battle for law and order.

The Home Ranch by Will James. Charles Scribner's Sons, 1935. When John B. Mitchell left Texas in a hurry with an "appropriated" herd of cattle, he headed north to create a ranch of his own. Fifty years later he owned the Seven X Ranch, a spread that was some sixty miles long and more than forty miles wide.

Seven Slash Range by Bennett Foster. William Morrow, 1936. The owner of the Seven Slash Ranch fought President Theodore Roosevelt's order that all fences on public domain in Arizona had to come down.

Pirates of the Range by B. M. Bower. Little, Brown 1937. Two Texas ranchers drove their herd into a green Montana valley and settled there. Then, one by one, their cattle begin to disappear.

Jubal Troop by Paul I. Wellman. Carrick, 1939. Jubal Troop was a Texas cowboy who eventually became a wealthy Oklahoma oilman. Along the way he made enemies—some thought he made love to an employer's wife, then killed her husband when he found out—but he also had friends such as his long-time partner who loved him like a son. Basis for the 1956 film "Jubal."

30,000 on the Hoof by Zane Grey. Harper and Brothers, 1940. Written from a woman's point of view, this unusual Zane Grey Western is an account of the hard life of an Arizona Tonto Basin ranch wife.

The Happy Man by Robert Easton. Viking Press, 1943. This novel describes life on a cattle ranch in California in the 1940s before World War II.

Powdersmoke Feud by William MacLeod Raine. Houghton Mifflin, 1945. A story of conflict between ranchers and nesters in Wyoming in the 1800s.

Trail Boss by Peter Dawson (Jonathan H. Glidden). Bantam Books, 1946. Santell was a trail boss, driving a herd of 30,000 cattle from Texas to Kansas. But he could not celebrate at the end of the trail, for he was being hunted by hired guns, a U. S. marshal, and the cavalry. He had to start a hunt of his own—for the man who framed him.

The Furies by Niven Busch. Dial Press, 1948. A novel of violence and primitive passions against the background of the New Mexico Territory in the bitter years before it had attained statehood. A cattle baron rejects the advice of his daughter and marries a socialite, then lets his ranch go to seed.

Blazing Guns on the Chisholm Trail by Bordon Chase. Random House, 1948. A rancher built a cattle empire with his adopted son, and together they began a massive cattle drive north from Texas to the Missouri railhead. But on the way, new information and the father's tyrannical ways caused his son to take the herd away from him and head to a new railhead in Kansas. The father, swearing vengeance, pursued. Basis for the 1948 film "Red River."

Flame of Sunset by L. P. Holmes. Pocket Books, 1948. Jeff Kennett had spent two hard years bringing 2,000 head of cattle from Texas to Sacramento. His men had climbed mountains and crossed deserts, fought Indians and renegades and still faced obstacles near the end of the trail.

Little Britches: Father and I Were Ranchers by Ralph Moody. W. W. Norton, 1950. The first of Moody's eight novels about growing up in the West. Little Britches (Moody) was eight when his family moved from New Hampshire to Colorado in 1906. This novel begins his saga of coming into manhood on a ranch amid Western people.

Winds of Morning by H. L. Davis. William Morrow, 1953. This is a story of love, murder and redemption set in eastern Oregon in the 1920's. The protagonist is a young man named Ross Tunison, whose father had left him thirty thousand acres of grass and hay land fronting on both sides of the Middle Columbia River. The novel combines elements of the popular Western and the mystery.

The Tall Men by Clay Fisher (Henry Wilson Allen). Houghton Mifflin, 1954. After the Civil War, two men left Texas for the gold fields of Montana. They teamed up with a cunning Yankee to drive a trail herd through the heart of the Seven Sioux Nations. Basis for the 1955 film.

The Maverick Queen by Zane Grey. Harper and Brothers, 1954. Based on Cattle Kate, an actual historical character who used her beauty to persuade cowboys to steal maverick cattle for her. Basis for the 1956 film.

The Fourth Horseman by Will Henry (Henry Wilson Allen). Random House, 1954. Based on the Graham-Tewksbury feud in Arizona in late the 1800s, this is the story of a war between cattlemen and sheepherders.

The Violent Land by Wayne D. Overholser. Macmillan, 1954. A gunman's loyalties were divided between the rancher he worked for and the nesters who lost their spreads to his land-hungry employer. Spur Award from Western Writers of America.

These Thousand Hills by A. B. Guthrie, Jr. Houghton Mifflin, 1956. Lat Evans, the grandson of Lije and Rebecca Evans from Guthrie's Pulitzer Prize novel *The Way West* (Houghton Mifflin, 1952), left Oregon in the 1800s to become a cattle rancher in Montana. Basis for the 1959 film.

Tall Wyoming by Dan Cushman. Dell, 1957. Control of the packing and shipping of cattle from the Montana frontier is the basis for this story of a big man who dealt himself into the game. He was called "Tall Wyoming."

Sweet Promised Land by Robert Laxalt. Harper and Brothers, 1957. Laxalt, a native Nevadan of Basque descent, has written a reminiscence of his father, who after a long life of herding sheep on the Nevada slope of the Sierras returned for a visit to his native Pyrenees. The old man yearned to stay there among the people of his childhood, but finally returned to Nevada, which had claimed him.

The Unforgiven by Alan LeMay. Harper and Brothers, 1957. On a lonely ranch in the Texas Panhandle in the 1870s, there was an Indian raid at the time of the "Kiowa Moon." They were not after cattle; they sought the return of one of their own. Basis for the 1960 film.

Elizabeth, by Name by Will Cook. Dodd, Mead, 1958. Setting up a trading post to take advantage of passing cattle herders during the early days of the Texas Territory, Elizabeth Retting found the land plagued by harsh weather, Indians, and lawless men, and she further found challenges in a long line of unwanted suitors.

The Big Country by Donald Hamilton. Dell, 1958. In 1886 Captain James McKay left the sea and came to Texas to claim his bride. He was alone and a stranger in a big country. Wearing a plug hat and carrying a carpet bag, McKay was out of place at her father's ranch. But he knew from experience that rough men either accept you on their terms or on yours. Source for the 1958 film.

Cowboy by Clair Huffaker. Gold Medal, 1958. Tom Reese was a living legend on the trail. When a cattle drive teamed him with Frank Harris, a tenderfoot from back East, he swore to make the kid a real cowboy. Source for the 1958 film.

Born of the Sun by John H. Culp. William Sloan, 1959. Shortly after the Civil War, a boy began a new life in the Concho country of Northwest Texas. This is a story of growing up on the frontier; of back-breaking labor, lawlessness, and in particular, the spring trail drive to Abilene.

The Feud by Amelia Bean. Doubleday, 1960. Set in Arizona's Tonto Basin in the late 1800s, this novel is about the Graham-Tewksbury Feud, the most violent in the history of the southwest.

Old Ramon by Jack Schaefer. Houghton Mifflin, 1960. A young readers' book about a boy whose father placed him in the care of an old sheepherder for a season. The boy learned about life as well as sheep from Old Ramon.

Sundown At Crazy Horse by Howard Rigsby. Gold Medal, 1961. The story of a cattle drive from Mexico to Texas, where tensions mounted as the herd neared Texas. The dramatic plot leads two of the participants to the brink of incest. Filmed in 1961 as "The Last Sunset."

Sun in Their Eyes by Henry Sinclair Drago. Pocket Books, 1962. Matt Harlan envisioned a fortune from the shorthorned cattle of Oregon if he could get them to the rich grazing lands of Wyoming. So with only a handful of men, he started a thousand miles trail drive across lava beds and desert, through hostile Indian territory, toward a country that was being ravaged by a notorious outlaw.

The Hi-Lo Country by Max Evans. Macmillan, 1962. The story of two cowboys who drank, fought, gambled, and rode the beautiful Hi-Lo country of New Mexico together, but were in love with the same married woman. Basis for the 1998 film.

The Home Ranch by Ralph Moody. W. W. Norton, 1962. One of Moody's eight books about his growing up in the West. This one covers his work on a Colorado cattle ranch when he was twelve.

One-Eyed Sky by Max Evans. Houghton Mifflin, 1963. This short novel is about the kinship of three survivors—an old cowboy, an ancient cow and an elderly coyote—the old cowpuncher reminiscing about his life before rounding up the last stray herd; the old cow calving for the last time; and the old coyote caring for her starving pups.

Scandalous John by Richard Gardner. Popular Library, 1963. John McCanless was a deranged old cattleman intent on driving his herd to market. The herd was a single skinny cow and his trail crew was a single Mexican hand, but McCanless pushed on, only to die tragically in a gun battle in Chicago. Basis for the 1971 film.

Wyoming Summer by Mary O'Hara. Doubleday, 1963. The third novel in O'Hara's story of the McLaughlin family and their Goose Bar Ranch. Ken, the boy who was the focus of *My Friend Flicka* (J. B Lippincott, 1941), is now a teenager. He helps another teen search for her valuable racing mare.

Monte Walsh by Jack Schaefer. Houghton Mifflin, 1963. The passing of the Old West in the late 1800s is observed through the lives of Monte Walsh and his buddy Chet Rollins, working cowboys on the Slash-Y Ranch in New Mexico Territory. Each chapter can stand alone, as if the author were writing a journal of the events in their lives. Basis for the 1970 film and the 2003 teleplay.

The Trail to Ogallala by Benjamin Capps. E. P. Dutton, 1964. This authentic story of the trail driving days follows a cattle drive from southwest of San Antonio up the Great Western Trail, across the Brazos and the Red River, through the reservations of the Kiowa, Comanche, Cheyenne, and Arapaho, to Oglala on the Platte River in Nebraska. Spur Award from Western Writers of America.

The Bright Feathers by John Culp. Holt, Rinehart and Winston, 1965. In 1871, three young cowhands set out on a 600-mile journey through the dangerous Oklahoma Territory. The three trail drivers encountered the notorious Belle Starr, the black bandit Blue Gum, and a Cherokee named Stanley Hightower, who had a degree in medicine.

Slaughter's Way by J. T. Edson. Toronto: Corgi, 1965. Texas John Slaughter was tough—very tough. For a small man, barely five foot nine in high-heeled boots, he usually had his way. And he wasn't about to let another Texas cattleman named John Chisum—later to be a New Mexico cattle baron—swallow up his stock.

The War on Charity Ross by Jack M. Bickham. Doubleday, 1967. A young widow had to fight to preserve her land and build up a ranch in the face of opposition from a greedy and unscrupulous neighbor.

To Be a Man by William Decker. Little, Brown, 1967. Roscoe Banks was orphaned at sixteen when his father was killed on suspicion of rustling in the preliminary skirmishing which led up to Wyoming's Johnson County War. He struck out on his own and drifted from ranch to ranch across the Southwest, becoming a competent cowboy. Finally, crippled and old, he settled in Coconino, Arizona. Roscoe himself sums up what "to be a man" really means to him when a friend reminds him that his kind isn't in demand anymore.

The Floating Outfit by J. T. Edson. London: Brown, Watson, 1967.

From Edson's *Floating Outfit* series. The Floating Outfit was a crew of top hands that worked for the O. D. Connected Ranch in West Texas. The outfit included Dusty Fog, a tough ex-Rebel cavalry officer; Mark Counter, the best-dressed man in the West; and the Isabel Kid, who was fast with a gun.

North to Yesterday by Robert Flynn. Alfred A. Knopf, 1967. Fifteen years after the last trail drive, an old, frail storekeeper named Lampassas assembles a straggly herd of longhorns and a scraggly crew, and starts them toward trails end. The old man risked all for one last, grand adventure. National Cowboy and Western Heritage Museum Western Heritage Award.

Will Penny by Tom Gries and Bob Thomas. Ballantine Books, 1968. Will Penny was a cowboy—a hired man on horseback. He had learned from his harsh life how to take care of himself. But he was getting old. Basis for the 1967 film.

Goodnight's Dream by J. T. Edson. London: Brown, Watson 1969. From Edson's *Floating Outfit* series. Charles Goodnight's dream was to drive cattle from Texas to Kansas, but there were many obstacles. He needed first-class help, and some boys from the Floating Outfit provided it.

The Outfit by J. P. S. Brown. Doubleday, 1971. This novel follows the adventures and conflicts of an "outfit" of hardworking cowboys as they race against time to round up the cattle before the winter snows begin.

The Cowboys by William Dale Jennings. Stein and Day, 1971. In 1877 a crusty old rancher's herd was ready for market when his cowhands left him for the gold fields. He assembled a crew of young schoolboys and started trailing the herd from his ranch at the base of the Montana Territory's Crazy Mountains to Belle Fourche in Dakota Territory. Along the way the schoolboys became cowboys. Basis for the 1972 film.

The Day the Cowboys Quit by Elmer Kelton. Doubleday, 1971. In 1883 the cowboys of the Canadian River country of Texas went on strike against the big ranches. Kelton used that little known incident to focus his novel on the changes brought to ranching by the big syndicates. They fenced the range and replaced traditions and trust with written rules of employment, such as dictating whether the cowboys could start herds and own land of their own while employed as punchers. Spur Award from Western Writers of America.

The True Memoirs of Charley Blankenship by Benjamin Capps. J. B.

Lippincott, 1972. During the days of the open range frontier, seventeen-year-old Charley Blankenship ran away from his Missouri home to learn about life as a cowboy on the trail and on a series of ranches. He came home for a visit after ten years, but would not stay long. He believed himself "too good a cowhand to give up the business."

Raton Pass by Tom W. Blackburn. Dell, 1973. The owner of one hundred thousand acres of New Mexico grassland had his cattle empire torn apart by a woman with a hunger for land.

Night of the Cattleman by Giles A. Lutz. Doubleday, 1976. A cattleman went to work for the largest sheep ranch in Wyoming and joined their side in the cattlemen- sheepmen's war.

The Stolen Steers by Bill Brett. Texas A&M University Press, 1977. Set in the Big Thicket of southeast Texas around the turn of the 19th century, this is the story of a young man, hurt in an oil field accident and down on his luck, who steals a small herd of steers and a horse and sets out to drive them to a distant market. National Cowboy and Western Heritage Museum Western Heritage Award.

The Good Old Boys by Elmer Kelton. Doubleday, 1978. In West Texas at the turn of the century, many cowboys settled into domesticity and became "nesters" with wife and family and a farm or small ranch. But Hewey Calloway was unable to give up the old free life. He wanted no part of land ownership or domesticity, although he was sorely tempted when he returned to his brother's ranch in 1906 for a visit. Spur Award from Western Writers of America. Basis for the 1996 teleplay.

The Kiowa Plains by Frank Ketchum. St. Martin's Press, 1978. Ben Hurley and Jeff Hill were hardworking, honest cattle freighters on the Kiowa Plains of lower Arizona. It was a hard life made made harder by ruthless raiders. When their livestock was stolen, Ben and Jeff swore to teach the outlaws a lesson they would never forget.

Short Grass by Tom W. Blackburn. Bantan, 1948. The free graze of Texas short grass drew cattlemen who built empires out of hard work and the use of guns. The town of Brokenbow had to take a stand against them. Basis for the 1950 film.

Sheepherding Man by Frank Roderus, Doubleday, 1980. "Most of the time I stayed clear of towns, preferring my own company and that of some animals to most people, but there are times when I enjoy getting to see some lights and to hear some noises I haven't made myself."

This Calder Range by Janet Dailey. Pocket Books, 1982. Across the Texas prairie, through treacherous Indian country, Benteen and Lorna Calder trailed their cattle to a new land. A romantic novel of the couple's efforts to harvest a fortune from the rich buffalo grass of Montana.

The Wranglers by Lee Davis Willoughby (house name). Dell, 1982. From Dell's *The Making of America* series. Set in Montana in the 1880s. A horse wrangler with a Harvard education helps a small rancher, an old classmate named Teddy Roosevelt, avoid a trap being set for him.

The Dakotas: At the Wind's Edge by Kathryn Davis. Pinnacle Books, 1983. The Marquis de Mores, an arrogant French aristocrat, and his wife Medora were determined to accumulate wealth and bring progress and prosperity to the Badlands of the Dakotas. But they were not prepared for the hostility they encountered.

The Dakotas: The Endless Sky by Kathryn Davis. Pinnacle Books, 1984. The enemies of the Marquis de Mores had caused his ruin and forced him to leave his beloved Dakota Badlands. In this novel his son Phillipe and his widow Medora return, determined to build the empire the Marquis had envisioned.

Stand Proud by Elmer Kelton. Doubleday, 1984. This story of the open-range cattle industry spans the period from the Civil War to the end of the century. Cattleman and Indian fighter Frank Claymore watched the land become settled until it was all fenced up, until he was surrounded by a society he didn't understand. He had once been a hero, a defender of the frontier during the Civil War, a forger of trails in the wilderness that had opened the Texas plains to civilization, and had built a cattle empire. But now, he was on trial for murder and vilified as an evil old man.

Dancing at the Rascal Fair by Ivan Doig. Atheneum, 1987. Angus McCaskill and Rob Barclay left Scotland in 1889 for a new life raising sheep in wind-swept Montana. This novel chronicles the next thirty years of their lives as they built homes and raised families in the Two Medicine country at the base of the Rocky Mountains.

The Savage Land by Matt Braun. Signet, 1988. Print Oliver, an ex-Confederate Texan, rounded up wild longhorns and drove them to markets from Galveston to Abilene, eventually establishing a major cattle operation.

South Texas by Ann Gabriel. Ballantine Books, 1989. In 1886 South Texas ranchers and farmers battled both a terrible drought and foreclosures on their properties.

Manifest Destiny by Brian Garfield. Penzler Books, 1989. The story of Theodore Roosevelt's coming of age as a small rancher in the wild Dakota Badlands of the 1880s.

Passage to Quivira by Norman Zollinger. Bantam Books, 1989. A ne'er-do-well, after years of drinking and brawling in the East, returns to the family ranch in the Ojos Negros Basin of New Mexico to face the terrible legacy of his family and try and find redemption.

The Blooded Stock by J. P. S. Brown. Bantam Books, 1990. The Cowdens were tough survivors. Their cattle grazed the Arizona range for three generations. They survived the Apache, bandits, and an Eastern cattle baron with barbed wire and hired guns.

The Breaking of Ezra Riley by James L. Moore. Lion, 1990. A Christian novel about coming of age in rugged Montana. As a cowboy, young Ezra Riley could not live up the the reputation of his father.

Home Mountain by Jeanne Williams. St. Martin's Press, 1990. Sixteen-year-old Katie MacLeod had to care for her siblings after her parents died. She moved them to Arizona and there become entangled with a cattle rustler and had to contend with the Apache. Spur Award from Western Writers of America.

The Big Lonely by Sam Brown. Walker, 1992. Two cowboys, working for the huge XIX Ranch in Texas, refused to look the other way when the ranch's cattle were rustled. The novel portrays the day-to-day life of the cowboy.

The Goodnight Trail by Ralph Compton. St. Martin's Press, 1992. Book 1 of Compton's *Trail Drive* series. After the Civil War, three former Texas Rangers rode with Charles Goodnight as he trailed a thousand longhorn cattle to Colorado.

The Chisholm Trail by Ralph Compton. St. Martin's Press, 1993. From Compton's *Trail Drive* series. Ten Chisholm, the half-breed son of Jesse

Chisholm, with a crew of cowboys and ex-soldiers rounded up a herd of wild longhorns in the Texas brakes and drove them a thousand miles through hostile Indian territory to open a new trail to Kansas.

Trail's End by Frederick Bean. Kensington, 1994. Twelve hundred Mexican longhorns were driven up the Chisholm Trail from Matamoros to Abilene. The trail boss had to contend with treacherous river crossings, storms, stampedes, outlaws, and an unruly crew of cowboys.

Shortgrass Song by Mike Blakely. Forge, 1994. Shortly before the Civil War, the Holcombs crossed the Great Plains to Colorado's sprawling Front Range country. Ab Holcomb, the father, became a powerful rancher, despite incredible obstacles. But two of his sons were dead, and the third had become a troubadour and a drifter.

Grass Kingdom by Jory Sherman. Forge, 1994. From Sherman's series about the Texas Baron clan. Family patriarch Matt Baron built a "grass kingdom" in the Texas panhandle.

The California Trail by Ralph Compton. St. Martin's Press, 1994. From Compton's *Trail Drive* series. Gold fever had hit California, and suddenly, there was a great demand for beef. For two Texas brothers, it meant the chance to sell well-grazed longhorns after years of hard ranching and a treacherous cattle drive up through Mexico. But between the Bandera Range and California, they faced a searing desert, swollen rivers, Indian attacks, and outlaws.

The Long Drift by Sam Brown. Walker, 1995. The plot follows middle-aged drifting cowboy Casey Wills as he moves from outfit to outfit, job to job, until he makes enough money to start a little ranch of his own.

Leaving the Land by James L. Moore. Thomas Nelson and Sons, 1995. A Christian novel, this is the sequel to *The Breaking of Ezra Riley* (Lion, 1990). Ezra faces an uncertain future as a Montana rancher.

Heart of the West by Penelope Williamson. Simon and Schuster, 1995. The story of a New England woman who found love on a Montana ranch—along with some rousing adventures.

Spanish Blood by Mike Blakely. Forge, 1996. In New Mexico in 1870, fortunes were made in land speculation on the old Spanish grants.

Death of an Eagle by Jonas Kirby. Howling Wolf, 1998. In 1883 a young Basque sheepherder was mauled by a grizzly and lost his flock to wolves. A mountain man found him and taught the boy survival skills, even though it was past the time of the mountain man in the Idaho wilderness.

Incident at Crazy Woman Creek by Frederick W. Boling. Bighorn, 2002. The culminating battle of the conflict known as the Johnson County Cattle War of 1892 was fought at the TA ranch compound located in a bend of Crazy Woman Creek. This is a story based on events leading up to and following the battle at the TA.

The Trail Brothers by Troy D. Smith. iUniverse, 2003. A powerful bond was formed between the Crown-H cowboys on an eventful trail drive. The cowboys were former Rebels, former slaves, and a half-Cherokee wrangler. They were willing to risk everything for a man some of them had once fought to keep in chains—a man who became their brother.

The Velvet Brand by Erv Bobo. Echelon Press, 2005. On a trail drive from Waco to Abilene, at least half the herd carried the Velvet brand, so named for a mysterious woman.

Dakota by Matt Braun. St. Martin's Press, 2005. After the loss of both his mother and his wife on the same day, Teddy Roosevelt went west to the Dakota Territory, where he established a ranch and hoped to recover from his devastating loss. Braun's suspense-filled plot is based on actual events. Spur Award from Western Writers of America.

A Lone Star Cowboy by Charles Angelo Siringo. Sunstone Press, 2006. Facsimile of the original 1919 edition. From Sunstone Press' *Southwest Heritage Series*. In 1916 Governor William C. McDonald persuaded Charlie Siringo to accept a commission as a New Mexico Mounted Ranger for the state Cattle Sanitary Board. The only thing unusual about that was Siringo's age, a ripe 61. Undaunted, he saddled up and with a pack horse started for his headquarters at Carrizozo in Lincoln County. His duty was to run down outlaws and stock thieves in southern New Mexico. *A Lone Star Cowboy* covers this period in his life but contains many of his earlier stories. In the preface Siringo said it was intended to replace *A Texas Cowboy* (1885).

Riata and Spurs: The Story of a Lifetime Spent in the Saddle as Cowboy and Detective by Charles Angelo Siringo. Sunstone Press, 2007. Facsimile of the 1927 edition. From Sunstone Press' *Southwest Heritage Series*. Siringo's third book based his adventures in the Old West. He wanted to include some of his daring adventures while serving with the Pinkertons, but the Agency threatened a lawsuit if he revealed any of their professional secrets. So the cowboy detective had to delete some of his best material.

Sam Hook by Richard S. Wheeler. Sunstone Press, 2008. Sam Hook was a cantankerous old man who raised longhorns in the midst of Montana's Hereford country. Since the grazing lands were open range, Hook's longhorn bulls reduced the value of the Hereford herds. The ranchers' association was determined to get rid of Sam and his longhorns. All that stood between the old man and a rope was a tin star pinned on a man who didn't care what kind of cattle any rancher had.

SELECTED REVIEWS

The Virginian: Horseman of the Plains
by Owen Wister
Macmillan, 1902

Trampas and the Virginian first met in Medicine Bow at a poker game. When the Virginian took his time in responding to Trampas' raise of twenty dollars, Trampas told him, "bet, you . . . ."

> The Virginian's pistol came out, and his hand lay on the table, holding it unaimed. And with a voice as gentle as ever, the voice that sounded almost like a caress, but drawling a very little more than usual, so that there was almost a space between each word, he issued his orders to the man Trampas:
> "When you call me that, smile !"

This line from Owen Wister's classic novel *The Virginian* is one of the most recognized in American literature.

Critic Stan Steiner believes *The Virginian* has long influenced how men think of themselves in the West. The character of the Virginian became the apotheosis of the heroic cowboy in later fiction.

Wister was an unlikely creator of this memorable Westerner. A Boston aristocrat, a Harvard man, a lawyer, an accomplished pianist, he made fifteen long journeys west, first for his health, later as an escape from the practice of law, and finally in search of literary materials.

His search paid off with a novel that's a milestone in American literature. Many worthy writers, most notably Zane Grey, capitalized on *The Virginian's* theme, setting, and characters and developed the Western as a truly American genre.

Set in the cattle country of Wyoming, the novel abounds with descriptive observations of the panorama of Western scenery, towns, and the cowboy life. Wister loved Wyoming:: "Nobody, nobody who lives on the Atlantic strip," he wrote in his journals, "has a notion of what sunrise and sunset and moonrise can be in his native land till he has come here to see." But he didn't totally view the region through rose-colored glasses. Speaking of the town of Medicine Bow, he wrote,

> [Towns such as Medicine Bow] littered the frontier from the
> Columbia to the Rio Grande, from the Missouri to the Sierras. They
> lay stark, dotted over a planet of treeless dust . . . they seemed to
> have been strewn there by the wind and to be waiting till the wind
> should come again and blow them away."

And this:

> Portable ready-made food plays of necessity a great part in the
> opening of a new country . . . The cow-boy has now gone to worlds
> invisible; the wind has blown away the white ashes of his camp-fires;
> but the empty sardine box lies rusting over the face of the Western
> earth.

These settings and Wister's exposition, based on his first-hand observations, account for much of the success of the novel.

The narrator, an Eastern dude who remains unnamed throughout the novel, was in awe of the Virginian. He described him as "a shy young man, more beautiful than pictures," who had set out at fourteen from his home in Virginia to see the country. At twenty-four, he had seen Arkansas, Texas, New Mexico, Arizona, California, Oregon, Idaho, Montana, and Wyoming. He's depicted as tall, strong, handsome, shrewd, gentle, courageous, incapable of meanness, polite and considerate of women; he's taciturn and uncommunicative; he minds his own business; he's proficient at roping, handling horses, tracking down thieves, and managing men; he's a fondness for the practical joke and is sentimental about his favorite mount. With the help of school marm Molly Wood, he learned to read and educated himself by reading her collection of classics.

The Virginian's romance with Molly is both tender and humorous. She was a descendent of, among others, Molly Stark, wife of Revolutionary War hero Captain John Stark. For generations her people had been gentlefolk, but then the mills in Vermont failed and Molly began to work, giving piano lessons and embroidering, and then she made the long trip west to teach school in Bear Creek, Wyoming.

The Virginian and Molly met when the stage she was traveling in became mired in a stream bed: "Then a tall rider appeared close beside the buried axles, and took her out of the stage on his horse so suddenly that she screamed. . . . Then the tall man withdrew, leaving her to become herself again." When she later saw him at a dance, Molly avoided the cowboy and pretended not to recognize him. "If you like to waltz, ma'am, will you waltz with me?" he asked. "You're from Virginia, I understand?" said Molly Wood, regarding him politely, but not rising. One gains authority immensely by keeping one's seat. All good teachers know this. When the Virginian first told Molly of his love for her, she replied airily: "I am not the sort of wife you want." On one occasion when he asked whether she had "anything different" to tell him about his marriage proposal, she said: "I wish to say that I have never looked on any man better than you. But I expect to." She wasn't an easy woman to court.

Molly's Eastern upbringing made it difficult for her to understand the Western man, who was molded by his harsh environment. The Virginian didn't believe all men were created equal: "Equality is a great big bluff . . . a man has got to prove himself my equal before I'll believe him." According to Wister, the East was decadent; American virtues had their last home in the West. "Now back East you can be middling and get along," observed the Virginian, "but if you try a thing in this Western country, you've got to do it well." When his friend Scipio meditated "I wonder what killing a man feels like," the Virginian replied: "Why—nothing to bother yu'—when he ought to have been killed." Leading a vigilante party and hanging his best friend for rustling or facing Trampas in a deadly gunfight seemed natural and was within the code of conduct the Virginian lived by, but it complicated his relationship with Molly Wood.

The Virginian has been adapted to the stage and screen. Both William S. Hart and Dustin Farnum played the title role on the stage. It's been filmed five times. There were three silent versions and two sound. Dustin Farnum starred in Cecil B. DeMille's 1914 silent film. Victor Fleming's 1929 version for Paramount was the first sound adaptation to film, and starred Gary Cooper in the title role and Walter Huston as Trampas. Fleming directed "Gone with the Wind" ten years after "The Virginian." The 1946 film starred Joel McCrea, supported by Brian Donlevy, Barbara Britton, and Sonny Tuffs. Both of the sound versions endure today as fine examples of Western cinema. A TNT original teleplay was aired in 2000, with a script by Larry Gross based loosely on Wister's novel.

In the foreword, Wister says "The world of the Virginian has vanished. The mountains are still there, far and shining, and the sunlight and the infinite earth, and the air . . . but where is the buffalo, the wild antelope, and where is the horseman with his pasturing thousands"? Well, they are in his novel, and the large body of Western literature it spawned—forever. Quoting a verse from Coleridge's *Rime of the Ancient Mariner*, the narrator comments that a half-great poet once had a wholly great day. Owen Wister is remembered as essentially a one book novelist (although he wrote others), but he had a wholly great day with *The Virginian*.

The Drifting Cowboy
by Will James
Charles Scribner's Sons, 1925

Will James wrote about cowboys. He wrote about real cowboys, working cowboys, about their lives and their spirit. He set his stories in the cowboys' West, the range country where they made their living. He wrote books about their work and the freedom they enjoyed, and glamorized their wandering lifestyle.

The Drifting Cowboy, a collection of stories originally published in *Scribner's*, *Saturday Evening Post*, and *Southwest Review*, is one of his best. A working cowboy named Bill narrates the stories, describing his experiences as he drifts from job to job across the Northern Plains to the Southwest. The freedom to go anywhere he wanted, when he wanted, was crucial to Bill, as it was to James. Jim Bramlett, a Will James biographer, wrote:

> There is something to be said about unfettered freedom . . . and Will
> James said it many times. He glamorized the "drifting cowboy"
> lifestyle. Open country always beckoned to him. After working for
> a while on a ranch, Will James would quit the outfit, saddle up a
> "toppy" saddlehorse, lash down his bedroll on another horse and ride
> off into the sunset: north in summer, south in winter.

This theme is central to all Will James' stories of the cowboy life, and nowhere does he say it better than in *The Drifting Cowboy*.

Perhaps the most illuminating aspect of the cowboy's work is in the contrast James' draws between riding the Northern Range and cowboying on the Great American Desert.

When the homesteaders started farming the prairie and the cow trails started being stopped by barbed wire, the cowmen had to look for places that couldn't be plowed to take his cattle. He went to the Badlands or alkali country of Montana and Wyoming. Bill was from Montana, and in the opening story he tells us about rounding up cattle in the fall on his home range:

I'm riding along, trying to look through the steady-falling drizzle snow for stock; it seemed to me that I was born and raised under a slicker, on a wet saddle, riding a kinky bronc, going through slush and snow, and facing cold winds. . . twelve to sixteen hours in the saddle, three to four changes of horses a day, covering from seventy-five to a hundred miles, and there's one to two hours night guard to break the only few hours left to get a rest in.

He would sometimes live outdoors in these conditions for as much as eight months.

But soon there were too many cows crowded into that country. So the cowmen looked west, to the desert.

The desert already had all the cattle it could hold, but the drifting stockmen dug out the springs, put in miles of pipeline, and ran in more cattle. Along with the herds came the cowboys. These newcomers had to learn from the desert cowboys how to practice their trade in this hard and unforgiving country.

Bill shipped down with a train load of cattle and, since he was raised a prairie cowhand, found it "mighty hard at first." He traded in his Angora chaps for batwings and started to get educated.

Since there were no hills to climb to look for cattle, he had to become an expert at reading tracks. And the land looked different. He could see for great distances, but was often fooled by joshuas, mistaking them for cattle at a distance. Then there were the malpais, and granite boulders with buckbrush twisted all around them that on the desert flats loomed up looking like stock. An experienced range rider looked for movement; he could tell a horse from a cow from ten or twelve miles away. So Bill learned to distinguish. True to his calling, he adjusted to the environment:

Taking in all what you have to contend with every day, the ponies, the cattle, and the long dry rides to nowheres wondering if there'll be water when you get to the other end, etc., makes it kind of aggravating, unless you're used to it . . . I used to cuss the desert at times and leave it . . . but when you live in it and ride all day long and part of the night . . . in all kinds of weather on all kinds of horses and handling the splitting cattle all by your lonesome, you get to feel you're part of that desert . . . that wide, unfenced sunburned country of the stunted sage.

The terrain where the cowboy works, the horses he rides, and the stock he tends are the fodder that distinguishes James' stories.

Will James was born Ernest Dufault in Southern Quebec Province in Canada. At age fifteen, he left home and worked for two years on Canadian ranches, then crossed the border into the American West, adopted the name Will James, and spent twelve years as a working cowhand. In this short time he learned a lot, and came out of it a top hand who was especially good at breaking horses and riding rough strings. He also learned to talk like a cowboy.

James' dialogue has enough authentic range jargon in it that the sometimes exaggerated cowboy vernacular is believable. The whimsical stories are backed up by his sound knowledge of the subject and give the reader a good dose of cowboying: Bill's narrative covers range riding, roundups, making camp, riding night guard, breaking horses, riding the grub line, rodeoing, and even working as a Hollywood cowboy.

James also became an artist of note, held in esteem by fellow Western artists, collectors, and others who appreciated his strong, bold style. His drawings captured horses and range stock in action, with nearly flawless accuracy. Many critics place his art above his writing. All of his books are illustrated; there are forty-four drawings in this book, adding immensely to the pleasure of reading the story.

The Drifting Cowboy is the second of Will James' twenty-four books. All of his work is an important contribution to the history of the American West, and provides a realistic account of the cowboy's role in that history. His writings and drawings introduced generations of readers to the American cowboy. He's so beloved by scholars and fans alike that the Will James Society celebrates his work and holds an annual convention in his name.

The Bad Lands
by Oakley Hall
Atheneum, 1978

Dakota Territory was wild and woolly in the early 1800s. Texas cattlemen had invaded the Bad Lands because they couldn't negotiate good grazing contracts with the Indian Tribal Councils in the Cherokee Strip and on the Arapaho-Cheyenne lands. Then the Homestead Law , which gave each settler 160 acres, brought farmers into a country best suited for open range.

Compounding the problem, Montana and Dakota ranchers were suffering heavy losses from cattle rustlers and horse thieves. The ranchers organized the Montana Stockraisers Association in April of 1883 to protect their property. The leader of the association was Granville Stuart, who formed a vigilante committee known as "Stuart's Stranglers." By the autumn of 1884, the Montana and Dakota ranges had been swept clean of stock thieves.

Some colorful characters were present in the Bad Lands during these turbulent times. Many wealthy Europeans moved there in 1883; one was the Marquis de Mores, a lordly Frenchman who was married to Medora von Hoffman, the daughter of a millionaire New York banker. With his father-in-law's money and his zeal for adventure, the Marquis left his mark on the territory.

During this same period a pale, slender, shy young man named Theodore Roosevelt arrived in Medora. While in the Bad Lands, he operated two ranches, wrote several books, and developed a philosophy of self-reliance that would someday carry him to the White House.

With apologies to Theodore Roosevelt and the Marquis de Mores, Oakley Hall drew on their experiences and the events that occurred while they were in Dakota Territory to write *The Bad Lands*, a novel of conflicting views on the best use of a beautiful but fragile land, and the tragedies that result from men's inability to accommodate.

George Eustace Balter, Lord Machray, was a giant Scotchman with a scarlet face and a mop of yellow hair. He was a military man, highly decorated for protecting the Queen's interests abroad. Machray was cherished by the men who worked on his Ring-cross Ranch. He could recite poetry by the hour and never repeat himself, his voice deep and low, or fast and bright, the thick Scottish accent making plain American sound barren. He once asked his cowboys if they understood the old Scots. "Nary a word!" a voice called back. "But she do sound grand."

The earlier residents of the Bad Lands didn't share this affection. Bill Driggs, a craggy hunter who had made his living from the once plentiful game of the Bad Lands, had little use for Machray:

> To begin with, he comes out here with something called script, that no one's ever heard of. Entitles him to grab land wherever he wants to grab it. Next thing, he has fenced him a piece of ground half the size of the territory, it looks like, and got claims and range rights out of more besides. He has fenced some fellows in, and some out. Some he has fenced out, like me, has been making a living here for twenty years wolfin' or shootin game for the railroad crews. He has got a fence across the only route a man can take downriver without fording deep water or fighting quicksand in the spring. And maybe you haven't seen yet what wire can do to a pronghorn, or a cow either, that gets messed up with it.

Yule Hardy, president of the Dakota Stockraisers Association, also disliked the Scotchman:

> I consider him my enemy. He is the enemy of the particular freedom of the Bad Lands. Of free range, free cooperation, free institutions. With his contempt for lessor men, and his schemes to enrich himself at their expense.

Cora Benbow, a woman of property, local madam, and confidant and lover to Machray, offered a different view:

> I have heard men out here claiming they love the idea of free range! . . . What they love is the idea of their own land, without the expense of buying or the trouble of fencing.

Lord Machray considered himself a man of progress working for the common good.

Andrew Livingston, like Roosevelt, was an easterner who came west on a hunting expedition and stayed for several years. He consulted Machray's ranch super on the prospects of ranching:

> Andy asked Johnny Goforth: "How many head would a prospective rancher need to purchase to have a paying proposition?"
>
> Goforth's cool eyes regarded him for a moment. "Why, no more than a hundred head, I'd say. But that is beside the point out here. There is a difference that is more than numbers between a man that runs a thousand head and one that runs a hundred."
>
> "What is that," Andrew asked.
>
> Goforth's teeth showed beneath his mustache in a thin grin. "The bigger fellow thinks the smaller one is a thief, and the smaller one thinks the bigger is a bully."

Nevertheless, Andy became a small rancher. And he became a friend of Machray's, Yule Hardy and the other large ranchers, and the grangers, acting as a bridge between them until he was forced to choose sides.

The Bad Lands is Oakley Hall's second in a trilogy of novels about the Old West. The first, *Warlock* (Viking Press, 1958), was nominated for a Pulitzer Prize. *The Bad Lands* didn't appear until twenty years later. Both it and the third, *Apache* (Simon and Schuster, 1986), won critical acclaim. He won a Spur Award from Western Writers of America for his short story *Horseman*.

Louis L'Amour's *Shalako* (Bantam Books, 1962) had a hunting party that included a German baron, a French count, and a senator's daughter. Responding to criticism that these were highly improbable people in his plains setting, L'Amour wrote,

> After living in the West much of my life, and years of research in the field, I can think of no Western cast I would consider improbable. One of the great charms of the West, and one of the things that cause me to continue to write about it, as well as one of the reasons

people like to read about it, was that the West was a place where the improbable happened every day.

Like *Shalako*, Oakley Hall's *The Bad Lands* shows the richness of the American West as a source of exciting historical fiction.

Duel in the Sun
by Niven Busch
Hampton, 1944

After the Civil War, Confederate Army Captain Jackson T. McCanlas promoted himself to colonel and followed the government surveyors into the Staked Plains country of Texas. He saw an empire waiting to be claimed, and he claimed it. At its peak, his Spanish Bit Ranch controlled over a million acres. He had also served in the senate, and was respectfully addressed as "Senator" by everyone, including his wife and children.

The senator was only five-two in high-heeled boots, a tiny man it seemed, to own so much land and be the father of four big sons.

Jesse was the oldest. His mother had made him a reader and his reading had led him to the practice of law and away from the Spanish Bit. Lewt, the second, was well-built, dark-haired, and extraordinarily handsome, but his face was mocking and vicious. He was his father's boy, and the senator spoiled him. The third son, Gil, was a strong and solid-looking boy who would one day take over the reins of the Spanish Bit when the senator grew older. The youngest, Ruck, was a slow-witted giant, nearly twice the size of his bantam father.

The senator had built the town of Paradise Flats and been pretty much a one-man law. But the railroad was coming. Most of the townspeople and ranchers wanted it; Senator McCanlas did not. Jesse stood against his father on this issue, for he was the lawyer for the railroad in Paradise Flats. But Jesse had grown up on the Spanish Bit, and understood the history of the area and his father's reservations:

Over the cattle trail in the last fifteen years had gone ten million cattle. They had swung up from the border, past Refugio and Goliad, across the Llano and up out of the live oak country, over the Colorado and the long hard stretch flanking Fort Griffin and the old Spur Ranch. Their eyes bulging like frogs' and their horns sticking out of the water like pickets, the hawking, howling herds got over the famous rivers—the Red, the Canadian, the Cimarron—on to Andarko Camp Supply, Dodge City, Abilene. Even then, many drivers still didn't stop to ship from the available railroad corrals but kept on into the rich grass of the Black Hills, the waters of gorges, the high, unused valleys of Montana.

Civilization had trailed the riders north. It had trotted behind the herds like a chuck-wagon dog, flea-bitten kind of civilization. Now it would come storming on an iron road-bed. It would ride in arrogantly, white-faced in plush seats, with starch-jacketed servants at its side. You didn't need to be a college professor to know that in a few months from now the Staked Plains country would face changes which had in other places had taken centuries.

The senator's life was further complicated by the arrival of Pearl Chavez in the spring of '93. She was twelve years old when Jesse McCanles met her at the stage stop in Paradise Flats. The girl wore a ragged old calico dress and was without shoes. Jesse took her to the store and bought her a new dress and some shoes before he drove her to the ranch. Pearl was a distant relative of Mrs. McCanles, who had asked her to live at the Spanish Bit after her father was hanged.

Pearl's father had been French, and her mother was a Mestizo woman from Laredo. She had long legs, and her Indian blood showed in her long ropy bluish-black hair. Everything about her was sensuous. For one so young, she had the air of sure feminine knowledge which is characteristic of some women, perceptible from the cradle on.

The senator didn't really welcome her, and Mrs. McCanlas knew intuitively that there would be trouble because of Lewt.

It didn't take long for Lewt to stake a claim on Pearl. He grabbed and kissed her during her first day at the ranch. They spent a lot of time together, rendezvousing at a sump hole where they'd swim and be alone. Only Mrs. McCanlas detected the complicated nature of the relationship between these two—the egoistic, spoiled, unstable boy and the sensuous girl who couldn't resist his advances.

Busch spins a dark, lurid tale of a passion that couldn't be controlled, set against the grim backdrop of the railroad's impact on Senator McCanlas' cattle empire. The division would widen between Jesse and his father, and Lewt would become a wanted man—tracked across the Texas Panhandle by Pearl, who was followed by Jesse. The conclusion is dramatic and violent.

There are sharp images of the wild Staked Plains country and the unbridled men who rode across it. This is Busch's description of a posse returning in the early morning after riding all night:

> The dawn was far away and the night over the plains was dark and solid, windless and noiseless except for the tired steps of the twelve horses. A little wind blew from the northeast; this wind had in it the wonderful fresh morning smell of the grass country. It had the dawn in it and the horses smelled it and picked up a little, tired though they were; at the same time they bunched together closer as if to make up for the shelter of the night which was leaving them.

Niven Busch was primarily a screenwriter. His Western screenplays included: *The Westerner* (1940); *Belle Starr* (1941); *Pursued* (1947); *The Furies* (1947); *The Man from the Alamo* (1953); and The *Treasure of Pancho Villa* (1955). His only other Western novel was *The Furies* (Dial Press, 1948). He didn't concentrate on a single genre and commented in 1952 that "The different kinds of fiction I have written have been of dubious advantage in building a literary reputation but I have chosen this course because I become bored if committed to work in a single genre." He considered *Duel in the Sun* his his most successful book (but not his favorite), due in part to the huge exposure from the film made of it.

When it was released in 1946, the film was the most commercially successful Western ever made. Produced by David O. Selznick and directed by

King Vidor, Busch's novel was brought to life by a superb cast. Jennifer Jones' erotic portrayal of Pearl Chavez captured her torment—her struggle between good and evil—and the ultimate surrender to her wild passions. Gregory Peck as the unstable Lewt and Joseph Cotton as his older brother Jesse lifted their characterizations directly from the novel. The fit was so good that one wonders if screenwriter Busch had a cast in mind when he wrote his book.

Lonesome Dove
by Larry McMurtry
Simon and Schuster, 1985

Larry McMurtry is an enormously popular author who's also considered a great writer by many critics. Some consider him the single finest writer who's ever written about the Old West. His crowning achievement is clearly *Lonesome Dove*, an 843-page tome that has generated an intense devotion to both the characters and the Spur Award and Pulitzer Prize-winning story.

The story of a cattle drive from south Texas to northern Montana in the early 1800s, the novel has a complex plot that chronologically unfolds. Captains Augustus McCrea and Woodrow Call, crankily aging former Texas Rangers, were partners in the Hat Creek Cattle Company in Lonesome Dove, Texas. When old companero Jake Spoon showed up after ten years, he was full of tales of a cattleman's paradise in a wilderness called Montana. Call, without outlaws and Indians to keep his mind off ghosts of the past, figured an adventure was just what he needed. He convinced McCrea to go along, and they assembled a herd by stealing longhorn cattle in Mexico that had been rustled in Texas.

The herd was trailed through Texas, Kansas, Nebraska, Wyoming, and into northern Montana, where the Hat Creek Cattle Company was reestablished. En route, the cowboys endured dust, hail, and wild raging rivers, as well as the arid plains stretching from Texas to Montana. They battled Indians, outlaws, stampeding cattle, and grizzly bears.

The settings include cowtowns (San Antonio, Fort Worth, Oglala), an Indian village, ranches, saloons, whorehouses, and an outlaw den.

McMurtry uses his settings not only to create the proper atmosphere for his story, but also to develop characters. For example, there's a character named Bolivar, the cook at the Hat Creek Cattle Company in Lonesome Dove. He had been a competent Mexican bandit before he ran out of steam and crossed the river. He had a murderous disposition; he was filthy in appearance and habits; he pissed off the porch in front of the rest of the outfit, to their disgust; he had a wife and nine daughters in Mexico; his skills didn't include cooking. Bolivar wouldn't appear real in any place much different from Lonesome Dove. He is, in fact, a product of the setting.

There are a raft of characters, approximately seventy-two. None of these are hazy stereotypes; all are full-blown three-dimensional people. Central are McCrea and Call, who had been friends and partners for many years. Although they shared many traits and characteristics—courage, loyalty, and a strong sense of duty—it's their differences that provide grist for the powerful story that evolves.

Woodrow Call was a taciturn, demanding man. He had such a single track mind that when he started a task—no matter what task: digging a well or tracking a man down to hang—he stayed with it until it was done.

The less talk Call had to listen to, the better his humor, whereas with Augustus it was just the opposite. His capacity for conversation was legend: "He'd rattle off five or six different questions and opinions, running them all together like unbranded cattle . . ." Call once said Gus would talk to a stump if no one was around to listen to him. Gus' aversion to work was also legend.

Whereas Call was short, dark, and intense to a fault, Augustus—Captain Gus, the men called him—was a tall man with a thick mane of white hair, which, along with his loquaciousness, embellished his image as a prairie sage. He was garrulous, philosophical, a lover of ribald argument and robust women.

Call is presented as a man who was the master of his own fate and a natural leader. He made decisions; he made things happen. McCrea, however, usually went along with Call because he had nothing better to do. But both were driven by a strong sense of duty, as are numerous other characters in the story. Augustus was never sure why Call wanted to drive a herd to Montana, much less why he went with him. But the drive became a "duty" once they started. Augustus and Call tracked down an old friend and hanged him because of "duty." The friend accepted his fate in stoic good grace because he realized they were performing their "duty." If there's a theme in *Lonesome Dove*, it's probably this sense of duty that's embedded in many of the characters. McMurtry has created a scenario that's full of danger and calamity, but because of an unswerving sense of something ill-defined as duty, the human spirit prevails against incredible odds.

There are numerous subplots, including several love stores, a vicious kidnapping, and three hangings. But all are carefully tied to and advance the main plot, the 2,500 mile trail drive to Montana.

One episode incidental to the main plot merits further discussion. The kidnapping of the whore Lorena and her rescue by Gus is the Western at its best. The reader's introduction to the renegade Blue Duck sets the stage for the chilling account that follows:

> The rider . . . . rode into camp. Gus had been right: he was an Indian. He had long, tangled black hair and wore no hat—just a bandanna tied around his head. . . . He looked at them without expression . . . Lorena wished Gus would say something, but he sat quietly, watching the man from under the brim of his old hat. The man had a very large head, squared and heavy.
>
> "I'd like to water," he said, finally. His voice was as heavy as his head. . . . The man looked at Gus calmly and a little insolently, it seemed to Lorena.
>
> "I'm Blue Duck," he said. "I've heard of you, McCrea, but I didn't know you was so old."
>
> "Oh, I wasn't till lately," Augustus said. It seemed to Lorena that he too had a touch of insolence in his manner. . . .
>
> "I guess Charlie Goodnight must have run you off," Augustus said, "otherwise you wouldn't be off down here in respectable country riding some dead Mexican's saddle."
>
> The man smiled a hard smile. "If you ever bring that goddamned ol' tongue of yours north of the Canadian I'll cut it out and feed it to my wolf pups," he said. "That and your nuts too."
>
> Without another word he rode past them and out of the camp.

Blue Duck later rode back and carried Lorena away. Augustus tracked them across the bleak Texas prairie into the staked plains north of the Canadian, and finally into an area known as the Valley of Tears, spoken of with anguish by many former white women captives of the Comanche. Blue Duck had retreated to this place and sold Lorena to a band of renegades who repeatedly raped and tortured her. He told the renegades:

> "There's an old man following me . . . I want you to kill him."
>
> "Hell, what is he?' Monkey John said. "Five against one is nice odds . . ."
>
> "Somebody better settle him," Blue Duck said. "Otherwise you'll all be dead."

But they did not settle him, and they all died, as Blue Duck predicted.

When *Lonesome Dove* was made into a television miniseries in 1989, it became the highest-rated in five years and the fifteenth of all time—and rightfully so. The series is as big, bountiful, and exciting as the novel itself. It's especially faithful to McMurtry's finely etched characters. Robert Duvall and Tommy Lee Jones shine as Captains McCrea and Call. The sterling cast also includes Anjelica Huston as Gus' one love Clara, Danny Glover as the scout Deets, Robert Urich as Jake Spoon, Diane Lane as Lorena, and Frederic Forrest as Blue Duck. It's fortunate that executive producer Suzanne de Passo chose the format of an eight hours miniseries. The sprawling story could never have been condensed into a two or even a three-hour movie format.

Authenticity makes the novel an important piece of work. When writers use historical characters and backgrounds in their work, they often exaggerate the sensational at the expense of the credible. *Lonesome Dove* has its exaggerations, but McMurtry maintains a balance in presenting people as they could have been and events as they might have happened. The novel spawned two prequels and a sequel, all best sellers, and has taken its place among the greats of the genre.

Sam Chance
by Benjamin Capps
Duell, Sloan, and Pearce, 1965

In 1865, at the end of the Civil War, ex-Confederate sergeant Sam Chance left his home in Tennessee and headed west. In Texas, Chance would become a cattle baron, eventually controlling close to a thousand square miles of range land. In a story that brings to mind the legendary cattleman Charles Goodnight, although there are significant differences in the lives of the two men, Benjamin Capps has written a classic on ranching in the West.

When Chance and his friend Lefores left Tennessee, they crossed the Red River, traveled through Arkansas and into Indian Territory. The land changed gradually as they entered the eastern edge of the Great Plains. Ridges replaced hills. There were no trees except a few that grew beside a stream bed; it was a land of chaparral bushes, prickly pear, Spanish dagger, and an occasional lone mesquite—a land vastly different from Tennessee.

They stopped at a stream Chance named Silver Creek, and he told Lefores, "We've come far enough." There he would build the Long C Ranch, which was initially

> . . . a crude stronghold of civilization thrust out into an almost uncharted land. To the north Indian country stretched away hundreds of miles, and civilization was represented in it only by small, widely scattered outposts of cavalry and some surveyors seeking a route for a railroad along the old Santa Fe Trail. To the west lay the Caprock, and beyond it the vast, desolate Llano Estacado, the Staked Plains, which had struck awe in the breast of every traveler since Coronado; and in that direction, west, lay no civilization at all until the far mountains in New Mexico Territory with their old Spanish settlements.

They built a herd catching Texas longhorns, wild creatures that could run almost as fast as a horse. After seventy-two days Chance had one hundred and fourteen animals under his brand and tame enough to handle in a herd.

During the early lean years, Chance had to supplement his income to keep the ranch solvent. One winter he and Lefores spent the three coldest months in a dugout, collecting pelts from the wolves and coyotes in the Silver Creek area. The wolves were thick-furred lobos, great gray wolves, weighing up to one hundred and fifty or two hundred pounds. They were scarce, and Chance and Lefores never got more than one shot at a single wolf. The next year they used poison, with much greater success.

He led a party of fourteen men into the rough country below the Caprock, into Comanche country, to slaughter buffalo for their hides. They were attacked by a war party, and in a battle reminiscent of the Second Battle of Adobe Walls, fought them off with the big Sharps .50 caliber rifles they used to kill buffalo.

Sam Chance is the central character—by far the dominant one, and the focus of the novel. Although a heroic figure, he had enough human failings, such as not seeing what prairie loneliness was doing to his wife, to seem like a real person. But even the most minor characters are interesting. There are two Mexican vaqueros that appear only briefly:

> He thought he had learned a great deal . . . about cattle, but the two Mexicans had skills and knowledge he had not dreamed existed. The young one was a reckless, even cruel, rider, of great ability with the lariat. The older one, who sometimes smiled a surprisingly white-toothed smile out of his brown-leather face, had a deep knowledge of cattle as wild beasts and as creatures of the human economy that could be controlled. He seemed able to smell them out, to know where they would be. He knew which way they would turn before they did themselves, how far they would wander in a morning, where they would bed. He knew which would be troublemakers and which good yoke oxen. When asked, he could not explain his knowledge, but Chance recognized that it existed and studied it.

Benjamin Capps' father and grandfather had worked as cowboys in the North Texas cattle country where he grew up. The real strength of the novel is Capps' insight into ranching: how Chance built his spread, protected it from the Comanche, and, when he heard there was a good market for Texas beef in Kansas, drove a herd to Abilene and later trailed it to Ellsworth, farther west. He had to cope with the introduction of "bob" wire in 1875, the encroachment of homesteaders, and the disappearance of free range. Unlike many of his contemporaries, he adjusted to change, even took advantage of it.

Nature was a sometimes a problem for the rancher that was as severe as advancing civilization. The drought and the "big die-up" of 1885-87 cruelly separated those who only dealt in cattle from the real cattlemen. The drought came subtly. In the summer there was trouble with prairie fires. It was cold through December and January. Ranchers had their skinning crews out gathering hides from stiff bodies. In early February the worst norther of the winter hit, bringing sleet and blowing snow.

> In mid afternoon they reached the cattle drift. Shorty hadn't exaggerated; an uneven band of gaunt cows as wide as a half-dozen trail herds stretched back into the north as far as the eye could see. They were cattle of every kind and color, with motley longhorns predominating. Here and there a spindly calf was trying to keep up with a mother that had forgotten him. Their backs each had its layer of snow, partly melted and refrozen into the hair. The backbone and hip points made a shiny cross of ice on every bony back. Their steamy breaths blew before them and were jerked and dissipated in the wind.

There were thousands, some from as far away as Kansas and Colorado.

Sam Chance isn't Capps' only classic Western. *A Woman of the People* (Duell, Sloan and Pearce, 1966) is one of the best captivity novels ever written. Many consider *The Trail to Oglala* (Duell, Sloan and Pearce, 1964) the best trail drive novel, even better than Andy Adams' *The Log of a Cowboy* (Houghton Mifflin, 1903), usually touted as the best on this subject.

A winner of the coveted Western Writers of America's Spur Award, *Sam Chance* is a sweeping novel of the cattle kingdom that merits space on any bookshelf dedicated to the American West.

The Sea of Grass
by Conrad Richter
Alfred A. Knopf, 1937

Colonel Jim Brewton's Cross B Ranch in the San Augustine Plains of New Mexico stretched a hundred and twenty miles north and south along the Rio Grande, and rolled "as far into the sunset as stock could roam." When young district attorney Brice Chamberlain asked Colonel Brewton if nester Andy Boggs had been run off and severely wounded because he wanted a mere one-hundred and sixty acres, Brewton replied:

> No. . . He was run off because of what he wanted to do with the land . . . I have sympathy for the pioneer settler who came out here and risked his life and family among the Indians. And I hope I have a little charity for the nester who waited until the country was safe and peaceable before he filed a homestead on someone else's range who fought for it. But . . . when that nester picks country like my big vega, that's more than seven thousand feet above the sea, when he wants to plow it up to support his family where there isn't enough rain for crops to grow, where he only kills the grass that will grow, where he starves for water and feeds his family by killing my beef and becomes a man without respect to himself and a miserable menace to the territory, then I have neither sympathy nor charity.

The colonel was right. The southwestern plains were perfect grazing range for cattle, but not suited to farming. The pioneer cattlemen in the later part of the 19th century controlled small empires, even though they didn't own all of their range. Their right to this range was challenged by an invasion of homesteaders from east of the Missouri. The cattlemen hated the nesters and everything associated with them. Hal Brewton, the colonel's nephew and narrator of the story, said:

> . . . what I heard in my brain was the clop, clop, clop of the cloven hoofs of oxen, crying babies and crates of cackling barnyard fowl, of

the baas of sheep and goats and all the rest of the despised chattels of nesters scattering like a victorious army over our range.

The homesteader's hatred and distrust of the ranchers were equally strong. Their war for possession of the prairie was supported by the United States government. But in the end, the land they fought so hard to win at last defeated them.

If the prairie was hard on the nesters, it was equally hard on Lutie Brewton, whom the colonel had fetched all the way from St. Louis to marry him. When she arrived in Salt Fork, the nearest town to the Cross B, there was a dead man swinging from the water tank, while the freighter he had killed lay on his back by his wagon. Lutie wasn't a frontier woman, but was able to take this in stride, never slowing her bubbling stream of polite conversation. It was the prairie, the endless sea of grass, that intimidated her. Driving her from Salt Fork to the ranch, Hal noted her aversion:

> . . . when we reached the top of the escarpment, there in front of
> us stretched the vast, brown, empty plain, dipping and pitching
> endlessly like a parched sea, she stopped as if she had run into
> barbed wire.

At the Cross B, Lutie coaxed the ranch hands to plant trees around the house, eventually forming a dense wall of cottonwoods and tamarisks between her and the dreaded grasslands.

She couldn't bear the isolation of her ranch house. Lutie let hardly a day pass without midday dinner guests or overnight guests or guests to stay the week. There were the sporting English owners of the Bar 44 and the dancing officers of Fort Ewing, the guests from Santa Fe and Albuquerque, and Judge White and Brice Chamberlain.

> But Colonel Brewton did not resent his wife's entertaining. He would
> come in from riding a cold range to warm, curtained rooms with
> Lutie bare-armed in a white silken gown, and a mellow atmosphere
> of company talking and laughing. He would bow with proud

courtesy to everyone, but would talk very little, preferring to sit there with a faint desert glow warming his weathered face. No matter how large the dinner, Lutie Brewton was the tireless pure flame burning in the center of it.

Her husband loved her absolutely, and forgave her excesses and indiscretions.

Colonel Brewton and Lutie are strong, memorable characters. Colonel Charles Goodnight can be seen in Richter's Jim Brewton, but an old pioneer who Richter saw in the Bernalillo courthouse one day was the inspiration for the character. When the old man was called to testify, his dramatic entrance and the look of scorn he gave the courtroom evolved into this image of Colonel Brewton:

> The Salt Fork County Court was stuffed and smelly as a stock corral . . . Then I heard a stir at the doorway behind us and presently I thought I could feel a wave of restrained excitement . . . I saw . . . moving erect and towering down the crowded aisle along the wall, a familiar, proud, almost insolent figure in a long gray broadcloth coat with tails and bulging on the side with what I knew was a holster capped with ivory handles, his coal-black eyebrows and mustache white with alkali dust, and in the abrupt quiet of the room the fall of his boot heels like the shots of a pistol.

Lutie was based on two women who lived in Albuquerque that Richter knew. One was Scottish-Mexican, full of gay animation, and the other was a New Zealander. Both, like Lutie, had been uprooted from the place and culture of their birth, and to a degree were repelled by their new surroundings

Richter "seldom felt myself the writer, but rather a kind of day laborer digging rocks from the New Mexican earth, hammering them roughly into shape, laying them into a semblance of walls for my house." Some critics have called his work the distillation of research and observations made during long residence in the Southwest. Loren D. Estleman and others speak of *The Sea of Grass* as a prose poem. His daughter, Harvena Richter, wrote:

The ability to compress the times and spaces of a country into tight mythic structure was, I believe, unique. At times it resembles the lost art of the ballad-maker. As in the ballad, all but the essential is pared away; details are significant, omissions tell volumes. The themes of endurance, of conflicts between peoples, generations, or ways of life, are universal. The emotional tone combines a sometimes harsh, sometimes gentle lament for times past with a constant affirmation of life in the face of death and violence.

In 1928 Richter settled in Albuquerque, New Mexico, where he produced a fine body of work about the westward expansion. *The Sea of Grass*, his first novel, was anticipated in the earlier short story *Smoke Over the Prairie* (1935) and was serialized in the *Saturday Evening Post*. His epic trilogy about the settling of the Ohio frontier was *The Trees* (Alfred A. Knopf, 1940), *The Fields* (Alfred A. Knopf, 1946) and *The Town* (Alfred A. Knopf, 1950), which won a Pulitzer Prize in 1951.

The Sea of Grass was filmed in 1946 by MGM. Directed by Elia Kazan with the screenplay by Marguerite Roberts and Vincent Lawrence, the film retained the major elements of the novel. Spencer Tracy and Kathryn Hepburn gave moving portrayals of Colonel and Mrs. Brewton. Although filmed in black and white and shot for the most part in the studio, it's notable for the cinematography of the prairie—the sea of grass—and the aftermath of farming.

The narrator Hal Brewton comments early in the story that "The free wild life we lived on that shaggy prairie was to me the life of the Gods." But Lutie and the nesters seemed to drown in this same luxurious sea of grass. In Richter's capable hands, the influence of the land on these people is compelling and profound.

The Rounders
by Max Evans
Macmillan, 1960

In the conclusion of Max Evan's riotous novel of contemporary cowboying, Wrangler Lewis tells his partner Dusty Jones that a bronc rider is "just a cowboy with his brains kicked out." This pretty much sums up Evan's story of two self-admitted dumb cowboys.

Although a comedy, the story has tragic undertones as Dusty and Wrangler try to break out of a tough and unrewarding existence. The two cowboys were bronc riders, working for a rancher named Jim Ed Love. Jim Ed wasn't a cowboy, but he was a cowman, carefully managing his pastures and hay, dickering aggressively for the best price for his beef, and, as Dusty observed, getting "more work and [giving] less pay to a cowboy than any other rancher."

Jim Ed told them, "Now, boys, I'm going to give you the chance of a lifetime" and asked them to spend the winter at his lower camp gathering a hundred or more strays that had gone wild. He said he would pay a five-dollar bonus for every head they gathered. When they agreed, Dusty allowed, "I never knew a couple of dumber cowboys than us."

Jim Ed's lower camp had been homesteaded long ago, but when Dusty and Wrangler took up residence it "was lonesome as hell." It was a big country out there. "You could look for a hundred miles in almost any direction except west. There the view was blocked by a long, rocky, piñon-covered mesa." Dusty knew they'd find the wild cattle on this mesa, and that gathering them in from the hundreds of brush-covered canyons was going to be hard on men and horses.

But they were good at their trade—naturally industrious and competent cowboys. They fixed up the old homestead shack and the corrals, and cleaned out the spring.

Then the serious work started.

First we jumped three mother cows and a four-year-old steer. They tore through the brush like a dose of salts. The broncs plowed right in after them, with me and Wrangler setting aboard ducking limbs, reining around boulders, feeling the brush pull and drag at us like the devil's own claws.

They gathered old thousand pound steers and big fat dry cows that were "wild as outhouse rats."

Their work included Dusty's battle of wills with Old Fooler, a roan horse that Jim Ed said was a fiver but Dusty placed him at nine years old. As horses go, this one wasn't impressive.

Old Fooler stood there half asleep; his eyelids drooped. He didn't even bother to switch his tail at a horsefly that was trying to swallow him whole. In fact, he was leaning so heavy on one side it looked like he might just fall over."

This old maniacal bronc tried his best to kill Dusty. The first time he tried to saddle the roan, Old Fooler bit him in the back. The second time he rode him, the horse kicked Dusty in the belly while the cowboy was opening a gate. On the next ride Old Fooler "fired" as he was topping a rise, sliding the saddle and Dusty off his rear end. On another ride he veered under the limb of a piñon tree while chasing a steer and Dusty busted some ribs.

This was a duel, though, and Dusty knew how to handle unruly broncs. He reciprocated:

The ground was rolling away under us so fast it made me dizzy. Right out ahead was another bunch piñon. I spurred him straight at them, leaning over just like I did before. Old Fooler was already bunching his muscles to jump the wrong way and break my crazy neck once and for all. Just as he thought it was time, I straightened up and pulled one foot out of the stirrup, yanking my leg up behind the cantle of the saddle. Then I jerked him into that tree at full speed. . . .

There must be a lot more wind in a horse than in a man. The air that came busting out of his lungs would have blown a Stetson hat around the world three times. That old horse staggered and fell. . . .

I hadn't killed him, though. He got up, and his eyes were rolling around in his head like a couple of gallstones in a slop jar. He wobbled on his legs.

Dusty would later swear he would sell the cantankerous horse for dogfood.

As if the wild cattle and old Fooler didn't provide enough excitement, the cowboys indulged in some outright dumb activities, like the time Dusty roped a bobcat.

He had always wanted to rope a coyote but had never been on a horse fast enough to run one down. But on Old Fooler he was able to whip out a loop and catch one. Encouraged, he roped a bobcat:

> When that cat hit end of the rope he went up in the air all right, but it was straight at Old Fooler's hindquarters. He was yowling to beat hell and he must have sunk them claws to the bone in Old Fooler's hind end because that horse snorted and started bawling and bucking at the same time. . . It was all I could do to stay on Old Fooler. . . .
>
> The next thing I knew I felt something digging in my back. It felt like an eagle with claws six inches long, but it was that bobcat. . . About that time Old Fooler ran under a low-hanging limb. I didn't see this limb. . . Old Fooler just kept going with that rope stringing out behind and that bobcat meowing on the other end.

When spring came, they had gathered a hundred head in all. Dusty thought, "Lord-a-mercy, a five-hundred dollar bonus and all that back pay coming!"

True to form, when their roundup was over and they had the most money either of them had ever had at one time, they quit their jobs and went to the Fourth of July celebration in Hi Lo. They bought drinks for nearly the entire Mexican village of Sayno, picked up two girls en route, competed in several rodeo events at Hi Lo, won some bets on Old Fooler's bucking ability, bet it all on a race between the crazy horse and old Ed Foster's black five-year-old. They were arrested twice, once for starting a fight because someone said something disparaging about Old Fooler. Wrangler told his partner, "You keep goin' on about what you are going to do with that horse when we get into Hi Lo. I'll bet you a month's wages that when the Good Lord sends you to hell you will be ridin' Old Fooler, and he will be buckin' to beat sixty."

The MGM film, directed by Burt Kennedy and starring Glenn Ford as Dusty, Henry Fonda as Wrangler, and Chill Wills as Jim Ed Love, was a box office success. It was fairly true to the novel, but Ernest Borgnine would have better fit the image of Wrangler than did Henry Fonda.

Max Evans, who has won numerous awards including two Western Writers of America's Spur Awards and their Levi Strauss Golden Saddleman Award for lifetime contribution to Western literature, and the National Cowboy and Western Heritage Museum's Western Heritage Award, has spent his entire life in the Southwest working as a cowboy, rancher, miner, painter, and writer. He's said that the behavior of people (and characters) is closely related to the land and its climate. The Hi Lo Country where *The Rounders* is set actually does exist. It consists, in Evan's words, "of the northeast quadrant of New Mexico, a slice of far West Texas, a bit of the Oklahoma Panhandle and another slice of the southeast bottom of Colorado—-both up and down. The Sangre de Cristos—part of the timbered Rockies—run through the western edge, and the great well-grassed rolling hills, malpai mesas and canyons cover most of the rest." It's a harsh and often beautiful land that's high and low physically and emotionally, and an integral part of the novel.

The Rounders is a humorous but sad story of contemporary range life, full of cowboying, rodeoing, and carousing. It's a comic tragedy that makes it difficult for the reader to decide whether to laugh or cry.

6

THE HUNTERS

INTRODUCTION

For five million years or so, man has been a hunter. He has hunted for survival, for profit, and for sport. The American West has been a bountiful host for all these activities. Few places on earth have the variety of big and small game, and deadly predators, as the plains, prairies, mountains and frozen northlands of the United States and the western regions of Canada and Mexico.

The American bison, or buffalo, was hunted by the plains Indians for survival. It provided more than just meat. It supplied virtually everything they needed, including clothing and shelter. General Philip Sheridan, who became commander of the Army's Division of the Missouri in 1869, and then Commanding General of the Army in 1884, looked the other way when the buffalo hunters fanned out across the Texas Panhandle, in violation of a treaty with the Indians, and started to slaughter the buffalo. He believed the only way to subdue the plains tribes was to destroy the great herds that kept them independent. He was right.

By the mid-1800s swarms of hunters, armed with Sharps .50 caliber rifles that could hit a target at fifteen hundred yards, started to kill the buffalo for profit. They only wanted the hides; the carcasses were left for scavengers or to rot on the prairie. By the late 1800s, the great herds were gone.

Other western big game has been hunted for profit. Bear, cougar, jaguar, wolf, coyote, bobcat, lynx, and fox at times had a bounty on them. These, along with deer, elk, moose, caribou, sheep, goat, antelope, and javelina, and all manner of small game, have been and still are hunted for sport and perhaps the meat or hide.

The early settlers and ranchers hunted predators to protect their livestock and sometimes their families. The big western cats—known as cougar, mountain lion, panther, puma, painter, catamount—are deadly predators, as are wolves. Contemporary ranchers in the West contend with these same threats.

The reader's guide in this section provides a selection of novels based on the wide-ranging hunting experience in the West. The selected reviews are *The Last Hunt* (Houghton Mifflin, 1954), by Milton Lott, a story about buffalo hunters, set in the midst of the final slaughter of the great herds, and *The Track of the Cat* (Random House, 1949), by Walter Van Tilburg Clark, which tells of the search for a large mountain lion that preyed on an isolated Nevada ranch during a blizzard. Both novels illustrate the drama and excitement of the hunt.

READER'S GUIDE

The Wolf Hunters by James Oliver Curwood. Bobbs-Merrill, 1908. An adventure tale set in the Canadian wilderness, where a city boy encounters wild animals, Indians, and a lost gold mine.

The Last of the Plainsmen by Zane Grey. Outing, 1908. In 1907 Zane Grey made a trip to the Grand Canyon and the Arizona Strip with Buffalo Jones, an accomplished hunter and "the last of the plainsmen." Jones was a living legend who practiced the dangerous sport of lassoing and capturing mountain lions alive. This trip provided rich material for the aspiring author.

The Thundering Herd by Zane Grey. Harper and Brothers, 1925. A story of how Buffalo Jones, a friend of Zane Grey, and the hide hunters in the Panhandle of Texas practically decimated the buffalo in the 1870s, destroying the Plains Indians' source of food, clothing, and shelter. Basis for the 1933 film.

Hound-Dog Man by Fred Gipson. Harper and Brothers, 1949. This story is structured around a three day raccoon hunt during which the narrator, a twelve-year-old boy named Cotton, was initiated into the ritual of the Texas Hill Country hunt and into some of the mysteries of adult life by Blackie Scantling, the "hound-dog man" of the title.

The Deer Stalker by Zane Grey. Harper and Brothers, 1949. Men's attempts to manipulate the balance of nature—ranchers demanded a bounty on mountain lions—had a deadly impact on the deer population on the north rim of the Grand Canyon in 1924. Without their natural predator, the herd became so large that forage would not support it and consequently faced starvation. A plan was devised to drive the deer through the Grand Canyon and into the forests of the south rim. The drama of the ill-fated drive is presented through the experiences of a young park ranger, who, against his will, became a deer stalker.

Buffalo Wagons by Elmer Kelton. Ballantine Books, 1956. By the summer of 1873, the great Arkansas River herd was gone, as was the Republican herd before it. The old hide hunters in Dodge City spoke of a vast herd south of the Cimarron in Comanche territory. But only a buffalo hunter like Gage Jameson would risk his life and head down that way. Spur Award from Western Writers of America.

Butcher's Crossing by John Williams. Macmillan, 1960. A young man from the East joined a buffalo hunt in Colorado. Following the hunt, he spent a snowbound winter and, after that ordeal, returned to town to find that the entire venture was futile because the hide market had failed.

Shalako by Louis L'Amour. Bantam Books, 1962. A hunting party of Europeans in New Mexico, guided by Shalako Carlin, are pursued by renegade Apaches. Basis for the 1968 film.

Last Hunt by Luke Short (Frederick D. Glidden). Bantam Books, 1962. Game warden and sheriff's deputy Lee McPhail searches for the man who shot a judge's horse out from under him on an elk hunt in the high country, then murdered the judge.

The Hard Time Bunch by Clifton Adams. Doubleday, 1963. Frank Beeler, an ex-U. S. deputy marshal in the Indian Territories, hired out as guide to a hunting party of wealthy dudes. But unknown to Beeler, the hunters were not after animal game, they were after men: some two-bit outlaws hiding in the hills of the Creek Nation. Beeler soon found himself human prey, along with the outlaws. But he had friends in the Creek Nation: Brother Duel Hooker, a preacher, and Captain George Forestman of the Creek Light Horse Police.

The Buffalo Runners by Fred Grove. Doubleday, 1968. In the spring of 1876, when the Western plains were brown with the migrating herds of buffalo, the guns of the buffalo hunters roared like thunder. Some of the hardest, most ruthless men in the West were there to profit from the slaughter. National Cowboy and Western Heritage Museum Western Heritage Award.

The Forests of the Night by J. P. S. Brown. Dial Press, 1974. Set in the high country of the Mexican Sierras, this is the story of a Mexican peasant's hunt for a jaguar, named El Yoco after the devil, who, when wounded, became a killer of man and a threat to the hunter's family.

Cimarron Jordan, by Matt Braun. St. Martin's Press, 1975. The thunder of hoofs mingled with the roar of rifles as hunters harvested the buffalo and faced the fierce Indian tribes on the Texas plains. Cimarron Jordan was one of the best of these plainsmen.

The White Buffalo by Richard Sale. Simon and Schuster, 1975. Two American icons, Wild Bill Hickok and Crazy Horse, dreamed of killing the last of the great white buffaloes, whose mystical presence haunted them. Both faced the beast's enraged charge in the novel's climax. Basis for the 1977 film.

The Hider by Loren D. Estleman. Doubleday, 1978. It was 1898, ten years after the last buffalo had been seen in Oregon. A young hunter and an old hider tracked the last one through what remained of the frontier.

The Wolfer by Loren D. Estleman. Pocket Books, 1981. In 1878 a journalist and a wolfer set out in pursuit of a black wolf, weighing over 100 pounds, that had been slaughtering herds of cattle and sheep in Idaho The wolfer intended to collect a large reward, but the cunning wolf was the only thing he really wanted.

The Hunt by James Powell. Doubleday, 1982. El Oso de Muerte, the Bear of Death, had been stalked in the San Juan mountains for over a decade by the best hunters in Colorado and New Mexico. Then, in the summer of 1895, an expedition from England came to hunt El Oso de Muerte for sport. But the hunters soon became the hunted.

Heart of the Country by Greg Matthews. W. W. Norton, 1985. A half-breed young man with a hunchback built a reputation as a buffalo hunter. His chosen vocation was good to him—until the herds started to become extinct.

Riley's Last Hunt by Frank Calkins. Doubleday, 1986. A wealthy Eastern businessman brought his spoiled son to the wild Wyoming Territory to go on a hunt to toughen and test him. He hired veteran hunter Riley as a guide, and together the three set out on a quest for the big game of the American wilderness: bull elk, buffalo, and—the most dangerous of all—the grizzly. But out in the unsettled territories, where there were all manner of outlaws and roughnecks, the hunter could become the prey.

Slaughter by Elmer Kelton. Doubleday, 1992. This is the story of the destruction of the vast buffalo herds and of the effects their destruction had on the white man and the red man alike. Spur Award from Western Writers of America.

Cheyenne Winter by Richard S. Wheeler. Pinnacle Books, 1992. From Wheeler's *The Rocky Mountain Company* series. When the beaver trade dried up, the mountain men came down to the plains to hunt the buffalo, whose hides brought a good price. They founded the great Rocky Mountain Company—an enterprise that would rival the legendary American Fur Company. One of these men was Brokenleg Fitzhugh (Broken Hand Fitzpatrick), who would survive a bitter winter trek across a frozen landscape in a desperate attempt to save the company.

Shadow of the Grizzly by Larry J. Martin. Doubleday, 1993. A rancher in early California's San Joaquin Valley was asked by the neighboring Indians to kill a child-murdering grizzly bear; the grizzly was revered by the Yocut, so their own braves could not kill the bear. The rancher's decision ultimately dragged him into a deadly battle with nature's most efficient predator and most vicious killer.

The Purification Ceremony by Mark T. Sullivan. Avon Books, 1997. Eight hunters were a thousand miles from civilization in the snowbound isolation of British Columbia. But they were not alone. They were being stalked and slaughtered like the animals they hunted. Their stalker would not rest until he purified the hunt by killing them all.

Blood Red River by Walter Lucas. Pinnacle Books, 2000. Led by a young Comanche war chief named Quanah Parker, the Comanche, Kiowa, Cheyenne, and Arapaho vented their anger against the buffalo hunters by attacking a small trading post in the Texas Panhandle called Adobe Walls. But the post had among its defenders the hunters with their big Sharps .50 caliber rifles, and these hunters included frontiersman Billy Dixon and Bat Masterson.

The Buffalo Hunters by Gary McCarthy. Leisure Books, 2001. Inspired by Buffalo Bill, a young greenhorn from Massachusetts headed west. When he heard of a reward for finding a surviving herd of buffalo, he was soon is searching for the nearly extinct beast.

SELECTED REVIEWS

The Last Hunt
by Milton Lott
Houghton Mifflin, 1954

Woodfoot, one of the colorful characters in Milton Lott's *The Last Hunt*, remembered traveling along the Arkansas in the fall of the year when the buffalo were "as thick as cattle at a roundup for two hundred miles or more." But in 1874 they were gone, all the buffalo in Kansas, clear to the Arkansas and Indian Territory, only their bones and rotten carcasses left wherever you looked. "It was something to remember even after he got used to it, the way it hit him then. The stinking carcasses and bones that whitened the ground like alkali, and the black spots of unskinned bull heads with dried shriveled noses. And in place of the buffalo, flies till a man was afraid to open his mouth."

Following the vanishing herds, a four man party was hunting buffalo on the Wyoming plains in the late 1800s. Lott's novel is the story of these men and their role in the extinction of the great American buffalo herds.

Sandy McKenzie was an older, experienced hunter who had participated in the last big organized buffalo hunt in the Canadian Red River country when he was only seven. In the spring of 1882, he had a permanent camp on Sand

River. One afternoon Charley Gilson rode into camp. He said he was also a buffalo hunter but had lost his outfit, and proposed they team up. Sandy, who was used to working alone, reluctantly agreed, and the new partners hired Woodfoot, so named because of a brightly painted foot at the end of his wooden leg, and a young red-headed half-breed named Jimmy O'Brian as skinners.

Charley knew he had done wrong to pass himself off as a buffalo hunter when about the only ones he had ever hunted had been for sport. He could shoot with anybody, but he had a lot to learn about the whole business. He knew he could learn from Sandy. Charlie deferred to Sandy, mining his knowledge until he learned to kill buffalo. Sandy, meanwhile, became sick of killing—the stinking carcasses, the whitened bones. He hoped to get enough money together to buy a little freight outfit and run a line off the railroad.

In the beginning, Sandy carried the load for the team, professionally killing enough to keep the skinners busy, while Charley made only a minimal contribution. He was good with a gun—when a wounded buffalo bull charged Sandy, Charley put three holes that he could cover with his hand into the animals skull—but did not know buffalo. But as he became more proficient, and Sandy became more disillusioned, the roles reversed. As Sandy's production became less and less, Charley began riding him more all the time.

One night their stock was stolen by four Blackfeet Indians. Two were squaws. Charley pursued the Blackfeet, killed three of them, and kept one of the squaws, who had a baby, as his "woman." Charley treated her crudely, and when Sandy engineered her escape, a confrontation was assured.

In addition to the main plot, there are four subplots that dwell on the four main characters—Sandy, Charley, Jimmy, and Woodfoot. A major subplot involves Charley and Woodfoot with two scientific researchers studying "the monarch of the plains" that ends in tragedy, while another concerns Jimmy's unsavory relationship with a prostitute and her gambler partner. But the bulk of the book is about hunting buffalo.

All hunters strove to get a "stand," to be able so kill a large number without scattering the herd. Early in the novel Charley heard shots, coming from the direction that buffalo had gone. He mounted and rode north along the ridge till he could see the mouth of the draw, still hearing the shots steady and spaced, about one a minute. Sandy had a stand.

The buffalo had stopped about a quarter of a mile out on the flats and were bunched up close now, milling and bawling—all but about ten head that were down around the edges. He could see Sandy about two hundred yards to the south of the herd, his rifle to his prong stick shooting, a little puff of smoke hanging over him in the quiet air.

While he watched, a bull detached itself from the herd and began hooking one of the downed animals. Even at that distance Charley could hear the flat, metallic bawl of buffalo that smelled blood. With the sound of a shot he saw the bull flinch and hump up, then turn to go back to the herd, and in turning fall.

It was the last bull in the herd. Sandy shot two more cows that started to lead off from the bunch, then stopped firing. He sat up and started cleaning his gun, and the animals moved off, not running. Charley counted sixteen dead ones. He saw the skinners pulling out from camp with the wagon before he turned and rode into the hills.

Then, after the kill, came the arduous task of skinning,

They worked in silence, the only sound their own breathing and the skinning sounds—the slicing whisper of the knives and the tearing sound of the hide giving from the flesh under a pull. There was the warm sweet smell of meat and the steam rising from the marbled flesh into the cold air.

They skinned out one side, then rolled the carcass over on the spread-out hide and skinned the other. Jimmy cut the hump meat off both sides and took the tongue . . .

The relationship between the four men was complex. All three liked Sandy, although Charley couldn't understand his attitudes toward Indians and killing buffalo, and would eventually turn on his partner. But he worked hard for Sandy's approval, like a kid, in some ways, Woodfoot thought. Charley, strangely, was also liked by the other three. It was odd the way Sandy felt about Charley. There was something inhuman about him, a machinelike quality of precision and untiring drive that Sandy could not understand. And yet he could not condemn him; he felt somehow akin to Charley, despising him and at same time feeling responsible for him. For Jimmy, there was something about Charley that drew him—or rather compelled him—and he could not understand it. For Woodfoot, "it was odd the way he had stuck with Charley. Not that he especially liked him—he had even disliked him at first and been a little afraid of him too. But if you knew a man well enough you got so you could handle him and it became sort of comfortable to be around him. You could always predict him even when you couldn't control him." Both Woodfoot and Sandy constantly teased Charley, who was completely humorless. It was a dangerous game, like playing with a rattler.

In one sense, *The Last Hunt* is a frontier morality play, a struggle between good (Sandy) and evil (Charley), two men engaged in the same deadly pursuit but with strikingly different attitudes about their profession. Sandy killed only the number of animals that the skinners could harvest, and longed for the day he could get the stench of death out of his nostrils. For him, killing buffalo was a living. He respected the shaggy beasts and felt their annihilation was a loss to the country. But when the buffalo were plenty, Charley hunted in all daylight, and Woodfoot and Jimmy could not keep up in skinning. When he finally got his stand, he killed nearly a hundred, and had to leave most of them for the wolves or to rot on the prairie. He loved killing. The slaughter of the huge animals gave him a thrill that he equated to "being with a woman." When the herds began to disappear, the fire went out of Charley.

Filmed in 1956 by MGM, "The Last Hunt" starred Robert Taylor as Charley Gilson, Stewart Granger as Sandy McKenzie, Lloyd Nolan as Woodfoot, Russ Tamblyn as Jimmy O'Brian, and Debra Paget as the Indian woman. U. S. government marksmen actually shot and killed buffalo during production as part of a scheduled herd-thinning.

Milton Lott was awarded the Houghton Mifflin Literary Fellowship award for *The Last Hunt*, his first novel. It is a fine account of of the American buffalo, of the endless herds that once thundered across the prairies from the Texas Panhandle to Montana and Canada, and of their impact on the Indians who depended on them for life itself, and to the white men who mercilessly slaughtered them for their hides.

The Track of the Cat
by Walter Van Tilburg Clark
Random House, 1949

Each year, with the coming of the first snow, a fleet and deadly mountain lion appeared at the Bridges' ranch in Nevada's Sierra mountains, ravaging the livestock, leaving behind a trail of senseless devastation.

Set in 1900, *The Track of the Cat* is the story of a dysfunctional family leading a lonely, divisive and destructive domestic life on their isolated Nevada ranch, of what happens to the family when it's faced with an evil it doesn't understand, and of the deadly hunt for the mountain lion.

The mother, Mrs. Bridges, was the source of the malignancy in the family. Self-righteous and domineering, she had destroyed the hopes and dreams of her husband and daughter. Old Mr. Bridges was a drunken leftover of the frontier days, who had been tainted by the civilization of San Francisco. He hadn't wanted to settle on a ranch, but had yielded to his wife. Arthur, the oldest son, was a dreamer who wanted nothing for himself. Curt was thirty-seven, the middle son. He had the utmost faith in himself, and little in anything else. Harold was the youngest, not quite twenty. He provided balance; he was part dreamer, like Arthur, with Curt's sense of practicality. Grace Bridges was a thirty-five-year-old spinster who lived with a disappointed heart. Her mother had made her quit her teaching job and come home to the ranch because she had taken up with an assayer, a "foreigner." She loved Arthur dearly, but hated Curt. She thought him a "cheap, dirty-mouthed bully."

Joe Sam, an ancient Paiute Indian, worked at the ranch for only his keep. He had been a brave when Frémont camped at Pyramid Lake, around sixty years ago, and was a war chief in 1860, when the Paiutes fought a big battle at the Truckee. After they lost that fight, Joe Sam took his family to up around Shasta. There, a black panther killed his wife and oldest daughter. The first snow would always upset Joe Sam. He would "see things" that would put him into a trance. He couldn't sleep, and he wouldn't eat. Arthur thought the black painter (Mrs. Bridges was southern; she used painter for panther, cougar, mountain lion, and the others picked up on it) was Joe Sam's personal evil spirit.

In the opening chapter, Arthur dreamed of a stalking black painter. He woke and heard a noise in the wind that sounded like something was after the stock. He and Curt went to investigate. They found three steers the cat had killed. "Killing for fun, the bastard," Curt said. "And running them like he was a wolf." Arthur was first to see the cat, a fearsome creature:

> [Arthur] was under the half-dome rock . . . when suddenly the mare neighed shrilly, in extreme terror . . . He fell into the stiff springing hedge of brush . . . and half entangled there saw the big cat above him, crouched on a slanting edge of rock, its hindquarters gathering under it, like pressed springs, for the leap, and its long, heavy tail lifted a little for balance and curling and uncurling slowly at the tip . . .

The premature Nevada winter was as terrible an adversary as the murderous cougar. Curt, an experienced tracker who knew this section of the Sierra Nevada, vowed to kill the cat: "No matter what color you are. No matter what color, or how big, or how long it takes." He began to track:

> [Curt] cradled the carbine in his right arm, and began to climb again. Out of old habit . . . he climbed slowly but steadily, keeping each step short enough to be easy, and flat-footed and a trifle pigeoned-toed, so that the soft pacs [of his bearpaws] gripped firmly in the snow or on stone. The same habit made him walk carefully beside the tracks of the cat and not in them, and glance up every now and then, to guard against ambush, and to be sure the trail made no big swing within sight.

But over time the severe weather began to exact its toll. His inner compass fell into disagreement with the compass of his reason. He turned sleepy and inattentive as well as weary. Twice he almost blundered into a tree, unable to see it until it loomed sudden and monstrous right before him. Each time the tree became, for an instant, a leaping black panther, but each time he forced the terrible fear down again.

There's a relation between the domestic destruction within the Bridges' home and the terror of the hunt. A theme of disorientation permeates both scenes. There are long dream sequences. Arthur tries to relate his dreams to events that are about to occur; he sees some meaning in them. Curt confidently fancied himself a man of hard-nosed practicality. He takes tough-guy pride in ridiculing dreams. A man cannot live on shadows, but must live on food, something of physical substance. The cat which is killing their cattle, he insists, is a physical cat; it can be killed with a regulation bullet. It is no spook, no black and mystic painter.

The cat that the Bridges hunted was a real beast; it had killed and mutilated cattle. But the cat which began to raise fear in Curt was an imaginary one. His mind couldn't deal with the panic his disorientation had unleashed within him.

Reared and educated in Nevada (his father was president of the University of Nevada), Clark's novels reflect an emphasis of the psychological effects of the land on man. *The Track of the Cat* isn't easy to read. Critics have long wrestled with the symbolism of the cat, the function of the dream sequences, and the importance of his use of black and white imagery throughout the hunt sequences. But it's nevertheless a rewarding reading experience, rich in suspense and drama and action.

Walter Clark is best known for *The Ox-Bow Incident* (Random, 1940), a landmark novel of mob violence set in the American West. But many critics consider *The Track of the Cat* his major work.

The 1954 Warner Brothers film was directed by William Wellman, who also earlier directed "The Ox-Bow Incident" (1943). It has a good cast, with Robert Mitchum as Curt, Teresa Wright as Grace, Tab Hunter as Harold, Diana Lynn as Harold's sweetheart Gwen, Philip Tonge as old Mr. Bridges, Beulah Bondi as Mrs. Bridges, William Hopper as Arthur, and Carl Switzer as the eerie Joe Sam. A. I. Bezzerides' script neatly balances the hunt for the cougar, which is never seen, with the family drama taking place inside the snow-bound Nevada ranch house. William H. Clothier's cinematography, in which the primary colors were bleached out, giving the resulting color images the look and feel of black and white, is extraordinarily effective.

Some scholars have compared T*he Track of the Cat* to Herman Melville's *Moby Dick* (Harper and Brothers, 1851). Others can find no novel at all with which to compare it. James C. Work describes it as an example of "novel of place," based on the theme that the West's natural world exerts a powerful psychological impact on human intruders. This is probably as clear a statement of Clark's purpose as any.

7

THE NATIVE AMERICANS

INTRODUCTION

Novels about the American Indians, or Native Americans, that are most familiar and have been the primary source of movie and television screenplays are those concerning the Indian Wars. But there are many other themes in a large body of literature. And the periods in these novels range from the seventeen hundreds, before the coming of the white man, through the Indian Wars and the turn of the century, to contemporary times. Further, there are a myriad of tribes and settings for writers to draw upon.

Many of these diverse Native Americans and their territories are found in novels in the readers guide. Best known are the Great Plains tribes—including the Cheyenne, Sioux, Comanche, Kiowa, Crow, Arapaho, and Pawnee—and the Southwestern tribes—the Apache, Navajo, and Pueblo Indians. But there are others, just as notable: the Blackfeet in the Rocky Mountains; the Flathead in Montana; the Ojibwa in Minnesota; the Paiute in California and Nevada; the Modoc in northern California; the Nez Percé in Oregon; the Mission Indians of Southern California; the Chippewa in North Dakota; the Cree in the Canadian West; the Creek and Cherokee nations in Oklahoma, and the Athabaskans in Alaska. There are, of course, many others.

The themes in novels about the American Indians are just as varied. Young men go on vision quests to achieve manhood. There are captivity stories. The stark realities of reservation life, and the attempts to adjust to it or escape from it are recurring themes. A prevalent contemporary theme is the conflict between the demands of modern society and the Indians' respect for their heritage. Many novels explore the myths and mysteries of Native Americans' beliefs. There are novels based on 20th century conflicts with the U. S. Government over tribal lands.

The novels I selected to review are Dorothy M. Johnson's *Buffalo Woman* (Dodd, Mead, 1977), the story of an Oglala Sioux woman who knew prosperity as a child, and then tragedy with the coming of the whites and the decimation of the buffalo. *Ramona* (Roberts Brothers, 1884), by Helen Hunt Jackson, addresses the injustices visited upon California's mission Indians when the white men came, and the impact their arrival had on the Mexican landholders. Frank Waters' *The Man Who Killed the Deer* (Farrar and Rinehart, 1942) is a classic novel of Pueblo Indian life. Finally, *Stay Away, Joe* (Viking Press, 1953), by Dan Cushman, is a hilarious look at contemporary life on a Cree-Chippewa reservation in Montana.

Novels concerned with the Indian Wars are addressed in Chapter 3, Boots and Saddles: The Army in the West and the Indian Wars.

READER'S GUIDE

Life Among the Modocs by Joaquin Miller. Bentley, 1873. Miller, a nature writer, was among the first to capture early California's wild beauty. *Life Among The Modocs* is based on his years in the mining towns and Indian camps of northernmost California during the tumultuous 1850s.

The Way of an Indian by Frederic Remington. Fox Dufield, 1906. The second and final novel by the noted Western artist tells the story of a Cheyenne boy who lived between the gold rush and the death of General Custer.

The Vanishing American by Zane Grey. Harper and Brothers, 1925. The story of an Indian boy who, at the age of seven, was abducted from the reservation. He was educated in the East, but returned to the reservation in the early 1900s as a young man to try to regain his identity as a Navajo. The title of the novel refers to the author's belief that the Indian, as a distinct group, was disappearing. Intermarrying with whites—as his young Navajo protagonist did—would eventually result in the disappearance of all Indian traits in their descendants.

Co-ge-we-a by Mourning Dove. Four Seas, 1927. The first novel published by a Native American woman. The half-Indian heroine Co-ge-we-a was drawn away from a mixed-blood cowboy suitor by an easterner after what he thought was her fortune. She felt marriage to the Indian cowboy would mean living "Indian," but she gradually recognized the importance of the values he represented.

Wild Horse Mesa by Zane Grey. Harper and Brothers, 1928. A Paiute girl who spent nine years in a government school returned to her reservation in Utah where her future was to become an Indian's number two wife.

Laughing Boy by Oliver La Farge. Houghton Mifflin, 1929. This Navajo love story, set in northern Arizona, won a Pulitzer Prize. Laughing Boy knew nothing of the white man, but Slim Girl did—too much. She saw in Laughing Boy her sole hope for salvation.

Wah'Kon-Tah: The Osage and the White Man's Road by John Joseph Mathews. University of Oklahoma Press, 1932. Based on the journal of Major Laban J. Miles, the first government agent for the Osage, Mathews tells of Miles's struggles to bring civilization, education, and agriculture to the Osage and of their struggles to retain the old ways while adapting to the new.

Silver Hat by Dane Coolidge. E. P. Dutton, 1934. This is a satire on Indian Westerns. Colorful characters include Lady Grace Benedict, known as Slender Woman; an old scout named Milton Buckmaster who passes as the Navajo called Silver Hat, and a young Hopi chieftain named Harold Chasing Butterflies, who went away to the white man's school and returned with only hatred in his heart.

Sundown by John Joseph Mathews. University of Oklahoma Press, 1934. A fictional account of Indian/White relations. Challenge Windzer was the son of a mixed blood father and an Osage mother whose conflicting views—his mother preferred the old Osage ways and his father looked to Washington and was betrayed—affected his life and assimilation.

Fig Tree John, by Edwin Corle. Liveright, 1935. A legendary White River Apache, living in a California's Salton Sea area at the turn of the century, is broken and embittered by encroaching whites. This great chief, killer of five white men, has to deal with his son's marriage to a white woman.

Brothers Three by John Milton Oskison. Macmillan, 1935. *Brothers Three* is set in Indian Territory and the major characters are part Indian. The novel describes the struggle by each of three brothers to break away from the farm established by their hardworking father and his quarter-Cherokee wife, and the failure of each to prosper by using family capital for investments. An underlying theme is the prejudice against mixed-bloods by even the shiftless poor whites in the territory.

The Surrounded by D'Arcy McNickle. Dodd, Mead, 1936. A young man, half Spanish and half Indian, returned from a federal Indian boarding school to his father's ranch on a Flathead Indian reservation in Montana, where he confronted assimilation and alienation from both the white way of life and traditional tribal culture.

People on the Earth by Edwin Corle. Random House, 1937. A novel of life on a Navajo Reservation, and of the failed attempts to Americanize the Indians.

The Enemy Gods by Oliver La Farge. Houghton Mifflin, 1937. A novel of Navajo versus white values in the education of an Indian. It recounts the return of Myron Begay to the Navajo reservation after ten years at the American Indian school. After many months, he was gradually rehabilitated into the ancient tribal ways and brought to acceptance once again of his native gods. By the end of the novel Myron possesses hard-won wisdom which he now wishes to share with his people: the Navajos can neither continue to follow the old Navajo ways nor walk in the white man's road, but must, in order to survive, learn to use all that is valuable in the white man's culture—and yet still remain Navajos.

Hawk Over the Whirlpools by Ruth M. Underhill. Augustin, 1940. Underhill, an anthropologist, wrote this sympathetic novel about the Navajo, and the impact of the depression on their lives.

The Last Frontier by Howard Fast. Duell, Sloan and Pearce, 1941. In August of 1879, a tiny village of three hundred half-starved Cheyenne left their stark reservation in the Oklahoma Territory and began an incredible 1,000-mile trek to their ancestral home in the Black Hills. The army's orders were to keep the Indians from breaking the white man's law, even if it meant killing them all.

Arrows in the Sun by Jonreed Lauritzen. Alfred A. Knopf, 1943. A story of the son of a mountain man and a Navajo-Spanish woman, who belongs in neither world, and of the conflict between Mormons and Navajo in the Arizona-Utah country, where life was dominated by the Rio Colorado.

When the Tree Flowered: An Authentic Tale of the Old Sioux World by John Neihardt. Macmillan, 1951. A novel of the Sioux Indians with details on social customs and battles against white men chronicled through the fictional experiences of an elderly Indian named Eagle Voice. It chronicles their traumatic transition period between pre-reservation days and the era of strife and repression at the hands of the U. S. Army.

Captives of the Desert by Zane Grey. Harper and Brothers, 1952. The effect of Anglo education on Indians is the theme of this novel, set in several locations on Hopi and Navajo reservations. The culture clash is symbolized by an Anglo-educated Navajo girl, whose education made her dissatisfied with traditional Navajo life, but not quite acceptable to the Anglos. Grey's Social Darwinism is reflected in the novel.

The Canyon by Jack Schaefer. Houghton Mifflin, 1953. A young readers' book. A young Cheyenne left his people because he would not fight— as was expected of him. He journeyed to an isolated canyon, where he found refuge. But his heart was heavy, until a warm and wise woman helped him find his way.

Conquering Horse by Frederick Manfred. McDowell, Obolensky, 1959. In this novel, set in the West of 1800 before the arrival of white settlers, a young Yankton Sioux grows to manhood and faces a terrifying test of his courage. His vision quest that would give him a warrior's name—Conquering Horse—requires him to conquer a wild white stallion, and then perform a deed that was horrible to contemplate. Book 1 of Manfred's *Buckskin Man Tales*.

Johnny Osage by Janice Holt Giles. Houghton Mifflin, 1960. Johnny Osage came by his name because of his close relationship with the Osage Indians. His story is told against the background of the old Osage homeland, the present state of Oklahoma, in the early 1900s. Johnny's love affair with a young school teacher, dedicated to teaching the Osage children, is set against a dark and bloody background of raids and massacres between the Osage and the Cherokee.

A Woman of the People by Benjamin Capps. Duell, Sloan and Pearce, 1966. A white woman, captured by the Comanche as a child and married to a warrior, is faced with a formidable choice: whether to return to her white family or stay with her adopted people as they go to an Oklahoma reservation.

Thunder Moon by Max Brand (Frederick Schiller Faust). Dodd, Mead, 1968. Brand's last novel. A Cheyenne brave kidnaps a white boy, who becomes known as Thunder Moon. The boy has to overcome the stigma of his lighter skin by leading a raid against the deadly Comanche.

The White Man's Road by Benjamin Capps. Harper & Row, 1969. Young Joe Cowbone, a half-breed Comanche living on the Fort Sill Indian Reservation around the turn of the century, sees a spiritual death for his people in "following the white man's road." To restore a sense of dignity within the tribe, he plans a daring horse raid. Winner of both the Spur Award from Western Writers of America and the Western Heritage Award from the National Cowboy and Western Heritage Museum.

The Temptations of Big Bear by Rudy Wiebe. McCelland and Stewart, 1973. As the buffalo vanished in the Canadian West, Big Bear had to find a way for his Cree nation to retain their way of life. But he resisted all efforts of the white Queen's people to give up the ancestral rights to their land and live on a reservation.

A Man Called Horse by Dorothy M. Johnson. Ballantine Books, 1974. This short story was originally published in a collection titled *Indian Country* (Ballantine Books, 1953). Captured by the Crow, he couldn't escape. He became the property of a screaming old squaw who humiliated him in front of the tribe. He was forced to carry burdens like a horse, to fight the dogs for his food. But one day he felt he might become a man again. One day he met the beautiful girl, Pretty Calf, and he knew he couldn't return to the White Man's world. Basis for the 1970 film.

The Manly-Hearted Woman by Frederick Manfred. Crown, 1975. Two Yankton Sioux, a man and a woman who are both outcasts in their tribe, join in a fight against the Omaha. The novel touches on changing sex roles, isolation, and religion.

Wind from an Enemy Sky by D'Arcy McNickle. Harper & Row, 1978. A novel about a small tribe of fictional Indians, the Little Elk, in northern Montana. They contend with the ever present encroachment of white settlers on their land, and the building of a dam leads to conflict between the tribe and the local whites. The novel focuses on the struggle between the two cultures to understand and accommodate one another.

Hanta Yo by Ruth Beebe Hill. Doubleday, 1979. Hanta Yo, which means "Clear the Way," is based on an actual Mahto Indian document discovered in 1865. Anthropologist Ruth Beebe Hill and her assistant, a seventy year old Dakotah Sioux named Chunksa Yuha, have captured in their translation the essence of the Lakota/Dakota Indians in this historic tale of Ahbleza and his rise to greatness and legend among the Mahto in pre-European America.

All the Buffalo Returning by Dorothy M. Johnson. Dodd, Mead, 1979. After the Battle of the Little Big Horn, Hunkpapa and Oglala Sioux flee to Canada with Sitting Bull in this sequel to Johnson's *Buffalo Woman* (Dodd, Mead, 1977).

The Windwalker by Blain Yorgason. Bookcraft, 1979. An aged Lakota (Sioux) warrior, though blind and infirm, learns that his greatest achievements need not be limited by age or physical condition. Basis for the 1961 film "Windwalker."

Creek Mary's Blood by Dee Brown. Holt, Rinehart and Winston, 1980. The saga of four generations of Creek Indians and their matriarch, known as Creek Mary. The novel follows Mary and her descendants from Georgia along the Trail of Tears to the Indian Territory in the 1830s, and eventually to the Great Plains in the second half of the 19th century. Dee Brown traces the life of her family, which over the decades through intermarriage forged roots in the Creek, Cherokee, and Sioux nations. Some of her descendants were even involved in the battle of Little Big Horn.

Woman Chief by Benjamin Capps. Doubleday, 1980. A novel based on the legends of an Indian woman who, defying the tradition of her people, became the undisputed leader of the Crow Nation.

Trail of the Spanish Bit by Don Coldsmith. Doubleday, 1980. Book 1 of Coldsmith's *Spanish Bit Saga*. In the early 16th century, Conquistador Juan Garcia rode into the heart of an unexplored continent. He discovered a people who showed him a new way of life. And he, in turn, brought them a talisman, the Spanish Bit, that introduced the horse culture and forever changed their lives. This novel begins the saga of the Elk-Dog People, the first American Indians of the Central Plains to tame the horse for use in hunting and war.

Buffalo Medicine by Don Coldsmith. Doubleday, 1981. From Coldsmith's *Spanish Bit Saga* series. Owl's father, Juan Garcia, had changed the lives of the People by bringing the horse from his native Spain. When they mastered the ways of the horse, the Elk-Dog band prospered. But now the younger son of that legendary chief must make his own contribution by learning the way of the buffalo from an ancient medicine man.

Ride the Wind by Lucia St. Clair Robson. Ballantine Books, 1982. Cynthia Ann Parker was captured by the Comanche in 1836, when she was nine years old. She became Comanche, and rode a horse called Wind. Although this is Cynthia Ann's story, is also a novel of the great Comanche nation. Spur Award from Western Writers of America.

The Woman Who Owned the Shadows by Paula Gunn Allen. Spinsters, 1983. This book starts where the rest of the world leaves Indians off: at the brink of death. Allen, who is Laguna Pueblo, Sioux, and Lebanese-American and was raised in New Mexico, seeks to reveal layers of culture and consciousness. Her novel is mythical in its telling of Native American origins.

Follow the Wind by Don Coldsmith. Doubleday, 1983. From Coldsmith's *Spanish Bit Saga* series. Don Pedro Garcia was an old man now, and he wanted to see his son who, rumor had it, was alive among the Indians of the Great Plains. But no matter how fast the Spaniards' search party tracked, the Indians always seemed to know their movements days in advance. Don Pedro did not know that his son was alive, now a chief of the Elk-Dog band.

Gone the Dreams and Dancing, by Douglas C. Jones. Holt, Rinehart and Winston, 1984. This is a story of how the Comanche, most warlike of all Indian tribes, laid down their arms and adapted to the ways of the white men and reservation life. Spur Award from Western Writers of America.

Back to Malachi by Robert J. Conley. Doubleday, 1986. Mose Pathkiller, a young Cherokee who loved the works of Lord Byron, was driven farther and farther from the white world and rebounded into his own private war to defend Cherokee rights, thus becoming the famous outlaw known as "Charlie Blackbird."

Fools Crow by James Welch. Viking Press, 1986. In 1870, Fools Crow had a vision at the annual Sun Dance ceremony. The young warrior saw the end of the Indian way of life and the choice that had to be made: resistance or humiliating accommodation. Through his eyes we watch the escalating tensions between the Blackfeet and the white men, who deliberately violate treaties.

A Dream Like Mine by M. T. Kelly. Toronto: Stoddard, 1987. This novel deals with the contemporary Ojibway in a Canadian wilderness setting. It is dark chronicle of native revenge for the white man's destruction of the environment, a haunting parable of retributive justice. Basis for the 1991 film "Clearcut."

The Land by Robert K. Swisher, Jr. Sunstone Press, 1987. Devil's Peak is the spiritual center of a certain section of dry, alkaline land in New Mexico, where centuries of men and women have lived and died. Symbolic of what this piece of earth means is the spear point made by Silver Moon and cast aside to be found by each successive generation. The spear point fills each possessor with the vision of the past and these ghostly visions have a determining effect on the fate of those who hold it in their hands.

Shoshone Mike by Frank Bergon. Viking Press, 1989. During 1910-1911 in frontier Nevada, four stockmen had been murdered by persons unknown. But a murderous posse composed of state troopers and vigilantes were absolutely certain that those "Injuns," the Shoshone, had committed the crime. They pursued and slaughtered the well-meaning, hard-working Shoshone Mike and his family.

The Ancient Child by N. Scott Momaday. Doubleday, 1989. Based on the ancient Kiowa myth of a boy who turned into a bear. A native American raised far from the reservation returns and is drawn irresistibly to the fabled bear-boy. Then he meets a beautiful medicine woman who is a visionary, fluent in both Kiowa and Navajo, who draws him into a magical world of ritual and turns his world upside down.

The Powder River by Win Blevins. Bantam Books, 1990. From Bantam Books's *Rivers West* series. The Northern Cheyenne had been banished by white men to the harsh Indian Territory. But they still called the Powder River country home. This is the story of the remnants of the nation, reduced to poverty and dying, who set out across 1500 miles of hostile land, pursued by thousands of soldiers, to return to their ancestral lands in the Powder River country.

Scalpdancers by Kerry Newcomb. Bantam Books, 1990. A Blackfoot shaman was driven in shame from the village of the Scalpdancers. Then the spirits gave him mysterious powers. The shaman and a rowdy sea captain—a captain without a ship whom fate had brought to the rugged Northwest—joined forces to defeat their respective enemies: an evil shaman and a ruthless pirate.

Beyond the Stars by David W. Ross. Simon and Schuster, 1990. Three white men searched for an abandoned gold mine on the wind-swept northern plains. There they encountered the plains tribes—Sioux, Cheyenne, Crow, Blackfeet, Pawnee, and Arapaho—engaged in a struggle for survival.

Buffalo Nickle by C. W. Smith. Pocket Books, 1990. In 1904 a Kiowa whom the missionaries had named David Copperfield left his Oklahoma reservation and entered the white man's world. He left behind his ancestors' sacred rituals and reverence for the land, and became enmeshed in a society that placed wealth above all else. When oil was discovered on his land, he became the world's wealthiest Indian. But as his ancestors had yielded to their conquerors, David had to develop a new vision for himself and his Indian heritage.

People of the Mesa by Ardath Mayhar. Diamond Books, 1992. A story of the Anasazi, who built their pueblos throughout the Southwest generations before the arrival of Columbus.

Song of Wovoka by Earl Murray. Tor Books, 1992. In the late 1800s a Paiute prophet named Wovoka promised the Sioux that buffalo would return and the white man would vanish if all would dance his Ghost Dance. But the dance led to more tragedy.

People of the Whistling Waters by Marci Oakley Medawar. Affiliated Writers, 1993. During the time when the Crow were struggling with change that would take away their ancient way of life, French-Canadian trapper Renee DeGeer married into the tribe. DeGeer became pivotal in the Crow's battle against other tribes who were competing for dwindling land and the white settlers who were trying to take over their lives.

Chaco: A Tale of Ancient Lives by Mark A. Taylor. Sunstone Press, 1993. The Great Houses of Chaco are in turmoil as the last survivors uncover the mystery and truth at the heart of their civilization. From the sandstone mesas of the Southwest to chambered catacombs hidden beneath the desert city, Chaco reveals a land of Indian sacrifice and other-worldly beauty shaken by a vision of the future.

Two Old Women: An Alaskan Legend of Betrayal, Courage and Survival by Velma Wallis. Epicenter Press, 1993. Based on an Athabaskan Indian legend passed along from mothers to daughters for many generations on the upper Yukon River in Alaska, this is the story of two elderly women abandoned by a migrating tribe that faced starvation brought on by unusually harsh Arctic weather and a shortage of fish and game.

Stone Song by Win Blevins. Forge 1995. The story of Crazy Horse, the great Sioux warrior who led his people to their greatest victory at the Greasy Grass, or the Battle of the Little Big Horn. Spur Award from Western Writers of America.

People of the Silence by Kathleen O. and W. Michael Gear. Forge, 1996. From the Gears' *The First North Americans* series. On his deathbed, the Great Sun Chief, leader of the 12th century Anasazi empire in the Southwest, discovered that his wife had been hiding a child named Cornsilk which she bore 15 years ago to another man, and he assigned a desperate killer to hunt down the girl and murder her.

To Be a Warrior by Robert Barlow Fox. Sunstone Press, 1997. Clay Walker is a Navajo boy who was taught the old ways of his people. He dreams of being a warrior, but is told that there are no more wars and there are no more warriors. He is selected to be one of the "code talkers" in the Marine Corps and becomes disillusioned with his dream.

Coyote Summer by W. Michael Gear. Forge, 1997. Set in 1825, against the grandeur of the Rocky Mountains and the cultural tapestry of the Sioux, Mandan, Crow, and Shoshone cultures, this is the story of a fur trader's keelboat trip up the great Missouri when the American interior was about to be opened and many native peoples stood on the brink of destruction

Zeke and Ned by Larry McMurtry and Diana Ossana. Simon and Schuster, 1997. Ezekiel Proctor and Ned Christie were the last Cherokee warriors. Following the Civil War, they sought to build a future in the Indian Territory east of the Arkansas River.

Mesa Verde by Gary McCarthy. Pinnacle Books, 1997. In the harsh landscape of desert Colorado, the ancient Anasazi built a great sanctuary into the walls of cliffs, a civilization that was lost for more than a thousand years, until two cowboys accidentally stumbled upon the magnificent ruins of Mesa Verde.

Deadly Indian Summer by Leonard A. Schonberg. Sunstone Press, 1997. When a critically ill Navajo boy fails to respond to modern medicine, a young physician must overcome the resistance of his colleagues when he turns to the ancient wisdom of the Navajo medicine men.

Comanche Dawn by Mike Blakely. Forge, 1998. The story of how the Comanche Nation evolved into the perhaps the best horsemen of all time and the most feared fighters on the southern plains.

The Antelope Wife by Louise Erdrich. Harper Perennial, 1998. This native re-creation tale begins long ago when a soldier deserts during a raid on an Ojibwa village in Minnesota to chase a dog with a cradle board on its back bearing a baby. Generations later, an Ojibwa woman is kidnapped from a powwow. The woman is part antelope, and she changes things. This is a story of the impact of her abduction on friends and family.

Pushing the Bear by Diane Glancy. Harcourt, Brace, 1998. A novel of the Trail of Tears. From October 1838 through February 1839, some 11,000 Cherokee walked 900 miles in bitter cold from the Southeast to Indian Territory. One-fourth died or disappeared along the way. This is the story of their forced removal from their ancestral lands by President Andrew Jackson's administration.

RavenShadow by Win Blevins. Forge, 1999. Joseph Blue Crow, who grew up in the Badlands but spent years of assimilation into white culture at a government boarding school, goes on a spiritual journey to reconcile the past and reclaim his Lakota heritage.

Killing Cynthia Ann by Charles Brashear. Texas Christian University Press, 1999. Captured by the Comanche from Parker's Fort in Texas in 1836, Cynthia Ann Parker married into the Noconi band and bore two sons and a daughter. One of the sons, named Quanah Parker, would write his own bit of Texas history. Her uncle was the legendary Judge Isaac Parker. She was rescued by Sul Ross and his Texas Rangers in 1860. This novel addresses the frustration of Isaac and the rest of the Parkers as Cynthia Ann grieves for her sons and attempts to hold on to her identity as a Comanche.

Gardens in the Dunes by Leslie Marmon Silko. Simon and Schuster, 1999. Dreams bring comfort and guidance to the independent characters in Silko's novel, which is an adventure tale about a young Native American woman, Indigo, who travels with her friend Hattie in the 1890's through the southwestern desert country, encountering Mexican revolutionaries, gypsies, opportunists of every kind, and an menagerie of animals—and then on a Grand tour of Europe.

The Dark Island by Robert J. Conley. Leisure Books, 2000. From Conley's series set among the Real People, the Cherokees of American prehistory. Marauding Spaniards have returned to the territory near the home of the Real People, leaving carnage and abandoned villages in their wake. Asquani, the son of an escaped slave and a Spaniard, must decide whether to join the Spaniards or defend the Cherokee homeland. Spur Award from Western Writers of America.

Ghost Warrior, by Lucia St. Clair Robson. Forge, 2002. The Chiricahua Apaches revered Lozen. One Apache described her as their patron saint. Victorio's beloved sister—shaman, warrior, healer, expert horse thief—is one of history's most remarkable individuals.

Buy the Chief a Cadillac by Rick Steber. Bonanza, 2003. In 1954, the U. S. government "incorporated" some Indian land on the Pacific coast and revoked the status of a number of tribes. In 1961, compensation came in the form of $43,000 payments per tribe member. This novel examines how three Klamath brothers react to the loss and the money they prepare to receive. Spur award from Western Writers of America.

Oblivion's Altar: A Novel of Courage by David Marion Wilkinson. New American Library. 2003. Ridge, a warrior and chief, was also a rich Cherokee farmer who believed in the treaties and the words of President Andrew Jackson. He did not understand, however, that the treaties were merely paper and that Jackson would not help the Indians in a vicious land dispute with the states. Even when the Cherokees won the court cases, they were driven from their lands by force, following the Trail of Tears westward. Spur Award winner.

Hombrecito's War by W. Michael Farmer. Llumina Press, 2005. Set in New Mexico from the early 1900s to modern times, the story describes the relationship between Henry, a physician, and his Apache surrogate father, Yellow Boy, who had saved young Henry's life after his father was murdered and the killers attempted to kill him.

Apache Shadows: A Novel of the West by Albert R. Booky. Sunstone Press, 2006. Set in the 19th century American Southwest at the time when both the Mexicans and Americans threatened to destroy the traditional ways of the Indians, *Apache Shadows* describes how these threats and dangers were met through the adventures of two mixed-blood Mescalero Apache brothers. From their Anglo mother they learned to reconcile two opposite cultures and accept a new way of life as more and more settlers moved westward.

SELECTED REVIEWS

Buffalo Woman
by Dorothy M. Johnson
Dodd Mead, 1977

Dorothy Johnson is usually the first name to come to mind when the subject of women writers of the Western genre is mentioned. Three of her short stories—*The Man Who Shot Liberty Valance* (1949), *The Hanging Tree* (1957), *A Man Called Horse* (1953)—have been made into first-rate films. Her writing is sharp yet poignant, and her stories look at the Western experience from a different angle.

Buffalo Woman shows us the Oglala Sioux, from 1820 through the Battle of the Little Big Horn in 1876, from the viewpoint of an Oglala woman. Through her eyes we see the daily routine and the rituals that were so important to Lakota life, and the devastation that came with the arrival and persistent advancement of white civilization.

Life was good for the Oglala before the coming of the white men, or Wasichus. They lived in a country rich with game, a land to which their nomadic lives were completely tuned. When a camp became muddy and dirty, they'd simply move to a new, unspoiled site, where there was plenty of grass for the horses.

Everyone in the camp had a role, vital to the survival and well-being of the band. The men were hunters and warriors. They provided meat and protection for the lodges. They did little else. The women did the work, even the heavy work. A man usually needed at least two wives to keep a lodge in order. But his first wife was his chief wife, his sits-beside-him wife.

Even children had their tasks. Little girls watched smaller children. Boys watched the pony herds.

> Sometimes boys and girls . . . played together quite peaceable, but mostly they squabbled and sometimes even fought. Little girls, playing house with their own miniature lodges and looking after babies assigned to them, might have their small play camp attacked by little boys riding in at a gallop on their ponies. The girls defended camp angrily with clubs. Or the boys might surprise them by bringing in small game, like rabbits, and yelling, "Cook a meal, you lazy women." The girls took pride in their skill in skinning and cooking such offerings while the boys sat around looking lordly and superior—more so than their fathers did at home.

On a cold bitter night in 1820 a girl baby was born to Many Bones Woman and Eagle Walks. "She was a puny baby. Her cry was no louder than a rabbit makes when a coyote kills it." The baby was named Whirlwind, in honor of her mother's father, who was a great warrior.

Eagle Walks was a man of standing in the camp; a good hunter, a brave fighter, a man who spoke wisely in meetings and was generous to the poor. He was rich in honor, and owned many horses. Many Bones Woman was gentle and quiet. She had lost her earlier babies, and her heartbreak had made her seem timid. Now she changed. She told her husband he should take another wife to help with the work. Eagle Walks bought a captive Crow woman and made her his second wife.

Rituals were important to the Sioux. As Whirlwind grew she witnessed important ceremonies, and the explanation of their meaning that she got from her elders gives us a clear, appreciative understanding of the beliefs that ruled Lakota life.

In the spring of 1825 all the separate small camps of the Oglala Sioux gathered for the great ceremony of the Sun-Gazing Dance. It was a sacred time of prayers and awesome rituals and glorious processions. Whirlwind's uncle Grey Bull danced, with Eagle Walks as his "captor." This was a torturous ceremony where the dancers' captor pierced his flesh in several places and fastened him to either a sacred tree or several heavy buffalo skulls. The dancer had to gaze at the sun all day, while he danced and blew constantly on a whistle. After dark he tore his flesh loose and completed the ceremony. Eagle Walks had danced it twice; the second was to thank the Great Mystery for Whirlwind's life. He explained the reason a man participated in the dance to Whirlwind:

> A man's body is his own, it is the only thing that really belongs to him. And his pain belongs to him. We can give the Great Mystery other presents, but that is where they come from in the first place. So we are giving back something the spirits gave us.

The people who lived in the lodge of Eagle Walks changed from year to year, as children were born, relatives moved out because of marriage, death or divorce. When Whirlwind was sixteen, after a courtship carried on within the rigid formality of Sioux custom, she married White Thunder, a handsome young warrior with scars from the Sun-gazing Dance on his body and an eagle feather in his hair. Two persons could hardly live in a lodge alone, unless they were very old and depended on the bounty of others. There was too much work to be done. So it was arranged that a widowed sister of White Thunder should live with them to help Whirlwind with the heavy work of homemaking. Her nine-year-old brother, Covers Up, would also live with them. There were plenty of small jobs for a small boy to do.

In 1845 there were five hunters living in White Thunder's lodge. Whirlwind's family should have been prosperous. But they weren't. The young men spent much of their time on the war trail or harassing the palefaces who traveled along the Overland Trail, or the Medicine Road, as the Lakota called it. There seemed to be no end of the enemy strangers who traveled on it. They were driving the buffalo herds away; they killed them for sport and wasted the meat.

The white men also brought smallpox and cholera with them. They stopped at Fort Laramie, and their stock ate the grass so that there was none left for the buffalo. In 1849 the emigrant trains left such devastation over so wide an area that the immense herds of buffalo no longer crossed the Medicine Road. Some grazed south of it and some grazed north of it, and the Indians found it harder to hunt for meat and robes. They tried to scare off the white man, but still he came.

By 1866 the Lakota were constantly harassed by the white men, or Wasichus. White Thunder was now head man of his village, which numbered only fifteen lodges. A few years ago it had been twice as big and much more prosperous. Along with other minor leaders, he refused to sign a treaty with the Wasichus in 1866, following Red Cloud's victories on the Bozeman Trail. They rode back to Powder River and resumed their lives. Among prominent leaders who refused to sign were Sitting Bull, Gall, and Black Moon of the Hunkpapa, and the young Oglala chief Crazy Horse.

Whirlwind lived through the good times, before the coming of the white man, as a girl, the gathering storm as a young woman, and the final devastation as an old woman. She saw Red Cloud ferociously defend the Oglala sacred lands, only to be subjugated in disgrace after the Wasichus broke treaty after treaty. She heard firsthand stories of the infamous Sand Creek Massacre. She was one of Crazy Horse's followers at the Battle at the Little Big Horn. She had a full, if tragic, life. She was also a warrior woman in her own right.

When she was fifty-six, she saved her grandson Jumps from a grizzly. Her other grandson, an untried youth of thirteen, killed the bear. Crazy Horse visited the lodge and asked to see the warrior woman. He kneeled beside the injured Whirlwind and said, "I give you a name . . . Grandmother. Your name is "Saved her Cub." She was now indeed somebody, a Buffalo Woman with a warrior's name, bestowed by the great chief Crazy Horse.

After the Battle at the Little Big Horn and a later attack that left her band homeless, Grandmother Whirlwind faced her greatest challenge. The band's journey through the snow to refuge in Canada is continued in *All the Buffalo Returning* (Dodd, Mead, 1979), Johnson's sequel to *Buffalo Woman*. Both novels are written in very simple prose—elegant in its simplicity. *Buffalo Woman* was awarded the National Cowboy and Western Heritage Museum's Western Heritage Award, richly deserved for a major contribution to Western literature.

Ramona
by Helen Hunt Jackson
Roberts Brothers, 1884

Ramona has long been recognized as one of the world's great love stories. But it is more. Helen Hunt Jackson has given us a capacious look at southern California in the mid-1800s that sharply contrasts the lifestyles of the wealthy Mexican landowners and the mission Indians. It is set against the backdrop of the coming of the Americans and the devastation they brought to both the Californios and the Indians. It's a landmark novel with moral substance.

Southern California during this period was idyllically pastoral, a paradise of beauty and abundance. The Mexican men and women of degree, under the rule of Spanish and Mexican Viceroys, led a "half-barbaric, half-elegant, wholly generous and free-handed life." It was picturesque, full of sentiment and gaiety, truly dramatic and romantic. "The aroma of it lingers there still."

The Señora Morena's house embodied this beguiling life. When it was built by her husband, General Moreno, he owned all of the land within a radius of forty miles (Jackson used Rancho Camulos in Ventura as a model). The Senora's household was like a little army. Nobody ever knew exactly how many women were in the kitchen, or how many men were in the fields. Her son Felipe knew to whom he paid wages, but not who was fed and lodged under his roof.

Señora Morena is the dominant character in the story. Her father was

Commandante of the Santa Barbara Presidio; her brother was the Superior of the Santa Barbara Mission. Her husband was beloved by both the Army and the Church. When the Americans came, she helped him buckle on his sword, and with dry eyes saw him go off to fight. They brought him home to her dead, killed in the last fight the Mexican forces made. After the war, she was left in the possession of a handsome estate, which she considered a pitiful fragment of her former holdings.

Since her husband's death, her son Felipe had been head of his mother's house. But, the Señora decided all questions. She was a tremendous force, but no stranger would suspect it, to see her gliding about, in her black gown, with her rosary hung at her side, her dark eyes cast down, and an expression of devotion on her face.

An older sister of the Señora had loved a seafaring man named Angus Phail, but had married a Mexican officer. Ramona was the product of a union between Angus and an Indian woman. Angus left her with the Senora's sister, who subsequently left her in the Senora's charge.

Ramona was sixteen when introduced to the reader. She had an olive tint to her complexion that enriched it. Her hair was much like her Indian mother's, heavy and black, but her eyes were steel-blue, like her father's. "The shepherds, the maids, the babies, the dogs, the poultry, all loved the sight of Ramona. All loved her except the Señora."

The rigid class structure prevented the Senora from loving a child with Indian blood. When she learned of Ramona's love for the Indian Allesandro, she thought she could force her to see the enormity of her offense. She could not.

Ramona's life with Allesandro was far removed from her idyllic existence at the Moreno rancho. But their love endured—grew—with each trial they faced. Ramona's faith in God and the Church never wavered. Although Allesandro was "by nature singularly pure-minded, open-hearted, generous, and full of veneration, he could not feel towards the saints as Ramona did. He believed they loved Ramona, but did not love Indians."

The Indians fared badly after the coming of the Americans. They were driven from their homes and villages. They banded into pueblos and tried to keep peace with the whites, but were still persecuted. When they could find work, they were only paid half-wages. Ramona said the Americans only think of money: "To get money, they will commit any crime, even murder . . . Mexicans kill only for hate . . . or in anger; never for gold." Allesandro replied: "Indians, also. Never one Indian killed another, yet, for money. It is for vengeance, always. For money! Bah! . . . they are dogs!"

The Californios also suffered. After the surrender of California, the United States Land Commission sifted and adjusted Mexican land titles. The Señora lost tract after tract of land. She hated the Americans. "[They] are running up and down seeking money, like dogs with their noses to the ground." She found the idea of having to wage war with peddlers monstrous.

In 1879, Helen Hunt Jackson heard Standing Bear, chief of the Ponca Indians, talk on tribal wrongs. Deeply concerned, she wrote *A Century of Dishonor* (1881), a bitter condemnation of the federal government's handling of Indian affairs. In 1850 she was part of a government commission that studied the living conditions of the mission Indians in southern California. No action was taken on the commission's report, so Jackson used the material to write *Ramona*, a novel intended to help the Indian cause. Its success may have accomplished the opposite of what Jackson envisioned. Her depiction of southern California was so inviting that Ramona is credited with luring many outsiders to the area, contributing to the region's land boom and compounding the Indian's problems with the Americans.

The novel has been issued in various editions over the last half-century or so, with over 135 printings. It's been filmed four times, played on the stage, adapted for a pageant, and may eventually provide the basis for a grand opera. The Ramona Pageant has lured nearly two million spectators to the small town of Hemet each spring since 1923. The films have been disappointing. Probably the best was the 1928 version, starring Warner Baxter as Allesandro and Dolores del Rio as Ramona.

The Man Who Killed the Deer
by Frank Waters
Farrar and Rinehart, 1942

Frank Waters was a regional author, writing entirely about his native Southwest. He never attained great popularity with the general public, appealing primarily to Western history buffs, people interested in ethnology and ecology, and the like. But some critics, including respected literary scholar John Milton, consider him one of the most distinguished Western writers of the 20th century.

He lived and worked throughout the Southwest, and in more than two dozen works of fiction and nonfiction he explored the past, present, and future of the region. He had a deep understanding of its three cultures-Indian, Hispanic, and Anglo-and wrote perceptively about each. *The Man Who Killed the Deer* is his classic novel about Pueblo Indian life.

Against a rich tapestry of Pueblo culture and religious ceremonies, this is the story of Martiniano, the "trouble-maker," the man who killed the deer. Torn between ritual ways of his tribe and the white man's culture, he searched for a true faith. He had been sent by the white man to away-school when he was young. He didn't want to go. His father didn't want him to go. Nor did the chief of the kiva he was about to enter for his religious training. But when he returned, he wouldn't follow the customs of his people; he wouldn't knock the heels off his boots nor would he cut the seat out of his trousers and wear them as imitation leggings, with a blanket wrapped around his middle. He was denied many privileges given to other members of the tribe. He complained to the government authorities, but was told the tribal council controlled the affairs of the pueblo. He endured two public lashings ordered by the council because of his refusal to recognize tribal authority.

In the opening chapter, Martiniano's friend Palemon lay awake in his hut, unable to sleep, for he could hear a beat, from deep within, from the heart of the world. Something was pulling his spirit, so strong that he arose, saddled his horse, and rode into the mountains. There he found Martiniano, lying injured near a deer he had killed out of season. He had been struck by a U. S. Forest Service Ranger. Palemon returned to the pueblo with Martiniano and the deer.

Martiniano had to defend himself before the old men of the pueblo council for killing the deer and not obeying the white man's law. He was sullen but respectful, for the old men were greatly respected in the pueblo.

> An old man was squatting on the ground against the sunny wall . . . His long brown fingers were bony and prehensile as the talons of a hawk. His tattered trousers tied round with a blanket held skinny, brittle limbs . . . But when he raised his face there was in it something one seldom sees now. Dark and wrinkled, at once kind and indomitable, it held the keen black eyes of a man who has known all the vagaries of weather and men's passions alike . . . He was the Governor of the pueblo.

Martiniano's quest for faith was long and arduous. He rejected the white man's religion that the other Indians had accepted—at least superficially. He felt the need to follow the teachings of his people, but rebelled at authority. When approached by one of the old men about participating in the annual Green Corn Dance, he said, respectfully, that something in his heart told him these dances were good, and he could dance when he felt like it, but not in response to his name being called from the housetops by the old men of the pueblo. "A man's religion is in his heart," he said. The old man replied: "There is only one great heart. Of our pueblo, our tribe. Of the whole world. We beat as one with all around us."

And there was the deer he killed, whose image kept appearing, both confusing and angering him. The Pueblo belief is that all things are a part of the greater whole. If you cut down a tree of kill an animal for the good of the whole, you must first ask its permission. Martiniano didn't do this. The deer haunted him. He began to see its image in his wife, and it drove a wedge between them. He sought council from his friend Palemon, a man respected in the pueblo and schooled in Indian beliefs and ceremonies. Palemon told him that he was separate and alone, and that must not be. He should be part of the greater whole. As for the deer, perhaps it was not for them to understand.

In parallel with Martiniano's struggle with himself, the council, and the white authorities, is the tribe's effort to have their sacred Dawn Lake restored to them. The federal government had made it a part of a national forest. When the government agent asked the old governor of the pueblo why he kept insisting on Dawn Lake's return, when the government had done so many other things for his people, such as sending Indian children to away-school and building a hospital, the old man answered patiently:

> They schools, but mebbe soon no children. They hospital, but mebbe soon people they dead . . . Dawn Lake our church. From it come all good things we get. The mountains our land, Indian land. The government promised. We not forget. This we say.

Waters paints a colorful but grim picture of the Pueblo Indian. He describes the pueblo:

> . . . when the sun was high a few Indians began to straggle out of the pueblo. A blanketed old man hobbling along with a stick between the wild plumb hedges. Boys kicking by on small, quick-stepping burros. An old springless wagon with an old boneless woman wrapped up in a turquoise shawl and shaking on the plank seat, and a man standing upright to the reins, his long hair braids wrapped in a pink ribbon hanging down his back. A lone dark horseman jogging past a group of women waddling spread-legged in snowy boots and flowered shawls. All small blotches of color against the gray-green sage and the stainless blue mountains. And all bobbing slowly along in the narrow river of dust curving out of the reservation to the village below.

Rudolfo Byers, a trader who had lived and worked with the Pueblo Indians his whole adult life, viewed them realistically. He knew their surface indolence and cunning, their dirt and filth and lice, their secretiveness and barbarity, ignorance and stubborn denial of change. But their life and their religion had a strange hold on him.

What held him he never knew, but it was always there. In the look of an eye, in a curious phrase, in the beat of a drum . . . They couldn't be thought about intelligently. They had to be either dismissed or taken on their own ground . . . Their premises of life were based . . . wholly on the instinctive and intuitive . . . The simple and ignored fact of how Palemon had known intuitively of trouble, and had gone without question or delay directly to Martiniano's aid. It seemed at once the very core of the mystery which ever held him.

Water's novel was based on the trial of Frank Samora, a Taos Pueblo Indian fined for shooting a deer out of season in the Carson National Forest. The book influenced political leaders to return 48,000 acres of the tribe's sacred Blue Lake land. In a 1987 interview, Waters said, "Anglos have always regarded the land and all nature as inanimate, and therefore to be used. Anglos speak of conquest, of empires, of taming and obtaining. The Indian ecology is a spiritual one. For an Indian, to cut a pine in a forest would be sacrilege unless he first got its permission to sacrifice itself for the common good." He used this as the theme for *The Man Who Killed the Deer*, arguably the finest novel ever written about the Pueblo Indians.

Stay Away, Joe
Dan Cushman
Viking Press, 1953

Dan Cushman, seldom mentioned in discussions of American Western literature, wrote fifteen Western novels; six were Book Club selections and one, *The Silver Mountain* (D. Appleton, 1957), won a Western Writers of America Spur Award. But his crowning achievement, the single work for which he's known, is *Stay Away, Joe*, a wildly humorous story of a Métis (French-Indian) family living on a reservation in Montana. This comic tour de force is populated with idiosyncratic characters whose differences create a chaos that delights readers.

Foremost among many is Big Joe Champlain, who returned from Korea with two toes missing and a Purple Heart.

He towered above everyone. He was six three or four; an extra two inches was added by the heels of his riding boots; and his huge white hat made him seem taller yet. He was broad and thick through, weighing about two hundred and ten pounds, with not an ounce of fat on him anywhere. He was slightly bowlegged—not in the hip-strung manner of a cowboy, but bowlegged as so many Indians are, starting with his toed-in feet and ending in his spread-apart hips. His legs were rather short in comparison with his trunk, which was very long. He was more Indian than anyone else in the family—his mother [was] . . . a full-blooded Assiniboin—and his face showed it, built in the classic lines of the warlike chiefs, with a low, slanting forehead, very high cheekbones, a huge nose, and a jaw that was square and big under the ears.

His father, Louis Champlain, was very proud of Joe. To celebrate his son's return, Louis drank several beers at Callahan's, then, feeling good, with tears coursing down his cheeks, made a little speech. In French, English, and Cree, he spoke fondly of his son by his first wife, a hero, with the Purple Heart, and with two toes gone, shot off by the Communists in Korea.

Annie (Mama), Louis' second wife, despised Joe. She knew he was a liar and a moocher. Joe's opinion of Mama was equally unfavorable: "Ha, that Mama . . . where did she come from? A Gros Ventre tepee, living on dog meat and turnips, that is where."

Grandpere, Louis' grandfather on his mother's side and Joe's great-grandfather, was a full-blooded Cree, one hundred and five years old. He remembered the old days.

They were great times when I was young, before railroad, before Ford skunkwagon, before Philco devilbox. Buffalo I have seen on Box Elder flats, many buffalo, as far as I could look, like black spots on the prairie, like the ducks that came in autumn in the old days.

His great-grandson reminded him of the Indians of old. Joe brought him back a scalp from Korea, a tuft of black hair attached to a dried and wrinkled piece of skin. "You are a chief!" said Grandpere. "You have taken coup from the Communists."

Joe professed to be a rodeo star. He claimed to have won a silver saddle in a rodeo at Madison Square Garden, but no one had ever seen it. He did win first money in bulldogging at the Blackfoot Rodeo in Browning, but spent his prize money before returning home, broke and hungry.

Before Joe returned from Korea, the government had given Louis a small herd, nineteen heifers and a young bull, as part of an experiment in Indian self-sufficiency. His friends at the reservation—Walt Stephenpierre, Connie Shortgun, Bix Red Eagle, Peter Old Squaw, Old Matthew Horse Chaser, and other colorful characters—started showing up to celebrate his good fortune. The gathering evolved into a whoop-up. Louis gave his friends permission to slaughter one heifer to feed the crowd. They killed the bull.

Joe's schemes to replace the bull nearly depleted the rest of the herd. He talked Louis into letting him trade two heifers to a friend in Great Falls for a bull; " . . . two days later Joe and his friend Bronc Hoverty set out for Great Falls in Hoverty's station wagon, with two heifers in a stock trailer behind. Joe was gone for four days and returned behind the wheel of a huge new emerald-green Buick sedan." Mama accused him of selling the cows and spending the money on the car. She asked to see the receipt for the bull. Joe said, "Oh, maybe I left it in my other pants." Grandpere said, "You are a chief. You have come with the greatest of all skunkwagons."

Joe and Mama continued to mix like oil and water. For Joe's meddling in his sister Mary's romantic affairs, Mama threw him out of the house: "Stay away, Joe." Joe moved into his Buick.

> Poor and friendless, Joe sat all day in his car, smoking the Bull
> Durham and playing the radio until the battery went dead. Finally
> he took the spare to Big Springs and sold it, together with the tube,
> for eighteen dollars. . . . Then, because the spare wheel was no good
> without a tire, Joe sold the wheel for seven dollars. He put the car
> on blocks and sold the other wheels, one by one, explaining to Louis
> that one of these days, when it pleased him, he would dig into his
> savings and replace all of them, because he would want the Buick

to be in first-class shape when he started out on the eastern rodeo circuit.

Joe is a big lout who doesn't generate much sympathy. He exaggerates his wartime exploits— "In Korea five thousand men with guns, and there is your Joe, all alone, crawling on his stomach with wounded feet, get out okay"—and takes an advantage of those who are closest to him. But neither does he engender animosity; his resourcefulness is admirable and you hope he'll come through on his promises, but doubt it.

Dan Cushman grew up on the edge of what's now the Rocky Boy Cree-Chippewa Reservation, northeast of Great Falls. This novel is an affectionate saga of these people he knew so well. It deals humorously with the very real problems caused by the influence of white culture and tribal tradition on contemporary Indians.

Stay Away, Joe became a best seller, a Book-of-the-Month-Club selection, and the Broadway musical *Whoop-Up* was based on it. A 1968 MGM film, of the same title, was directed by Peter Tewksbury and starred Elvis Presley. It was a bad film. It's a shame something better wasn't made from Dan Cushman's minor masterpiece.

8

The Glory Trail: The Church in the West

Introduction

As early as 1598 Spain had established Catholic missions in what is now New Mexico. Over the next seventy-five years their presence would extend to all northern Mexico, Texas, Arizona, and California. By 1773 the brown-robed Franciscans, led by Fray Junipero Serra, had five missions and two Presidios in California.

The French Catholic missionaries arrived in the Pacific Northwest around 1838. In 1840 Father Pierre DeSmet, known by the Indians as "Black Robe," established a Jesuit mission in the Bitterroot Valley, and then missionized the interior portion of the Oregon Country.

In 1836 Protestant missionaries came to the Oregon Country. The Whitman-Spalding party established missions near Fort Walla Walla and at Lapwai. These missions were a failure, ending in tragedy for the missionaries. But many Protestant denominations sent preachers west to establish churches and spread Christianity. Many Protestant ministers became circuit riders, traveling great distances to preach at frontier towns each Sunday.

After persecution in Missouri and Illinois, the Mormons journeyed west in 1838 to a wilderness area that would become the state of Utah. Under the leadership of Brigham Young, they would build a faith-based civilization that, despite many obstacles and atrocities on their part, endures to this day.

Religion played an important role in both exploring and settling the West. Novelists have used the characters and events associated with the spread of the word of God and the establishment of his churches in the West to develop a fine body of American literature. The novels reviewed in this category are two of the best. Willa Cather's *Death Comes for the Archbishop* (Knopf, 1927), based on the efforts of two 19th century French priests to establish a diocese in the territory of New Mexico, is considered by many to be her masterpiece. Zane Grey's *Riders of the Purple Sage* (Harper and Brothers, 1912), a traditional Western set in Mormon Utah in the 1870s, is perhaps the most recognized Western novel ever written.

READER'S GUIDE

The Lions of the Lord by Harry Leon Wilson. Lothrop, 1903. The protagonist, Joel Rae, moved from the persecutions in Illinois, across the plains with the handcart companies, through the Utah-U. S. A. war, and to the Mountain Meadows Massacre. He struggled to maintain his moral integrity and remain a faithful Mormon.

We Must March: A Novel of the Winning of Oregon by Honoré Willsie Morrow. Frederick Stokes, 1905. In 1836 Protestant missionaries Marcus and Narcissa Whitman, with another missionary couple as traveling companions, journeyed west to establish missions in the Pacific Northwest. The Whitmans started a mission near Walla Walla, Washington, where a great tragedy would eventually find them. Narcissa and the other female missionary, Eliza Spalding, were the first white women to cross the Rocky Mountains. This novel is based on Narcissa's journal, published in a report of the Oregon Pioneer Association in 1892.

The Sage Brush Parson by A. B. Ward. Little, Brown, 1905. In May of 1881, a young man dressed in clerical black stepped off the train in Battle Mountain, Nevada. The itinerant preacher from Gainsborough, England, was absolutely alone on the expansive plains. He was there to spread the word of God.

The Heritage of the Desert by Zane Grey. Harper and Brothers, 1910. Mormons give refuge and aid to an easterner who is ill, and, in turn, he helps them defend their land against those who would take it. Set in northern Arizona and southern Utah.

The Rainbow Trail by Zane Grey. Harper and Brothers, 1915. The sequel to *Riders of the Purple Sage* (Harper and Brothers, 1912). An Illinois preacher comes to the northern Arizona-southern Utah locale, one of Grey's favorite settings, to track down a legend concerning Lassiter, Jane Withersteen, and Fay Larkin—three characters from *Riders of the Purple Sage*—and a hidden valley. In his search the easterner visits Mormon villages, where plural wives are common.

The Chariot of Fire by Benard DeVoto. Macmillan, 1926. A story about a midwestern frontier prophet with similarities to the Mormon prophet Joseph Smith.

The Fighting Danites by Dane Coolidge. E. P. Dutton, 1934. A lieutenant in the Third Dragoons was sent west when Brigham Young founded the State of Deseret and defied the United States Government. The lieutenant, through a series of events, would become a spy in the infamous Danites, and eventually capture the leader of the Mountain Meadows Massacre of 1857.

The Devil's Highway by Richard A. Summers. Thomas Nelson and Sons, 1937. A novel based on the explorations and missionary work of Father Kino, the Jesuit priest who spread Christianity through much of what is now Arizona and Sonora, Mexico.

Children of God: An American Epic by Vardis Fisher. Harper and Brothers, 1939. A novel about Mormonism, covering their beginnings in the 1920s, their persecution, heroism, their migration across the frontier, and their settlement in Utah. Considered by many to be Fisher's finest work, and the best novel on the subject.

Arizona Jim by Charles Alden Seltzer. Doubleday, Doran, 1939. A novel about a mild-spoken preacher from Arizona who used his guns to protect his flock from an outlaw's reign of terror.

The Giant Joshua by Maurine Whipple. Houghton Mifflin, 1941. A story of Mormon life in southern Utah from 1860 to 1886. The protagonist, Clorinda (Clory) McIntyre, knew what was wrong in her life but was helpless to change anything. Clory was a victim of both heritage and environment, born a Mormon, married in polygamy, and trapped in the isolated area of southern Utah.

A Little Lower than the Angels by Virginia Sorensen. Alfred A. Knopf, 1942. A story of the early days of Joseph Smith and his Mormon church's struggles, with women and their problems in the church accentuated.

The Mormon Trail by Tom Curry. Gateway Books, 1942. From Curry's *Rio Kid* series. Persecuted in the East, devout Mormon people emigrated to Utah in 1847 and founded Salt Lake City. But joining the migration was a small group of evil men—cold-blooded killers.

The Power and the Glory by Graham Greene. Viking Press, 1946. Originally published by Viking in 1940 under the title *The Labyrinthine Ways*. In the late 1930s in a remote section of Mexico, in a state where the church has been outlawed, an alcoholic Mexican Catholic priest, having a tortuous spiritual struggle, becomes the quarry in an organized hunt.

Stars in My Crown by Joe David Brown. William Morrow, 1947. The parson emphasized the seriousness of his sermons on the golden rule by brandishing two pistols. His faith had been forged in a score of Civil War battles and skirmishes. He had ridden with Quantrill's Raiders on the Missouri-Kansas border—men who were as unchristian as they were bold. Now he was determined to spread God's word. Affectionately narrated by the parson's young grandson. Basis for the 1950 film.

Dust on the King's Highway by Helen C. White. Macmillan, 1947. Spanish missionary Father Francisco Garcés (1738-1781), who made a series of entries into the land of the Hopi and Havasupais and beyond the San Joaquin Valley in California, is the focus of this novel. He was martyred by the Yuma near the junction of the Gila and the Colorado in 1781, when the Indians became disillusioned with the economic benefits of Christianity.

The Peaceable Kingdom by Ardyth Kennelly. Houghton Mifflin, 1949. In Salt Lake City in the 1890s in the era of polygamy, the second wife of a Mormon man, who has born him several children, struggles with the very difficult battle between love for her husband and jealousy of the first wife.

Doctor in Buckskin by T. D. Allen. Harper and Brothers, 1951. Missionaries Dr. Marcus Whitman and his wife Narcissa served as physician and teachers to the Indians living in the Oregon territory in the mid-1800s. But the warlike Cayuse tribe held the missionaries responsible for diseases that ravaged their communities, leading to a catastrophe.

Cry of Utah by Samuel O. Sisco. Hollywood, 1956. A story of the Mormons' struggle to establish their home in Utah, and of a rugged old bishop who faced all manner of problems and danger.

The Fancher Train by Amelia Bean, Doubleday, 1958. A novel based on the Mountain Meadows massacre in Mormon Utah. Spur Award from Western Writers of America.

Battalion of Saints by Richard Wormser. David McKay, 1961. While the Mormons were still en route to the West, a full year before the first party arrived in Utah, the United States Army asked them to provide 500 volunteers to help in the Mexican War. The Mormon Battalion, commanded by Brigadier General St. George Cooke, was promptly organized and marched 2,000 miles, following the Santa Fe Trail through the Southwest and on to what is now San Diego, California.

The Franciscan by Forrester Blake, Doubleday, 1963. A story of the struggles of a Franciscan missionary, Padre Lorenzo de Escalona, who in 1675 arose to defend oppressed Indians in Spanish New Mexico.

The Cross and the Sword by Jonreed Lauritzen. Doubleday, 1965. Father Junîpero Serra, the Catholic priest who founded missions in California from San Diego to San Francisco, and Juan Bautista de Anza, a professional soldier who established the presidio of San Francisco, were both men who strove to conquer California for Spain, but their methods were decidedly different.

My Brother John by Herbert Purdum. Doubleday, 1966. Frank Niles had promised his dying mother that he would look after his soft-spoken brother John. But that was no easy task because the Reverend John Niles became a circuit rider on the Western frontier. His calling required an abundance of faith, since he would confront some of the most ruthless killers in the West. Spur Award from Western Writers of America.

Hellfire Jackson by Garland Roark and Charles Thomas. Doubleday, 1966. During the age of Sam Houston, Santa Anna, the Alamo, and the Texas Revolution, Horatio Jackson was a preacher whose furious fire-and-brimstone style earned him the nickname of "Hellfire." Spur Award winner.

Angel Range by John Reese. Doubleday, 1973. The Mooney County minister was a man of God who had served time in prison. When an outbreak of robberies and murders struck the frontier community where he tended his flock, the only man who could help him to stamp it out was the one who had sent him to jail.

Saints by Orson Scott Card. Tor Books, 1984. This novel follows the Mormon church from its inception to the tragedy at Nauvoo, and on to Salt lake City with Brigham Young. The chief protagonist is Dianah Kirkham, a Mormon woman in the 1800s who was devoted to her beliefs.

Salt Lake City by A. R. Riefe. Signet, 1989. From Riefe's *Fortunes West* series. The Catton family came to the forbidding Utah territory, following its Mormon leader Brigham Young. But Mormons would face the U. S. Army on the edge of deadly conflict before the desert would bloom and blossom into God's kingdom as Brigham Young envisioned it.

Sanctuary by Gary D. Svee. Walker, 1990. In the 1880s, Sanctuary, Montana, was controlled by a fire and brimstone preacher, whose staples were fear and hate, and a rancher who hated Indians. A wandering preacher, who preached and exemplified love of neighbor down to the most lowly, arrived and conflict ensued. Spur Award from Western Writers of America.

The High Missouri by Win Blevins. Bantam Books, 1994. From Bantam Books' *Rivers West* series. A would-be priest from the East signed up with the Northwest Company to bring God to the Indians. As he traveled across the Saskatchewan in the company of a mystical wanderer called the Druid, he saw acts of violence and evil he could never have imagined.

Wild Plum at Night: A Novel of Betrayal by Jamie Wheelas. Sunstone Press, 1996. A young priest turns his back on his powerful and wealthy family's privileged world to become parish priest of an impoverished Indian pueblo church near Santa Fe, New Mexico. Caught in a relationship with a young male hedonist, he breaks his vow of celibacy and feels he must leave the priesthood. A benevolent archbishop offers a solution to the young man's agony.

Red Water by Judith Freeman. Pantheon, 2002. In 1857, a wagon train of migrants from Arkansas crossed into Mormon Utah. The Mormons were almost at war with the government at that time. Joseph Smith, their prophet, had been murdered. John D. Lee, a prominent Mormon, engineered an attack the wagon train, leading to more than 120 people, the majority of them women and children, being murdered. John Lee was executed in 1877 for his role in the massacre. *Red Water* tells the story of the Mountain Meadows Massacre from the viewpoints of three of Lee's nineteen wives—Emma, Anna, and Rachel.

Blood Atonement by J. D. Harkleroad. Publish America, 2004. Eighteen-year-old Hart McKeon was caught in a comprising situation with the teenage daughter of Mav Thulin, a religious fanatic and deputy sheriff of Prophet, Utah. Hart was beaten by Thulin, arrested for rape, and spent ten years in prison. When paroled, he returned to the vicinity of Prophet, to Bryce Canyon National Park where he worked a wilderness guide. Then history began to repeat itself. The dark side polygamy in modern Utah is the underlying theme of Harkleroad's novel.

Mysterious Ways by Terry Burns. River Oak, 2005. A Christian Western. The protagonist, Amos, was a stagecoach robber who rode into town dressed in a parson's garb that he stole off a clothes line. He had never been in a church in his life, but he found himself in a situation where he had to preach a sermon. He was unfamiliar with the Bible, and was not anxious to rectify his ignorance of the Good Book. But if he refused to preach, then the sheriff could become suspicious.

SELECTED REVIEWS

Death Comes for the Archbishop
by Willa Cather
Alfred A. Knopf, 1927

The New Mexico country was evangelized in fifteen hundred by the Franciscan Fathers. It was allowed to drift for nearly the next three hundred years but wasn't yet dead. *Death Comes for the Archbishop* tells of the missionary efforts of a French Bishop, Jean Marie Latour, and his Vicar, Father Joseph Vaillant, to establish a diocese in the territory of New Mexico. The travels of these dedicated missionary priests over a desert region of sand, arroyos, towering mesas, and bleak red hills, and the accounts of their work and the hardships they endured to establish the order and authority of the church in a wild land provide the framework for this epic novel. The novel also gives a vivid picture of a particular region and culture, including tales and legends from Spanish colonial history and from the primitive tribal traditions of the Hopi and Navajo.

Father Latour was thirty-five when appointed Vicar of New Mexico in 1850. He had been out of the seminary but nine years. Cather's austere style captures the scholarly religious devotion that composes Father Latour's character, and is at the heart of his personality and at the heart of the book.

Father Joseph Vaillant was the Bishop's boyhood friend who made the long journey to Santa Fe with him. He's an intriguing character. Short, skinny, and ugly, there was nothing in his appearance to suggest the fierceness and fortitude and fire of the man. His personality was in startling contrast to that of Father Latour, who was an intellectual. Father Vaillant was his opposite, a hearty man with more good humor and physical vitality than eloquence. This served him well in the new country.

Before Father Latour's arrival, Padre Antonio José Martinez had been dictator to all the parishes in northern New Mexico, and the native priests at Santa Fe were all under his thumb. He was the richest man in the parish. Kit Carson said of him: "Padre Martinez at Taos is an old scapegrace . . . he's got children and grandchildren in almost every settlement around here." He was a vigorous but arrogant priest: "He was rather terrifying, that old priest, with his big head, violent Spanish face, and shoulders like a buffalo . . ." It was common talk that Padre Martinez had instigated the revolt of the Taos Indians, when Bent, the American governor, and a dozen other white men were murdered and scalped.

When his Bishop first visited Taos, Padre Martinez met him wearing buckskin breeches, high boots and silver spurs, a wide Mexican hat, and a great black cape about his shoulders. But the Bishop found him deeply versed, not only in the scriptures, but in the Latin and Spanish Classics. He told the Bishop that

> celibacy may be all very well for the French clergy, but not for ours
> . . . our native priests are more devout than your French Jesuits.

We have a living church here, not a dead arm of the European church . . . We pay a filial respect to the person of the Holy Father, but Rome has no authority here . . . The church the Franciscan Fathers planted here was cut off; this is the second growth, and is indigenous. Our people are the most devout left in the world. If you blast their faith by European formalities, they will become infidels and profligates.

Young Bishop Latour eventually had to deal with the Padre and his loose interpretation of the church's mission.

This isn't just a story of the church and two devoted priests. It's also the story of the people who inhabited this vast territory. There were the Mexicans, whom Father Latour immediately liked. He felt at ease with them. Their voices were gentle; their gaudily decorated altars reflected the high color that was in the landscape. And there were the Indians, the Hopi and the Navajo. Father Latour was convinced that neither the white man nor the Mexicans in Santa Fe understood anything about Indian beliefs or the working of the Indian mind. And the Americans, who were intensely disliked by the Mexicans and Indians alike. Jose, a young man in the little village of Agua Secreta, told Father he would never be an American: "They say in Albuquerque that now we are all Americans, but that is not true . . . They are infidels . . . They destroyed our churches . . . and now they will take our religion from us."

Other characters present the whole spectacle of frontier life. There's the legendary Kit Carson, who said he became a Catholic only as a manner of form, as Americans usually did after they married a Mexican girl, but he became a valued friend of the Bishop. Señora Carson, a tall woman, slender, with drooping shoulders and lustrous black hair and eyes, was very religious; she was also cheerful and had a pleasant sense of humor. The Bishop thought her handsome. Eusabio was one of the most influential men among Navajo people, and one of the richest in sheep and horses. Don Manuel Chavez was a handsome man who boasted his descent from two Castilian knights. He was jealous of Kit Carson's fame as an Indian fighter, declaring that he had seen more Indian warfare before he was twenty than Carson would ever see.

The Bishop's middle years in New Mexico were clouded by the

persecution of the Navajo and their expulsion from their own country. It was Kit Carson who finally subdued the last unconquered remnant of that people, who followed them into the depths of Canyon de Chelly, where they made their last stand. He laid waste to their stores, their cornfields, and their orchards. The Navajo lost heart. They didn't surrender; they just ceased to fight.

The simple story is fleshed out with a number of graphic episodes. The legend of Fray Balzar tells how the Acoma Indians disposed of an overbearing priest, a tyrant, "whom on the whole they liked very well." Father Latour visited the dying pueblo of Pecos, the once rich and populous (some six thousand souls) Cicuyé of Coronado's expedition. It was from here, the story went, that the Spaniards set forth on their ill-fated search for the seven golden cities of Quivera, taking with them slaves and concubines from the Pecos people. There were less than one hundred adults in Pecos, all that was left. There are other episodes, each adding immensely to the flavor and substance of the novel.

The setting establishes the tone of the narrative. Life is intimately related to the landscape, mostly a dry desert plain. For example, Father Joseph loved the tamarisk above all trees:

> Wherever he had come upon a Mexican homestead . . . out of the sun-baked earth . . . the tamarisk waved its feathery plumes . . . The family burro was tied to its trunk, the chickens scratched under it, the dogs slept in its shade, the washing was hung on its branches . . . he loved it merely because it was the tree of the people, and was like one of the family in every Mexican household.

Willa Cather was born in Virginia, but moved to Red Cloud, Nebraska, when she was nine, and later graduated from the University of Nebraska. *O Pioneers!* (Houghton Mifflin, 1913) was the first of her great novels about pioneer life in Nebraska. *My Antonia* (Houghton Mifflin, 1918) followed. Both are great novels, highly acclaimed, about the pioneer era. *One of Ours* (Knopf, 1922), a lesser novel, won a Pulitzer Prize.

When Cather discovered a rare little book on the life of Father Mechebeauf, who had worked with the great Archbishop Lamy of New Mexico, she dropped everything to write *Death Comes for the Archbishop*.

Vaillant is modeled after Father Joseph Machebeuf. Latour is based on Bishop Jean Baptist Lamy, the first Archbishop of Santa Fe. Paul Horgan's *Lamy of Santa Fe: His Life and Times* (Farrar, Straus and Giroux, 1975), a biography inspired by Cather's novel, won a Pulitzer Prize.

Willa Cather's masterpiece gives an exciting history of New Mexico during the last half of the 19th century. J. Frank Dobie, in his *Guide to Life and Literature in the Southwest* (Southern Methodist University Press, 1952), wrote: "While the Southwest can hardly claim Willa Cather, of Nebraska, her *Death Comes for the Archbishop*, which is made out of New Mexico life, is not only the best known novel concerned with the Southwest but one of the finest in America."

Riders of the Purple Sage
by Zane Grey
Harper and Brothers, 1912

Riders of the Purple Sage is the most recognized, and considered by many the best Western novel ever written. All of the elements—setting, plot, and characterization—combine in an exciting romance, filled with action, that literally gallops to an astounding conclusion.

Set in southern Utah in the 1870's, *Riders* flawlessly blends the plot into the magnificent locale. Grey's sensitivity to the beauty of Utah is obvious in descriptive narrative throughout the novel, such as:

> The sage about him was breast high to his horse, oversweet with its warm, fragrant breath, gray where it waved to the light, darker where the wind left it still, and beyond the wonderful haze-purple left by the distance.

In the midst of this scenic beauty lay the Withersteen Ranch, owned by Jane Withersteen.

Jane, like many of Grey's heroines, was a strong and idealistic woman. Her father had been a leader in the Mormon church, and Jane was humble and obedient until his death. But she became the only woman among thousands to rebel against the church's authority. She didn't yield to persuasion or threats, so her churchmen set out to break her.

Into the fray rode Lassiter, a legendary gunman known throughout Utah. His face "had the characteristics of the range rider: leanness, red burn of the sun, and the set changelessness that come from years of solitude." Lassiter was the first of the dreaded mysterious gunfighters who have appeared in hundreds of Western novels. His confrontation with Elder Tull, Jane's primary tormenter, and the treacherous Bishop Dyer was, in the words of Jane's rider Judkins, the "awfulest" of many "soul-rackin' scenes" he had witnessed on the Utah Border.

In parallel with Jane and Lassiter's conflict with the Mormons is the story of Bern Venters. Venters was a Gentile who had his own small ranch in southern Utah until he lost it because of depredations committed against him by the Mormons. He became a hired hand for Jane Withersteen, and then her lead rider. His loyalty to Jane led him to the discovery of a beautiful, secluded valley while tracking rustlers. In "Surprise Valley" he also learned the secret of the rustler leader Oldring's "Masked Rider." Venters eventually had his own showdown with the Mormons. This is a complex plot, with startling climaxes that are never predictable.

The characters have perhaps over the years become stereotypical, but weren't when Grey conceived them. All stood out. Elder Tull and Bishop Dyer and their abuse of the power of their church make them omnipresent, evil villains. Jane, Lassiter, and Venters are strong protagonists. There are no weak characters—all are larger than life. For example, the rustler Oldring, present only in a few pages, is memorable because of his strength:

> He had a large brow, large black eyes, a sweeping beard, as dark as the wing of a raven, an enormous width of shoulder and width of chest, and a presence charged with vitality and strength.

> The clash of adversaries such as these provides exciting reading.
> In fact, the action scenes in *Riders* have never been beaten in the genre.

There's a chapter titled *Wrangle's Race Run*. Wrangle was a large, raw boned sorrel that Jane gave to Venters. He was half-wild, and could run for hours without tiring. But the love of Jane's life was her "racers," Night and Black Star. *Wrangle's Race Run* describes Bern Venters' pursuit of Jerry Card, a frog-like little man reported to be the best rider in Utah, who had stolen Night and Black Star.

Venters was trailing the racers following their theft. "Wrangle's long, swinging canter was a wonderful ground gainer. His stride was almost twice that of an ordinary horse, and his endurance was equally remarkable." He "whistled his pleasure at the smell of the sage." When Venters sighted Jerry Card riding Black Star and leading Night, he cried "Wrangle, the race is on!" He knew he "bestrode the strongest, swiftest, most tireless horse ever ridden by any rider across the Utah uplands." He recalled Jane's devoted assurance that "Night could run neck and neck with Wrangle, and Black Star could show his heels to him." But Bern knew, "in ten miles Wrangle could run Black Star and Night off their feet, and in fifteen he could kill them outright." So he held the sorrel in. But in a few miles of his swinging canter, Wrangle had closed the gap appreciably. Jerry Card looked over his shoulder, and when he saw how the sorrel had gained, he put Black Star to a gallop. The racers lengthened out into a run. "Now, Wrangle," cried Venters, "run, you big devil, run!" And run he did. *Wrangle's Race Run* speeds to an unexpected conclusion, but en route it's one of the most exciting action chapters in Western fiction.

Grey had trouble getting *Riders* published because it was considered anti-Mormon. True, it attacked polygamy and the blind faith that caused so much trouble in the early frontier days. Jane told Lassiter the men of her creed were unnaturally cruel: "They have been hated, driven, scourged 'till their hearts have hardened." Lassiter had no use for Mormon men, but believed Mormon women to be "the best, the noblest, the most long-suffering, and the blindest, unhappiest women on earth." But *The Heritage of the Desert* (Harper and Brothers, 1910), which is also set in Utah and preceded *Riders* by two years, is as pro-Mormon as some claim *Riders* is anti-Mormon.

Pearl Zane Grey was born in Zanesville, Ohio, in 1872. He graduated from the University of Pennsylvania Dental School and practiced dentistry in New York before succumbing to the lure of the West. He became the favorite author of two generations of Americans, producing eighty-nine books in his lifetime. Fifty-six of these were novels of the West.

Since 1918 more than forty-five of Grey's books have been made into motion pictures; many have been made two, three, or four times—yielding a staggering total of over a hundred films. *Riders* has been filmed four times and was the source for a 1996 TNT teleplay. Because of the popularity of Grey's novels, the studios attempted to retain the value of his stories and the films were closely adapted to the books.

Zane Grey's biographer, Frank Gruber, said it best: *Riders of the Purple Sage* is a magnificent epic of a land, a people, and a way of life.

9

HOME ON THE RANGE: SETTLING THE WEST

INTRODUCTION

The mountain men harvested a rich bounty of beaver pelts in the West. The Forty-Niners and others exploited the region for its natural treasures. The cattlemen spread their vast herds over the abundant grasslands, but brought only a meager number of people, not enough to civilize the Wild West.

It was the homesteaders—and the army of people who followed and built the infrastructure to support them—who settled the West. The homesteaders were farmers; they came to till the land. They had only an oblique interest in building settlements or towns. But those who followed—lawyers, doctors, ministers, merchants, millers, bankers, blacksmiths—built homes, schools, churches, and towns where they could make their living providing goods and services.

The settling of the West is a big story. There are many pioneer tales, where immigrants struggle to survive and prosper on the harsh Midwest prairies. There are stories of the town builders: the newspaper editors, merchants, and professionals who had visions of cities, and of those who tamed the wilderness by building telegraph lines to connect with the rest of the nation and massive dams to tame the rivers and provide power to a growing population. There were epic events that hastened the settlement of the West, including the Homestead Act of 1862 and the Oklahoma Land Rush of 1889. All together, this provides a rich and varied background for novelists to mine.

The development of transportation also contributed greatly to the settling of the West. This topic is covered separately in Chapter 11, Transportation in the Early West: People, Freight, and Mail.

The three books selected for review illustrate the breath—and the quality—of novels set against the background of the settling of the West. Bess Streeter Aldrich's *A Lantern in Her Hand* (D. Appleton, 1928) is the heart-rending yet joyous story of a pioneer woman's life on a Nebraska homestead in the 1800s. *Cimarron* (Doubleday, Doran, 1929), by Edna Ferber, is an exciting story of the Oklahoma Land Rush. And finally, the grim *Welcome to Hard Times* (Simon and Schuster, 1960), by E. L. Doctorow, is about a town builder who sees his work destroyed by a wandering outlaw known as "the bad man from Bodie."

READER'S GUIDE

The Chosen Valley by Mary Hallock Foote. Houghton Mifflin, 1892. In Idaho's Boise Valley, an unscrupulous engineer attempted to construct an irrigation dam by profitable but dangerous methods.

The Rose of Ducher's Cooley by Hamlin Garland. Stone, 1895. Garland's heroine Rose, born on a farm, wearied of the monotony of farm life and dreamed of escape. When she left the farm, Rose felt guilt toward her father, whom she left behind.

The Octopus by Frank Norris. Doubleday, Page, 1901. An epic based on the turn-of-the-century struggle between California's San Joaquin Valley wheat growers and the railroad—the "octopus."

The Winning of Barbara Worth by Harold Bell Wright. Book Supply, 1911. Set in the Imperial Valley of California in the early 1900s, this historical novel is backgrounded against the reclaiming of desert land by the diversion of water from the Colorado River. Basis for the 1924 film.

O Pioneers! by Willa Cather. Houghton Mifflin, 1913. Life on the Nebraska frontier is the subject of this novel, Cather's first, where immigrants face the harshness of the vast American prairie and make it a prosperous farmland. Basis for the 1991 and 1992 teleplays.

My Antonia by Willa Cather. Houghton Mifflin, 1918. This novel, which Cather considered her best, depicts the violent yet inspiring existence of foreign and native-born settlers of Nebraska in the early 1900s. The protagonists, Jim Burden and Antonia Shimerda, grew up together on the Nebraska prairie, but their lives diverged unhappily when they grew older. Basis for the 1995 teleplay.

The Sagebrusher by Emerson Hough. D. Appleton, 1919. An Eastern girl answers a matrimonial ad, and goes out West to the hills of Montana to find her mate. Source for the 1920 film.

Druida by John T. Frederick. Alfred A. Knopf, 1923. Druida Horsfall is placed in the position of having to decide between the farm and the city. She renounces the attractions of an urban career, marries a farm boy, and settles for homesteading in Montana.

So Big by Edna Ferber. Doubleday, Page, 1924. A young woman struggles to survive in the Midwest after her father dies, first as a school teacher and then as the wife of a truck farmer, in this Pulitzer Prize-winning novel. Source for the 1924, 1932, and 1953 films.

The Rim of the Prairie by Bess Streeter Aldrich. D. Appleton, 1925. A story of life in a small pioneer town in Nebraska, made more interesting by just a touch of mystery.

Giants in the Earth: A Saga of the Prairie, by O. E. Rölvaag. Harper and Brothers, 1927. Translated from the Norwegian. Per Hansa, a Norwegian immigrant, moved his family to the Dakota prairie in the last part of the 19th century. They were homesteaders, bound to the cruel and unforgiving land; this is a narrative of their pioneer hardship and heroism.

Our Daily Bread by Frederic Phillip Grove. Macmillan, 1928. John and Martha Elliot, pioneers on the Saskatchewan prairie, believed farming was the only truly legitimate occupation for human beings. Their ten children failed to inherit their parents' value system. Some tried to farm and others migrated to the city. But all were maladjusted.

Toilers of the Hills by Vardis Fisher. Houghton Mifflin, 1928. Fisher's first novel is the story of pioneers who leave behind everything they know to make a life in the Antelope Hills region of Idaho.

Pender Victorious: A Tale of the Pioneers Twenty Years Later by O.

E. Rölvaag. Harper and Brothers, 1929. Translated from the Norwegian. The second novel in Rölvaag's prairie saga, this novel centers on the struggles of Per Hansa's son Pender, who was only four at the end of *Giants of the Earth.*

Their Father's God by O. E. Rölvaag. Harper and Brothers, 1931. Translated from the Norwegian. This final novel in Rölvaag's prairie saga brings the struggle of the Norwegian immigrants into the 20th century.

Let the Hurricane Roar by Rose Wilder Lane. Longmans, Green, 1933. Reissued in the 1970s as *Young Pioneers.* In the late 1800s David Beaton and his 16-year-old bride Molly homesteaded a section of Dakota land. Their soddy was comfortable and their wheat fields were lush. But a natural disaster sent David east to find work and left Molly and their new baby alone to face the fierce Dakota winter. Basis for the 1972 teleplay "Young Pioneers."

Ma Jeeter's Girls by Dorothy Thomas. Alfred A. Knopf, 1933. Ma Jeeter was a Nebraska farm woman with six daughters, Ella, Bell, Lena, Laura, Lizzie, and Evie. This is her story, and an account of the shotgun weddings of five of her girls.

Honey in the Horn by H. L. Davis. Harper and Brothers, 1935. A story of homesteading in Oregon during the first decade of the 20th century. The novel is filled with rascals, scoundrels, romantic misfits, Indians, thieves, land exploiters, and assorted homesteaders, all searching for the metaphorical "Honey in the Horn." Winner of the 1935 Harper Prize and 1936 Pulitzer Prize.

Little House on the Prairie by Laura Ingalls Wilder. Harper and Brothers, 1935. A young readers novel. From Wilder's *Little House* series. After selling their Wisconsin log cabin, the little house in the big woods, the Ingalls family set out by covered wagon for Kansas—Indian territory. There Pa Ingalls built their little house on the prairie. Source for the television series.

The Home Place, by Dorothy Thomas. Alfred A. Knopf, 1936. A Nebraska farm story, covering a year with a very large family in a very small house.

Free Land by Rose Wilder Lane. Longmans, Green, 1938. This is a continuation of the story of David and Molly Beaton, which began in Lane's *Let the Hurricane Roar* (1933), and their struggle to survive on the Dakota prairie. They found "free land" had a tremendous price.

Western Union by Zane Grey. Harper and Brothers, 1939. Hiram Sibley, head of the Western Union Telegraph Company, convinced President Abraham Lincoln to seek funding to stretch a telegraph wire across the Great Plains and the Rocky Mountains to the Pacific. Sibley's chief engineer, Edward Creighton, took on the difficult job that he knew could be done.

Wind Without Rain by Herbert Kraus. Bobbs-Merrill, 1939. Set in the early 1900s in the narrow valleys of western Minnesota ("Pockerbrush," as Kraus called the region), this is a story of the German immigrant farmers of western Minnesota, who had little material wealth and fewer cultural possessions. The plot revolves around the Vildvogel family—a brutal father, a gentle mother, four rebellious sons—and their complicated relations with their neighbors.

She Came to the Valley by Cleo Dawson. William Morrow, 1943. Inspired by the life of her mother, who helped establish the settlement of Mission, Texas, Cleo Dawson wrote this novel set in the Rio Grande Valley of Texas in the early 20th century, when pioneers come to the valley and created an agriculture oasis along the Rio Grande. Basis for the 1977 film.

The Golden Bowl by Feike Feikema (Frederick Manfred). Webb, 1944. Manfred's first novel is set in the "Dust Bowl" era of the 1930s. A young man, a victim of the Dust Bowl, rejected farming but then met a farm family and helped them through a bad time, only to escape again from the land. He eventually returned again and accepted the land and his responsibilities.

The Thresher by Herbert Krause. Bobbs-Merrill, 1946. Set in western Minnesota, as was Krause's *Wind Without Rain* (1939), the scene is Pockerbrush and once again the central character is Johnny Black, the owner of first one and finally three steam engine threshing machines that he uses to exploit the wheat farmers of the region. But eventually gasoline tractors begin to replace steam, ending his dominance in harvesting wheat.

This Is the Year by Frederick Manfred. Doubleday, 1947. Set in Siouxland—the corners of Minnesota, South Dakota, Nebraska, and northwest Iowa—this Midwestern farm novel has as its theme the neglect and abuse of the land.

Uncovered Wagon by Hart Stilwell. Doubleday,1947. By age sixteen, Frank Endicott had killed a man, driven cattle up the Chisholm Trail, served as a Texas Ranger, fought Indians, worked in gambling halls, and trapped mustangs. Then he spent his later years helping to turn Texas land west of the Brazos into a multi-million-dollar garden.

Mountain Time by Benard DeVoto. Little, Brown, 1947. Set in Custis, an imaginary town in the mountain West, this story is about a brilliant young doctor in the early 1900s who left New York to practice medicine in the West of his childhood.

The Edge of Time by Loula Grace Erdman. Dodd, Mead, 1950. This is a rare look at homesteading—as opposed to ranching—in the Texas Panhandle, with the focus on women.

The Adventurers by Ernest Haycox. Little, Brown, 1954. In 1865, three shipwreck survivors tried to build a life on the Oregon frontier. One built a stage line and a sawmill, only to lose both. Another comitted murder for the third, a lovely woman named Clara Dale.

The Curlew's Cry by Mildred Walker. Harcourt, Brace, 1955. This novel traces a Montana town's growth from pioneer days to the era of dude ranching.

Miss Morissa: Doctor of the Gold Trail by Mari Sandoz. McGraw-Hill, 1955. Morissa Kirk graduated from medical school and set up her practice in the valley of the North Platte River on the brawling Nebraska frontier of the 1870s. She was twenty-four and unmarried—and a much-sought-after professional woman in man's land of cowboys, farmers, prospectors, and outlaws.

Buffalo Grass by Frank Gruber. Rinehart, 1956. Two Civil War veterans returned to Kansas and built a booming railroad cow town with captured Confederate gold. Basis for the 1957 film "The Big Land."

South of the Angels by Jessamyn West. Harcourt, Brace, 1960. In the 1920s two elderly Quaker couples—one from Kentucky and another from Colorado—attempted to build a new town south of Los Angeles, in still unsettled Southern California.

The Shadow Catcher by James David Horan. Crown, 1962. A novel of the journey in the 1830s of a band of men and women, led by Captain Mark Dana, who made their way westward and founded the first settlement of Americans in the Oregon territory. National Cowboy and Western Heritage Museum Western Heritage Award.

Boulder Dam by Zane Grey. Harper & Row, 1963. Men of vision, courage, and strength harness the power of the Colorado River.

They Came to a Valley by Bill Gulick. Doubleday, 1967. Spanning 1863 to 1868, this is a novel of the settlement and development of the Idaho Territory. The story begins with a wagon train and ends in the gold fields of Boise.

Founder's Praise by Joanne Greenberg. Holt, Rinehart and Winston, 1976. Three generations of Colorado farmers encounter hardship and grief while searching for a "new Eden."

The Land Rushers by Elizabeth Zachary (Hugh Zachary). Dell, 1979. From *The Making of America* series. A romantic novel set during the Oklahoma Land Rush of 1889, when otherwise sane people acted otherwise in their lust for free land.

Plains Song: For Female Voices by Morris Wright. Harper & Row, 1980. Three generations of Midwestern women relate to each other through a form of unison singing in unmeasured time known as plainsong. The plot follows the female members of a family living in Nebraska from the late 1800s to modern times.

The Valiant Women by Jeanne Williams. Simon and Schuster, 1980. Volume one of *The Arizona Saga*. An historical Western romance about the struggles, rewards and aspirations of the early settlers of the territory of Arizona. Spur Award from Western Writers of America.

Western by Frank Yerby. Dial Press, 1982. Ethan Lovejoy, a Harvard-educated Yankee, came to Kansas in 1886 to homestead free land. He became one of the biggest landholders in the state, but his success was marred by bad memories from the Civil War, his wife's battle with madness, and his love for a young Kansas schoolgirl.

Sarah, Plain and Tall by Patricia MacLachlan. Harper & Row, 1985. A young reader's book that won a Newbery Medal. In the late 19th century, a young woman from Maine responded to a midwestern farmer's newspaper ad for a wife. The farmer and his two children came to love Sarah—plain and tall. Basis of the 1991 teleplay.

Son of Manitou by Albert R. Booky. Sunstone Press, 1987. In this story of the early days when control of the West was still unsettled, Indians, outlaws, mountain men and settlers all played their part in determining its future. The ensuing dramatic events are told from the viewpoint of one family and in particular, Sam Sidwell, a young hunter and trapper who anticipated the changes that were to come about after the Civil War.

Mattie by Judy Alter. Doubleday, 1988. Born into poverty, a young woman through grit and determination becomes a doctor and sets up her practice in rural Nebraska. Spur Award from Western Writers of America.

Blowing in the Wind: The Fury of Frontier War by Bernice M. Chappel. Wilderness Adventure Books, 1990. Set in the 1850s, this is the story of two German families who crossed the Atlantic and homesteaded land in the Minnesota territory

The Journey Home by Isabelle Holland. Scholastic, 1990. A novel for young readers. Two orphaned sisters, ages seven and twelve, join an orphan train west to a new life on the Kansas prairie.

Skylark by Patrica MacLachlan. HarperCollins, 1994. MacLachlan's sequel to *Sarah, Plain and Tall* (1985). The farm family contends with drought and a prairie fire and Sarah takes the children to Maine for a visit. Basis for the 1993 Hallmark teleplay.

Children of the Dust by Clancy Carlile. Random House, 1995. An historically accurate tale of the Oklahoma land rush of the 1880's. The central character is a mixed-blood black-Cherokee, who is also a deadly gunfighter and lawman. The theme of the novel is racism. Basis for the 1995 film.

A Sweetness of the Soul by Jane Kirkpatrick. Questar, 1995. An inspirational novel about life in Oregon in the late 19th century, where a young pioneer woman has an unusual and touching romance with a dreamer sixteen years her senior, struggles to make peace with an emotionally distant mother, and fights to build a family of her own.

Flint's Gift by Richard S. Wheeler. Forge, 1997. From Wheeler's *Sam Flint* series. In 1877 a young editor, Sam Flint, opened *The Payday Pioneer* in the idyllic Southwestern town of Payday. His fledgling newspaper brought settlers, but not the kind Sam had in mind.

Second Lives by Richard S. Wheeler. Forge, 1997. Denver in the 1880s was in its formative years, a robust young city that promised wealth and fame. Memorable characters in this novel include a mining magnate, a lawyer trying to redeem himself, a farm girl who momentarily has a fortune, a consumptive poet, and some of Denver's legendary figures, including Horace and Baby Doe Tabor.

Liar's Moon: A Long Story by Phillip Kimball. Henry Holt, 1999. A mythic story of the settling of Kansas during and after the Civil War, when former slaves, cattle drovers, immigrating farmers, and Indians came together to form a complex society on the swirl of the Great Plains.

When the Sky Rained Dust, by Patrick Dearen. Eakin Press, 2005. Set in 1934 during the Great Depression. A fourteen-year-old boy watched his family struggle to make a living on their small farm in the middle of the Dust Bowl in Central Texas and wondered why they were hanging on.

SELECTED REVIEWS

A Lantern in Her Hand
by Bess Streeter Aldrich
D. Appleton, 1928

When Abbie Deal was an old woman, she told her granddaughter Kathrine, "You can't describe love, Kathie, and you can't define it. Only it goes with you all your life. I think that love is more like a light that you carry. At first childish happiness keeps it lighted and after that romance. And then motherhood lights it and then duty . . . and maybe after that sorrow. You wouldn't think that sorrow would be a light would you, dearie? But it can. And then after that service lights it. Yes . . . I think that's what love is to a woman . . . a lantern in her hand." And Abbie kept the lantern lighted her whole life, under the harsh conditions that pioneer women endured when they left safety and comfort behind to battle blizzards and fire, droughts and locusts, loneliness and deprivation—and create homes, schools and churches on the windswept prairies.

Abbie Mackenzie was eight years old when her mother drove a wagon west to Blackhawk, Iowa. Her father was dead and the family was dirt poor, but all her life she had been told the story of her aristocratic father who married her peasant mother, then lost the family fortune. Abbie's dream was to be like her aristocratic grandmother, Isabel Anders-Mackenzie, whose image was in a portrait which had hung in the great hall of the family home in Scotland. She had reddish-brown hair like Abbie, and she had pretty hands and long slender fingers that tapered at the ends—like Abbie's. Abby had only seen the painting in her imagination, but her dream was to be like her grandmother— a fine lady—and to develop her lovely singing voice.

When Abby was not quite nineteen, she married twenty-three year-old Will Deal on a winter's day in 1865. Will was a farmer, but didn't want to spend his life as a hired man for his successful father. He wanted to homestead in Nebraska.

In July 1868 the young couple started west with an ox team, a wagon, and one child in tow. The half section of Nebraska prairie land that Will an Abbie would homestead was about thirty-five miles from Nebraska City and about ten miles from Weeping Water. The county seat, Plattsmouth, had a hotel and some houses and a grist mill. Their land lay in long rolling swells, with nothing to be seen in any direction but the prairie grass and the few native trees along the banks of Stove Creek. The undulating land was covered with prairie grass, a vast, lonely landscape. A coyote howled. Other than that, there was complete silence. "Silence, so deep, that it roared . . . ." Abby felt insignificant in its vastness.

Will built a sod house, or "soddie," and planted his first crop. Life was hard. It was six years before Will produced a promising crop, a crop that a black cloud of grasshoppers promptly ate up. Will and Abbie would suffer summer droughts, winter storms, and a prairie fire. But they endured, and their children, who finally numbered five, were healthy, bright, and happy. The narration speaks of a Christmas on the prairie in those hard times, when all the gifts were homemade:

Historians say, "The winter of 'seventy-four to 'seventy-five was a time of deep depression." But historians do not take little children into consideration. Deep depression? To three children on the prairie it was a time of glamour. There was not much to eat in the cupboard . . . The presents were pitifully homely and meager. And all in a tiny house, a mere shell of a house, on a new raw acreage of the wild, bleak prairie. How could a little rude cabin hold so much white magic? How could a little sod house know such enchantment?

Abbie eventually gave up her dreams of art and music and writing. Her daughter Grace told her that she should have done something with her talents. Abbie replied wistfully, "No . . . I was only meant to appreciate it, . . . not do it." Instead, she passed her aspirations on to her children and grandchildren. In her old age, Abbie said to her granddaughter Laura, "I've dreamed dreams, Laura. All the time I was cooking and patching and washing, I dreamed dreams. And I think I dreamed them into the children . . . and the children are carrying them out . . . doing all the things I wanted to and couldn't. Margaret has painted for me and Isabelle has sung for me. Grace has taught for me. . . and you, Laura . . . you'll write my book for me I think."

In Bess Streeter Aldrich's hands, ordinary people become engaging characters. Will Deal was a solid, hardworking farmer who believed that Nebraska had the finest, blackest loam on the face of the earth, and that those who stuck it out would see more rains and not so much wind, and Nebraska would be the richest and most productive state in the Union. Grandma Deal, Will's mother, was a born pessimist to whom life meant nothing but work. When "Grandma's restless spirit took its final grumbling flight, [she sputtered] a little at the Lord for the time spent upon her demise." Abbie's friend Christine Reinmueller "seemed as stolid as the oxen, her face as patiently expressionless. One could not have told whether she was old or young. Her colorless hair was braided in small braids and wound flat from ear to ear, looking like a small oval-shaped rug pinned on the back of her head." At first Abbie didn't like Christine; she found her uncouth, not quite clean. But Christine would deliver two of her children, save her life during a snowstorm, and become her friend for life. But there is one character in the story who is not ordinary, and her introduction soars.

You will remember that Basil Mackenzie [Abbie's father], an aristocratic young Scotchman, of Aberdeen, riding to the hares and hounds, wooed and won Maggie O'Conner from the whins and silver bazels of Ballyporeen. But what you do not know is that several generations later, the good Saints, up in high heaven's court, gave that couple three chances each to mold the life of a descendant . . . a baby girl . . . just born upon earth. Basil Mackenzie first crowned her with hair like the mist around the mountains of Glencoe when the sun shines through,—and immediately Maggie O'Conner gave her eyes the color of the blue-black waters at Kilkee. Then the man, remembering sensibly that the outward appearance is not all, endowed her with a keen Scotch mind, but the woman smiled and slipped an Irish heart into her. For a long time Basil pondered cannily, wondering how he might use his last chance and finally gave her the sturdiest of Scotch chins—but Maggie O'Conner laughed and pressed a roguish V-shaped cleft into the center of it.

Practical folks there are, who will not believe this; but here, nineteen years later, was Katherine Deal with her misty Glencoe hair and her blue-black Kilkenny eyes and her gay great-granny's dimple in the middle of her dour great-grandfaither's chin. Sure, and what more proof could a body be needin'? Here she was,—Katherine, the only daughter of Mackenzie Deal—this warm summer afternoon, stretched out in her Grandmother Deal's hammock on the screened-in sitting-room porch of the farmhouse, . . .

And flippant Katherine, disrespectful and not in the least interested in her grandmother's stories of hardships on the prairie, would make one of Abbie's most cherished dreams come true.

Aldrich writes lovingly of the prairie in all its moods. Following a fierce winter, when "the winds, blew hard from the open country to the north and west, and dried tumbleweeds rolled over the prairie like great platoons of charging cavalry," a miracle occurred:

Spring came over the prairie,—not softly, shyly, but in great magic strides. It was in the flush of green on the elders and willows by Stove Creek. It was in the wind,—in the smell of loam and grasses, in the tantalizing odor of wild plums budding and wild violets flowering. Nature, the alchemist, took them all, the faint odors of the loam and the grasses, the willow buds and the little wild flowers, and mixing them in her mortar, threw them over the prairies on the wings of the wind.

Aldrich, a Midwesterner, set some fine novels in the heartland prairies, including *The Rim of the Prairie* (D. Appleton, 1925), *The Cutters* (D. Appleton, 1926), *White Bird Flying* (D. Appleton, 1931)—the sequel to *A Lantern in Her Hand*, and *The Lieutenant's Lady* (D. Appleton, 1942). *Lantern* was the basis for a poorly adapted 1995 CBS teleplay titled "A Mother's Gift," starring Nancy McKean and Adrian Pasdar.

Like *Lantern*, all of Bess Streeter Aldrich's novels are unpretentious, sentimental, romantic, strangely optimistic, and address high matters of the human heart.

Cimarron
by Edna Ferber
Doubleday, Doran, 1929

No one tells the story of the American people better than Edna Ferber. Five of her novels were set in the American West: *So Big* (Doubleday, Page 1924), *Cimarron*, Great Son (Doubleday, Doran, 1945), *Giant* (Doubleday, 1952), and *Ice Palace* (Doubleday, 1958). Some of these novels had a significant impact on the reading public. *Giant* formed the image of Texas that many people hold. Some credit *Ice Palace* with helping Alaska achieve statehood—which occurred in the same year as the book's publication. Ferber won the Pulitzer Prize in 1925 for *So Big*.

The overt theme of *Cimarron* is the settlement of the Oklahoma territory. But Ferber's purpose was to show the triumph of materialism over spirit in America. It contains paragraphs and even chapters of satire and bitterness. She was disappointed that many critics and thousands of readers took it as a colorful romantic Western novel.

Satire aside, *Cimarron* is an extraordinarily colorful and romantic Western novel. In her foreword Ferber tells us "only the more fantastic and improbable events contained in the book are true." In many cases she discarded research material because it was too absurd for fiction.

Aristocratic Sabra Cravat defied her family and rode off to the wild Oklahoma territory with a husband whose past was clouded with myths and surmises. No one really knew him. They called him Yancey Cravat. He came out of Texas and the savage Cimarron country.

Yancey was a bizarre, glamorous figure. No room seemed big enough for his gigantic frame. First, you noticed his head, huge like a buffalo's, so heavy it seemed to loll of its own weight. He was verbose, frequently even windy, but a born orator, with a vibrant, flexible voice, great charm, and beautiful hypnotic eyes under long lashes.

He had made the first run into the central district of Oklahoma in '89. He did not homestead, but returned to Kansas to take Sabra and their young son Cimarron to the territory. Sabra was reluctant, her genteel family was strongly opposed, but Yancey was insistent. Sabra's former teacher Mother Bridget summed it up for her:

> He's going for the adventure of it. They always have, no matter
> what excuse they've given, from the holy grail to the California gold
> fields. The difference in America is that the women have always gone
> along . . . The history of England is a joust . . . When Lady Guinevere
> had pinned a bow of ribbon on her knight's sleeve, why, her job was
> done for the day. But here in this land, Sabra, my girl, the women,
> they've been the real hewers of wood and drawers of water . . .

Sabra went with Yancey to Osage (a composite of five Oklahoma cities). In this primitive settlement, she learned many outstanding things in her first few days. Among the most terrifying were the things she learned about her husband. She learned that Yancey Cravat was famed as the deadliest shot in the Southwest. She also learned, despite her Southern upbringing in a tradition where the man was always right, always to be deferred to, that the male of the species might be fallible.

Sabra's husband had always treated her tenderly, as a charming little fool, a role she meekly accepted. But in Osage she began to suspect that men, as a sex, were often mistaken, and that Yancey, as an individual, was almost always wrong. He was a visionary, a great planner, but too impatient to carry any undertaking, however noble, through to completion.

Yancey was a lawyer and a newspaper editor. He could have been the greatest criminal lawyer of his day. His practice yielded him nothing. His newspaper, the Oklahoma Wigwam, would have yielded approximately the same had it not been for Sabra. She emerged slowly from her role as charming little fool. By degrees she took more and more of a hand in reporting the local news and getting the paper out on time, while Yancey wrote fiery editorials advocating, among other inflammatory subjects, that reservation Indians be allowed to live anywhere they wanted.

Sabra and Yancey differed sharply in their views of the Indian Nation. Yancey was their champion. He considered the government's dealing with them deplorable (In Ferber's exposition she contends their plight wasn't as pitiable as Yancey painted it: "He cast over them a gleam of his own romantic nature. The truth was they themselves cared little. They hunted a little, fished, slept, visited from tribe to tribe, gossiping, eating, holding powwows, . . .). Sabra despised them: "Oh, my heavens, Yancey! Indians! You and your miserable dirty Indians! You're always going on about them as if they mattered. The sooner they're all dead the better. What good are they? Filthy, thieving, lazy things. They won't work . . . They just sit there, rotting." It was ironic that years later Sabra, not Yancey, as a representative from Oklahoma, introduced a bill in Congress that advocated the abolition of the Indian reservation system.

Ferber had her critics. Mediocre to bad reviews were common. Some reviewers suggested she curb the platitudes and probe her characters a little deeper. This is a fair criticism. But in *Cimarron* she develops a cast that figuratively leaps off the page. In addition to Yancey and Sabra, there's Sol Levy, the "town Jew," a person apart, who had walked to Oklahoma and made his fortune in mercantile; young Cimarron Cravat, who had his father's look and temperament but not his heroic bulk; Ruby Red Elk, Sabra's housekeeper, the insolent daughter of an Osage Chief, who would break Sabra's heart; Donna Cravat, viperous daughter of Yancey and Sabra; and little black Isaiah, who stowed away in the Cravat's wagon for the trip to Oklahoma and met a terrible fate because of his color. There are others—lawmen, outlaws, prostitutes—who illustrate Ferber's ability to paint the American scene. Perhaps they could have been probed deeper, but each makes an impression.

The novel was filmed twice, first by RKO in 1931 and again by MGM in 1960. Both followed the book closely. Richard Dix was superb as Yancey Cravat in the 1931 version and Irene Dunn was equally effective as Sabra. The 1960 film starred Glen Ford and Maria Schell. The 1931 version was the first Western to win an academy award for best picture.

Edna Ferber's friend Rudyard Kipling expressed the reading public's interpretation of her story of the Oklahoma Land Rush: "I am reading *Cimarron* . . . That's a big piece of work and a damn good atmosphere . . . Of course it's melodramatic, but so was (and is) Oklahoma and how well she describes the merciless pressure of the respectable women pulling their men folks into line—like mothers chasing up bad boys which, indeed, I suspect all men are."

Welcome to Hard Times
by E. L. Doctorow
Simon and Schuster, 1960

One reviewer commented that *Welcome to Hard Times* is deceptively simple, more fable than story, more ballad or parable than traditional novel. Whatever the form, Doctorow has created an image of the West that is brutally capitalistic, selfish, and cruel. The tone is set in our introduction to the Bad Man from Bodie in the opening paragraph:

> The Man from Bodie drank down a half bottle of the Silver Sun's best; that cleared the dust from his throat, and then when Florence, who was a redhead, moved along the bar to him, he turned and grinned down at her. I guess Florence had never seen a man so big. Before she could say a word he reached down and stuck his hand in the collar of her dress and ripped it down to her waist so that her breasts bounded out bare under the yellow light.

He raped and killed the redheaded whore before he burned the town to the ground and rode away.

But the novel isn't about the Bad Man; rather it's a character study of his effect on two who survived and remained in Hard Times.

Blue was the unofficial mayor of Hard Times, a pitiful little town in the starkest of landscapes in Dakota Territory in the late 1800s. He is the narrator, providing the only perspective on Hard Times, and is obsessed with recording the events that take place in his tiny frontier hamlet. Blue's first ledger is a history of the town and of its destruction by the Bad Man. The middle ledger recounts the rebuilding, and the third its final destruction.

When he first came west he was a young man with expectations. In time the expectations faded, and he learned it was enough to stay alive. He began to believe "Bad Men from Bodie weren't ordinary scoundrels, they came with the territory, and you could no more cope with them than you could with dust and hailstones." Like the other citizens of Hard Times, Blue simply stood by and watched the Bad Man carry out his depredations.

Molly Riordan was a whore the Bad Man brutalized and left for dead. Blue found her in the rubble of the saloon and nursed her back to health. But because he hadn't stood up to the Bad Man, Molly regarded him as she would a lizard: " . . . if I had a knife now I would stick it in you and watch the yellow flow."

The town began to recover and even grow. Blue was a town-builder and despite incredible odds, he could see a prosperous town and a good life. Molly, however, was haunted by the memory of the Bad Man and knew his return was inevitable.

The novel presents a bleak view of their experiences. There's terrifying hopelessness in Blue's attempt to build a civilization out of the rubble left by the maniacal outlaw and Molly's obsession with being prepared for his eventual return.

This hopelessness is intensified by the desolation of the Dakota prairie that surrounds Hard Times. On three sides—east, west, south—there was nothing but miles of flats. To the north were hills of rocks where the mines were that gave an excuse for the town. Doctorow created the image of an arid, rocky, empty landscape without life, and ultimately, without hope. He's quoted as saying "I could spin the whole book out one image. And I did."

The characterizations, like the Dakota setting, are powerful. There's a drifter named Jenks, whose "head was not much thicker than a broom handle" and whose "sly yellow eyes made you think of a wolf's cunning. But really he was a stupid man." In the winter he wore a hat made out of prairie dog fur which came down to his eyes. "You could just about make out his wolfy grin under that cap."

Jenks spent most of his time oiling his gun and holster. When Molly asked him if he could shoot, he replied, "Well, yess'm, ah can shoot whur yew kin see." And he could. A representative from the governor's office appointed Jenks deputy sheriff because the town would need a "shootist" if it began to prosper. When the Bad Man from Bodie returned, Molly pleaded, cajoled, and finally persuaded Jenks to go after him. Doctorow puts the reader squarely in the foolish deputy's corner:

> By and by Jenks was spinning his colt and checking each chamber, his simpleton pride rising like manhood to her promises . . . The wolfly fool licked the syrup of her words and was marching up the street . . . he was trotting like a hero . . . He marched up the steps holding his polished pistol and pulled one of the doors back. "Hey!" he cied, raising the gun to sight . . . there was a rush for the door . . .

There are other characters who are equally interesting: Zar, the Russian who opened a bar and whorehouse in Hard Times; Adah, the madam of Zar's whores; and young Jimmy Fee, the only child in town, who Molly would try to use as she had Jenks.

Doctorow was an editor at both New American Library and Dial Press, where he reviewed many Westerns. *Welcome to Hard Times*, his first novel, written when he was only twenty-nine, was an experiment with the genre. The result is a sparse, finely constructed novel that takes the romance out of the Western Experience. Doctorow is now a successful, well-known writer, but hasn't returned to the Western genre which launched his career.

The film, "Welcome to Hard Times," released in 1967, was scripted and directed by Burt Kennedy. It starred Henry Fonda and Janice Rule, and featured Aldo Ray as the Bad Man from Bodie. Like the novel, it is a cold, angry Western.

10

Wealth of the West: Gold, Silver, Oil, Timber and Lost Treasures

Introduction

T he lure of treasure enticed hundreds of thousands of men and women from all over the world to travel to remote areas of the American West in hope of claiming some of the riches discovered in California, Nevada, Colorado, the Dakotas, Montana, Idaho, Alaska, and neighboring Canada and Mexico. Of those who made it through the hardships of the trip, nine out of ten came away with nothing, while a few made fortunes.

The search for these riches began with the conquistadors, military adventurers who led the Spanish exploration and conquest of the New World during the 16th century. Fierce and ruthless, they were motivated both by missionary zeal and greed for gold and other riches. Among the most famous was Francisco Vazquez de Coronado, who led an expedition from Mexico City in 1540 to search the Southwest for the fabled Seven Golden Cities of Cibola and the riches of Gran Quivira. He returned to Mexico in 1542, where his expedition was regarded as a failure. It is now recognized, however, as one of the greatest North American explorations. The exploits of the conquistadors are covered in Chapter 13, The Spanish West.

The greatest gold rush in the history of the United States began with the discovery of gold at Sutter's Mill on the American River in northern California in 1848. When news of the discovery spread, thousands of Californians flocked to the region. The great rush, however, began in 1849. California's population grew from about 14,000 in 1848 to 100,000 in 1850. That number increased to 250,000 by late 1852 and to 380,000 by 1860. Ramshackle mining camps with names like Poker Flat, Hangtown, Whiskey Bar, and Placerville sprang up almost overnight.

The earliest 49ers mined stream beds for eroded gold in the form of dust, flakes, and nuggets. This supply was quickly exhausted, and eventually deep mines were dug, rock was hauled to the surface, crushed, and treated to extract the precious dust. Extraction techniques like this required capital beyond the means of the placer miners, so they were forced to work as laborers for large mining companies, or wander on to subsequent strikes in Colorado, Nevada, Idaho, Montana, and Arizona.

The gold rush drew not only fortune hunters but also merchants, artisans, farmers, gamblers, prostitutes, and outlaws to the American West. This boom in turn encouraged construction of wagon roads and railroads and attracted essential outside capital.

Between 1858 and 1875 miners spread into the mountainous regions of Colorado and Nevada, across the deserts of Arizona, over the inland empire of Oregon, Washington and Idaho, and through the wilds of Montana to the domed Black Hills of South Dakota. They found a fortune in gold and silver, and left behind a partly settled country.

It began in 1858, when "pay-dirt" was struck near present-day Denver. The following year, some 100,000 "fifty-niners" were in the Pike's Peak country. The Pike's Peak gold rush of 1859 was a fiasco. But the fortunate few who stayed on in Denver struck it rich. Then new mines were opened as prospectors uncovered beds of silver ore near Leadville and deposits of gold on Cripple Creek a few years later.

The discovery of the fabulous Comstock Lode in Nevada's Carson River Valley in 1859 made "penniless millionaires," men who owned claims they could not mine until Eastern capital flowed in to purchase and operate the heavy mining equipment needed to extract the gold from the quartz veins it was locked in. During the next decade mine after mine was opened. In 1873 miners bored through 1,167 feet of flinty rock to the heart of the Comstock, or the "Big Bonanza," a fifty-four feet wide vein filled with gold and silver, the richest find in the history of mining.

Most of these prospectors came from west to east, or from California.

They had gone there in the gold rush of 1849, at a time when gold nuggets or "dust" were relatively easy to obtain. But by the middle of the 1850s most rich "diggins" had already been appropriated, and the area had been thoroughly prospected.

The Klondike is a sparsely populated area in west central Yukon territory in Canada, near the Alaskan border. Gold was discovered at Rabbit Creek in 1896, and a gold rush began in 1897. More than 30,000 people streamed into the area. Dawson, still the major town of the Klondike, served the needs of the prospectors. By 1910, when the great strike was over, more than $100,000,000 worth of gold had been taken from the Klondike.

In 1899 gold was found on the beach at Nome, and quickly an Alaskan gold rush was under way. By mid-1900 about 10,000 gold seekers were in Nome. Important gold discoveries were made around Fairbanks in 1902, in the Yellow and Iditarod river valleys (near the modern town of Flat) in 1906-10, and along the Yukon near Ruby in 1907-10. Novels based on Canadian and Alaskan gold strikes are included in chapter 14, The Land Beyond.

Our southern neighbor Mexico has been mined for centuries, dating back to prehistoric times. The mines of Zacatecas, Arizpe, Guanajuato, Pachuca, Batopilas, Fresnillo, Puebla and Taxco are world renowned for rich ore deposits. The silver mines of Mexico have produced perhaps as much as a third of the silver that the world has ever used.

In addition to mining, the search for lost treasures has lured prospectors to the West. In present-day New Mexico and Arizona, the driving out of the Spaniards and the capture by bandits of hundreds of loads of treasure bound for Mexico City provide a fertile field for the countless tales of lost mines and cached plants of silver and gold. It is the same throughout the Southwest: buried vaults stacked with gold bars, secret caches of coins and jewels plundered from the Spaniards and the Church, exposed veins of ore with nuggets the size of turkey eggs. Guarded by the bones of dead men, the legendary treasures of the Southwest still wait for those foolhardy or desperate enough to seek them. These legends include the Lost Dutchman Mine in the Superstition Mountains of Arizona, The Lost Breyfogle in California, The Lost Adams Diggings in New Mexico, The Lost San Saba Mine in Texas, and the Lost Tayopa of the Sierra Madre in Mexico.

The West held, and still holds, treasures richer than gold and silver: its oil and timber. From California's giant redwoods to the Douglas fir and Sitka spruce found farther north along the rugged Pacific coastline, to the sequoias and ponderosa pines found in the mountain ranges, the West is rich in timber. The 1849 California Gold Rush, and the many strikes that followed, created a huge demand in the region for lumber. A new breed of entrepreneurs met that demand, and built empires that drew from the forests of the West.

The Indians in Texas and Oklahoma territory had long been familiar with a brown fluid that seeped from the earth. The seeps were surround by an invisible gas in the air that would burn brightly, forever. Then in 1894 an oil well was bored by accident while drilling for water in Texas, and the first oil boom in the West was off and running. It has never stopped.

Novelists have not ignored this treasure-trove as a source for plots and colorful characters. Two of the best novels of the search for riches I have chosen for review: *The Travels of Jaimie McPheeters* (Doubleday, 1958), by Robert Lewis Taylor, is the story of a boy and his father who journey along the Oregon-California Trail, with a detour and winter stay in Salt Lake City, to the gold fields of California in 1849. B. Traven's *The Treasure of the Sierra Madre* (Alfred A. Knopf, 1935), revolves around three American adventurers who hunt for gold in the rugged Sierra Madre region of Mexico.

READER'S GUIDE

M'liss: An Idyll of Red Mountain by Bret Harte. 1863. This novella tells the story of spunky and bucolic M'liss, who fashioned a life for herself in the rough mining world of the Sierra Nevada mountains. Basis for the 1918 film "M'liss," and the 1922 film "The Girl Who Ran Wild."

The Led-Horse Claim by Mary Hallock Foote. Osgood, 1883. Foote's first novel is the story of a young man and woman who learn to love each other despite the violent claim disputes dividing a Colorado mining camp.

Coeur D'Alene by Mary Hallock Foote. Houghton Mifflin, 1894. The story of a malicious laborers' strike at the Idaho mines of Coeur d'Alene.

Woodsmen of the West by Martin Allerdale Grainger. Toronto: McClelland and Stewart, 1908. Grainger, a miner, logger, and eventually Chief Forester of British Columbia, wrote this novel, set in rugged, turn-of-the-century British Columbia, about the drama of the coastal logging camps and small boom towns where a forturne could be won and lost.

The Riverman by Stewart Edward White. McClure, 1908. A story of the early loggers on the Northwest coast riverways who called themselves the rivermen.

Cavanaugh: Forest Ranger by Hamlin Garland. Harper and Brothers, 1910. A novel that deals with the conflict between the newly established Forest Service and Westerners, especially cattlemen, who resented the "locking up" of natural resources that they wished to exploit.

Gold by Stewart Edward White. Doubleday, McClure, 1913. A fictionalized first-person account of the 1849 California Gold Rush.

Overland Red by Henry Herbert Knibbs. Houghton Mifflin, 1914. Overland Red, a tramp prospector, and a boy he has befriended stumble across an aged miner in the last stages of starvation, whose pockets reveal the map of a secret mine and a bag of gold dust. The two bury the old man, the gold and the map, only to be accused by an unscrupulous sheriff and his posse of murdering the old miner. Basis for the 1920 film of the same title, and the 1924 film "The Sunset Trail."

Life's Lure by John G. Neihardt. Kennerly, 1914. In this novel poet John Neihardt portrays the lives of Black Hills miners and the card sharps and desperadoes who preyed on them.

The Border Legion by Zane Grey. Harper and Brothers, 1916. The California Gold Rush drew a horde of lawless ruffians west. Then, when gold was found at Alder Creek on the southern border of Idaho, those criminals descended on that rich strike. The Border Legion was a band of outlaws disguised as miners, trying to take over the richest claims. Filmed in 1930 and 1940, with the same title.

Desert Valley by Gregory Jackson. Charles Scribner's Sons, 1921. Intrigue and doublecrossing over a gold prospector's claim in the Southwest desert leads to a fearful confrontation.

The Saga of the Comstock Lode by George Lyman. Charles Scribner's

Sons, 1934. During 1859-1865 thousands of Californians rushed to Sun Mountain, Nevada, to stake their claims in the rich veins of silver. A horde of miners from across the continent and from Europe followed them.

The Guard of the Timberline by George Washington Ogden. Dodd, Mead, 1934. A novel based on the most destructive fire in the history of forestry, which the author witnessed on the national reserves in Idaho in 1910.

City of Illusion by Vardis Fisher. Harper and Brothers, 1941. Virginia City, Nevada, sprang up after the discovery of the Comstock Lode in the spring of 1859. The rich silver deposits drew all sorts of people seeking wealth, including Eilley Bowers. Eilley's greed and desire to be "Queen of the Comstock," achieved on the backs of the mine workers who labored under dangerous conditions, made her wealthy before it caused her downfall.

Alder Gulch by Ernest Haycox. Little, Brown, 1942. A fugitive and a lady who had known better days made their way to Alder Gulch, a mining town in Montana. In 1863, Alder Gulch was far from civilization and any kind of law. In the midst of violence and tragedy, the man panned for gold and the woman began a strange, new life. Partial basis for the 1954 film "The Far Country."

Canyon Passage by Ernest Haycox. Little, Brown, 1942. Men drunk with gold fever fought each other to gouge riches from the Oregon wilderness. The story centers on Logan Stuart; a respected mediator until one of his friends was accused of robbery. Source for the 1946 film.

Tracey Cromwell by Conrad Richter. Alfred A. Knopf, 1942. A frontier madam left Socorro, New Mexico, and became the wife of a gambler in the Arizona copper mining town of Bisbee, where she attempted to become respectable.

The Timber Beast by Archie Binns. Charles Scribner's Sons, 1944. A novel set in the 1940s in the logging communities of Port Townsend and Puget Sound in the Pacific Northwest. The story is of a hardboiled old logging operator, his sons and his attractive and restless young second wife, and of the "cut and get out" attitude of the "timber beast" conflicting with the new ideas of his sons.

Colorado by Louis Bromfield. Harper and Brothers, 1947. Louis Bromfield was a popular novelist who won a Pulitzer Prize in 1926. *Colorado* is his only Western story. It is set in Silver City, a fictional Colorado town that prospered during the silver bonanza sometime around 1859. A beautiful woman named Mademoiselle La Belle da Ponte turned Silver City upside down from the moment she stepped off the train. Within a week she had captured the hearts of most of the male population and started more trouble than the rough mining town had ever seen.

Foxfire by Anya Seton. Houghton Mifflin, 1951. A young woman abandoned her Eastern debutante life to marry a mining engineer in the bleak little town of Lodestone in post-depression Arizona. Her husband's Apache heritage led them on a quest for a lost gold mine.

Lost Pueblo by Zane Grey. Harper and Brothers, 1954. A millionaire's feisty daughter was kidnapped in the 1920s and forced by her captor to join his archaeological expedition in Arizona. Beckyshibita, the ruin of a past civilization, is the setting for this romance of the spoiled eastern girl by a serious young archeologist.

Sierra Baron by Tom W. Blackburn. Random House, 1955. A tough Irishman from the slums of Boston jumped ship in Monterey during the Gold Rush. He clashed with the Spanish aristocrats who controlled California, but eventually he became known as the "Sierra Baron." Basis for the 1958 film.

The Treasure of Pleasant Valley by Frank Yerby. Dial Press, 1955. In 1849, two young men from the South joined the California Gold Rush and ended up in the shanty town of San Francisco. There, they were in a world of utter lawlessness, a land swarming with misfits and dreamers, with men driven mad by hardships and scarcity of women.

The Silver Mountain by Dan Cushman. D. Appleton, 1957. During the late 1890s in Montana "The Mountain" paid out a million dollars a month. It made John Ballard and his equally poor partner Grattan O'More millionaires almost overnight. But both fell in love with the same ruthless young woman, and she shortened the life of one and changed forever that of the other. Spur Award from Western Writers of America.

Desert Gold by Steve Frazee. Dell, 1957. He had survived as a trapper, hunter, cowhand, and prospector. And then a muddy river had yielded the gold, and he had crossed and recrossed trackless miles of desert to hide his fortune. Source for the 1961 film "Gold of the Seven Saints."

The Hanging Tree by Dorothy M. Johnson. Ballantine Books, 1958. The title story in a collection with the same title. This short novella is based on an actual piece of Montana history. In the gold camp of Skull Creek, a mysterious doctor/gunman saves a boy from the law, then enslaves him. He also treats a temporarily blinded Eastern girl, then falls in love with her. Source for the 1959 film.

MacKenna's Gold by Will Henry (Henry Wilson Allen). Random House, 1963. This novel about the legend of the Lost Adams Diggings in Arizona is based on J. Frank Dobie's *Apache Gold and Yaqui Silver* (Little, Brown, 1939). Somewhere, "eight days toward the sunset," lay the Adams diggings, with nuggets the size of eggs and secret caches of gold bars and coins and jewels plundered from the Spaniards and the Church. In Henry's novel, his protagonist reluctantly leads a pack of scoundrels to the treasure, at their peril. Source for the 1968 film.

Red Mountain by David Lavender. Doubleday, 1963. Lavender's novel of the rich silver strikes between Ouray (Argent) and Silverton (Baker), Colorado, tells how protagonist Johnny Ogden built what is now the Million Dollar Highway to connect Argent with the booming Red Mountain Mining District. Red Mountain portrays the excitement and optimism of the silver boom days of Colorado, as well as the doom and despair that followed after the collapse of the price of silver.

Sometimes a Great Notion by Ken Kesey. Viking Press, 1964. A story of three generations of Oregon loggers and of the clan's bitter battle with the union, the town, and the forces of nature. Basis for the 1971 film.

Gold in California! by Todhunter Ballard. Doubleday, 1965. A novel based on California gold history, beginning with the organization of wagon trains for the trips across the plains, moving on to the mining camps and towns in California. Spur Award from Western Writers of America.

Maximilian's Gold by Jane Barry. Doubleday, 1966. In 1867, after the Civil War had robbed the South of its past, the goal of five former Confederate soldiers and one mountain man was a cave in Mexico—a cave guarded by a nest of rattlesnakes and filled with gold.

Calico Palace by Gwen Bristow. Crowell, 1970. The forty-eighters were already in California when the gold rush of forty-nine brought thousands of people seeking their fortunes. One woman with a talent for card games saw her opportunity and at a mining camp called Shiny Gulch she set up a gambling tent called the Calico Palace.

Black Apache by Clay Fisher (Henry Wilson Allen). Bantam Books, 1976. A betrayed black West Point officer became a renegade Apache and waged war against his former comrades, then hooked up with a mestizo priest who dreamed of gold.

Treasure in Hell's Canyon by Bill Gulick. Doubleday, 1979. Legend placed the Golden Girl mine at the bottom of Hell's Canyon—a no-man's-land bordered by mile-high rock cliffs. The only way in was through miles of Snake River killer rapids.

Golden Dreams by Gwen Bristow. J. B. Lippincott, 1980. A story of the California Gold Rush.

The Treasure of Jericho Mountain by Cameron Judd. Leisure Books, 1980. Two ex-Confederate soldiers sought to recover a fortune in stolen gold hidden deep in the mountains of Colorado.

Comstock Lode by Louis L'Amour. Bantam Books, 1981. The Comstock Lode was the Great Bonanza—no place on earth was richer in silver. It drew wealth-seekers like the miners and builders, and the vultures. They built a legendary boomtown called Virginia City.

The Forty-Niners by John Toombs. Dell, 1981. From Dell's *The Making of America* series. In 1849, when gold was discovered at Sutter's Mill near Sacramento, California, thousands of people from all over the country headed for the Mother Lode; among them an assortment of prospectors, gamblers, frontiersmen, and down on their luck gentry.

Challenge at Castle Gap, A Novel of the West by Ben Douglas. Sunstone Press, 1984. Danger, love, treasure-hunting and history are all in this Western gothic set in Texas in 1912, where life on a ranch is complicated by intrigue and mystery in the search for Maximilian's treasure.

Pike's Peak: A Mining Saga by Frank Waters. Swallow Press, 1987. This novel is based on a trilogy Waters published in the 1930s, using the same themes and characters. It is an account of the Rogier family, who moved to the Pike's Peak, Colorado, region soon after the Civil War, and it covers the mining boom and the union organization of the miners.

The Old Timers in the Sangre de Cristo by Jim Miller. Dell, 1988. Near Taos, New Mexico, a fortune lay hidden in the Sangre de Cristo Mountains, deep in hostile Apache country. The only people brave enough—or crazy enough—to attempt to find it and bring it out were two tough old gunfighters.

Maximilian's Gold by Gordon D. Shirreffs. Fawcett, 1988. A Civil War veteran named Dave Hunter searches for the legendary lost treasure of Maximilian, ill-fated emperor of Mexico. The treasure is somewhere near Horsehead Crossing on the Pecos River in West Texas, and Hunter must deal with the Mescalero Apache ahead of him, and the murderous bounty hunters following him.

The Treasure of Rudolfo Fierro by St. George Cooke. Doubleday, 1990. After the Mexican Revolution, General Pancho Villa's bloodthirsty right-hand man, Colonel Rudolfo Fierra, was rumored to have shipped a trainload of stolen treasure to Deming, New Mexico, and to have buried it nearby. In 1923, eight years later, six men, each with a piece of a map showing the treasure's location, were in Deming plotting to get the other five pieces.

Pinto and Sons by Leslie Epstein. Houghton Mifflin, 1990. Set in 1846 against the backdrop of the California Gold Rush. A young man named Pinto, thrown out of Harvard Medical School for an unfortunate anesthesia accident, goes to northern California where he helps discover the Neptune Mine and tutors his "sons," children of the Modoc Indians who are virtual slaves to the gold mine.

The Walking Sands by Gordon D. Shirreffs. Fawcett, 1990. Sequel to *Maxmilian's Gold* (Fawcett, 1988). Dave Hunter and his partner Ash Mawson hear a story of buried treasure beneath the sands of an old mission church from a man who staggered into their desert camp. But there are others who are interested in the buried treasure, and are willing to kill for it.

What Law There Was by Al Dempsey. Tor Books, 1991. The 19th century gold camp of Bannock, Montana, was crowded with every type of humanity—good and bad—and growing rapidly. They needed a sheriff. The lawman they selected was Henry Plummer, a notorious gunman/outlaw who would organize an efficient and ruthless gang to terrorize and plunder the region.

Honor at Daybreak by Elmer Kelton. Doubleday, 1991. Caprock, Texas, was a sleepy cow town until oil was discovered in the 1920s. Suddenly thousands of people poured in seeking their fortune—some were honest, many were not.

Paint the Wind by Cathy Cash Spellman. Dell, 1991. Fancy was born Francoise Deverell of the Deverells of Louisiana. In Spellman's romantic novel, she is swept from her family's Louisiana plantation during the Civil War to a wide-open Colorado mining town. There Fancy used her beauty to strike it rich.

The American River by Gary McCarthy. Bantam Books, 1992. From the *Rivers West* series. John Augustus Sutter came to the wild California country destined to build an empire at the confluence of the Sacramento and the American rivers. But while Sutter followed his fortunes, the ill-fated Donner party had become mired in the deadly grip of winter in the Sierra Nevada.

Bluefeather Fellini by Max Evans. University Press of Colorado, 1993. Bluefeather Fellini was born in New Mexico in 1918, the son of an Indian mother and an Italian father. Although he would be a cardsharp, a World War II soldier, and a salesman, his calling was the earth. He became a prospector, roaming the Southwest with a humorous spirit guide, returning often to Taos, the home of his Pueblo Indian mother.

Goldtown by Rita Cleary. Sunstone Press, 1996. In 1867 in the mining boomtown of Varina, Montana, an ex-Confederate army captain and professional gambler searched for the woman he once loved. He found her as a good woman who was not quiet respectable. She was also the object of a violent man's lust, a man whose jealousy of the captain turned to obsessive hatred.

Sierra by Richard S. Wheeler. Forge, 1996. Against the backdrop of the California Gold Rush of 1849, two adventurers sought their fortune in the gold camps of the Sierra Nevada. The settings include isolated gold camps, the fever jungles of Panama, and the raucous new city of San Francisco. Spur Award from Western Writers of America.

Shorty Harris, or the Prince of Gold by William H. Bevis. University of Oklahoma Press, 1999. The story of a legendary desert prospector who spent his whole life searching for gold and, when he found it, gave it away and in 1934 died broke. The novel begins during the gold rush of 1849, and the settings include the Nevada boom towns of Rhyolite and Harrisburg, and Death Valley.

The Curse of Dunbar's Gold by Johnny D. Boggs. Avalon, 1999. A fortune in stolen gold had been lost in the mountains of the Wyoming territory for four years. An escaped convict, wrongfully accused of having taken part in the robbery, and a woman whose father was murdered because he may have found the gold, were captured by the killer and his gang and forced to lead them to the treasure. But there was a terrifying legend that a spirit guarded the stolen gold and would kill those who sought it—the curse of Dunbar's gold.

Sun Mountain: A Comstock Memoir by Richard S. Wheeler. Forge, 1999. A young man named Henry Stoddard drifted west to Virginia City, Nevada, in the 1860s and became a reporter on the fabled *Territorial Enterprise.* Among his acquaintances was a young fellow reporter named Sam Clemens, who would later become Mark Twain. There were also visionaries, mining titans, speculators, and bankers who collectively deluged the world with silver and gold during this heady period.

Treasure of the Templars: A Western Story by Tim Champlin. Five Star, 2000. While evacuating an ancient Scottish castle in 1897, archaeologist Roddy McGinnis discovered a journal written a member of the Knights Templar entrusted with concealing their treasure horde. The Templar had taken it to what is now the Southwestern United States. The journal pointed to its exact location, and McGinnis set out to recover the treasure.

Wayfaring Stranger by Tim Champlin. Five Star, 2000. Champlin tells the story of the California Gold Rush by following the routes three different parties took to the gold fields. The first route was around Cape Horn at the tip of South America, the second was by sternwheeler through the Gulf of Mexico and across the Isthmus of Panama, and the third was overland by wagon train. The lives of the primary characters on each route were entwined before their journey, and the story comes together when they meet in California.

Discovery Tree: A Western Novel by Glen Onley. Sunstone Press, 2001. Young Ben Logan, his family lost in the Civil War, sold his Texas ranch and headed to Fort Union in the New Mexico territory, where he eventually bought a ranch. He scaled Mount Baldy in Moreno Valley and found a Ponderosa pine with the word DISCOVERY freshly carved in its bark and streambed sediment piled beside a nearby creek. In the spring, Ben and two partners returned and struck gold. When the Colfax County War erupted, Ben's ranch was targeted.

Rivers of Stone by Robert Pruitt. Sunstone Press, 2002. A mining engineer and his buddy search Utah's deserts and canyon country for diamonds from a lost mine.

Pecos Queen by Barbara Spencer Foster. Sunstone Press, 2003. Grace Shockey, a spoiled Texas girl, finds herself a reluctant inhabitant of a mining town in the Sangre de Cristo Mountains north of Santa Fe, New Mexico, where her father has taken a job at the mine. When the miners go on strike, Grace is pulled between her father, who doesn't join the striking miners, and her friend Jimmy, who has sympathy for the workers.

Vengeance Valley by Richard S Wheeler. Pinnacle Books, 2004. A down-on-his-luck miner discovers gold beneath a Sisters of Charity miners' hospital, a discovery that pits him against ruthless mining barons. Spur Award from Western Writers of America.

Rocks in My Bed by Craig Nettleton. Sunstone Press, 2007. When the granddaughter of an elderly outlaw asks Philip Habib, an Arab American private investigator, to find the source of her grandfather's money, he encounters the legend of the Lost Adams Diggings. His request for help from a female ranger intern at the Malpais National Monument in the lava beds of New Mexico leads to more than information. A skinhead biker becomes convinced that Habib and his friend, an alcoholic geologist, are members of a terrorist cell who are looking for nuclear materials for a dirty bomb in the uranium country in Cibola County. His misplaced patriotism escalates into violence.

SELECTED REVIEWS

The Travels of Jaimie McPheeters
by Robert Lewis Taylor
Doubleday, 1958

In 1848 the discovery of gold at Sutter's Fort, engulfed by present-day Sacramento, California, marked the opening of the first great American gold rush. In 1849, around 90,000 aspiring millionaires left their homes, farms, and businesses behind to seek their fortunes in California. Two of those were Dr Sardius McPheeters and his thirteen-year-old son, Jaimie.

Looking back from an older age, Jaimie narrates their adventures. His account is fleshed out by the letters and journals of his erudite father, providing counterpoint to Jaimie's sometimes judgmental observations. The plot is an off-told tale, except for the beginning and the ending, refined by the author's use of humor, subtlety, and charm.

The story begins in Louisville, Kentucky, the home of the McPheeters family. Dr. McPheeters was a Scotsman, a graduate of the University of Edinburgh, and a doctor in very good standing, medically speaking, but with a weakness for gambling and alcohol. Because of his gambling, he was deeply in debt. He became excited about the gold fields in California after reading Joseph E. Ware's *Immigrant Guide to California*, so when a number of his creditors banded together with the intention of serving an attachment, he and Jaimie skipped town in May of 1849 and headed for the gold fields of California.

In Independence, Missouri, they joined the "Beaver Company," a group that banded together and hired a trail guide for the trek west. On the trail they endured severe hardships, testing both body and spirit. There were long, dry stretches of prairie, with its scarcity of water. Jaimie was captured and held for ransom by the Pawnee. The company was attacked by a Crow war party. In Utah, they had to contend with the dreaded Danites. But they eventually reached beautiful California. On May 9, 1859, Dr. McPheeters wrote in his journal that they had at last arrived in the Sacramento Valley. The weather was mild, there was grass, and there was water.

. They camped on a branch of the Feather River, near some other emigrants, not far from a collection of huts called Marysville, where the Yuba came into the Feather. Sixty miles farther down, the latter ran into the Sacramento, and the town of Sacramento lay about twenty miles below that. They were deep in the middle of the diggins. Miners were strung out up and down all the streams, because gold was supposed to be there, and in canyons, gulches and ravines.

Jaimie and his father give a good recounting of gold mining in the Sierras during this period. They first used a gold washer with a sieve, then a cradle, upgraded to a Long Tom, and finally, seventy feet of sluice boxes.

They experienced anger and confrontation when their claim was jumped and their cradle stolen by a bullying Frenchman named Le Chat and his gang of ruffians. There was the joy of a near strike, when Jaimie found a ravine with large chunks of gold visible in the crevices of the walls. And then there was disappointment and dejection when, about the time their claim played out, they were swindled out of their money by a pair of grifters who sold them a salted claim.

This familiar but highly entertaining plot is bookended by two defining episodes; the first sets the stage for much of the plot, and the second rings down the curtain. En route to Independence, Jaimie fell off a riverboat and was captured by John Murrel, a Tennessee highwayman (based on John Murrell, a mid-1800s bandit sometimes called "The Land Pirate" who operated along the Mississippi River stealing slaves, among other depredations)) who usually killed his victims. Jaimie used his wits and escaped, but Murrel—an old man, tall and sallow, dressed in gamblers black, extruding evil—reappeared several times in the plot to make life perilous for the boy.

In the final episode, Dr. McPheeters and Jaimie left the company and journeyed to San Francisco. Their existence there was hand-to-mouth. They did day labor, ran a pitiful sundry stand on the street, and Dr. McPheeters practiced some medicine. People knew he was a doctor, but didn't take him seriously because he had returned to the bottle. This episode wends its way to a satisfying, albeit sad, conclusion to the story.

Into this plot Taylor infuses many memorable characters; chief among them are the stalwarts of Beaver Company.

Our narrator, Jaimie McPheeters, was a natural-born liar who could spin out a whopper without even thinking. His father said he was "basically fine, plenty of common sense, good bone structure, but [without] an ounce of learning capacity. Head's solid concrete, more like a gorilla than a human." Jaimie was also a smart-aleck. When his father tried to teach him Latin, Jaimie said, "I'm not apt to be transacting business with dead Romans, so why bother?" His father explained slowly, "Latin is the basis for our own richly eloquent language of English." "Oh well, them," responded Jaimie, smartly, "in that case, hand me the book. I hadn't realized we might switch back." But Jaimie's quick wit and fast tongue served him well on his California odyssey.

Dr. McPheeters, despite his weakness for strong drink and gambling, and his windy dissertations on any subject imaginable, was the glue that held Beaver Company together. His leadership was imbedded in a great enthusiasm for the journey and for the search for gold, and his bubbling optimism, which was contagious. On August 12, 1859, on a particularly tough stretch of the Oregon Trail approaching Chimney Rock, he wrote to his wife Melissa:

> I write from an exuberance of spirits, occasioned by the fact of everything proceeding so splendidly. The trail, while not actually improving, and even deteriorating in some trifling respects (the wheels now sinking into the sand to a distance of ten inches), still is passable. The oxen, though not refreshed to the point of rambunctiousness (some numbers of them dropping by the wayside from time to time), continue to pull the wagons with commendable zeal, considering the absence of both grass and good water. . . . Ahead lies gold, gold to wallow in, to fling out of the carriage as one proceeds (with credit restored) over the streets of Louisville. By Fort Laramie, only a comparatively brief distance up the trail, we shall have gone halfway! After that it is only a pleasant stroll across a few deserts, some salt flats, and then the Rocky Mountains. Could any prospect be more enticing!

Other members of Beaver Company who stayed together and made the entire journey were the Kissels, Jennie Brice, Henry Coe, and their trail guide, Buck Coulter.

Matt Kissel was "about three pounds heavier than an ox, standing six and a half feet, with mild, clear-blue eyes, and a half-smile on his face." He and his family were farmers, drawn into gold mining only because the trip used up their resources. Jennie Brice was an eighteen or nineteen-year old-girl who was a captive of John Murrel when Jaimie became his prisoner. Dr. McPheeters observed, "This girl Jennie is as fresh and sparkling as a rosebud, . . . [but] the lovely petals are protected by a thorn. Masked over by an innocent smile, she has a caprice of steel." Jaimie considered her just plain bossy. Henry Coe was a wealthy Englishman who wore white kid gloves, striped trousers, and a black coat. Henry was an unlikely hero who would save the company's mining claim from the villainous Le Chat, and ultimately ensure the success of the expedition.

In a novel of unlikely heroes, Buck Coulter stands out as a man of the West who knew how to live by its rules. As described by Dr. McPheeters, he was " a paragon of trail lore, . . . who was hired in the dual roles of hunter and trail 'boss.' I find him a tolerable companion though gruff and unsuggestible, even something of a tyrant in his way. There can be no question that he fancies his knowledge of pioneering to exceed that of the Almighty himself . . ." But Coulter would get them through to California, saving their lives numerous times, as in Jaimie's narration of his rescue from the Pawnee:

> I must have drifted off to sleep; when I woke up, smelling something wrong, bright starlight winked down through the smokehole. Outside, the camp was deathly still; then I heard a horse whinney. For some reason, my heart began to thump and I made to sit up. But a rough hand fastened over my mouth.
>
> "Quiet, quiet."
>
> It wasn't any more than a hiss. I knew the voice, but I couldn't find him in the dark. Then he shifted into the starlight, soft as a snake, and it was Coulter, right enough. Even here I could see the old sardonic look on his face. No matter what he did, he seemed to despise you for doing it.
>
> "What . . . ?" I started, but he clapped his hand on my mouth again. He didn't do it easy, either; the palm hit me like a slat.
>
> "Raise up slow and careful—don't bump anything."
>
> Then I thought, by George we're not alone in here, and at that second I saw Sick from Blackberries [one of his Indian captors] sitting up and watching us from across the tent. I could make out his eyes shining, a kind smile on his face.
>
> I gasped, pointing, "Look out!"
>
> Coulter's voice had its usual sting. "He won't mind—there ain't any way for him to move his head without it falling off."

Then there were the villains. In addition to Murrel and Le Chat, already mentioned, their was Brother Muller, a brutish Mormon, built like a gorilla, who developed a lust for Jennie during the company's stopover in Salt Lake City. He was thoroughly whipped by Matt Kissel in a public wrestling match, but with the dreaded Danites he followed the company when they resumed their journey. Again, Coulter, with his friend Jim Bridger, protected them, and saved Jennie from a terrible fate.

Robert Lewis Taylor's lines are full of the flavors and odors of St. Louis, Independence, the Oregon Trail, Indian camps, frontier forts, Mormon Utah, the California gold camps, and San Francisco. Though largely forgotten, this Pulitzer Prize winning novel is still enormously readable.

The Travels of Jaimie McPheeters was the basis for a television series in 1963-1964, with the same title.

The Treasure of the Sierra Madre
by B. Traven
Knopf, 1935

B. Traven, who wrote in German and translated his own work into English, guarded his identity his whole life. Though his life is shrouded in mystery, it's known that he lived his later years in Mexico, and had a love for the country and the people.

A recurring theme in his work is the exploitation of working men, of forgotten men and underdogs. His major work is *The Caoba Cycle*, a series of six novels about the violent conditions that led to the Mexican Revolution of 1910.

The Treasure of the Sierra Madre is his best known work. The plot has three down-on-their-luck Americans hunting for gold in the rugged eastern Sierra Madre region of Mexico. Traven shows basically decent men being slowly transformed, brutalized, and finally turned against each other—pushed on by their growing lust for gold.

Dobbs was a derelict living in Tampico, surviving on handouts from fellow Americans. He drifted to the oil fields in Tuxpam, where he and his new-found friend Curtin were cheated out of their wages after a near slave-labor stint with a contractor.

Back in Tampico, they met Howard, an old man who had prospected for gold many years. He had been a member of a party that searched for the famed La Mina Agua Verde, the Green Water mine, which lay along the border of Arizona and the Mexican state of Sonora. He spoke of fabulous wealth that could come from the wilds of Mexico, but he also warned them of the effect gold can have on men:

> Anyway, . . . gold is a very devilish sort of a thing, believe me, boys. In the first place, it changes your character entirely. When you have it your soul is no longer the same as it was before. No getting away from that. You may have so much piled up that you can't carry it away; but, bet your blessed paradise, the more you have, the more you want to add, to make it just that much more. Like sitting at roulette. Just one more turn. So it goes on and on and on. You cease to distinguish between right and wrong. You can no longer see clearly what is good and what is bad. You lose your judgment. That's what it is.

Dobbs and Curtin paid little attention to the old man's warning. Curtin hadn't come to Mexico to work in the oil fields; he came to search for gold. Dobbs was ready to try something different and Howard's stories excited him. And Howard, though he was old, and decrepit in the other two's opinion, was eager to go prospecting again.

They became partners and journeyed to the Sierra Madre. Howard knew what he was doing; the other two knew nothing about prospecting or mining. The old man told them:

> We have to go where there is no trail. We have to know where we can be positive that no surveyor or anybody who knows something about mining has ever been before. The best spots are those where you feel sure that anybody who is paid for his job would be afraid to go and would not think it worth while to risk his hide for the salary he gets. Only at such spots is there a chance that we might find something.

So they went deep into the mountains, miles west of Durango, to a crater like valley, where Howard found pay dirt. But the mountains were not friendly to the miners:

> One should not forget that though the Sierra Madre is in
> fact a sister to the Rocky Mountains, it is in the tropics. There is no
> winter, no snow and ice, and consequently all plants, shrubs, insects,
> and animals keep alive all the time, and very much alive at that.
> There were mosquitoes biting day and night. The more you
> sweat, the more they like sucking your blood. There were tarantulas
> the size of a man's hand, and spiders the same size, not very pleasant
> to have for permanent neighbors. And then there was the real genuine
> pest, a little yellowish-reddish scorpion the sting of which kills you
> within fifteen hours.

And there were other tribulations. A mysterious stranger followed Curtin to the camp after a supply trip to the nearest village. Uninvited and even threatened with death, he wouldn't leave. But there were other more threatening visitors.

All of Mexico was plagued by bandits, mostly mestizos and Indians who were so bold and ruthless that, when captured, they were quickly executed without a trial. Fifteen of them found the mine:

> All the men carried guns on their hips—guns of different types and
> calibers. Four men carried shotguns, and two had rifles. All were
> in rags and had not washed or shaved for weeks; for months they
> had had no haircuts. Most of them wore the usual sandals; a few
> had boots, but ripped open and with torn soles; some had on leather
> pants like those worn by cowboys or cattle-farmers. All carried cheap
> woolen blankets over their shoulders.

> They were a motley lot, but their purpose was deadly.

> Then there was the hellish task before the miners of getting their pay

dirt safely back to Durango. But the worst problem they faced was the changes the gold made in the partners, primarily Dobbs.

The three had never been close friends; they were joined together only for the pursuit of wealth. They became troubled by the miserable life they led, and began to distrust each other. As Howard had predicted, the lust for gold slowly transformed basically decent men and turned them against each other. Howard watched relations between his young partners disintegrate. Dobbs lost control over his actions and became a man capable of murder. Curtin tried to be a voice of reason, but wouldn't be intimidated by Dobbs. Howard had seen it all before. This is a grand adventure story, but it's also a brilliant psychological study of human greed.

Traven lived much of his life in Mexico and respected the Indians and Mestizos. But he castigates the Catholic Church in Mexico for its power over them. He was an anarchist who believed even the state is better able to rule its citizens than the church, which is more interested in money than justice. He even, to a degree, excused the deadly bandits who, with their war-cry "Long live Jesus," murdered and plundered across the country. He argues in his exposition that they were trained from childhood by their church for this life, doing and thinking only what they had been taught—only the cruelest and the bloodiest and the most repulsive parts of the Catholic religion.

Traven's novels are revered in Mexico. Noted Chicano author Rudolfo Anaya wrote, "The cantineros and taxi drivers in Mexico City know about him as well as the cantineros of Spain knew Hemingway; or they claim to." But his work wasn't a commercial success in the United States. He was largely unknown until the late 1960s and early 1970s, when a concerted effort was made to publish most of his novels.

His American popularity received a boost from the 1948 film version of *The Treasure of the Sierra Madre*, which secured Oscars for John Huston for direction and screenplay, and for Walter Huston, who received the Best Supporting Actor award for his portrayal of the old prospector Howard. It's the only film for which a father and his son have won Oscars. Humphrey Bogart as Dobbs and Tim Holt as Curtin also gave memorable performances. The film and the novel are recognized today as classics.

11

TRANSPORTATION IN THE EARLY WEST: PEOPLE, FREIGHT, AND MAIL

INTRODUCTION

In the mid-1800s the settlement of the West began in earnest. With the discovery of gold in California in 1848, and subsequently in other regions, towns started dotting the Western landscape almost overnight. These towns needed to connect with each other, and with Eastern populations and markets. The need was met by riverboats, overland freight wagons, stagecoaches, the Pony Express, and finally the railroad.

Beginning with the Lewis and Clark Expedition, the Missouri River provided access to the West. Trappers and traders paddled dugout canoes and bullboats in and out of the depths of the wilderness. Thousands of prospectors heading west to the gold and silver strikes in California, Nevada, and the Rocky Mountain regions rode the hundreds of steamboats that plied its waters.

Other major Western rivers served as channels for transportation and commerce. Rivermen traveled into Oklahoma on the Arkansas; the Army used Colorado River steamboats to supply their forts in the Southwest; the Sacramento and the San Joaquin carried the Forty-Niners on their search for gold. The Columbia, 1,210 miles of it through the Pacific Northwest, transported trappers, prospectors, settlers, and freight that were second in number only to the Missouri. These rivers and others floated a broad array of vessels providing transportation for westward expansion, including canoes, flatboats, keelboats, and steamboats—each uniquely suited to its task.

Bull whackers and muleskinners drove their lumbering wagons

throughout the West, hauling goods overland across the Great Plains and from riverboat ports and, later, from railroad terminals, to supply army posts and frontier merchants. Lucrative army contracts helped develop this capability. The freighters' wagons rolled across the plains into the early 20th Century.

Just as the army contracts had subsidized the freight haulers, U. S. Government mail contracts were used to develop overland stage routes. The first major contract for an overland route was awarded to John Butterfield in 1857. His contract was to transport U. S. Mail "from the Mississippi River to San Francisco, California, as follows: From St. Louis, Missouri, and Memphis, Tennessee, converging at Ft. Smith, Arkansas, thence to El Paso, Tucson, Fort Yuma, Los Angeles and San Francisco, California, and back twice a week . . ." Butterfield established way stations about 20 miles apart, though the distances ranged from as few as nine to as much as sixty miles. He had 250 Concord coaches at each end of the route, and as many as 1,800 horses and mules. The first westbound mail arrived in San Francisco in just under twenty-four days.

The Civil War forced suspension of Butterfield operations on the Southern Route, and personnel and equipment were transferred to the more northerly Central Route. Other operators, including the Leavenworth & Pike's Peak Express Company, the Central Overland, California, & Pike's Peak Express (the company actually painted C. O. C. & P. P. on their stagecoach doors), Wells Fargo, and the Holladay Overland Mail and Express would establish various routes to provide safe and dependable transportation from East to West and from West to East. But by 1869 the coming of the telegraph and railroad brought an end to the transcontinental stage routes.

The freighting and express firm of Russell, Majors, and Waddell established a brief (April 1860 to October 1861) rapid mail delivery service from Missouri to California that will forever be remembered as an exciting piece of American history—the fabled Pony Express. The pony riders cut the delivery time from St. Joseph to Sacramento to ten days, half of the time by overland stagecoach. But the Pony Express service ended after 18 months, when the overland telegraph became operational.

The event that cemented the connection between east and west was the completion of the transcontinental railroad. It became a reality on May 10, 1869, when the tracks of the Union Pacific, spanning westward from Omaha, met those of the Central Pacific, running eastward from San Francisco, at Promontory, Utah. This magnificent feat was accomplished against incredible odds. Rails had to be shipped to the Central Pacific by sea from the east coast, whereas the Union Pacific had to ship crossties from Wisconsin to cross the Great American Desert. On the western segment, construction crews had to tunnel through the high Sierras, while those coming west contended with hostile Plains Indians. Roughly 25,000 workers were used by the two lines, primarily Irish immigrants by the Union Pacific and Chinese laborers by the Central Pacific.

Of the many novels written about riverboats, freighting, stagecoaches, the Pony Express, and the railroad, I have chosen two for review that are representative as well as fine reading. Janet Holt Giles' *Six-Horse Hitch* (Houghton Mifflin, 1969) is the story of a young stagecoach driver who drove the nineteen hundred miles of the Overland line. It is packed with meticulously researched detail on staging, as well as the history of the industry. *The U. P. Trail* (Harper and Brothers, 1918) is a Zane Grey novel of romance, treachery, and captivity set against the background of the building of the Union Pacific Railroad.

READER'S GUIDE

Heart's Desire by Emerson Hough. Macmillan, 1905. The railroad changed the West. This is the story of its effect on one little settlement.

Vanguards of the Plains: A Romance of the Old Santa Fe Trail by Margaret McCarter. Harper and Brothers, 1917. A romantic novel of the Santa Fe Trail, encompassing its clearing, building, and defense.

The Pony Express by Henry James Forman and Walter Woods. Grosset and Dunlap, 1925. A romantic adventure novel about the Pony Express, based on the question of California joining the Union or remaining a separate empire. The protagonist is John Weston, who helped secure California for the United States, and the villain is the notorious Jack Slade. Source for the 1925 film.

Fighting Caravans by Zane Grey. Harper and Brothers, 1929. With help from his friend Kit Carson, a youngster drove supplies up and down the Santa Fe Trail, fighting Indians and a mean and dangerous man set on raiding his wagons.

Trouble Shooter by Ernest Haycox. Popular Library, 1936. A trouble shooter for the Union Pacific Railroad had to contend with hostile Indians, outlaws, and power-hungry opponents of the line as he struggled to get tracks laid across a thousand miles of rugged terrain. Source for the 1939 film "Union Pacific."

Buckskin Empire by Henry Sinclair Drago. Doubleday Doran, 1942. An overland freight hauler fights against the advance of the railroad into his territory. His daughter falls in love with the railroad builder and his right-hand man defects in protest over the thugs he has hired. Basis for the 1942 film "Buckskin Frontier."

Long Storm, by Ernest Haycox. Little, Brown, 1946. Riverboat captain Adam Musick was the owner of the only independent vessel in Portland, Oregon. During the "Long Storm," or Civil War, he resolved to protect his independence and his position in the port. But as gold prospectors poured into Portland, Confederate agents came with them, and Musick immediately detected the danger to the Union.

You Rolling River by Archie Binns. Charles Scribner's Sons, 1947. Set in Astoria in the Pacific Northwest at the mouth of the Columbia River following the opening of the Pacific Territories in the 1800s. The river shapes the lives of a sea pilot and his family.

Jubilee Trail by Gwen Bristow. Crowell, 1950. In 1844, when California was still under Mexican rule, a young woman and her trader husband transported goods by mule team from California to Santa Fe, along the Jubilee Trail. Source for the 1955 film.

One Way to Eldorado by Hollister Noble. Doubleday, 1954. A railroad trouble shooter had to fight blizzards, avalanches, and man-made destruction 8,000 feet up on the Great Western's stretch of rail over Eldorado Pass.

West with the Missouri by Cliff Farrell. Random House, 1955. An adventure novel of the Montana gold fields and the steamboats that the prospectors took to get there.

Steamboat Up the Missouri by Dale White (Marian T. Place). Viking

Press, 1958. A young readers novel about an apprenticed riverboat pilot. Spur Award from Western Writers of America.

Last Stage West by Frank Bonham. Dell, 1959. A story centered on the last stage journey west before the outbreak of the Civil War.

Bitter Trail by Elmer Kelton. Ballantine Books, 1962. A teamster whose wagons hauled cotton from Mexico into Texas became caught up in the Civil War that was raging throughout the South.

Cast a Long Shadow by Frank Bonham. Simon and Schuster, 1964. A novel that deals with the rivalry between two competing stage lines. Basis for the 1959 film.

The Muleskinner by Robert MacLeod. Fawcett, 1967. Because of his size and reputation, muleskinner Ben Davis was a target for every brawler on the frontier. Although only a fool would brace him in a fair fight, the killers who wanted him out of the way were anything but fools.

Texas Guns by Ray Hogan. Prestige Books, 1969. A southern teamster and his crew contracted to deliver a wagon train load of rifles to the Confederacy. But before they could deliver the guns, the war ended. With no buyer, the wagonmaster pointed his wagons toward Mexico and a violent revolution.

Bold Passage by Frank Bonham. Berkley, 1978. Bullwhackers and their freight wagons encounter hostile Indians and gunrunners on the Bozeman Trail.

The Builders by Jeanne Sommers. Dell, 1979. Sixth book in Dell's *The Making of America* series. In the 1860s those building the western end of the transcontinental railroad—Leland Stanford, Collis P. Huntington, Mark Hopkins, and Charles Crocker, known as "the Big Four" in railroad history—were impeded by private feuds, labor strife and sabotage until a mystery woman named Liberty Lee and her even more mysterious "friend" became involved in their high stakes race with the Union Pacific.

The Great Yellowstone Steamboat Race by Robert J. Steelman. Doubleday, 1980. On a six-day trip to deliver supplies to Fort Mahone, Alec Munro's reputation preceded him all along the banks of the Upper Missouri and Yellowstone Rivers: He was a stubborn Scot who piloted the fastest sternwheeler in the territory.

The Cherokee Trail by Louis L'Amour. Bantam Books, 1982. During the Civil War Mary Breydon's Virginia home was burned to the ground. Then her husband was killed on his way to Colorado for a new start. So Mary Breydon took his place and went west, to manage an isolated stagecoach station on the Cherokee Trail. Basis for a 1981 teleplay.

Pony Express by Donald Clayton Porter (house name). Bantam Books, 1983. As the threat of Civil War raged throughout the country, Pony Express rider Ted Henderson was chosen to deliver an important letter from President Lincoln to the commander-in-chief of the Union forces in the Pacific area. A great responsibility rested on the shoulders of this lone rider carrying the mail through bitter weather, treacherous terrain and hostile Indian country, relying only on himself and his horse.

Iron Trail by Tim Champlin. Ballantine Books, 1987. When the gold and silver boom swept over the Colorado Rockies, the Denver & Rio Grande line grappled with the Santa Fe Railroad for the right to build tracks through the vital Royal Gorge. An undeclared and historic rail war was underway.

Palo Pinto by G. Clifton Wisler. Zebra Books, 1987. From the *Texas Brazos* series. When the Ft. Worth & Western Railroad began operating in Texas in 1888, it extended the frontier rapidly. Settlers poured into the town of Palo Pinto, on the Brazos River. But rails linking Texas to Kansas City and Chicago spelled the end of the cattle trails, and the settlers challenged the freedom of the open range.

Union Pacific by Donald Clayton Porter (house name). Bantam Books, 1988. As the Union Pacific forged its way toward Promontory, Utah, President Andrew Johnson chose legendary scout Ted Henderson to protect the line and its construction crews. Henderson recruited the best men on the frontier to help him contend with hired guns and renegade Indians determined to stop the building of the railroad.

Shotgun and Sagebrush by Jim Miller. Fawcett, 1989. The driver on the St. Louis to Denver stage was transporting a load of greenhorns on a trip west. He would find out a lot about his passengers before his dangerous drive was over.

Esmeralda by G. Clifton Wisler. Walker, 1989. In 1880 trains carrying Colorado gold, Texas cattle, and settlers turned the far western Kansas settlement of Esmeralda into a boomtown. But along with the good came the bad and the ugly—thieves who would prey on Esmeralda's prosperity.

The Pony Express War by Gary McCarthy. Bantam Books, 1992. From McCarthy's *Derby Man* series. In 1860 the Pony Express deepened the divide between the North and the South. Depredations against the Express blamed on the Paiute were actually the treachery of white men engaged in a broader conflict.

Grayfox by Michael Phillips. Bethany House, 1993. A Christian novel from *The Journals of Corrie Belle Hollister* series. When the stories of the first Pony Express riders hit California's newspapers, young Zack Hollister jumped at the chance to get away from home and be independent. But he found that the Pony Express held much more than adventure, independence, and great pay, It was a challenging and dangerous occupation.

Cody's Ride by Stan Wiseman. Walker, 1993. Set in Missouri in 1860, this is the story of a Pony Express Rider who chases a brutal outlaw and a beautiful captive as they head for Texas. The novel contains a detailed portrayal of the Pony Express.

The Red River by Frederic Bean. Bantam Books, 1997. Flatboat pilots Eli McBee and Seth Booker left the rough-and-tumble life of the Mississippi River, headed across the High Plains and into the uncharted wilderness, their sights set on the rich, fur-trapping lands along the banks of the Red River. But as they navigated its treacherous currents, they learned why the Red River ran the color of blood.

The Wagon Wars by James A. Ritchie. Walker, 1997. When Ben Hawkins and his friends started a freight operation with some old wagons, their competitor wasn't about to let anyone take business away from him.

Riding the Wind by Brix McDonald. Avenue, 1998. A young readers novel, the first in a series that introduces fifteen year old Carrie Sutton, living in Wyoming in 1860. At sixteen, she realizes her dream and becomes a Pony Express rider.

Pony Express Christmas by Sigmund Brouwer. Tyndale House, 2000. A Pony Express rider, despite the urgency of delivering the mail on time, stops to help a family in need.

Dark Voyage of the Mittie Stephens by Johnny D. Boggs. Five Star, 2004. This novel recreates the fateful February 1869 voyage of the Mittie

Stephens, a sidewheel steamboat bound from New Orleans to Jefferson, Texas. Its cargo includes a $100,000 payroll for the Federal barracks in Jefferson.

Whispering Smith by Frank Spearman. Sunstone Press, 2008. Origionally published in 1906. Whispering Smith, a troubleshooter for the railroad, went after an old friend who was wreacking havoc on the line's mountain division, burning bridges and holding up trains. The story is based on the true-life experiences of Joe LeFors, the famous Wyoming peace officer who trapped Tom Horn. Source for the 1949 film.

SELECTED REVIEWS

Six-Horse Hitch
by Janice Holt Giles
Houghton Mifflin, 1969

When the great transportation era on the Overland Trail began in 1859, the Missouri River was the jumping-off place to all the West. St. Joseph and Westport (now Kansas City) on the Missouri side of the river, Fort Leavenworth and Atchison on the Kansas side, were four of the most important towns in the history of the West.

A remarkable breed of men operated out of those towns. There was William Russell and Alexander Majors and William Waddell who combined to form the huge freight company of Russell, Majors and Waddell. There were dozens of other freight companies. In 1860; there were forty-one traders and freighters doing business out of Atchison alone.

And there was Ben Holladay, a wealthy freighter who would become the stagecoach king of the world.

Starr Fowler, the narrator in Janet Holt Giles' novel of these heady days of staging, was only nineteen when he climbed to the box of a mainline stage and threaded the reins of a six-horse hitch between his fingers. It was the summer of 1859 and he was at Fort Kearney, on the first leg of a long freight haul, working for his brother Matt, when he hired on as a relief driver with the Leavenworth & Pike's Peak Express, a line that belonged to Russell, Majors and Waddell. This was the beginning of a long career in which he would also drive for the Central Overland California & Pike's Peak Express, the Overland Stage Company, and Wells, Fargo & Company. Starr would also own a "home" station, where horses were changed and passengers fed, manage a division of the Overland, and, finally, in 1869 when the railroad killed the long overland routes, buy some Wells, Fargo surplus equipment and open his own stage line to the mining centers up in the mountains. During his career, Starr was virtually involved in every aspect of stagecoach transportation.

At Plumb Creek Station, just west of Fort Kearney, Nebraska, Starr met Ed and Emma Westmoreland, who ran the station. They had a nine-year-old daughter, Mary Buchanan, or Bucky, who adored Starr. Later, Emma's beautiful sister Bernie arrived from the East, and troubled Starr's dreams but would spurn him because he was a stage driver: "You're a reckless lot. All of you drink too much and you gamble too much and you're on the road too much." The two girls would be captured by the Sioux, and a major plot line concern's Starr's efforts to negotiate their return.

The period the novel covers is from 1859 through 1869, and the events and the actual characters who lived in the West during that time provide the framework for the plot. One historical personage who has a prominent role in the novel is Jack Slade.

Slade was the division manager at the Leavenworth & Pike's Peak Express who hired Starr and gave him a regular run from Fort Kearney to Plumb Creek. Slade told him, "Nothing on earth must ever stop the United States Mail," and Slade lived by that rule and was considered the best division agent on the line. When he shot and killed a drunken teamster for trying to borrow an old mud wagon from the stage line, his stock went up with the company for protecting their property.

When he was not drinking Slade was a gentleman, with a quiet courteous manner and a soft voice. But when he was drinking, he became wild and reckless. He eventually turned into a killer—killing for the pleasure of it. He killed twenty-six men in just three years, and had an inglorious end to his life. Jack Slade was, arguably, the original bad man of the West.

The essence of the novel, however, is Starr's narration about staging.

He gives us a history of the enterprise, from its beginning to its demise when the railroad came. He lovingly describes, in great detail, the coaches, with their gleaming paint, beautiful scrollwork and the lettering, straw-yellow running gear, a body slung on wide, heavy leather thoroughbraces instead of springs, and sides cambered up as "pretty and as graceful as the curves of a woman's hips . . . Nothing but a Clipper ship was ever as graceful as one of Abbot & Downing's coaches." The horses that pull the coaches get equal treatment:

> I moved around among them. They were the prettiest stock I'd ever seen. The wheelers were big fellows, running twelve hundred pounds at least. The swings were a little lighter, and the leaders, always the lightest of a team, were around eight hundred pounds. They weren't matched. It was several years before staging on the Overland got fancy enough for that. But they were fine horses.

Both horses and mules were used on different runs. Starr explained the difference:

> A mule is a critter and the best of them is not a particularly handsome animal. If you've worked with horses and mules all your life you get to where you either hate animals, or come to have a feeling for them almost like they were human beings. A mule has really got more sense than a horse. A horse will kill himself for you. A mule won't, not without a lot of punishment and then sometimes he'll die of the punishment without giving you an extra mile. In Indian country, I wouldn't want to bank on mules running long enough and hard enough to get me out of a scrape. Horses, on the other hand, will go till their hearts quit. But in heavy sand, pulling heavy loads, mules last better.

Few people realize that a stage company was a big operation. Starr tells us that Ben Holladay's Overland needed five hundred stages, about the same number of freight wagons, and five thousand horses, mules and oxen. There was an army of about 150 drivers, and about 300 hostlers and stock tenders.

There were fifty stations between Atchison and Denver, fifty-one between Denver and Salt Lake, and fifty-five between Salt Lake and Placerville.

At the beginning of Chapter 13, Starr invites readers to "Come ride with me," and takes us on a mile by mile, stop by stop trip from Atchson on the Missouri to Denver, a jolting trip of some nineteen hundred miles. The fare is $100 and you will be allowed thirty pounds of luggage free. There are three seats that hold nine passengers, The front seat, facing backwards, is the most comfortable. About a half hour out you will meet the inbound stage, an event you will look forward to on each leg. Somewhere along the way you will see a Pony Express rider, materializing from a small speck on the horizon into a lithe young man on a galloping horse, a picture that will sear into your memory. The stage will stop at swing stations, where you can get out and stretch your legs while the team is being changed. Within three minutes the stage will roll again. At home station stops, you will be served dinner and it will cost you fifty cents. Quality varies from station to station. At each home station, you will change drivers, and the stage will roll day and night. The trip is not easy on passengers.

> The passengers began piling out, looking like they'd been wallowing
> in mud. Summers are blistering hot on the plains and the inside of
> a stage was like a baking oven. Cram it full of people of different
> sizes and shapes, and it wasn't long till they were sweating so hard
> it was like they had been dunked in the river. Dust turned to mud
> almost as soon as it settled on them. The more they wiped at it, the
> more streaked it got. Add to that the natural dirt from several days'
> traveling without a bath, some whiskey fumes and food spills over
> their clothes, and it was the rare passenger who could emerge from a
> stage looking or smelling like a human being.

Starr's narration is at its best, however, when he is on the box, driving the stage, employing the skills required to handle a six-horse hitch.

> It is to be remembered that the driver of six horses holds three reins
> in each hand. The near horses of the team are those on the left side of

the hitch. The line to the near leader is the top line, the one between your first and middle fingers, in your left hand. The line to the near swing is next, between the middle and third fingers, and the line to the near wheel horse is the bottom line, between your third and little fingers. The same is true in your right hand, with the reins to the off horses. The horses are hitched as a team and they must work as a team, but the lines to each horse, held separately and worked separately, give a driver separate control of each individual animal. Directions are given to any horse in the team by means of slipping, or letting out his line, or by climbing, taking in the line. It is a very fine skill, requiring perfect muscular control of each finger of both hands. The driver sits on the right side of the box. The brake comes up tall and broad and he drives with his right foot always resting on it, because he drives almost as much with the brake as with the reins. When you use the brake, even a fraction of an inch, it slackens the lines slightly. The horses feel that slight slack before the lines are climbed and they are alerted to the tightening of the reins. They are ready for whatever the driver is going to ask of them.

Forbears of Starr Fowler have delighted readers since the publication of *The Kentuckians* (Houghton Mifflin, 1953), the first of Giles' *American Frontier* series, and in such works as *The Great Adventure* (Houghton Mifflin, 1967), *Hannah Fowler* (Houghton Mifflin, 1956), and *Johnny Osage* (Houghton Mifflin, 1956). *Six-Horse Hitch* is a dashing, romantic adventure of the spectacular era of American stagecoaching, a massive enterprise that overcame primitive roads, bad weather, highwaymen, and Indian ambushes to deliver passengers and mail on schedule.

The U. P. Trail
by Zane Grey
Harper and Brothers, 1918

The idea of a transcontinental railroad to connect California to the East was not considered feasible by most Americans as late as the 1850s. There were doubts that construction crews could overcome the physical challenges of the American West. There was the sheer distance, 2,000 miles of sparsely populated wilderness from Missouri to California. There was the dry and deadly desert to cross, and formidable mountain ranges, with snow-packed passes and steep river canyons, and the Indians, who had already taken their toll of advance survey parties. But with the help of federal loans and land grants, a handful of visionaries, entrepreneurs, engineers, and an army of Chinese, Irish, and Black laborers accomplished the improbable.

Against this background, Zane Grey wrote *The U. P. Trail*, a fictional account of the building of the eastern half of the railroad—the Union Pacific. It is a novel of romance, treachery, and captivity that revolves around Allie Lee, a young woman who survived an Indian massacre of a wagon train only to later be captured by the Sioux. She escaped her captors, then became a captive of the arch villain of the novel, a gambler named Durade who had taken her mother and Allie from Omaha to California. Allie's mother left Durade and, with Allie, was bound east on the wagon train when the Indians attacked and she was killed.

The protagonist is Warren Neale, a young surveyor and engineer who ran the particularly difficult surveys for the Union Pacific. Neale found Allie Lee following the Sioux massacre and, along with a grizzled trapper named Slingerland, nursed the young woman back to health and fell in love with her. He would twice lose her to the evil Durade, and her rescues from these abductions is the framework of the plot.

Allie Lee's tribulations and Neale's heroics are played out within the grand scale of the building of the Union Pacific, including the funding (the use of the "Credit Mobilier" which gave rise to one of the most serious political scandals in the history of the United States Congress), survey, and construction. Here is bit of narrative on the construction:

The engine puffed smoke and bumped the cars ahead, little by little as the track advanced; men on the train carried ties and rails forward, filling the front cars as fast as they were emptied; long lines of laborers on the ground passed to and fro, burdened going forward, returning empty-handed; the rails and the shovels and the hammers and the picks all caught the hot gleam from the sun; the dust swept up in sheets; the ring, the crash, the thump, the scrape of iron and wood and earth in collision filled the air with a sound rising harshly above the song and laugh and curse of men.

We follow the surveyors across the Wyoming hills as they run the line on into Utah, where they met the surveying party working in from the Pacific. We see the camps and towns that spring up and flourish, like mushrooms, in a single night as the railroad progresses westward. Here is Grey's Benton, east of Medicine Bow, six hundred and ninety-eight miles from Omaha:

The sun set, the twilight fell, the wind went down, the dust settled, and night mantled Benton. The roar of the day became subdued. It resembled the purr of a gorging hyena. The yellow and glaring torches, the bright lamps, the dim, pale lights behind tent walls, all accentuated the blackness of the night and filled space with shadows, like specters. Benton's streets were full of drunken men, staggering back along the road upon which they had marched in. No woman now showed herself. The darkness seemed a cloak, cruel yet pitiful. It hid the flight of a man running from fear; it softened the sounds of brawling and deadened the pistol-shot. Under its cover soldiers slunk away sobered and ashamed, and murderous bandits waited in ambush, and brawny porters dragged men by the heels, and young gamblers in the flush of success hurried to new games, and broken wanderers sought some place to rest, and a long line of the vicious, of mixed dialect, and of different colors, filed down in the dark to the tents of lust.

The story and the characters are fictional, but the building of the railroad was real.

The plot is played out with a host of interesting characters. There is Larry King, Neale's partner and friend, a gunfighter from Texas whose brother was the infamous King Fisher. Durade was a blue-blooded Spanish adventurer who did not love gold, but loved games of chance. General Lodge, Chief Engineer for the Union Pacific, had been a major-general in the just ended Civil War. Allison Lee, a railroad commissioner and crooked contractor, was revealed to be Allie Lee's father. Beauty Stanton was a beautiful woman who operated the largest and most popular saloon and brothel in Benton. And Ancliffe, a pale, slender English gentleman, who came from no one knew where, did not go to extremes in gambling or drinking, and was attached to Beauty Stanton. All these characters are somewhat stereotypical but nevertheless believable. Consider the gambler Place Hough (Grey had a way with names):

> . . . a gambler in black, immaculate in contrast to his companions, [Hough] had a white, hard, expressionless face, with eyes of steel and thin lips. His hands were wonderful. Probably they never saw the sunlight, certainly no labor. They were as swift as light, too swift for the glance of an eye. But when he dealt the cards he was slow, careful, deliberate.

Near the end of the novel, there is a tribute to the workers whose arduous labor made the Union Pacific a reality. When the last spike was driven at Promontory Point, Utah, on a summer day in 1869,

> Their hour was done. And they accepted that with the equanimity with which they had met the toil, the heat and thirst, the Sioux. A splendid, rugged, loquacious, crude, elemental body of men, unconscious of heroism. Those who had survived the five long years of toil and snow and sun, and the bloody Sioux, and the roaring camps, bore the scars, the furrows, the gray hairs of great and wild times.

Their work brought great changes to the West. The trapper Slingerland hated the railroad. Every ringing hammer blow had sung out the death-knell of his kind and the Indian. It spelled the end of wilderness. The grass of the of the plains would be burned, the forests blackened, the fountains dried up in the valleys, and the wild creatures of mountains driven and hunted and exterminated.

Zane Grey's highly successful writing career produced some eighty Westerns. His novels contain minute observations and powerful descriptions, vividness, sometimes mawkish dialogue, heroic manly values, strong female characters, overt racism against Mexicans, Orientals, and Blacks, and an overall Darwinist philosophy. *The U. P. Trail* certainly has all these characteristics. On the whole, however, it is an exciting novel, full of detail on one of the grandest undertakings in American history.

12

The Civil War in the West

Introduction

In the 1850s the slavery controversy in the United States reached its bloody climax in a civil war, a conflict that pitted the northern states of the American Union against the southern states in a violent war that raged for four years (1861-65).

In general, the West confronted the same wartime problems as Americans farther east: divided loyalties, subversive activities, shortages, and disruption of civil life.

The border states felt the brunt of the war. Missouri was critical to both sides but belonged to neither. In 1862 Union forces pressed Confederate defenders back into Arkansas. But in Western Missouri and Kansas, northern "Jayhawkers" and southern "Bushwhackers" forayed back and forth across the border, engaging in bloody guerrilla warfare that harassed the general population on both sides. William Clarke Quantrill was a notorious Confederate guerrilla leader during the war whose bushwhackers burned and looted Union strongholds in Kansas and Missouri, diverting thousands of Union troops. On August 21, 1863, Quantrill's Raiders pillaged Lawrence, Kansas, killing more than 150 civilians.

In Texas, Governor Sam Houston was a Unionist, whereas the majority sentiment was southern. Over his veto, the state legislature voted for succession and Houston was forced to resign.

In 1864 Union forces embarked upon the "Red River Campaign," as it became known, to open new sources of cotton for New England mills. Nearly 30,000 troops, supported by Union gunboats, began an ascent of the Red River in Texas. They were vigorously engaged by Confederate forces and sent back downriver. General Sherman called the campaign a disaster.

That titanic four-year struggle touched the remote Far West only lightly. The region generally remained loyal to the Union, with the notable exception of New Mexico.

New Mexico's sparse population was in the main southerners who would doubtless have joined the Confederacy if not for 1,200 federal troops garrisoned there. Confederate leaders decided to send an army into the Southwest. The loyal southerners there would support an expedition, they reasoned. If successful, this would give the South an outlet in the Pacific, room for slavery expansion, and access to mineral wealth needed for the war effort. The Confederate invaders briefly occupied Albuquerque and Santa Fe, but were then repulsed by Union forces, aided by California and Colorado volunteers. The Confederate invasion of New Mexico was the only major military activity in the Far West.

Two highly readable novels based on the Civil War in the West are reviewed in this section. They are Frank Gruber's *Quantrell's Raiders* (Ace, 1953), a story of guerrilla leader Willam Clark Quantrell (Gruber's spelling) and his depredations along the Missouri-Kansas border; and *Glorieta Pass* (Forge, 1999), P. G. Nagle's novel set in 1862, when Union troops, assisted by Colorado volunteers, turned back a Confederate attempt to march north from Texas along the Rio Grande and capture the gold fields around Pikes Peak, a victory called "the Gettysburg of the West."

READER'S GUIDE

The Dark Command by W. R. Burnett. Alfred A. Knopf, 1938. Set in Kansas in 1859 as the political tension between the states was growing, this is a fictional account of the depredations of Quantrill's Raiders. Source for the 1940 film.

Past All Dishonor by James M. Cain. Alfred A. Knopf, 1946. A young Confederate spy in Virginia City, the great mining town at the height of its boom period, became infatuated with one of the camp's sporting girls.

Incident at Sun Mountain by Todhunter Ballard. Houghton Mifflin, 1952. The "Golden Circle" was a group of Southern sympathizers who planned to seize the silver mines in Sun Mountain, Utah, and use the wealth to help finance the Confederate cause.

Company of Cowards by Jack Schaefer. Houghton Mifflin, 1957. During the Civil War, Union Army rejects were sent to the Western territories to fight Indians. Company Q had in it eight "cowards," each one court-martialed and convicted, each one hated by the world and by himself. Theirs was the worst war—they had to fight for the honor of the Union Army, and even harder for their own betrayed honor. Basis for the 1964 film "Advance to the Rear."

The Missourian by Brad Ward (Samuel L. Peebles). Macmillan, 1957. Dan and Rob Jory had ridden with Quantrill in the last bitter days of the Civil War. When the war ended, they returned home to a murderous Yankee occupation. The war wasn't really over for Dan and Rob; it was just beginning.

The Bushwhackers by Frank Gruber. Rinehart, 1959. An artist made an on-the-spot sketch of the horrifying scene when Quantrill's Raiders hit a small Kansas town. Long afterward, many Bushwhackers could be recognized by what the artist had drawn. Strangely, Phil Bokker found his own face pictured with the killers. But Bokker was not one of the raiders.

By Dim and Flaring Lamps by Alan LeMay. Harper and Brothers, 1962. Set in the time of the Jayhawkers and the bloody raids in Kansas and Missouri, of the closing of traffic on the Mississippi, and the fall of Fort Sumter, this is the story of mule drover Shep Daniels.and his own private war with the wealthy man who killed his father.

Desperation Valley by Todhunter Ballard. Macmillan, 1964. The Cherokees in Oklahoma split their support during the Cival War. This novel addresses the serious difficulties they faced because of this division after the war ended.

Long Way to Texas by Lee McElroy (Elmer Kelton). Doubleday, 1976. A long way from Texas, the remnants of the once-proud Second Texas Mounted Rifles were badly mauled by the Union Army and in retreat. Then they stumbled upon an incredible opportunity: the chance to seize ten wagonloads of munitions secretly stored in Mexico.

The Galvanized Reb by Robert J. Steelman. Doubleday, 1977. A "galvanized reb" was a Confederate soldier who switched sides in the Civil War. David Chantry renounced his family and the rebel cause, but was working as a Confederate spy to undermine the Union Army by stirring up the Oglala Sioux against the North.

Elkhorn Tavern by Douglas C. Jones. Holt, Rinehart and Winston, 1980. The central event of this novel is the battle of Pea Ridge in the Ozarks with Captain Phil Sheridan and a Federal scout called Wild Bill Hickok among the supporting characters.

Glorieta Pass by Gordon D. Shirreffs, Fawcett, 1984. This story of mountain man Quint Kershaw, his two sons and his lonely daughter is set in the New Mexico territory at the outbreak of the Civil War.

Dark Thicket by Elmer Kelton. Doubleday, 1985. Owen Danforth, a wounded Confederate soldier, returned home to Texas, to a place more savagely divided than the nation itself, with secessionist "home guards" and staunch Union loyalists conducting their own war. Against his will, Owen joined his father and a band of Union guerrillas in the dense thicket that afforded protection from the murderous home guards.

Woe to Live On by Daniel Woodrell. Holt, Rinehart and Winston, 1987. Set in the 1860s in Missouri and Kansas, this novel is about two young men who join the "Bushwhackers," irregulars who are loyal to the South. Basis for the 1999 film "Ride with the Devil."

Strange Company by Robert J. Conley. Pocket Books, 1991. Dhu Walker, a mixed-blood Cherokee, was fighting for the Confederacy in the Civil War by direction of his tribal elders. While attempting to escape during the battle of Pea Ridge in Arkansas, he fell into the hands of the sadistic Confederate officer "Old Ham" Early. Walker was compelled to fight another prisoner, Ben Franklin Lacey, an Iowa farm boy, for the amusement of their captor's troops. They were able to escape and conceived a plan to ally with others and ambush Early, who would be returning from Mexico with a troop escorting gold bound for the Confederate treasury.

Savage Frontier by Frank Burleson. Signet, 1995. In the East, tensions between the North and the South were pulling the country apart in 1854. But in the West, the Apache posed a different threat. First Lieutenant Nathanial Barrington was a vetran of the Indian Wars, but nothing had prepared him for the violence that flamed in the shadow of the gathering storm of the Civil War.

Burn, Missouri, Burn by Randal L. Greenwood. Forge, 1995. In Missouri during the Civil War, no one was safe. While the Kimbrough sons fought with Colonel Joe Shelby's Confederate Cavalry, the rest of the family was forced to fight off the depredations of occupying Federal troops.

Kansas, Bloody Kansas by Randal L. Greenwood. Forge, 1996. The War Between the States was no longer thought of as a glorious conflict; for the Kimbrough men it was a bitter struggle for honor and survival. For the Kimbrough women, it was a struggle to keep their hope and love alive.

Blood on the Plains by Robert Vaughan. St. Martin's Press, 1996. Two West Point cadets, sent by the President on a secret mission to the burning Kansas-Missouri border, would become enemies when caught up in the maelstrom of the Civil War.

South Wind by Don Coldsmith. Bantam Books, 1998. The Kansas territory was being torn apart by insurrection and the Civil War. During the war, abolitionists were set upon by Quantrill's savage raiders. And , after the war, new battle lines were drawn between Indian warriors and the army sent to destroy them.

The All-True Travels and Adventures of Lidie Newton by Jane Smiley. Alfred A. Knopf, 1998. The narrator, Liddy Newton, married Thomas Newton, an abolitionist, and moved with him to Kansas, a hotly contested territory in the 1850s slavery debate. There she encounterd slaves, slave owners, abolitionists, political activists, and all sorts of border ruffians, and found empathy among all of them. Spur Award. from Western Writers of America.

Into the Far Mountains by Fred Grove. Five Star, 1999. Confederate Captain Jesse Wilder was wounded at the battle of Shiloh and taken prisoner. He chose to fight Indians on the Plains as a "galvanized Yankee" rather than wait out the war in a Union prison, but his family and neighbors viewed this as treason. So Jesse joined other ex-Confederates in Mexico, helping the Juaristas to liberate their country from Maximilian, and then undertook two rescue missions for the U. S. Army.

Charissa of the Overland by Phyllis de la Garza. Royal Fireworks, 1999. A young adult novel. Based on the true story of the woman known as Charley Parkhurst, the novel focuses on Parkhurst's enlistment with Quantrill's Raiders, with the intention to kill the guerrilla leader to avenge the deaths of her husband, child, and a young Union soldier. Before her enlistment she was Charissa, but she disguised herself as a boy to carry out her plan.

Dark Trail by Hiram King. Leisure Books, 1999. When the Civil War ended, many men returned from the conflict to find their homes destroyed and their families scattered. Bodie Johnson, a black man, found that his family had been packed up like cattle and shipped west on a slave train. He set out to find whatever remained of them. Spur Award from Western Writers of America.

First Cherokee Rifles by Karl Lassiter. Kensington, 1999. In the American Civil War, the Cherokee Nation was torn between the Union and the Confederacy. The Ross Party, led by John Ross, aligned themselves with the Union. The Ridge Party, led by the fierce Cherokee warrior Stand Watie, were bound to the Confederacy.

Wildwood Boys by James Carlos Blake. William Morrow, 2000. "Bloody Bill" Anderson was the deadliest killer among Quantrill's Raiders, a band of "bushwhackers" who spread terror along the Kansas-Missouri border during the Civil War. This is the story of who he was and why he did such deeds.

The Guns of Valverde by P. G. Nagle. Forge, 2000. Sequel to *Glorieta Pass* (Forge, 1999). Union Captain Alastar O'Brien retook some heavy cannons captured by Confederate troops from Texas. He turned the Rebel column, but his unwitting general ordered a retreat. Then a young woman O'Brien loved inadvertently provided a Confederate officer with an opportunity to get the guns back.

Pray for Texas by Cotton Smith. Leisure, 2000. Rule Cordell was a gunfighter turned Confederate cavalryman fighting for his beloved Texas. Deep inside he was also fighting his abusive, tyrannical father, a Texas preacher. After General Lee surrendered, Cordell joined a band of guerrillas in a war they refused to abandon. Eventually, he faced his unrepentant father.

Galveston by P. G. Nagle. Forge, 2002. Nagle's sequel to *The Guns of Valverde* (Forge, 2000). Young Confederate soldier Jamie Russell returned home from Valverde to accompany his grieving sister, Emma, who lost a husband in battle, to their aunt's home in Galveston, Texas. The city was attacked by the Union Army, and Jamie took part in a Confederate plan to retake the city.

The Underground River by Jeanne Williams. Thorndike Press, 2004. The first of Williams' *Beneath the Burning Ground* trilogy. In "Bleeding Kansas" in the days leading up to the Civil War, the Ware family was caught between the Border Ruffians out of Missouri, and John Brown's abolitionists. The underground river in the title was a haven for a runaway slave who sought shelter with the Wares. But aiding a runaway was not only a very serious crime; it was one that divided the community.

Camp Ford by Johnny D. Boggs. Five Star, 2005. Win McNaughton joined the Union Army at 17 and became a prisoner of war at Camp Ford, Texas, the largest camp west of the Mississippi River. There he helped organize a baseball game between the Union prisoners and their Confederate guards, which soon became a mini-Civil War. Spur Award from Western Writers of America.

Selected Reviews

Quantrell's Raiders
by Frank Gruber
Ace, 1953

The Civil War didn't spare the West. But those who lived closer to the seat of war were more involved. Missouri, whose outlook was western, didn't belong to either the North or the South, but was vitally important to each side. The bitterest western fighting of the Civil War predictably took place along the Kansas-Missouri border, the region that set the standards for brutality.

There were pro slavery southern guerrillas, or bushwhackers, who ambushed, shot from behind, and always attacked in surprise from cover. Free-state extremists were called jayhawkers. The most famous of these border ruffians was William Clarke Quantrill, who came to Kansas a few years before the war and had ridden with the jayhawkers for a time. Early in 1862 he formed his own band of Missouri bushwhackers and began to plunder Kansas towns. His army—the majority were teenagers—grew until he commanded a force of approximately 300.

Quantrill adopted the name Charlie Hart in 1858. He used this name in Lawrence in 1859 or 1860. The name "Charlie" stuck with him until his death. In Missouri he was known as Charlie Quantrill. In most books by Missourians his name is given as Charles William Quantrill. Many newspaper reports spelled his name "Quantrill." Gruber used Charles William Quantrill.

Tall, thin, with blond, almost white hair, this sometime schoolteacher was a blight upon the land. The scum of the border rode with him: William Haller, George Todd, Bill Gregg, Frank James (there is some uncertainty as to whether his brother Jesse ever rode with Quantrill), and in particular Bloody Bill Anderson, who was more savage than a mad wolf. They raided Kansas and plundered and burned. Quantrill gave no quarter and he asked none.

Frank Gruber, a self-taught historian of the Civil War, was a prolific and successful writer of formula Westerns. He wrote some 60 novels, 25 or more were popular Westerns. Many of his stories were set in Kansas and Missouri during and in the aftermath of the Civil War. His characters in these stories were often ex-Civil War officers or former Quantrill raiders trying to escape their pasts.

The protagonist in *Quantrell's Raiders* is Doniphan Fletcher, who graduated from West Point at the beginning of the Civil War and was commissioned a second lieutenant in the United States Army. Awaiting orders for his first duty assignment, he returned to his home in Lees Summit, Missouri. He killed a jayhawker who had murdered one of his father's slaves. The Union Army court-martialed him and sentenced him to death. But he escaped and returned home. When his father was killed by jayhawkers, Doniphan became a guerrilla and rode with Quantrell's Raiders. In an interesting plot, Lieutenant Fletcher is given a chance by the army to redeem himself.

The bushwhackers were a scary lot. William E. Connelley, in his biography of Quantrill, wrote:

No more terrifying object ever came down a street than a mounted guerrilla wild for blood, the bridle-reins between his teeth or over the saddle-horn, the horse running recklessly, the rider yelling like a Comanche, his long unkempt hair flying wildly beyond the brim of his broad hat, and firing both to the right and left with deadly accuracy.

Quantrill's destruction of Lawrence, Kansas, is perhaps the most infamous incident of the Civil War.

Lawrence was the headquarters of the Emigrant Aid Society, the embodiment of anti-slavery sentiment of the North—abolitionism. The Missourian believed that in fighting Lawrence he was battling against national abolitionism. Quantrill, who cared nothing for slavery nor abolition, seized upon this feeling to gratify his thirst for blood and plunder.

Mounted, the detachment pressed forward at an increased pace. It was a race with the dawn, but when they reached Franklin, four miles from Lawrence, the huge ball of fire that was the sun had already shot up over the horizon.

"Column of fours!" the command rang down the line. "And gallop!"

Not a breath of air was stirring; the day was clear without the least bit of haze. Here and there, on the prairie, straight columns of smoke from the chimneys indicated the morning cooking fires. And straight ahead was the smoke of Lawrence. Lawrence, the metropolis of the plains, a village of two thousand souls, the seat of the free-state government of Kansas, . . .

Incredible as it seems, the guerrillas marched fifty miles into Kansas without opposition, destroyed a town of 2,000 population and killed more than one hundred and fifty of its citizens—and then began a retreat of almost a hundred miles, during which they burned almost every farmhouse they passed, killed dozens more, and outbluffed and outfought 1,200 to 1,500 troops and militia. And in the end the guerrillas dispersed completely. Only a few were ever captured.

Although Frank Gruber remains firmly classified as a Western genre writer, there's realism and excitement in his workmanlike prose based on the border wars. *Quantrell's Raiders* has all the drama of the Civil War—father against son, brother against brother—and is a realistic portrayal of the bushwhackers and jayhawkers' trail of blood and destruction. It was serialized in Adventure magazine in 1940 under the title *Quantrell's Flag*, but it wasn't until 1954 that it was published as a paperback original titled *Quantrell's Raiders*.

Glorieta Pass
by P. G. Nagle
Forge, 1999

The Civil War in the West was not confined to the border states. In 1861 Federal troops were recalled from the West to fight in the East, leaving the way open for Confederates to invade New Mexico and obtain a route to Colorado's gold and San Francisco's unblockadeable sea coast.

A Confederate Army, led by Brigadier General Henry Hopkins Sibley, was assembled in Texas in 1862 and marched into the Union Southwest. After a series of early victories, fortune turned against the Confederates, and the war in the Southwest proved to be short, sharp, and bloody for both sides.

In New Mexico, General Sibley's Texas Confederates were opposed by a Union army under Colonel E. R. S. Canby. Before the war, Sibley and Canby were friends who had been classmates at West Point. Both served in the New Mexico Territory before the Civil War and at Sibley's wedding, Canby was his best man. Now they were torn apart by politics and geography.

The most significant battle in the Far West was for control of Glorieta Pass, in the Sangre de Cristo Mountains near Santa Fe. That engagement, known as the "Gettysburg of the West," pitted Sibley's Texas Brigade against a Union force primarily made up of New Mexican and Coloradan volunteers. In a fierce fight, the Confederates were defeated and their hopes of advancing to the Pacific ended

In Nagle's story, all of the principals are present: Sibley and Canby and their staff and field officers; the Colorado volunteers, or "Pike's Peakers," led by Colonel John Slough and Major John Chivington; Colonel Manuel Chavez and his 2nd New Mexico Volunteers; and Colonel Christopher "Kit" Carson and his 1st New Mexico Volunteers. Their personalities and their actions were carefully researched and ring true.

But the author put the historical figures in the background and developed fictional characters to carry the narrative and advance the plot. The primary protagonists are: (1) Captain Alastar O'Brien, a rough miner turned soldier leading a company of 1st Colorado Volunteers; (2) Laura Howland, a resilient young lady from Boston, recently orphaned and brought to Santa Fe by a rascally uncle and caught up in the conflict and forever changed by what she sees; (3) Lieutenant Jamie Russell, a store clerk from Texas serving as a quartermaster in Sibley's Brigade; (4) Lieutenant Lacey McIntyre, a West Point-educated officer serving as a member of Canby's staff who impulsively abandons the Union when the Rebels capture him; and (5) Lieutenant Charles Franklin, a bright, genteel Colorado Volunteer with an astonishing secret. In the maelstrom of war, as they struggle with patriotism and survival, their lives converge in a realistically inevitable way.

The chronology of the battles, the actual participants and the fictional characters are woven into a complex plot that requires close attention to follow. But Nagle, who was born and raised fifty miles from Glorieta Pass, through careful research and attention to detail has created a strong sense of place. The underlying theme, as in many Civil War novels, is the anguish of split loyalties suffered when countrymen go to war against countrymen. Lacey McIntyre had to make a difficult decision when many of his comrades were leaving the Union Army to join the Confederacy. When he was asked if he would switch sides and fight for the Rebels, he was conflicted. His father would disown him. But this was a war, which he wanted no part of, but it looked like the only choice he would have was which side to fight on.

Loyalty and friendship were often conflicting emotions and accommodations had to be made. Before the Rebel incursion, Colonel Canby received a letter from Sibley which caused this exchange between Mrs. Canby and Laura Howland:

"You met Henry Sibley, didn't you, Miss Howland?"
Laura nodded. "Briefly. At Fort Union"

"Yes, I thought so. He and Richard were once great friends. He's a Confederate general now . . Do you still plan to return to Boston?"

"Yes."

"Best go soon," Mrs. Canby said. A sob escaped her . . .

"I think you must have had some bad news," Laura said lightly, "so I wouldn't dream of going to Boston now."

Mrs. Canby laughed. "How ridiculous. No, you must go." Her face became serious again. "Henry's brought his army near Fort Craig. He plans to march up the Rio Grande. He was warning Richard to send me to safety."

Laura's lips parted in surprise, and Mrs. Canby nodded grimly. "You must go now,' she repeated.

The effect of the war on her characters and their reactions and interactions is the thrust of Nagle's novel, but this is a war story, and she doesn't neglect the battle itself.

There is much detail on the logistic tail of the Confederate brigade—the long march, the plodding mules, the ill-tempered teamsters, the shortage of water, rations and supplies, and the constant pressure on a young quartermaster named Jamie Russell to meet the needs of a force of around 3,500 tired, hungry troops. And eventually, Lieutenant Russell got his first taste of battle.

It was thunder and hell. Jamie's hands shook as he clutched the shotgun he'd borrowed from one of the teamsters. Out ahead the first line was getting shot to pieces by the Federal cannon and supporting troops . . . Captain Shropshire, waving his sword over his head, strode on, and the second line followed. Jamie forced his feet to move . . . "Down!" Shropshire screamed, and Jamie dropped with the rest of the line, covering his head as the hail of balls shrieked overhead . . . Major Lockridge came up, a bull of a man, shouting "Charge' The line rose, and a wordless howl burst from them as they ran toward the Yankees . . . A wave of bullets hissed toward them, and the shouting of the Federal cannoneers promised another deadly round of canister. Jamie's throat and nostrils burned with the smell of powder. . .

Glorieta Pass is the first of Nagle's two novels of the New Mexico Campaign. The second installment, *The Guns of Valverde* (Forge, 2000), picks up the narrative as the Confederates, yielding to the pressure of Union forces and the collapse of their own expectation of certain victory, begin to withdraw to Texas.

This fine first novel from a talented writer precedes a series of stories about the Civil War in the West that should find a place in the library of any devotee to Western fiction.

13

THE SPANISH WEST

INTRODUCTION

Mexico has a tumultuous history. In the early 1500s, Hernán Cortés, with only 600 soldiers, destroyed the Aztec Empire, whose accomplished warriors and citizens numbered in the millions, and claimed the country for Spain. During the early 1800s Mexicans fought and won a war of independence from Spain. Texas declared its independence from Mexico in 1836, and by 1846 Mexico was at war with the United States. In the end, Mexico lost over half of its territory, including the present states of Texas, California, New Mexico and Northern Arizona. During the mid-1800s the French sought to establish a Mexican empire under the Austrian prince, Maxmilian. Mexican liberals, led by Benito Juarez, resisted bitterly, and the French withdrew in 1817, leaving Emperor Maxmilian and his wife Carlotta to face execution by firing squad. The Revolution of 1910, a revolt against President Porfirio Diaz' monopoly of political power, was a bloody affair fought between government forces and the followers of Francisco (Pancho) Villa in the north and Emiliano Zapata in the south. In 1914 the United States recognized Venustiano Carranza as head of the Mexican government. In 1921, Carranza was overthrown in a military coup.

The influence of Spain in the southwest United States, as in Mexico, was profound. By 1540 Spanish expeditions had visited considerable parts of the present American Southwest. Most impressive was the expedition of Francisco Coronado (1540-1542), which included three hundred horsemen in burnished armor. He searched for the fabled Seven Golden Cities of Cibola, and traveled as far as present Kansas in search of imaginary wealth. Representatives of the church traveled with the army, intending to save pagan souls from damnation. They established towns, garrisons, and churches. Father Junipero Serra, backed by the army, journeyed up the Pacific Coast and established San Francisco in 1776, the year of American independence.

The Spaniards' march across the American landscape, from the eastern border of Texas through the southwest and up and along the nine hundred mile sweep of today's California, left thousands of Spanish place names, and throughout the Southwest today you see Spanish architecture, eat Mexican cuisine, and listen to Mexican music.

The Spanish expeditions into the New World, Mexico's violent past, and the involvement of Americans with our southern neighbors have been the source of many novels. Chosen for review in this section are *The Iron Mistress* (Doubleday, 1951), Paul I. Wellman's biographical novel of Jim Bowie, one of the heroes of the Texas Revolution; Norman Zollinger's *Not of War Only* (Forge, 1994), an account of two Americans caught in the tragedies and triumphs of the Mexican Revolution in 1914; and Tom Lea's *The Wonderful Country* (Little, Brown, 1952), the story of an American expatriate who rode as a paid pistolero in Mexico during the late 1800s, between the Mexican-American War and the Mexican Revolution.

READER'S GUIDE

The Californians by Gertrude Atherton. Lane, 1898. Life in California at the turn-of-the-century as seen through the experiences of the shy, plain daughter of a Spanish grandee and the vivacious, beautiful daughter of a San Francisco entrepreneur.

Isidro by Mary Hunter Austin. Houghton Mifflin, 1905. A Novel of Alta California in the early 19th century, the last days of the Catholic missions. Action revolves around Spanish and Portuguese settlers and Indians, and the loves of Isidro and the Commandante's lost daughter.

Desert Gold by Zane Grey. Harper and Brothers, 1913. Along the Arizona-Mexican border, with the Mexican Revolution as a backdrop, a young American tenderfoot comes West in search of adventure, rescues an aristocratic Spanish girl from revolutionary bandits, falls in love with a rancher's daughter, becomes a border ranger, and as the revolution grows more intense, is forced to flee into the Sonoran desert.

The Light of Western Stars by Zane Grey. Harper and Brothers, 1914. A wealthy New York society girl bought a ranch near the turbulent Mexican border during the Revolution, was abducted by Mexican guerrillas, and rescued by the the legendary El Capitan, an American who was respected by Mexican forces on both sides.

The Blood of Conquerors by Harvey Fergusson. Alfred A. Knopf, 1921. Spanish-Mexican and Anglo-American relations in New Mexico in the early 19th century are at the heart of Harvey Fergusson's first novel. It follows the decay of traditional Spanish life in Albuquerque after the influx into the Southwest of entrepreneurial Anglos. The Dons are replaced by modern businessmen.

The Mark of Zorro by Johnston McCulley, Grosset and Dunlap, 1924. Originally published as a serial in a pulp magazine and titled *The Curse of Capistrano* in 1919, this novel created an enduring character who would appear through the years in numerous films and television shows. The story is set in the 1820s, when California was under Spanish rule. A seemingly frivolous caballero, Don Diego de la Vega, returned home from Spain to find a new military commandante subjugating the people of the pueblo of Reina de Los Angeles. Diego, assisted by his deaf-mute servant Bernardo, donned a black mask and cape and rode to protect the people of Los Angeles as Zorro. Notable film versions were the 1940 release with the same title, and the 1998 film "The Mask of Zorro."

Paso Por Aqui by Eugene Manlove Rhodes. Houghton Mifflin, 1927. Released together with *Once in the Saddle* under one cover for the first edition in 1927, this short novel is a sentimental story about an outlaw who risks capture and his life by nursing a Mexican family who are near death with diphtheria. Basis for the 1948 film "Four Faces West."

In Those Days: An Impression of Change by Harvey Fergusson. Alfred

A. Knopf, 1929. Following the life of a young man who settled in Albuquerque after a long journey from Connecticut to the Southwest and down the Santa Fe Trail, this novel presents a portrait of the changes brought about by commerce, the railroad, and the automobile in the Anglo-Spanish Southwest.

Flowering Judas by Katherine Anne Porter. Harcourt, Brace, 1930. This novella, the title story in a collection of ten, is about Laura, an idealistic woman who traveled to Mexico from Arizona at the age of twenty-two to help the Obregon Revolution, and Braggioni, a Mexican revolutionary, a man who had "taken pains to be a good revolutionist and a professional lover of humanity." But Laura, the "gringita" he pursued, loved the revolution without being in love with any man in it.

Ranchero by Stewart Edward White. Doubleday Doran, 1933. The second book in White's Andy Burnett series. Mountain man Andy Burnett reached California in the autumn of 1832. The survivor of an Indian massacre, he would enjoy the golden life of California in the days before the Gold Rush.

Tortilla Flat by John Steinbeck. Covici-Friede, 1935. The shabby district of Tortilla Flat, which lay above the town of Monterey on the California coast, was home to a group of paisano (a mixture of Spanish, Indian, Mexican and Caucasian bloods) friends, who lived in squalid poverty and blissful idleness. They led a wholly boisterous life until they were eventually done in by a climactic fire. Basis for the 1941 film.

People of the Valley by Frank Waters. Farrar and Rinehart, 1941. Set in the late 19th and early 20th centuries, this is a story of how an isolated Spanish-speaking people in northern New Mexico's Mora Valley confronted Anglo newcomers who wanted to build a dam in the name of progress.

The Road to San Jacinto by L. L. Foreman. E. P. Dutton, 1943. In 1836 Sam Houston and the Mexican general Santa Anna were engaged in a deadly war over the fate of Texas—the Texas of the ill-fated Alamo and the last desperate battle of San Jacinto.

Captain from Castile by Samuel Shellabarger. Little, Brown, 1944. In 1518 Captain Pedro de Vargas was a member of Hernán Cortés' conquistadors, five hundred men who were out to conquer a continent. This story of Captain de Vargas' adventures is based on the historic facts of Cortés conquest of Mexico. Basis for the 1947 film.

The Seven Cities of Gold by Virginia Davis Hersch. Duell, Sloan and Pearce, 1946. A romantic account of the Coronado expedition of 1540 to find the Golden Cities of Cibola, which proved to be the Zuñi pueblos of New Mexico and not the cities of fabulous riches the Spanish explorers were seeking.

Wetback by Claud Garner. Coward-McCann, 1947. This is the story of a man's struggle to gain legal immigrant status in the United States. Presented from the point of view of Dionesio, a young Mexican "wetback" who crossed the Rio Grande into South Texas.

The Caballero by Johnston McCulley. Samuel Curl, 1947. In Old California, Caballero Don Fernando Venegas, scion of a wealthy Castilian family, killed a man in a duel and accepted the penance imposed by the church. For three months he lived as a peon, enduring toil and humiliation, and emerging as a champion for the downtrodden.

The Yogi of Cockroach Court by Frank Waters. Farrar and Rinehart, 1947. In a violent Mexican-American border town, a young half-breed orphan is taken in by an old Chinese shopkeeper who practices yoga. Other major characters are a mestizo dancer in a local cantina and her American friend, a "percentage girl." These characters interact in a bordertown environment which includes open prostitution, gambling, and drugs, which eventually destroys each of them.

The Wind Leaves No Shadow by Ruth Laughlin. McGraw-Hill, 1948. An historical novel of the upper Rio Grande Valley from 1811 to 1822, based on the life of Doña Tules Barcelo, the gambling queen of territorial Santa Fe and the mistress of Governor Armijo.

The Brave Bulls by Tom Lea. Little, Brown, 1949. The bullfight is about bravery, glory, and death. The protagonist in this story is Luis Bello, "The Swordsman of Guerreras," whose profession was violent death. He was the greatest bullfighter in Mexico. He had everything—family, friends, mistresses, money, and courage. But one day, Luis faced the brave bulls—and felt terror! Source for the 1951 film.

Grant of Kingdom by Harvey Fergusson. William Morrow, 1950. In 1841, the huge Maxwell Land Grant in northern New Mexico had a profound effect on those who possessed the land and those who wanted it. The grant shaped their futures, and led to a baronial life for some.

Time of the Gringo by Elliott Arnold. Alfred A. Knopf, 1953. A novel of Manuel Armijo, the last Mexican governor of New Mexico, and of his efforts to contain the tide of Anglos during the American conquest.

The Conquest of Don Pedro by Harvey Fergusson. William Morrow, 1954. Following the Civil War, New Mexico was on the verge of change—balanced between the new ways and the old. The peddler Leo Mendes had traveled throughout the Southwest, building a flourishing trade in the small towns and outposts. But in Don Pedro he found that powerful Spanish families still ruled and Gringo storekeepers were not welcome.

They Came to Cordura by Glendon Swarthout. Random House, 1958. Set against the background of the Pancho Villa campaign, this is a story of five brave men, a coward, and a woman suspected of treason on a strange and violent journey across the Mexican desert. Basis for the 1959 film.

The Cactus and the Crown by Catherine Gavin. Doubleday, 1962. In the late 1860s the ill-fated Maximilian von Hapsburg and his beautiful wife Carlota became Emperor and Empress of Mexico. During their reign Sally Lorimér and her brother came to Mexico to claim an inheritance and became players in the fate of that nation.

The Hands of Cantu by Tom Lea. Little, Brown. 1964. A narrative of a 17th century Spanish rancher's pursuit of a prized horse herd which had fallen into the hands of an Indian tribe in the Big Bend country of present-day Texas.

Massacre at Goliad by Elmer Kelton. Ballantine Books, 1965. When the news came that the Alamo had been overwhelmed in San Antonio, a pall of gloom descended upon at the garrison at Goliad. But few really thought it could happen at Goliad. Then the Mexicans came.

Below the Rio Grande by William H. Fear. Bridbooks, 1966. In this traditional Western, a ragged Americano youth, who was a fleeing Rebel soldier following the Civil War, was caught on the dusty plains of southern Mexico by the Mexican Army. He was flogged and then sent to rot in a stinking prison at Puebla. There he swore an oath of revenge.

The King's Fifth by Scott O'Dell. Houghton Mifflin, 1966. A young reader's book. In 1541, near Vera Cruz, New Spain (Mexico), seventeen-year-old Esteban de Sandoval was about to stand trial. Esteban was a cartographer who had traveled with a band of conquistadors to the seven golden cities of Cibola, where they found and secretly kept an amazing treasure. But, the king wanted his obligatory fifth.

Sam Houston: A Biographical Novel by Noel Gerson. Doubleday, 1968. This novel follows Sam Houston as he fought with Andrew Jackson at Horseshoe Bend and as he defeated Santa Anna at San Jacinto, to the turbulent times leading up to the Civil War where he chose a different road than the Texans he had so gallantly served.

Bless Me, Ultima by Rudolfo Anaya. Berkley, 1972. Antonio Marez grew up in a New Mexican household divided by the traditions of his cowboy (vaquero) father and his farm-bred mother. Ultima, a curandera (one who cures with herbs, faith, and magic), helped Tony find his way among the conflicting ties of family, culture, and religion.

The Manhunters by Elmer Kelton. Ballantine Books, 1974. This novel was inspired by the story of controversial Mexican fugitive Gregorio Cortez. In 1901 Cortez, a young horseman, shot a sheriff during an argument, leading to the largest concerted manhunt in Texas history. As he fled to the sanctuary of Mexico, Kelton's protagonist, based on Cortez, was unaware of the fuel he had added to the already simmering racial hatreds in and around the quiet town of Domingo, Texas. He became a folk hero to his people and a dangerous fugitive to a group of zealous lawmen.

The Adelita by Oakley Hall. Doubleday, 1975. This novel, which spans the years from 1913 to the present (1975), tells the story of the son of an American oil tycoon who was prospecting in Mexico until the outbreak of the Revolution. He joined his late mother's vaqueros fighting against the Federal troops. And with them was the beautiful soldadera called the Adelita.

The Blazing Dawn by James Wakefield Burke. Pyramid Books, 1975. The saga of men and women entangled in the the bloody struggle for a free Texas, including Davy Crockett, Jim Bowie, William Travis, and Santa Anna, the enemy—tyrannical, obsessive, perverse, and feared. These men were joined forever at the Alamo.

Chihuahua 1916 by Otis Carney. Prentice-Hall, 1980. In the desert of Chihuahua in 1916, General "Black Jack" Pershing prepared to lead a futile punitive expedition against Pancho Villa.

Aztec by Gary Jennings. Atheneum, 1980. A story of the great Aztec civilization of Mexico, told in the words of an Aztec who was a scribe, a warrior, and a traveling merchant.

Two for Texas by James Lee Burke. Pocket Books, 1982. Two escaped convicts, one old and one young, exit a Louisiana hell hole of a prison and move south into Texas, ending up with Sam Houston's forces fighting in the Texas Revolution. Basis for the 1998 film.

Tom Mix and Pancho Villa by Clifford Irving. St. Martin's Press, 1982. In his youth, Tom Mix rode in the Mexican Revolution with Pancho Villa. This is a fictional account of that association.

Curandero: A Spanish Legend by José Ortiz y Pino III. Sunstone Press, 1983. Complete with folklore on the art of mystic healing in the lost mountains of Northern New Mexico, this cuento, a legend, is first and foremost a love story. Antonio is also infatuated with Marianela. Will Antonio remain in the village of San Lucas, wed Marianela and become a farmer to support their future? But everything in his life directs him toward a calling he cannot ignore. Antonio will become a curandero, Northern New Mexico's version of a healer, a mysterious individual schooled in the magic of collecting and combining herbs with convalescent powers.

The Lizard Woman by Frank Waters. Thorp Springs, 1984. First published in 1930 under the title *Fever Pitch*, *The Lizard Woman* is Frank Waters' first novel. A young American engineer and a mestizo bar-girl journeyed deep into the Baja California desert to assay what may have been a huge deposit of gold. Their destination was a enclosed by "The Lizard Woman," a circular wall of mountains whose rim resembled a serpent—a serpent that didn't welcome the interlopers.

Old Gringo by Carlos Fuentes. Farrar, Straus and Giroux, 1985. Ambrose Bierce was a noted journalist and short story writer whose "Prattle" column in the *San Francisco Examiner* was popular on the West Coast. Bierce eventually retired and traveled to Mexico. Although a mystery surrounds his death, many believe he was killed during the siege of Ojinaga during the revolutionary war in 1914. This novel is based on that mystery. Basis for the 1989 film.

Blood Meridian by Cormac McCarthy. Random House, 1985. Based on historical events that took place on the Texas-Mexico border in the 1850s, where Indians were murdered for a Mexican bounty on their scalps.

Death of the Fifth Son by Robert Somerlott. Viking Press, 1987. An historical novel of the conquistador Hernán Cortés, who toppled the Aztec Empire on behalf of Spain.

Remember the Alamo by Amelia Barr. Dodd, Mead, 1988. The most severe sufferings caused by war are the suffering of families. Before a shot had been fired in the war of Texan independence, the battle had begun in a Texas household.

Of Arms I Sing: A Novel of the Settlement of the American West by Joseph J. Bohnaker. Sunstone Press, 1990. A fictionalized history of New Mexico, where in the 16th century Don Juan Oñate established the first permanent settlement in the American West, on behalf of Phillip II of Spain. The story is told through the eyes of Onate's staunchest supporter, Captain Villagra, who writes from his prison cell in Seville years after Onate's conquest.

The Bear Flag: A Novel of the Birth of California by Cecelia Holland. Houghton Mifflin, 1990. A woman, widowed on the terrible trek west in the early 1840s, was in California when the Bear Flag, proclaiming California a free republic, was hoisted in Sonoma on June 14, 1846. She witnessed the real struggle that followed, from Sonoma to Monterey to Los Angeles.

Eyes of Eagles by William W. Johnstone. Zebra Books, 1990. Jamie Ian MacCallister, orphaned at the age of seven and adopted by Ohio Shawnee, grew up in the wilderness. But when he struck out westward, across the Arkansas territory into Texas, he found himself in the middle of a war. Texans like Jim Bowie and Sam Houston were waging a fierce struggle against Santa Ana's Mexican army, and Jamie MacCallister made the perfect scout for the fledgling volunteer force. What lay ahead of them was a place called the Alamo.

Duel of Eagles by Jeff Long. William Morrow, 1990. A novel of the Mexican and U. S. fight for the Alamo, what led to it, and the war for Texas that followed.

The Eagle and the Raven by James A. Michener. State House Press, 1990. The revolution of 1876 which severed Texas from Mexico had as leaders Sam Houston for the Texans and Santa Ana for Mexico. Both were charismatic men, each flawed but able to inspire and lead their countrymen.

Against the 7th Flag by Larry J. Martin. Bantam Books, 1991. Traveling across Alta California in the mid-1800s as the rumblings of war grew in Mexico City, Los Angeles, and Washington, John Clinton Ryan found himself caught in the wrong place at the wrong time.

Gringos by Charles Portis. Simon and Schuster, 1991. An odd assortment of American expatriates in Mexico are observed by Jimmy Burns, who earns his living as a trucker and as a private investigator who looks for missing persons. Jimmy is a keen observer of his fellow gringos, who include a wave of "hippies," who bring serious problems with them.

Cutting Stone by Janet Burroway. Houghton Mifflin, 1992. A novel based on an event in August of 1914, when the United States government gave permission for Pancho Villa, Alvaro Obregon, and a limited number of troops to travel over American territory by Southern Pacific rail from El Paso to Nogales to settle a border incident.

All the Pretty Horses by Cormac McCarthy. Alfred A. Knopf, 1992. The first novel in McCarthy's *Border Trilogy*. At sixteen, John Grady Cole found himself at the dying end of a long line of Texas ranchers. With two companions, he went to Mexico, a beautiful and desolate land, but cruelly civilized. John Grady's love for horses and a knowledge of them gained him employment on a Mexican cattle ranch, but a romance with the rancher's daughter landed him and his companions in a hell-hole Mexican jail. Source for the 2000 film.

Mexico by James A. Michener. Random House, 1992. An American journalist, in Mexico to report on a celebrated duel between two matadors, is also on a journey of discovery to trace his family's history. His journey captures all the drama and tragedy of Mexico's long and tumultuous history.

Border Crossings by David L. Fleming. Texas Christian University Press, 1993. During a 1916 raid on Columbus, New Mexico, by Mexican revolutionaries, one of Pancho Villa's bandits kidnapped the daughter of a New Mexico rancher. Three ranch hands, two of them ex-Texas Rangers, went in pursuit of the bandits and the girl.

Empire of Bones by Jeff Long. William Morrow, 1993. A revisionist novel of the Texas Revolution, where Sam Houston is presented as an ordinary man, swept along by events, who doubts both himself and his control over the ragtag Texas army of 1836. Spur Award from the Western Writers of America.

Promised Lands: A Novel of the Texas Rebellion by Elizabeth Crook. Doubleday, 1994. Crook retraces the movement of General Santa Anna's Mexican Army in 1836 as it sweeps north intending to end the Texas Rebellion. The men of the Kenner family, a doctor and his two sons, leave home to help defend the Alamo and are ultimately involved in the atrocities at Goliad. The Kenner women—the doctor's mother, his wife, and their daughter—become refugees.

Fair Laughs the Morn: An Historical Romance of the Anza Expedition to California 1775-76 by Genevieve Gray. Sunstone Press, 1994. At the time of the Boston Tea Party, a rebellious convent orphan in Mexico City named Gabriella Salagado plots to escape from her post as the indentured companion of a nobleman's spoiled daughter. She is befriended by Elias Martinez and becomes his wife. Dreams of a new beginning lead Elias and Gabriella to follow Colonel Juan Bautista de Anza on a thousand-mile trek from Nueva Espana's northern frontier to the California coast.

The Crossing by Cormac McCarthy. Alfred A. Knopf, 1994. The second book in McCarthy's *Border Trilogy*. In the 1930s on the eve of World War II, Billy and Boyd Parham set out from New Mexico into the remote regions of northern Mexico to recover horses which had been stolen from their parents' ranch by Indians.

The Rio Grande by Jory Sherman. Bantam Books, 1994. From Bantam's *Rivers West* series. The Rio Grande rises in the Rocky Mountains of western Colorado, flows through the vast deserts of the Southwest to the Gulf of Mexican. In the early 1800s, when a young America challenged the Spanish for control of the region, Matthew Caine, an agent of the American government, made friends with the Shoshone and other tribes and mapped the river from its source to Santa Fe—even though a Mexican officer had sworn to bring him to the gallows.

Pancho and Black Jack by Frederick Bean. Pocket Books, 1995. In 1916 President Woodrow Wilson ordered General John J. "Black Jack" Pershing to go into Mexico and capture Pancho Villa and punish him for a raid on a New

Mexico town. The legendary Villa, however, was innocent of the raid.

Chapultepec by Norman Zollinger. Forge, 1995. A veteran French Foreign Legion officer, who was haunted by the shameful Battle of Chapultepec, returned to Mexico to defend and uphold Austrian archduke Maximilian's dubious claim to the title of emperor of Mexico. The novel covers the period from 1847 to 1867.

The Friends of Pancho Villa by James Carlos Blake. G. P. Putnam's Sons, 1996. Told from the viewpoint of the notorious General Rodolfo Fierro, this is the story of Pancho Villa and the Mexican Revolution.

Blood of Texas by Will Camp (Preston Lewis). HarperCollins, 1996. Rubio Portillo was a Mexican living in San Antonio in 1835 who joined the fight for Texas independence. That meant losing not only his friends, but his betrothed. He would have to fight with the white man who doubted his loyalty, while confronting the hatred of his own people. Spur Award from Western Writers of America.

Texas Glory by Robert Vaughan. St. Martin's Press, 1996. In an adobe-walled fortress called the Alamo, a small army of independence, though outnumbered forty-to-one, stood in the way of Santa Anna's best troops.

In the Rogue Blood by James Carlos Blake. Avon Books, 1997. Two teenage sons of a whore mother and a homicidal father were driven from their home in the Florida swamplands after killing the father. They headed for Texas, became separated, and eventually found themselves in Mexico, fighting in the Mexican-American War.

Hacienda by Albert R. Booky. Sunstone Press, 1997. This historical novel begins in the 1840s in New Mexico when young Simon Gomez's breathtaking adventures begin to fulfill his obsessive dream for success.

Two Lives for Oñate by Miguel Encinias. University of New Mexico Press, 1997. An historical novel about Oñate and his failed governorship of Spanish New Mexico from 1598 until 1610.

The Crystal Frontier by Carlos Fuentes. Farrar, Straus and Giroux, 1997. Translated from the Spanish by Alfred MacAdam. This novel in nine stories explores the transparent border between Mexico and the United States through the life and violent death of a ruthless fifty-year-old businessman who earns big profits from directing human traffic across the border.

Aztec Autumn by Gary Jennings. St. Martin's Press, 1997. Set one generation after the rich culture of the Aztecs was all but destroyed by invading Spaniards. Their capital city of Tenochtitlan had been renamed Mexico City. One young Aztec secretly began to recruit an army of insurrection.

Mountains of the Blue Stone by Dorothy Cave. Sunstone Press, 1998. Fleeing his plush decaying world and a marriage gone stale, Drake Cavanaugh is badly injured while staging his own death. Found unconscious, he is carried to the tiny Hispanic village of Descano, high and remote in the mountains of New Mexico. Here, in this "forgotten pocket of God's overalls," begins his cure—physical, metaphysical, and intellectual. Here he becomes increasingly part of a strange world of saints and witches and ancient gods, of murder, mysticism, and miracles. And from here he eventually returns with a truth that is not what he sought.

Bowie by Randy Lee Eickhoff and Leonard C. Lewis. Forge, 1998. A retelling of the Jim Bowie legend through a set of (fictional) interviews with his former slave, his mother, his brother, the Shakespearean actor Edwin Forrest, Sam Houston, and Caiaphas K. Ham, who fought with Bowie during the Texas War for Independence.

The Sun He Dies: A Novel About the End of the Aztec World by Jamake Hightower. Replica Books, 1999. A novel of the Spanish invasion of Mexico, where Cortés, with only 600 soldiers, destroyed an Indian empire whose warriors and general population numbered in the millions.

Fearless by Lucia St. Clair Robson. Ballantine Books, 1999. Sarah Bowman, the heroine in this novel, was an imposing figure, around six feet tall with flaming red hair. The strong-willed Tennessee woman had participated in the Florida campaign against the Seminoles. Then, in 1845, when Mexico and the U. S. prepared for war, Sarah signed on as a laundress and cook and bivouacked with General Zachary Taylor's army in Corpus Christi.

The Gates of the Alamo by Stephen Harrigan. Alfred A. Knopf, 2000. In this retelling of the oft-told Battle of the Alamo, strong fictional characters—a botanist and a widowed innkeeper and her son who find themselves inside the mission during the nearly two weeks battle, and a Mexican sergeant trying to keep his men alive—are used to present a view of life inside and outside the fortress during the siege. Spur Award from Western Writers of America.

Gone for Soldiers by Jeff Shaara, Ballantine Books, 2000. A novel of the Mexican-American War that blends fiction with fact. The two main characters are General Winfield Scott, a short-tempered, vain man, and Robert E. Lee, an aristocratic, dignified engineer who had never seen combat.

The Salt War: Unrest in El Paso by Ira Compton. iUniverse, 2001. An historical novel of the 1877 El Paso Salt War. Although acceptable under American law, the Mexicans felt that no one person should own a mineral deposit. Under Spanish law, the commodity was placed there by God and was free to everyone. When they challenged Charlie Howard's authority to place a tariff on the salt in the dry lakes at the foot of Guadeloupe Peak, mob action ensued, leading to a Texas Ranger surrender and the execution of an American judge.

Sam Houston Is My Hero by Judy Alter, Texas Christian University Press, 2003. For young readers. A fictional account of fourteen-year-old Catherine Jennings, who actually rode across Texas to recruit soldiers for Sam Houston's army following the fall of the Alamo.

Santa Fe Passage by Jon R. Bauman. St. Martin's Press, 2004. An historical novel where the protagonist traveled westward from Missouri into the world of Santa Fe traders, Mexican aristocrats, mountain men, prostitutes, and Comanche. The novel recreates the powerful social and political forces in New Mexico in 1846, at the end of the Santa Fe Trail.

North With De Anza by Dorothy Ward Erskine. University of New Mexico Press, 2004. For young reader. First published in 1958. A fictionalized account of thirty families who traveled from present-day Arizona north to California. Led by Don Juan Bautista de Anza, the group founded San Francisco in the 18th century.

Jericho's Road by Elmer Kelton. Forge, 2004. From Kelton's *Texas Ranger* series. Cattle baron Jericho Jackson owned an enormous ranch just above the Rio Grande, and Mexican cattle baron Guadeloupe Chavez owned an equally large ranch south of the Rio Grande in Mexico. Jackson hated Mexicans and Chavez hated gringos. Only the Texas Rangers, determined to keep the peace on the Rio Grande, stood between the two ranchers.

A Nation of Shepherds: A Novel Based on a True Story by Donald L. Lucero. Sunstone Press, 2004. Driven into exile in 1577 from Carmena, Spain, to escape the threat of death by the Inquisition, the Robledo family immigrated first to New Spain and then joined the Oñate colonial expedition in 1596 to New Mexico. In the tragic year of 1598, the family suffered the deaths of two family members, one as the result of an Indian attack at the Pueblo of Acoma. Lacking adequate harvests, and semi-dependent upon their Pueblo Indian neighbors into whose villages they had moved, the colonists were eventually reduced to eating roasted cowhides even as the Indians were eating dirt, coal, and ashes. In the end, some family members returned to New Spain in 1601.

War Lovers by Jason Manning. Signet, 2004. Timothy Barlow was a war hero, a congressman, and close friend of Andrew Jackson. The new president, James K. Polk, asked him to again serve his country, this time in the Republic of Texas. Barlow arrived in Texas in time to witness the impending Mexican-American War, and was sent to Mexico on a secretive mission to find out how much support there was for the American cause, and to make a rough estimation of Mexican troop strength.

Zorro by Isabel Allende. Harper Perennial, 2005. Allende has resurrected Johnston McCulley's early California swashbuckling hero (*The Mark of Zorro*, 1924), focusing on the childhood of Don Diego de Vargas, his education in Spain, and his return to the pueblo of Los Angeles to anonymously challenge the Spanish rulers' abuse of indigenous people.

The Diezmo by Rick Bass. Houghton Mifflin, 2005. Bass' novel is based on an infamous episode in early Texas history that became known as the Mier Expedition. To counter occasional Mexican invasions along the border, Texans formed raiding units that pillaged and slaughtered south of the border. When they laid siege to the Mexican village of Mier, the Texans surrendered after a bloody battle and were taken prisoners by the Mexican army. The central part of this story is the ensuing ordeal of the captured Texans, which would persist for nearly two years. The title refers to the execution of prisoners.

Sons of Texas by Elmer Kelton. Forge, 2005. The first novel in a trilogy that follows the Lewis family through the Alamo and Texas Independence. This tale is set largely in Mexican-ruled Texas. In 1816, the patriarch of the Lewis clan left Tennessee planning to capture Texas wild horses and bring them back to sell. His sixteen-year-old son Michael sneaked off and joined him. When Michael's father was murdered by a Mexican patrol, he was left to die on the prairie, but survived and returned home. Five years later, he and a younger brother returned to Texas to settle the score and stake out new lives for themselves.

Doña Lona: A Novel Based on the Life of Doña Tules by Blanche Chloe Grant. Sunstone Press, 2007. Facsimile of original 1941 edition. Doña Lona is a story based on actual history and the life of the famous gambling queen, María Gertrudis Barceló, better known as Doña Tules. During the time of turbulence, turmoil and trouble that culminated in the Mexican War and the American Army occupation of what had been part of Mexico since their independence from Spain in 1821, Doña Lona was a woman of wealth and importance in New Mexico and, as the owner of a gambling hall, was involved in the politics of the time.

The Plumed Serpent by D. H. Lawrence. Sunstone Press, 2008. Originally published in 1926. Set in Mexico in the 1920s, during an era of political turmoil, this novel centers on a revolutionary movement to revive the religion of the ancient Aztecs.

SELECTED REVIEWS

The Iron Mistress
by Paul I. Wellman
Doubleday, 1951

Some deeply flawed men achieve greatness. Such a man was James Bowie. British historian and essayist Thomas Carlyle wrote of Bowie, "The Texans ought to build him an altar." But Carlyle was speaking of Bowie's heroic deeds in securing Texas independence, not his other side as a sometimes less than honest land speculator, gambler, frontier brawler, and slave trader.

Paul Wellman's romantic narrative of Jim Bowie's adventurous life is filled with detail of the period and the settings, as Bowie builds his reputation and moves westward to Texas. The saga begins in New Orleans, which in the year 1817 remained a self-contained extension of Europe: "Its languages were

French and Spanish; manners, arts, cuisines, and customs were Continental; and New Orleans didn't forget that it had been what it was for a full century before its vicissitudes threw it to the upstart young Republic of the north."

In New Orleans Bowie met beautiful Judalon de Bornay, an upper-class Creole who believed that a woman's happiness rested on her power to control men. She would complicate his life for many years. He fought his first duel because of Judalon, going against a fencing master's sword with a knife, locked in a dark room.

In 1818, in his continual search for wealth, Bowie sought out Jean Lafitte in his stronghold on Galvaz Island, off the coast of Mexican Texas. Here the despicable institutions of piracy and slavery met. He purchased slaves from the pirate for one dollar a pound. During his first visit, Bowie had an interlude with Lafitte's beautiful mistress, Catherine Villars.

The year 1827 found Bowie in Natchez, on the banks of the Mississippi. Natchez was actually two cities, separate and distinct. The river had carved out from its eastern bank a high cliff. At the bottom was Natchez-under-the-bluff, a collection of weathered, run-down buildings where the dregs of the river drank, gambled, and consorted with prostitutes. Above the bluff was Natchez-on-the-hill, where rich gentlemen with stately manners dealt in cotton and slaves, and paid extravagant compliments to ladies who dwelled in "unmatched luxury and ease, waited upon by whole retinues of black servants, attended and flattered and spoiled by courtly men, beautiful, idle, sparkling, willful, and very useless."

Jim Bowie was equally at home in both cities, enhancing his reputation above and below the bluff. He killed Major Norris Wright during a duel on the infamous Vidalia Sand Bar, where he and Wright weren't primary participants. Then, below the bluff, he fought Bloody Jack Sturdevant, a murderous, rough-and-tumble fighter who had killed six men.

But it was in Texas that Bowie found immortality. By 1829 the American tide had flowed over into Mexican Texas. Jim Bowie followed it to San Antonio de Bexar, the queen city of Texas, serenely a city of the Mexican people. "Mexican leisure, Mexican laughter, Mexican happiness characterized Bexar. Not for a time yet was it to be violently jarred out of its peaceful existence" by the American settlers and merchants who came at the encouragement of the Mexican government, with the twin requirements that they become Catholics and Mexican citizens.

Bowie did both, again enhancing his reputation and elevating his position in life. He married Ursula de Veramendi, the daughter of the vice governor of the state of Coahuila and of Texas.

In the Texas Revolution, Bowie made the greatest decision of his life: he wrote to General Sam Houston that "The salvation of Texas depends on keeping [San Antonio de Bexar] out of the hands of the enemy" and that he "would rather die in these ditches than give it up to the enemy . . ." He will forever be remembered as one of the gallant defenders who died at the Alamo.

Wellman tells Bowie's story with rich detail: the settings set the stage for the plot; the characterizations, most based on historical personages, are powerful and memorable; and the action is sometimes intense. He describes San Antonio:

> Very much he liked the adobe houses with their soft pastel tints, the quaint old bridges spanning the San Antonio River—which meandered through the town, the gardens and orchards, the carved front doors, the barred windows of the greater casas, behind which one sometimes caught a glimpse of a cloud of dark hair and bright eyes flashing, and the market with its awnings of skin or canvas, beneath which vendors squatted sleepily beside their wares. He became accustomed to the groaning of the ungreased wooden wheels of the carretas, and the sight of tiny burros almost concealed beneath huge loads of mesquite or live-oak firewood, with the master, almost larger than the beast, perched like as not on top of the heap.

Jean Lafitte's quadroon mistress, Catherine Villars, is one of many memorable characters:

> Every movement she made was graceful, her manners pretty, her face delicate and lovely. Yet the majesty of her beauty was veiled by the shadow of her mixed blood. Perhaps the distant strain from the

African race had endowed her with that added luxuriance of dark hair, the soft fullness of lips, the tropic warmth of eyes. Such exotic perfections sometimes resulted from the combination of Creole and Negro parentages. The girl was fit for an emperor: and she could never hope to be more than she was—this outlaw's mistress.

Bowie's knife duel with Jack Sturdevant provides rousing action:

Sturdevant growled, "They tell me you call yourself a knife fighter. Knives—in a circle?"
Bowie nodded. "And left wrists strapped together?"

Sturdevant used a foot-long splinter of steel known as an "Arkansas Toothpick" and Bowie used his famous Bowie Knife, with its eleven inch blade, an inch and a half wide, curved to the point convexly from the edge and concavely from the back, with both curves as sharp as the edge of the blade itself. This fight made James Bowie a name to be feared.

The major characters of the Texas revolution are present: Sam Houston, Stephen F. Austin, Lieutenant Colonel William Barrett Travis, Davy Crockett, Santa Anna, and many lesser participants. Their relationships (Austin didn't like Bowie, Travis and Bowie had a command conflict), strategies, and the defense of the Alamo are discussed. *The Iron Mistress* is a superb blend of biography and fiction, a feat Wellman would repeat with *Magnificent Destiny* (Doubleday, 1962), a novel that deals with Sam Houston's exploits and Andrew Jackson's presidency.

James R. Webb's screenplay for the 1952 film "The Iron Mistress" significantly shortened the novel's plot, deleting the slave-trading episode and the battle of the Alamo. But the abbreviated result is still an exciting film. Alan Ladd gives a good portrayal of James Bowie, even though he was physically an exact opposite.

Paul Wellman wrote ten fine Western novels and a good body of Western history. *The Iron Mistress* represents his best work.

Not of War Only
by Norman Zollinger
Forge, 1994

In April of 1914 Jorge Martinez, a young Mexican-American, was chased into Mexico by Corey Lane, the sheriff of Chupadera County, New Mexico. Charges against Jorge were subsequently dropped, but not knowing this, he enlisted in the army of the revolution to fight injustice in Mexico.

Corey Lane, the protagonist in two previous Zollinger novels, the award-winning *Rage in Chupadera* (Bantam Books, 1991) and *Corey Lane* (Ticknor & Fields, 1981), was recruited by the state department to observe and report on events developing in Mexico; that is, to spy. Although they were no longer adversaries, his and Jorge Martinez' paths would cross and finally merge as Zollinger reconstructs the revolution.

The intriguing plot is fleshed out with an array of characters who range from the comic to the heroic. There's Fergus Kennedy, a diminutive Scotsman who was an agent for the British Empire and became Corey Lane's closest ally. Sargento Paco Durán was a giant Villista soldier who trained Jorge Martinez and continued to call him "Capitan Cockroach" even after Jorge became his commanding officer and his son-in-law. Juanita Durán followed her father in Villa's army until she became Jorge's *soladara* (soldier's woman). Doña Lusia Montenegro, a beautiful rica (wealthy Mexican), had a complicated relationship with Corey Lane. Major Trinidad Álvarez, a student as well as a practitioner of war, who, unlike most of Villa's soldiers and commanders, had always been a soldier. There are others. Even the most obscure are interesting, such as a federalist escort assigned to Corey Lane and Fergus Kennedy at the battle for Zacatecas:

> . . . an arrogant, talkative captain named Morales—no more than five feet two inches tall, not happy about wasting his valuable time on a pair of foreign rubbernecks. Morales explained his garrison's defensive position: "This is not the best terrain for Pancho Villa's horsemen, but that has never stopped the fat, stupid pig before," the dwarfish captain said. "I suppose he is waiting for the trains to get

his infantry in position. Of course, we have no fear of the bandit's infantry. They will fade like the sunset when they face General Barrón's real soldados. This will not be Paredón or Torreón." He almost grew taller as he spoke, and his eyes sparkled until Corey thought his pomaded head might go up in flames.

Captain Morales was wrong.

The legendary figures of the revolution are here. Emilio Zapata, General Alvaro Obregón, Venustiano Carranza, and the towering figure of Pancho Villa.

Americans were fascinated by Villa, who had backed the revolution of Francisco Madero (1910) against Porfiro Diaz and contributed considerably to Diaz' fall. The "Tiger of the North" moved with a "physical grace that was at odds with his top-heavy, ungainly body" He was at his best on horseback. His Division del Norte included, by some accounts, the finest light cavalry to ever take the field. "Pancho Villa dismounted wasn't truly Pancho Villa."

Differing views are expressed on the causes and the objectives of the Revolution. Corey Lane, who came to love Mexico, was bothered because the ricos seemed so little affected by the war. Luisa Montenegro preferred to change the existing system rather than dismantle it. She told Corey, "I think I have as much sympathy for the lot of the poor as you do. I just think there is a better way to care for them than by chaos and killing. Our way of life has gone awry." Zapata's "Plan de Ayala" would take a third of every hacienda for the peasants. Professor Narcisco Trujillo, an anthropologist with Mexico's Ministry of Culture, viewed the Revolution as a fiesta:

> We have something here I do not believe you have in your country, Corey. La fiesta. Certainly you have celebrations, holidays, but there is a vast difference between a función—a mere party—and a true fiesta. A fiesta is an explosion of the soul, an orgasm, a death—and a concepción. It is the one thing that breaks the ritual, but even in breaking it, it renews it.
>
> The Revolution is such fiesta, a festival of blood and death and life. It is a great howling grito of joy and sorrow, a release that perhaps eludes you in your Calvinism.

Professor Trujillo understood his country.

The two protagonists give us different views of the war. Lane's was an observer's. He watched the politics—the lack of a grand design for the revolution, the friction among its generals over who would get to Mexico City first. He studied the strategy and tactics—Villa's brilliant use of trains as tactical devices, his futile hurling of cavalry against General Obregón's dug-in infantry at Celya.

Major Jorge Martinez had a soldier's view. He led a charge at Celya, where General Villa commanded twenty-two thousand troops against an enemy of like size. With a heavy heart, he spearheaded the attack on Columbus, New Mexico. Through Jorge, we have a close-in view of the bloodiest North American conflict of the 20th Century.

Norman Zollinger, who has won two Golden Spur Awards from the Western Writers of America, understands war. He flew fifty-one heavy bombardment missions during World War II with the 15th Air Force in Italy. His sensitivity to the doubts and fears of men in combat adds dimension to the horrible experiences of the men who fought on both sides of the revolution.

Not of War Only just may be the finest novel ever written about the Mexican Revolution.

The Wonderful Country
by Tom Lea
Little, Brown, and Company, 1952

Selected by the Western Writers of America in 1985 as one of the top twenty-five western novels of all time, *The Wonderful Country* is El Paso writer and artist Tom Lea's story of two civilizations that meet along the west rim of Texas, an awesome land of mesquite, vast stretches of prairie, and jagged mountains. The novel captures the sweep of a period when Mexico's internal affairs and relations with her Texas neighbors were tumultuous and violent, and played out against a backdrop of greed, government chicanery, and bloody Indian warfare.

Set in the late 1800s between the Mexican-American War and the

Mexican Revolution, *The Wonderful Country* is the story of Martin Brady, an American expatriate who swam the Rio Grande to the safety of Mexico after killing the murderer of his father. Only a boy at the time, Brady was befriended by a kindly vaquero who raised him as his son. On reaching manhood, he rode as a pistolero for Ciprano Castro, the tyrannical governor of Chihuahua. Ciprano, his brother General Marcos Castro, and their cohorts were an ominous evil that permeated the "wonderful country." Martin's adoptive father, Mateo Casas, called them "the sorrow of my Mexico." Inevitably, the Castros become the sorrow of Martin Brady.

Martin became Mexican in appearance—Mexican boots, sombrero, frayed jacket, Mexican breeches—and demeanor. When asked his profession, he replied "I ride." However,

> Brady was a pistolero to fill his belly. It was that simple. He never had time to think beyond his belly. But he was tired of being a stranger, tired of walking with eyes in the back of his head. And people saying sideways "Do you speak English?"

And he wondered what would become of him when the Castros no longer needed or wanted his services. Would they drop a rock on his head and leave him dead by the side of the road? They were capable of it. Governor Castro's "Rurales," a private police force that enforced his mandates, held court and executed unfortunate transgressors on the spot. Cruelty was embedded in many of Mexico's officials during this turbulent period.

But Lea's Mexican characterizations, unlike those of many Western writers, aren't stereotypical. In contrast to the evil Castros are estimable individuals such as Mateo Casas and, in particular, Santiagio Santos. Santos was the owner of Bavanuchi, a grand ranch in the heart of the Sierras. He was a man of stature:

> Santiago Santos stood by the branding fire. Martin knew he was the patron [boss] the moment he saw him; authority stood written in the set of his head on his shoulders. It was a working authority, inherent in the stamp of the man. The leather cloths that cased him bore the

rips of rough rides and the stains of many camps.

The Santos had lived at Bavanuchi since the time of King Carlos III, who had granted them the land. A Santos had been Marques of Sonora. "But," Santiago said, "we do not produce any dammed Marques in this time . . . My grandfather said it is better to own land than to govern it. We Santos produce rancheros."

Near the Santos ranch Martin saw the handiwork of another bane of the wonderful country, the dreaded Apache.

The Apaches' raids deep into the heart of Chihuahua were frequent and chilling. Martin witnessed the aftermath of their viciousness at a ranch they had raided, where men, women, and children were butchered. In this attack, the Apaches were engaged by a troop of black soldiers from Fort Jefflin, north of the border (the black troopers, called "Buffalo Soldiers" by their Indian antagonists, fought frequently and hard in the plains wars). Following the engagement, Martin assisted the troop and returned to Texas with them. He eventually participated in a campaign that jointly pitted the Rangers, the U. S. Army, and Mexican forces against the Apache chief Fuego and his warriors. A similar event actually occurred in 1880, when in a rare instance of cooperation, the U. S. and Mexican governments worked together to track down and kill the renegade Chiricahua Apache Victorio and his band.

Lea, whose mother and father were born "at the pass" (El Paso), knows the country of which he writes. An accomplished artist, his sensitivity to the beauty of the Sierras, the starkness of the Texas prairie, and the diversity of the people who live there comes through in the narration. His writing appeals to all the senses, as in this description of a trail meal during a roundup:

> There were succulent yams, new and good to Martin's taste, and fiery
> meat floating in chili on the tin plates. There were tender dainties
> to pick from a bull's head that had been roasted cooked in clay and
> buried in hot coals since dawn. There was coffee in milk and sugar in
> tin cups. There was a scarred little cask of mescal for the cups when
> the coffee was gone.

Lea pays attention to detail; his writing has a ring of authority. For example, a large Mexican freight cart is prominent in the plot. An image of the freight cart, the oxen that pulled it, and the Mexican peon Pablo who drove the oxen is carefully developed:

> It was afternoon when the big oxen stood with the yokes strapped to their horns. The chains clinked as Pablo set them to the yoke rings . . . Pablo had brought the wheel oxen to the cart tongue . . . The cart wheels screeched a dry duet as they unrolled their dry tracks along the furrows of the road. The yoke straps squeaked chafing on the horns. The big splayed hooves moved slowly along the dust.

There is a sketch of the oxcart (Lea illustrates his books), pulled by the plodding oxen, with Pablo trudging alongside, that seals the image developed in the narrative.

In 1959 Robert Mitchum's DRM Productions filmed "The Wonderful Country." Mitchum is excellent as Martin Brady. It's reasonably true to the novel, and is a memorable Western film.

Overall, *The Wonderful Country* is a rugged and spirited adventure in the tradition of the best of Western fiction. It's a powerful, well-written novel that illuminates an important period in Western history.

14

THE LAND BEYOND: ALASKA AND WESTERN CANADA

INTRODUCTION

Canada is the world's second largest country after Russia. Alaska, the largest of the United States of America, is separated from the lower forty-eight by Canada. Both have vast regions of pristine wilderness and awesome beauty. Both have fierce winters that can be deadly to the unprepared.

Western Canada has historical similarities to the Western United States. Washington Irving observed in 1836 that it was the fur trade that gave early sustenance and vitality to the Canadian provinces. Before Canada was a country or even a dominion, it was controlled by Hudson's Bay Company, the "Company of Adventurers." When voyageurs from Hudson's Bay and rival North West Company set forth in search of beaver, they used a 3,000 miles network of waterways, linked by occasional portages, to set up a chain of trading posts, several of which would develop into major cities of the Canadian West.

In 1860 British Columbia, like its neighbor to the south, had a gold rush that lured thousands to the colony. By 1871 the boom was over, and the restless prospectors moved on.

In the decades following Canada's unification in 1867, the offer of 160 acres of virgin farmland lured settlers from the Ukraine, Scandinavia, Germany, and Holland. Thousands of pioneers poured into her prairies. By 1911 the population of Canada's West had soared from a few thousand to more than a million.

From its earliest days Canada has had its share of lawlessness. And just as the American West had its steely-eyed marshals and Texas Rangers to bring law and order, Canada had the mounties.

In 1872 the central prairie of Canada was populated by American whiskey traders, discontented Indians, and struggling settlers. It was to bring law to this untamed land that the Mounties were created. The Royal Canadian Mounted Police (RCMP) was established as the North West Mounted Police (NWMP) in 1873. Its mission was to police on horseback the vast western plains known then as the North-West Territories, which are now Manitoba, Saskatchewan and Alberta. During the next few years, after driving out the whiskey traders, they made friends with the Indians and persuaded them to sign treaties with the Canadian government. Then they set up police posts and protected incoming settlers from lawlessness. To this day, the scarlet-uniformed Mounties with their legendary reputation for persistence and bravery personify Canada.

Alaska, like Canada and the American Northwest, was exploited by fur traders. As early as the mid-1700s Russians were trapping in the Aleutian Islands, depleting the stock of many fur-bearing animals. Sitka was founded in 1799 and became the capital of Russian Alaska. During the first half of the 19th century, the Hudson's Bay Company and American traders were very active in Alaska. In 1867 the United States purchased Alaska—a land of snowcapped mountains, glaciers, and vast expanses of rolling tundra—from Russia for only $7.2 million.

In 1897-98 southeastern Alaska served as a gateway to the Klondike gold fields in neighboring Canada. Skagway, Valdez, and other Alaskan villages grew as way stations. In 1899 gold was found on the beach at Nome, and quickly an Alaskan gold rush was under way. Other important discoveries were made in the early 1900s around Fairbanks, in the Yellow and Iditarod river valleys, and along the Yukon near Ruby.

Novelists have capitalized on the rich history and the fierce, pristine landscapes of Canada and Alaska. Two of the best are by writers who used northern settings for many of their stories. *The Spoilers* (Harper and Brothers, 1905), by Rex Beach, is set in Nome during the gold rush. The plot of *The River's End* (Rinehart, 1919), by James Oliver Curwood, has a dying mountie give his identity to the man he is pursuing. Both novels depend heavily on their far north settings for their plots.

READER'S GUIDE

The Silent Places by Stewart Edward White. McClure Phillips, 1904. This novel, set in the Canadian wilderness near James Bay, is a tale of the Hudson's Bay Company and the search for Jingoss, an Ojibway who reneged on his debt to the company.

The Barrier by Rex Beach. Harper and Brothers, 1908. A love triangle, set in the wild Yukon in the early 1800s, involving the mixed-blood daughter of a trading post owner, an Army officer in command of troops at the local garrison, and a French trapper who is the girl's ardent admirer. Source for the 1926 and 1937 films.

The Silver Horde by Rex Beach. Harper and Brothers, 1909. A story set in and around the salmon fisheries of Bristol Bay, Alaska. Basis for the 1920 and 1930 films.

Burning Daylight by Jack London. Macmillan, 1910. The Yukon in 1893 was a wild and merciless land. This is the story of a gambler who came over the Chilkoot Pass and made his fortune before the gold seekers came, only to lose it when he returned to the States.

The Trail of '98 by Robert Service. Toronto: Ryerson Press, 1910. Robert Service is best known as the "Poet of the North," the author of classics such as *The Spell of the Yukon, The Cremation of Sam McGee,* and *The Shooting of Dan McGrew.* But Service also wrote some novels. This one is a story of the trail "to the Golden North, to the land of the Midnight Sun, to the treasure-troves of the Klondike Valley."

Philip Steele of the Royal Northwest Mounted Police by James Oliver Curwood. A. L. Burt, 1911. The son of a multimillionaire Chicago banker became Private Phil Steele of the Northwest Mounted Police. He learned fast, and his chief sent him on a mission involving a dangerous and beautiful woman. Basis for the 1925 film.

Corporal Cameron of the Northwest Mounted Police by Ralph Conner (Reverend Charles Gordon). George H. Doran, 1912. A tale of the McLeod Trail. A young Scotsman, newly arrived in Canada, worked as a surveyor in the wilderness before joining the famed Mounties at McLeod Barracks.

God's Country and the Woman by James Oliver Curwood. Doubleday, Page, 1915. A novel about women—how they were treated and accepted in the early Canadian wilderness, or "God's Country." In the plot two rival lumber companies clash and a man helps a woman defend against the wiles and lechery of an outlaw gang. Basis for the 1916 and 1937 films.

The Yukon Trail by William MacLeod Raine. Houghton Mifflin, 1917. The ruthless and brutal "big man of the North" was challenged by a young government agent, who believed in conservation rather than exploitation. Basis for the 1928 film "The Grip of the Yukon."

The Courage of Marge O'Doone by James Oliver Curwood. Doubleday, Page, 1918. Originally titled *The Girl Beyond the Trail*. The story of a train being snowbound in the frozen Canadian North Woods. Basis for the 1919 film.

The Flaming Forest by James Oliver Curwood. Cosmopolitan, 1921. Traveling northward on the trail of a killer named Black Roger, David Carrigan of the Royal Canadian Mounted Police found himself a prisoner in the camp of St. Pierre, a wealthy trader who recognized no authority. No one had ever seen St. Pierre, though tales of his power were legendary.

Renfrew of the Royal Mounted by Laurie York Erskine. D. Appleton, 1922. The first title in the series featuring Douglas Renfrew of the Royal Mounted, and his various thrill-packed adventures in the Canadian wilderness. Source for the 1937 film.

Wild Geese Calling by Stewart Edward White. Doubleday, Doran, 1940. John Murdock rode into an Oregon town a bachelor and left later that day with a wife who helped him carve out a home in the Alaskan wilderness.

Great Son by Edna Ferber. Doubleday, Doran, 1945. Four generations of the Melendy family wrested their fortunes from the rich Alaskan gold fields. They grew in wealth and influence as Seattle grew from a small wilderness town to a great city of gleaming skyscrapers.

Peace River Country by Ralph Allen. Doubleday, 1958. A story the

Sonderns—two children and their mother—who traveled to Canada's Peace River Country, where the plains meet the mountains, and of the father they could never quite manage to leave behind.

Ice Palace by Edna Ferber. Doubleday, 1958. Set during the territory's struggle for statehood, this is the story of a fifty-year battle between two titans trying to dominate Alaska's future. And here, too, are the men from "The Outside" determined to exploit a fabulously rich Alaska for their own gains. Source for the 1960 film.

Sitka by Louis L'Amour. Bantam Books, 1958. Adventurer Jean LaBarge found a life or death challenge in Sitka, on the rugged coast of the Alaska territory, which was chartered to the Russians. But Russia was in upheaval and a ruthless man had seized control of the fur trade both in and out of the territory. LaBarge was ready to fight to win Alaska for America.

The Goldseekers by W. R. Burnett. Alfred A. Knopf, 1962. A novel of Alaska at the turn of the century during the Gold Rush years.

The White Dawn: An Eskimo Story by James Houston. Harcourt, Brace and Jovanovich, 1971. On a spring day in 1896, several men in a small boat from a New England whaling ship were missing and presumed lost in the icy, arctic sea. There was tremendous excitement when three strangers, unlike any men the Eskimos had ever seen, were brought back to the camp. They were nursed back to good health and became a delightful curiosity to the Eskimo people. But during the long arctic winter, misunderstandings and distrust arose.

The Temptations of Big Bear by Rudy Wiebe. Toronto: McClelland and Stewart, 1973. In 1876, as the buffalo vanished from the Canadian plains, Big Bear led his Cree nation across the prairie in search of a means of retaining their free way of life. He refused to sign away his people's land to the White Queen and go onto a reservation.

Tisha: The Story of a Young Teacher in the Alaskan Wilderness by Robert Specht. St. Martin's Press, 1976. In 1927 young Anne Hobbs trekked across the northern tundra to become schoolmarm in the remote Alaskan gold-rush settlement of Chicken. There she endured the relentless Alaskan winter and pitted herself against the village residents' demands that she conform to their standards.

"Dot It Down": A Story of Life in the NorthWest by Alexander Begg. Toronto: University of Toronto Press, 1978. Originally published in 1871. The Hudson's Bay Company sold its vast territories to Canada in 1869. The Métis, led by the charismatic Louis Riel, violently resisted what they saw as the final threat to their rights. The events leading to the Red River Rebellion, including the role played by Americans pressing for annexation of the region, are the background for this novel.

The Great Alone by Janet Dailey. Poseidon Press, 1986. A beautiful Indian woman fell in love with a Cossack hunter. From their union sprang seven generations of native Alaskans—a proud mix of Russian, English, Indian and American blood.

Alaska by James A. Michener. Random House, 1988. Like many Michener novels, *Alaska* ranges from the near-forgotten past to the present. It tells the story of the native peoples of Alaska, of their confrontation with a fierce wilderness. He combines historical and fictional characters, and tells how two unlikely Americans brought the first justice to Alaska.

The Northern Lights by Howard Norman. Simon and Schuster, 1988. In the frigid wilderness of northern Manitoba, two boys explore their domain of Cree Indians, trappers, missionaries, and fugitives.

The Last Exile by Charles Durham. Ballantine Books, 1989. Gabriel Dublanche, with his wife Celeste, fled the turmoil of religious war and pestilence in France for a new start in Canada. There, in a moment of blind fury, he committed an act that forced him to seek refuge in the harsh wilderness of the Chippewa Indians.

The Journey by James A. Michener. Random House, 1989. In 1897 gold fever sent thousands scurrying to the Klondike. This novel recounts the adventures of four aristocratic Englishmen and their Irish servant, who chose the most difficult route to the gold fields: north from Edmonton down the forbidding Mackenzie River. That decision was the first of many wrong judgments.

Running West by James Houston. Crown, 1989. An historical adventure set in the Canadian North of the early 1700s, where a young Scotsman, an indentured clerk to Canada's Hudson's Bay Company, met a young Indian woman and together they were sent "running west" into an uncharted wilderness in search of gold.

Ashana by E. P. Roesch (Ethel and Paul Roesch). Random House, 1990. In the 1790's, during the reign of Catherine the Great, Russian fur traders claimed the rich Alaskan wilderness for imperial Russia. A young Athabascan woman, Ashana, was torn from her husband to become the mistress of the Russian leader of the traders. Based on a true story recorded in 1843, the novel unfolds a little-known era of Alaskan history.

Valley of a Thousand Smokes by Dan Cushman. Five Star, 1996. A white lie helps Tom Flynn secure a position as a sergeant with the Royal Canadian Mounted Police. His investigation of the murder of a boy at an Indian mission leads him into a potentially deadly conflict with Pere Brissaud, the ruler of the Valley of a Thousand Smokes. And then there is a possible revolt against the Canadian government he must counter. He may or may not live to regret his white lie.

The Winter Wolf by Richard Parry. Forge, 1996. Fifty-year-old Wyatt Earp brought his wife to the Alaskan boomtowns of Skagway and Nome, hoping to strike it rich in the Alaskan gold fields. They were followed by young Nathan Blaylock, the son of Wyatt and Mattie Blaylock, Wyatt's common-law wife in Tombstone. Nathan intended to kill his father.

The Englishman's Boy by Guy Vanderhaeghe. St. Martin's Press, 1996. An historical novel that interleaves two parallel, linked narratives: the history of the Cypress Hills massacre of Assiniboine by U. S. wolfers in 1873—one of the bloodiest, most brutal events of the 19th century Canadian West and one of the formative events for the North West Mounted Police—and a fictional rendering of Hollywood's fixation with Westerns during the 1920s.

Whispers of the Wind by Tom Hron. Signet, 1997. From Hron's series set in the Far North featuring United States Marshal Eli Bonnet. In this story, Marshal Bonnet uprooted his family to the frozen Yukon to join legendary Marshal Wyatt Earp in search of an aging prospector. But then Bonnet's daughter was kidnapped, and the two lawmen had to search for the prospector and the child.

The Last Crossing by Guy Vanderhaeghe. Toronto: McClelland and Stewart, 2002. Two Englishmen were ordered by their tyrannical father to find their brother who had gone missing in the 19th century American West. Their search took them from Oxford to the dusty whiskey trading posts of the American and Canadian West.

Selected Reviews

The Spoilers
by Rex Beach
Harper and Brothers, 1905

Robert Service, the acclaimed "Poet of the North," wrote eloquently of a beautiful, pristine, but unforgiving land where only the strong survive. Its riches attracted every sort of adventurer from all over the world, as well as boatloads of ne'er-do-wells. The weak could not win this land, wrote Service. It could only be won by the strong. This is the story of two men, one good and one bad, both with the hearts of Vikings, who fought ferociously for the treasures the land reserved for the strong.

The Nome gold rush in Alaska started in the winter of 1898-99. The frontier village, which had only one narrow street, quickly grew into a bustling boomtown, with twenty saloons to make life bearable. Men from every land came, most of them living in corrugated iron buildings and canvas tents. All were set on making a fortune.

During the summer life moved at a furious pace. Two shifts worked the mines twenty-four hours a day: "For there is no respite here—no night, no Sunday, no halt, during the hundred days in which the Northland lends itself to pillage."

Rex Beach heard about Nome while in law school in Chicago, and he went there in June of 1900. In three years he failed to make his fortune, and returned to Chicago broke. But from his Far North observations he wrote *The Spoilers* and the book was a huge success.

The arch villain in the novel is Alec McNamara, based on an actual scoundrel who schemed to misappropriate most of Nome's gold. He was an impressive, resourceful man with courage and great physical strength. McNamara had his pal, a federal district judge who owed his appointment to him, issue injunctions on the largest production mines around Nome. The judge appointed his benefactor the receiver for each mine and McNamara took over the mines, continued to work them and harvested an enormous fortune.

Beach gave his villain a worthy adversary; a raw boned young miner named Roy Glenister. He and his partner Dextry owned the Midas Mine on Anvil Creek, the main object of McNamara's scheme. The Midas had made Dextry and Glenister wealthy, but the life of a rich miner wasn't something to be envied, as Dextry explained:

> Well, bein' as me and Glenister was gougin' into the bowls of Anvil Creek all last summer, we didn't really get the fresh grub habit fastened on us none. You see, the gamblers down-town cop out the few aigs an' green vegetables that stray off the ships, so they never get as far as the creek none; except, maybe, in the shape of anecdotes."

Glenister was tall and athletic, college educated, and self-confident. Although he had Service's heart of a Viking, he was ruled by his emotions. The source of most of his emotional turmoil was Helen Stillman, the niece of Alec McNamara's crooked judge. Helen was attracted to him, but didn't understand the wild North as he did. Glenister explained it to her:

> It calls to a fellow in some strange way that a gentler country never could. When once you've lived the long, lazy June days that never end, and heard geese honking under a warm, sunlit midnight; or once you've hit the trail on a winter morning so sharp and clear that the air stings your lungs, and the whole white, silent world glistens like a jewel; yes—and when you've seen the dogs romping in harness till the sled runners ring; and the distant mountain ranges come out like beautiful carvings, so close you can reach them—well, there's something in it that brings you back—that's all, no matter where you've lost yourself.

Helen wanted the law to take hold in Nome, because order wasn't possible without it. Glenister told her:

> There isn't half the disorder you think there is. There weren't any

crimes in this country till the tenderfeet arrived. We didn't know what a thief was . . . I like the old way best . . . a survival of the fittest.

He tried to change to please Helen, but "the wilderness . . . the wild rage of desperation; the exhalation of victory—can make a man a savage."

Glenister and McNamara were on a collision course, and they eventually met in a fearsome fist fight that shocked even rough and rowdy Nome. The narrator set the stage:

Men may fight duels calmly, may shoot or parry or thrust with cold deliberation; but when there comes the jar of body to body, the sweaty contact of skin to skin, the play of iron muscles, the painful gasp of exhaustion—then the mind goes skittering back into its dark recesses while every venomous passion leaps forth from its hiding-place and joins in the horrid war.

Beach then staged maybe the best fight scene in Western literature. Certainly, its translation into cinema is classic. It has been the center-piece for five rip-roaring film versions of the novel.

There was a silent version in 1914. The first sound version was made in 1930. The 1942 release is the best known. It starred John Wayne, Randolph Scott, and Marlene Dietrich. The screenwriter revised the plot to accommodate Dietrich's character. The elaborately staged fistfight between Wayne and Scott is the film's highlight. A routine remake of the 1942 version was released in 1956.

The strike at Nome and the subsequent gold rush was the most remarkable in the Far North. Rex Beach has preserved this phenomenal event in a novel that's rich in action, humor, and local color.

The River's End
by James Oliver Curwood
Rinehart, 1919

In the early 1900s Canadian law was enforced by His Majesty's Northwest Mounted Police—the legendary Mounties. "Don't come back unless you get your man, dead or alive," was their creed. These scarlet-coated policemen had enormous courage and stamina, often pursuing a criminal across the vast Canadian wilderness for months, living on limited rations and whatever the land could provide. With true British chivalry and persistence, they won their battles—bringing in a desperado or quelling an Indian uprising—more by their presence than by force.

Constable Derwent Conniston had followed his prey John Keith for twenty-seven months along the rim of the Arctic. But a strange thing happened during the pursuit. Although Conniston followed him for over a thousand miles with the tenacity of a ferret, Keith passed up scores of opportunities during the chase to kill the Mountie—even though capture meant the hangman. When Conniston caught up to him, Keith couldn't take advantage even when the frost got the Mountie's lung. The hunted tried to nurse the hunter back to health. A mutual admiration and a strong bond developed between the two.

The story begins with Keith and Conniston holed up in a cabin north of the Arctic circle, waiting for Conniston to die:

> Over their heads the Arctic storm was crashing in a mighty fury, as if striving to break down the little cabin that had dared to rear itself in the dun-gray emptiness at the top of the world, eight hundred miles from civilization. There were curious wailings, strange screeching sounds, and heart-breaking moanings in its strife, and when at last its passion died away and there followed a strange quiet, the two men could feel the frozen earth under their feet shiver with the rumbling reverberations of the crashing and breaking fields of ice out in Hudson's Bay.
>
> There was plenty of time to get to know one another.

Although Keith had been tried and convicted of killing a man, Judge Kirkstone, he was not sure that he had committed the murder. His captor began to believe that a man of Keith's character couldn't have perpetrated such a crime. Because of a strong physical resemblance between the two, and because he had no family in Canada, Conniston proposed that, after his death, Keith go "back to God's Country" as Derwent Conniston of the Northwest Mounted Police.

Conniston died and Keith buried his friend under the floor of the cabin to keep the foxes away. He had a simple plan; he would serve out the short remaining time of Conniston's enlistment, then follow the Saskatchewan to the base of the Rocky Mountains—to the beautiful country at the river's end. With the Mountie's clothes and pack, he started south. Ahead was eight hundred miles of wilderness between him and the little town on the Saskatchewan where Inspector McDowell commanded F Division of the Royal Mounted. On the sixth day he saw the sun, for the first time in many months.

When Keith reached Prince Albert, he straightaway reported to Inspector McDowell. The inspector recognized him as Derwent Conniston, and welcomed him back heartily. Keith breathed more easily. But he had forgotten Shan Tung, the Chinaman.

Shan Tung possessed an unholy power, the ability to remember faces. Once he looked at a face, it was photographed in his memory for years. He recognized Keith and left a note in his cabin, asking if he had killed Derwent Conniston. But he kept his knowledge to himself.

Shan Tung didn't expose Keith because he coveted Miriam Kirkstone, the murdered judge's daughter, and thought Keith could help him get Miriam. But the Inspector, from afar, admired Miriam Kirkstone and unofficially put Keith on the Chinaman's trail.

This elaborate plot is further complicated by the arrival from England of Mary Josephine Conniston, the eighteen-year-old sister of the dead Mountie. She hadn't seen her brother in years, and readily accepted Keith as Conniston. In time, Keith began to feel love for her, and it made the big lie he was living almost unbearable:

A strong man, a man in whom blood ran red, there leaped up in him for a moment a sudden and unreasoning rage at that thing which he had called fate. He saw the unfairness of it all, the hopelessness of it all, the cowardly subterfuge and trickery of life itself as it had played against him, and with tightly set lips and clenched hands he called mutely on God Almighty to play the game square. Give him a chance.

With these odds, Keith would have to earn his freedom. Conniston never told him it would be easy.

If *The River's End* were published today, it would be widely condemned for its racism. Although Shan Tung is an arch villain, evil to the core, his characterization reflects the occidental's early 1900s view of the oriental. McDowell thought him to be, "Either an exiled prime minister of China or the devil in a yellow skin." Shan Tung told Keith, " . . . like my yellow-headed goddess, you hate me because of my skin. . . ." Keith realized that "it was her [blond] hair that roused the venom in him when he thought of her as the property of Shan Tung. If it had been black or even brown, the thought might not have emphasized itself so unpleasantly in his mind. But that vivid gold cried out against the crime . . ." But just as it is important to view history in its temporal context, fiction must be read with respect to the period in which it's set.

James Oliver Curwood wrote numerous exceptionally good novels and short stories of Alaska and the Canadian Northwest. Some of his best include *Steele of the Royal Mounted* (Bobbs-Merrill, 1911), *Kazan* (Bobbs-Merrill, 1914), *The Grizzly King* (Doubleday, Page, 1916), *Back to God's Country* (Cosmopolitan, 1920), *The Country Beyond* (Cosmopolitan, 1922), and *The Alaskan* (Cosmopolitan, 1923).

Many of his novels and short stories have been adapted to film. There have been three movie versions of *The River's End*. There was a silent film made in 1922, and two later sound features. Michael Curtiz' 1930 film was a remake of the 1922 silent version. It used the silent plot line, which was unsuitable for sound. The 1940 film, directed by Ray Enright, was superior to the earlier ones.

The River's End places interesting characters in an exciting plot, set in "God's Country." It is one of a fine author's best works.

15

HIGH NOON: THE ROMANTIC WEST

INTRODUCTION

When casual readers use the term "Western," they are usually referring to a novel that author Matt Braun describes as the "Traditional Western." These novels are founded on the mythology of the Old West, and as Braun defines them, typically run 60,000-70,000 words in length. This short length limits multiple subplots and the number of characters.

A lot of scholarly effort has gone into distinguishing between "Westerns" and "genuine" Western literature. Some of it is quite harsh. John R. Milton describes "Westerns" as a "sub literary form." James C. Work, in his anthology *Prose and Poetry of the American West* (University of Nebraska Press, 1990), had the following statement in his preface:

Because the Western is so popular, and because it is usually a perennial source of confusion in the discussion of western American literature, it is the first topic we need to clarify before going on. The fact is, this book has almost nothing to do with Westerns. In the entire volume there are only four or five stories about cowboys. There are no ex-Confederates trailing stolen cattle in Texas, no marshals playing stud poker in Arizona, and no horses named Cherokee or Comanche or Blue Boy. In deference to serious literature of the American West, I have seriously avoided anthologizing the Western.

C. L. Sonnichsen contends Owen Wister's *The Virginian* (Macmillan, 1902) divided the high road from the low road of popular Western novels, with popular writers of traditional Westerns on the low road. Irwin R. Blacker said a writer must avoid having his novel based on the Western myth judged as "a Western in the popular sense of the word—a tale of two dimensional figures moving without motivation through a series of violent incidents to destroy an obvious evil."

Yet many traditional Westerns do have literary merit. And some of those that don't have a sense of place and history and are rip-roaring action-packed good stories that have been read and reread by a loyal audience. Novels by Zane Grey, Max Brand, Luke Short, and other popular Western writers have been reissued many times, and still have a significant readership. There are many fine authors today who are still writing traditional or commercial Westerns.

You will find many traditional Westerns scattered throughout the other sections of this reader's guide, so categorized because of plot and setting considerations.

There have been literally thousands of Westerns written, starting in the 1800s and still going strong. Many authors wrote a multitude of books; Max Brand (Frederick Schiller Faust) alone wrote over 180 Westerns. I have attempted to give a good sampling of their work, but have necessarily included only a few entries of the more prolific writers.

For review, I selected *Bar-20* (Outing, 1907), by Clarence E. Mulford; *Destry Rides Again* (Dodd, Mead 1930), by Max Brand; *Hondo* (Fawcett, 1953), by Louis L'Amour; *Hombre* (Ballantine Books, 1961); by Elmore Leonard; and *Shane* (Houghton Mifflin, 1949), by Jack Schaefer. These fine novels clearly represent the best of traditional Westerns.

Francis Berrian by Timothy Flint. 1826. The story of a theological student who left his studies at Harvard for the early Southwest, where he fell in love with a Spanish girl and led a dangerous, exciting life.

Lin McLean by Owen Wister. Harper and Brothers, 1898. Lin McLean was a tall, easy-going cowboy who had something that set him apart. He had a genius for trouble. Basis for the 1918 film "A Woman's Fool."

John Ermine of the Yellowstone by Frederic Remington. Macmillan, 1902. A novel by the famed artist, set in the Yellowstone country of Montana, about a white child raised by the Crow who eventually becomes a scout for the army.

Chip of the Flying U by B. M. Bower. G. W. Dillingham, 1906. B. M. (Bertha Muzzy) Bower's first novel introduces a woman-shy cowboy who is part of "The Happy Family," a Montana bunkhouse gang. In the romantic plot, a young woman doctor enters Chip's life. The Happy Family reappears in Bower's later books. Source for the 1914, 1926, and 1939 films.

Sundown Slim by Henry Herbert Knibbs. Houghton Mifflin, 1915. Washington Hicks was a homely six-foot-four hobo-cowboy-cook-philosopher of good humor who preferred to be called Sundown Slim. His story is set in the midst of cattlemen-sheepmen conflict in central Arizona. Basis for the 1920 film of the same title, and the 1925 film "The Burning Trail."

The Man from Bar-20 by Clarence E. Mulford. McClurg, 1918. Johnny Nelson left the Bar-20 looking for adventure and joined the CL Ranch. While punching cattle for the CL, he found a hidden valley with over 200 head of CL cattle rebranded QE. He also found a gang of rustlers and a deadly gunfighter looking to cut him down. He should have left, but his friend Hopalong Cassidy had never taught him to run from trouble.

The Untamed by Max Brand (Frederich Schiller Faust). G. P. Putnam's Sons, 1919. *The Untamed* was Max Brand's first Western. The protagonist is the mysterious Whistlin' Dan Barry, who rode a black stallion named Satan and was followed by a wolf dog named Black Bart. Barry would appear in several Brand novels. Basis for the 1920 film.

Judith of Blue Lake Ranch by Jackson Gregory. Charles Scribner's Sons, 1919. Judith Sanford, with the help of soft-spoken horse handler Bud Lee, packs her own six-guns and goes on a rough and ready campaign to drive out the scheming killers who menace her Blue Lake Ranch.

The Ridin' Kid from Powder Ridge by Henry Herbert Knibbs. Houghton Mifflin, 1919. The kid acquired a good knowledge of horses, along with a wide range of profanity, while he was still very young. Then Pop Annersley taught him more civilized ways but he watched as Pop was brutally murdered. Then a sheepherder taught him to use a gun, and the Kid turned into an outlaw.

Oh, You Tex by William MacLeod Raine. Houghton Mifflin, 1920. Texas Ranger Jack Roberts had saved the Panhandle from the looting and killing that ravaged Dodge City and the vulnerable towns of New Mexico. Then the ruthless Dinsmore Gang came to his domain and challenged the law, determined to take over the rich cattle country of West Texas.

Temescal By Henry Herbert Knibbs. Houghton Mifflin, 1925. An adventure in Mexico, featuring a mysterious traveler captured by bandits, and his subsequent escape to become leader of a band of followers.

The Gentleman from Virginia by Charles Alden Seltzer. Doubleday, Page, 1926. A gentleman from Virginia settles in the savage country of the old Southwest, builds a Virginian mansion, and fights off a gang of outlaws.

The Killers by Max Brand (Frederick Schiller Faust). Macaulay, 1931. Geraldi, a young gambler and gunman who lived by his wits, was persuaded by Louise Asprey to search for her father—a rich mine owner who was now wanted by the law for shooting a man in a gambler's brawl. But there was another on her father's trail: a notorious killer whose job it was to ensure her father did not return.

Hopalong Cassidy and the Eagle's Brood by Clarence E. Mulford. Doubleday, Doran, 1931. Hopalong Cassidy and his gunslingers hunt down a band of outlaws who have killed a woman—a terrible crime almost unheard of in the West and seldom seen in the plot of a traditional Western.

Beyond the Rio Grande by William MacLeod Raine. Houghton Mifflin, 1931. Jack Hadley found the murderer of his father in Mexico, riding as an officer in a rebel army of the Revolution. At his back Hadley had only the pitifully few guns of the cow outfit he worked for, while the man he hunted commanded an outlaw army.

A Son of Arizona by Charles Alden Seltzer. Doubleday, Doran, 1931. When Bob Blakeslee returned home after an eleven-year absence he found his father had been robbed and killed while carrying home the fall payroll. He further found the old man's great Circle B ranch under the control of a powerful neighbor. The hot-tempered, fast-drawing prodigal had to avenge his father and claim what was his.

Riders of the Night by Eugene Cunningham. Houghton Mifflin, 1932. Set on the Texas range, this is the story of young Burk Yates and Myra Yarborough, whose fathers were cowmen "out of the old rock," and of a fierce struggle for law and order in the cow country. In *Riders*, Cunningham introduced a trio of gunfighters he called the "Three Mesquiteers." He used a different trio in a later novels, and William Colt MacDonald picked up the title for a trio he created in *Law of the Forty-Fives* (Covici-Friede,1934).

Arizona Ames by Zane Grey. Harper and Brothers, 1932. Arizona Ames was a drifting cowboy who was also a gunman. He used his deadly skill to help people he met during his wanderings.

Don Jim by Charles H. Snow. Macrae, Smith. 1932. A young woman is kidnapped, and a young cowhand sees an opportunity to rescue her and earn her respect. But things don't go quite so smoothly.

Buckaroo by Eugene Cunningham. Houghton Mifflin, 1933. Three Texas Rangers battle three hundred villians.

Idaho by Paul Evan Lehman. Macauley, 1933. A stranger known only as Idaho hired on and became the best ranch foreman John Endicott ever had. He knew cattle and his deadly gun gave Endicott an edge in his range feud with Clint Hollister. But Idaho was unaware of a family relationship that could have complicated his loyalties.

Law of the Forty-Fives by William Colt MacDonald. Covici-Friede, 1934. The novel that introduced Tucson Smith, Stony Brooke, and Lullaby Joslin, the "Three Mesquiteers," a trio that would appear in a series of MacDonald novels and numerous B-Western films.

Diamond River Man by Eugene Cunningham. Houghton Mifflin, 1934. Lit Taylor, heir to the Bar B Ranch in Diamond River, goes into outlaw territory to pick up some stolen cows. The trail of the stolen beef points to Frenchy Leonard's rustlers and leads to the wealthy rancher King Connell.

Powdersmoke Range by William Colt MacDonald, Covici-Friede, 1934. MacDonald's "Three Mesquiteers"—Tucson Smith, Lullaby Joslin, and Stony Brooke—purchased an old Spanish ranch and learned that the former owner had been murdered and the stock ran off. Investigation brought the trio into conflict with the self-appointed cattle king and dictator of that section of the cow country. Basis for the 1935 film.

Riders of the Whistling Skull by William Colt MacDonald. Covici-Friede, 1934. Tucson Smith and the other Mesquiteers rescue a Mexican beauty from a gang of gunmen. Basis for the 1937 film.

The Trail of Danger by William MacLeod Raine. Houghton Mifflin, 1934. In the days following the American conquest of California, a young sailor jumped ship and found refuge in the home of an old Spanish gentleman who opposed violence and accepted the Americans. Others did not. One swore to kill the young sailor.

Singing Lead By George C. Henderson. Greenberg, 1936. A Spanish grandee, turned outlaw to find the killer of his mother and sisters, rode with a ruthless American who had a strange power over women. The Spaniard knew he was about to be betrayed by his companero of the trail.

Comanche Kid by E. B. (Edward Beverly) Mann. William Morrow, 1936. Dallas Spain was the son of one of the most feared men in the Southwest. A slender kid who drank lemonade instead of liquor, he set out to clear his father's name of the charges of murder and robbery.

Rustler's Roundup by E. B. (Edward Beverly) Mann. William Morrow, 1936. The deeds of the man known as "The Whistler" were known to all men throughout the West; his face was known to none. But when The Whistler was summoned to end the robbing and killing of violent Blaze Tremaine, two men arrived who whistled. One was The Whistler, the other an impostor.

The Lone Ranger by Fran Striker. Grosset and Dunlap, 1936. Created for a radio show in Detroit, the Lone Ranger and his companion Tonto would ride across many novels, movies, and television screens and become part of the American culture. "An Indian and a white man rode slowly in silvery moonlight across a rolling plain. The Indian, mounted on a paint horse, was known as Tonto, but no one knew the name of his companion who rode a snow white stallion. The white man wore a mask which was as much a part of his equipment as the brace of ivory handled Colts holstered on his hips."

Riding Gun by Eugene Cunningham. Houghton Mifflin, 1938. Lorn Moray, a Texas Ranger in the border country accused of killing a sheriff in cold blood, received the promise of a pardon in exchange for a dangerous errand to an outlaw town.

Mavericks of the Plains by Bliss Lomox (Henry Sinclair Drago). Greenberg, 1938. The Hatton brothers struck in broad daylight, faces uncovered, their identity almost as potent a weapon as their guns. They would rob a bank or train, dodge sheriffs and marshals, and then retreat to the security of the Cherokee Strip, a place peace officers feared to tread.

The Tree of Death by Frederick R. Bechdolt. Caxton House, 1939. A novel about the ruthless ruler of the border country where a great cottonwood tree called "The Tree of Death" stood where three trails met near its spreading boughs.

Peace Marshal by Frank Gruber. William Morrow, 1939. The town of Broken Lance, astraddle the Chisholm Trail, with great droves of Texas cattle bawling down the main street, and wild, drunken, gun-toting cowboys, needed a peace marshal. But the only man who was gunfighter enough to pacify Broken Lance had hung up his guns, sworn never to shoot another man for pay. Source for the 1943 film "The Kansan."

The Lone Ranger and the Outlaw Stronghold by Fran Striker. Grosset and Dunlap, 1939. From Striker's *Lone Ranger* series. The Lone Ranger and Tonto were on their way to Durango to help settle a long-standing feud between Flint Greggson and Tom Carling over a silver claim. En route they found Carling dead. It seemed obvious who the killer was, but the ranger wasn't so sure.

Brand of Empire by Luke Short (Frederick D. Glidden). Collins, 1940. U. S. senator and powerful cattleman Matt Waranrode controlled the law, the territory, and everyone in it. When the local newspaper got out of line, he sent his killers after it. When one of his cowboys objected, the man was horse-whipped and beaten senseless. The senator made a mistake in not killing him, a forty-a-month cowboy who would challenge the lord of the Ute River.

Sheriff of Yavisa by Charles H. Snow. Macrae, Smith. 1941. Lawlessness was rampant in Yavisa when young Bob Jackson was sworn in as sheriff. His predecessor had been murdered. It was up to Bob to find the killer. It helped that his father had been a sheriff before him and had taught him the ropes.

Gunman's Chance by Luke Short (Frederick D. Glidden). Doubleday, Doran, 1941. Jim Garry was a hired gun, a man who killed for money. But when the Sun Dust combine brought him to Massacre Basin, he found their contract included deeds that were too dirty even for a hired killer. Republished in paperback as *Blood on the Moon*. Basis for the 1948 movie with the that title.

Silvertip by Max Brand (Frederick Schiller Faust). Dodd, Mead, 1942. Restlessness and a chance meeting with the bandit Bandini led Jim Silver, the legendary Silvertip—one of Max Brand's most heroic protagonists— to Haverhill Valley, where he found more action and excitement than he expected.

Long Ride by Peter Dawson (Jonathan H. Glidden). Dodd, Mead, 1942. In Agua Verde, the line was drawn between cattlemen and sheepmen, and an ex-convict was given the responsibility for resolving the conflict.

Boss of Panamint by Leslie Ernenwein. Leisure Books, 1942. Searching for the killer who had ambushed his father, Lee Beauregarde rode into Panamint, and into the midst of a range war. When he killed a man to stop a fight, Lee found himself in the middle of a showdown, with the identity of his father's killer at stake.

Ride the Man Down by Luke Short (Frederick D. Glidden). Doubleday, Doran, 1942. Most of the huge Evarts spread was open range, land that belonged to anyone who could take it. On Phil Evarts' death, his foreman Will Ballard was left to defend the ranch against an army of well-armed intruders intent on driving their cattle onto the Evarts' range. Basis for the 1952 film.

Useless Cowboy by Alan LeMay. Farrar and Rinehart, 1943. In this comical novel, LeMay pokes fun at cowboy clichés. When Melody Jones arrived in Payneville, strangers called him "sir" and bought him drinks. Needless to say, it was a case of mistaken identity. But Jones liked the attention, and so he continued with his new identity. What Melody didn't know was that he bore a striking resemblance to Monte Jarrad, the most feared killer in the southwest.

Source for the 1951 film "Along Came Jones."

Corner Creek by Luke Short (Frederick D. Glidden). Macmillan, 1946. All that remained after the Apache raid was a silk dress, enough for Chris Danning to track his intended bride's killer. This is the grim story of his manhunt. Basis for the 1948 film.

Sheriff of Lonesome by Burt Arthur (Herbert Arthur Shappiro). Belmont Books, 1948. Cocky young Hank Wilson left his home in the Texas Panhandle and rode north, intent on seeing some of the rest of the world. Shortly, he found himself sheriff of a wild, bloody town, where he would be severely tested.

High Vermilion by Luke Short (Frederick D. Glidden). Houghton Mifflin, 1948. Larkin Moffit came to the mining town of High Vermilion looking to change his ways and become an honest man. But he ran up against the scoundrel who owned most of the town and most of the people in it, who tried to buy him and then tried to kill him. Basis for the 1951 film "Silver City."

Passport to Perdition by Gunnison Steele. Better Publications, 1948. From the *Rio Kid* series. Bob Pryor, the Rio Kid, combats outlaws who are attacking and looting steamboats on the Colorado River carrying gold from the boomtowns of the Rockies to California vaults.

Fiddlefoot by Luke Short (Frederick D. Glidden). Houghton Mifflin, 1949. Frank Chess was a drifter, a "fiddlefoot." He never stayed around long enough to take a stand on anything. But when he finally did take a stand, he was ready to destroy anything that stood against him. Basis for the television series with the same title.

The Lobo Legion by Jackson Cole (House Name). Popular Library, 1950. Ranger Jim Hatfield rode beyond the Texas state line, into the land of the Lobo Legion, the raiding marauders who preyed on the great cattle drives. When Hatfield crossed into their country, his star was worthless and he left all help behind.

Vengeance Valley by Luke Short (Frederick D. Glidden). Houghton Mifflin, 1950. Two brothers strode into town with a grim announcement: they were going to kill the man who had dishonored their sister down in Texas. But they came up against a ranch foreman who covered up for his wayward foster brother. Basis for the 1951 film.

Ranger's Luck by William MacLeod Raine. Houghton Mifflin, 1950. In Arizona territory a young ranger accidentally stumbled upon the loot from a train robbery, was confronted by a headstrong young young woman pointing his own revolver at him, and had to tangle with a killer and an unscrupulous lawyer to get to the bottom of the robbery.

Tall Man Riding by Norman A. Fox. Dell, 1951. Madden came back to Montana sworn to kill Tucker Ordway for the bullwhip scars across his back. Instead, he found a whole town that wanted to destroy the ruthless old rancher, and by a strange twist of fate he had to defend the man he hated. Source for the 1955 film.

Land of the Lawless by Les Savage. Doubleday, 1951. An old Indian in Mexican Hat stood accused of murdering a white man, and the local citizens were lynch-crazy. But Lee Banner knew the real killer was still free, and that one of three possible witnesses was an Indian named Adakhai who would not hesitate to kill a white man.

Johnny Guitar by Roy Chanslor. Simon and Schuster, 1953. An ambitious woman built a gambling saloon on land wanted by the railroad. She romanced an outlaw who was the former lover of a cattle queen who despised her. Then the saloon owner's old lover—the title character—showed up and defended her when the cattle queen stirred up the townspeople. Source for the 1954 film.

Dig the Spurs Deep by Peter Field (House Name). Pocket Books, 1953. When Pat Stevens' cattle started disappearing, their trail led through the high country to the fabled Bluestem Ranch, where strangers were not welcome.

Night Raid by Frank Bonham. Ballantine Books, 1954. A story of trouble between Texans and a Mexican bandit, set in the Big Bend country of Texas.

Follow the New Grass by Cliff Farrell. Random House, 1954. A fugitive from Texas hires on to protect the grazing lands near a Cheyenne reserve.

The Man from Laramie by Thomas T. Flynn. Dell, 1954. The man from Laramie rode a thousand miles down into New Mexico territory to kill a man he'd never met, a gunrunner who sold guns to the Apaches who slaughtered the cavalry detachment led by his brother. Source for the 1955 film.

Bitter Sage by Frank Gruber. Rinehart, 1954. In 1877 a new railroad brought a frenzy of activity to a small western town in Kansas. It also brought Wes Tancred, fleeing the disbelief of others that he killed a man in self defense—a man who, legend had it, robbed from the rich to give to the poor. It didn't matter that the legend was false. For the first time in years Tancred was forced to pick up a gun again. Basis for the 1956 film "Tension at Table Rock."

Smoky Valley by Donald Hamilton. Fawcett, 1954. A skinny Easterner who went West to recover from war wounds had to show some toughs that looks can be deceiving. Source for the 1955 film "The Violent Men."

The Border Jumpers by Will C. Brown (Scott Boyles). E. P. Dutton, 1955. Link Jones was a respected family man with a past. Then he and a dance-hall girl named Billie accidentally tangled with the Dock Tobin gang of border jumpers. Link thought they would be it all right, because Dock Tobin was his uncle—and Link had once ridden with the gang. But after a few days he began to feel that he was still one of them. Basis for the 1958 film "Man of the West."

Cast a Long Shadow by Wayne D. Overholser. Macmillan, 1955. The story of a land dispute between a large company, which claimed ownership through an old Mexican land grant, and the land's settlers, who had lived and worked on the land so long that they believed it belonged to them—and of a man caught in the middle. Basis for the 1959 film.

The Law and Jake Wade by Marvin H. Albert. Fawcett, 1956. The story of a reformed outlaw trying to escape his past. Jake Wade, now a respected sheriff who is trying to go straight, runs into his former gang. Source for the 1958 film.

The Night of the Tiger by Al Dewlen. McGraw-Hill, 1956. A man came home to his small Texas frontier town after eleven years of hunting buffalo with a small fortune, but was beaten, robbed, and accused of cattle rustling. Then he sought revenge on those who had ruined his life. Filmed in 1966 as "Ride Beyond Vengeance."

He Rode Alone by Steve Frazee. Fawcett, 1956. A boy walked out of the wilderness in the summer of 1855, leaving three graves behind him, with a determination to hunt down and kill a family named Snelling.

Return of the Texan by Burt Arthur (Herbert Arthur Shappiro). Leisure Books, 1956. When Johnny Canavan returned to Cuero, Texas, he landed in the middle of a battle between cattlemen and homesteaders.

Stirrup High by Walt Coburn. Julian Messner, 1957. Coburn aimed this autobiographical novel at young adult readers. It tells of a fourteen-year-old boy's adventures on a Montana ranch in the summer of 1903.

The Square Shooter by Walt Coburn. Belmont Books, 1957. Boone was a tough young cowboy who didn't know where he came from or even his real name. He rode with a drunken outlaw named Jawbone Smith, who had raised him, knew who he was, and planned to turn him into a ruthless killer.

The War Wagon by Clair Huffaker. Fawcett, 1957. Originally titled *Badman*. Two brothers, one just out of prison, ambushed an armored stagecoach that promised a fortune to anyone who could take it. Basis for the 1967 film.

Last Stand at Saber River by Elmore Leonard. Dell, 1957. The story of an ex-Confederate soldier whose real war for his land was just beginning. With his strong-willed wife and their two children, the former rebel returns to his Arizona home to resume a quiet life. Instead, he finds Union sympathizers have taken possession his small spread. He faces one more battle. Basis for the 1997 teleplay.

The Hard Riders by Noel Loomis. London: Priory, 1957. Jim Carlson took a position against his father and his sweetheart when he sided with the homesteaders rather than the cattlemen. But he knew that sooner or later Mad Horse Dam would be built and the range land would have to be farmed.

The Bounty Killer by Marvin H. Albert. Fawcett, 1958. Jose Gomez, a brutal Mexican outlaw, with the help of a beautiful young woman escaped capture and returned to his hometown. Soon Luke Chilson, a bounty hunter, was dispatched to track down and recapture Jose. The people of the small town despised bounty hunters and gave no aid to Chilson as he searched for the bandit. Source of the 1966 film.

Saddle Tramp by Todhunter Ballard. Popular Library, 1958. A drifter took a job as ramrod at a ranch and became involved in a campaign of terror in a ranch feud.

Guns of the Rio Conchos by Clair Hufffaker. Gold Medal, 1958. Riot Holiday escaped a Comanche onslaught with an arrowhead in his chest. Now he intended to settle the score, even if it meant taking on the Comancheros, the Mexican army, and the whole Comanche nation. Filmed in 1964 as "Rio Conchos."

Man in the Saddle by Ernest Haycox. Little, Brown, 1958. Owen Merritt lost his woman and his land to the richest man in the country. His enemies branded him a coward and a killer, and he went into hiding. But he came back. They neglected to kill him. Basis for the 1958 film.

Posse from Hell by Clair Huffaker. Crest Books, 1958. When the bandits rode into Paradise, they destroyed what they couldn't take and carried a girl away. Seven men pursued them, crazy with revenge—a "Posse from Hell." Basis for the 1961 film.

Short Cut to Red River by Noel Loomis. Macmillan, 1958. Ross Phillips rode north from Santa Fe at the head of a wagon train carrying a million dollars in gold bullion bound for Red River, Arkansas. He was establishing a new trade route through a thousand miles of Comanche-infested wilderness. But when he came up against a Comanche war chief who held white women captives, he came to a dead halt. Spur Award from the Western Writers of America.

The Mad Marshal by William Colt MacDonald. Pyramid Books, 1958. A town marshal joins forces with a brothel madam and together they swindle the citizens.

The Bravados by Frank O'Rourke. London: Heinemann, 1958. Three prisoners escaped from jail in Rio Arriba, taking Emma Steinmetz as a hostage. Jim Douglas had been doing time too, but events put him charge of the high country hunt for the convicts. Basis for the 1958 film.

Long Run by Nelson Nye. Macmillan, 1959. Will Howlett set his guns aside and rode a thousand miles from Texas to leave his past behind. But because of a woman trying to hang on to her ranch, he had to buckle on his gunbelt again. Spur Award from the Western Writers of America.

Holster Law by Bradford Scott (A. Leslie Scott). Pyramid Books, 1959. From Scott's *Walt Slade* series. On a trail drive from Texas to the cattle market at Dodge City, the herd owner and his range boss were found murdered. Suspicions flared, and a range war was in the making when Texas Ranger Walt Slade entered the conflict.

Day of the Hunter by Ann Ahlswede. Ballantine Books, 1960. A mixed-blood searches for the murderer of of the couple who raised him in this story of racial prejudice.

The Stars in Their Courses by Harry Brown. Alfred A. Knopf, 1960. A western tragedy of a feud that did not end until the blood of many deaths had washed away the sin of pride. Basis for the 1966 film "El Dorado."

Flint by Louis L'Amour. Bantam Books, 1960. With only a short time to live, wealthy New York financier James T. Kettleman came to a place described to him years before over a small campfire by the only friend he ever had—cold, hard-eyed paid assassin Jim Flint. When he found himself in the middle of a range war, he surprised his past and present enemies as well as his new friends and acquaintances when they learned that this man they thought they all knew was one of the most feared gunmen ever.

Night Marshal by L. P. Holmes. Dodd, Mead, 1961. Chris Waddell was a lawman, one of the best. But in Midas Hill, toughs and hired guns ran the town and killed at will. So from the moment he pinned on the marshal's badge, Waddell knew his only hope was to move fast, shoot faster, and try to stay alive.

The Honyockers by Giles A. Lutz. Doubleday, 1961. They came from Wisconsin and Minnesota, from Iowa and Missouri. They were farmers who were met with hostility by the cattlemen and sheepmen. The first arrivals were Slavic people from Minnesota, and the Montanans soon lumped them all together with the contemptuous term "Honyockers." Spur Award from the Western Writers of America.

The Savage Land by Ann Ahlswede. Ballantine Books, 1962. story of a boy growing up wild in Mountain View, California, who becomes a convenient victim for the townspeople when they need a suspect for a murder, and faces frontier justice and a hangman's rope.

Hanging at Comanche Wells by Benjamin Capps. Ballantine Books, 1962. This is Capps' first novel, a traditional Western, set around 1883 in a small Texas frontier town, based on the experiences of Tom Horn, the well-known frontiersman, former Pinkerton detective, and later killer-for-hire for cattlemen in Wyoming in the late 1890s and the early 1900s.

The Dangerous Days of Kiowa Jones by Clifton Adams. Doubleday,

1963. Kiowa Jones was a drifter who let a dying marshal talk him into taking four prisoners to Fort Sill. One was Bobby Jack Wilkes, still little more than a boy but dangerous as a snake, who let the word get out that he'd pay double bounty to the man who'd free him. Source for the 1966 film.

Invitation to a Hanging by Walt Coburn. Lancer Books, 1963. For years Lee Jackson had been an outlaw, with a bounty on his head. Now he was in jail, sentenced to hang for a murder he hadn't committed. Only the real killer knew Jackson was innocent.

Ramrod by Walt Coburn. Lancer Books, 1963. Hod Cutter was the most feared man on the range, known as "King of the Cougar Mountains." But a gunfighter with an icy smile named Tom Barlow was not afraid. He joined Hod's gang of rustlers and relations among them became deadly.

The Girl from Fort Wicked by Dee Brown. Doubleday, 1964. Captain Westcott lost his fiancée in a wagon train ambush led by the renegade Yaneka Snell. Blind with rage, Westcott followed Snell into Platt Indian territory. Then a sassy little girl from Fort Wicked became Snell's next target, and the Captain headed for a final showdown with the renegade killer, intent on saving the girl's life.

A Mule for the Marquesa by Frank O'Rourke. William Morrow, 1964. In 1916, during the sixth year of the Mexican revolution, Angelina Grant was kidnapped. Her abductor was China Eye Raza, who along with 150 other renegades, had established headquarters in an almost impenetrable natural fortress in the high desert area of Mexico, 150 miles south of the Texas border. Rather than pay the ransom Raza demanded, Angelina's wealthy husband hired Henry Farden to lead a daring dash by five men to Raza's stronghold and return his wife. Basis for the 1956 film "The Professionals."

High Fury by Harry Whittington. Ballantine Books, 1964. An innocent but wanted man rode into the town of Sage Crossing carrying a half-demented girl who had been raped by one or more men high in the badlands country. The wanted man had been on the run for three years—all the while looking for the outlaw who could clear him. And then he discovered that one of the rapists was the man he was after.

Thundering Guns by Bradford Scott (A. Leslie Scott). Pyramid Books, 1965. From Scott's *Walt Slade* series. As the railroad tried to push a line through cow country, violence flared in Brownsville, Texas. A masked gang fanned the bitter feud between the railroad and ranchers. Texas Ranger Walt Slade almost had the situation under control until he became the target of a killer.

The Stalking Moon by Theodore V. Olsen. Doubleday, 1965. Army scout Sam Vetch had no way of knowing that his wife had once been the woman of Salvaje, the notorious Apache chieftain known as The Ghost, and that she had borne two sons by him. When Salvaje came to claim what was his, a deadly duel began between two men of strong will, courage, and honor. Basis for the 1968 film.

The Holdout in the Diablos by Louis Trimble. Ace Books, 1965. For two years Marne had trailed Lowden Doncaster, an ex-Confederate wanted for sedition and treason. Through cow camp and boom town, desert and border village, Doncaster managed to keep ahead of him, leaving Marne with only disturbing rumors. Rumors of guns and ammunition being cached along the border. Rumors of a private army of outlaws and hardcases. Rumors of deals with renegade Indians. Now Marne had found him.

The Hardy Breed by Giles A. Lutz. Doubleday, 1966. In a wide-open town in the badlands of Texas, the hired guns laughed at the dude in his suit and fine English boots. But they found the greenhorn to be a dangerous man who could hold his own—with or without a gun.

The Californio by Robert MacLeod. Fawcett, 1966. The Gringo on the big red horse was known as "the Californio." Throughout the Southwest border country Mexican peasants, half-starved Indians, and ruthless rurales had heard of the reckless stranger who would not look the other way when innocent people were being killed.

Single Action by Nelson Nye. Ace Books, 1967. Eighteen-year-old Pearly Adams' first assignment in the Arizona Rangers stranded him in hell's half-acre, in the middle of a range war.

Jory by Milton R. Bass. G. P. Putnam"s Sons, 1969. In the afternoon of his fourteenth birthday when Ab Evans kicked his pa to death in the Trail End Saloon, Jory became a gunslinging orphan, violence bound. Basis for the 1972 film.

West of Cheyenne by Lee Hoffman. Doubleday, 1969. When Eben headed to Wyoming, he thought he could leave the past behind. He had killed men in the Civil War and afterwards done time in prison. But west of Cheyenne, a rancher and his hired toughs tried to burn him out of his homestead.

Trail to Tucson by Ray Hogan. Signet, 1969. It was Apache country, and the girl was alone. Frank Gault was a loner who had no use for the girl—nor for the $20,000 she was carrying in her saddlebags. But the only other white men around were her brutal, cowardly "fiancé" and the half-dozen outlaws who had smelled the money.

The Last Days of Wolf Garnett by Clifton Adams. Doubleday, 1970. Frank Gault had spent more than a year tracking the notorious outlaw Wolf Garnett, determined to revenge the brutal murder of his young wife, only to find that his prey was dead. At least everyone agreed that the corpse just buried in a local cemetery was Wolf Garnett. But Gault had seen Garnett in Indian territory four days earlier and knew he had not been dead for two weeks. Spur Award from Western Writers of America.

Buzzard Ridge by Phillip Ketchum. Ballantine Books, 1970. Up in the Blackfoot Hills, somewhere in Wyoming territory, there was the town of Tavener. Remote as it was, wagon trains had learned to avoid it because many people who went into Tarvener never came out.

Valdez is Coming by Elmore Leonard. Fawcett, 1970. The quiet, respectable Valdez at one time had been a man who could track over parched ground, hide where there was no cover and rise up and kill an enemy with one shot. But that was in the past. Then Tanner and his personal army shamed him, tortured him, and left him half dead. Now Valdez was coming for them. Source for the 1971 film.

The Apple Dumpling Gang by Jack M. Bickham. Doubleday, 1971. The story of a sheriff in an isolated town in the far West who was trying to cope with three gangs of outlaws when the town drunk left him with five children. Their mischief earned them the name of "The Apple Dumpling Gang." Source for the 1971 film.

Track of the Hunter by Lewis B. Patten. Signet, 1971. When Frank Latham died with a bullet in his back, the town said that no one was to blame, that Latham was a murderer and deserved just what he got. But his wife and his two half-Apache sons mourned his death. Then they buried him and set out to avenge his death against the town and the professional gunman who had killed him.

The Fastest Gun in the Pulpit by Jack Ehrlich. Pocket Books, 1972. When outlaw Ernie Parsons found the body of Reverend Frank Fleming, he took the reverend's horse, supplies, and identity. He was hired to be the parson in Castle Walk, Colorado. But the job required Ernie to be as handy with his guns as with the gospel.

The Guns of Ellsworth by Dwight Bennett (Dwight Bennett Newton). Doubleday, 1973. Two years in prison had made Vern Balance a bitter man. He was not looking for trouble when he rode into the dusty Kansas cowtown of Ellsworth to collect an old debt that he hoped would be the start of a new life, but trouble came in an unexpected showdown with the family of the man he went to jail for killing.

Dutch Uncle by Marilyn Durham. Harcourt, Brace and Jovanovich, 1973. Jake Hollander was an aging gunfighter and professional gambler who, through unusual circumstances, became a town marshal in a small New Mexico mining town. He also was saddled with the care of two Mexican children.

Sun on the Wall by Wayne D. Overholser. Ballantine Books, 1973. In the 1870s Jim Glenn went to Cheyenne, a new town in the southeastern corner of Wyoming that was going to be a division point on the Union Pacific. There he found a "city" of tents and muddy walks and vigilante justice.

They Don't Shoot Cowards by John Reese. Doubleday, 1973. "Honker" Cahoon was a coward, but his gaunt satanic face, with its drooping mustache the scar across his cheek, along with his foghorn voice, created an impression on strangers that safely got him out of many dangerous encounters. But when a young kid took him for a famous gunfighter, his good sense deserted him and led to a situation where false courage was replaced by fear and despair.

High Plains Drifter by Ernest Tidyman. Bantam Books, 1973. A stranger with a fast gun was all that stood between the town and a trio of ex-convicts who had whipped their sheriff to death in the middle of main street. Basis for the 1973 film.

The Man from Yuma by Hal G. Evarts. Pocket Books, 1974. A vicious band of Army deserters came out of their lair in the mountains—robbing and killing, terrorizing settlers,then scurrying back to safety. The army sent John Hazard to put an end to their depredations. But first, he had to desert and join the band.

A Hanging in Sweetwater by Stephen Overholser. Doubleday, 1974. A story of the Old West when homesteaders and ranchers clashed over land ownership in 1879 Wyoming. Spur Award from the Western Writers of America.

The Name's Buchanan by Jonas Ward (William Ard). Gold Lion, 1974. From Ward's *Buchanan* series. When a girl was violated and a family's honor tarnished in Agry County, Tom Buchanan from West Texas strapped on his gunbelt and went after the criminals responsible. Source for the 1958 film "Buchanan Rides Alone."

Get Buchanan! by Jonas Ward (William Ard). Gold Medal, 1974. When Buchannan knew her years ago, she was just a ranch wife. Now her husband was dead and she had become the tyrannical ruler of the whole county. Her son and Buchanan were the only ones in the entire county to oppose her, and now she had the whole town gunning for them.

Gone to Texas by Forrest Carter. Delacorte Press, 1975. Josey Wales lost his young wife and child to pre-Civil War destruction and joined the guerrilla soldiers of Missouri. A hunted fugitive with a price on his head, Josey and his friend, Lone Watie, set out for Texas through the dangerous Comanchero territory. Partial basis for the 1976 film "The Outlaw Josey Wales."

The Terrible Teague Bunch by Gary Jennings. W. W. Norton, 1975. An old trail boss, L. R. Foyt, decided while driving a herd off the Texas caprock in the blizzard of 1902 that "there's got to be an easier way for a man to make a living." He drifted to East Texas and formed a gang, with the intent to rob a train. But they were failures as outlaws. However, they become Good Samaritans when a widow and her daughter needed help.

The Vengeance Trail of Josie Wales by Forrest Carter. Delacorte Press, 1976. The sequel to Carter's *Gone to Texas* (Delacorte Press, 1975). Escobedo and his brutal Mexican Rurales had raped, murdered, and rampaged through Santo Rio, and among his victims were friends of Josie Wales, leading Josey to embark on a vengeance trail. Partial basis for the 1976 film "The Outlaw Josey Wales."

Raiders of the Valley by Tom Curry. Popular Library, 1976. A *Rio Kid* Western. Originally published in a pulp magazine in 1946. Manfred Von Wohl was a Prussian cattle baron who was using the murderous methods he brought from Europe in a beautiful California valley. Then Bob Pryor, the Rio Kid, came on the scene, determined to stop the carnage.

The Devil's Playground by Cliff Farrell. Doubleday, 1976. The notorious Haskell gang kidnaps the daughter of one of the West's richest men—deep in the heart of the treacherous Mojave Desert.

Long Way to Texas by Lee McElroy (Elmer Kelton). Doubleday, 1976. A long way from Texas, the remnants of the once-proud Second Texas Mounted Rifles were badly mauled and in retreat. Then they stumbled upon an incredible opportunity—the chance to seize ten wagon loads of munitions secretly stored in Mexico.

Search for the Fox by Stephen Overholser. Doubleday, 1976. Benjamin Fox's father was legendary Confederate General John Fox, the Southern hero who, while still in uniform in 1865 rode into Richmond and robbed the Atlanta Bank and Trust. Then "The Fox" fled Richmond, headed west, and became a notorious outlaw. In the summer of 1882, seventeen-year-old Benjamin set out from Richmond in search of his elusive heritage, not knowing what he would find.

Trail Through Tascosa by Peter Field (House Name). Pocket Books, 1977. Pat Stevens and his friends Sam and Ezra, recurring characters in the Field Westerns, enlisted the services of some rough men to fulfill an army contract to drive some choice horses to Texas.

Omaha Crossing by Ray Hogan. Ace Books, 1977. Sheriff John Glade got along fine with the citizens of Omaha Crossing—until he was forced to kill the son of the town's most prominent citizen. The town turned on him. But when it was threatened by a revenge-seeking gang, Glade was the only one who could help.

Swimming Man Burning by Terrence Kilpatrick. Doubleday, 1977. Clay Benton was cornered in a deadly Indian ambush and spared by his attackers only to be forced to escort four Indian warriors—chosen from the four most powerful plains tribes—to Washington, D. C. to meet with President Ulysses S. Grant. Spur Award from the Western Writers of America.

Rattlesnake by Theodore V. Olsen. Doubleday, 1978. The Apache wars had taken almost everything from Indian Jim Izancho. Now a powerful politician wanted his land. Only Sheriff Frank Tenney, the Apache's boyhood friend, would try to help him.

The High Rocks by Loren D. Estleman. Doubleday, 1979. During the worst winter Montana ever had, a peace treaty was needed with the Flatheads. But the Indians wouldn't talk until Bear Anderson was gone from the Bitterroots. A seven-foot giant, Anderson was collecting Flathead scalps to avenge the slaughter of his family. Deputy Page Marshall, Anderson's boyhood friend, had to hunt the legend, somewhere up in the high rocks, and end the scalpings.

Hard Trail to Santa Fe by Tom West (Fred East). Zebra Books, 1980. Volunteers were sought to open the new trading route from Texas to Santa Fe. Renegades, ex-soldiers, and cowboys came—seeking glory, gold, or adventure, each with his own motive. One of them was Red Blake, whose wife had been taken by the Comanche. Hs only hope of finding her was to search in the great Taos slave market.

The Manhunter by Matt Braun. Pocket Books, 1981. From Braun's *Luke Starbuck* series. Luke Starbuck's gun was for hire. A wealthy banker hired him to bring down Jesse James and his gang, the toughest challenge Starbuck had ever faced.

Broomtail Basin by Lee Floren. Leisure Books, 1981. The first night Lemanuel Bates assumed the duties of presiding judge in the town of Broomtail Basin, a dynamite explosion destroyed a nearby water reservoir. The vandals were cattlemen who were violently opposed to a proposed railroad through their profitable Broomtail ranches. Only the Judge and his friend and protector Tobacco Jones stood against a threat of war that loomed larger every day.

The Appaloosa by Robert MacLeod. Walker, 1981. Set in 1874 Texas, this story tells of a man's attempts to recapture a stolen horse. Source for the 1966 film.

The Long Rider's Winter by Frank Calkins. Doubleday, 1983. When ranch hand Bob Lee was fired, young Tom Lavering also quit and rode out with Lee for a season of hunting. But Lee was out for more than deer. He had his eye on Chun Kwo's Fan-Tan Parlor in Wyoming, and he meant to ride off with Kwo's money. National Cowboy and Western Heritage Museum Western Heritage Award.

Leaving Kansas by Frank Roderous. Doubleday, 1983. Harrison Wilke is not an admirable protagonist. Weak-willed and indecisive, he lets a con man lead him into an act that endangers his future inheritance of the sprawling Running W Ranch. Then he unwittingly accuses three men of rustling, leading up to the novel's title. Spur Award from the Western Writers of America.

The Shadow Riders by Louis L'Amour. Bantam Books, 1985. When Dal and Mac Traven, who fought on opposite sides of the Civil War, rode home together to start rebuilding the family ranch they found their sister and Dal's girlfriend had been abducted by a band of guerrillas. With their brother Jesse and their Uncle Jack, Dal and Mac set out to rescue the girls—four Travens against thirty killers. Basis for the 1992 film.

Luke Sutton: Bounty Hunter by Leo P. Kelley. Doubleday, 1985. From Kelley's *Luke Sutton* series. Virginia City hired bounty hunter Sutton to bring back Ted Kimball—dead or alive. Sutton tracked him from Chinatown to the wild Barbary Coast, but discovered that there was more to Kimball's disappearance than met the eye.

Shadow of the Wolf by F. M. Parker. Doubleday, 1985. Jubal Clason, a Union Army deserter, and Ghost Walker, an Arapaho Indian, were unlikely partners who roamed the rugged Colorado territory in the 1860s, robbing and killing—one out of greed, the other out of pure hatred. But when the homicidal pair ambushed rancher Luke Coldiron and left him for dead, they became the target of a quest for revenge by a man with courage, strength, and endurance—whether he was pitted against the harsh elements of nature or a pair of murderous rogues.

Texas Anthem by James Reno. Signet, 1986. Texan Johnny Anthem was left to die in the Mexican desert by a rival suitor. But he did not die nor did his love for the girl claimed by his rival.

Crush by Del Beman. M. Evans, 1988. Judge Sherman O'Dell gave former lawman Farley Dant a choice; be hanged or become his marshal in Crush, Texas. Based on a true event in Texas history.

Mojave Showdown by Larry J. Martin. Kensington, 1988. Mangas Saragosa, the "Demon of the Desert," was a giant, tatoo-covered Indian sworn to avenge the murder of his family. And anyone, guilty or otherwise, who got in his way was fair game. He was leading eighteen head of stolen prize borax mules across the blistering, man-killing Mojave. The Mojave was out of Sheriff Ned Cody's jurisdiction, but two of his friends were being carried face down across a couple of Saragosa's mules. Rescuing them meant entering the "demon's" territory.

Rogue River by James Reno. New American Library, 1988. Cole Anthem had to join forces with a vicious army scout he had sworn to kill to steer a band of men and women to safety down the treacherous Rogue River. In close pursuit was an Indian chief whose warriors knew every trick of terror.

The Intruders by Kirk Winkler. Walker, 1988. Cora Diemert was homesteading a strip of land in New Mexico, a difficult undertaking for a widowed woman with three young children. Cora was being harassed by the crew of a nearby ranch who wanted to take over her land when two strangers rode into her life. Each was potential help or a possible threat.

Bitterroot by Cameron Judd. Bantam Books, 1989. The Civil War never ended for Simon Cain. He became a notorious outlaw who hunted down and killed the former Union soldiers who murdered his family. Now, saved from a lynch mob by John Crosston, he is asked to lead Crosston into the heart of the Bitterroot Mountains in Montana territory and to a showdown with a half-mad half-breed and a team of bounty hunters.

Bad News by Giles Tippette. Berkley, 1989. When a brutal murder occurred in 1894 in Bandera, Texas, the law looked for a scapegoat and tried to beat a confession out of Justa Williams. But back in Matagorda County, Justa had two brothers tough enough to take on the sheriff and the whole town.

Among the Eagles by G. Clifton Wisler. Fawcett, 1989. Will Delamer had a strong sense of right and wrong. That was why he sided with the Sioux when white hunters raided their territory. Delamer found peace among the Indians and was soon a trusted member of their tribe. Spur Award from the Western Writers of America.

Duel on the Mesa by Bill Dugan. Harper, 1990. Dalton Chance was a small rancher in New Mexico whose family was massacred by band of drunken Apache. Lone Wolf, General Crook's Indian scout, convinced Chance that the Indians were crazy on illegal white man's whiskey, and they joined forces to wipe out the whiskey smugglers.

A Passage of Seasons by Douglas Hirt. Doubleday, 1990. A seventeen-year-old boy, with his kid brother in tow, disembarks from a train in Cripple Creek, Colorado, intent on becoming a man. Seventy-two-year-old U. S. Marshal Devon also disembarks at Cripple Creek. there to pick up a notorious prisoner and bring him back to Texas for imprisonment. Devon knows what the boys are up to, and he knows that Cripple Creek, with its vice dens and bawdy houses, is too dangerous for two green kids. But he can't stop them. All he can do is keep an eye out.

Rustler's Venom by W. W. Lee. Walker, 1990. Jefferson Birch, a former Texas Ranger, traveled to Rattlesnake, Montana, to help recently-widowed Mattie Quinn find out who was trying to drive her off her ranch.

Firewind by Bill Pronzini. Ballantine Books, 1990. The logging town of Big Tree in northern California became a raging inferno when a single gunshot sparked a wildfire. The only escape was on an old locomotive that had to outdistance the flames and reach an old wooden trestle before the fire.

Riders of the Silver Rim by Brock and Bodie Thoene. Bethany House, 1990. A Christian novel from the Thoene's *Saga of the Sierras* series. A tragic accident sent Joshua Roberts west to find peace. Instead, he became a constable, with the responsibility to bring order to a rowdy frontier mining town.

Riders of the Monte by L. J. Washburn. M. Evans, 1990. Dirt-poor farmer turned outlaw Curtis Daniels fled to the dusty cantinas on the rough mountain terrain south of the border and rode with the bandido Ignacio Guerrero until he was double-crossed. Then Daniels avenged himself and the young girl orphaned by Guerrero.

The Old Boys by Kirk Winkler. Walker, 1991. A group of wily old lawmen rally to try and clear the name of one of their comrades charged with the murder of a saloon girl.

Tubar: A Western Adventure by John Tilley. Sunstone Press, 1992. A cool ale in a Baltimore tavern plus a Micky Finn turned young Tubar Lane's student world into hell. Bounced out of school and disgraced, he could not return home to a strict father. He walked to the railroad yard where he met a train-hopping gunman. And that was the beginning of Tubar's long trek to wild and wooly Dodge City. It was 1872—the year of the great buffalo herds, of Indians, gunslingers, outlaws and renegades.

Frontier Lady by Judith Pella. Bethany House, 1993. A Christian novel. Deborah Graham escaped from the ravages of the Civil War to the plains of Texas, to marry a handsome young man who would inherit wealth and influence from his cattle-baron father. But a murderer's bullet changed everything. Deborah was almost hanged for her husband's murder.

St. Agnes' Stand by Tom Eidson. G. P. Putnam's Sons, 1994. Fleeing through the territory of New Mexico to avoid a hanging, Nat Swanson came upon two overturned wagons surrounded by about 30 Apaches and felt compelled to help. Sister St. Agnes, a 76-year-old nun, believed that he had been sent by God to save them. This placed a burden on Nat that he had never before felt; it also forced him to act beyond his normal expectations as he attempted to pull off a miracle. Spur Award from the Western Writers of America.

Stoner's Crossing by Judith Pella. Bethany House, 1994. A Christian novel, the sequel to Pella's *Frontier Lady* (1993). Thirteen years ago, Deborah Stoner had been accused of the murder of her husband, and was almost executed in Stoner's Crossing, Texas. Miraculously, she escaped—but now the past has caught up with her.

The Last Ride by Tom Eidson. G. P Putnam's Sons, 1995. This story opens in the New Mexico territory of the late 1880s, as the terminally ill Samuel Jones, a 76-year-old Indian fighter, shows up on the doorstep of his daughter Maggie, seeking to make amends for deserting his family 30 years earlier to live with an Apache squaw. She refused to acknowledge him. But soon after Jones's appearance, Maggie's daughter Lily was kidnapped by a grotesquely deformed Apache witch. Maggie and Samuel, who was still a formidable warrior, were forced to form an alliance to pursue and reclaim Lily. The basis for the 2003 film "The Missing."

The Devil on Horseback by Lauran Paine. Walker, 1995. In Calabasas, New Mexico, a prosperous merchant committed murder to hide a dark past. Saloon Keeper Jim Rourke found out about the murder, and became the target of a hired killer. A Mexican priest in Calabasas told Rourke the killer, known as Halcón, was not human, but the "devil on horseback."

Potter's Fields by Frank Roderus. Bantam Books, 1996. Joe Potter was a cold-blooded killer who hid behind a badge. But Joe could not outrun his demons. His moment of truth came when an Indian woman and her child forced him to face his past.

Black Gold by Frederic Bean. Forge, 1997. Texas Ranger Lee Garrett was sent to Longview to investigate the murder of a small-time oil wildcatter and uncovered the first East Coast organized crime racket in Texas.

Old Marsden by Frank Roderus. Leisure Books, 1999. Ol' Cap Marsden had been a mountain man in his youth, but that was long ago. But when his granddaughter was murdered, Cap trailed her killers to Virginia City, and was wounded so bad he had to get about in a wheelchair. He could still shoot, though, good enough to kill the three murderers when he caught up with them.

Barjack by Robert J. Conley. Leisure Books, 2000. Barjack was the name of a scrappy sheriff who was just five-foot-seven in cowboy boots and hat. But he was ornery. He didn't take anything from anybody. When he arrived in Asininity, Barjack didn't intend to stay for long, let alone take on the job of sheriff, but soon enough he was doing both, and taking on the dreaded Benson brothers as well.

The Lawless Land by Dusty Richards. St Martin's Press, 2000. An Arizona territorial Marshal named Sam T. Mayes was after the vicious Border Gang, whose deprecations endangered statehood. He was accompanied by an alcoholic, ex-army scout named Jesus Morales, and the Apache Too-Gut and his woman. Not exactly the best colleagues for his dangerous task, but Mayes would work with what he had.

Cuts No Slack by Tom Whatley. Sunstone Press, 2000. A *Reed Haddok* Western. Having to be a man before his time on a ranch in 1850s Texas, Bud Haddok was traveling west to see the country his rambling father had described so often. He was now in Arizona and someone was trailing him. But why?

Gabriel's Story by David Anthony Durham. Doubleday, 2001. The protagonist in this story of a black pioneer family in the late 1870s is Gabriel, a young man who moved from the urban North with his mother and younger brother to join his stepfather, a homesteader in Kansas. When he ran away to become a cowboy, he found only trouble.

Miss Emily: The Yellow Rose of Texas by Ben Durr and Anne Corwin. Sunstone Press, 2001. Miss Emily Morgan, once known as Rose, charmed every man who crossed her path and helped set the future of the Republic of Texas.

The Survivor by Tim Champlin. Leisure Books, 2002. Marcel Dupre excaped from a French Guiana prison and found his way to America. Dupre's journal, which piques the interest of New York publishers, also stirs interest within the governments of France and Mexico. Dupre, a one-time member of the French Foreign Legion, not only can expose the cruelty of the French prison colony, but also knows some potentially embarrassing things about French support of Mexican monarch Maximilian. Jay McCraw, a young Wells Fargo agent, is assigned to Dupre and told to get the Frenchman and his manuscript to New York.

He Ain't Dead by Tom V. Whatley. Sunstone Press, 2002. A *Reed Haddok Western*. The sequel to *Cuts No Slack* (Sunstone Press, 2000). Beecham had planned to control the territory and its rich gold deposits around Prescott, Arizona, but was stopped dead in his tracks a young man from Texas named Reed Haddok. So he placed a large price on Haddok's head payable to whoever killed him.

Guns of Wolf Valley by Ralph Cotton. Signet, 2004. Sloane Mosely was determined not to be added to the harem of Preacher Jessup, a banker and religious fanatic who confiscated any recent widow and her property as well. So she had a wounded gunman named C. C. Ellis pose as her husband, who had rode away and disappeared a year ago.

Winter Kill by Cotton Smith. Leisure Books, 2004. Some of Old Titus Branson's Bar 6 cattle were missing, and he knew they had been rustled by Bass Manko. He sent men to town to apprehend Manko, but there was a problem: Titus' youngest son Cade was Manko's best friend. He was not going to be able to hang Bass Manko without going through Cade

Ride to Raton by Marsha Ward. iUniverse, 2004. James Owen left home for Colorado because his fiancée married his brother. He was looking for work in the mines, but events had him set upon, shot, jailed, married, caught in a battle between Mexican and white factions, and finally, embarked on a trail of vengeance.

Ghost Runner by Tom V. Whatley. Sunstone Press, 2004. A *Reed Haddok Western*. Tall Tree, an Indian who had saved Reed Haddok's life, is now the wounded captive of an Apache war party. Haddock immediately sets out to save his new friend. The rescue, escape, and trek back to Tall Tree's hidden village takes a series of riveting, fast paced turns.

Sawyer's Quest by Will Cade. Leisure Books, 2005. A general store clerk in Kansas needed money to send his daughter back East for an operation. He found a valuable manuscript belonging to a famous writer, and planned to return it, hoping for a finder's fee. But his luck was bad—masked bandits took the manuscript from him. Could he still help his daughter?

Twice as Good by Tom V. Whatley. Sunstone Press, 2005. A *Reed Haddok Western*. Beecham bought the Two Butte Ranch under the alias Jake Lansford and, surrounded by seven gunslingers, waited to hear that his nemesis Reed Haddok was dead. But Haddok was very much alive, and soon whittled down the odds a bit.

Marshal of Medicine Lodge by Stan Lynde. iUniverse, 2006. In 1886 U. S. Deputy Marshal Merlin Fanshaw arrived at the Crow Indian Reservation in Montana territory with orders to restore law and order. But when a shocking murder rocked the town, tension and violence escalated between the Crows and the settlers.

Appaloosa by Robert B. Parker. Putnam, 2005. This novel, crime novelist Parker's second Western, concerns two Old West lawmen, Marshal Virgil Cole and his deputy, in the mining and ranching town of Appaloosa. They arrested a rancher who ordered the killing of the previous marshal and his deputy and saw him tried and sentenced to hang. But a jailbreak and a long chase through Indian territory precedes the story's final confrontation.

Riders of Deathwater Valley by James C. Work. Five Star, 2005. From Work's *Keystone Ranch* series. A gang of rustlers raids a picnic and kidnaps the women and children. Incensed, the ranchers join together and prepare for an armed confrontation with the rustlers.

Telegraph Days by Larry McMurtry. Simon and Schuster, 2006. The story starts in 1876, the year of George Custer's massacre. Nellie Courtright and her brother Jackson buried their father, who committed suicide after settling on a plain in what is now the Oklahoma panhandle near New Mexico. Finding themselves alone, the Virginia-born orphans migrated over to the nearby town of Rita Blanca to start a new life. Nellie became the telegraph operator, and Jackson hired on as the sheriff's deputy. Many historical characters who appeared in McMurtry's previous Old West novels resurface in *Telegraph*

Days. The main historical character is William "Buffalo Bill" Cody, but Wild Bill Hickok and Billy the Kid also ride through the novel.

The Final Tally by Richard S. Wheeler. Sunstone Press, 2007. Santiago Toole is the sheriff at Miles City in frontier Montana. He is also a doctor but he can't make a living at it. He soon finds that enforcing the law and practicing medicine intertwine in startling ways, and there is as much danger from sick or crazed people as there is from men who heed no law on earth.

Fears No Man by Tom V. Whatley. Sunstone Press, 2007. Half-breed Cherokee warrior Tse-quo-ni fears no man. But his greatest frustration comes from his hatred of the white blood racing unwanted through his veins. Primarily, he hates Matthew McCloud, the white man his mother revealed to be his father just before her death. He hates the deceitfulness of all whites, and what has happened to the once proud Cherokee nation because of their rush to live like white people. During the time of the removal of the great Cherokee nation from North Georgia and the Carolinas, he slips away and journeys West to keep the promise he made to himself the moment he learned about Matthew McCloud.

SELECTED REVIEWS

Bar-20
by Clarence E. Mulford
Outing, 1907

William Boyd appeared in over sixty motion pictures and a long running television series as a silver-haired, gentlemanly, upright Western character immaculately dressed in black named Hopalong Cassidy. But the celluloid Hoppy bore little resemblance to the cussing, drinking, rowdy, illiterate introduced as one of the Bar-20 cowboys in Clarence E. Mulford's novel:

> The outfit of the Bar-20 was, perhaps, the most famous of all from
> Canada to the Rio Grande. The foreman, Buck Peters, controlled

a crowd of men (who had all the instincts of boys) that had shown no quarter to many rustlers, and who, while always carefree and easygoing (even fighting with great good humor and carelessness), had established the reputation of being the most reckless gang of daredevil gunfighters who ever pounded leather . . . sheriffs and marshals of many localities had received from their hands most timely assistance—and some trouble. Wiry, indomitable, boyish and generous, they were splendid examples of virile manhood; and, surrounded as they were with great dangers and a unique civilization, they should not, in justice, be judged by opinions of the commonplace.

The most reckless of the bunch was Hopalong Cassidy.

At twenty-five, Hopalong was a combination of irresponsibility, humor, good nature, love of fighting, and nonchalance in the face of danger. He had been crippled some years before in a successful attempt to prevent the assassination of a friend. He was sensitive about his limp and his height; one sure way to provoke a fight was to call him gimpy or a runt. Hopalong's antics made the others laugh, but they grumbled at his recklessness, and weren't tempted to emulate him.

Mulford relates Hopalong's adventures with vigor and humor. He and his friends are wild and woolly. The Bar-20 boys are hard to warm up to. At first, they come across as a bunch of unruly and deadly hoodlums. Eventually, though, their good-natured banter becomes infectious. For example, during a gun battle with some renegade Indians, Hopalong was wounded:

> "Where'd he git yu?" [Skinny] asked.
> "In the heart, yu pie-faced nuisance. Come over here and corral this cussed bandage an' gimme some water . . ."
> "Close your yap; yore worse than a kid! Anybody'd think yu never got plugged afore," said Skinny indignantly.

Behind this bravado is a code for the cowboy that Mulford lays out in his exposition:

He must tolerate no restrictions of his natural rights, and he must not restrict; for the one would proclaim him a coward, the other a bully; and both received short shrifts in that land of the self-protected. The basic law of nature is the survival of the fittest.

In the series of episodes that stand in for a plot, the central theme seems to be that a cowboy must always even the score.

About midway through the novel, Mulford started using a semi-formal tone—addressing his characters as Mr. Buck Peters, Mr. Hopalong Cassidy, . . . This gives a mock seriousness to the narrative, and provides an unusual change of pace.

The Bar-20 cowboys are ordinary, never intended to be heroes. None are presented as an ideal man—in looks or deeds. C. L. Sonnichson said that with Hopalong as a model, the specification for a hero was quite simple: all he needed was guts.

An Illinois-born Easterner, Clarence E. Mulford began writing his series about the Bar-20 cowboys in 1905. The short stories and novels would eventually fill eighteen books. He retired from writing in the early 1940's. Doubleday reissued most of his books, abridging some, but the market was still unsatisfied. Four new books were commissioned from Louis L'Amour, writing as "Tex Burns." This was early in his writing career and he was at that time trying to break into the hardcover market. L'Amour's stories were initially written more in the Mulford style, but the character descriptions were changed prior to publication to reflect the Boyd persona. L'Amour later disavowed the works.

Destry Rides Again
by Max Brand
Dodd, Mead, 1930

Max Brand is the best known pen name of Frederick Schiller Faust, who wrote over 300 novels under several pseudonyms. He was an intellectual, steeped in the classics, who wrote spy novels, medical drama, romance, fantasy, and poetry, as well as some of the most popular and enduring genre Westerns. A poet, soldier, novelist, magazine and screen writer, Faust was a handsome, charming, six-foot-two man with a deep resonant voice who charmed his audience when he read poetry. He led an adventurous life, ending at age fifty-one on the Italian front, where he was killed in 1944 while covering World War II as a war correspondent.

Although his Dr. Kildare series were popular, he's best known for his Westerns. Some critics say he distorted and degraded the Western, and is largely responsible for discrediting it as serious literature. Others say he put it where it belongs, in the realm of myth. Faust linked his Westerns to mythology through similes, metaphors, and poetic tone to achieve classical values of remoteness and timelessness. This, in the opinion of his biographer Robert Easton, is his unique contribution to the Western. His lifelong preoccupation with Arthurian knights and Greek gods provided the structure for his highly romantic fiction.

Destry Rides Again, the most successful Max Brand Western and one of the most popular novels of all times, is based loosely on Homer's *Odyssey*. It is the story of Harry Destry, a man who was framed and sent to prison. When he entered jail, Destry was bronzed, hard, and contemptuous of those who judged him. He returned pale and beaten. He was met with insult and scorn. But the town cowered and trembled before he was done enjoying the sweet taste of revenge.

Whereas his predecessors Owen Wister and Zane Grey set their stories in the real West and described it in glorious detail, Faust used a generic West. *Destry* unfolds in Wham, an imaginary town so named because when cowpunchers gathered there from all directions their meeting was explosive. Wham existed only in Faust's imagination. By developing his setting to fit the plot, he could tell a story unconstrained by everyday reality.

Harry Destry was a fighter by taste, cultivation, and habit. The judge who passed sentence on him summarized his life: "You have been found guilty . . . not for a first offense, in my estimation, but for the culmination of a life of violence, indolence, and worthlessness." But Destry possessed great courage and a strong sense of fairness.

His adversary Chester Bent was a big man, with a seal-like slickness. Beneath the slickness was ample strength, and behind his habitual smile was the will of a fighter. He had been whipped by Destry when they were boys, and never forgot it.

There are other characters, sketched quickly, who pave the way for the eventual showdown between Destry and Bent. There is Charlie Dangerfield, who loved Destry and waited for him while he was in prison. There is Sheriff Ding Slater, a prototype for competent but low-key sheriffs who have since appeared in hundreds of Western stories. And there is Willie Thornton, a boy who showed extraordinary courage while twice saving Destry's life.

Charlie Dangerfield is important to the story only because she's coveted by Bent. She is briefly described as "a pretty girl with hair down her back, and the pigtail faded to straw color." Like women, Mexicans and "niggers" don't seem worthy of character development and are used only for background. The are treated harshly and are generally presented as lazy, lying, cheating and treacherous. For example, Brand describes Mexican rider Jose Vedres as " . . . a venomous looking specimen of his race, slinking, yellow-eyed, with nicotine ingrained to his very soul." Unfortunately, this same stereotype has appeared in the works of many other popular Western writers.

As a young man, Faust studied the social sciences at Berkeley. His observations on human behavior are liberally sprinkled about. On shame, he says:

> Shame, after all, is a human condition. The elephant knows no shame when it flees from the mouse, and the lion runs from the rhinoceros without a twinge of shame.

On the subject of conscience, he observes:

Too much is made of guilty conscience. They generally begin to
work on criminals after the stern hand of the law has grasped them
by the nape of the neck. They prepare for a holy death to make up for
a bad life, only after the hangman is assured.

We're always able to understand why a Max Brand character takes a
particular course of action.

Much of *Destry's* continued popularity is rooted in its success in film
and on the stage. It's formed the basis (loosely) for three motion pictures,
featuring in turn Tom Mix (1932), James Stewart (1939), and Audie Murphy
(1954) in the title role. In 1959 it was the subject of a David Merrick musical
comedy on Broadway.

Frederick Faust was a huge success as a Western novelist. But he didn't
take his work too seriously. *The Untamed* (G. P. Putnam's Sons, 1919), his first
published book, was so successful that readers demanded three sequels. Faust
is quoted as saying of it, "Daily I thank God in three languages that I write
under a pen name." He was unquestionable a man of enormous and diverse
talent. Some of his work was superb; some was just passable. But the reading
public has decided his place in literature. More than twenty million Max Brand
books have been sold in the U. S. alone in the past quarter-century, and are still
on the shelves of bookstores and supermarkets across America.

Hondo
by Louis L'Amour
Fawcett, 1953

Louis L'Amour was an American treasure. He wrote 86 novels; most
of them were set in the American West. There were nearly 200 million of his
books in print at his death in 1989; forty-five or more of them have been made
into feature films or TV shows. He was the only novelist to be awarded both
the National Gold Medal by Congress and the Presidential Seal of Freedom.

Hondo, L'Amour's first novel published under his own name, is the
story of three people caught in the frightening web of a bloody Indian uprising.

Hondo Lane was a big man, tough without cruelty. He was a fighting man, the kind Indians recognized and admired. He was fiercely independent, as could be seen in his relationship with Sam, a huge mongrel dog, a dog he didn't own, just a dog who traveled with him. He explained this to Angie Lowe when she asked to feed Sam:

"What can I feed your dog?"
"Nothin', thanks. He makes out fine by himself. He can outrun any rabbit in the territory."
"Oh, its no trouble . . ."
"If you don't mind, ma'am, I'd rather you didn't feed him."
"Oh, I understand. You don't want him to take food from anyone but you.
"No ma'am. I don't feed him either . . . Sam's independent. He doesn't need anybody. I want him to stay that way."

Hondo's own independence included minding his own business. If asked for advice, he would tell people to "do what you think you should," even when this could result in disaster.

He was riding dispatch for General Crook when his horse was shot from under him by the Apache. He arrived at Angie Lowe's ranch on the fringe of the New Mexico desert carrying his saddle and his rifle.

Angie and her young son, Johnny, had been deserted by her husband, but she kept a fragile hold on her home. L'Amour doesn't give a good physical description of Angie, but Hondo found her beautiful, and she was guiltily attracted to him.

Vittoro was Chief of the Mescalero Apache. He was off the reservation with his fighting men, leading his people into a war he knew they couldn't win. Because of an act of bravery by young Johnny Lowe, Vittoro made him a blood brother and protected the Lowe ranch from the Apache.

The plot places these central characters—Hondo Lane, Angie Lowe, Vittoro—in conflict, providing grist for a superb traditional western structured along a single impelling storyline.

Hondo is a romantic novel in the tradition of Scott, Hawthorn, Kipling,

Cooper, and Grey. The situation is at times hopeless, Hondo is bigger than life, and Angie is vulnerable. Their subdued passion is understated and in keeping with the period. In one of their more romantic exchanges, Hondo tells Angie Indians can smell white people:

> You baked this morning . . . I can smell fresh bread on you.
> Sometime today you cooked salt pork . . . you smell all over like a
> woman. A woman's got a different smell from a man. Not salty and
> sharp, but rich and warm. I could find you in the dark, Mrs. Lowe,
> and I'm only part Indian."

The dialogue is sparse, but sprinkled with dry humor, as when Hondo tells Angie of the time he almost ate Sam:

> Wasn't he an ugly cuss, that Sam? Mean as a catamount in
> the breeding season. I almost ate him once. Up on the Powder. Quick
> freeze caught us, and after I'd been three days without rations, I took
> to looking at Sam.

Louis L'Amour was keenly attuned to the beauty and the starkness of the American West. When he sketched a scene, the effect was sometimes remarkable.

> Before them stretched the vast and rolling plain of sand,
> rock, and cactus that is the desert of the southwest. Desert . . . but
> a desert strangely alive. Not a dead land, but a land where all life is
> born with a fire, a thorn, a sting.

His readers feel they've actually walked the land where his stories take place.

Hondo shows a particular respect for both the Apache and the U. S. Cavalry, and carefully relates their virtues. The Apaches are treated sympathetically. Although he realistically portrays them as cruel and vicious fighters, we also see them as an honorable, unselfish people. There's high praise for the cavalry and the young West Pointers who lead the troops. Consider this bit of thoughtful and provocative exposition as a company of cavalry rides out to engage the enemy:

> No man knows the hour of his ending, nor can he choose the place or the manner of his going. To each it is given to die proudly, to die well, as this is, indeed, the measure of the man. The forty-seven men of Company C rode with an awareness of death . . .

This bit of discourse anticipates the extraordinary courage Company C will display in their deadly duel with the Apache.

The film "Hondo," released in the same year as the book, cast John Wayne as Hondo and Geraldine Page as Angie. Wayne's characterization of Hondo Lane, along with the Ringo Kid ("Stagecoach"), Ethan Edwards ("The Searchers"), and Rooster Cogburn ("True Grit"), is his best work. Page received an academy award nomination for her portrayal of Angie Lowe.

Hondo is a solid action western. It treats the antagonists with respect, and captures the temper of the Southwest during the Plains Indian Wars. It will surely please aficionados of the Western genre.

Hombre
by Elmore Leonard
Ballantine Books, 1961

The classic white-flag scenario has the opposing sides facing each other with guns, at a standoff. Someone waves a truce flag, and they decide to talk. The heavy will try to use the truce to his advantage. The good guy always honors the truce.

In the introduction to *Hombre*, Elmore Leonard said this bothered him. It seemed that in this life or death situation, the good guy acted foolishly. So he wrote a scene, his own white-flag situation. The good guys are cornered in an assay shack, up on the side of a deserted mine works. The lead heavy ascends the hill under a truce flag, and promises food and water in exchange for a bag of money the good guys are holding. He makes several threats, then turns to go. One of the good guys says "I got a question." The heavy looks back over his shoulder. The good guy puts a Spencer carbine dead on him and asks: "How are you going to get down that hill?" Out of this simple, direct question a novel began to take shape. The novel that emerged from this pivotal scene was *Hombre*, the story of a stagecoach holdup in southern Arizona. A character named John Russell was born; a man with a highly unusual personality and an intriguing point of view—a man who didn't allow custom or emotion to alter his perspective.

The Hatch and Hodges Stage Line was making its final run from Sweetmary south to Bisbee. The passengers were Dr. Alexander Favor, the Indian Agent at the San Carlos Reservation; his wife Audra; Kathleen McLaren, a pretty girl of seventeen or eighteen who had been held captive by the Chiricahuas for four or five weeks before she was rescued; Carl Allen, a young employee of the stage line and narrator of the story; Frank Braden, who eventually reveals himself as leader of the holdup gang; and John Russell. The stage was driven by Henry Mendez, the Hatch and Hodges division manager at Sweetmary. The bandits were after money that Dr. Favor had swindled from the Reservation and was taking with him to Mexico.

All of the characters are sketched quickly but clearly. The narrator introduces Henry Mendez:

> From a distance you could never tell he was Mexican. He never
> dressed like one, everything white like their clothes were made out
> of bedsheets. He usually didn't act like one. Except that his face,
> with those tobacco-stained looking eyes and drooping mustache, was
> always the same and you never knew what he was thinking. When
> he looked at you, it was like he knew something he wasn't telling, or
> was laughing at you, no matter what it was he said. That's when you
> could tell Henry Mendez was Mexican.

The image of outlaw leader Frank Braden is more succinct:

> He was tall, with the thin, stringy look of a rider and the ching-ching
> sound of spurs, with dust and horse-smell on him.

But the intriguing character is John Russell.

Russell was a young man, not more than twenty-one, of mixed Anglo and Mexican blood, who had been captured by the Apaches when he was a child and raised as an Indian. When first introduced to the reader, he was a mustanger. He and two White Mountain Apaches would capture and break wild horses, sell them to Henry Mendez, then deliver the ones Mendez didn't need to other relay stations. When narrator Carl Allen first saw him, Russell was wearing a stained, dirty looking straight-brim hat and a cartridge belt across his chest. He had a dark face and long hair. Except for his blue eyes, he looked Apache.

Because of this, he was used to angry looks and rude behavior. These he endured on the stagecoach journey, particularly from Dr. Favor and his wife. Following the holdup, Russell killed one of the bandits and fled cross-country on foot to escape the others. The stage passengers followed Russell across the harsh and hostile southern Arizona desert, laboring to keep him in sight as he moved easily through the rough and brushy terrain. Russell didn't wait; Dr. Favor claimed he was deliberately trying to lose them. But the McLaren girl said no, he didn't care if they followed or sprouted wings and flew; he was thinking of Braden and his men on horseback and was making it as hard for them as he could, making them get off their horses and walk if they wanted to follow him. In the final showdown at the abandoned mine their lives would depend on this strange and aloof man they didn't understand.

Elmore Leonard is currently a very successful mystery writer. But his roots are in the Western genre, in which he worked before turning to mysteries. He's the author of many classic Westerns, including several that have been made into genuinely good movies—*Valdez is Coming* (Hale, 1969), *3:10 to Yuma* (short story), 1955—and the screenplay for *Joe Kidd* (1972). *Hombre* was chosen in 1985 as one of the "Twenty-Five Best Westerns of All Time" by the Western Writers of America.

The novel was finished in 1959 and rejected by publishers for nearly two years before Ballantine Books brought it out in 1961. Five years later 20th Century Fox acquired screen rights and in 1967 Paul Newman appeared as John Russell. Richard Boone, as Frank Braden, came up to the assay shack with the white flag tied to his Winchester, leading to Russell's classic question:

"How are you going to get down that hill?"

Hombre is a thoughtful, absorbing western, full of action—a tale of classic confrontation.

Shane
by Jack Schaefer
Houghton Mifflin, 1949

Those who don't like Westerns will find in *Shane* all the elements they don't like—conventions, stock characters, a guardian angel hero, gunfighting and violence—that account for much of the Western's popularity.

Those who do will love it. In 1985 the Western Writers of America voted it best Western of all time.

Jack Schaefer's first novel, it evolved from a three-part serial published in Argosy magazine entitled *Rider from Nowhere*. When he wrote *Shane*, Schaefer had never been west of his native Cleveland. He researched the book by reading old newspapers and diaries at Yale University. The success of the novel and the subsequent movie allowed him to move to a small ranch near Santa Fe, New Mexico.

Schaefer develops his protagonist Shane along mythic lines. The myth begins with the arrival of a lone rider at the Starretts' Wyoming homestead in the summer of 1889. Young Bob Starrett, the narrator, describes the stranger:

> As he came near, what impressed me first was his clothes. He wore
> dark trousers of some serge material tucked into tall boots and held
> at the waist by a wide belt, both of a soft black leather tooled in
> intricate design. A coat of the same material as the trousers was
> neatly folded and strapped to his saddle-roll. His shirt was finespun
> linen, rich brown in color. The handkerchief knotted loosely around
> his neck was black silk. His hat was not the familiar Stetson, not
> the familiar gray or muddy tan. It was a plain black, soft in texture,
> unlike any hat I had ever seen, with a creased crown and a wide
> curling brim, swept down in front to shield the face.

He was not much above medium height, almost slight in build. But for all his slim build he was solid and compact.

And he didn't carry a gun, although most men at that time, in that country, did not feel fully dressed without one.

When Joe Starrett introduced himself and his son Bob, the stranger simply said, "Call me Shane." The Starretts quickly learned that "his past was as tightly fenced as our pasture." But whatever his past was, Shane would be unable to escape from it. Near the end of the novel he would tell Bob, "A man is what he is, Bob, and there's no breaking the mold. I tried that and I've lost."

Joe Starrett and his wife Marian immediately liked Shane. Marian cooked a good meal, and they talked. Starrett told Shane of his plans. Starrett knew the days of the open range were dying. It was a poor business in terms of the resources going into it. Though his place was small, he had already raised stock that averaged three hundred pounds more than range stock.

The only cloud over his place and the entire valley where it was located was recurrent trouble between Luke Fletcher and the homesteaders. Fletcher owned a large ranch that sprawled across most of the valley. He had range rights on a lot more acres than he had cows for, but he would lose these acres as homesteaders moved in. Starrett asked Shane to stay on and help him get things in shape for winter. Shane agreed, even though he knew it was partly because Fletcher was crowding his friend.

That was the happiest summer of Bob's life. It was plain to see that Shane was beginning to enjoy living with the Starretts' and working the place. Little by little the tension in him was fading out. Bob also noticed that his mother and father were more vibrant since Shane arrived.

But at the end of summer, Fletcher received a large government beef contract. He needed the whole range and said the homesteaders would have to go. Chris, one of Fletcher's cowboys, braced Shane in the saloon and Shane walked away, giving the impression he had backed down. Marian detected that Shane was worried about what he might do if there was any fighting because of Fletcher. Later, when Shane rode into town with the Starretts and went into the bar for a drink, he was jumped by Fletcher's foreman and four cowboys. Shane and Joe Starrett soundly thrashed all five. Fletcher left town and returned with a gunman named Stark Wilson.

He was tall, rather broad in the shoulders and slim in the waist. He carried himself with a sort of swagger. He had a mustache that he favored and his eyes were cold and had a disturbing glitter . . . He was something of a dude about his clothes. When he turned, the coat he wore matching his pants flapped open and he was carrying two guns, big capable forty-fives, in holsters hung low and forward. Those holsters were pegged down at the tips with thin straps fastened around the man's legs.

Wilson goaded a hot-tempered homesteader named Ernie Wright into a fight, then gunned him down when Wright went for his pistol. Shane rode into town to challenge Wilson.

He was dressed as he was that first day when he rode into our lives . . . But what caught your eye was the single flash of white, the outer ivory plate on the grip of the gun, showing sharp and distinct against the dark material of the trousers. The tooled cartridge belt nestled around him, riding above the hip on the left, sweeping down on the right to hold the holster snug along the thigh, just as he had said, the gun handle about halfway between the wrist and elbow of his right arm hanging there relaxed and ready.

Bob followed him and watched the ensuing events. Shane confronted Wilson and asked for Fletcher. Wilson responded by asking for Starrett. His words went past Shane as if they had not been spoken. "I had a few things to say to Fletcher," he said gently. "That can wait. You're a pushing man, Wilson, so I reckon I had better accommodate you." There's not a better climax in Western fiction.

A unique feature of the novel is that the story is told from a young boy's perspective. Schaefer understood that the Western is an American boy's dream of the world as it should be.

Before Shane came, Fletcher's cowboys had been Bob's heroes. His father, of course, was special all to himself. There could never be anyone quite to match him. He wanted to be like him, just as he was. But first he wanted, as his father had done, to ride the range, to have his own string of ponies and take part in an all-brand round-up and in a big cattle drive and dash into towns with just such a rollicking crew and with a season's pay jingling in his pockets.

Now he wanted to be like Shane.

There's a love triangle, so intermingled with admiration and respect that those involved—Joe and Marian Starrett and Shane—are all willing to go against their true feelings for the good of the others.

The highly successful film "Shane" was released by Paramount in 1953. Directed by George Stevens with the screenplay by A. B. Guthrie, it starred Alan Ladd as Shane, Jean Arthur as Marian Starrett, Van Heflin as Joe Starrett, Brandon DeWilde as Bob Starrett, and Jack Palance as the gunfighter Stark Wilson. The screenplay followed the book closely, even the dialogue, which accounts for much of its success.

Monte Walsh (Houghton Mifflin, 1963), Schafer's only long novel, is considered by many to be the high point in his writing. But *Shane* has achieved a place in American Western literature that can't be surpassed, even by its author.

Shane is a poignant yet heroic Western. John Milton wrote, "Schafer takes the mysterious avenger as hero as far as the man in black with no past and no future . . . can be taken. It is the perfection of the stereotype, and done so skillfully there is no need to do it again."

16

HOOKED ON AN EIGHT SECOND RIDE: RODEOS AND WILD WEST SHOWS

INTRODUCTION

In 1883 Colonel William F. Cody organized *Buffalo Bill's Wild West Show*, which came to symbolize the Old West for millions and firmly established the American frontier myth.

Cody had a colorful background. During the Civil War, he served as a Union scout in campaigns against the Kiowa and Comanche. In 1863 he enlisted with the Seventh Kansas Cavalry, which saw action in Missouri and Tennessee. After the war he stayed with the Army as a scout and dispatch rider. In 1867, he became a buffalo hunter for the Kansas Pacific Railroad, providing meat for the construction crews and earning the nickname "Buffalo Bill." In 1868, he became chief scout for the Fifth Cavalry and was awarded the Congressional Medal of Honor for his service. He became a national hero through the efforts of pulp novelist Ned Buntline, who created the legend of Buffalo Bill through narration of the exciting real and imaginary exploits of William F. Cody.

Buffalo Bill's Wild West Show dramatized life in the Old West. It had a buffalo hunt with real buffalos, an Indian attack on the Deadwood stage with real Indians, a Pony Express ride, and a reenactment of *Custer's Last Stand*. He would later add sharpshooter Annie Oakley, Chief Sitting Bull, and other notable western characters. The show toured the country for three decades and played to enthusiastic crowds across Europe.

Cody's show spawned many imitators, but none were even nearly as successful. One of the last was the Miller Brothers 101 Ranch Show. When it went bankrupt in 1931, the Wild West shows' popularity waned and they were replaced the newest representation of the Old West—the rodeo.

Working cowboys originated the rodeo. After the hard work of a roundup, they would hold competitions in cowboy working skills and bet their wages. The first rodeo with an admission charge for spectators was held in Prescott, Arizona, in 1888.

The standard rodeo events are bareback bronc-riding, saddle bronc-riding, bull-riding, calf-roping, and steer-wrestling, sometimes called bull-dogging. The cowboys are not paid a fee or wages; they compete solely for prize money. Some of the more prominent rodeos are the Frontier Days Celebration in Cheyenne, Wyoming; the Roundup in Pendleton, Oregon; the California Rodeo in Salinas, California; the Stampede in Calgary, Alberta, Canada; and the National Finals Rodeo in Las Vegas, Nevada.

I reviewed Ken Kesey's *Last Go Round* (Viking Press, 1994), based on the first All Round Championship Rodeo that took place in Pendleton, Oregon, in 1911. It features actual competitors Jonathan Spain from Tennessee, George Fletcher, a black man who rode the most wicked broncs as if he were at a picnic, and Jackson Sundown, a Nez Percé Indian, who would win a championship in 1916 when he was fifty years old. An older Buffalo Bill Cody plays a role in the plot. This novel captures the excitement of the Wild West as entertainment.

READER'S GUIDE

The Diamond Hitch by Frank O'Rourke. William Morrow, 1956. Based on the life of bronc rider Doughbelly Price, this novel follows riders from show to show throughout the Southwest, as they dream of a respectable job, a decent home, nice things for a wife and children. They hoped the rodeo would make this possible—if they didn't get hurt.

The Bronc People by William Eastlake. Harcourt, Brace, 1958. From Eastlake's Bowman family trilogy. Black, intellectually oriented Alastair Benjamin's white adoptive brother Saint Bowman decided to become a bronc rider on the western circuit. Meanwhile. Alastair, the only survivor of a gunfight that cost him his home, his father and his identity, looked for resolution through retribution.

When the Legends Die by Hal Borland. J. B. Lippincott, 1962. Thomas Black Bull was an orphaned Indian boy forced into the white man's world, transplanted to the rodeo arena. He became Tom Black—known as Killer Tom because he would ride a horse to death—and lost all sense of his tribal identity. How he found his way back is the theme of Borland's novel. Basis for the 1972 film.

Moving On by Larry McMurtry. Simon and Schuster, 1970. A young, beautiful woman and her shiftless husband drift through the honkytonk glitz of the rodeo circuit in the 1960s American West.

Cherokee Rose: A Novel of America's First Cowgirl by Judy Alter. Bantam Books, 1976. Tommy Jo Burns was raised on an Oklahoma ranch where she learned to rope and ride. When she was only fourteen Teddy Roosevelt called her America's first cowgirl. She became a member of Colonel Zack Miller's 101 Ranch Show, where she gained fame as "Cherokee Rose."

Cowboy by Grady Rankin and Aaron Fletcher. Belmont Books, 1977. Clay Tyler was a top hand who had rodeoed his way to fame throughout the Southwest. But he didn't like the way the West was changing, with ranches being run by accountants and cowboys turned into clerks. Then Clay met the girl from Denton, and together they found that the West was still alive in the rodeo—and nowhere else.

Wild Times by Brian Garfield. Simon and Schuster, 1979. The years between the Civil War and Prohibition were wild times that produced men like Hugh Cardiff—sharpshooter, Indian fighter, actor, buffalo hunter, pioneer moviemaker, and lover of many women, including the sister of an Apache chief and the wife of a U. S. Senator. He was the star of thousands of spectacular arena entertainments in the days when the Wild West Show was America's favorite entertainment. Basis for the 1980 teleplay with the same title.

The Secret Annie Oakley by Marcy Heidish. New American Library, 1983. At the height of her popularity as a sharpshooter with Buffalo Bill's Wild West Show in the summer of 1903, Annie Oakley's fame was threatened with scandal. Her husband Frank Butler had to search back through her life to find the secret that she jealously guarded, even from him.

Winterkill by Craig Lesley. Houghton Mifflin, 1984. A contemporary novel set in Oregon, this is the story of a Nez Percé drifter and rodeo rider whose career was flagging, and of his reunion and growing relationship with his teenage son. Medicine Pipe Bearer Award from Western Writers of America.

The Magic Wagon by Joe R. Lansdale. Doubleday, 1986. This elegy to the Wild West centers on a traveling medicine show's strange odyssey across East Texas at the turn of the century. After narrator Buster Fogg's family was wiped out by a tornado, Buster joined Billy Bob Daniels, a patent-medicine pusher and trick shooter, a kindly ex-slave named Albert, and Rot Toe, a wrestling ape. Their adventures on the road included swiping the mummified remains of Billy Bob's "pa" and swindling settlers with their concoction of watered-down whiskey.

Buffalo Girls by Larry McMurtry. Simon and Schuster, 1990. Calamity Jane, who was living as a "Buffalo Gal" in her friend Dora's bawdy house in Miles City, hooked up with her old friend and rival, Buffalo Bill Cody, who cast her as a member of his Wild West Show. They would reenact in Europe the drama of the American West. Basis for the 1995 teleplay.

Virgin of the Rodeo by Sarah Bird. Doubleday, 1993. When Sonja Getz was twenty-nine, her mother remarried and kicked her out of their Texas home. The dour young woman hired a quarrelsome trick roper named Prairie Jones to help her find her absent father, whom she believed to be a Navajo trick roper. Sonja and Jones traveled across Texas and New Mexico in Jones' rusty van, ducking into various rodeos along the way.

Hey, Cowboy, Wanna Get Lucky? by Baxter Black. Crown, 1994. This novel, the first by noted cowboy poet Baxter Black, is the story of two rodeo cowboys named Lick and Cody and their quest to qualify for the National Finals in Oklahoma City sometime in the late 1980s. Lick and Cody competed in the roughstock events, specializing in bull riding.

Biting the Dust: The Wild Ride and Dark Romance of the Rodeo Cowboy and the American West by Dirk Johnson. Simon and Schuster, 1994. The author spent a year with cowboys on the rodeo circuit, watching them risk broken bones for fame and fortune in an eight second ride. The resulting novel recounts the struggles of men such as Joe Wimberly, a bull rider in desperate financial straits with a wife and three small kids, hoping for a chance to ride a ferocious 1,700-pound Brahma that had never been rode, and of Craig Latham, trying to measure up to the memory of an older brother who was a rodeo legend, and others who were willing to risk all for a big payoff.

Lady Buckaroo by Suzanne Lyon. Five Star, 2000. In the 1920s barnstorming cowgirl Lael Buckley followed her dream and became a rodeo professional. From Madison Square Garden to Hollywood, this is the story of rodeo life from the time women were allowed to compete on an equal basis with men.

The Heartsong of Changing Elk by James Welch. Doubleday, 2000. Welch's novel is based on the true story of an Oglala Sioux who was plucked from the reservation to perform in Buffalo Bill's Wild West Show. After a while, Changing Elk didn't feel guilty about participating in the white man's sham—in fact, the troupe became the only family he had left.

East of the Border by Johnny D. Boggs. Five Star, 2004. The story of the Buffalo Bill Combination, a precursor to Buffalo Bill's Wild West Show. A trio of Buffalo Bill Cody, Wild Bill Hickok, and Texas Jack Omonundro plus Indians and a dancing girl toured the East in a Wild West melodrama.

The Honorable Cody: A Novel of the Famous Showman by Richard S. Wheeler. Sunstone Press, 2006. When Buffalo Bill Cody died early in 1917, he continued to live on because his family, colleagues and rivals were not done with him. His family, friends and associates squabbled over his legacy, his money and where he would be buried. The Cody that emerges from Wheeler's fictional anecdotes is a flawed but good man.

Selected Review

Last Go Round
by Ken Kesey, with Ken Babbs
Viking Press, 1994

Ken Kesey is best known for his remarkable best seller *One Flew*

Over the Cuckoo's Nest (Viking Press, 1962) and as the subject of Tom Wolfe's widely read *The Electric Kool-Aid Acid Test* (Farrar, Straus and Giroux, 1968), which chronicles Kesey's role in the California psychedelic revolution in the 1960s. Critics note that understanding his public excesses lends a necessary dimension to understanding his work. But you don't need this background to enjoy *Last Go Round*, a rip-roaring story of the first All Round Championship Rodeo that took place in Pendleton, Oregon, in 1911.

In that year the little prairie town looked a lot like it does today, the streets laid out neatly north and south, east and west. Indian teepees bordered the Round Up grounds; their sawtooth skylines looked wild and threatening. The town was swollen with visitors, and chock full of colorful characters with whom Kesey populates his novel.

The first two were George Fletcher, the hometown favorite to win the All Round, and Jackson Sundown, his Nez Percé nemesis. Both were old cowboys, George around fifty-one and Sundown about forty-five, and had competed neck-in-neck at Pendleton for years.

George was a black man who was famous for his jubilant manner in riding the meanest outlaws as if he were at a party. Known for his merry grin, floppy yellow hat, and wool chaps, everything about him seemed to dance.

Sundown was his opposite. A Nez Percé Indian, thin and straight, wearing a flat-brimmed hat and a thin-lipped scowl, he usually wore a severe three-piece suit and a starched white shirt. He was lean and ramrod stiff, with eyes that bored like carbon-tipped drills, and glossy black hair braided down each side of his face, then tied under his chin, like a necktie. He claimed to be Chief Joseph's last living relative, son of the chief's brother. He was as formal in his riding competition as George was casual.

George and Sundown arrived in Pendleton by train. The welcoming committee cheered as the ramp on the open stock car they were riding was dropped, and the two bronc riders passed in review:

> Sundown had put sheepskin chaps on over his blue serge trousers. Gauntlet gloves covered his coat cuffs, a beadwork red rose on the back of each glove. The saddle on his paint horse was painstakingly decorated and tooled. George's old army saddle was pitiful by

comparison—drab and tattered. To spruce things up he'd spread the zigzag Indian blanket over the back of his bay gelding, and he'd tied [an] orange-and-green silk sash around his throat for a bandana. Crowned with his butter-gold Stetson, it's doubtful many even noticed the shabby saddle.

The third member of the trio who would become a finalist disembarked virtually unnoticed. He was Jonathan Spain, a calf roper from Tennessee. Tall and skinny, only seventeen, he would become known as the southern gentleman cowboy, and in this Roundup would prove a worthy opponent for the two old timers who were favored. An older John Spain narrates the story.

These are the good guys in this Western. There are, of course, the bad guys, led by a national icon, Buffalo Bill Cody. Kesey's Buffalo Bill was an old man, but still a striking figure with his pearl-white hair down to his shoulders and mustache and goatee to match, but by this time primarily a businessman whose goal was to take over the rodeo. He told the Pendleton organizers, "I've seen shows come and go. . . If you brush poppers hope to keep this punkin rolling you positively must have outside investors and experienced promoters." They rebuffed him; "This ain't show business. What us brush poppers have here isn't an investment, it's a tradition!" But Cody didn't give up.

His henchman was the star attraction in Buffalo Bill's Wild West Show, a sadistic wrestler named Frank Gotch. He was a huge man with penetrating blue eyes, completely hairless, a man Jack London said looked as if he were turned inside-out. John Spain had seen heavy blue stares like Frank Gotch's before, through eyeholes in white sheets. Gotch turned his stare on George Fletcher, telling him that no one had ever heard of "cowboys and niggers," and trying to coerce George into the ring with him. Instead, he got Sundown's cousin, a Yakima Indian named Parson Montanic, an eloquent preacher with fine teeth and a jaw like a snapping turtle.

There are a lot of well-defined, interesting characters, but the rodeo dominates the story. The action is lively and illuminating:

The stands are as twitchy as the mare by now, straining to imagine the nuptial vows being exchanged in the blood-blessed chapel before them: "Do you Sundown take this mare? Do you Whirlwind take this buckaroo?" Man and animal nod together. The snubbing rope is flipped free from one side as the blindfold is jerked away from the other. "We now pronounce you cowboy and bronc. Let 'er buck!"

Sundown rocks backward and rowels the neck and shoulders. The mare makes a mighty kick at the sky. The crowd thunders to its feet and we're in business. Sundown is leaned so far back the mare's high-kicking rump knocks his hat off. Man and mare are both impossibly perpendicular for a heart-stopping tick—the mare actually walking on her front hooves, like a circus acrobat walking on his hands; the rider standing straight up in the stirrups, hatless, his Wild West coxcomb flaring. When the mare's hind hooves come back to earth she plants them very neatly to the right of the prints left, by her fore-hooves. She paws at the clouds, then jackknifes back down, twisting her forequarters to the left with a sling of her head. She does it again. And again. And again! Teeter-tottering up and down, round and round, more like a Brahma bull than a horse, spinning counterclockwise, faster and faster . . . Then the mare plunges out of the [dust] cloud and takes off in a last-gasp run across the arena, bucking double-hard in a straight-legged, spine- jarring series of bounds that makes your kidneys ache just watching. The rider is raking just as hard. Rake and buck, spin and spur. The nuptials are obviously over and so is the honeymoon. Still, Sundown doesn't allow the contest to degenerate into a mere domestic squabble. On and on he rides, stone faced and straight up, and curiously considerate. Every watching wife is uplifted; every husband's heart made proud. . . The crowd roared acclaim as the Indian rode from the arena with Whirlwind beneath him, obedient but unbent. Dignified. Sundown hadn't broken her, exactly—he had instructed her. As they passed I got another look into the horse's eyes. The storm had passed and her craziness was cured. Her bucking-bronc seasons were over as well. Last I saw Whirlwind she was pulling a milk wagon for The Dalles Creamery, and letting school kids sit on her back.

Other events and other riders are presented with equal vigor, leading up the famous last go round for All Round Cowboy between George Fletcher, Jackson Sundown, and John Spain. The text is supplemented with archival photographs of Pendleton and the actual participants, collected by Ken Babbs.

Ken Kesey's roots are in the West; he was born in Colorado and his parents moved to Oregon when he was about eleven. He studied writing at Stanford under Wallace Stegner, among others. Kesey first heard the story of the Pendleton *Last Go Round* and the three legendary finalists from his father, seated around a sagebrush campfire in Oregon. In a disclaimer, he states, "If we offend the facts with our tall tale, pray accept our contrition and our excuse: A short little stub of a tale just would not serve." He was right. His polishing of the bare facts has given us a rollicking novel with keen insight into the event, the characters, and the times.

17

FOUR-LEGGED AND FEATHERED WESTERNERS: LIVESTOCK, DOGS, PREDATORS, AND GAME

INTRODUCTION

Many novels have Western animals or birds as central characters. Some authors are poetic when they write about a cowboy and his horse, although this relationship is more practical than romantic. There are some great dog stories, such as Fred Gipson's *Old Yeller* (Scholastic, 1988). Wildlife—bears, wolves, mountain lions, hawks, and others—often take center stage in Western fiction. There are even stories told from an animal's point of view.

For review I chose Jack London's classic *The Call of the Wild* (Macmillan, 1903), a novella about the dog Buck and his master during the Klondike Gold Rush. It represents the best of the Western animal stories.

READER'S GUIDE

White Fang by Jack London. MacMillan, 1906. He was born a large gray cub among a litter of red-haired puppies, with a quicker bite and heavier paw. Men determined he was half-dog, half-wolf, and named him White Fang. When a sadistic owner took advantage of his massive size and tremendous strength to pit him in to-the-death dog fights, White Fang was driven near mad, until a young man came along and offered him kindness and friendship, a kindness the wolf dog did not know how to accept. Basis for the 1925, 1936, 1975, and 1991 films.

Kazan by James Oliver Curwood. Cosmopolitan, 1914. Set in the Canadian wilderness in 1910, this is a tale of a "quarter-strain wolf and three quarters husky" who survives by his wits against the harsh climate and cruel humans. Basis for the 1921 film with the same title, and the 1934 film "Ferocious Pal."

Wildfire by Zane Grey. Harper and Brothers, 1917. Lin Slone tracked the wild stallion he called Wildfire across the desert to the swift Colorado River. The horse is the central figure in this novel, set on a ranch near the Lee's Ferry Colorado River crossing. Basis for the 1949 film "Red Canyon."

The Grizzly King by James Oliver Curwood. Grosset and Dunlap, 1918. The story of a bear cub and a giant grizzly, and the two hunters who tracked them in the rugged Canadian Rockies in the 1880s. Later published as *The Bear*, and the basis for the 1988 movie with that title.

Smoky, the Cow Horse by Will James. Charles Scribner's Sons, 1926. A young reader's book that won a Newbery Medal, *Smoky the Cowhorse* is one horse's story, from his birth on the open range, through his "breaking," to his outlaw rodeo star and saddle horse years. Basis for the 1926, 1933, 1943, and 1966 films titled *Smokey*.

The Pinto Horse by Charles Elliott Perkins. Wallace Hebberd, 1927. *The Pinto Horse* is a novel about a horse that roamed the Montana range in the late 1880s, surviving wolves and blizzards, but never quite blending into the herd. This is an animal biography; Perkins does not humanize his spotted horse.

Sand by Will James. Charles Scribner's Sons, 1929. A cowboy's lone duel with a wild black stallion, a horse with "sand," is at the heart of this novel.

Scorpion by Will James. Charles Scribner's Sons, 1929. Scorpion was a working horse. This is the story of his work, and of his relationship with the cowboys.

The Phantom Bull by Charles Elliott Perkins. Houghton Mifflin, 1932. Bulls don't have the appeal of horses and dogs for most people. But the bull in

Perkins's story is sympathetic, especially when the scene shifts from Montana ranching country to a Mexican bullring, where Perkins gives the surly Phantom Bull's point of view instead of the Spanish matador's. This is a companion volume to *The Pinto Horse* (1927), linked by the Montana setting and the time—both begin in 1888.

The Trail Boss by Walter Gann. Houghton Mifflin, 1937. On a trail drive, the lead steer Sancho dominates the action, earning the admiration of cowhand Bill Sanders.

The Red Pony by John Steinbeck. Corvice-Friede, 1937. Set in California, this is the story of a sorrel colt that was the center of a boy's big dreams. Source for the 1948 film and the 1973 teleplay.

My Friend Flicka by Mary O'Hara. J. B. Lippincott, 1941. A story of a boy's love for a horse. Ken McLaughlin was a youngster whose father, an ex-Army officer, raised blooded horses on his sprawling Goose Bar ranch in Wyoming. The colt, Flicka, was a wild and beautiful filly who had not yet been broken to the saddle. Against the advice of his father and of seasoned ranch hands, Ken chose Flicka for his very own. Basis for the 1943 film.

Green Grass of Wyoming by Mary O'Hara. J. B. Lippincott, 1946. Ken McLaughlin, the boy who wanted his own colt in O'Hara's *My Friend Flicka* (J. B.Lippincott, 1941), has grown into a sturdy, self-reliant youngster. O'Hara's familiar setting is the Goose Bar Ranch. The plot involves the search for a valuable racing mare, owned by an attractive teenage girl, that has been taken into the brood of Thunderhead, a wild stallion. Thinderhead is an offspring of Flicka, Ken's "very own colt" in O'Hara's earlier novel. Basis for the 1948 film.

The Black Bull by Frank Goodwyn. Doubleday,1958. The tale of a young Mexican cowboy obsessed with catching the clever El Toro Moro. The vaquero cannot bring himself to hold the black bull captive after conquering him, which leads to tragedy.

The Valdez Horses by Lee Hoffman. Doubleday, 1967. Chino Valdez was ugly, withdrawn, a devil when drunk—but everyone respected his ability as a horseman. No man knew breeding and training better. Spur Award from the Western Writers of America. Basis for the 1976 film "Chino."

Mavericks by Jack Schaefer. Houghton Mifflin, 1967. This novel deals with the end of wildlife in the West, following the earlier course of the buffalo. Jake, the protagonist, is confronted by the dwindling herds of wild horses.

The Crossbreed by Allan W. Eckert. Little, Brown, 1968. The crossbreed was the offspring of a house cat who had reverted to the wild and a Wisconsin bobcat. The combination of the finest qualities of both breeds gave him strength and intelligence. He made a thousand-mile trek to find the boy who had once rescued him from a flash food.

The Bears and I by Robert Franklin Leslie. E. P. Dutton, 1968. A young prospector, panning for gold in northern British Columbia, found and cared for three orphaned bear cubs. But the bears discovered a painful truth: Though a man was their friend and protector, man could also be a deadly foe.

Cry Wild: The Story of a Canadian Timberwolf by R. D. Lawrence. Toronto: Thomas Nelson and Sons, 1970. A wolf cub named Silverfeet grew to maturity in the remote forests of northern Canada. Then, one hot July, a fire raged through the forest, driving Silverfeet and his pack far to the south, where a trapper saw in the wolf an opportunity for financial gain.

Incident at Hawk's Hill by Allan W. Eckert. Little, Brown, 1971. Set In the Red River country north of Winnipeg, Canada, in 1870, this is the story of a shy, undersized boy, obsessed with wildlife, who survived in the wild for most of a summer, adopted, protected and cared for by a female badger. It is based on an actual incident.

Baker's Hawk by Jack M. Bickham. Doubleday, 1974. Young Billy Baker nursed an injured red-tailed hawk back to health and they became attached to each other. A reclusive mountain man became their friend, and this unusual trio had some good times until the prejudices of the citizens of the Colorado town where Billy lived threatened them with disaster. Source for the 1976 film.

Match Race by Fred Grove. Doubleday, 1982. Quarter horse racing presented a challenge and thrill that few men in the Old West could resist. An unlikely threesome, Dude McQuinn, Coyote Walking and Uncle Billy Lockhart were no exception, as they rode from town to town, cleverly matching and trading racehorses. Spur Award from Western Writers of America.

Steeldust by J. P. S. Brown. Walker, 1986. Bill Shane left home at the High Lonesome Ranch in 1917 to join the Marines. When he returned from

France, his parents had died and the ranch had been sold. He became a hired hand for the new owner. But a sorrel colt named Steeldust would help Bill to start raising horses, as his father had done. The book was originally published in 2 volumes, *Steeldust I* and *Steeldust II—The Flight*.

The Mustangers by Gary McCarthy. Doubleday, 1987. In Nevada in the early 1860s, mustanging—the breaking and selling of wild horses—was a profitable trade. An apprentice mustanger at the Cross T Ranch set out to capture Sun Dancer, a fabulous palomino, to win the favor of the ranch owner's daughter.

Old Yeller by Fred Gipson. Scholastic, 1988. When his dad left on a cattle drive from Texas to Kansas, fourteen-year-old Travis became the man of the house. With his "Old Yeller" dog, Travis would contend with a bear attack on his kid brother and a terrifying disease that turned animals and humans into mad creatures. Source for the 1957 film.

The White Puma by R. D. Lawrence. Henry Holt, 1990. In the snowy mountains of western Canada, a mountain lion was tracked by two hunters who had already killed his mother and sister. But unknown to the hunters, the cat was tracking them.

The Horse Whisperer by Nicholas Evans. Delacorte Press, 1995. When a teenage girl on horseback was hit by a forty-ton truck, her mother tried to save her maimed daughter and the horse, driven mad by pain. Her search for help brought her to the Horse Whisperer, a Montana rancher whose voice could calm wild horses and his touch could heal broken spirits. Source for the 1998 film.

The Loop by Nicholas Evans. Delacorte Press, 1998. Helen Ross, a young government biologist, was sent to the Rocky Mountain ranching town of Hope, Montana, to protect a pack of wolves from ranchers who sought to destroy them. Protected as an endangered species, the wolves were both feared and hated by those in the livestock industry.

Yellow Bear Lodge: A Montana Dude Ranch Adventure, by Bryant C. Blewett and Ellen Marshall. Sunstone Press, 2004. This romantic novel is set on a Montana dude ranch in the Absaroka-Beartooth Wilderness, forty-two miles from the closest town. The scenery is spectacular and the abundance of beauty and wildlife frames the adventures of the diverse ranch crew and the local populace they encounter. An ancient Indian folktale about a menacing yellow grizzly bear in this valley is entwined with the rampaging descendent of that magnificent creature. The authors own and operate a dude ranch in Montana.

SELECTED REVIEW

The Call of the Wild
by Jack London
Macmillan, 1903

> Buck did not read the newspapers, or he would have known that trouble was brewing, not alone for himself, but for every tide-water dog, strong of muscle and with warm, long hair, from Puget Sound to San Diego. Because men, groping in the Arctic darkness, had found a yellow metal, and because steamship and transportation companies were booming the find, thousands of men were rushing into the Northland. These men wanted dogs, and the dogs they wanted were heavy dogs, with strong muscles with which to toil, and furry coats to protect them from the frost.

Thus begins *The Call of the Wild,* one of the most beloved animal stories ever written, which takes place during the Alaska-Yukon gold rush near the end of the nineteenth century, where large, strong dogs were in demand to pull the heavy sleds between Skagway on the Pacific coast and Dawson, a trip hundreds of miles long through bitterly cold weather and treacherous terrain.

Buck, a 140-pound offspring of a St. Bernard and a Scotch sheep dog, was kidnapped from his comfortable home in Southern California and shipped to the Northland, where he was bought by two French Canadian mail couriers, Francois and Perrault , who forcefully introduced him to his new life as part of a sled dog team. Buck learned many hard lessons: the lesson of the leash, of near-starvation and cruelty, the strenuous routines of hauling the sled and running with the pack, and the harsh "law of club and fang," all the while adjusting to the fierce climate. To survive, he had to find in himself those instincts and traits possessed by his ancestors.

From the start Buck was different from the other dogs in the sled team: more intelligent, more resourceful, fiercer, far more cunning, and most of all, more courageous. A natural leader, he usurped the authority of the savage lead sled dog Spitz, a husky the size of a full-grown wolf. A rivalry developed, and Buck defeated Spitz in a ferocious fight and took his place as the lead dog.

While carrying the Canadian mail, the dogs traveled twenty-five hundred miles in less than five months. For a fourteen day period they averaged forty miles a day. After a return trip to Skagway, Francois and Perrault left for other pursuits.

Buck passed from master to master during his time as a sled dog. Some were fair in their treatment of dogs, but all were cruel taskmasters until John Thornton. Thornton nursed Buck back to health after a particularly cruel and inept driver nearly killed him with overexertion, and Buck became lavish in his love for the kind man. From Thornton he learned the power of love and loyalty. Yet always, even at the side of the human he loved, he felt a pull in his bones, an urge to answer his wolf ancestors as they howled to him.

Buck accompanied his new master and his party to a remote mine to search for gold. The expedition turned out badly for the men, though, when they were attacked by Indians. It was then that Buck headed the call of the wild, and joined the wolf pack.

> There is an ecstasy that marks the summit of life, and beyond which life cannot rise. And such is the paradox of living, this ecstasy comes when one is most alive, and it comes as a complete forgetfulness of living, comes to the artist, caught up and out of himself in a sheet of flame; it comes to the soldier, war-mad on a stricken field and refusing quarter; and it came to Buck, leading the pack, sounding the old wolf-cry, straining after the food that was alive and that fled swiftly before him through the moonlight. He was sounding the deeps of his nature, and of the parts of his nature that were deeper than he, going back into the womb of Time. He was mastered by

the sheer surging of life, the tidal wave of being, the perfect joy of each separate muscle, joint and sinew and that it was everything that was not death, that it was aglow and rampant, expressing itself in movement, flying exultantly under the stars and over the face of dead matter that did not move.

Despite his pampered early life in California, Buck's transformation from a creature of comfort to a beast of burden to a wolf pack leader seemed natural, partly because of his physical makeup.

But for the stray brown on his muzzle and above his eyes, and for the splash of white hair that ran midmost down his chest, he might have well been mistaken for a gigantic wolf, larger than the largest of the breed. From his St. Bernard father he had inherited size and weight, but it was his shepherd mother who had given shape to that size and weight. His muzzle was the long wolf muzzle, save that it was larger than the muzzle of any wolf; and his head, somewhat broader, was the wolf head on a massive scale.

He became known by those who saw him with the pack as the legendary "ghost dog of the Klondike."

Humans only play a supporting role in the story, so there is little dialogue. In its place, Buck is personified with human tendencies like pride, achievement, love, hate, and anger.

A gust of overpowering rage swept over him. He did not know that he growled, but he growled aloud with a terrible ferocity. For the last time in his life he allowed passion to usurp cunning and reason, . . .

The story of Buck's life is unique in the sense that the narrator tells the story from the dog's point of view. Buck is a strong protagonist and London skillfully weaves the plot around him. The other sled dogs are given distinctive personalities but do not share the human characteristics of Buck.

The Call Of The Wild is an extraordinarily well-written adventure story with grand descriptions of its bleak and forbidding Far North setting. There are brutally riveting scenes in which Buck and his canine rivals and antagonists fight nearly to the death. It portrays the thin line between wild and tame that separates dog and wolf.

The novel has been compared to Robert Louis Stevenson's *Robinson Crusoe* (Stockdale, 1790), where the main protagonist was marooned on an island and became increasingly savage as he adapted to his new environment. But Crusoe's goal was to return to civilization, whereas Buck drifted into the wild state of his ancestors. Some reviewers find a relation to Anna Sewall's *Black Beauty* (Jarrold, 1877), where the animal protagonist also passed through through several owners, good and bad. And although the novel has long been considered a children's book, many literary scholars have argued that the novel's complexities warrant close analysis, especially its relationships to the philosophy of the "survival of the fittest." It is clear, however, that for novels with animal protagonists, *The Call of the Wild* is a literary conflagration.

Jack London (1876-1916), a native of San Francisco, California, spent a restless youth as an oyster pirate, sailor, mill worker, vagabond, and student before heading to the Klondike during the gold rush of 1897. His experiences in Alaska gave him the material for his best known stories, including *The Call of the Wild* and *White Fang* (Macmillan, 1906). *The Call of the Wild* first appeared in serial form in the *The Saturday Evening Post* in 1903. It is widely regarded as Jack London's masterpiece.

The novel has been adapted to the screen three times (1935, 1972, 1992) and was the basis for a 1996 Hallmark Hall Of Fame teleplay. The 1992 film and the Hallmark teleplay were fairly faithful to the book, with good production values.

18

THE CONTEMPORARY WEST

INTRODUCTION

The Old West may have passed, but the vibrant New West is the setting for a plethora of contemporary novels. The themes are varied: ranching, the environment, farming, race relations, immigration—presented over a wide range of comedy, drama, and tragedy.

This range is depicted in the reader's guide and in the novels reviewed. Wallace Stegner's *Big Rock Candy Mountain* (Duell, Sloan and Pearce, 1943) follows Bo Mason and his family all up and down the West, along the vanished frontier, from Nevada to Saskatchewan in search of the Big Rock Candy Mountain. Edward Abbey's *The Brave Cowboy* (Dodd, Mead 1956) is about a taciturn, self-reliant cowboy at odds with the contradictions and technologies of modern society. *Keep the Change* (Houghton Mifflin, 1989), by Thomas McGuane, tells of a man's efforts to revive his family's rundown ranch, as he faces himself—and his past—as well as the forces of nature. Ivan Doig's *Ride with Me Mariah Montana* (Atheneum, 1990), set in Montana in the centennial summer of 1989, is the story of a grizzled sheep rancher who sets out in a Winnebago with his daughter Mariah and her obnoxious ex-husband to explore the character of the Big Sky land and to define his legacy. These novels illustrate the breadth and depth of fiction set in the contemporary West.

READER'S GUIDE

The Valley of the Moon by Jack London. Macmillan, 1913. This novel is London's paean to the pastoral life and to his ranch in Glen Ellen, California, in Sonoma Valley, the "Valley of the Moon." The central characters of the novel, Saxon and Billy Roberts, lose their first child through stillbirth in the ugly, strike-ridden city of Oakland; but they find Eden in the Valley of the Moon.

A Lost Lady by Willa Cather. Alfred A. Knopf, 1923. Niel Herbert was a motherless boy who idealized the beautiful young wife of the town of Sweet Water's outstanding citizen, Captain Forrester, who was an invalid. Marian Forrester was both a romantic and maternal figure to Niel, and the most important influence of his boyhood. As the Captain's health deteriorated, she turned for help to Ivy Peters, who drained and turned into a wheatfield a beautiful marshland the Captain valued aesthetically. After the Captain died, Marian's apparent surrender to Peters caused Niel to leave Sweet Water with contempt for her in his heart.

Prairie Fires by Lorna Doone Beers. E. P. Dutton, 1925. Set in North Dakota early in the second decade of the 20th century, this is a novel about farmers, exploited by merchants and bankers, who established "the League" to advance their interests.

The Professor's House by Willa Cather. Alfred A. Knopf, 1925. Professor Godfrey St. Peter was disillusioned with his materialistic life and felt choked to death by the rootless and mundane post-WWI world. Alienated more and more from his family, he reflected on his experiences with former student Tom Outland, who had stepped into his life from an earlier West. The central part of the novel is the professor's recollection of Tom's account of his discovery of cliff dweller ruins at Blue Mesa, when Tom followed a steer into the mesa and looked up at the sleeping stone city from the floor of the canyon and recognized an otherworldly quality.

Code of the West by Zane Grey. Harper and Brothers, 1934. A 1920s flapper, who wore her skirts too short and painted her face, was sent West to live with her sister, a schoolteacher in Arizona's Tonto Basin. She wreaked havoc among the young men of the three Thurman families with whom her sister and she boarded. The flighty girl came to realize that the simple Western values—the code of the West—revealed the loss of morality in the East.

In Dubious Battle by John Steinbeck. Covici-Friede, 1937. Steinbeck's novel deals with the efforts of a seasoned labor organizer and a political neophyte to organize an uprising among the migrant farm workers in California's Torgas Valley.

Of Mice and Men by John Steinbeck. Covici-Friede, 1937. This tragic story is about the complex bond between George Milton and Lennie Small, two migrant laborers. The novel is set near the Salinas River south of Soledad, California, where the two worked as farm laborers. Lennie was a big, powerful man who wasn't very smart, but easily pleased. George, a little man, acted as his friend's brain, guiding him and keeping him out of trouble. When Lennie accidentally killed a flirtatious woman, George protected him the only way he could. Basis for three films (1940, 1981, 1992) with the same title.

Burro Alley by Edwin Corle. Random House, 1938. A story of Santa Fe, New Mexico, during the tourist season. The plot follows the adventures of some unusual characters hanging out in a tavern in Burro Alley—Easterners, Westerners, Mexicans, and Indians.

The Grapes of Wrath, by John Steinbeck. Covici, Friede, 1939. Steinbeck's Pulitzer Prize-winning classic is the story of the Joad family, "Oakies" who during the Great Depression traveled from the Dust Bowl of the American Southwest to California in search of a better life. Basis for the 1940 film.

Cannery Row by John Steinbeck. Viking Press, 1945. A tale of some disreputable loafers, drunks, fancy ladies, benign bums and social-outcast philosophers, *Cannery Row* is set in Monterey, California, during the Depression. The novel celebrates lowlifes who are poor but happy. The title derives from a section of Monterey that processed fish harvested by the sardine industry. Basis for the 1982 film.

Border City by Hart Stilwell. Doubleday, Doran, 1945. This novel has at its heart the social conflict of Americans and Mexicans on the Texas-Mexico border. A young newspaperman caught the look of terror and hurt in the eyes of Chelo Moreno, who had been seduced by the political boss of Border City, and nothing could be done about it, since American justice was not for Mexicans. Heartache and tragedy were inevitable when the idealistic newspaperman and the Mexican girl began an Anglo-Mexican love affair.

Giant by Edna Ferber. Doubleday, 1952. A tale of Texas in the 20th century, *Giant* is the story of the powerful Benedict family, who owned the two and one-half million acre Reata Ranch. Bick Benedict, who ruled this empire, brought a new wife from back East to share his 50-room house. She was stunned by the hugeness of the ranch, and slowly came to realize that the enormously wealthy Texas men, of which her husband was one, lived and dreamed bigness in all their endeavors. Basis for the 1956 film.

The Actor by Nevin Busch. Simon and Schuster, 1955. Dan Prader had once been the greatest Western star in pictures. His arrogance had lost him that, and now the few pay checks he earned as a stuntman were quickly gone. But his wife Jill did not mourn for their prosperous past. Her heartbreak was caused by the deep bitterness that lay between Dan, the aging actor on his way down, and Harold, their only son, a brilliant young director on his way up.

Go in Beauty by William Eastlake. Harper and Brothers, 1956. William Eastlake's first novel. In a trilogy of the modern West he chronicles the lives of the Bowman brothers and their relationship with the Navajo in northern New Mexico.

The Bone Pickers by Al Dewlen. McGraw-Hill, 1958. A novel of one Texas family: the Mungers of Amarillo. The six Munger siblings were the heirs of hard-drinking, hardscrabble farmer Cecil Munger, who in one generation brought his family from Dust Bowl poverty to unfathomable wealth in the oil-rich Texas Panhandle of the late 1950s.

The Elbow of the Snake by Sarah Lockwood. Doubleday, 1959. Emily and John Bradford had expected to find a lush, green land in the valley of Idaho's Snake River. What they found was a harsh country of endless miles of bone dry sagebrush. This is the dramatic story about 20th century pioneers who, long after the covered wagons, turned a desert waste into productive farm land.

The Children of Sanchez: Autobiography of a Mexican Family by Oscar Lewis. Random House, 1961. This book is about a poor family in Mexico City: Jesús Sánchez, the father, age fifty, and his four children: Manuel, age thirty-two; Roberto, twenty-nine; Consuelo, twenty-seven; and Marta, twenty-five. Author Oscar Lewis says in the introduction that his purpose is to give the reader "an inside view of family life and of what it means to grow up in a one-room home in a slum tenement in the heart of a great Latin American city which is undergoing a process of rapid social and economic change."

Horseman, Pass By by Larry McMurtry. Harper and Brothers, 1961. Homer Bannon was an old-time cattleman with the frontier virtues of honesty and decency. Homer's strength of character was in marked contrast with that of his unscrupulous son, Hud. The novel portrays the contemporary West in sharp conflict with the Old West. Basis for the 1963 film "Hud"

Fire on the Mountain by Edward Abbey. Dial Press, 1962. An elderly rancher whose land bordered the U. S. Air Force's White Sands Missile Range was told he had to sell his ranch to the government. The stubborn old man, who had lived his whole life on his New Mexico spread, found himself confronting the county sheriff, the Department of the Interior, the Atomic Energy Commission, and the U. S. Air Force. National Cowboy and Western Heritage Museum Western Heritage Award. Basis for the 1981 film.

The Bones of Plenty by Lois Phillips Hudson. Little, Brown, 1962. In this story of farm life in the 1930s on the prairies of North Dakota, George Armstrong Custer is handicapped by some of the personality traits associated with his famous namesake. He is rash, impulsive, and overly optimistic—not good qualities for combating the recurring farm problems of drought and depression.

Portrait of an Artist with Twenty-Six Horses by William Eastlake. Simon and Schuster, 1963. From Eastlake's Bowman family trilogy. Ring Bowman, mired in quicksand that threatened to take his life, quietly gazed at the painting his friend Twenty-Six Horses had painted on the face of the mountain. Episodes of his life passed through his mind, as he remembered that he and his Indian friend left home because his father, the trader George Bowman, took a young Indian girl into his hogan.

Leaving Cheyenne, by Larry McMurtry. Harper & Row, 1963. This novel interweaves the lives of three West Texas people in a story of love and loss, set against the backdrop of the old Fort Worth cattle world, with its stockyards and cowboy hotels. The title reference is to an old cowboy ballad, not Cheyenne, Wyoming. Basis for the 1974 film "Lovin' Molly."

House Made of Dawn by N. Scott Momaday. Harper & Row, 1968. This Pulitzer Prize novel tells the story of a young Kiowa veteran who, after returning from World War II, struggles to reconcile the traditional ways of his people with the demands of the 20th century. Growing up on a New Mexico reservation, he reveled in the sounds of nature and the dawning sunrise. But while living in Los Angeles after the war, alcohol and laziness began to threaten the beliefs and understanding of his youth. The novel explores this aspect of Native American struggles in a modern society.

Red Sky at Morning by Richard Bradford. J. B. Lippincott, 1968. While waiting with his mother in the New Mexico hill town of Sagrado for his father to return from service in the Navy during World War II, a young man comes of age. Characters like Marcia, the foul mouthed daughter of the preacher, contribute to the complexities of the life of a teenage boy trying to find his place in the world. Basis for the 1971 film.

The Last of the Mountain Men by Harold Peterson. Charles Scribner's Sons, 1969. The story of Sylvan Hart, better known as Buckskin Bill, who lived the mountain man lifestyle of the mid-19th century in the contemporary 20th century wilderness of Idaho. Hart lived alone for 35 years on Five Mile Bar, beside the River of No Return in the Idaho Rockies.

Jim Kane by J. P. S. Brown. Dial Press, 1970. Jim Kane ventured from Arizona into Mexico to buy and sell cattle. His deals throughout northern Mexico were complicated by the shadowy complexity of Mexican commerce. Every man of power in every town had to have his palm is greased to allow the passage of cattle. Basis for the 1972 film "Pocket Money."

Play It As It Lays by Joan Didion. Farrar, Straus and Giroux, 1970. Set in Los Angeles, Las Vegas and the barren Mojave Desert, this novel is a dissection of American life in the late 1960s. The central character in the drama is Maria Wyeth, an emotional drifter who found herself, in her early thirties, divorced from her husband and her past, almost anesthetized against pain and pleasure, living in a culture characterized by emptiness and boredom.

Arfive by A. B. Guthrie, Jr. Houghton Mifflin, 1970. Arfive, a small Montana town, was home for Benton Collingsworth, newly arrived from Indiana to become head of the district school, where he had to test his own beliefs against the mores and prejudices of the townspeople in this story set at the edge of America's involvement in World War I.

Bless the Beasts and Children by Glendon Swarthout. Doubleday, 1970. "Send us a boy and we'll send you a cowboy," bragged the Arizona boy's camp. In Swarthout's novel, six adolescent "misfits" discover something important about being men while at the camp.

Black Sun by Edward Abbey. Simon and Schuster, 1971. A forest ranger fell in love with a woman half his age and introduced her to his wilderness of woods and canyons. Then she disappeared, plunging him into a deep gloom.

The Bushwhacked Piano by Thomas McGuane. Simon and Schuster, 1971. On a demented mission of courtship, Nicholas Payne went from from Michigan to Montana, where his antics included a ride on a homicidal bronco. By no reasonable standard could Nicholas be considered a solid citizen or even completely sane.

The Time It Never Rained by Elmer Kelton. Doubleday, 1973. In the 1950s, West Texas suffered the longest drought in the memory of most men then living. Rancher Charlie Flagg, old and overweight but self-sufficient and courageous, refused to accept defeat and endured the seven year drought in his determination to stay on the land he loved. Winner of both the Spur Award from the Western Writers of America and the National Cowboy and Western Heritage Museum's Western Heritage Award.

Thin Men of Haddam by C. W. Smith. Grossman, 1973. Raphael Mendez was orphaned as a child and reared by an Anglo family. Now he is neither de la raza nor Anglo. In this novel of Chicano life in eastern New Mexico in the 1970s, Mendez is the foreman of a ranch who must contend with his penniless cousin, the father of six starving children and unable to find work, who out of desperation choses the other side of the law.

The Milagro Beanfield War by John Nichols. Holt, Rinehart and Winston, 1974. Volume I of Nichol's *New Mexico Trilogy*. This contemporary novel is set in a tiny Spanish-speaking village in rural northern New Mexico. It is a socially-conscious story of water and land rights conflicts and racism, and the troubles that follow protagonist Joe Mondragòn's illegal diversion of an irrigation ditch to water his beanfield. Source for the 1988 film.

Yonnondio: From the Thirties by Tillie Olsen. Delacorte Press.

Yonnondio (the title taken from a Walt Whitman poem) follows the Holbrook family during the late 1920s through Great Depression as they move from the coal mines of Wyoming to a tenant farm in western Nebraska, ending up finally on the killing floors of the slaughterhouses and in the wretched neighborhoods of the poor in Omaha, Nebraska. The effect of poverty on each member of the family reveals what the Depression meant to a whole generation.

Winter in the Blood by James Welch. Harper & Row, 1974. Set in Montana as the nation neared its bicentennial year, the story concerns a few days in the life of a thirty-two-year-old man, a descendant of Indians and living in two worlds: his mother's home on the reservation and the dreary bars and hotels of nearby Havre and Malta. His days and nights blended together in an alcoholic haze until he began to come to terms with his heritage—and his dreams.

The Monkey Wrench Gang by Edward Abbey. J. B. Lippincott, 1975. Vietnam veteran George Washington Hayduke III, feminist saboteur Bonnie Abbzug, wilderness guide Seldom Seen Smith, and Doc Sarvis, M. D., join forces to wage war on the man-made eyesores that blight Abbey's beloved Southwestern wildernesses.

Dancers in the Scalp House by William Eastlake. Viking Press, 1975. A contemporary novel set in New Mexico about a struggle by the Navajo against a land developer and the government. The plot centers on attempts by the Navajo to blow up a dam built to provide recreational facilities for the whites in northern New Mexico.

The Last Valley by A. B. Guthrie, Jr. Houghton Mifflin, 1975. After World War II a young newspaperman in Arfive, Montana, created controversy concerning the land and its uses in the fifth book in Guthrie's *American West* series.

Northern Lights by Tim O'Brien. Delacorte Press, 1975. A story of the relationship between two brothers: one who went to Vietnam and one who stayed home and protested against the war. On a cross-country skiing trip, as the two brothers struggled against an unexpected blizzard in Minnesota's remote north woods, they discovered things about themselves and each other that changed them forever.

A River Runs Through It and Other Stories, by Norman MacLean.

University of Chicago Press, 1976. The title work of his collection, a novella, is about fly fishing. A Montana clergyman has taught his two sons the sport and considers it a ritual of perfection. One of the sons, the narrator, left home, but the other remained, to devote himself intensely to fly fishing on wild Montana rivers. His life has a hopeless beauty and ends abruptly when he is beaten to death in an alley after a barroom quarrel.

The Last Cattle Drive by Robert Day. G. P. Putnam's Sons, 1977. A novel about a Kansas cattleman who, in 1973, decided to drive his 250 head of cattle to the Kansas City stockyards to save shipping costs.

The Last Cowboy by Jane Kramer. Harper & Row, 1977. Henry Blanton, a foreman on a ranch, lived his life as a cowboy, following a time-honored code of conduct. But the Old West he knew was passing, replaced by agribusiness and college educated ranch managers who mocked his way of life.

Ceremony by Leslie Marmon Silko. Viking Press, 1977. A young Native American returned to his New Mexico Laguna Pueblo after surviving a Japanese prisoner of war camp in World War II. He found himself estranged from his people, and sought comfort and resolution through acceptance of the Laguna beliefs and a curative ceremony to relieve his despair.

Comes a Horseman by Dennis Lynton Clark. Dell, 1978. Set in Montana in 1945, this is the story of a young man home from the war, who revered the Old West and wanted to start a ranch. But a declining cattle baron and the oilmen wanted his land. He and a young woman in the same predicament joined forces to market their cattle and save their ranches. Source for the 1978 film.

Continental Drift by James D. Houston. Alfred A. Knopf, 1978. In northern California in the early 1970s, the return of a shaken and confused son from Vietnam coincides with a series of bizarre killings in this novel where the dreaded San Andreas Fault is both a real and a metaphorical player.

The Magic Journey by John Nichols. Holt, Rinehart and Winston, 1978. Volume II of Nichol's *New Mexico Trilogy*. An old bus loaded with dynamite blew up in the little southwestern town of Chamisaville, creating a giant gushing hot spring. Local entrepreneurs recognized the possibilities, and within a year, the little town was flooded with tourists, even though the rest of the country was in the Great Depression.

The Holdouts by William Decker. Little, Brown, 1979. A ranch in 1964 was faced with rustling in this contemporary Western. After fifteen head of Rocking R cattle were found with altered brands at an auction hundreds of miles from the ranch, the foreman was determined to solve the problem himself, without the sheriff's help. Spur Award from the Western Writers of America.

Recapitulation by Wallace Stegner. Doubleday, 1979. Bruce Mason, who left Salt Lake City as an embittered young man at the conclusion of Stegner's *Big Rock Candy Mountain* (Duell, 1943), returns nearly fifty years later. Now a successful statesman and diplomat, he must confront the ghosts of the past who darkened his childhood.

The Death of Jim Loney by James Welch. Harper & Row, 1979. Jim Loney was a half-breed Indian living in a small Montana town. He was thirty-five years old, and slowly going mad. In this novel Welch, a Blackfoot Native American, depicts the trials of a modern American Indian, with no tribe and no home in nature available to him.

Chase a Tall Shadow by John Ell. Tower Books, 1981. A white renegade had been living peacefully as an Apache in the mountains of Arizona until his sanctuary was invaded by a motorcycle gang. He killed two of them and drove the others away and became the target of a massive desert manhunt.

The Nirvana Blues by John Nichols. Holt, Rinehart and Winston, 1981. Volume III of Nichol's *New Mexico Trilogy*. After the seventies, the once-tight Chicano community of Chamisaville had changed. The Anglos controlled almost everything. Joe Minver, a husband and father, needed money to buy the land he worked and launched an illegal scheme to raise it.

Texas Dawn by Phillip Finch. Seaview Books, 1981. Two teenagers, as a history project, examine the colorful life of a Texas ranchwoman.

Nobody's Angel by Thomas McGuane. Random House, 1981. Patrick Fitzpatrick was a veteran, a fourth-generation cowboy, and an alcoholic. His life in Deadrock, Montana, was deathly dull until he met Claire and Tio, who pulled him into their strange world, where he saw a darker, uncontrollable side of life.

English Creek by Ivan Doig. Atheneum, 1984. This is the second novel in Doig's *McCaskill Trilogy*, which began with *Dancing at the Rascal Fair*

(Atheneum, 1987). Set on a sheep ranch in northern Montana in the summer of 1939, where teenager Jick McCaskill discovers his connection to the land when his brother decides to forgo college for the life of a cowhand and a painful rift occurs in the family.

Stones for Ibarra by Harriet Doerr. Viking Press, 1984. An American husband and wife came to the small Mexican village of Ibarra to reopen a copper mine abandoned by the husband's grandfather fifty years before. The only foreigners in Ibarra, the two Americans lived among people who both respected and misunderstood them.

Love Medicine by Louise Erdrich. Henry Holt, 1984. Beginning with the death of a young high-spirited, hard-drinking Chippewa woman in the snow of a North Dakota reservation, this is a multigenerational portrait of those who left the Indian land and those who stayed behind.

Leaving the Land by Douglas Unger. Harper & Row, 1984. In the desolate western Dakotas, family farming was giving way to corporate farming and agribusiness. This novel views the change through the eyes of the daughter of a turkey farmer.

The Blind Corral by Ralph Beer. Viking Press, 1986. A contemporary novel about a large rancher who fences off a waterhole, denying access to the cattle of small ranchers, because he wants additional land, not for his stock, but for a housing development he is planning. Spur Award from the Western Writers of America.

Incident at Big Sky by Johnny France and Malcolm McConnell. W. W. Norton, 1986. This is a true modern-day mountain man story. On July 15, 1984, Sheriff Johnny France received a message that a woman was reported missing while jogging on a isolated Montana mountain trail. The abductors were father and son survivalists who had lived alone for years in the wilderness. This is Sheriff France's own story of a hunt that would climax in a desperate confrontation when he went up into the mountains alone to take out the killers.

Flight from Fiesta by Frank Waters. Rydal Press, 1986. Set in Santa Fe in the mid-1950s at fiesta time, this novel tells of an interesting relationship that developed between an elderly Pueblo Indian and a young Anglo girl attending the fiesta. The ten-year-old girl, unhappy with her mother, maneuvered the old

Indian into taking her away with him. When she disappeared, a posse mentality developed in the town.

Wanderer Springs by Robert Flynn. Texas Christian University Press, 1987. When a native son returned to a dying town in northwest Texas, one of that string of dusty towns left to wither away when the highway from Fort Worth to Amarillo bypassed them, he began a physical and imaginative journey through his and the town's history. Spur Award from the Western Writers of America.

Cactus Thorn by Mary Hunter Austin. University of Nevada Press, 1988. Written in 1927, this slim novella was previously unpublished. Set primarily in the lonesome southwest desert lands of the 1920s, the plot revolves around Grant, a socialist politician who flees from his pressure-ridden life in New York City, and a remarkable woman, Dulcie, a girl as skilled as an Indian tracking in the desert where she was raised. Their relation seems to promise a happy ending. But subtle clues signal otherwise: the eponymous cactus thorn, a tiny dagger with which Dulcie kills a snake rearing toward Grant, and Dulcie's conviction that one must act according to one's belief—beliefs that she thinks Grant's socialism espouses and that his own life should reflect.

The Bean Trees by Barbara Kingsolver. Harper & Row, 1988. A Kentucky woman named Taylor Greer headed west to change her life. By the time she reached the outskirts of Tucson, Arizona, and pulled up at an auto repair shop called "Jesus Is Lord Used Tires," she had "inherited" an American Indian girl named Turtle, who did indeed change her life.

The Man Who Rode Midnight by Elmer Kelton. Doubleday, 1988. Jim Ed Hendrix was a college dropout whose father sent him to Big River, Texas, to convince his grandfather to sell his ranch to developers who wanted to build a recreational lake for free-spending tourists. Jim Ed's grandfather, Wes Hendrix, was one of the few men to ride and stay on the legendary bucking horse Midnight. Wes vowed to save his land, and as Jim Ed watched his stubborn old grandfather fight for what he believed in, a bond began to develop between them.

Border Patrol by Alvin Edward Moore. Sunstone Press, 1988. During the 1920s the problems that the U. S. Border Patrol agents faced along the

Texas-Mexican border were smugglers, illegal aliens, and shoot-outs—pretty much the same as today.

The Heirs of Franklin Woodstock by Benjamin Capps. Texas Christian University Press, 1989. The disappearance of "Papa" Woodstock from a local nursing home in West Texas plunges his five children into a battle over what to do with the ranch. The descendants search for their missing father while finagling for his ranch.

Hayduke Lives! by Edward Abbey. Little, Brown, 1989. Ex-Green Beret George Washington Hayduke, the industrial development saboteur introduced in Abbey's *The Monkey Wrench Gang* (J. B. Lippincott, 1975), presumed dead by his enemies, resurfaces to wage eco-war on the world's largest mobile earth-moving machine, now eating its way through the the canyon lands and desert country of Arizona and Utah.

A Gentleman's Guide to the Frontier by Joanne Meschery. Simon and Schuster, 1990. Two wildly different men, Andrew Marsh and Reg Vickers, set out together in the fall of 1982 on a journey from the suburbs of San Francisco to the vast expanses of the Great Plains. The two trace, in reverse, the westward migration of Reg's father, a lone black man struggling toward his own place in the West. Meschery reveals a world where the frontier spirit has given way to superhighways, missile silos and trailer parks. By segueing to the wild adventures of Reg's father, she shows how the past and present converge.

From the River's Edge by Elizabeth Cook-Lynn. Arcade, 1991. In the Missouri River country of the Sioux in the early 1960s, Joe Tetekeya, a Dakotah and a cattleman, looked for justice in the white man's court of law when forty-two of his steers were stolen.

Wolfsong by Louis Owens. West End Press, 1991. Set in the Cascade range of Northwest Washington, this novel is about a contemporary American land rights controversy. A young Native American named Tom Joseph decided to act against a copper mine for a complex of reasons, largely having to do with his own identity.

Almanac of the Dead, by Leslie Marmon Silko. Simon and Schuster, 1991. A Native American woman who had lived in the reckless world of the drug dealers returned to the Southwest to search for her child. In Tucson, she became the companion of an old woman with the gift of "second sight" who was transcribing, from ancient notebooks, a history of her people, a Native American "Almanac of the Dead." A large cast of off-beat characters contributes to this, as one reviewer called it, "moral history of the Americas from the conquered viewpoint."

A Thousand Acres by Jane Smiley. Ballantine Books, 1991. Pulitzer Prize and the National Book Critics Circle Award. Shakespeare's King Lear set on an Iowa farm. An aging patriarch of a rich, thriving farm in Iowa decided to retire and offered his land to his three daughters. For the two who lived there with their husbands, it made sense as a reward for years of hard work. But the youngest was disinherited when she had the nerve to be less than enthusiastic about her father's generosity. Basis for the 1997 film.

Young Men and Fire by Norman MacLean. University of Chicago Press, 1992. The 1949 Mann Gulch fire in Montana claimed the lives of 12 smoke jumpers. This is MacLean's story of that wildfire, the firefighters and fire scientists, and of their terrible collision.

The Temptations of St. Ed and Brother S by Frank Bergon. University of Nevada Press, 1993. A novel about people caught in a contemporary conflict between nuclear and spiritual energy. The battle for the book's fictional Shoshone Mountain, the site of a proposed nuclear waste dump, becomes a reflection of the battle going on in the souls of the modern monks St. Ed and Brother S in their struggles with the temptations of this world. Backed by an assortment of Native American activists, desert rats, a BLM ranger, and dropout kids, the monks find themselves up against talk-show hosts, technicians, and bureaucrats of the Department of Energy.

Consider This, Señora by Harriet Doerr. Harcourt Brace, 1993. A contemporary story about four North American expatriates living in a small Mexican village.

Green Grass, Running Water by Thomas King. Houghton Mifflin, 1993. This comic postmodern novel by Cherokee author Thomas King satirizes revered American literature from the native American point of view. Coyote and four old Indians from the indigenous, oral tradition assist their grandchildren from the Blackfoot nation in setting the world back in balance. The narrative is a word war for the rights to tell the real story of North America. Canadian and

U. S. history and literature are reconstructed in terms of indigenous witnesses and storytellers from the past and the present.

Pigs in Heaven by Barbara Kingsolver. HarperCollins, 1993. A continuation of the story of Taylor Greer and her adopted American Indian daughter Turtle, which began in Kingsolver's *The Bean Trees* (Harper & Row, 1988). An Indian-activist lawyer recognizes Turtle as a missing child from the Cherokee Nation in Oklahoma, placing Taylor's adoption of the child in jeopardy.

Death Walk at Acoma by Gregory D. Kincaid. Sunstone Press, 1993. A law student drops his studies to search for his eccentric grandfather who has set out on a dangerous ritual desert journey, known to the Indians in a remote New Mexico tribe as the Death Walk.

La Maravilla by Alfredo Véa, Jr. Penguin, 1993. During the 1950s, there was a squatters settlement located to the east of Phoenix, in the city's "unofficial trash heap." It was inhabited by an aristocratic Spanish-Catholic curandera, Yaqui Indians, Blacks, Whites, Chicanos, Okies, Arkies, and Asians; a place of juke joints, transvestites, prostitutes, and the ghosts of wandering hoboes. The author grew up in that world, and this is his story of the passions and relationships that existed there.

Face of an Angel by Denise Chavez. Farrar, Straus and Giroux, 1994. Life in a small southern New Mexico town is viewed through the eyes of Soveida Dosamantes, a once-divorced, once-widowed waitress, who brings to life the day-to-day world of the Hispanic working class through her customers, coworkers, and extended family.

Chamisa Dreams by Robert B. Salter. Sunstone Press, 1994. The comfortable world of a well-regarded Santa Fe based archaeologist is turned around by the realities of reservation life and death, in the shadow of corporate uranium mining on Indian lands.

Wild Game by Frank Bergon. University of Nevada Press, 1995. *Wild Game* follows the pursuit of a modern-day mountain man by an aggressive, tough Nevada state wildlife biologist. The biologist is a man powerfully shaped by the myths and mythologies of the West. Bergon relates both the pursued and the pursuer to the western history which has produced each of them.

The Tortilla Curtain by T. Coraghessan Boyle. Viking Press, 1995.

Cándido and América Rincón crossed the Mexican border and slipped into Southern California in search of the American dream, only to live in a makeshift camp deep in a ravine, fighting off starvation. At the top of the ravine, Topanga Canyon, Los Angeles liberals Delaney and Kyra Mossbacher lead an ordered life in a gated community. A freak accident brings Cándido and Delaney into intimate contact, and this becomes the story of how their opposite worlds intersect.

Border Music by Robert James Waller. Warner Books, 1995. Texas Jack Carmine and Linda Lobo didn't know each other, but left by the back door of a place called the Rainbow Bar in Dillon, Minnesota, got in a pickup truck, drove all day, and ended up in bed in a motel room. This was the kind of thing Jack was famous for doing. *Border Music* is the story of his and Linda's wild relationship.

Bucking the Sun by Ivan Doig. Simon and Schuster, 1996. The Duff family was driven from their Montana bottomland to relief work on the New Deal's project to dam the Missouri River. This willful family was as unpredictable as the river itself. Around them swirled a huge cast of unsavory characters, drawn there to prey on the workers who labored on the project. And then there was the restless river, flowing ceaselessly toward tragedy. To "buck the sun" is to push on against the glare of sunrise or sunset.

Sun Dancer by David London. Simon and Schuster, 1996. In 1971 twenty members of the American Indian Movement (AIM) occupied Mount Rushmore. They were protesting the U. S. Government's violations of the 1868 Laramie Treaty, which granted the Black Hills of South Dakota to the Sioux. Their protest was quickly suppressed by the federal government. Novelist David London moved the event into 1990 to form the basis for this novel, which is a blend of history and fiction.

Son of Durango: A Contemporary Novel by Laurance L. Priddy. Sunstone Press, 1996. Jesus Camacho, driven by poverty and pride, leaves his family on their small farm in the Mexican State of Durango and follows his younger brother, Miguel, to work illegally in Texas. But Miguel has disappeared, and Jesus must struggle with the greed and hostility of both Texans and other Mexicans. Constantly threatened with deportation and torn by conflict, Jesus will need all the strength he can muster and good luck to find Miguel and support his family while making a new life in an alien land.

Montana Sky by Nora Roberts. G. P. Putnam's Sons, 1996. Three half-sisters who don't know one another must share their late father's ranch for one year in order to inherit his fortune. But their father also left behind enemies who are determined to deny the women their inheritance. Basis for the 2007 teleplay.

Heaven's Gold by Giles Tippette. Forge, 1996. Wilson Young was one of the most notorious outlaws of his day, but was pardoned by the governor of Texas in 1888. In 1916 the fifty-eight-year-old former gunslinger, whose only child was flying with the Lafayette Escadrille in France, found out about a shipment of $250,000 in gold bars to the Federal Reserve Bank in San Antonio, and decided to go after it. Wilson claimed his intent was to teach the U. S. government a lesson and keep America out of the war.

Cities of the Plain by Cormac McCarthy. Alfred A. Knopf, 1998. The third novel in McCarthy's *Border Trilogy*. John Grady Cole, the protagonist in *All the Pretty Horses* (Alfred A. Knopf, 1982), and Billy Parham, from *The Crossing* (Alfred A. Knopf, 1994), work together in the fall of 1952 on a New Mexico ranch, where there is a threat of takeover by the U. S. military. They repeatedly cross the Mexican border in their leisure time in response to the pressures of social change.

Keep the Wind in Your Face by John D. Nesbitt. Endeavor Books, 1998. A contemporary big-game hunting story focused on a hunter-outfitter named Del Watters. "Del had the satisfaction of knowing that he brought out [hunters] year after year, to ruin the things he loved the best. And he couldn't blame it on them."

Brokeback Mountain by Annie Proulx. London: Fourth Estate, 1998. In this short novella two young men spend the summer of 1963 together herding sheep on a Wyoming ranch. They embark on an intimacy that they feel is their own business. The summer ends, they separate and return to their respective lives. But four years later their affair picks up where it left off during that summer on Brokeback Mountain. Source for the 2005 film.

The Buffalo Commons by Richard S. Wheeler. Forge, 1998. Laslo Horoney, his wealth immeasurable, had a dream—to establish a national grassland over tens of thousands of square miles of the high plains of eastern

Montana and to restore the damaged and eroded prairie. He wanted a place where buffalo could graze and multiply as they did before the advent of civilization, a "buffalo commons." But Laslo faced many obstacles, thrown up by radical environmentalists, ranchers, and county, state and federal government bureaucrats.

Mine Work by Jim Davidson. Utah State University Press, 1999. Set in the 1940s and 50s in Colorado mining towns and the Navajo Reservation in the Four Corners region of the Southwest, this story tells of a man's search for the truth behind his family's troubled past. In his search he finds a troubling story of race politics and murder, linked to his grandfather and his father. His search leads him to the tragic experiences of the oppressed working-class Colorado miners, and to emotional devastation faced by the economically poor Navajo. Spur Award from Western Writers of America.

Mountain Time by Ivan Doig. Scribner, 1999. A story of family feuds, *Mountain Time* brings together lovers, sisters, and father and son for long-overdue confrontations. Set in Montana mountain country, members of the clan from Doig's *McCaskill Trilogy* are prominent in the cast of characters.

Fencing the Sky by James Galvin. Henry Holt, 1999. Set in the 1990s in upland Wyoming, when greedy developers like Merriwether Snipes divided up the old ranches and sold them as 40-acre ranchettes, Galvin's first novel opens with a cowboy roping the pistol-packing Snipes and snatching him from his vehicle, breaking the developer's neck in the process. The novel then directs its attention to events leading up to the incident, and how the cowboy deals with the consequences.

Plainsong, by Kent Haruf. Alfred A. Knopf, 1999. On the Colorado high plains east of Denver, in the small town of Holt, a high school teacher raises his two boys alone, while out in the country, two brothers, elderly bachelors, work the family homestead and care for a pregnant teenage girl who has nowhere else to go. Like the title, reviewers have called Haruf's story a "simple and unadorned melody."

Dark River by Louis Owens. University of Oklahoma Press, 1999. A Choctaw from Mississippi, following his return from the Vietnam war, worked as a tribal ranger on an Apache reservation in eastern Arizona, where he lived among people far different from his own. Among the odd assortment of characters he encountered was a right-wing militia group, training secretly on reservation lands.

Southwest of Heaven by Giles Tippette. Forge, 2000. In 1924, Willis Young is back in Texas after flying combat in France during WW I. He and his former mechanic drill for oil on the 200,000 useless acres of West Texas that Willis owns. They strike water instead, which will turn the dry Texas plains into heaven. But there are questions over who will control the water well.

The Last Report on the Miracles at Little No Horse by Louise Erdrich. HarperCollins, 2001. Father Damian had seen the Little No Horse Reservation in North Dakota through its most severe crises. He had lived and serviced the Ojibwa people as a man of the cloth, but also as a woman. Now, nearing the end of his life, he dreaded discovery and had to wrestle with demons from his past and the secret of his own identity—among other things—in his revelatory last report to the Pope.

The Smoke Jumper by Nicholas Evans. Delacorte Press, 2001. The fire that was to change so many lives started with a single bolt of lightning. Soon it engulfed an entire mountain and exacted a deadly toll. Into this inferno came the smoke jumper, like an angel of mercy from the sky.

South of Eden by Earl Murray. Forge, 2001. Murray's novel is about the establishment of the Forest Service in 1905 and the conflict between the Service and the cattle ranchers who grazed their animals on Forest Service land. The plot also has a shadowy figure who loves to brutally kill young women and bury their bodies in a ritual manner.

The Sheep Queen, by Thomas Savage. Back Bay Books, 2001. Originally published as *I Heard My Sister Speak My Name* (Little, Brown, 1977). The narrator, Tom Burton, remembers his mother and grandmother when he receives a letter at his house on the Maine coast from a woman claiming to be his sister. His grandmother, Emma Russell Sweringen, was known as the "Sheep Queen of Idaho," and at one time on a large ranch 30 miles south of Salmon, her sheep numbered 7,000. But she had a daughter who disappointed her, marrying Tom's father, leading to Tom's dilemma in dealing with a woman in Washington State searching for details about her birth parents.

Boy's Pond by Warren J. Stucki. Sunstone Press, 2001. Set in 1953, when a nuclear test rained burning radioactive particles on southern Utah. This event, plus an ill-fated volcano prank that killed two men and left another critically injured, changed the lives of J. T. Kunz and Mick Graff forever. They were charged with manslaughter in the volcano prank. Additionally, Mick was diagnosed with acute myeloblastic leukemia, ostensibly from the radiation fallout. Faced with the prospect of his own death, Mick turned to God. J. T., on the other hand, became more cynical and disillusioned by God's apparent indifference to Mick's plight.

The Buffalo Soldier by Chris Bohjalian. Crown, 2002. A flash flood in rural Vermont drowned the 9-year-old twin daughters of state Highway Patrol Sgt. Terry Sheldon and his wife Laura. The Sheldons took in a foster child to fill the void, a 10-year-old African-American boy named Alfred. A neighbor let Alfred ride his horse and gave him a book about the Buffalo Soldiers, black U. S. cavalrymen and infantrymen who helped patrol the Great Plains after the Civil War. Alfred was inspired by one of the Buffalo Soldiers, Sgt. George Rowe. Rowe's wife was a 16-year-old Comanche mother of two named Popping Trees. Their unlikely love story unfolds in counterpoint to the Sheldons' efforts to create a new family on the ruins of their old one.

Song on a Blue Guitar by Dorothy Cave. Sunstone Press, 2002. An old promise, a new ghost, and a resurgent mystery send rancher Joe Steele in search of Toro Duran, his army buddy of some fifty years ago. In a northern New Mexico barrio called Tuceros Joe finds himself sucked into a fight Toro and his offbeat amigos are waging to save their cantina and its wildly decorated outhouse—"best little privy on the Rio Grande"—from a Dallas developer.

Perma Red, by Debra Magpie Earling. Bluehen Books, 2002. A novel set on Montana's Flathead Reservation in the 1940s. In the tiny town of Perma, Louise White Elk struggles with a passion for Baptiste Yellow Knife. Their love-hate relationship is complicated by Charlie Kicking Woman, the local police officer who admires Louise. Baptiste and Louise's passions finally lead to murder. Spur Award from Western Writers of America.

Girl of the Manzanos by Barbara Spencer Foster. Sunstone Press. 2002. Mardee's father Ben had built an empire deep in New Mexico territory. But Mardee was searching eagerly past the narrow borders of their mountain home. And when she met Jeff Corbin, a young ambitious lawyer from Socorro, her heart was set on fire. When New Mexico became a state in 1912, Jeff went to work for the new governor in Santa Fe and promised to help Mardee get a job in the same office. Would she make her mark on this wild new state?

Summer of Fifty-Seven: Coming of Age in Wyoming's Shining Mountains by Stephen C. Joseph. Sunstone Press, 2002. Steve Jonas is 19 years old in the summer of 1957, riding his thumb north and west. He hitches into the two-horse town of Jackson, Wyoming in a June snowstorm, and comes face to face with the Grand Teton Range. He finds work in the National Park, building the mountain trail that is to shape the course of his coming-of-age. It is the late 1950s, a more innocent and sweeter time than the turbulent decades to come.

That Old Ace in the Hole, by Annie Proulx. Scribner, 2002. Young Bob Dollar was out of college and aimless when he took a job with Global Pork Rind. His task was to locate big spreads of land in the Texas and Oklahoma panhandles that could be purchased by the corporation and converted to hog farms. In a Texas town called Woolybucket, Dollar learned the hard way how vigorously the old owners would hold on to their land, even though their children wanted no part of it.

The Miracle Life of Edgar Mint by Brady Udall. W. W. Norton, 2002. The trials of Edgar Presley Mint began on an Arizona reservation at the age of seven, when the mailman's jeep accidentally ran over his head. Half-Apache orphaned Edgar was taken from his home and began a long journey from the hospital to a school for delinquents to a Mormon foster family and an eventual, unexpected return home. Spur Award from the Western Writers of America.

The Lucky by H. Lee Barns. University of Nevada Press, 2003. At fourteen Peter Elkins becomes the legal ward of Willy Bobbins, the hard-drinking owner of The Lucky casino in Las Vegas. Willy hopes Peter will go to college, become a lawyer, and help him run his casino, but Peter would rather be a cowboy on Willy's Montana cattle ranch.

Prairie Nocturne by Ivan Doig. Scribner, 2003. Susan Duff, the headstrong schoolgirl from Doig's *Dancing at the Rascal Fair*, now a middle-aged voice teacher in Helena, Montana, is at the center of this story, set in the 1920s, that incorporates a vast amount of fascinating historical material into a personal drama.

Hunted Past Reason by Richard Matheson. Forge, 2003. Two old friends were hiking through the wilderness toward a remote cabin in the woods of northern California. But the isolation of the hike soon brought out long-hidden resentments between the two men, until finally these resentments erupted into a terrifying life-or-death battle for survival.

Man on the Border by Dave Austin. Berkley, 2004. Near the beginning of the 20th century, young Billy Delisle hired on as a border patrol agent for the U. S. government. He learned that his partner was Tuck Adler, legendary gunfighter, rumored to be as fast as Wild Bill Hickok or Wyatt Earp. But Billy learned that legends sometimes lie. Austin paints a gritty portrait of the Texas-Mexico border and the illegal traffic that crisscrosses it.

The Ghost Ocean by Richard Benke. University of New Mexico Press, 2004. The title refers to the ancient sea beds that were once southwestern New Mexico. Set in the border area between southwestern New Mexico and northern Mexico, the remote Gila Wilderness, *The Ghost Ocean* is a story of modern-day crime and violence.

Useful Girl by Marcus Stevens. Algonquin Books, 2004. When a construction crew uncovers the remains of a Cheyenne girl, the foreman's daughter, Erin Douglass, assists Charlie White Bird in his quest to rebury the remains in a sacred place. In parallel with a developing relationship between Erin and Charlie, Stevens re-creates the life of the young Cheyenne girl and the circumstances that led to her death.

Following the Harvest by Fred Harris. University of Oklahoma Press, 2004. In 1943 a sixteen-year-old boy left his home town of Vernon, Oklahoma, to travel to Rhame, North Dakota, with his father's wheat harvesting business. Adventure and tragedy awaited him. Not everyone returned home from following the harvest.

Charley Sunday's Outfit by Stephen Lodge. Behler, 2004. Charley Sunday decided to drive a herd of Texas longhorns from Golden, Colorado, to Juanita, Texas, just a little east of Del Rio. Never mind that it was the 21st century and the herd had to cross 1,000 miles of country crisscrossed with highways and railroads and dotted with towns and cities. Charley wanted to impart the American Cowboy legacy to his only grandchild.

Last day in Paradise by Robert K. Swisher Jr. Sunstone Press, 2004. Banjo Ortega, an old Mexican bandit who hates white people, and Rodney

Slugger, a down on his luck white cowboy from Montana, are both men who know they are living relics of the old West. But no matter what, they must hang onto what they are no matter the hardships. They become unlikely allies in stopping the new owner of the 167,000 acre Last Day in Paradise Ranch from acquiring Banjo's land for a subdivision.

The Only Road There Is by Rebecca Bailey. Texas Review Press, 2005. In this novella, Brenda Marlene Simpkins, aka Starflower Jade-Eagle, drove her eighty-year-old computer junkie mother to Cooke City, Montana, to visit Brenda's brother Dennis, who believed he was a mountain man. Upon seeing Dennis after a decade or more, Marlene suspected the man calling himself her brother was an impostor.

The Divide by Nicholas Evans. G. P. Putnam's Sons, 2005. The body of a young woman is found embedded in ice on a mountain in Montana. The body is identified as that of the daughter of an upper middle-class family back East who was involved romantically with an eco-terrorist. The title refers to the distance she put between herself and her family. At the time of her death, the girl was pregnant and wanted for murder.

High Country by Willard Wyman. University of Oklahoma Press, 2005. During the Great Depression, young Ty Hardin became a packer, guiding mule trains into mountains where wagons could not travel. After being wounded in World War II, he returned home to Montana and packed into the mountains to heal, then left for the Sierra Nevada, the highest, most rugged country of all. Spur Award from the Western Writers of America.

The Whistling Season by Ivan Doig. Harcourt Brace, 2006. In the late 1950s, Paul Milliron, the narrator, who was superintendent of the Montana schools, came to Great Falls to make a sad announcement. In pursuit of greater efficiency, the state has decided to close all its one-room schoolhouses. As the burden of making that speech weighed on him, Paul remembered his own experience in a one-room school 43 years earlier, and that reverie forms the body of the novel.

The Willow Field by William Kittredge. Alfred A. Knopf, 2006. In his first novel, noted memorist and story writer William Kittredge tells the story of Rossie Benasco, a true son of the West. Beginning in the 1930s and covering most of the twentieth century, the novel follows Rossie on a trail drive from a Nevada ranch to Calgery, to the Montana farm of an extraordinarily wealthy family, through World War II, and on his quest for the governorship of Montana.

Midnight Cactus by Bella Pollen. Grove Press, 2006. A young mother arrived in Arizona to oversee the renovation of some decrepit property in a ghost town into a resort. In the remote desert country she had to contend with a harsh climate filled with deadly wildlife, illegal immigrants, immigrant traffickers and vigilante border guards.

How Far the Mountain, by Robert K. Swisher, Jr. Sunstone Press, 2007. *How Far The Mountain* is the story of a man, a woman, and a mountain. The woman, from the city, must go to the mountain to discover who she is after her husband's death from cancer. The man, a cowboy, must force himself to go to the mountain and make a shrine from the bones of "Texas Lady," the horse his wife was riding when she was killed by lightning.

SELECTED REVIEWS

The Big Rock Candy Mountain
by Wallace Stegner
Duell, Sloan and Pearce, 1943

Harry "Bo" Mason was born with an itch in his bones. He was always looking for a land of Canaan, some Big Rock Candy Mountain where life was effortless and something could be had for nothing. But others had been before him at all the Canaans he migrated to. Yet, he would never quite grant that all the good places were filled up. So he kept moving.

Elsa Mason knew her husband was a rambler, and that the responsibilities of marriage and a family would never sit easily on his back. So she and their two sons followed him on his western odyssey, enduring a life they despised and hated.

The Big Rock Candy Mountain is clearly autobiographical. It deals with an asteroid-like family on the Western frontier, and is almost Stegner's exact view of his early years. He wrote, "My themes are mainly of the American West, in which I grew up. I grew up without history, in a place where human occupation had left fewer traces than the passage of buffalo herds. I early acquired the desire to find some history in which I myself belonged, and some tradition in which I might have a self-respecting part."

This view is reflected in Elsa, who "dreamed of quiet streets, apple trees heavy with fruit or white with blossoms, her children scuffling leaves under the maple and running to meet Bo when he came down the sidewalk with his coat on his arm and the six o'clock sun on his face. She didn't want much."

But she had married Bo Mason, and these things were not to be. Bo was "a man who was never satisfied, who was born disliking the present and believing in the future." He wasn't, by any orthodox standard, a good husband or a good father. His younger son Bruce (Stegner) hated him: "My hatred seems to arise from two things: his violence to me [Bo had once, in anger, rubbed the child Bruce's face in the child's own excrement], and his unwillingness to see he was misusing my mother." His mother, however, loved Bo absolutely and had resigned herself to his restlessness.

This restlessness carried the family throughout the West—a West that was still a primitive frontier in the early 1900s. Elsa met Bo in 1904 in Hardanger, North Dakota, where he ran a bowling alley. He and his partner Jud Chain bought a hotel in Grand Forks and endured seven years of hard times, including the crash of 1907. Then, hearing stories of a wild paradise, Bo moved his family to Washington, where he bought a cafe in Richmond. Then to Saskatchewan, where Bo started running whiskey. Then back to Great Falls, where he continued to run whiskey and prospered for a while. Then they moved to Salt Lake City, where Bo continued his whiskey business. There, the Masons lived in twelve houses in the first four years—a man who drove a big car but never seemed to have regular working hours created suspicion among the neighbors. Bruce and his brother Chet graduated from high school in Salt Lake City. After being arrested for possession and transportation, Bo became a partner in a gambling hall in Reno, where he had a summer cottage on Lake Tahoe nestled on the east slope of the Big Rock Candy Mountain. Finally, they returned to Salt Lake City.

Long afterward, Bruce looked back on the rootlessness of his family. He wasn't sure where "home" was. Tahoe? Salt Lake City? In truth, he was a Westerner. Anywhere beyond the Missouri was home.

One critic considers Stegner only peripherally a Western writer; a writer to whom setting is irrelevant in his fiction. Not so. In describing Bo's search for the Big Rock Candy Mountain, Stegner takes us through North Dakota wheat towns, Saskatchewan prairie hamlets and homesteads, Washington logging camps, and the cities of Seattle, Salt Lake, Reno, and a lot of country seen on the fly between them. The sight, sound, smell, and feel of these Western settings are central to the novel. Stegner writes of fall in North Dakota:

> There weren't any trees to change, for one thing. The land just got brown, then gray, and at night it froze, and then it rained and froze again so that the road was ridged with hardened tracks, and ever change from summer to winter made the place look more desolate than it had before, and the wind blew interminably, holding you back, hustling you along, sweeping at you from around corners

This grim setting accents the misery Elsa and the boys endured while following Bo on his ramblings across the West.

Stegner was a respected professor of literature at Stanford whose students included Thomas McGuane, Edward Abbey, N. Scott Momaday, Tillie Olsen, Robert Stone, Larry McMurtry, Ernest Gains, Max Apple, Ken Kesey, and numerous other highly successful writers. His own writing is sober and reproduces persons, settings, and experiences as they actually existed. Robert Stone said Stegner wasn't an eccentric stylist at all; his writing was tremendously sound and clear and good. In fact, his writing is a delight. Consider this description of a farmer chasing a boy on a bicycle:

> Frankie had fifty yards to go before he hit the trail and ground smooth enough to ride on, and Angus, coming down at an angle, had a good chance to cut him off. Frankie sprinted, bouncing the wheel, his bare legs and fallen stockings twinkling, but Angus was coming like a thunderbolt . . . Frankie hit the road and made a

running leap onto the seat. It looked as if Angus could reach out in one more stride and grab him. He had looked terribly fast before, coming uphill. Now, going down, he was all legs. He opened clear up to the neck, like a clothespin, he ate up twenty feet at a stride. Frankie's head went down, his feet on the peddles were a blur, his shirt was ballooning out behind, but he did not open up any daylight between himself and Angus. One bump, one spill, and Frankie was a goner. But he didn't spill, and he didn't let up, and even the tracks, where with providential carelessness he had left both gates open, he peddled right on, bumped perilously over the planks of the crossing, and legged it out the other side and up the road to town. Angus stopped at the fence.

Robert Stone is correct. This is tremendously sound and clear and good writing.

Dr. Stegner taught at Stanford twenty-six years, then quit at age sixty-two to write full time. He won the Pulitzer Prize in 1972 for *Angle of Repose* (Doubleday, 1971), and the National Book Club Award in 1977 for *The Spectator Bird* (Doubleday, 1976). *Where the Bluebird Sings to the Lemonade Springs: Living and Writing in the West* (Random House, 1992) was written when he was in his mid-eighties—and he was still at the top of his form.

Stegner's sizable body of work includes not only novels and volumes of short stories but also historical works such as *Mormon Country* (Duell, Sloan and Pearce, 1942), *Beyond the Hundredth Meridian* (Houghton Mifflin, 1954), and *The Gathering at Zion: The Story of the Mormon Trail* (McGraw Hill, 1964). These latter works reveal a serious scholar who saw the past as a permanent part of the present American experience.

The Brave Cowboy
An Old Tale in a New Time
by Edward Abbey
Dodd, Mead, 1956

Edward Abbey is at his best describing the American wilderness in crisp, vivid language, as in *Desert Solitaire* (McGraw, 1968). But *Brave Cowboy* isn't about the wilderness, nor is it about Abbey's well-known obsession with preserving the wilderness; rather it's about American individualism.

When he wrote *Brave Cowboy* in the summer of 1955, Abbey was a practicing and preaching anarchist. His philosophy, and his doubts, are embodied in Paul Bondi, a veteran who choses to go to prison for two years rather than register for the draft. Bondi is philosophically an anarchist, but knows it won't work in the real world:

> Did I call myself an anarchist? Well, that's a metaphor, not a
> description of my politics. I see clearly enough the utter hopelessness
> of the anarchist ideal: everything is against it—the massive pressure
> of overpopulation, industrialization, militarization, the weight
> of sentiment, the momentum of history. My anarchism is just a
> sentimentality; I'm a good sound citizen.

And Bondi even has doubts about his defiance. He wrangles with himself: "My emotions become ideas, my ideas emotions. But here I lie, a victim of both. Should be home milking the goddamned goat."

His friend Jack Burns rides down from the hills to see what he can do; he assumes freedom is dear to Paul and serving time in prison unthinkable. Burns is a loner, a self-sufficient individualist, whose companions are nature, his guitar, and his horse, Whiskey. He's out of step with the modern age. His clash with the regimentation of society is inevitable.

Set in Duke City (Albuquerque), New Mexico, in the early 1950s, the story begins with the cowboy enjoying the simple, easy pleasures of his solitary, unencumbered life: a warm fire; a simple trail meal of coffee, dried mutton, and bacon; a smoke; and a wilderness to roam. Abbey writes of the

New Mexico landscape with a sure sense of place:

> ... the vast sweep of desert around him, the sky singing overhead. The five volcanoes to the south, lined up like old ruined tombs, swung slowly around on his wheeling horizon. Riding into the brush of greasewood, live oak, mesquite, he flushed a covey of quail; they rose in unison from the desert floor, shrilling and fluttering, flew ahead for a distance and dropped in unison to the ground again.

The contrast is striking when the cowboy intentionally violates the law, and the police toss him into jail. But Burns has no fear of authority, only contempt. When his jailers ask where he lives, he defiantly replies, "Anywhere I like." He carries no social security card, no driver's license, and although he's a decorated veteran, no draft registration card. He maneuvers into a cell with Bondi, and unveils his plan: "Come with me. We'll go up high in the Rockies—maybe the Shoshone Forest in Wyoming." It's ironic that the friend he wants to help escape is in prison by choice.

Understanding Edward Abbey isn't easy. He was an ardent environmentalist whose book *The Monkey Wrench Gang* (J. B. Lippincott, 1975) inspired *Earth First!* and other hard-line environmental groups. But, he sometimes tossed his empty beer cans out the window as he drove through the starkly beautiful desert country he loved. He believed the population had to be reduced drastically, yet he married five times and fathered five children. There was contempt on a personal level for causes he cared for dearly. This is evident in his characterization of Paul Bondi, who's willing to serve two years in prison to make a statement about his beliefs, but doesn't intend to live up to them after his release.

The cowboy, however, isn't a preaching, practicing anarchist. He's simply a rugged individualist who gets run over by modern society. In a prelude to the novel, Abbey gives us a poem *Ballad of the Brave Cowboy*, which closely resembles the traditional cowboy ballad *Utah Carroll*. In Abbey's poem, a cowboy named Burns died saving a friend during a stampede. This kind of man was eulogized in song and legend in the Old West. In the New West, the brave cowboy is ground under the heel of stampeding social order while trying to save his friend. He's made a fugitive instead of eulogized. Abbey hated the order imposed by society, as this metaphor for Duke City illustrates:

> After awhile they went on, still eastward, following the unpaved street past a big new graveyard laid out like a model housing project, past a big new housing project laid out like a model graveyard . . .

The cowboy acts out his little drama against a backdrop of other interesting characters. There's Bondi's wife Jerry, left to struggle and support their young son while Paul makes his statement, and Sheriff Morey Johnson, a big, plain man, given to scratching himself wherever he itches, but a savvy sheriff who knows his country. When Burns becomes a fugitive, Johnson relentlessly tracks him. However, the sheriff is sympathetic to his quarry and doesn't let the posse turn the manhunt into a "coon hunt." And there's Whiskey, the cowboy's horse, half Appaloosa and half range stock, who Burns can't leave behind even as he flees for his life.

"Lonely Are the Brave," a film based on the novel, was released by Universal in 1962. David Miller directed it, and Dalton Trumbo wrote the screenplay. Trumbo changed Bondi's crime to helping "wetbacks," which probably elicited more sympathy in 1962 than defying the draft laws. Kirk Douglas was cast as Jack Burns, Michael Kane as Paul Bondi, Walter Matthau as Sheriff Johnson, and Gena Rowlands as Jerry Bondi. Douglas and Matthau are especially convincing in their roles. Abbey liked the film; in his foreword to the 1971 Ballantine Books edition, he thanked Kirk Douglas for helping keep the story alive.

Edward Abbey has been called "America's crankiest citizen." In *Brave Cowboy*, his displeasure with a society that demands conformity is eloquently presented through the neutering of Paul Bondi and the squashing of the cowboy. The novel is an American tragedy.

Keep the Change
by Thomas McGuane
Houghton Mifflin, 1989

Russell Martin, in his introduction to *Writers of the Purple Sage* (Viking, 1984) classifies Thomas McGuane as an immigrant writer living in the interior West—one of those who came west because it seemed to be a good place to write. He says their work is less hopeful than that of the natives. They tend to supplant optimism with nagging doubt, and attention to familial detail is often abandoned in favor of displaced individuals. This is a good assessment of McGuane's novels, and in particular this one.

In this contemporary Western the protagonist, Joe Starling, is a misfit who's lost all interest in success. He recognizes that his character is composed almost totally of things he hates in other people, and knows that he's increasingly losing the ability to distinguish between love and hate.

Joe left Montana to study art at Yale. He became a successful artist, but painted from memory and lost his ability to remember. After a couple of years in New York, he moved to Florida, where he met Astrid. They began living together, and Joe made a living as a freelance illustrator of operations manuals, working mostly for his friend Ivan Slater.

Joe's father had left him the family ranch in Montana, in care of his Aunt Lureen. The income from a grazing lease allowed him some selection in the jobs he took. Astrid blamed the payments for his not painting; she called them his food stamps. Then the lease money stopped coming; none of the explanations from Aunt Lureen made sense. And Joe wasn't getting along with Astrid. He borrowed her car, a small pink convertible, to go to the grocery store. Instead, he headed for Montana.

Joe hoped to find meaning in restoring the run-down ranch. But his romantic memories of the Old West quickly evaporated as he faced the realities of the task before him in the New West:

> When Joe's father began leasing the pastures to the Overstreets, the
> ranch began to go downhill. The house started toward its present
> moldering state; the fences were kept in what minimal condition

would hold cattle but where the property joined the lessors, the fences were allowed to fall and be walked into the ground by herds of cows. The pastures were eaten down year after year until the buck brush, wild currants and sage had begun to advance across their surfaces, with the result that the carrying capacity dropped and with it, the grazing fees. Evaporation from the stripped ground reduced the discharge of the good springs to trickles; the marginal springs had long since been milled to mud by cattle and finally the mud itself had dried up and sealed the springs. But the worst problems of the ranch existed at the level of paper, where liens and assumptions clouded its title.

Joe and his Aunt Lureen stocked the ranch with two hundred and fifty head of cattle, and Joe started to work. The narrator asks, "Where had people gone wrong in the West?" Joe began to understand the latest regional joke, where leaving a ranch to one's children was called child abuse.

McGuane populates his novels with strange and sometimes bizarre characters. Joe's Cuban girlfriend, Astrid, "had been raised in a conventional Cuban-exile household in Florida, and had duly celebrated her quince in the tarted-up strumpet costumes that suggested the elders were putting their daughters on the open market." He met her in Florida, riding on the front of a 1935 Rolls-Royce, wearing nothing but gold spray paint. She was going to a costume party as a hood ornament. Ivan Slater, his only true friend and sometimes employer, was a successful, if unconventional, businessman who's typical of McGuane's odd characters.

The silver doors of the elevator opened and Ivan Slater stepped out, wearing the latest Italian fashions, wide shoulders, a kind of one-button roll, really an old fashioned hoodlum suit but made in the bright shades of a discount carpet barn. The shirt was green and the tie was red. He wore great spatulate suede shoes and his pants were held up with what appeared to be a pajama string. His proximity to the fashion centers entitled him to spend a fortune to look like a fool . . . [His] round, pumpkinlike head and piercing black eyes seemed to say "Stop the music!"

There are others, just as vivid. Overstreet, who owned the property surrounding the Starling place on three sides, was an old man who had "aged to a kind of papery fierceness like a hornet" and coveted Joe's ranch with a passion. His daughter Ellen and Joe had met when Joe worked for Overstreet one summer while in school, and had "lapped tongues while their bodies moved in vague figure eights." Ellen would complicate Joe's life. Her husband Billy Kelton, a decorated Vietnam veteran and a former top five saddlebronc rider in the Northern Rodeo Association two years in a row, is about the only remotely admirable character in the novel, depending, of course, on your values. Joe's weak and devious Uncle Smitty, who had his own plan for the ranch's profits, is a pathetic antagonist.

In 1992 Turner Pictures broadcast "Keep the Change," a teleplay directed by Andy Tennant. John Milgis' script used the framework of the novel, but deleted a key character (Ivan Slater) and greatly enhanced the role of another. His greatest sin was not using enough of McGuane's biting dialogue. The cast included William Peterson as Joe, Rachel Ticotin as Astrid, Lolita Davidovich as Ellen, Jeff Kober as Billy, Buck Henry as Smitty, and Jack Palance as Overstreet.

Keep the Change has a solid plot, with some surprising turns, and interesting characters, written by an author who's been compared to Ernest Hemingway. Its particular appeal to me, accounting for its inclusion in this collection, is McGuane's ability to contrast the romance of the Old West with the realities of the New West.

Ride with Me, Mariah Montana
by Ivan Doig
Atheneum, 1990

Montana became a territory in 1864 and was admitted to the Union in 1889. Ivan Doig chose its centennial year to complete his trilogy recounting the history of the McCaskills of Montana. It began with *Dancing at the Rascal Fair* (Atheneum, 1987), when in 1889 Angus McCaskill migrated from Scotland to a windswept homestead in northern Montana. During the next three decades,

Angus built a home and raised a family in the Two Medicine country at the base of the Rocky Mountains. In the second part of the trilogy, *English Creek* (Atheneum, 1984), the story jumps forward to the summer of 1939, where teenager Jick McCaskill discovered his connection to the land.

At sixty-five, Jick McCaskill narrates *Ride with Me, Mariah Montana*, the closing chapter of the saga. In 1989 Jick was still ranching the land passed down from Angus, not getting rich, but hanging on. His lanky, flame-haired daughter Mariah (dubbed Mariah Montana in college back East) coaxed him into using his motorhome—all expenses paid—to drive her and her "whistledick" ex-husband Riley Wright around Montana for four months. They were to do a series of articles on the state for the Montanan newspaper during the centennial. Riley wrote a column for the paper and Mariah was a photographer. Jick resisted; he didn't like Riley. But his daughter said "Jick, I need you along," and since the end of her marriage had been an explosion instead of a breakup, he agreed to go.

Ivan Doig is clearly one of the better authors writing about the West today. His style is witty during the dialogue, wistful or even elegiac during much of Jick's narration, and elegant when Riley puts his thoughts and observations on paper for his weekly column.

The dialogue sparkles. Riley spoke of the vigilantes in Virginia City making "windchimes out of outlaws," and of "a statue of General Meagher on horseback with sword uplifted like he was having it out with the pigeons." Jick spoke of greeting an old neighbor, Amber Finletter, and getting back "the merest little picklepuss acknowledgment." Mariah and Riley's acrid exchanges were full of spice and vinegar. They sometimes made Jick uncomfortable, but he could hold his own—Jick's wisdom and wit usually exceeded that of his offspring and her ex.

There is a series of episodes as the trio lurched around the state looking for stories that fit into a centennial theme. They stopped at a national Bison Range, where a buffalo attacked Jick's Winnebago. In Virginia City, Riley wrote a piece about bartenders; particularly, a young brunette named Kimi. In Butte, they addressed the deaths that have happened from copper mining. In Shelby, the start of the High Line Country, they viewed the site and reviewed the circumstances of the Jack Dempsey and Tommy Gibbons fight in

1923. There are two episodes that are especially interesting: the relocation of a grizzly and their visit to the Chief Joseph battleground.

At the Pine Butte Swamp Preserve, protected and maintained by The Nature Conservancy, they watched a wildlife biologist and his assistant relocate a grizzly bear. Jick had once trapped a grizzly on his place and then killed it when the bear tried to tear its foot loose from the trap. He remembered the terrifying encounter and why he shot the bear:

> No sheep rancher has any reason to welcome a grizzly . . . my mind flew automatically to the bunches of ewes and lambs scattered across the ranch . . . But before that thought was fully done, the feel of invasion of our family was filling me . . . Nor was I personally keen on being out on some chore and afterward all they'd ever find of me would be my belt buckle in a grizzly turd.

His caution was justified. During release of the grizzly at the relocation site, there was an equipment failure and the bear charged the biologist.

Out beyond Havre, across miles and miles of grassland and at last almost into the Bearpaw Mountains, they visited the Chief Joseph Battleground. Even though the Nez Percé had fought and lost their final battle there in 1877, Jick felt the place was "still in a bad mood." As they tromped around, hunching in a cold wind, examining the trenches and rifle pits, every sense told him what nasty country this was to fight in. Riley wrote,

> . . . craters of war heal over, don't they? . . . Combat pits nowadays are greatly deeper in the prairie south of the Bearpaws, where the Nez Percé ghosted across the center of Montana on their route to defeat . . . Missile silos . . . Two hundred Minuteman missile silos across Montana . . . So no, warpox does not heal . . . in the heart of the West today, you can meet the next shift-change of missile crews in their Air Force vans, blue taxies to Armageddon."

Their travel provides an offbeat history of Montana that's intriguing and the banter between the trio is engaging. But the underlying theme of the novel is serious. Jick is sixty-five. He wants to keep the ranch started by his ancestors in the family, but neither Mariah nor his other daughter Lexia wants it. Riley wrote an article titled *Twilight of the Rancher?* for his column that could have been written as Jick's obituary:

> From a life spent under a Stetson, he has his divided mind written on his forehead, the tanned lower hemisphere where wind and sun and all other weathers of the ranch have reached and then above the hatline equator an oddly shy indoor paleness. When he was younger, that line of pearly-white forehead made him stand out at the Saturday night dances . . . Now worry fits on that line. The rancher starts his day with the usual choice of frets . . .weather . . . Checks the commodities page and calculates one more time what the latest disappointment in livestock prices is going to cost him (Of all of Montana's hard weather, the reliably worst has been its economic climate) . . . Runs on through the wish list to where he always ends up, damning his bones for their increasing complaint against the daylight-to-dark ranch life, yearning with everything in him for someone to shoulder all this after he soon can't. . . . [He] goes back and forth in his mind—give it up, tough it out . . . He rubs at that ellipse-line across his forehead and wonders how he and his way of life have ended up this way, forgotten but not gone.

The Double W, a ranch owned by a big land conglomerate back east, offered Jick top dollar for his spread. Riley told him to take it. Mariah told him it was his decision—alone. The way Jick faced up to his decision and how he was able to reach a resolution that would satisfy him and his ancestors is a fitting climax to the McCaskill saga.

Ivan Doig grew up in northern Montana along the Rocky Mountain front where his McCaskill trilogy is set. He was the son of a sheeptender, descended from a family of homesteading Scots who settled into the gray Montana foothills. He grew up on a succession of sheep and cattle ranches, and in little one-street towns. This is his literary turf, and is reflected in the richness of his characterizations, the real-life problems of today's ranchers, and the picturesque landscape of Montana he eloquently paints.

19

WESTERN SAGAS

INTRODUCTION

The selections in this chapter are novels that deal with such things as family histories, myths and legends, or the evolution of a state, region, or the entire West. Also included are those where the plot takes the reader across a wide range of the West, and biographical novels about individuals whose lives have embraced a large part of the history of the West.

Selected for review are Thomas Berger's *Little Big Man* (Dial Press, 1964), which gives us a good tour of the places, events, and characters that were the American West in the late 1800s, and *Centennial* (Random House, 1974), James Michener's celebration of America in a massive historical novel that begins in Colorado three billion, six hundred million years ago and details the development of the West to contemporary times. Both novels give a panoramic view of the West and its history—Berger's somewhat tongue-in-cheek and Michener's a detailed history brimming with the glory and greatness of the American West.

READER'S GUIDE

East of the Giants by George R. Stewart. Henry Holt, 1938. A novel of California in mid-nineteenth century. From the early "hide-and-tallow" years, the story moves through various Indian troubles, the revolution against Micheltorena, the Bear Flag revolt, the Conquest, the Gold Rush of '49, and finally the beginnings of California big-business in the later fifties.

The Tom-Walker by Mari Sandoz. Dial Press, 1947. The patriarch of the Stone clan was Milt Stone, the Tom-Walker, circus slang for man on stilts, so called because he lost a leg fighting in Grant's army. After the war he took his family west to the Missouri country, where he became a passionate defender of the little man. He lived to see his son and grandson fight in World War I and World War II, respectively, and return home maimed, like him.

Men to Match My Mountains by Irving Stone. Doubleday, 1956. Stone's novel, subtitled *The Monumental Saga of the Winning of America's Far West*, ranges in time from 1840 to 1900 and takes the reader through the building of Los Angeles, San Francisco, Denver and other great Western cities. Also covered are the discovery, development, and impact of the West's unique mineral resources, the building of the railroads, the development of agriculture under near impossible conditions, and the contributions of many diverse immigrant groups. Spur Award from Western Writers of America.

Angle of Repose by Wallace Stegner. Doubleday, 1971. In the author's words, this is "a novel about Time, as much as anything—about people who live through time, who believe in both a past and a future." Set in the North American West—California, the Dakotas, Colorado, Idaho, Mexico—it covers four generations in the life of an American family (1860-1970), people who had a hand in shaping whole areas of western life. The theme of the novel deals with the relations of a man with his ancestors and his descendants. Pulitzer Prize.

The Kincaids by Matt Braun. Putnam, 1976. The Kincaids founded an empire on cattle, land and oil in Oklahoma territory. Three generations of Kincaids transformed the Western wilderness into the American dream and forged a dynasty. This novel encompasses early wide-open cow towns, the arrival of the railroad and then the settlers, the opening of the Cherokee Strip, the discovery of oil and the resulting boomtowns, Oklahoma statehood, and the impact of World War I on the region. Spur Award from Western Writers of America.

The Warriors by John Jakes. Jove Books, 1977. Volume 6 of Jakes' *Kent Family Chronicles*, an American Bicentennial Series. As the Civil War draws to its climax, the divided Kent family migrates to new arenas—the West and its lusty, brawling towns; the plush eastern mansions of the robber barons—Gould, Fisk, and Drew; and the seething enclaves of the new trade unions.

Riders to Cibola by Norman Zollinger. Museum of New Mexico Press, 1977. In this saga beginning in the days of Pancho Villa, Ignacio Ortiz, an orphan and a runaway searching for his past, lives through eras of intense change, including two world wars and the beginning of the modern West. As these turbulent events serve as backdrop to his life, Ignacio's loyalties will be tested by the passions of his tempestuous employers—the MacAndrews clan. Spur Award from Western Writers of America.

The Proud Breed: A Three Generational Saga of California by Celeste De Blasis. Coward, McCann and Geoghegan, 1978. This is a romance novel about Californios and their nineteenth century struggle with outsiders who would annex the territory and alter their way of life.

The Lawless by John Jakes. Jove Books, 1978. Volume 7 of Jakes' *Kent Family Chronicles*, an American Bicentennial Series. In 1876, when America was 100 years old, the changes sweeping the nation were also engulfing the Kent family. Postwar prosperity had thrust the Kents into the daring occupations of our country's most reckless and corrupt era—feverish speculation in the east, the cattle boom in the west, rip-roaring Abilene and Deadwood.

The Americans by John Jakes. Jove Books, 1980. Volume 8 of Jakes' *Kent Family Chronicles*, an American Bicentennial Series. At the turn of the century, the Kents—Eleanor, Carter, Will—are heirs to land they have never earned and must face the challenge of immigrant America. *The Americans* takes the Kent family into the 1890s, to the frenetic San Francisco political scene, to the tragedy of the Johnstown flood, and to the crushing poverty of a New York slum. These three young Kents struggle to find their place in a rapidly changing world and, like their ancestors, keep faith with America.

Chance Fortune by Bill Starr. Pinnacle Books, 1981. In 1849, as America surged west to the California gold fields, two men were destined to play major roles in the region's explosive history: Chance Malcolm, who would stop at nothing to win a fortune, and David Wheeler, a God-fearing man of the soil. This is the saga of the dynasties they forged and of the squalid Mexican pueblo that grew into the city of Los Angeles.

This Old Bill by Loren D. Estleman. Doubleday, 1984. Buffalo Bill Cody had done it all: cowboy, Pony Express rider, Indian fighter, Union soldier, scout for General George Custer, slayer of Tall Bull and Yellow Hand—and had made way for the railroad through the nation's rugged frontier. But now, in his final hours, old Bill Cody faces the last great challenge of his life.

From Sea to Shining Sea by James Alexander Thom. Ballantine Books, 1984. The saga of the Clark family of Virginia, who fought for our nation's independence (George Rogers Clark) and explored the continent (William Clark) from sea to shining sea.

Texas by James A. Michener. Random House, 1985. Spanning four and a half centuries, this expansive (over 1,000 pages) saga of Texas begins in the early 1500s, when the first Spaniards—Cabeza de Vaca and Francisco Vásquez de Coronado—explored parts of it, and ends with Texas' present-day eminence as one of America's most powerful states.

Republic: A Novel of Texas by E. V. Thompson. Franklin Watts, 1985. In 1838, following Sam Houston's defeat of General Santa Anna and his Mexican legions, the newborn Republic of Texas faced the grim prospect of bankruptcy, was plagued by Indian unrest, and was not yet accepted by the nations of the world.

Prairie by Anna Lee Waldo. Berkley, 1986. Charles Burton Irwin was an American legend, an adventurer and a leader of men. From the wagon trains and cattle drives of the Old West, to the birth of the railroads, he helped shape America's destiny.

Red River Story by Alfred Silver. Ballantine Books, 1988. In Canada's northern Great Plains, where the Assiniboine joined the Red, settlers dreamed of a home of their own and land to farm. The half-Indian buffalo hunters dreamed of a land kept open for their wild, free way of life. And the great fur companies dreamed only of profit.

California Gold by John Jakes. Random House, 1989. From 1886 to 1921, this novel explores the lure and the legends of California, charts its change from a frontier to a modern state, and sweeps across the events that shaped the Golden State after the end of the Gold Rush. The protagonist, Mack Chance, moves from the high Sierras to the mansions and clubs of San Francisco society to Los Angeles during the great land boom of the 1890s and to Riverside in the heyday of the millionaire citrus growers. He becomes involved in the struggle of early environmentalists to preserve the wilderness, endures the terror of the San Francisco earthquake of 1906, fights the railroad monopoly known as the Octopus, invests in silent movies, and is caught up in the labor wars in the fields of the great Central Valley.

Outlaw by Warren Kiefer. Donald. I. Fine, 1989. *Outlaw* is a picaresque novel that spans nearly a century of American history. The narrator and protagonist is Lee Oliver Garland, a grizzled, semiliterate old man of eighty-nine, who has seen and done it all: rustler, wildcatter, Rough Rider with Teddy Roosevelt, ambassador to Mexico—as well as the trenches of the Argonne, the mansions of Fifth Avenue, and the Teapot Dome Scandal.

Cross a Wide River: A Western Novel by Paul R. Stevenson. Sunstone Press, 1989. This epic novel begins in pre-Civil War Georgia and ends in New Mexico. Free men, slaves and slave owners, settled their differences on the battlefields in this saga of the westward expansion of the United States and the families who braved the hardships of frontier life.

Lord of the Plains by Alfred Silver. Ballantine Books, 1990. In Canada's Northwest Territories in 1885, the Indians were starving on their reservations. The mixed-blood peoples were being swindled out of their ancestral lands. The corrupt Ottawa government would not hear their pleas. Gabriel Dumont and his wife, Madeleine, leaders of the Métis, the half-Indian culture of the plains, and their friend Louis Riel, a visionary who would face the hangman's rope, stood in the eye of the storm.

Silver Light by David Thomson. Alfred A. Knopf, 1990. *Silver Light* redraws the American West from its late-nineteenth-century heyday to its early-twentieth-century decline through the life stories of two "relics" of the Old West: Susan Garth, a reclusive octogenarian photographer, and her longtime friend Bark Blaylock, an equally reclusive seventy-five-year-old writer of western comic books. Their life stories, coaxed from them by a young Santa Fe gallery curator, ranges across the West. Susan and Bark have been witness to, among other events, the slaying of Billy the Kid, the last cattle drive along the Chisholm Trail and the 1906 San Francisco earthquake. They've crossed paths with Judge Roy Bean, Willa Cather, Howard Hawks, and numerous other Western notables.

Brules by Harry Combs. Lyford Books, 1992. Cat Brules' long, eventful life embraced the whole short, turbulent history of the West—as a cow puncher, Indian fighter, gunman, and lover—from an 1867 cattle drive to Hays, Kansas, to the death of his beloved Shoshone wife in 1891.

Shortgrass Song by Mike Blakely. Forge, 1994. Shortly before the Civil War, Ab Holcomb brought his family to Colorado's sprawling Front Range country. During the war, Ab lost a leg fighting the Confederates in New Mexico. But in the 1870s and 1880s the Holcombs become powerful ranchers until land-hungry homesteaders subdivided the open range. Two of Ab's sons were killed, and the third, Caleb, became a drifting troubadour.

The Scout by Harry Combs. Delacorte Press, 1995. The sequel to *Brules* (Lyford Books, 1992). By 1900 the Old West was vanishing. By then the legendary Cat Brules had shut himself and his secrets away in a cabin on Colorado's Lone Cone Peak. Only one person knew his real story, a boy of eleven who became his friend and heard his extraordinary tales in 1909.

Too Long at the Dance by Mike Blakely. Forge, 1996. In this sequel to Blakely's *Shortgrass Song* (Forge, 1994), cowboy musician Caleb Holcomb is joined by a young sidekick named Kinchloe and the two cowboys become embroiled in a Holcomb family feud, Wyoming's Johnson County War, and the Arapaho uprising. The novel takes us through the West's bloody cattle wars, the last great cattle drives, and the wild, lawless land rushes that settled the Indian territory.

The Legend of the Painted Horse by Harry Combs. Delacorte Press, 1996. In 1917, when he returned from the war, Steven Cartwright, by a Rocky Mountain campfire, told a young woman the story of Cat Brules—legendary Indian scout, mountain man, storyteller, and teacher. Looking back over 30 years, he wove together stories of Cat Brules and his own life, spanning the taming of the Old West to the frontiers of aviation.

Tallgrass by Don Coldsmith. Bantam Books, 1997. This is a collection of stories unified by their setting—the tallgrass region of Kansas. The tales begin in the 16th century with the arrival of the first Spanish conquistadors and their conflicts with the native Americans already there— Osage, Pawnee, Comanche, Cheyenne, and others. This is the saga of the warriors, priests, trappers, traders, explorers, schemers, and other pioneers who passed through the tallgrass.

The Return of Little Big Man by Thomas Berger. Little, Brown, 1999. The sequel to Berger's *Little Big Man* (Little, Brown, 1964), published 35 years later. This sequel continues the reminiscences of a 112-year-old man. Jack Crabb says he grew up among the Cheyenne, who named him Little Big Man; knew Wyatt Earp and Wild Bill Hickok; and is the only white survivor of Custer's Last Stand. He resumes his story shortly after that battle, where he continues his adventures with Hickok, Bat Masterson, Buffalo Bill, Sitting Bull, Annie Oakley, and other Western notables—all across the West.

Liar's Moon: A Love Story by Phillip Kimball. Henry Holt, 1999. A novel set in the West in the years following the Civil War and culminating in 1890 at Wounded Knee. *Liar's Moon* shows how history slid into legend to become the defining myth of America.

River of Souls by Ivon B. Blum. Sunstone Press, 2000. Novel of the American Myth. Sixteen-year-old Pedro Cortez came of age during the bloody Pueblo revolt of 1847. He witnessed the murder of his father by Taos Pueblo Indians and returned home to find his mother brutally mutilated. His search for his father's murderer led him and two mountain men friends to the California gold fields and then back home.

Bound for the Promise-Land by Troy D. Smith. Writers Club, 2000. The novel's protagonist, Alfred, illuminates what conditions must have been like as a slave, a civil war soldier, a free man, and a buffalo soldier. Spur Award from Western Writers of America.

Sin Killer by Larry McMurtry. Simon and Schuster, 2002. Book 1 of McMurtry's *Berrybender Narrative*. In 1830, the wealthy, aristocratic English Berrybender family started up the Missouri River to see the American West. They were accompanied by a large and varied collection of retainers. As they journeyed, they encountered dangers and difficulties, viewed awesome natural scenery, and met Indians, pioneers, mountain men, and explorers, both historical and fictional. Central to the plot is young Tasmin Berrybender's developing relationship with Jim Snow, a frontiersman, ferocious Indian fighter, and part-time preacher, known up and down the Missouri as "the Sin Killer."

Legacy by Leonard Schonberg. Sunstone Press, 2002. An epic novel spanning three generations of the Schneider family, unfolding the lives of three unforgettable women: Hannah, Pearl, and Sarah. After emigrating from Europe in 1913, Hannah ends up in the rough and tumble mining town of Butte, Montana, becoming a prostitute. Pearl, the mixed-race child borne by Hannah as the result of rape, grows up in an orphanage knowing nothing about her parents. Tormented by her abandonment as an infant, Pearl finds it difficult to bond with her own daughter, Sarah, whose life is a mess. When Sarah receives word that her mother is dying. she discovers the secret of Pearl's past and this makes it possible for her to take control of her life.

The Wandering Hill by Larry McMurtry. Simon and Schuster, 2003. The second novel in McMurtry's *Berrybender Narratives*. This novel starts where *Sin Killer* (Simon and Schuster, 2002) left off. The aristocratic English family the Berrybenders are waiting out the oncoming winter at a high plains trading post. They have to contend with one another in the close confines, as well as their assortment of retainers and the rough trappers wintering at the fort. Tasmin is pregnant, and there is conflict between her and her stoical, evangelical mountain man husband Jim Snow, the Sin Killer.

By Sorrow's River by Larry McMurtry. Simon and Schuster, 2003. The third book in McMurtry's *Berrybender Narratives*. This novel is set on the Great Plains of Wyoming and Colorado. Lord Berrybender is on a hunting expedition in the shadow of the Rocky Mountains, protected by an accompanying group of mountain men. As the hunting party slowly travels from its winter camp in the north, southward toward Santa Fe, they survive Indian attacks and encounter a murderously insane Mexican army captain, among other travails. The relationship between Indian fighter Jim Snow and Tasmin Berrybender worsens.

SELECTED REVIEWS

Little Big Man
by Thomas Berger
Dial Press, 1964

Most casual readers of this tongue-in-cheek history of the Old West will thoroughly enjoy it, but may dismiss Thomas Berger's comic masterpiece as nothing more than delightful satire. If evaluated primarily on historical accuracy, *Little Big Man* won't quite measure up. But the novel, as Roger Ebert says in his review of the film version, captures the *flavor* of the times.

This is the story of Jack Crabb, told in his own words, who was in 1952 a nursing home resident who claimed to be 111 years old and a survivor of Custer's Last Stand and just about every other momentous occasion that took place in the wild West. Major events he claimed to have participated in include the Washita Massacre, the building of the Union Pacific Railroad, and the killing off the buffalo herds. He professed to have had an encounter with Wyatt Earp—"the meanest man I ever met"— and to have even survived a gunfight with Wild Bill Hickok. Other historical characters who make an appearance include Calamity Jane, Kit Carson, Black Kettle, Sitting Bull, Crazy Horse, Gall, Hump, Elizabeth Custer, Tom Custer, Major Reno, Captain Benteen, and Scout Mitch Bouyer.

The action spans the West. Settings include Independence, the California Trail, Fort Laramie, Fort Leavenworth, Denver, the Indian Nations in Oklahoma, the Powder River Country in Wyoming, Santa Fe, the Texas Panhandle, and Cheyenne. Berger's descriptions of these settings add to the flavor:

> In a day or so I reached Santa Fe, down in the valley among the mountains, with its Mex women in their bright colors and naked shoulders, and Pueblo Indians sitting around selling their junk and a Ute or two with red blankets walking arrogant around, and Spanish cowboys in their tight pants slitted at the ankle, along with the more

usual types you might see anywhere. This was quite a town for the time and place . . .

Crabb was, at various times, a mule skinner, buffalo hunter, gambler, business man, gold miner, and gunfighter. But it was his life among the Cheyenne that gives his tale its unique allure.

When he was about fifteen, Jack and his sister Caroline were captured by a band of Northern Cheyenne. Caroline subsequently stole a pony and slipped away. Jack's position in the band was that of an orphan attached to the chief's lodge, which gave him the right to benevolent consideration from the whole family, just as if he were related to them by blood. For an act of bravery, Jack was given the Cheyenne name "Little Big Man."

The chief of the band was Old Lodge Skins, one of the most finely etched characters in all of Western fiction. He was a peace chief—as opposed to war chief—who was highly respected by the Cheyenne but appeared buffoonish around whites. Old Lodge Skins and Jack Crabb's observations and dialogue concerning the Cheyenne and the white man and their differences are the focus of the novel. Berger's dry humor and understatement in these exchanges are sometimes profoundly moving. For example, Little Big Man (Crabb) asked the old chief why he didn't keep his band up north where there were few whites. Old Lodge Skins replied:

A Human Being [In their spoken language the Cheyenne call themselves "the People" or "the Human Beings."] has always gone wherever he wished, and if someone tried to stop him, he rubbed them out or was killed by them. There are many fine young men in this band . . . They have decided to fight the white men whenever they can find them, and rip up those iron rails and drive away the fire wagons. Once that is done, they will kill all the remaining Americans . . .

Jack asked him: "Grandfather, do you honestly think that can be done?"

"My son," said Old Lodge Skins, "If it cannot, the sun will shine upon a good day to die."

Old Lodge Skins also observed that ". . . the white men are coming in ever greater numbers . . . Whatever else you can say about the white man, it must be admitted that you cannot get rid of him. He is in never-ending supply."

Crabb drifted back and forth between the two worlds, always welcome in Old Lodge Skin's tepee but frequently forced by circumstances, usually to save his skin, to return to the white world.

> There couldn't have been a worse time for running with the Cheyenne. They was being chased throughout the whole frontier, and whenever they eluded their pursuers, would commit some new outrage against the whites. So I would be on the one hand a renegade to join them in danger of my whole race. On the other hand, I was under a constant threat from the Cheyenne themselves, for to many of them the very sight of a white face was the occasion for mayhem . . .

He complained in his narrative that the whites never asked him about his life with the Indians, and the Cheyenne never asked him for his views on the whites, even when they were being destroyed by them.

Crabb found almost nothing to admire in his own race. He felt that the Cheyenne had a better grasp of what was important and what was not, but he also held a white man's opinion of his adopted brothers:

> I would be feeling right good and then see a little band of redskins riding along and then fall into melancholy. I could never remember how shabby Indians was until I saw some. Not because they was always poor; there was something awfully seedy about an Indian when he was in his lights dressed to the nines. Old Lodge Skins in his best turn-out looked like something the cat drug in by white standards. Now I never noticed this much till I had been to the Missouri settlements and back.

Although there's plenty of hyperbole in Berger's narrative, there's also dramatic vigor. Following Custer into the Battle of the Little Bighorn, Scout Jack Crabb tells us:

We entered the gorge at a fast trot, the five troops in formation, column of fours, . . . Within each company of the Seventh, the men rode matched mounts: Tom Custer's C Troop on sorrels; Troop E, gray horses; and the other three commands on fine bay animals. The guidons was swallow-tailed American flags with concentric circles of gilt stars within the blue field. They fluttered throughout the columns, amid the rising dust as we descended that dry coulee, hearing naught but our own hoof-thunder.

Arthur Penn directed the 1970 film "Little Big Man" based on Berger's novel. Phil Hardy's *Encyclopedia of Western Movies* (Woodbury Press, 1984) calls it a "major Western." Both TV Guide and film critic Roger Ebert rate it four stars. Dustin Hoffman ages from fourteen to 111 years in a sterling performance as Jack Crabb. Chief Dan George perfectly captures the wit and wisdom of Old Lodge Skins in one of the best portrayal of an Indian leader in cinema.

Thomas Berger isn't identified with any particular genre. *Little Big Man* and its sequel, *Little Big Man Returns* (Little, Brown, 1999) are his only Westerns. Both clearly demonstrate an ability to paint on the American West in prose, and will surely endure despite criticism of historical inaccuracies.

Centennial
by James A. Michener
Random House, 1974

Centennial may be intimidating for readers not familiar with the work of James Michener. First, there's the sheer length, some 909 pages. Then there are the tutorials—geology, anthropology, paleontology—interlaced with voluminous detail on flint knapping, sugar beets, dryland farming, guns, irrigation, birds, and other subjects Michener researched while writing the novel. But for those who like their fiction buttressed with facts, Michener's copious exposition will add immensely to their reading experience.

There are 14 chapters; many of them are complete enough to be short novels. In *Texas* (Random House, 1985), another Michener novel on the same scale as *Centennial*, his editors cut a chapter on Sam Houston and

Santa Anna, feeling it was more history than fiction and didn't fit. Michener published it separately as *The Eagle and the Raven* (State House Press, 1990). But *Centennial* is big and engrossing, with a narrative framework that gives Michener space for digressions and exhaustive background details.

The many episodes are anchored by the primary setting—northern Colorado, bordering eastern Wyoming and western Nebraska on the north, and the Rocky Mountains on the west. Four notable rivers had their birth in the Colorado uplands—the Platte, Arkansas, Rio Grande, Colorado—and what happened there determined life in neighboring states like Kansas, Nebraska, Texas, New Mexico, Arkansas, California, and even Old Mexico. The heart of the novel is the South Platte, and the life it supported. The fictional town of Centennial, which becomes the focus of the plot, would stand at a spot where a man could look eastward and catch the full power of the prairie, or westward to see the Rockies.

The story begins three billion, six hundred million years ago, after the crust of the earth had formed. Michener carries us through the development of the Ancestral Rockies, their demise, and the formation of the current Rockies. We observe the appearance and evolution of the great dinosaurs, the horse, a great shaggy beast that would become the bison, or American buffalo, and early man. The great land bridge leading from Asia to Alaska was open 40,000 years ago, after which it melted. It was open again about 28,000 years ago, and for the last time, about 13,000 years ago, closing about 10,000 years ago. When it was open, it's easy to imagine humans living in eastern Siberia following mammoths and other large animals into Alaska. Michener says one can speculate that the American Indian descended from such men.

In the year 1756 a sliver group of Arapaho, holding tentatively to the land between the two Plattes, faced a crisis. The Indians surrounding them (the fearful Dakota to the north, the unspeakable Ute to the west, the Comanche to the south, and the Pawnee to the east) had horses and would soon have guns; they had neither. A young brave named Lame Beaver, with two friends, raided a Comanche village and stole twenty-nine horses, changing their people's lives forever.

Lame Beaver was the first Arapaho to have contact with white men, Pasquinel and Alexander McKeag, two traders who entered the Arapaho land in

1799 to trade for beaver pelts. They were allowed to cross Pawnee and Arapaho territory without being killed only because they moved with authority, without any visible fear. Pasquinel was a unique character, one of many frontier types made fresh and unforgettable in *Centennial*.

He was a small, dark Frenchman, who dressed like an Indian but wore the red knitted cap of Quebec. Pasquinel was a coureur de bois, one who runs the woods, a solitary trader with the Indians, and there were none better. When he was 26 years old in the spring of 1795, and weighed somewhat less than 150 pounds, he fastened a buffalo strap across his forehead and suspended two bales of beaver pelts from it; each weighed just under a hundred pounds. Then he walked two hundred miles through the wilderness to where his canoe was cached.

In this early period of Colorado's history, roughly 1756-1829, Michener draws vivid portraits of the Arapaho, the Pawnee, and the traders and trappers who plied their trade in Indian territory. In 1828, in one of the coincidences of history, the beaver was largely exterminated in the mountains at the exact time when the fashion changed in the cities, and the pelts were no longer in demand. The era of the mountain man had ended.

Fictional accounts that parallel the actual development of the West follow. There are wagon trains, bound for Oregon; a massacre such as the actual one at Sand Creek; a massive cattle drive from Texas to Colorado, and the establishment of the 5,760,000 acre Venneford Ranch; the introduction of sheep and the resulting range wars; the buffalo hunters and their extermination of the great herds; the coming of irrigation and the sugar beet industry; and the development of dryland farming. A few actual historical characters appear, such as Charles Goodnight and the Shoshone chief Washakie. But there are numerous fictional characters you'll recognize as legendary Westerners, including mountain man and guide Old Bill Williams, Colorado militia commander Colonel John Chivington, Cheyenne Chief Black Kettle, General O. O. Howard, and black cowboy Nat Love.

Michener's critics say he has trouble in dealing with emotion and the nuance of human behavior. He responds that "psychological" novels just aren't his style. His style is that of a master narrator. Consider this description of the various tribes arriving for the great convocation at Fort Laramie in 1851:

In all previous American history there had been nothing like the gathering at Fort Laramie that summer . . . in later years the Indians would be dispersed . . . But in late August of 1851 they stood at the apex of their power, and as they assembled from all points they were majestic.

First the mighty Sioux came from the northeast, the many tribes glistening in paint and feathers . . . They were the powerful Indians, willing to engage eight different enemy tribes at once . . . Each tribe had its own special characteristics— Brulé, Ogalalla, Minniconjou, Hunkpapa—but all were members of the same warlike society. . .

From the northwest came the Assiniboin, slim men . . . [who] rode like centaurs. To see them coming across an open prairie was to see motion and dust and waving grass frozen together for a moment, then dissolving as the procession came closer. These Indians wore no headdresses; their dignity resided in their solemn character . . .

Up the Platte came the Cheyenne, tallest of the tribes and incomparably the noblest in appearance. They . . . sat like graven images . . . and impressed the assembly with the beauty of their headdresses and the fineness of their garments. They were the nobility of the plains, the men of arrogance and self-assurance. For two hundred years they had defended themselves against any combination, and now they rode as if they possessed the prairies. . .

From the north came the strangers, the Mandan, the Hidatsa and the Arikara . . . They were ill-at-ease, so far south . . . They were shorter than the plains Indians . . . they had been in contact with the white man since the days of Lewis and Clark.

From the west came . . . a small group . . . of dark-skinned Shoshone, moving cautiously, each with a loaded rifle across his arms. . . their chief was Washakie, who would play a notable role in subsequent history . . .

And from the southwest . . . came the poets of the prairies, the tall, quiet, hesitant Arapaho, less arrogant than the Cheyenne, less imposing than the Sioux. They were handsome men . . . philosophers . . . artists, the ones who listened when the others spoke, but they were men and women of terrible determination, . . . They were not a tribe to be trifled with, these Arapaho, for they were men and women with an inner dignity that had never so far been subdued. . .

Riding from the west . . . came an enormous contingent of three thousand Crow, who many considered the ideal braves. They were not so dark as some of the other tribes; they were a moody people, vacillating between gravity and exhilaration . . . They were a mighty nation, prowling the northern Rockies and holding tenaciously to valleys that had long been theirs.

Descriptions of a cattle drive, a buffalo hunt, and even dryland farming are equally as dynamic and dramatic as the gathering of the tribes.

James A. Michener has been described as one of the foremost deans of American belles lettres. He won the Pulitzer Prize in 1948 for *Tales of the South Pacific* (Macmillan, 1947). Some of his books have been made into notable films, including *Tales of the South Pacific* (filmed as "South Pacific"), *The Bridges at Toko-Ri* (Random House, 1953), *Sayonara* (Random House, 1954), and *Hawaii* (Random House, 1959).

NBC adapted *Centennial* to a momentous twenty-four-hour miniseries. The all-star cast included Robert Conrad as Pasquinel, giving probably the best performance of his career as the little French trapper. Other notable performances included Richard Chamberlain as his partner Alexander McKeag, Dennis Weaver as trail boss R. J. Poteet, Alex Karras as beet farmer Hans Brumbaugh, Richard Crenna as militia commander Colonel Frank Skimmerhorn, William Atherton as cowboy Jim Lloyd, Lynn Redgrave as English heiress and Venneford Ranch owner Charlotte Buckland, and Brian Keith as Sheriff Alex Dumire. This epic television series faithfully transferred the massive novel to the screen. Michener himself introduced the series.

Centennial, Colorado, and the nation celebrated their birthdays in 1976; the nation its 200th, Centennial its 100th. The novel *Centennial* is an enthralling celebration of both—a stunning panorama of the West, past and present.

20

WESTERN MYSTERIES

INTRODUCTION

The first mystery story was possibly Edgar Allen Poe's *The Murders at the Rue Morgue*, written in 1843. Since then, the mystery genre has grown to become the most read form of fiction in the world—surpassing even our beloved Western.

But western settings, with their stark, often isolated landscapes and romantic towns and villages provide a unique backdrop for the mystery story. These settings have drawn successful novelists from other genres west, while some Western writers use mystery as the theme in their novels.

I differentiate between mystery and crime novels; most novels set in the West have elements of crime—gunfights, brawls, cattle rustling, and so on. Western mysteries are meant to baffle the reader, to build suspense to the end of the novel.

Many writers are highly successful in both the Western and the mystery genres, most notably Elmore Leonard and Loren D. Estleman. Others, like Tony Hillerman and J. A. Jance, have written highly successful mystery series set in the West. Some well-known novelists, such as Raymond Chandler, set their mysteries in Western cities but focused on urban crime. These novels are not included in the reader's guide.

The two reviews in this section are both by New Mexico authors. Tony Hillerman's *Coyote Waits* (Harper & Row, 1990) is from his acclaimed *Navajo Mystery* series. *Zia Summer* (Warner Books, 1995) is from Rudolfo

Anaya's series of mysteries featuring Chicano private eye Sonny Baca. Both are excellent reads.

READER'S GUIDE

The Proud Sheriff by Eugene Manlove Rhodes. Houghton Mifflin, 1935. Spinal Maginnis was proud to be the law in Hillsboro, a Southwest mining town. He had been sheriff for eight years and had made his few arrests without even using his gun. Then came a shocking double murder and circumstantial evidence piled up against an innocent boy. But the killer didn't allow for the savvy of the proud sheriff.

Tumbling River Range by W. W. Tuttle. Houghton Mifflin, 1935. From Tuttle's series featuring range detective Hashknife Hartley. Joe Rich, sheriff of Pinnacle City, hadn't shown up for his own wedding because he was so drunk he couldn't get up, much less walk a bride down the aisle. Embarrassed, he decided to leave town. But the very next day, his bride-to-be's father was found dead. Things were looking none too good for Rich until Hashnife Hartley arrived.

Lincoln McKeever by Eleazar Lipsky. Appleton, 1953. Set in in Cuatro Rios, New Mexico territory, before the turn of the century. No one knew knew why Justice Douglas Hanna was murdered. News of the killing reached Lincoln McKeever in Denver where the brilliant Eastern lawyer had retired. Although barely forty, he wanted to give up his career as a trial lawyer. But when McKeever realized that justice, as well as the life of a Spanish aristocrat set on martyring himself, was at stake, he "heard the trumpets" and answered their call.

El Rancho Rio by Mignon G. Eberhart. Random House, 1970. A beautiful woman, alone at her husband's isolated ranch west of nowhere, found a bloody railroad spike out on the trail, next to a dead man. And when her husband and guests arrived at the ranch, the murderer struck again.

Wild Pitch by A. B. Guthrie, Jr. Houghton Mifflin, 1973. Buster Hogue was killed by a sniper at the annual county picnic. Chick Charleston, the sheriff in this small Montana county, had no experience in this kind of case, nor did his county office have the equipment to identify the criminal. He had to rely on patience, persistence, and his sharp understanding of human nature to solve the crime.

Weapon Heavy by John Reese. Doubleday, 1973. From the series featuring frontier detective Jefferson Hewitt. Hewitt was smart and tough, but had more enemies than friends. When he rode into Dunsmuir, Kansas, on the trail of two suspected killers, he quickly came up against pressures that were at the boiling point.

Thief Hunt by William O. Turner. Doubleday, 1973. A Cherokee lighthorse policeman investigated a theft from the Cherokee Nation treasury, a quest made difficult because he had no authority nor protection of the law when he was off tribal lands.

The Wrong Case by James Crumley. Random House, 1975. Hard-bitten Montana private eye Stag Milo Milodragovich, a recurring protagonist in Crumley's stories, is introduced in this novel. Milo is from a pioneer Montana family that has fallen on bad times. Here he investigates the death of a homosexual young man who was involved in a drug scam.

The Genuine Article by A. B. Guthrie, Jr. Houghton Mifflin, 1977. Sheriff Chick Charleston and his young deputy Jason Beard investigated the murder of Frank Grimsley, a prominent but unpopular Montana cattleman. Under suspicion were Indians Grimsley had accused of rustling his cattle, as well as their chief, old Eagle Charlie, whose beautiful young wife Rosa had been sharing her favors with Grimsley. But only a few days later Eagle Charlie himself was found dead—killed in the same manner and apparently with the same weapon.

The Last Good Kiss by James Crumley. Random House, 1978. This novel introduces private eye C. W. Sughrue, who was hired to find and babysit a well-known poet who tended to get drunk and drift from bar to bar. The plot takes Sughrue from Montana to California to Colorado to Oregon to Idaho and back to several of those places.

"A" Is for Alibi by Sue Grafton. Henry Holt, 1982. The first book in Grafton's *Kinsey Millhone Alphabet Mystery* series. In the picturesque town of Santa Teresa (Santa Barbara), California, a ruthless divorce attorney was

murdered and his young and beautiful wife was convicted of the crime. Eight years later and out on parole, she hired private investigator Kinsey Millhone to find out who really killed her husband.

Playing Catch-Up by A. B. Guthrie, Jr. Houghton Mifflin, 1985. Montana Sheriff Chick Charleston and his deputy, Jason Beard, investigate the gruesome murder of a local call girl. Their task is complicated when a big oil company gets involved and uncooperative rival cops block the potentially explosive investigation.

Dead Kachina Man: A Mystery by Teresa Vanetten Pijoan. Sunstone Press, 1986. Police Captain Dominique Rios begins an investigation inside an Indian Pueblo in modern New Mexico to determine who—or what—killed Ray Hava, the best Indian kachina doll carver in the country. During his investigation he finds more violence and a string of mysterious events that border on the supernatural.

Fool's Gold by Ted Wood. London: Collins Crime Club, 1986. In Canada the biggest gold strike ever has turned Olympia into an instant mecca for prospectors, chopper pilots, construction workers, and drifters, all eager to get rich. Then a geologist is found dead—apparently mauled by a bear—and Reid Bennett is called to the scene. It starts out like an open-and-shut case, but Bennett soon has his suspicions. There hasn't been a mauling in years. In fact, no one has even spotted a bear recently. Could it have been murder?

Skinwalkers by Tony Hillerman. Harper & Row, 1987. From Hillerman's Navajo Mysteries series. The first book to unite Tribal Policemen Lieutenant Joe Leaphorn and Officer Jim Chee draws them deep into the realm of Navaho witchcraft as they investigate three murders connected only by their lack of motive and their methods—all reminiscent of "skinwalkers" or witches. Basis for a 2002 teleplay. Spur Award from the Western Writers of America.

The Haunted Mesa by Louis L'Amour. Bantam Books, 1987. The sudden disappearance from the face of the earth of a race of Southwestern cliff dwellers the Navajo called the Anasazi has baffled historians for centuries. .Summoned to a dark desert plateau by a letter from an old friend, renowned investigator Mike Raglan is slowly drawn into a world of mystery and violence, where he will ultimately learn the astonishing legacy of the Anasazi.

The New Mexico Heritage by Lauran Paine. Walker, 1987. Dr. George

Brunner was unprepared for the life he found in the New Mexico territory working with old Dr. Homer Hudspeth. Most of his patients preferred to be treated by curanderas, old native women whose treatments included disemboweled chickens and yucca root poultices. When Maria Antonia Gallegos Lord was shot by a sniper as she stood at her father's graveside, Brunner asked a lot of questions. That almost proved fatal for the doctor—and his patient.

Spirit of the Hills by Dan O'Brien. Crown, 1988. In this first novel, three individuals are drawn to the beauty and violence of the stark South Dakota landscape: a Vietnam vet who hunts the Black Hills for the man who killed his brother; a wolf trapper who comes out of retirement to stalk a predator that has been killing livestock; and an Indian woman who returns to her South Dakota homeland to join peaceful Sioux political activists trying to reclaim the Black Hills, which once belonged to their ancestors. But a militant faction of the group plans to blow up Mount Rushmore.

Talking God by Tony Hillerman. Harper & Row, 1989. From Hillerman's *Navajo Mysteries* series. A grave robber and a corpse reunite Navajo Tribal Police Lieutenant Joe Leaphorn and Officer Jim Chee and sends them to Washington, where they must confront the white world on its own terms as they search for a nefarious museum conservator suspected of ransacking the sacred bones of his ancestors.

Ghost Dancing by James Magnuson. Doubleday, 1989. Legendary film director Jeremiah Gage discovered that his son Peter, who disappeared in the radical underground of the late sixties, could still be alive. He searched for him through ghost towns resurrected by the counterculture, through the isolated mountain villages of northern New Mexico. The closer Gage came to finding answers, the more the violence escalated.

The Laying Out of Gussie Hoot by Margot Fraser. Southern Methodist University Press, 1990. The irascible Gussie Hoot was murdered while counting her money, which she did daily. The quest for her killer provides a colorful purview of life in a small Texas ranch town.

"G" Is for Gumshoe by Sue Grafton. Henry Holt, 1990. From Grafton's *Kinsey Millhone Alphabet Mystery* series. Kinsey is hired to find an elderly lady missing from her trailer home on the edge of the Mojave Desert, and finds

herself on ex-con Tyrone Patty's hit list. She hires a bodyguard, Robert Dietz, and becomes involved in a romantic entanglement.

The Indian Lawyer by James Welch. W. W. Norton, 1990. Although he was raised in poverty on a Blackfeet reservation, Sylvester Yellow Calf became a prominent lawyer and a successful businessman and politician. But a disgruntled convict, denied parole, threatened to destroy his career.

The Search for Temperance Moon by Douglas C. Jones. Henry Holt, 1991. At the turn of the century, former federal marshal Oscar Schiller investigated the violent slaying of Temperance Moon, the legendary female outlaw. Set in the Indian territory and Arkansas, this is a story of jealousy, blackmail, and deceit.

Murder by Reference by D. R. Meredith. Ballantine Books, 1991. Brad Hemphill, curator of the Texas Panhandle-Plains Historical Museum, was found in a museum display perched on a dinosaur—as dead as the dinosaur. While local legend says the museum is haunted by the spirit of a pioneer woman, only a human hand could have swung the blunt object that cracked the curator's skull. Peerless attorney John Lloyd Branson and his trusted legal assistant Lydia Fairchild seek to identify the killer.

Alburquerque by Rudolfo Anaya. University of New Mexico Press, 1992. A young boxer from Alburquerque's (Anaya uses the original Spanish spelling) barrio named Abrán Gonzalez was summoned to the deathbed of his biological mother, a woman he had never known. He learned he was the son of this wealthy Anglo woman and an unknown Mexican man. His search for his father led him into the highest circles of Alburquerque society, where he confronted bigots, avaricious businessmen, and driven politicians.

Track of the Cat by Nevada Barr. G. P. Putnam's Sons, 1993. The first in Barr's series of novels featuring Ranger Anna Pigeon, who fled New York to work as a ranger in the country's national parks. In the remote back country of West Texas, a fellow ranger was mysteriously killed, presumably by a mountain lion. But Anna thought the deep claw marks across the ranger's throat and the paw prints surrounding the body were too perfect to be real.

The Mexican Tree Duck by James Crumley. James Cahill, 1993. Freewheeling Montana private investigator C. W. Sughrue was hired to track down the vanished wife of the Republican special envoy to Mexico. The complicated plot encompasses drug deals, sex, salted oil wells involving the DEA and the FBI, an undercover New Mexico sheriff, links to buddies who served with Sughrue in Vietnam, and rival Mexican gangs.

Friends by Charles Hackenberry. M. Evans, 1993. Two Scalp was a peaceful town until someone torched old Nell Larson's place, leaving two people dead. Now a deputy is tracking a mysterious killer clear across the Dakota territory and fighting a friend who had forgotten justice—a man with bloody vengeance on his mind. Spur Award from the Western Writers of America

The Shaman Sings by James D. Doss. St. Martin's Press, 1994. A brilliant female graduate student is brutally murdered in a southwestern Colorado town. The police chief, a former Chicago cop, enlists the aid of an aged Ute shaman to help solve the murder. She takes him into the realm of the spirit—of ancient and sacred magic.

Desert Kill by Phillip Gerard. William Morrow, 1994. A chief of police and his college professor nephew conduct a multiple murder investigation in the hot landscape of the Arizona desert. Several mutilated bodies turn up, and the search for the murderer leads across the parched terrain to an abandoned gold mine, where a psychotic killer lurks.

"N" Is for Noose by Sue Grafton. Henry Holt, 1994. From Grafton's *Kinsey Millhone Alphabet Mystery* series. This story takes Kinsey away from her Southern California coastal town of Santa Teresa to the small mountain community of Nota Lake in the Sierras, where the wife of a policeman hires her to find out what had been bothering her husband before he died from a heart attack.

Tombstone Courage by J. A. Jance. William Morrow, 1994. From Jance's series featuring Cochise County, Arizona, Sheriff Joanna Brady. When an assassin's bullet left Joanna Brady's policeman husband to die in the Arizona desert, the young widow brought the killers to justice and won the job of Cochise County Sheriff. Then she had to battle the prejudice and hostility of a male-dominated police force and solve a grisly double homicide.

The Sharpest Sight by Louis Owens. University of Oklahoma Press, 1994. Deputy Sheriff Mundo Morales of Amarga, California, found the corpse of his Vietnam buddy floating down the river. The dead man was a mixed-blood Choctaw who had been confined to a mental institution after brutally murdering his white girlfriend. Ghosts and Choctaw soul eaters move through the story, assisting Deputy Morales with the search for his friend's murderer.

Ill Wind by Nevada Barr. G. P. Putnam's Sons, 1995. An *Anna Pigeon* mystery. Colorado's Mesa Verde National Park is noted for its well-preserved cliff dwellings, the sole legacy of the Anasazi civilization, which vanished without any other trace in the twelfth century. In these quiet ruins, Park Ranger Anna Pigeon contends with a high number of medical rescues, the unexpected death of an asthmatic child, and the death of a fellow ranger, who is found neatly curled up in one of the ancient kivas.

The Eagle Catcher by Margaret Coel. University of Colorado Press, 1995. First of Coel's *Arapaho Indian Mysteries* series, set in the Arapaho Nation in Wyoming. The protagonist is a Catholic priest, Father John O'Malley, who solves crimes on the side. Arapaho attorney Vicky Holden is usually his partner. The trail leads them into the Wind River Reservation and the fraud infested world of Indian oil and land deals.

The Edge of the Crazies by Jamie Harrison. Hyperion, 1995. The first novel in a series set in Blue Deer, Montana, a small town bordering Yellowstone, and featuring Sheriff Jules Clement. When a screenwriter was shot as he worked on his newest screenplay, the killer was assumed to be his wife, who was angry since her discovery of her husband's many affairs. But, soon there were more killings and longer lists of possible suspects for Sheriff Clement to tnvestigate.

Shoot! Don't Shoot by J. A. Jance. William Morrow, 1995. From Jance's series featuring Cochise County, Arizona, Sheriff Joanna Brady. Attending a police training course in Phoenix, Sheriff Brady is drawn into the mystery of an imprisoned husband her gut tells her did not murder his estranged wife. But her impromptu investigation draws a serial killer too close for comfort.

Rio Grande Fall by Rudolfo Anaya. University of New Mexico Press, 1996. During the annual Hot Air Balloon Fiesta de Albuquerque, a body plummets from the sky. Four black feathers, the calling card of Raven, a recurring Anaya villain, were found by the body. Albuquerque P. I. Sonny Baca was offered a handsome reward by the Fiesta to find the killer before the local police or the FBI—an attempt to avoid bad publicity. But Raven possesses strengths no mortal can match; he can acquire the powers of his nagual, his animal spirit. Sonny will need his own guardians, the coyotes, as well as a curandera, a healer, to guide him to Raven's lair.

Bordersnakes by James Crumley. Mysterious Press, 1996. *Bordersnakes* brings together two of Crumley's orneriest characters. In barren West Texas, C. W. Sughrue is licking his wounds after being gut shot in a suspicious bar fight. Milo Milodragovitch's dead father's fortune has been plundered by a white-collar scoundrel. They join forces to claim revenge in a tangled plot.

The Fallen Man by Tony Hillerman. HarperCollins, 1996. From Hillerman's *Navajo Mysteries* series. After climbing gear and skeletal remains are discovered by a climbing party, Navajo policeman Jim Chee and retired Lieutenant Joe Leaphorn investigate the decade-old death of a man on Ship Rock, 1700 feet above the desert floor.

Hotshots by Judith Van Gieson. HarperCollins, 1996. A *Neil Hamel Mystery*. Albuquerque lawyer/sleuth Neil Hamel investigates the death by flames of a wildfire firefighter, or "hotshot," in the Colorado wilderness.

Cimarron Rose by James Lee Burke. Hyperion, 1997. Billy Bob Holland, a former Texas Ranger turned lawyer, agreed to defend Lucas Smothers, knowing that the boy was his illegitimate son and realizing that the trial would bring pain to both of them. Defending his son took Billy Bob toward a confrontation with the intolerant, hate-filled citizenry of Deaf Smith, Texas, and deep into the past to revisit his great-grandfather Sam, a Texas pioneer who had fought Indians and cow thieves.

The Original Adventures of Hank the Cowdog by John R. Erickson. Gulf, 1997. First in a series of stories about the adventures of Hank, a cowdog who is Head of Ranch Security on a West Texas ranch. In this story, Hank investigates a vicious murder on his ranch and finds himself the number one suspect.

Skeleton Canyon by J. A. Jance. William Morrow, 1997. From Jance's series featuring Cochise County, Arizona, Sheriff Joanna Brady. Brianna "Bree" O'Brien came to Skeleton Canyon for a romantic tryst with her boyfriend Ignacio. That terrible night she met a cruel death. Bree's distraught parents were convinced Ignacio was the killer. But other startling revelations suggested to Sheriff Brady that there was much more involved in this case than passionate anger and forbidden love.

A Spider for Loco Shoat by Douglas C. Jones. Henry Holt, 1997. Seven-year-old Jay Bird Joey Schwartz, an orphan living in a Ft. Smith bordello, in the summer of 1907 discovered the murdered body of one of western Arkansas' most powerful citizens. Former Deputy Federal Marshal Oscar Schiller found it odd that the sheriff's office was so quick to close the case and brush off Jay Bird Joey's observations. Suspecting foul play, Schiller set out in search of answers.

Mexican Hat by Michael McGarrity, W. W. Norton, 1997. A *Kevin Kerney* novel. Kevin Kerney, ex-Santa Fe chief of detectives, in this novel is working as a seasonal forest ranger in the Gila Wilderness. Despite the deadly antics of the county militia, Kerney looks forward to a quiet summer in the high mountains. But the poaching of wildlife, the murder of a Mexican tourist, and the discovery of a disoriented old man in the wilderness thrust Kerney into a dangerous investigation.

Big Black Dog in Vallarta by Mary Branham. Sunstone Press, 1998. A *Sydney Reardon Mystery*. Hoping to prevent her best friend's suicide, Sydney Reardon rushes to Puerto Vallarta, Mexico, where she becomes entangled with witchcraft, a handsome Gringo lawyer, a New York cop, a huge black dog— and murder.

The Dream Stalker by Margaret Coel. Berkley, 1998. From Coel's *Arapaho Indian Mysteries* series. Father John O'Malley and Arapaho lawyer Vicky Holden join forces to search for a killer who stalks his victims, driven by his own nightmarish dreams.

The Devil's Backbone by Robert Greer. Mysterious Press, 1998. Denver-based bail bondsman and sometime bounty hunter C. J. Floyd searched Colorado's high mountain country for the murderer of a retired black rodeo star and the secrets of a place called the Devil's Backbone.

Ambrose Bierce and the Queen of Spaces by Oakley Hall. University of California Press, 1998. In San Francisco in the late 1800s, a Jack the Ripper type killer started butchering young women, leaving a spade playing card with each body. For reporter Tom Redmond, who feared for the safety of a particular young woman, it was a major mystery. For crusading journalist

Ambrose Bierce, it was an opportunity to continue his war on the mining and railroad monarchs.

An Unfortunate Prairie Occurrence by Jamie Harrison, Hyperion, 1998. From Harrison's series set in Blue Deer Montana, featuring Sheriff Jules Clement. In mid-October, a camper's discovery of old bones threatens to open up secrets that have long been buried. Sheriff Clement begins a casual investigation that leads to long-simmering enmities, love affairs, arson, and murder.

The First Eagle by Tony Hillerman. HarperCollins, 1998. From Hillerman's *Navajo Mysteries* series. Acting Lieutenant Jim Chee of the Navajo Tribal Police caught a Hopi eagle poacher huddled over the bloody body of a fellow tribal police officer. It was open-and-shut until retired Lieutenant Joe Leaphorn blew Chee's case wide open.

Rattlesnake Crossing by J. A. Jance. William Morrow, 1998. From Jance's series featuring Cochise County, Arizona, Sheriff Joanna Brady. When a gun dealer died violently in Bisbee and his stock of high-powered weapons was missing, suspicion fell upon a rancher who was an armed separatist at war with the federal and local government. But Joanna wasn't convinced he was guilty.

Serpent Gate by Michael McGarrity, Scribner, 1998. A *Kevin Kerney* novel. Now deputy chief of the New Mexico State Police, Kevin Kerney is monitoring the town of Mountainair, a place some call God's Country. But six months ago, on the opening night of the annual town rodeo, Patrolman Paul Gillespie left the calf-roping finals, headed toward the police station, and was murdered. Kerney suspects that Robert Cordova, a schizophrenic who rambles on about "Serpent Gate," saw something that memorable night.

The Blue Corn Murders: A Eugenia Potter Mystery by Nancy Pickard. Delacorte Press, 1998. In Eugenia Potter, the late Virginia Rich created one of the mystery genre's most endearing sleuths. After collaborating with Rich on one Eugenia Potter mystery, Nancy Pickard has continued the series on her own. This story has Eugenia out West, where she visits the Medicine Wheel Archaeological Camp near Cortez, Colorado, hoping to glean the wisdom of the ancients, and see some exciting ruins. But trouble appears when a busload of youngsters disappears without a trace, with an eerie connection to the lost Anasazi tribe of so many years before.

El Camino del Rio by Jim Sanderson. University of New Mexico Press, 1998. U. S. Border Patrol officer Dolph Martinez, working out of Presido, Texas, is led by circling buzzards to a corpse in Red Wing boots with an expensive haircut. Dolph realizes this is no ordinary norteño trying to cross the desert border from Mexico. The dead man may be connected to Sister Quinn, a nun who practices curanderismo and helps Central American political refugees find sanctuary. It is Dolph's job to find out.

Coachella by Shelia Ortiz Taylor. University of New Mexico Press, 1998. In 1983 in California's Coachella Valley, Yolanda Ramirez, a lowly phlebotomist at the Palm Springs hospital, had a hunch. Gay men, hemophiliacs, and women scarred by cosmetic surgery were dying. Safe blood, like water keeping the desert green, was a lie.

Incident at Twenty-Mile by Trevanian. St. Martin's Press, 1998. In 1898 at Twenty-Mile, a dying silver-mining town in the hills of Wyoming, a mysterious stranger shows up and insinuates himself into the lives of the townfolk. Then three more strangers arrive. During a harrowing mountain storm, the people of Twenty-Mile are held hostage by the four, who are escaped convicts.

Coyote Revenge by Fred Harris. HarperCollins, 1999. In Oklahoma in 1937, during the last days of the Dust Bowl, Okie Dunn and his father, Hudge, scraped out a living farming and trading cattle. When the Cash County sheriff was murdered, Okie took the job and set out to find the killer. The author is a former senator from Oklahoma.

Hunting Badger by Tony Hillerman. HarperCollins, 1999. From Hillerman's *Navajo Mysteries* series. In 1998 when three heavily armed "survivalists" came out of the Four Corners canyons, murdered a policeman, had a shootout with pursuers, and then eluded a massive manhunt, Sergeant Jim Chee and retired Lieutenant Joe Leaphorn of the Navajo Tribal Police connected the crime to the exploits of a legendary Ute hero-bandit.

Outlaw Mountain by J. A. Jance. William Morrow, 1999. From Jance's series featuring Cochise County, Arizona, Sheriff Joanna Brady. An elderly widow was found dead in the Arizona desert. The prime suspects were teens caught driving her car across the Mexican border. But the victim was a free spirit with a lover twenty years her junior and enough money for her children to fight over. So Sheriff Brady had to dig deeper, sifting through some ugly land disputes and political graft and corruption to solve the case.

The Lost Bird by Margaret Coel. Berkley, 2000. From Coel's *Arapaho Indian Mysteries* series. The murder of his elderly assistant propels reservation priest Father John O'Malley into a partnership with Arapaho lawyer Vicky Holden, and together they set out to hunt down the killer.

Devil's Claw by J. A. Jance. William Morrow, 2000. From Jance's series featuring Cochise County, Arizona, Sheriff Joanna Brady. A missing teenager and an octogenarian were found dead of apparently natural causes. A thin connection between the two events was enough for Sheriff Brady to solve both cases.

Kiss of the Bees by J. A. Jance. William Morrow, 2000. The Walkers of Tucson, Arizona, were an Anglo family with solid ties to the legends and history of the Tahono O'othham Indian nation. Twenty years ago a personified evil named Andrew Carlisle, a psychopathic college professor, brought terror to the family, nearly murdering Diana Ladd Walker and her young son. But Diana fought back, blinding and crippling her assailant. In later years, in an uneasy collaboration with her would-be killer, she wrote a book about the horrific events that nearly destroyed her and her family. The book made her famous. When Carlisle died in prison, the Walkers believed their nightmare was finally over. They were wrong.

The Judas Judge by Michael McGarrity. E. P. Dutton, 2000. A *Kevin Kerney* novel. When six murders were committed at remote campgrounds in south central New Mexico, the evidence pointed to the work of a spree killer. But Deputy State Police Chief Kevin Kerney saw peculiarities at one crime scene suggesting another possibility: that five random people had been shot to death to cover the premeditated murder of the sixth victim.

Thunderhead by Douglas Preston and Lincoln Child. Warner Books, 2000. Since the days of Coronado, explorers have been captivated by the search for Quivira, the fabled Lost City of Gold, abandoned by the Anasazi centuries before. In this novel, a young associate professor of archaeology at the Sante Fe Institute of Archaeology received a letter from her long dead father giving its location. The expedition she directed to the site found it a sinister place, and they unearthed evidence of human sacrifice, cannibalism and the evil cult of the skinwalkers.

Safe Passage by Jim Sanderson. University of New Mexico Press, 2000. Jerri Johnson worked for Sam's Investigating Services in downtown San Antonio, tracking down bail jumpers and serving subpoenas. Her former lover Vincent Fuentes, a Mexican intellectual, had returned to San Antonio and was trying to enlist her in a plot involving running guns across the border. Her friend Joe Parr, an aging Texas Ranger, kept an eye on Jerri, Vincent Fuentes, and Vincent's father, Palo, a retired gangster who had become a solid citizen of San Antonio's West Side.

Buckskin and Satin, A Novel of the Wild West, by Romain Wilhelmsen. Sunstone Press, 2000. On July 14, 1882, the notorious Texas gunman, John Peters Ringo, was found beneath a blackjack oak tree some distance from Tombstone, Arizona, with a bullet in his head. Colonel Henry Hooker, Billy Breakenridge, Wyatt Earp, Doc Holliday, and Frank Buckskin Leslie were all suspected of doing him in, but charges were never brought against anyone. Was this going to be an unsolved mystery?

The Tobermory Manuscript by James C. Work. Five Star, 2000. A story about the murder of James Nugent, better known as Mountain Jim, in the Estes Park region of Colorado in 1874, shortly after a trip up Long's Peak with Isabella Bird. A hundred years later a professor in Colorado, David McIntyre, became interested in the story, including the rumor that Mountain Jim had been writing a history of the Estes Park region at the time of his death. After the murder, the manuscript vanished. Professor McIntyre traced it to Scotland, to a small cottage in Tobermory where Isabella Bird, a British travel writer, had once lived.

Open Season by C. J. Box. Putnam, 2001. A *Joe Pickett* novel. In this first novel of the series, Joe Pickett, a rookie game warden in Twelve Sleep, Wyoming, must enforce laws his neighbors have no intention of obeying. He faces a crisis when three elk hunters are killed under suspicious circumstances, and he must contend with a scam involving an oil pipeline and an endangered species.

Bitterroot by James Lee Burke. Simon and Schuster, 2001. This is Burke's third book featuring former Texas Ranger, now lawyer Billy Bob Holland. In this one, Holland visits war buddy Doc Voss in the Bitterroot Valley area of Montana. The visit turns ugly when Voss' daughter is the victim of a violent rape and three suspects turn up dead.

Potshot by Robert B. Parker. Putnam, 2001. From Parker's *Spenser* series. Tough PI Spenser and his sidekick Hawk usually solve crimes back east, but this mystery is set in the desert town of Potshot, Arizona. Spenser is hired by a woman to find out who killed her husband, but his investigation is hindered by thugs who control the town. Spenser rounds up his own hired guns from all over the country to take on the gang of toughs.

Cannibal Plateau: A Mystery Novel by Joe Wise. Sunstone Press, 2002. On a spring day in 1874, a reporter for Harper's Weekly, traveling with a surveying party on a wilderness road through a remote mountain valley in Colorado's San Juan Mountains, wandered onto an abandoned campsite where he found the mutilated and rotting bodies of five men. Immediately a search began for Alfred Hammit (Packer), a hapless drifter and the sole survivor of the ill-fated prospecting expedition, suspected of murdering the five men and living off their bodies during the severe winter weather that had trapped them. This novel is based on actual events surrounding his trial. Packer is the only American ever to be convicted of cannibalism.

Deception on All Accounts by Sara Sue Hoklotubbe. University of Arizona Press, 2003. A *Sadie Walela* mystery. Set in the Cherokee Nation and surrounding areas of northeastem Oklahoma. The protagonist is Sadie Walela, a contemporary mixed-blood Cherokee woman who works as a bank officer in a nearby small city. The story line explores Sadie's confrontations with her mother, her abusive ex-husband, and institutional racism and sexism, as well as the central mystery of the plot that revolves around a daring bank robber.

A Grave at Glorieta by Michael Kilian. Berkley, 2003. A mystery set in the West during the Civil War. Pinkerton spy Harrison Raines and fellow detective Joseph "Boston" Leahy travel to territorial New Mexico to uncover the plans of the Confederacy in the West.

Trophy Hunt by C. J. Box. Putnam, 2004. A *Joe Pickett* novel. The Wyoming game warden is a member of a special task force investigating mutilations—game, cattle, and human. Some county residents fear aliens are responsible—a theory Joe calls "woo-woo crap."

The Clovis Incident: A Mystery by Pari Noskin Taichert. University of New Mexico Press, 2004. Quirky Sasha Solomon bids on a PR project for the

Clovis, New Mexico, Chamber of Commerce after being fired from her job as the PR director at Albuquerque's only holistic HMO. While she waits for a response, she visits a close friend in Clovis, an eccentric dairy farmer who is preoccupied because there is a body in her stock tank. Sasha has a lot to do and many distractions—particularly the space aliens.

Silver Lies by Ann Parker. Poisoned Pen Press, 2004. Inez Stannert was the owner of the Silver Queen Saloon in Leadville, Colorado, during the 1879 silver boom. A frozen corpse that turns up in the alley behind the saloon puts Inez and her partner at odds with a crooked lawman, an infamous madam, a spurned suitor and the mysterious stranger who rides into town as the new minister.

A Title to Murder: The Carhenge Mystery by James C. Work. Five Star, 2004. When Professor David McIntyre returned to Alliance, Nebraska to teach a summer course at the community college, he learned that one of his students from the previous summer had vanished and the man she had been living with was found murdered. The murder and disappearance followed the plot of a 19th century English novel used in the class the girl had taken from him. "Carhenge" in the title refers to a full-scale replica of Stonehenge, crafted out of old auto bodies, that is a significant part of the novel's setting.

Jemez Spring by Rudolfo Anaya. University of New Mexico Press, 2005. When the governor of New Mexico was found drowned in the bath house at Jemez Springs, Alburquerque private eye Sonny Baca was called in to investigate. Was this the work of terrorists or Sonny's old nemesis, Raven?

Cory's Feast by Sallie Bingham. Sunstone Press, 2005. Cory is a divorced middle-aged Easterner who moves to Taos, New Mexico, and buys a famous old house and turns it into a crucible for the transformation of her guests. She finds her guests, mainly skiers and tourists, bewildered by her particular philosophy, which she calls "The School of As-If." Then her long-time friend is found murdered and Cory is suspicious of the local police's half-hearted attempts to find the murderer. Involving herself in trying to solve the case, her unleashed power leads to surprising and even terrifying results.

Wounded by Percival Everett. Graywolf Press, 2005. In this mystery set in contemporary Wyoming, the body of a gay college student, "strung up like an elk with his throat slit," is found near the ranch of John Hunt. The chief suspect is one of Hunt's ranch hands, and Hunt is recruited by the sheriff to act as a go-between for the friendless, inept young man. The plot has both homophobic and racial (Hunt is black) elements.

SELECTED REVIEWS

Coyote Waits
by Tony Hillerman
HarperCollins, 1990

Tony Hillerman has made the starkly beautiful Four Corners country where Utah, Colorado, New Mexico, and Arizona come together the setting for a unique series of mystery novels. Using Navajo Tribal Policemen as his protagonists, he supports his complex plots with a liberal helping of Native American lore. He's said he wants his readers to gain a respect for the Navajo culture from his books; beliefs he admires for their central goal of being in harmony with surrounding circumstances, and the high value they place on family and the extremely low value they place on material possessions.

The Navajo, with almost a quarter million members, is by far the nation's largest tribe. There are twenty-five thousand square miles that they call the Big Rez. Names given the geography—Coyote Wash, Standing Rock, Carrizo Range, Chivato Mesa, Chuska Mountains, Turquoise Mountain—and the Navajo clans—Bitter Water, Streams Come Together, Towering House, Slow Talking—give the Four Corners setting a strange and wonderful allure.

Coyote Waits is the eleventh novel of the series. All of the earlier novels except one featured either Lieutenant Joe Leaphorn or Officer Jim Chee of the Tribal Police, or both. These popular characters differed in their approach to their work and in their view of Navajo culture. Leaphorn was a person of the forties, a pragmatist, a rationalist, keenly aware of his ancestral culture, but a man who looked through the mythology at the reason the mythology was created. He lived almost exclusively in the biligaana (white man's) world of twentieth century America. Chee was a young man—tall slender, and dark—who wore his hair tied in a knot at the back of his head and looked like an Indian. He felt stronger ties to the old ways, and dreamed of becoming a tribal shaman, one who acts as a medium between the visible world and an invisible spirit world, someday. Leaphorn considered Chee an unusually bright young man, clever, with some good qualities. "But he had what might be a fatal flaw for a policeman. He was an individualist, following the rules if and when they agreed with him. On top of that, he was a romantic. He even wanted to be a medicine man." Leaphorn considered the two professions, tribal policeman and shaman, utterly incongruous. Chee considered Leaphorn "sort of our supercop. Old as the hills. Knows everybody. Remembers everything. Forgets nothing. I worked with him a time or two before. Everybody does sooner or later because he handles the tough investigations wherever they are."

Leaphorn and Chee became reluctant but respectful allies in a case that started with the defacement of an old volcanic site that was traditionally believed to be a meeting ground for witches, followed by two murders. Their trail led through the dark side of academic life to the last days Butch Cassidy. And all through the investigation, Coyote, the mythical embodiment of bad fortune, was waiting.

In *Talking Mysteries* (University of New Mexico Press, 1991) Hillerman's friend and critic Ernie Bulow tells us, " . . . in the real world there are no Navajo policeman of the sort Hillerman invoked. In reality they are used primarily as traffic cops and for crowd control at Reservation functions and little else. Crimes of any consequence come under someone else's jurisdiction—county, state, or federal—and any homicide is automatically the province of the FBI." But consider this Associated Press Release:

> Police in Kayenta [Arizona] don't like to admit it, but it terrifies them to think of how Officer Hoskie Gene died—his crumpled, beaten body left in the dirt like trash along the remote highway in the silent desert night.
>
> Gene was the only officer on duty when he headed off alone on a robbery call an hour away on the sprawling Indian reservation . . . Soon after, he lost communication with the

dispatcher. Hours later, he was found strangled amid broken beer bottles, his weapon and vehicle stolen.

He died as he worked: alone. (Associated Press 02/23/97)

This piece could have been lifted from a Tony Hillerman novel. In *Coyote Waits*, on a lonely stretch of road near the old volcanic site believed to be the witches' meeting ground, a tribal policeman named Delbert Nez was shot and his patrol car burned with Nez inside. The remoteness of the Four Corners country can provide a dangerous environment for the Tribal Police, both in Hillerman's novels and in real life.

Officer Jim Chee's good friend Delbert Nez lay dead in his burned-out patrol car, and a whiskey-soaked Navajo shaman was found with the murder weapon. The old man was Ashie Pinto. He was quickly arrested for the homicide and defended by Janet Pete, a public defender and Chee's romantic interest. But when Pinto wouldn't utter a word of confession or denial, Lieutenant Leaphorn began an investigation. Soon, he and Chee unraveled a complex plot of death involving an historical find, a lost fortune—and the mythical Coyote, who was always waiting, and always hungry.

Hillerman differs from many mystery writers because he emphasizes motive rather than identity. He also differs from most contemporary novelists in that he avoids sex and graphic violence in his books. But it is his sense of place and his descriptions that truly set him apart, as in this depiction of twilight in the Four Corners country:

North, over Sleeping Ute Mountain in Colorado, great thunderheads were reaching toward their evening climax. Their tops, reflecting in the direct sun, were snowy white and the long streamers of ice crystals blown from them seemed to glitter. But at lower levels the light that had struck them had been filtered through the clouds over the Chuskas and turned into shades of rose, pink, and red. Lower still, the failing light mottled them from pale blue-gray to the deepest blue. Overhead, the streaks of high-level cirrus clouds were being ignited by the sunset. They drove through a fiery twilight.

This is Georgia O'Keefe country, painted in prose.

A 2003 PBS teleplay starred Adam Beach as Jim Chee and Wes Studi as Lieutenant Leaphorn. Like the novel, it is fine entertainment.

Tony Hillerman is a World War II veteran who was awarded the Silver Star, two Bronze Stars, and the Purple Heart. He's a past president of the Mystery Writers of America, and has won their coveted Edgar Allen Poe Award. In 1987 his *Skinwalkers* (Harper & Row, 1986) won the Western Writers of America's Spur Award for the Best Novel Set in the West.

Zia Summer
by Rudolfo Anaya
Warner Books, 1995

> *As a Chicano writer I am part of a community which for the first time in our contemporary era produced enough literary works to create a literary movement. Prior to the 1960s western literature was written about us, but seldom by us. Now the world has a truer insight into our world; the view is now from within as more and more Chicano and Chicana writers explore their reality.*
>
> Rudolfo Anaya

With Mexican and Indian blood ties, Rudolfo Anaya is truly a Chicano writer. He is best known for *Bless Me, Ultima* (Quinto Sol, 1972), a major contribution to the growing body of literature that emerged during the Chicano Movement of 1965-75. This critically-acclaimed novel is the story of a Mexican-American, or Chicano, boy growing up on the eastern plains of New Mexico during the 1940s. The boy struggles with his identity, torn between the free vaquero life on the Llano that his father had enjoyed, and his mother's wish that he become a priest. In *Alburquerque* (University of New Mexico Press, 1992), Anaya moves to the ethnically and culturally diverse world of New Mexico in the 1990s. The protagonist, Abrán Gonzalez, born of a Mexican father and a Gringa mother, is Anaya's new Chicano. *Alburquerque*—notice the use of the original Spanish spelling—introduced many characters that appear in *Zia Summer*, including Sonny Baca.

Sonny was a small-time private eye, whose great-grandfather, El Bisabuelo, was Elfego Baca, the most famous lawman New Mexico ever produced. His great-grandfather, known and revered by his people throughout New Mexico, had rid the country of many dangerous desperadoes. Sonny made his living looking for debtors who had skipped, missing persons, divorce surveillance, and the like. Although he carried El Bisabuelo's Colt 45, he wondered if he had his great-grandfather's courage.

Zia Summer is a mystery steeped in Chicano culture, in the same vein as Tony Hillerman's Navajo Tribal Police mysteries. Sonny's cousin Gloria Dominic, his beloved prima, was murdered. She had met a ghastly end; her body had been drained of its blood and a Zia sun symbol had been etched around her navel.

Gloria's mother, Sonny's Tia Delfina, hated Frank Dominic, Gloria's husband. Frank was a powerful Alburquerque politician, a candidate for mayor. An immigrant from back east, of uncertain ethnic origin, he wanted to build a Venice on the Rio Grande, with a canal close to the river, bounded by casinos, and turn Alburquerque into one of the fabled Cities of Cibola.

> Dominic longed to be the new duke of Alburquerque. He yearned
> to be connected to royalty, anything that had to do with the Spanish
> blue blood of the first conquistadors. The names of Oñate and de
> Vargas were heroic in his mind, they were the Españoles who led the
> colonization of New Mexico, northern New Spain.

Tia Delfina was certain Dominic had killed her daughter. She hired Sonny for twenty dollars to find Gloria's killer. The murder's trail led Sonny not only to a confrontation with Dominic, but also to deadly encounters with evil brujos, or witches, who worshiped the Zia.

The search for cultural identity in Anaya's earlier novels continues. Sonny was keenly aware of his roots:

> The Nuevo Mexicanos had been in the Rio Grande for centuries, so

Indian blood flowed in their veins . . . Not only the history of Spain but the history of the Nile was his inheritance . . . Some of his friends said he looked Arabic. Maybe he had a drop of Jewish blood also, the legacy of the crypto Jews who came to New Mexico with the Oñate expeditions centuries before. The Marranos, the Catholics called them. He probably also carried French-Canadian trapper blood, German merchant blood, Navajo, Apache, you name it. Here a grand mestizo mixture took place. The Nile of the desert southwest. All bloods ran as one in the coyotes of Nuevo Mexico.

Although a modern Chicano, Sonny didn't dismiss the old ways. He had a girlfriend, Rita, who interpreted his dreams. He sought the help of a curandera, or good bruja (witch), to help him deal with Gloria's susto, or spirit, which he believed had entered his body. And he tracked an evil, mysterious character, called Raven by his followers, who Sonny sometimes believed had the power of the old brujos.

Anaya's novels show a deep respect for Chicano elders. Sonny thought the Chicano children had lost the way, but the old people kept the universe in balance. There are three characters in *Alburquerque*, central to the plot, who called themselves "Snap Crackle, and Pop." Their leader, Don Eliseo, was Sonny's eighty-year old neighbor, from whom he drew strength:

> The old man smiled. "You're a good man, Sonny," he said, returning the abrazo [hug] with strong arms, then placing his forehead against Sonny's forehead.
> "The kiss of life," the old man said, The energies of their souls met for a moment, and the old man's light flooded through Sonny. He felt the old man's strength enter his body.
> "Gracias," Sonny whispered.

Don Toto was an old pachuco from the forties, once the terror of the gray-haired bingo ladies at Our Lady of Sorrows, until Father Joe ruled the bingo games off limits to him. Doña Concha had outlived both don Toto and don Eliseo's wives, and now she had them to herself. She walked with a cane, touched peroxide to her gray hair to give it a slash of red, and wore falsies that continually fell to her waist. "If you've got it, flaunt it" she was fond of saying. Snap, Crackle, and Pop were Sonny's friends and his confidants, who saved his life and found the key to the puzzle of Gloria's murder. They're finely etched characters that Anaya presents with respect.

Western writers reflect their landscape, the bond they have with the environment. Anaya understands and eloquently expresses the effect of the forces of nature—wind, rain, sun, seasons—on the lives of desert people. He weaves the environment into the lore handed down by Chicano oral storytellers, as in the legend of La Llorona, the ubiquitous, seductive, ever-searching, weeping or wailing woman, who is often encountered in his fiction.

> Wind. The llaneros had as many ways to describe wind as did
> the Eskimos for describing snow . . . There were dry winds and
> wet winds, male winds and female winds, winds for every mood,
> tormenting winds that drove people crazy, . . . but always the wind
> was constant. Yes, a constant companion . . . La Llorona rode the
> wind, the weeping woman rode the Llano wind, her keening cry like
> the cry of the wind.

Add to this his descriptions of Chicano Alburquerque—Rita's restaurant "served Mexican food, and its specialty was menudo, sheep tripe thoroughly cleaned, cut in small pieces, and cooked overnight with small posole corn. Served in large, steaming bowls with lots of hot red chili and oregano, the dish was a delicacy. It was the best food for those who woke up crudos [hung-over] . . ." —and vivid Southwestern images emerge.

Because Sonny didn't dismiss the old ways, he knew that the sign of the sun was the work of brujas, of evil witches. He sensed a mysterious connection between the past and present. The Aztecs, he reasoned, used blood to feed the sun. Was Gloria's stolen blood also a gift to the sun? Before the mystery was solved, he held the fate of Alburquerque in his hands, and had to fight for his life three times. Before the Zia summer was ended, Sonny Baca could judge if he had his El Bisabuelo's courage.

21

Unusual Western Themes

Introduction

Stories that can be told in a western setting are so numerous and diverse that some are not easily categorized. This chapter presents some of these "peculiar" Westerns, with a potpourri of themes centered on utopian communities, movie stars, dancing bears, orphan trains, journeys through time, boxing, prophesying, earthquakes, and other not easily classified settings and themes.

My review is of Matt Braun's *Bloodsport* (St. Martin's Press, 1999), a novel based on a heavyweight prizefighting championship that took place on the Rio Grande River in 1896, when prizefighting was illegal throughout most of the country.

Reader's Guide

McTeague by Frank Norris. Doubleday, McClure, 1899. McTeague was a massive, slow-witted man, an unlicensed dentist who would sometimes pull teeth with his bare hands. He was a violent man, whose brutality was intensified by alcohol, a man who eventually became a murderer.

Rezanov by Gertrude Atherton. Authors and Newspapers Association, 1906. In 1806, Rezanov was a diplomatic agent of the Russo-American company, imperial inspector of the extreme eastern and northwestern dominions of the emperor of Russia. He was a man of ambition, who dreamed of dominion in the sun-soaked land of California, lazily held in the lax grasp of Spain.

Three Godfathers by Peter B. Kyne. George H. Doran, 1913. A Christmas story about three bank robbers who escape into the desert. When they find a newborn infant and its dying mother, they rescue the infant, carrying it across the wastelands without water, at the cost of their freedom. Basis for the 1948 film—and five previous ones.

Slogum House by Mari Sandoz. Little, Brown, 1937. In the pioneering days of Nebraska, Gulla Slogum sought to amass a fortune. Her base was her evil family and Slogum House, a saloon, brothel, and outlaw's haven.

The Magic of Limping John by Frank Goodwyn. Farrar and Rinehart, 1944. The story of of a Mexican fiddler who could not cope with his friends' belief that he was a wizard. Then he began to believe in his own magic powers.

The Turquoise by Anya Seton. Houghton Mifflin, 1946. Santa Fe Cameron's mother was high born Spanish, her father a Scot. On her seventeenth birthday her home was a New Mexico slum, nine years later she was the wife of one of the wealthiest men on Wall Street. In the 1870s, Gotham society welcomed this strange and beautiful Western woman. Only a handful knew the truth about her background. Then one of them attempted to destroy her.

The Lady by Conrad Richter. Alfred A. Knopf, 1957. Doña Ellen was the beautiful and refined daughter of a Mexican mother and an English father, a wealthy New Mexican woman with life's material advantages. Then a series of shattering events culminated with the loss of her property in the Panic of 1893. But throughout her trials and adversity, she was always "The Lady."

The Staked Plains by Frances X. Tolbert. Harper and Brothers, 1958. Llano Estacado Nabors was the son of a plainsman and his Indian wife. He found little that pleased him in the Anglo world of his father below the caprock and the Staked Plain; he much preferred life among the Antelope Comanche Indians of his mother. In the rugged country that was the Texas frontier in the 1860s and 1870s, Nabors was a hunter, not merely of animals but of a man as well—the killer of his father and his Indian stepmother.

The Hallelujah Train by Bill Gulick. Doubleday, 1963. The colonel was an officer and a gentleman, trained to obey orders, whatever they might be. But now he had a new assignment, guarding a wagon train filled with whiskey and besieged by temperance women and thirsty tribesmen. Source for the 1965 film.

King of Spades by Frederick Manfred. Trident Press, 1966. A tale of incest and murder, often compared to *Oedipus Rex*, is played out on the American plains in the 1870s. A young man mistakenly slept with his mother. His father, presumed dead, figured out the infamy, and deep in the Dakota frontier territory in Deadwood during the Black Hills Gold Rush, the family tragedy erupted into a shattering conclusion. The plot carries the story from England to Sioux City, to Chicago, to Cheyenne, and finally to Deadwood.

Ride a Northbound Horse by Richard Wormser. Scholastic, 1966. A young readers novel. The story of thirteen-year-old Cal Rand, who traveled alone on the road from Alabama to Texas with the family cart and Bo and Billy, the oxen. Cal was determined to become a cattleman. Spur Award from the Western Writers of America. Source for the 1969 film.

Brothers of Uterica by Benjamin Capps. Meredith Press, 1967. In the mid-neneteenth century a band of European and American idealists undertook a noble but improbable experiment in founding a utopian community amidst the harsh realities of the Texas frontier. But they failed to reckon with such things as unpredictable weather, drouth, Indians, and principally, their own selfish motives.

The Power of the Dog by Thomas Savage. Little, Brown, 1967. Two bachelor brothers, Phil and George Burbank, lived on a Montana ranch in the 1920s. Phil was a bullying, repressed homosexual. When George married a widow, her arrival shattered an already uneasy peace. Phil terrorized his new sister-in-law, and when her teenage son came to the ranch, things got even more tense.

A Roaring in the Wind by Robert Lewis Taylor. Putnam, 1967. In 1857 a young man left Harvard College in search of adventure and nature in the mountains of Montana. He encountered miners, mountain men, thieves, Indians, saloon girls, gamblers, quack doctors and vigilantes, along with drinking, gambling, dueling, killing, and a young, beautiful girl of the West.

Down the Long Hills by Louis L'Amour. Bantam Books, 1968. After escaping an Indian massacre, a seven-year-old boy and a three-year-old girl were stranded on the prairie, with only a horse and a knife to sustain and protect themselves. They were up against starvation, marauding Indians, savage outlaws, and wild animals. Spur Award from the Western Writers of America.

Yellow Back Radio Broke-Down by Ishmael Reed. Doubleday, 1969. This novel is set in the western town of Yellow Back Radio and features a black outlaw, the Loup Garow Kid, and his nympho mail-order bride Mustache Sal, in a satire of the "frontier" myth.

Tom Mix Died for Your Sins by Darryl Ponicsan. Delacorte Press, 1975. This is a fictional account of the life and times of the colorful cowboy actor, a larger-than-life Western character who lived a full and adventurous life.

Seven Rivers West by Edward Hoagland. Summit Books, 1976. A novel set in the 1880s involving Cecil Roop, who dreams of capturing a grizzly cub to show on the vaudeville circuit.

California Bloodstock by Terry McDonnell. Macmillan, 1980. In this dark novel that spoofs the history of California, a fifteen-year-old heroine, searching for the men who had savaged her, attempted to cover up the discovery of gold and refused to marry Zorro. Passing through the novel's landscape are the Donner Party, Joaquin Murietta, the Bear Flaggers, and other historical figures, as well as the the Perfect Worm Eaters, the Animal People, the keeper of the buckskin known as His-Own-Ghost, and Guatemalan apes dressed as Mexican soldiers.

Thousand Pieces of Gold by Ruthanne Lum McCunn. Design Enterprises, 1981. In 1871 a young Chinese girl named Lalu Nathoy, whom her father called his treasure—his "thousand pieces of gold," was sold into slavery by her poverty-stricken family and auctioned off in the American West. This biographical novel tells of Lalu's struggle to get out of servitude.

Soledad by R. G. Vliet. Texas Christian University Press, 1986. Originally published in 1977. Set in the Texas Hill Country and Edwards Plateau. In 1881 a cowboy killed a Mexican stranger for reasons he himself did not fully comprehend. From the stranger's pocket he removed a smudged photograph of a young woman in a white dress. His first glimpse of the photograph was the beginning of an obsessive search for the woman.

Dead in the West by Joe R. Lansdale. London: Kinnell, 1986. A Western horror story. Mud Creek, Texas, was a town overshadowed by a terrible evil. An Indian medicine man, unjustly lynched by the people of Mud Creek, had put a curse on the town: When darkness falls, the dead walk and they will be hungry for human flesh. The only one that can save the town is Reverend Jebediah Mercer, a gun toting preacher who has lost his faith in the Lord and turned to whisky.

The Last Days of Horse-Shy Halloran by Bill Pronzini. M. Evans, 1987. Henry W. Halloran, better known as Horse-Shy Halloran, rode into San Francisco looking for rich widows and soft beds.

The Rough Rider by Jack Cummings. Walker, 1988. Lew Axford and Jess Gault were close friends who joined Teddy Roosevelt's Rough Riders and charged up San Juan Hill side by side, where Lew earned the Medal of Honor for saving Jess' life. Lew used his hero status and ran over other men to get elected governor, but his old friend Jess broke with him when killing became part of the deal.

Under Outlaw Flags by James Reasoner. Berkley, 1988. In 1917, when the Wild West was only a memory, the Tacker Gang was still making a dishonest living in the wide-open spaces. Then the law caught up with them— and offered the gang a choice: serve your country by fighting in the war in Europe, or serve 20 years.

Lady of No Man's Land by Jeanne Williams. St. Martin's Press, 1988. Kirsten left her home in Sweden at seventeen to make a place for herself on the American frontier. There she discovered that she had a rare talent, a gift for turning ordinary country cloth into works of grace and beauty. She found the vast, unsettled stretch of prairie just north of the Texas Panhandle was a land of limitless possibilities.

South of the Border by John Byrne Cooke. Bantam Books, 1989. The narrator is Charles Siringo, the famous Pinkerton detective who spent a number of years pursuing the infamous Butch Cassidy. The time is just after the end of World War I and before the Roaring Twenties and Prohibition. The place is Hollywood. Into this land of fantasy rides the outlaw Butch Cassidy, thought by all to be dead. He encounters Siringo, and soon both men are bound for the deserts of Mexico with the beautiful Victoria Hartford and her film crew. There they come face-to-face with Pancho Villa's revolution.

Moon Dance by S. P. Somtow. Tor Books, 1989. A horror novel that brings the ancient werewolf legend to the American West. During the European expansion into the West in the late 1800s, a pack of Viennese werewolves emigrated to Dakota territory. But unknown to them, the territory was already home to a clan of Lakota Sioux who become wolves by the light of the full moon.

The Falconer: A Novel of Mysticism and Adventure by Jorge Gutierrez and James K. Omiya. Sunstone Press, 1991. Mauro, a history teacher in South Texas, often watched the frequent storms that swept the beaches on the Gulf of Mexico. But this time things were different. The violence of wind, sand and sky contained visions of Arab warriors and explorers of centuries past. Could he have been touched by the mythical spell of the Falconer, an Arab of the Middle Ages, and could the Falconer's power reach up to him from a forgotten time to reveal some reality long hidden?

Deadwood Dick and the Code of the West by Bruce H. Thorstad. Pocket Books, 1991. In the 1800s, hoping to join up with his hero, dime novel character Deadwood Dick, Mortimer Ridley Chalmers III, a 14-year-old boy, runs away from his Philadelphia home to the Black Hills of Dakota territory. But instead of Deadwood Dick, he finds Coffee Arbuckle, an ex-slave and former cavalry sergeant who disappoints Mortimer by not following the Code of the West.

The Living by Annie Dillard. HarperCollins, 1992. Bellingham Bay lies ninety miles north of Seattle, on the northwest coast of Washington State. A rough settlement founded in the 1850s became the town of Whatcom. This is a tale of the men and women of Whatcom, whose hopes rose and fell as they struggled to clear the forests and fish and farm for their subsistence—and to commit murder. All this took place over a hundred years ago, when they were "the living."

Anasazi and the Viking: A Novel of the Southwest by A. Tanner Smith. Sunstone Press, 1992. In this fantasy novel a Viking warrior wanders into a settlement of Anasazi Indians in southwestern Colorado over 800 years ago. Within this improbable setting the author weaves a story of Norsemen and Anasazi ways of life that eventually leads to a hunt for something more precious than gold.

Power in the Blood by Greg Matthews. HarperCollins, 1993. In 1869, following their mother's death, three children from New York were sent out West on one of the so-called orphan trains—a cruel philanthropy of the time which provided household and farm help to pioneer families. The children were separated, adopted by couples in three different states, and lost contact with one another. Sixteen years after their separation and the divergent trails their lives took, they have a bizarre and tragic reunion in Colorado.

Redeye: A Western by Clyde Edgerton. Algonquin Books, 1995. In turn-of-the-century Colorado, frontier entrepreneur Billy Blankenship aimed to turn the newly discovered Native American cliff dwellings of Mesa Largo into America's first roadside attraction. The story has three narrators. One is a pit bull named Redeye.

Angels in Tesuque by Michael Glasco. Sunstone Press, 1995. Young Ben Touchstone, a half-breed, was born with pale skin, straw colored hair and cobalt eyes, Rejected by the pueblo and regarded as an oddity by Anglos, Ben feels forsaken in a strange limbo between the cultures. But on Christmas Eve, in the mysterious chapel at Chimayo, his angel appears and promises him she will intervene and council him at every crossroad of his life. But does she?

Out of Eden by Kate Lehrer. Harmony, 1995. Two women, an American and a French, in 19th century Paris moved to the Kansas plains, determined to create an independent women's community. They discovered that along with freedom come hardships and costly decisions.

The Mercy Seat by Rilla Askew. Viking Press, 1997. In early February of 1887, two brothers, John and Lafayette Lodi, fled Kentucky in the middle of the night, heading west into Indian Territory. One was a mule thief and a bootlegger, the other a blacksmith whose daughter had visions. The clairvoyant child's gift made her the object of a tug-of-war between Christians and Native Americans and ignited a blood feud between her father and her bootlegging uncle. This mystical tale is set against the harsh backdrop of 1880s Oklahoma and is centered on a disintegrating family and the Native American spirit world.

Spirits of the Ordinary by Kathleen Alcala. Harcourt Brace, 1998. In northern Mexico in the 1870s, the Caraval family had long been clandestine Jews, and when Zacarias abandoned religion to wander the desert, his wife took the bold step of declaring herself independent.

Journey of the Dead by Loren D. Estleman. Forge, 1998. When Pat Garrett killed Billy the Kid, he had no idea what a terrible emotional price he would pay. Haunted by memories of Billy, he wandered the New Mexico desert in a fruitless pursuit of peace. Deep in the same desert, an ancient Spanish alchemist searched for the fabled philosopher's stone. Together and separately, Garrett and the alchemist journeyed through time and history searching for answers to their ancient questions. Spur Award winner.

In the Arms of the Sky by Earl Murray. Forge, 1998. In 1873 an Englishwoman named Isabella Lucy Bird came to Colorado territory to see Estes Park, a magical valley at the foot of Longs Peak, a towering natural wonder in the rugged wilderness of the Rockies. "Belle" Bird was a rarity in the Victorian age, a woman who traveled the world alone and feared nothing, not even the notorious outlaw, Jim Nugent, a formidable, self-appointed "protector" of Estes Park.

Brass by Robert J. Conley. Leisure Books, 1999. *Brass* is a horror tale set the West with themes of ecology and Native American lore. It opens in a small midwestern town where a major environmental project involved the draining of a fetid stretch of water. Buried in the middle of the water was a pole, guarded by two crows that were hostile toward the workers. The pole impaled Brass or Untsayi, an ancient Native American demon, and a shape shifter. When the pole was removed, the demon was released to satisfy his evil desires.

The Hell Benders by Ken Hodgson. Pinnacle Books, 1999. The Bender family turned murder into a way of making a living. Those who stayed the night at the Benders' ramshackle inn outside of Parsons, Kansas, on the Osage Mission Trail, stayed forever.

Prophet Annie by Ellen Recknor. Avon Books, 1999. Subtitled *Being the Recently Discovered Memoir of Annie Pinkerton Boone Newcastle Dearborn, Prophet and Seer*. In 1881, at age 22, Annie left Iowa for the wild Arizona territory and married a prosperous "old geezer" 54 years her senior. He died in bed on their wedding night, but then took up residence in her mind and body and began "prophesying," giving speeches through her to audiences eager to hear his visions of the future. Spur Award winner.

Aftershocks by Richard S. Wheeler. Forge, 1999. On April 18,1906, the devastating San Francisco earthquake leveled one of the great American cities. Wheeler takes the reader into the midst of the earthquake in which thousands died, and tens of thousands were left homeless and destitute.

Where the Buffalo Roam by Michael Zimmer. Pinnacle Books, 1999. Clay Little Bull was born into slavery on an East Texas cotton plantation. He was captured by the Kiowa as a small child and raised among the tribes until he broke away at the age of twenty. An outcast among whites, blacks, and Indians, Clay joined forces with a buffalo hunter named Ty Calhoun and led a band of freed men and a young Indian woman across the plains in search of a place where he belonged.

Ride South to Purgatory by James C. Work. Five Star, 1999. From Work's *Keystone Ranch* series. The protagonist, Pasque, attending a Christmas party at his uncle's Keystone Ranch, was confronted by a giant of a man who issued a peculiar challenge. The mystical stranger was Death and New Life, and his challenge would send Pasque on a mysterious journey that would end in exactly one year. This series is influenced by the King Arthur legend.

The Colony: A Suspense Novel for the Young Reader by Thomas L. Carroll. Sunstone Press, 2000. Lawrence Bell, a young boy who's bullied by other boys at school, runs away into the American southwestern desert, a forbidden place filled with tarantulas, rattlesnakes, and wandering coyotes. In the face of almost unbelievable events, he finds protection in an ant colony and becomes a member of their army.

Eagle's Cry by David Nevin. Forge, 2000. A novel of the Louisiana Purchase, *Eagle's Cry* covers the election of 1800 until the time of the purchase in 1803. The major figures involved are all present—Thomas Jefferson, James Madison, Aaron Burr, Napoleon Bonaparte—as America made a move that turned it into a global nation.

The Borderland by Edwin B. Shrake. Hyperion, 2000. Subtitled *A Novel of Texas*. The story is set in 1839, three years after the Alamo fell. President Lamar decided to move the capital of the Republic from Houston to a valley in central Texas—Comanche country—and gave birth to the new city of Austin. The repercussions were enormous; it set off the largest Comanche war party of all time. The Texas Rangers sent a desperate, ragtag force against the Comanche warriors on the plains south of Austin. Meanwhile, a mythical character—a half-Cherokee physician descended from Jonathan Swift—went on a quest to find a mysterious, otherworldly creature said to live in a cave full of Spanish gold.

A Deeper Wild by William L. Sullivan. Navillus Press, 2000. A novel of the Oregon frontier that follows the adventures of Joaquin Miller—the pony express rider, gold miner, outlaw, and county judge who galloped to worldwide fame as the "Poet of the Sierras."

Chanchers by Gearld Vizenor. University of Oklahoma Press, 2000. Centered on the volatile issue of the repatriation of Native American skeletal remains, *Chanchers* follows a group of student Solar Dancers who set out to resurrect Native remains housed in the Phoebe Hearst Museum of Anthropology at the University of California, Berkeley. In a gruesome ritual, they sacrifice faculty and administrators associated with the collection and storage of Native remains. The Dancers replace stored Native skulls with those of the academics, and the resurrected Natives become the Chanchers.

The Witness by Richard S. Wheeler. Signet, 2000. Set in 1890s Colorado, this is the story of a man who must resist pressure to tell a lie in court. This would violate his ethical standards, but refusing would jeopardize his job, his family's security and his future.

Summer of Pearls by Mike Blakely. Forge, 2001. Ben Crowell was fourteen during the Great Caddo Lake Pearl Rush of 1874, and his home, the riverboat community of Port Caddo, Texas, was dying. But the irregular and discolored pearls found in local freshwater mussels brought it back to life. By the end of the summer, the pearl boom was over. Port Caddo was doomed, and people turned their attention to an unsolved murder. It took Ben forty years to solve the mystery. Spur Award from the Western Writers of America.

Bodie Gone: A Science Fiction Novel of Suspense by Bill Hyde. Sunstone Press, 2001. Frances "Tip" DeQuill—affluent housewife, mother, and sometimes newspaper writer—had been obsessed trying to unravel the mystery of the strange things that had happened close to Bridgeport and the nearby ghost town of Bodie, California. Her quest for a story would take her back in time to the gold rush days and urge her to chronicle the stories of eight strangers who had struggled to reach Bodie seeking gold, love, lust, adventure or revenge. Her strangers would interact with some of the best known characters from the Old West and they would experience many historical happenings. But nothing they suffered would prepare them for their bizarre departure from Bodie.

Code of the West by Aaron Latham. Simon and Schuster, 2001. Latham's novel transplants the legend of King Arthur, Guinevere, Lancelot, and Merlin to the Old West. It begins with young Jimmy Goodnight visiting a county fair and pulling a deeply imbedded ax out of an anvil, a feat of strength that forever changes his life. It leads to a friendship with Jack Loving, and together they make a formidable team. The story cleverly interweaves Western history (Loving and Goodnight) and Arthurian legend.

The Chili Queen by Sandra Dallas. St. Martin's Press, 2003. Set in New Mexico in the 1880s. When Emma Roby's prospective husband failed to show at the train station, Addie French sheltered Emma at her brothel, The Chile Queen. Addie broke all her rules to shelter the girl, but once Emma entered Addie's life, both women began to question everything they thought they knew. Spur Award from the Western Writers of America.

The Hebrew Kid and the Apache Maiden by Robert J. Avrech. Seraphic Press, 2004. The story of a thirteen-year-old Jewish boy who wants a bar mitzvah. But Ariel lives in Arizona territory in the 1870s and besides his family there are no Jews in town. Ariel's father is a rabbi, and when Ariel and his family are captured by Lozen, the sister of the Apache chief Victorio, he tells her that his father is a holy man, a healer.

Field of Honor by D. L. Birchfield. University of Oklahoma Press, 2004. In this novel, a secret underground civilization of Choctaws, deep beneath the Ouachita Mountains of southeastern Oklahoma, has evolved into a high-tech culture. P. P. McDaniel, a half-blood Choctaw Marine Corps deserter from the Vietnam War, stumbles into this idyllic world and becomes entangled in political intrigue. Spur Award from the Western Writers of America.

Crofton's Fire by Will Camp (Preston Lewis). Putnam, 2004. In 1876 a green second lieutenant named Crofton barely escaped Little Bighorn, where he saw Custer killed by his own enraged men. This was only the beginning of his adventures. After being shot in the chest by a French whore he was attempting to rescue during a "whore's war" in Kansas, he saw action in revolutionary Cuba, shot his way out of a Ku Klux Klan siege, toiled behind a desk in Washington, D. C., and fought alongside gallant British comrades in the East African Zulu War.

People of the Raven by Kathleen O'Neal Gear and Michael Gear. Forge, 2004. From the Gears' *The First North Americans* series. In this entry, based on recent evidence, the Gears posit that there were Caucasoids—light-skinned people—in North America between 9,000 and 11,000 years ago. The story is of of rival cultures in the Pacific Northwest at a time of momentous change. Spur Award from the Western Writers of America.

The Reluctant Assassin by Preston Darby. Five Star, 2005. The new owner of a long vacant piece of land outside San Angelo, Texas, found a mummy inside a derelict stone storage shed, and inside the mummy was a diary wrapped in leather. It was the diary of John Wilkes Booth, recounting the assassination of Lincoln, Booth's escape from his pursuers, and his subsequent life.

The Undertaker's Wife by Loren D. Estleman. Forge, 2005. Richard Connable was an undertaker, an artist restoring the dead in the frontier West to a life-like appearance. But the protagonist is Lucy, Richard's wife, who followed him from town to town, always there to listen, although he was usually as quiet as the dead that provided their livelihood. Spur Award winner.

No Country for Old Men by Cormac McCarthy. Alfred A. Knopf, 2005. This dark-themed novel is set in 1980 southwest Texas, where Llewelyn Moss, while hunting antelope near the Rio Grande, stumbles across several dead men, a bunch of heroin and $2.4 million in cash. Moss takes the money and goes home, but he is not the only player in the game. He is pursued by an ex-Special Forces agent employed by a powerful cartel, and a psychopathic murderer armed with a cattle gun and a dangerous philosophy of justice.

High Plains Tango by Robert James Waller. Random House, 2005. A young drifter from California, a master carpenter with a Stanford degree, arrived in the almost deserted town of Salamander, South Dakota, looking for solitude. But all was not peaceful in Salamander. Unexplained deaths had occurred on Sioux sacred ground on the adjoining reservation and the townspeople felt that black magic was to blame. As the young carpenter plied his trade, he met a mysterious woman who intrigued him, and then strange and violent things began to occur.

SELECTED REVIEW

Bloodsport
by Matt Braun
St. Martin's Press, 1999

    Matt Braun is a prolific author who has written about nearly every major historical character in the West. His body of work deals with lawmen like Bill Tilghman in *One Last Town* (St. Martin's Press, 1997), gunmen such as John Wesley Hardien in *Noble Outlaw* (St. Martin's Press, 1996), and mountainmen, cattlemen, gamblers, and other familiar Western types. *Bloodsport* is somewhat of an excursion from his other books. It is based on a heavyweight prizefighting championship that took place on the Rio Grande River in 1896.

    The protagonist is Daniel Stuart, a gambler by profession. In Dallas, he was acknowledged as a high roller without equal. His game was poker, and for twenty years, he'd been known to bet a fortune on the single turn of a card. But in 1894 he saw a different kind of opportunity.

    At that time, prizefighting was illegal throughout most of the country. The statutes varied, but in many states it was a felony that carried a prison sentence.

    The reigning heavyweight champion was Gentleman Jim Corbitt, who had defeated the mythical John L. Sullivan and captured the heavyweight crown. Corbitt was an inordinately vain man, educated and well spoken, who had natural gift for the sport. He was twenty-nine, and unbeaten in nineteen fights. But he had defended his title only once in fifteen months, devoting himself instead to Broadway and the stage. The public was clamoring for a fight between Corbitt and and the number one contender, Bob "Ruby Rob" Fitzsimmons. In November of 1894 Stuart signed Corbitt and Fitzsimmons to fight in Dallas for a $25,000 winner-take-all purse.

    But it was not to be. The Texas governor declared the fight illegal, as did the governors of Arkansas and New Mexico, followed by the Secretary of the Interior with the same decree for the Indian Territories.

Stuart set up shop in El Paso, intending to stage the fight across the border in Juarez. The fight was expected to draw over 20,000 people, an economic bonanza for both El Paso and Juarez. But, at the urging of Governor Culberson of Texas and Mexico President Portfirio Diaz, Governor Ahumada of Chihuahua refused to allow the fight , and came to Juarez with a force of 500 Rurales to enforce his decision.

At about the same time Texas Adjutant General Woodford Mabry arrived in El Paso with four Ranger captains and a force of forty Rangers, with orders to ensure that no fight took place. Mabry was a determined man. So was Stuart. Their first meeting was less than cordial

Mabry seated himself before the desk. . . Stuart took the swivel chair behind the desk. "What can I do for you . . . ?" he said, lighting a cigar. "I presume you're not here for tickets to the fight."

"Let me be blunt," Mabry said sharply. "I consider you a scalawag and a man who holds himself above the law. I would like nothing more than to arrest you on the spot."

"Well, so much for the amenities. Is that your personal opinion, or do you speak for the governor?"

"We are here at the direct order of Governor Culberson. He has authorized the Rangers to take whatever measures necessary to enforce the law."

Stuart blew smoke at him. "You've made a long trip for nothing, Mr. Mabry. At last count, I haven't broken any laws."

"You will," Mabry said with certainty. "Unless you intend to cancel this prizefight."

"I assure you that won't happen."

"Then it will give me great pleasure to place you in irons."

And then there were other major problems that plagued the promotion. Corbitt retired from the ring and refused to honor his contract. Stuart replaced him with Peter Maher, a burly, thick necked Cornishman with oxlike shoulders who had fought Fitzsimmons two years earlier. He went twelve rounds before his nose was broken and he lost on a technical knockout. During training for

Stuart's fight, Maher damaged his eyes while running during a sandstorm and the fight had to be delayed.

The thrust of the factually-based plot deals with the multitude of obstacles placed in the way of the promotion and how Stuart dealt with them. His formidable adversaries included a strange alliance between the Texas Rangers and the Mexican Rurales. In addition, there is a major subplot that has three outlaws with designs on the estimated one million dollar gate the fight would bring.

As in all of Braun's novels, numerous historical characters appear. In addition to those already mentioned, there are Bat Masterson, welterweight champion Joe Walcott, legendary heavyweight champion John L. Sullivan, Judge Roy Bean, and several noted Texas Rangers. Braun's spare prose defines the characters quickly and without fuss, and then gets on with the action. Here he introduces Captain Bill McDonald:

> McDonald was whipcord lean, with slate-gray eyes and a soup-strainer mustache. At forty-three, he had been a lawman most of his life, working as a deputy sheriff and a deputy U. S. marshal before he became a Ranger. His calm demeanor belied the tough, nononsense attitude of a religious man who wore a badge and smote lawbreakers with something approaching the wrath of God. He was not a man to be crossed.

He gets mileage out of most supporting players. Lea Osborn, the leader of the three outlaws, was formally a saloon girl in Fort Worth's infamous Hell's Half Acre. A woman of innate intelligence, she could subtly dominate men. She used her wiles to extract information on the gate receipts from Bat Masterson, Stuart's chief of security. She had a natural gift for firearms and an uncanny ability to sling lead at rapid-fire and still hit her target.

> Lea saw the [Breckenridge] bank door open. Stovall stepped out, pistol in one hand and gunnysack in the other. Directly behind him was Taylor . . . She swung into the saddle as they crossed the sidewalk, vaguely aware of the gunnysack, stuffed full with cash.

The door suddenly burst open, and a man attired in a business suit and vest rushed outside, brandishing a revolver. He drew a bead on Taylor's back. Her reaction was of pure reflex; she pulled her right-hand Colt and fired in the same motion. She knew he was dead even as she tripped the trigger.

The fight was finally held on the Rio Grande adjacent to Langtry, which lay in squalid isolation almost 400 miles east of El Paso, a fourteen hour train ride. There was not a Rurale within a three-day ride. The dusty little Texas town was the domain of Judge Roy Bean, the "Law West of the Pecos," and a legend along the border, who "dispensed justice with the whimsical hand of a buccaneer."

The actual fight is covered briefly in the narrative—finally crowning Corbitt's successor as Heavyweight Champion of the World. When the opening bell rang,

Fitzsimmons sprang from his corner. He rushed forward eager for the scrap, his pale blue eyes glinting in the sun. Maher lumbered out, head tucked low behind cocked fists, his arms rippling with muscle. There was no hesitation, no sparring to feel the other man out. Maher launched a roundhouse right and Fitzsimmons slipped the blow, countering with a sharp left-right combination. They clinched, wrestling about with brute strength, and [the referee] ordered them to break. . . . Before Fitzsimmons could retreat, Maher waded in, landing a right to the body and a sizzling left hook to the mouth. . . . Fitzsimmons was on the verge of going down, . . . Then, with a nifty sidestep, Fitzsimmons slid off the ropes and dodged a murderous right cross. . . . they moved again to the center of the ring . . .

The outcome surprised Stuart, and it will surprise readers who are not familiar with boxing history.

Bloodsport has interesting expository comment on the early years of boxing interlaced with an unusual bit of Texas history that will please both the fight fan and those who enjoy a good Western

Selected Bibliography

Blacker, Irwin R. *The Old West in Fiction*. New York: Ivan Obolensky, 1961.

Braun, Matt. *How to Write Western Novels*. Cincinnati: Writer's Digest, 1988.

Cancellari, Mike. *Checklist of Western and Northern Fiction*, 1900-1980. Self-Published, 1988.

Davis, Robert Murray, ed. *Playing Cowboys: Low Culture and High Art in the Western*. Norman: University of Oklahoma Press, 1992.

Dobie, J. Frank. *Guide to Life and Literature of the Southwest*. Rev. ed. 1975. Dallas: Southern Methodist University Press, 1952.

Dobie, J. Frank. *Prefaces*. 1975. Austin: University of Texas Press, 1982.

Dobie, J. Frank. *Out of the Old Rock*. Austin: University of Texas Press, 1988.

Dunaway, David King, ed. *Writing the Southwest*. New York: Plume/Penguin, 1995.

Erisman, Fred and Richard W. Etulain, eds. *Fifty Western Writers*. Greenwood, 1982.

Estleman, Loren D. *The Wister Trace: Classic Novels of the American Frontier*. Ottawa: Jameson Books, 1987.

Etulain, Richard W. *Re-Imagining the Modern American West: A Century of Fiction, History, and Art*. Tucson: University of Arizona Press, 1996.

Folsom, James K. *The American Western Novel*. New Haven: College and University Press, 1966.

Hardy, Phil. *The Encyclopedia of Western Movies*. Minneapolis: Woodbury Press, 1984.

Henderson, Lesley, ed. *Twentieth-Century Romance and Historical Writers*—Second Edition. Chicago: St. James Press, 1990.

Lyon, Thomas J., ed. *A Literary History of the American West*—Second Edition. Fort Worth: Texas Christian University Press, 1999.

Magill, Frank N, ed. *Masterpieces of Latino Literature*. New York: HarperCollins, 1994.

Martin, Russell and Marc Barasch, ed. *Writers of the Purple Sage: An Anthology of Recent Western Writing*. New York: Penguin, 1984.

Martin, Russell, ed. *New Writers of the Purple Sage: An Anthology of Contemporary Western Writing*. New York: Penguin, 1992.

Mead, Jean. *Maverick Writers: Candid Comments by Fifty-Two of the Best*. Caldwell: Caxton, 1989.

Milton, John R. *The Novel of the American West*. Lincoln: University of Nebraska Press, 1980.

Quantic, Diane Dufva. *The Nature of the Place: A Study of Great Plains Fiction*. Lincoln: University of Nebraska Press, 1995.

Riegel, Robert E. and Robert G. Athearn. *America Moves West*—Fifth Edition. New York: Holt, Rinehart, and Winston,1971.

Starrett, Vincent. *Best Loved Books of the Twentieth Century*. New York: Bantam Books, 1955

Snodgrass, Mary Ellen. *Encyclopedia of Frontier Literature.* New York: Oxford University Press, 1999.

Sonnichsen, C. L. *From Hopalong to Hud: Thoughts on Western Fiction*. College Station: Texas A&M University Press,1978.

Tuska, Jon. *The American West In Fiction*. Lincoln: University of Nebraska Press, 1988.

Tuska, Jon and Vicki Piekarski, eds. Encyclopedia of Frontier and Western Fiction. McGraw-Hill, 1983.

Tuska, Jon and Vicki Piekarski, eds. *The Frontier Experience: A Readers Guide to the Life and Literature of the American West*. Jefferson: McFarland, 1984.

Vinson, James, ed. *Twentieth Century Western Writers*—Second Edition. Farmington Hills: Gale, 1992.

Work, James C., ed. *Prose and Poetry of the American West*. Lincoln: University of Nebraska Press, 1990.

The Western Writers Series, published by Boise State University in Boise, Idaho, contains more than 140 in-print titles. The majority focus on the life and work of individual writers who have made significant contributions to Western American literature. These booklets provide biography, critical interpretation, and discussion of the full range of an author's work.

INDEX BY TITLE

Index By Author

www.ingramcontent.com/pod-product-compliance
Lightning Source LLC
Chambersburg PA
CBHW030924020726
47498CB00001B/102